GOLDEN AGE DETECTIVE STORIES

GOLDEN AGE
DETECTIVE STORIES

Edited by Marie Smith

This is a Parragon Book published 2002

Parragon
Queen Street House
4 Queen Street
Bath BA1 1HE, UK

This collection first published in the UK as
The Mammoth Book of Golden Age Detective Stories
by Robinson Publishing Ltd, 1994

A copy of the British Library Cataloguing in Publication Data
is available from the British Library

ISBN 0-75257-429-9

Printed and bound in the EC

10 9 8 7 6 5 4 3 2 1

CONTENTS

CONTENTS

Introduction

And Edgar Allan Poe begat the Chevalier Dupin, and Dupin begat Lecoq, and Lecoq begat Sherlock Holmes, and Sherlock Holmes begat – oh, dozens and dozens of detectives, and the Golden Age of the Detective Story was upon us.

I'm probably in trouble already. The Golden Age is generally taken to be the period between the two World Wars, that idyllic (for some) era when such writers as Agatha Christie, Dorothy L. Sayers, John Dickson Carr, Margery Allingham, Ellery Queen, S. S. Van Dine and others were pouring out whodunnits that now seem classic, and for the mystery *novel* probably was an era as Golden as it has been painted. But the period that is covered in this collection – roughly the late-Victorian and Edwardian age – offers not only the complete canon of Sherlock Holmes short stories, the first and best of Father Brown, The Old Man in the Corner, the blind detective Max Carrados, Raffles, Uncle Abner, John Silence, Dr Thorndike and the "inverted" detective story, Prince Zaleski, "The Thinking Machine", Arsène Lupin, Craig Kennedy, and Inspector Hanaud, but many more besides, and there has surely never been a more gilded age for the detective *short* story. And that is not to mention *The Hound of the Baskervilles, The Big Bow Mystery, Trent's*

Last Case, The Thirty-Nine Steps and other classic novels of the same vintage.

It was a time of lively and intense experimentation. Sherlock Holmes had the good fortune to make his début in *The Strand Magazine* at precisely the time when, as a result of the Education Act, there was suddenly a large, newly-literate public looking for something to read. Holmes was what they chose, and writers were not slow to try and feed this new and voracious appetite for detective fiction. Some of their detectives were modelled closely on Holmes, as Sexton Blake was, while others were made as unlike him as possible. And so there were plump detectives, immobile detectives, female detectives and even the aforementioned blind detective, Max Carrados. As far as most of the writers and readers were concerned, this form was a brand-new one and the rules of the game were not yet clear. (They would not be formally stated until the 1920s, when Ronald Knox formulated them in his typically whimsical manner.) Writers often did not trouble too much about "playing fair" with their readers, feeling that it was thrill enough just to watch one of their sleuths on the scent, with the result that all too often the clues were seen by the detective but not disclosed to the readers, who accordingly had no chance of solving the mystery for themselves.

This probably troubles us more than it did them, but in making this selection from the period I have borne modern tastes in mind and on the whole avoided stories where the reader is offered no clues and is *still* expected to gasp in wonderment when the detective reveals his solution. If this has excluded some of the so-called Great Detectives of the era, well there it is. I have also avoided most of those hackneyed tales that crop up time and time again in anthologies; as a reader of such things myself I now scream when I am confronted yet again with "The Red-Headed League", "The Hands of Mr Ottermole", "The Problem of Cell 13", "The Lodger" and a handful of others. I am also puzzled as to why these stories recur so often when there are so many other good ones to choose from – though this is perhaps naïve: anthologists anthologize from other anthologies, of course.

In this anthology I have tried not to do that. I have very deliberately *not* duplicated any of the stories in Sir Hugh Greene's excellent *Rivals of Sherlock Holmes* series, or any in Michele B. Slung's pioneering *Crime on Her Mind* – or, indeed, from any collection from this period that has come my way. Instead I have chosen stories that reflect the liveliness and experimentation of these exciting years, and together they perhaps offer a somewhat different view of the period from the conventional one.

The stories are arranged in chronological order, as far as I have been able to establish it. Most of them appeared in magazines before they were collected into books, and I have not always been able to track down the dates of those first magazine appearances; the order may therefore be a little approximate here and there, but I think that the overall pattern is clear enough. Each story is prefaced by a short introduction giving some details of the author and his or her work, which leaves me with no more to say here except that in researching the book I have convinced myself at least that this was indeed the Golden Age of the Detective short story. I hope you will agree.

Marie Smith, 1994

A. Conan Doyle

A Scandal in Bohemia

Sherlock Holmes made his début in A Study in Scarlet, *which was first published in* Beeton's Christmas Annual *for 1888, but it was not until his appearance in a series of short stories in* The Strand Magazine *that he really caught the imagination of the new reading public. Then the whole world became captivated by the idea of the Great Detective and clamoured for more and more and more until his creator, the doctor with literary aspirations, gave up in despair and plunged him over the Reichenbach Falls: a false end, as it turned out, just as* A Study in Scarlet *had proved to be a false start.*

"A Scandal in Bohemia" was the first of the Holmes short stories, appearing in the Strand *in July, 1891. Poe may have invented the detective story in his tales of the Chevalier Dupin and others may have created sleuths before Sherlock Holmes, but as far as popular taste was concerned they were just rehearsals: for the world at large the detective story began with* this *story.*

I

TO SHERLOCK HOLMES she is always *the* woman. I have seldom heard him mention her under any other name. In his eyes she eclipses and predominates the whole of her sex. It was not that he felt any emotion akin to love for Irene Adler. All emotions, and that one particularly, were abhorrent to his cold, precise, but admirably balanced mind. He was, I take it, the most perfect reasoning and observing machine that the world has seen: but, as a lover, he would have placed himself in a false position. He never spoke of the softer passions, save with a gibe and a sneer. They were admirable things for the observer – excellent for drawing the veil from men's motives and actions. But for the trained reasoner to admit such intrusions into his own delicate and finely adjusted temperament was to introduce a distracting factor which might throw a doubt upon all his mental results. Grit in a sensitive instrument, or a crack in one of his own highpower lenses, would not be more disturbing than a strong emotion in a nature such as his. And yet there was but one woman to him, and that woman was the late Irene Adler, of dubious and questionable memory.

I had seen little of Holmes lately. My marriage had drifted us away from each other. My own complete happiness, and the home-centred interests which rise up around the man who first finds himself master of his own establishment, were sufficient to absorb all my attention; while Holmes, who loathed every form of society with his whole Bohemian soul, remained in our lodgings in Baker-street, buried among his old books, and alternating from week to week between cocaine and ambition, the drowsiness of the drug, and the fierce energy of his own keen nature. He was still, as ever, deeply attracted by the study of crime, and occupied his immense faculties and extraordinary powers of observation in following out those clues, and clearing up those mysteries, which had been abandoned as hopeless by the official police. From time to time I heard some vague account of his doings: of his summons to Odessa in the case of the Trepoff murder, of his clearing up of the singular tragedy of the Atkinson brothers at Trincomalee, and finally of the mission which he had accomplished so delicately and successfully for the reigning family of Holland. Beyond these signs of his activity, however, which I merely shared with all the readers of the daily press, I knew little of my former friend and companion.

One night – it was on the 20th of March, 1888 – I was returning from a journey to a patient (for I had now returned to civil practice), when my way led me through Baker-street. As I passed the well-remembered door, which must always be associated in my mind with my wooing, and with the dark incidents of the Study in Scarlet, I was seized with a keen desire to see Holmes again, and to know how he was employing his extraordinary powers. His rooms were brilliantly lit, and, even as I looked up, I saw his tall spare figure pass twice in a dark silhouette against the blind. He was pacing the room swiftly, eagerly, with his head sunk upon his chest, and his hands clasped behind him. To me, who knew his every mood and habit, his attitude and manner told their own story. He was at work again. He had risen out of his drug-created dreams, and was hot upon the scent of some new problem. I rang the bell, and was shown up to the chamber which had formerly been in part my own.

His manner was not effusive. It seldom was; but he was glad, I think, to see me. With hardly a word spoken, but with a kindly eye, he waved me to an armchair, threw across his case of cigars, and indicated a spirit case and a gasogene in the corner. Then he stood before the fire, and looked me over in his singular introspective fashion.

"Wedlock suits you," he remarked. "I think, Watson, that you have put on seven and a half pounds since I saw you."

"Seven," I answered.

"Indeed, I should have thought a little more. Just a trifle more, I fancy, Watson. And in practice again, I observe. You did not tell me that you intended to go into harness."

"Then, how do you know?"

"I see it, I deduce it. How do I know that you have been getting yourself very wet lately, and that you have a most clumsy and careless servant girl?"

"My dear Holmes," said I, "this is too much. You would certainly have been burned had you lived a few centuries ago. It is true that I had a country walk on Thursday and came home in a dreadful mess; but, as I have changed my clothes, I can't imagine how you deduce it. As to Mary Jane, she is incorrigible, and my wife has given her notice; but there again I fail to see how you work it out."

He chuckled to himself and rubbed his long nervous hands together.

"It is simplicity itself," said he; "my eyes tell me that on the inside of your left shoe, just where the firelight strikes it, the leather is scored by six almost parallel cuts. Obviously they have been caused by someone who has very carelessly scraped round the edges of the sole in order to remove crusted mud from it. Hence, you see, my double deduction that you had been out in vile weather, and that you had a particularly malignant boot-slitting specimen of the London slavey. As to your practice, if a gentleman walks into my rooms smelling of idioform, with a black mark of nitrate of silver upon his right forefinger, and a bulge on the side of his top hat to show where he has secreted his stethoscope, I must be dull indeed if I do not pronounce him to be an active member of the medical profession."

I could not help laughing at the ease with which he explained his process of deduction. "When I hear you give your reasons," I remarked, "the thing always appears to me to be so ridiculously simple that I could easily do it myself, though at each successive instance of your reasoning I am baffled, until you explain your process. And yet I believe that my eyes are as good as yours."

"Quite so," he answered, lighting a cigarette, and throwing himself down into an armchair. "You see, but you do not observe. The distinction is clear. For example, you have frequently seen the steps which lead up from the hall to this room."

"Frequently."

"How often?"

"Well, some hundreds of times."

"Then how many are there?"

"How many! I don't know."

"Quite so! You have not observed. And yet you have seen. That is just my point. Now, I know that there are seventeen steps, because I have both seen and observed. By the way, since you are interested in these little problems, and since you are good enough to chronicle one or two of my trifling experiences, you may be interested in this." He threw over a sheet of thick pink-tinted notepaper which had been lying open upon the table. "It came by the last post," said he. "Read it aloud."

The note was undated, and without either signature or address.

"There will call upon you to-night, at a quarter to eight o'clock," it said, "a gentleman who desires to consult you upon a matter of the very deepest moment. Your recent services to one of the Royal Houses of Europe have shown that you are one who may safely be trusted with matters which are of an importance which can hardly be exaggerated. This account of you we have from all quarters received. Be in your chamber then at that hour, and do not take it amiss if your visitor wear a mask."

"This is indeed a mystery," I remarked. "What do you imagine that it means?"

"I have no data yet. It is a capital mistake to theorize before one has data. Insensibly one begins to twist facts to suit theories, instead of theories to suit facts. But the note itself. What do you deduce from it?"

I carefully examined the writing, and the paper upon which it was written.

"The man who wrote it was presumably well to do," I remarked, endeavouring to imitate my companion's processes. "Such paper could not be bought under half-a-crown a packet. It is peculiarly strong and stiff."

"Peculiar – that is the very word," said Holmes. "It is not an English paper at all. Hold it up to the light."

I did so, and saw a large E with a small g, a P, and a large G with a small t woven into the texture of the paper.

"What do you make of that?" asked Holmes.

"The name of the maker, no doubt; or his monogram, rather."

"Not at all. The *G* with the small *t* stands for 'Gesellschaft,' which is the German for 'Company.' It is a customary contraction like our 'Co.' *P*, of course, stands for 'Papier.' Now for the *Eg*. Let us glance at our Continental Gazetteer." He took down a heavy brown volume from his shelves. "Eglow, Eglonitz – here we are, Egria. It is in a German-speaking country – in Bohemia, not far from Carlsbad. 'Remarkable as being the scene of the death of Wallenstein, and for its numerous glass factories and paper mills.' Ha, ha, my boy, what do you make of that?" His eyes sparkled, and he sent up a great blue triumphant cloud from his cigarette.

"The paper was made in Bohemia," I said.

"Precisely. And the man who wrote the note is a German. Do you note the peculiar construction of the sentence – 'This account of you we have from all quarters received.' A Frenchman or Russian could not have written that. It is the German who is so uncourteous to his verbs. It only remains, therefore, to discover what is wanted by this German who writes upon Bohemian paper, and prefers wearing a mask to showing his face. And here he comes, if I am not mistaken, to resolve all our doubts."

As he spoke there was the sharp sound of horses' hoofs and grating wheels against the curb, followed by a sharp pull at the bell. Holmes whistled.

"A pair, by the sound," said he. "Yes," he continued, glancing out of the window. "A nice little brougham and a pair of beauties. A hundred and fifty guineas apiece. There's money in this case, Watson, if there is nothing else."

"I think that I had better go, Holmes."

"Not a bit, Doctor. Stay where you are. I am lost without my Boswell. And this promises to be interesting. It would be a pity to miss it."

"But your client – "

"Never mind him. I may want your help, and so may he. Here he comes. Sit down in that armchair, Doctor, and give us your best attention."

A slow and heavy step, which had been heard upon the stairs and in the passage, paused immediately outside the door. Then there was a loud and authoritative tap.

"Come in !" said Holmes.

A man entered who could hardly have been less than six feet six inches in height, with the chest and limbs of a Hercules. His dress was rich with a richness which would, in England, be looked upon as akin to bad taste. Heavy bands of Astrakhan were slashed across the sleeves and fronts of his double-breasted coat, while the deep blue cloak which was thrown over his shoulders was lined with flame-coloured silk, and secured at the neck with a brooch which consisted of a single flaming beryl. Boots which extended half way up his calves, and which were trimmed at the tops with rich brown fur, completed the impression of barbaric opulence which was suggested by his whole appearance. He carried a broad-brimmed hat in his hand, while he wore across the upper part of his face, extending down past the cheek-bones, a black vizard mask, which he had apparently adjusted that very moment, for his hand was still raised to it as he entered. From the lower part of the face he appeared to be a man of strong character, with a thick, hanging lip, and a long straight chin, suggestive of resolution pushed to the length of obstinacy.

"You had my note?" he asked, with a deep harsh voice and a strongly marked German accent. "I told you that I would call." He looked from one to the other of us, as if uncertain which to address.

"Pray take a seat," said Holmes. "This is my friend and colleague, Dr Watson, who is occasionally good enough to help me in my cases. Whom have I the honour to address?"

"You may address me as the Count Von Kramm, a Bohemian nobleman. I understand that this gentleman, your friend, is a man of honour and discretion, whom I may trust with a matter of the most extreme importance. If not, I should much prefer to communicate with you alone."

I rose to go, but Holmes caught me by the wrist and pushed me back into my chair. "It is both, or none," said he. "You may say before this gentleman anything which you may say to me."

The Count shrugged his broad shoulders. "Then I must begin," said he, "by binding you both to absolute secrecy for two years, at the end of that time the matter will be of no importance. At present it is not too much to say that it is of such weight that it may have an influence upon European history."

"I promise," said Holmes.

"And I."

"You will excuse this mask," continued our strange visitor. "The august person who employs me wishes his agent to be unknown to you, and I may confess at once that the title by which I have just called myself is not exactly my own."

"I was aware of it," said Holmes dryly.

"The circumstances are of great delicacy, and every precaution has to be taken to quench what might grow to be an immense scandal and seriously compromise one of the reigning families of Europe. To speak plainly, the matter implicates the great House of Ormstein, hereditary kings of Bohemia."

"I was also aware of that," murmured Holmes, settling himself down in his armchair, and closing his eyes.

Our visitor glanced with some apparent surprise at the languid, lounging figure of the man who had been no doubt depicted to him as the most incisive reasoner, and most energetic agent in Europe. Holmes slowly reopened his eyes, and looked impatiently at his gigantic client.

"If your Majesty would condescend to state your case," he remarked, "I should be better able to advise you."

The man sprang from his chair, and paced up and down the room in uncontrollable agitation. Then, with a gesture of desperation, he tore the mask from his face and hurled it upon the ground. "You are right," he cried, "I am the King. Why should I attempt to conceal it?"

"Why, indeed?" murmured Holmes. "Your Majesty had not spoken before I was aware that I was addressing Wilhelm Gottsreich Sigismond von Ormstein, Grand Duke of Cassel-Felstein, and hereditary King of Bohemia."

"But you can understand," said our strange visitor, sitting down once more and passing his hand over his high, white forehead, "you can understand that I am not accustomed to doing such business in my own person. Yet the matter was so delicate that I could not confide it to an agent without putting myself in his power. I have come *incognito* from Prague for the purpose of consulting you."

"Then, pray consult," said Holmes, shutting his eyes once more.

"The facts are briefly these: Some five years ago, during a lengthy visit to Warsaw, I made the acquaintance of the well-known adventuress Irene Adler. The name is no doubt familiar to you."

"Kindly look her up in my index, Doctor," murmured Holmes, without opening his eyes. For many years he had adopted a system of docketing all paragraphs concerning men and things, so that it was difficult to name a subject or a person on which he could not at once furnish information. In this case I found her biography sandwiched in between that of a Hebrew Rabbi and that of a staff-commander who had written a monograph upon the deep sea fishes.

"Let me see," said Holmes. "Hum! Born in New Jersey in the year 1858. Contralto – hum! La Scala, hum! Prima donna Imperial Opera of Warsaw – Yes! Retired from operatic stage – ha! Living in London – quite so! Your Majesty, as I understand, became entangled with this young person, wrote her some compromising letters, and is now desirous of getting those letters back."

"Precisely so. But how – "

"Was there a secret marriage?"

"None."

"No legal papers or certificates?"

"None."

"Then I fail to follow your Majesty. If this young person should produce her letters for blackmailing or other purposes, how is she to prove their authenticity?"

"There is the writing."

"Pooh, pooh! Forgery."

"My private notepaper."

"Stolen."

"My own seal."

"Imitated."

"My photograph."

"Bought."

"We were both in the photograph."

"Oh dear! That is very bad! Your Majesty has indeed committed an indiscretion."

"I was mad – insane."

"You have compromised yourself seriously."

"I was only Crown Prince then. I was young. I am but thirty now."

"It must be recovered."

"We have tried and failed."

"Your Majesty must pay. It must be bought."

"She will not sell."

"Stolen, then."

"Five attempts have been made. Twice burglars in my pay ransacked her house. Once we diverted her luggage when she travelled. Twice she has been waylaid. There has been no result."

"No sign of it?"

"Absolutely none."

Holmes laughed. "It is quite a pretty little problem," said he.

"But a very serious one to me," returned the King, reproachfully.

"Very, indeed. And what does she propose to do with the photograph?"

"To ruin me."

"But how?"

"I am about to be married."

"So I have heard."

"To Clotilde Lothman von Saxe-Meningen, second daughter of the King of Scandinavia. You may know the strict principles of her family. She is herself the very soul of delicacy. A shadow of a doubt as to my conduct would bring the matter to an end."

"And Irene Adler?"

"Threatens to send them the photograph. And she will do it. I know that she will do it. You do not know her, but she has a soul of steel. She has the face of the most beautiful of women, and the mind of the most resolute of men. Rather than I should marry another woman, there are no lengths to which she would not go – none."

"You are sure that she has not sent it yet?"

"I am sure."

"And why?"

"Because she has said that she would send it on the day when the betrothal was publicly proclaimed. That will be next Monday."

"Oh, then, we have three days yet," said Holmes, with a yawn. "That is very fortunate, as I have one or two matters of importance to look into just at present. Your Majesty will, of course, stay in London for the present?"

"Certainly. You will find me at the Langham, under the name of the Count Von Kramm."

"Then I shall drop you a line to let you know how we progress."

"Pray do so. I shall be all anxiety."

"Then, as to money?"

"You have *carte blanche*."

"Absolutely?"

"I tell you that I would give one of the provinces of my kingdom to have that photograph."

"And for present expenses?"

The King took a heavy chamois leather bag from under his cloak, and laid it on the table.

"There are three hundred pounds in gold, and seven hundred in notes," he said.

Holmes scribbled a receipt upon a sheet of his note-book, and handed it to him.

"And mademoiselle's address?" he asked.

"Is Briony Lodge, Serpentine-avenue, St John's Wood."

Holmes took a note of it. "One other question," said he. "Was the photograph a cabinet?"

"It was."

"Then, good-night, your Majesty, and I trust that we shall soon have some good news for you. And good-night, Watson," he added, as the wheels of the Royal brougham rolled down the street. "If you will be good enough to call to-morrow afternoon, at three o'clock, I should like to chat this little matter over with you."

II

At three o'clock precisely I was at Baker-street, but Holmes had not yet returned. The landlady informed me that he had left the house shortly after eight o'clock in the morning. I sat down beside the fire, however, with the intention of awaiting him, however long he might be. I was already deeply interested in his inquiry, for, though it was surrounded by none of the grim and strange features which were associated with the two crimes which I have elsewhere recorded, still, the nature of the case and the exalted station of his client gave it a character of its own. Indeed, apart from the nature of the investigation which my friend had on hand, there was something in his masterly grasp of a situation, and his keen, incisive reasoning, which made it a pleasure to me to study his system of work, and to follow the quick, subtle methods by which he disentangled the most inextricable mysteries. So accustomed was I to his invariable success that the very possibility of his failing had ceased to enter into my head.

It was close upon four before the door opened, and a drunken-looking groom, ill-kempt and side-whiskered, with an inflamed face and disreputable clothes, walked into the room. Accustomed as I was to my friend's amazing powers in the use of disguises, I had to look three times before I was certain that it was indeed he. With a nod he vanished into the bedroom, whence he emerged in five minutes tweed-suited and respectable, as of old. Putting his hands into his pockets, he stretched out his legs in front of the fire, and laughed heartily for some minutes.

"Well, really!" he cried, and then he choked; and laughed again until he was obliged to lie back, limp and helpless, in the chair.

"What is it?"

"It's quite too funny. I am sure you could never guess how I employed my morning, or what I ended by doing."

"I can't imagine. I suppose that you have been watching the habits, and perhaps the house, of Miss Irene Adler."

"Quite so, but the sequel was rather unusual. I will tell you, however. I left the house a little after eight o'clock this morning, in the character of a groom out of work. There is a wonderful sympathy and freemasonry among horsey men. Be one of them, and you will know all that there is to know. I soon found Briony Lodge. It is a *bijou* villa, with a garden at the back, but built out in front right up to the road, two stories. Chubb lock to the door. Large sitting-room on the right side, well furnished, with long windows almost to the floor, and those preposterous English window fasteners which a child could open. Behind there was nothing remarkable, save that the passage window could be reached from the top of the coach-house. I walked round it and examined it closely from every point of view, but without noting anything else of interest.

"I then lounged down the street, and found, as I expected, that there was a mews in a lane which runs down by one wall of the garden. I lent the ostlers a hand in rubbing down their horses, and I received in exchange twopence, a glass of half-and-half, two fills of shag tobacco, and as much information as I could desire about Miss Adler, to say nothing of half a dozen other people in the neighbourhood in whom I was not in the least interested, but whose biographies I was compelled to listen to."

"And what of Irene Adler?" I asked.

"Oh, she has turned all the men's heads down in that part. She is the daintiest thing under a bonnet on this planet. So say the Serpentine-mews, to a man. She lives quietly, sings at concerts, drives out at five every day, and returns at seven sharp for dinner. Seldom goes out at other times, except when she sings. Has only one male visitor, but a good deal of him. He is dark, handsome, and dashing; never calls less than once a day, and often twice. He is a Mr Godfrey Norton, of the Inner Temple. See the advantages of a cabman as a confidant. They had driven him home a dozen times from Serpentine-mews, and knew all about him. When I had listened to all that they had to tell, I began to walk up and down near Briony Lodge once more, and to think over my plan of campaign.

"This Godfrey Norton was evidently an important factor in the matter. He was a lawyer. That sounded ominous. What was the relation between them, and what the object of his repeated visits? Was she his client, his friend, or his mistress? If the former, she had probably transferred the photograph to his keeping. If the latter, it was less likely. On the issue of this question depended whether I should continue my work at Briony Lodge, or turn my attention to the gentleman's chambers in the Temple. It was a delicate point, and it widened the field of my inquiry. I fear that I bore you with these details, but I have to let you see my little difficulties, if you are to understand the situation."

"I am following you closely," I answered.

"I was still balancing the matter in my mind, when a hansom cab drove up to Briony Lodge, and a gentleman sprang out. He was a remarkably handsome man, dark, aquiline, and moustached – evidently the man of whom I had heard. He appeared to be in a great hurry, shouted to the cabman to wait, and brushed past the maid who opened the door with the air of a man who was thoroughly at home.

"He was in the house about half an hour, and I could catch glimpses of him, in the windows of the sitting-room, pacing up and down, talking excitedly and waving his arms. Of her I could see nothing. Presently he emerged, looking even more flurried than before. As he stepped up to the cab, he pulled a gold watch from his pocket and looked at it earnestly. 'Drive like the devil,' he shouted, 'first to Gross & Hankey's in Regent-street, and then to the church of St Monica in the Edgware-road. Half a guinea if you do it in twenty minutes!'

"Away they went, and I was just wondering whether I should not do well to follow them, when up the lane came a neat little landau, the coachman with his coat only half buttoned, and his tie under his ear, while all the tags of his harness were sticking out of the buckles. It hadn't pulled up before she shot out of the hall door and into it. I only caught a glimpse of her at the moment, but she was a lovely woman, with a face that a man might die for.

"'The Church of St Monica, John,' she cried, 'and half a sovereign if you reach it in twenty minutes.'

"This was quite too good to lose, Watson. I was just balancing whether I should run for it, or whether I should perch behind her landau, when a cab came through the street. The driver looked twice at such a shabby fare; but I jumped in before he could object. 'The Church of St Monica,' said I, 'and half a sovereign if you reach it in twenty minutes.' It was twenty-five minutes to twelve, and of course it was clear enough what was in the wind.

"My cabby drove fast. I don't think I ever drove faster, but the others were there before us. The cab and the landau with their steaming horses were in front of the door when I arrived. I paid the man and hurried into the church. There was not a soul there save the two whom I had followed, and a surpliced clergyman, who seemed to be expostulating with them. They were all three standing in a knot in front of the altar. I lounged up the side aisle like any other idler who has dropped into a church. Suddenly, to my surprise, the three at the altar faced round to me, and Godfrey Norton came runing as hard as he could towards me.

" 'Thank God!' he cried. 'You'll do. Come! Come!'

" 'What then?' I asked.

" 'Come, man, come, only three minutes, or it won't be legal.'

"I was half dragged up to the altar, and before I knew where I was, I found myself mumbling responses which were whispered in my ear, and vouching for things of which I knew nothing, and generally assisting in the secure tying up of Irene Adler, spinster, to Godfrey Norton, bachelor. It was all done in an instant, and there was the gentleman thanking me on the one side and the lady on the other, while the clergyman beamed on me in front. It was the most preposterous position in which I ever found myself in my life, and it was the thought of it that started me laughing just now. It seems that there had been some informality about their licence, that the clergyman absolutely refused to marry them without a witness of some sort, and that my lucky appearance saved the bridegroom from having to sally out into the streets in search of a best man. The bride gave me a sovereign, and I mean to wear it on my watch chain in memory of the occasion."

"This is a very unexpected turn of affairs," said I; "and what then?"

"Well, I found my plans very seriously menaced. It looked as if the pair might take an immediate departure, and so necessitate very prompt and energetic measures on my part. At the church door, however, they separated, he driving back to the Temple, and she to her own house. 'I shall drive out in the Park at five as usual,' she said as she left him. I heard no more. They drove away in different directions, and I went off to make my own arrangements."

"Which are?"

"Some cold beef and a glass of beer," he answered, ringing the bell. "I have been too busy to think of food, and I am likely to be busier still this evening. By the way, Doctor, I shall want your co-operation."

"I shall be delighted."

"You don't mind breaking the law?"

"Not in the least."

"Nor running a chance of arrest?"

"Not in a good cause."

"Oh, the cause is excellent!"

"Then I am your man."

"I was sure that I might rely on you."

"But what is it you wish?"

"When Mrs Turner has brought in the tray I will make it clear to you. Now," he said, as he turned hungrily on the simple fare that our landlady had provided, "I must discuss it while I eat, for I have not much time. It is nearly five now. In two hours we must be on the scene of action. Miss Irene, or Madame, rather, returns from her drive at seven. We must be at Briony Lodge to meet her."

"And what then?"

"You must leave that to me. I have already arranged what is to occur. There is only one point on which I must insist. You must not interfere, come what may. You understand?"

"I am to be neutral?"

"To do nothing whatever. There will probably be some small unpleasantness. Do not join in it. It will end in my being conveyed into the house. Four or five minutes afterwards the sitting-room window will open. You are to station yourself close to that open window."

"Yes."

"You are to watch me, for I will be visible to you."

"Yes."

"And when I raise my hand – so – you will throw into the room what I give you to throw, and will, at the same time, raise the cry of fire. You quite follow me?"

"Entirely."

"It is nothing very formidable," he said, taking a long cigar-shaped roll from his pocket. "It is an ordinary plumber's smoke rocket, fitted with a cap at either end to make it self-lighting. Your task is confined to that. When you raise your cry of fire, it will be taken up by quite a number of people. You may then walk to the end of the street, and I will rejoin you in ten minutes. I hope that I have made myself clear?"

"I am to remain neutral, to get near the window, to watch you, and, at the signal, to throw in this object, then to raise the cry of fire, and to wait you at the corner of the street."

"Precisely."

"Then you may entirely rely on me."

"That is excellent. I think perhaps it is almost time that I prepared for the new role I have to play."

He disappeared into his bedroom, and returned in a few minutes in the character of an amiable and simple-minded Nonconformist clergyman. His broad black hat, his baggy trousers, his white tie, his sympathetic smile, and general look of peering and benevolent curiosity were such as Mr John Hare alone could have equalled. It was not merely that Holmes changed his costume. His expression, his manner, his very soul seemed to vary with every fresh part that he assumed. The stage lost a fine actor, even as science lost an acute reasoner, when he became a specialist in crime.

It was a quarter past six when we left Baker-street, and it still wanted ten minutes to the hour when we found ourselves in Serpentine-avenue. It was already dusk, and the lamps were just being lighted as we paced up and down in front of Briony Lodge, waiting for the coming of its occupant. The house was just such as I had pictured it from Sherlock Holmes' succinct description, but the locality appeared to be less private than I expected. On the contrary, for a small street in a quiet neighbourhood, it was remarkably animated. There was a group of shabbily-dressed men smoking and laughing in a corner, a scissors grinder with his wheel, two guardsmen who were flirting with a nurse-girl, and several well-dressed young men who were lounging up and down with cigars in their mouths.

"You see," remarked Holmes, as we paced to and fro in front of the house, "this marriage rather simplifies matters. The photograph becomes a double-edged weapon now. The chances are that she would be as averse to its being seen by Mr Godfrey Norton, as our client is to its coming to the eyes of his Princess. Now the question is – Where are we to find the photograph?"

"Where, indeed?"

"It is most unlikely that she carries it about with her. It is cabinet size. Too large for easy concealment about a woman's dress. She knows that the King is capable of having her waylaid and searched. Two attempts of the sort have already been made. We may take it then that she does not carry it about with her."

"Where, then?"

"Her banker or her lawyer. There is that double possibility. But I am inclined to think neither. Women are naturally secretive, and they like to do their own secreting. Why should she hand it over to any one else? She could trust her own guardianship, but she could not tell what indirect or political influence might be brought to bear upon a business man. Besides, remember that she had resolved to use it within a few days. It must be where she can lay her hands upon it. It must be in her own house."

"But it has twice been burgled."

"Pshaw! They did not know how to look."

"But how will you look?"

"I will not look."

"What then?"

"I will get her to show me."

"But she will refuse."

"She will not be able to. But I hear the rumble of wheels. It is her carriage. Now carry out my orders to the letter."

As he spoke the gleam of the sidelights of a carriage came round the curve of the avenue. It was a smart little landau which rattled up to the door of Briony Lodge. As it pulled up one of the loafing men at the corner dashed forward to open the door in the hope of earning a copper, but was elbowed away by another loafer who had rushed up with the same intention. A fierce quarrel broke out, which was increased by the two guardsmen, who took sides with one of the loungers, and by the scissors grinder, who was equally hot upon the other side. A blow was struck, and in an instant the lady, who had stepped from her carriage, was the centre of a little knot of flushed and struggling men who struck savagely at each other with their fists and sticks. Holmes dashed into the crowd to protect the lady; but, just as he reached her, he gave a cry and dropped to the ground, with the blood running freely down his face. At his fall the guardsmen took to their heels in one direction and the loungers in the other, while a number of better dressed people who had watched the scuffle without taking part in it, crowded in to help the lady and to attend to the injured man. Irene Adler, as I will still call her, had hurried up the steps; but she stood at the top with her superb figure outlined against the lights of the hall, looking back into the street.

"Is the poor gentleman much hurt?" she asked.

"He is dead," cried several voices.

"No, no, there's life in him," shouted another. "But he'll be gone before you can get him to hospital."

"He's a brave fellow," said a woman. "They would have had the lady's purse and watch if it hadn't been for him. They were a gang, and a rough one too. Ah, he's breathing now."

"He can't lie in the street. May we bring him in, marm?"

"Surely. Bring him into the sitting-room. There is a comfortable sofa. This way, please!"

Slowly and solemnly he was borne into Briony Lodge, and laid out in the principal room, while I still observed the proceedings from my post by the window. The lamps had been lit, but the blinds had not been drawn, so that I could see Holmes as he lay upon the couch. I do not know whether he was seized with compunction at that moment for the part he was playing, but I know that I never felt more heartily ashamed of myself in my life than when I saw the beautiful creature against whom I was conspiring, or the grace and kindliness with which she waited upon the injured man. And yet it would be the blackest treachery to Holmes to draw back now from the part which he had entrusted to me. I hardened my heart and took the smoke rocket from under my ulster. After all, I thought, we are not injuring her. We are but preventing her from injuring another.

Holmes had sat up upon the couch, and I saw him motion like a man who is in want of air. A maid rushed across and threw open the window. At the same instant I saw him raise his hand, and at the signal I tossed my rocket into the room with a cry of "Fire." The word was no sooner out of my mouth than the whole crowd of spectators, well dressed and ill – gentlemen, ostlers, and servant maids – joined in a general shriek of "Fire." Thick clouds of smoke curled through the room, and out at the open window. I caught a glimpse of rushing figures, and a moment later the voice of Holmes from within, assuring them that it was a false alarm. Slipping through the shouting crowd I made my way to the corner of the street, and in ten minutes was rejoiced to find my friend's arm in mine, and to get away from the scene of the uproar. He walked swiftly and in silence for some few minutes, until we had turned down one of the quiet streets which lead towards the Edgeware-road.

"You did it very nicely, Doctor," he remarked. "Nothing could have been better. It is all right."

"You have the photograph!"

"I know where it is."

"And how did you find out?"

"She showed me, as I told you that she would."

"I am still in the dark."

"I do not wish to make a mystery," said he, laughing. "The matter was perfectly simple. You, of course, saw that every one in the street was an accomplice. They were all engaged for the evening."

"I guessed as much."

"Then, when the row broke out, I had a little moist red paint in the palm of my hand. I rushed forward, fell down, clapped my hand to my face, and became a piteous spectacle. It is an old trick."

"That also I could fathom."

"Then they carried me in. She was bound to have me in. What else could she do? And into her sitting-room, which was the very room which I suspected. It lay between that and her bedroom, and I was determined to see which. They laid me on a couch, I motioned for air, they were compelled to open the window, and you had your chance."

"How did that help you?"

"It was all-important. When a woman thinks that her house is on fire, her instinct is at once to rush to the thing which she values most. It is a perfectly overpowering impulse, and I have more than once taken advantage of it. In the case of the Darlington Substitution Scandal it was of use to me, and also in the Arnsworth Castle business. A married woman grabs at her baby – an unmarried one reaches for her jewel box. Now it was clear to me that our lady of to-day had nothing in the house more precious to her than what we are in quest of. She would rush to secure it. The alarm of fire was admirably done. The smoke and shouting was enough to shake nerves of steel. She responded beautifully. The photograph is in a recess behind a sliding panel just above the right pull. She was there in an instant, and I caught a glimpse of it as she half drew it out. When I cried out that it was a false alarm, she replaced it, glanced at the rocket, rushed from the room and I have not seen her since. I rose, and, making my excuses, escaped from the house. I hesitated whether to attempt to secure the photograph at once; but the coachman had come in, and as he was watching me narrowly, it seemed safer to wait. A little over-precipitance may ruin all."

"And now?" I asked.

"Our quest is practically finished. I shall call with the King to-morrow, and with you, if you care to come with us. We will be shown into the sitting-room to wait for the lady, but it is probable that when she comes she may find neither us nor the photograph. It might be a satisfaction to His Majesty to regain it with his own hands."

"And when will you call?"

"At eight in the morning. She will not be up, so that we shall have a clear field. Besides, we must be prompt, for this marriage may mean a complete change in her life and habits. I must wire to the King without delay."

We had reached Baker-street, and had stopped at the door. He was searching his pockets for the key, when some one passing said:

"Good-night, Mister Sherlock Holmes."

There were several people on the pavement at the time, but the greeting appeared to come from a slim youth in an ulster who had hurried by.

"I've heard that voice before," said Holmes, staring down the dimly lit street. "Now, I wonder who the deuce that could have been."

III

I slept at Baker-street that night, and we were engaged upon our toast and coffee when the King of Bohemia rushed into the room.

"You have really got it!" he cried, grasping Sherlock Holmes by either shoulder, and looking eagerly into his face.

"Not yet."

"But you have hopes?"

"I have hopes."

"Then, come. I am all impatience to be gone."

"We must have a cab."

"No, my brougham is waiting."

"Then that will simplify matters." We descended, and started off once more for Briony Lodge.

"Irene Adler is married," remarked Holmes.

"Married! When?"

"Yesterday."

"But to whom?"

"To an English lawyer named Norton."

"But she could not love him?"

"I am in hopes that she does."

"And why in hopes?"

"Because it would spare your Majesty all fear of future annoyance. If the lady loves her husband, she does not love your Majesty. If she does not love your Majesty, there is no reason why she should interfere with your Majesty's plan."

"It is true. And yet −! Well! I wish she had been of my own station! What a queen she would have made!" He relapsed into a moody silence which was not broken until we drew up in Serpentine-avenue.

The door of Briony Lodge was open, and an elderly woman stood upon the steps. She watched us with a sardonic eye as we stepped from the brougham.

"Mr Sherlock Holmes, I believe?" said she.

"I am Mr Holmes," answered my companion, looking at her with a questioning and rather startled gaze.

"Indeed! My mistress told me that you were likely to call. She left this morning with her husband, by the 5.15 train from Charing-cross, for the Continent."

"What!" Sherlock Holmes staggered back, white with chagrin and surprise. "Do you mean that she has left England?"

"Never to return."

"And the papers?" asked the King, hoarsely. "All is lost."

"We shall see." He pushed past the servant, and rushed into the drawing-room, followed by the King and myself. The furniture was scattered about in every direction, with dismantled shelves, and open drawers, as if the lady had hurriedly ransacked them before her flight. Holmes rushed at the bell-pull, tore back a small sliding shutter, and, plunging in his hand, pulled out a photograph and a letter. The photograph was of Irene Adler herself in evening dress, the letter was superscribed to "Sherlock Holmes, Esq. To be left till called for." My friend tore it open, and we all three read it together. It was dated at midnight of the preceding night, and ran in this way:

My Dear Mr Sherlock Holmes,

You really did it very well. You took me in completely. Until after the alarm of fire, I had not a suspicion. But then, when I found how I had betrayed myself, I began to think. I had been warned against you months ago. I had been told that if the King employed an agent, it would certainly be you. And your address had been given me. Yet, with all this, you made me reveal what you wanted to know. Even after I became suspicious, I found it hard to think evil of such a dear, kind old clergyman. But, you know, I have been trained as an actress myself. Male costume is nothing new to me. I often take advantage of the freedom which it gives. I sent John, the coachman, to watch you, ran upstairs, got into my walking clothes, as I call them, and came down just as you departed.

"Well, I followed you to your door, and so made sure that I was really an object of interest to the celebrated Mr Sherlock Holmes. Then I, rather imprudently, wished you good-night, and started for the Temple to see my husband.

"We both thought the best resource was flight when pursued by so formidable an antagonist; so you will find the nest empty when you call to-morrow. As to the photograph, your client may rest in peace. I love and am loved by a better man than he. The King may do what he will without hindrance from one whom he has cruelly wronged. I keep it only to safeguard myself, and to preserve a weapon which will always secure me from any steps which he might take in the future. I leave a photograph which he might care to possess; and I remain, dear Mr Sherlock Holmes, very truly yours,

IRENE NORTON, née ADLER.

"What a woman – oh, what a woman!" cried the King of Bohemia, when we had all three read this epistle. "Did I not tell you how quick and resolute she was? Would she not have made an admirable queen? Is it not a pity she was not on my level?"

"From what I have seen of the lady, she seems, indeed, to be on a very different level to your Majesty," said Holmes, coldly. "I am sorry that I have not been able to bring your Majesty's business to a more successful conclusion."

"On the contrary, my dear sir," cried the King. "Nothing could be more successful. I know that her word is inviolate. The photograph is now as safe as if it were in the fire."

"I am glad to hear your Majesty say so."

"I am immensely indebted to you. Pray tell me in what way I can reward you. This ring – " He slipped an emerald snake ring from his finger, and held it out upon the palm of his hand.

"Your Majesty has something which I should value even more highly," said Holmes.

"You have but to name it."

"This photograph!"

The King stared at him in amazement.

"Irene's photograph!" he cried. "Certainly, if you wish it."

"I thank your Majesty. Then there is no more to be done in the matter. I have the honour to wish you a very good morning." He bowed, and, turning away without observing the hand which the King had stretched out to him, he set off in my company for his chambers.

And that was how a great scandal threatened to affect the kingdom of Bohemia, and how the best plans of Mr Sherlock Holmes were beaten by a woman's wit. He used to make merry over the cleverness of women, but I have not heard him do it of late. And when he speaks of Irene Adler, or when he refers to her photograph, it is always under the honourable title of *the* woman.

Israel Zangwill

Cheating the Gallows

Israel Zangwill (1864–1926) was one of the handful of authors who had ventured into the field of mystery fiction before Sherlock Holmes made it his own. The Big Bow Mystery *appeared just before the first of the Holmes short stories, and it remains one of the minor classics of the period – though it was not, as some have claimed, the very first locked-room mystery. Zangwill drew on his East London background in other books like* Children of the Ghetto *and* The King of the Schnorrers, *and was busy as a journalist and as a worker for Jewish causes in the early years of the century.*

"Cheating the Gallows", first published in 1893, is an ingenious tale with a strangely modern theme by this excellent writer, which deserves to be better known than it is.

THEY SAY THAT a union of opposites makes the happiest marriage, and perhaps it is on the same principle that men who chum together are always so oddly assorted. You shall find a man of letters sharing diggings with an auctioneer, and a medical student pigging with a stockbroker's clerk. Perhaps each thus escapes the temptation to talk "shop" in his hours of leisure, while he supplements his own experience of life by his companion's.

There could not be an odder couple than Tom Peters and Everard G. Roxdal – the contrast began with their names, and ran through the entire chapter. They had a bedroom and a sitting-room in common, but it would not be easy to find what else. To his landlady, worthy Mrs Seacon, Tom Peters's profession was a little vague, but everybody knew that Roxdal was the manager of the City and Suburban Bank, and it puzzled her to think why a bank manager should live with such a seedy-looking person, who smoked clay pipes and sipped whiskey and water all the evening when he was at home. For Roxdal was as spruce and erect as his fellow lodger was round-shouldered and shabby, he never smoked, and he confined himself to a small glass of claret at dinner.

It is possible to live with a man and see very little of him. Where each of the partners lives his own life in his own way, with his own circle of friends and external amusements, days may go by without the men having five minutes together. Perhaps this explains why these partnerships jog along so much more peaceably than marriages, where the chain is drawn so much more tightly and galls the wedded rather than links them. Diverse, however, as were the hours and habits of Peters and Roxdal, they often breakfasted together, and they agreed in one thing – they never stayed out at night. For the rest, Peters sought his diversions in the company of journalists, and frequented debating rooms, where he propounded the most iconoclastic views; while Roxdal had highly respectable houses open to him in the suburbs and was, in fact, engaged to be married to Clara Newell, the charming daughter of a retired corn merchant, a widower with no other child.

Clara naturally took up a good deal of Roxdal's time, and he often dressed to go to the play with her, while Peters stayed at home in a faded dressing-gown and loose slippers. Mrs Seacon liked to see gentlemen about the house in evening dress, and made comparisons not favourable to Peters. And this in spite of the fact that he gave her infinitely less trouble than the younger man. It was Peters who first took the apartments, and it was characteristic of his easy-going temperament that he was so openly and naïvely delighted with the view of the Thames obtainable from the bedroom window, that Mrs Seacon was emboldened to ask twenty-five per cent more than she had intended. She soon returned to her normal terms, however, when his friend Roxdal called the next day to inspect the rooms, and overwhelmed her with a demonstration of their numerous shortcomings. He pointed out that their being on the ground floor was not an advantage, but a disadvantage, since they were nearer the noises of the street – in fact, the house being a corner one, the noises of two streets. Roxdal continued to exhibit the same finicking temperament in the petty details of the ménage. His shirt fronts were never sufficiently starched, nor his boots sufficiently polished. Tom Peters, having no regard for rigid linen, was always good-tempered and satisfied, and never acquired the respect of his landlady. He wore blue-check shirts and loose ties even on Sundays. It is true he did not go to church, but slept on till Roxdal returned from morning service, and even then it was difficult to get him out of bed, or to make him hurry up his toilette operations. Often the mid-day meal would be smoking on the table while Peters would still be smoking in the bed, and Roxdal, with his head thrust through the folding doors that separated the bedroom from the sitting-room, would be adjuring the sluggard to arise and shake off his slumbers, and threatening to sit down without him, lest the dinner be spoiled. In revenge, Tom was usually up first on week-days, sometimes at such unearthly hours that Polly had not yet removed the boots from outside the bedroom door, and would bawl down to the kitchen for his shaving water. For Tom, lazy and indolent as he was, shaved with the unfailing regularity of a man to whom shaving has become an instinct. If he had not kept fairly regular hours, Mrs Seacon would have set him down as an actor, so clean shaven was he. Roxdal did not shave. He wore a full beard, and being a fine figure of a man to boot, no uneasy investor could look upon him without being reassured as to the stability of the bank he managed so successfully. And thus the two men lived in an economical comradeship, all the firmer, perhaps, for their incongruities.

It was on a Sunday afternoon in the middle of October, ten days after Roxdal had settled in his new rooms, that Clara Newell paid her first visit to him there. She enjoyed a good deal of liberty, and did not mind accepting his invitation to tea. The corn merchant, himself indifferently educated, had an exaggerated sense of the value of culture, and so Clara, who had artistic tastes without much actual talent, had gone in for painting, and might be seen, in pretty smocks, copying pictures in the Museum. At one time it looked as if she might be reduced to working seriously at her art, for Satan, who still finds mischief for idle hands to do, had persuaded her father to embark the fruits of years of toil in bubble companies. However, things turned out not so bad as they might have been; a little was saved from the wreck, and the appearance of a suitor, in the person of Everard G. Roxdal, insured her a future of competence, if not of the luxury she had been entitled to expect. She had a good deal of affection for Everard, who was unmistakably a clever man, as well as a good-looking one. The prospect seemed fair and cloudless. Nothing presaged the terrible storm that was about to break over these two lives. Nothing had ever for a moment come to vex their mutual contentment, till this Sunday afternoon. The October sky, blue and sunny, with an Indian summer sultriness, seemed an exact image of her life, with its aftermath of a happiness that had once seemed blighted.

Everard had always been so attentive, so solicitous, that she was as much surprised as chagrined to find that he had apparently forgotten the appointment. Hearing her astonished interrogation of Polly in the passage, Tom shambled from the sitting-room in his loose slippers and his blue-check shirt, with his eternal clay pipe in his mouth, and informed her that Roxdal had gone out suddenly.

"G-g-one out," stammered poor Clara, all confused. "But he asked me to come to tea."

"Oh, you're Miss Newell, I suppose," said Tom.

"Yes, I am Miss Newell."

"He has told me a great deal about you, but I wasn't able honestly to congratulate him on his choice till now."

Clara blushed uneasily under the compliment, and under the ardour of his admiring gaze. Instinctively she distrusted the man. The very first tones of his deep bass voice gave her a peculiar shudder. And then his impoliteness in smoking that vile clay was so gratuitous.

"Oh, then you must be Mr Peters," she said in return. "He has often spoken to me of you."

"Ah!" said Tom, laughingly, "I suppose he's told you all my vices. That accounts for your not being surprised at my Sunday attire."

She smiled a little, showing a row of pearly teeth. "Everard ascribes to you all the virtues," she said.

"Now that's what I call a friend!" he cried, ecstatically. "But won't you come in? He must be back in a moment. He surely would not break an appointment with you." The admiration latent in the accentuation of the last pronoun was almost offensive to her.

She shook her head. She had a just grievance against Everard, and would punish him by going away indignantly.

"Do let me give you a cup of tea," Tom pleaded. "You must be awfully thirsty this sultry weather. There! I will make a bargain with you! If you will come in now, I promise to clear out the moment Everard returns, and not spoil your tête-à-tête." But Clara was obstinate; she did not at all relish this man's society, and besides, she was not going to throw away her grievance against Everard. "I know Everard will slang me dreadfully when he comes in if I let you go," Tom urged. "Tell me at least where he can find you."

"I am going to take the 'bus at Charing Cross, and I'm going straight home," Clara announced determinedly. She put up her parasol, and went up the street into the Strand. A cold shadow seemed to have fallen over all things. But just as she was getting into the 'bus, a hansom dashed down Trafalgar Square, and a well-known voice hailed her. The hansom stopped, and Everard got out.

"I'm so glad you're a bit late," he said. "I was called out unexpectedly, and have been trying to rush back in time. You wouldn't have found me if you had been punctual. But I thought," he added, laughing, "I could rely on you as a woman."

"I was punctual," Clara said angrily. "I was not getting out of this 'bus, as you seem to imagine, but into it, and was going home."

"My darling!" he cried remorsefully. "A thousand apologies." The regret on his handsome face soothed her. He took the rose he was wearing in the buttonhole of his fashionably-cut coat and gave it to her.

"Why were you so cruel?" he murmured, as she nestled against him in the hansom. "Think of my despair if I had come home to hear you had come and gone. Why didn't you wait a few moments?"

A shudder traversed her frame. "Not with that man, Peters!" she murmured.

"Not with that man, Peters!" he echoed sharply. "What is the matter with Peters?"

"I don't know," she said. "I don't like him."

"Clara," he said, half sternly, half cajolingly, "I thought you were above these feminine weaknesses. You are punctual, strive also to be reasonable. Tom is my best friend. There is nothing Tom would not do for me, or I for Tom. You must like him, Clara; you must, if only for my sake."

"I'll try," Clara promised, and then he kissed her in gratitude and broad daylight.

"You'll be very nice to him at tea, won't you?" he said anxiously. "I shouldn't like you two to be bad friends."

"I don't want to be bad friends," Clara protested; "only the moment I saw him a strange repulsion and mistrust came over me."

"You are quite wrong about him – quite wrong," he assured her earnestly. "When you know him better, you'll find him the best of fellows. Oh, I know," he said suddenly, "I suppose he was very untidy, and you women go so much by appearances!"

"Not at all," Clara retorted. "'Tis you men who go by appearances."

"Yes, you do. That's why you care for me," he said, smiling.

She assured him it wasn't, that she didn't care for him only because he plumed himself, but he smiled on. His smile died away, however, when he entered his rooms and found Tom nowhere.

"I daresay you've made him run about hunting for me," he grumbled unhappily.

"Perhaps he knew I'd come back, and went away to leave us together," she answered. "He said he would when you came."

"And yet you say you don't like him!"

She smiled reassuringly. Inwardly, however, she felt pleased at the man's absence.

If Clara Newell could have seen Tom Peters carrying on with Polly in the passage, she might have felt justified in her prejudice against him. It must be confessed, though, that Everard also carried on with Polly. Alas! it is to be feared that men are much of a muchness where women are concerned; shabby men and smart men, bank managers and journalists, bachelors and semi-detached bachelors. Perhaps it was a mistake after all to say the chums had nothing patently in common. Everard, I am afraid, kissed Polly rather more often than Clara, and although it was because he respected her less, the reason would perhaps not have been sufficiently consoling to his affianced wife. For Polly was pretty, especially on alternate Sunday afternoons, and when at ten p.m. she returned from her outings, she was generally met in the passage by one or the other of the men. Polly liked to receive the homage of real gentlemen, and set her white cap at all indifferently. Thus, just before Clara knocked on that memorable Sunday afternoon, Polly, being confined to the house by the unwritten code regulating the lives of servants, was amusing herself by flirting with Peters.

"You are fond of me a little bit," the graceless Tom whispered, "aren't you?"

"You know I am, sir," Polly replied.

"You don't care for anyone else in the house?"

"Oh, no sir, and never let anyone kiss me but you. I wonder how it is, sir?" Polly replied ingenuously.

"Give me another," Tom answered.

She gave him another, and tripped to the door to answer Clara's knock.

And that very evening, when Clara was gone and Tom still out, Polly turned without the faintest atom of scrupulosity, or even jealousy, to the more fascinating Roxdal, and accepted his amorous advances. If it would seem at first sight that Everard had less excuse for such frivolity than his friend, perhaps the seriousness he showed in this interview may throw a different light upon the complex character of the man.

"You're quite sure you don't care for anyone but me?" he asked earnestly.

"Of course not, sir!" Polly replied indignantly. "How could I?"

"But you care for that soldier I saw you out with last Sunday?"

"Oh, no sir, he's only my young man," she said apologetically.

"Would you give him up?" he asked suddenly.

Polly's pretty face took a look of terror. "I couldn't, sir! He'd kill me. He's such a jealous brute, you've no idea."

"Yes, but suppose I took you away from here?" he whispered eagerly. "Some place where he couldn't find you – South America, Africa, somewhere thousands of miles away."

"Oh, sir, you frighten me!" whispered Polly, cowering before his ardent eyes, which shone in the dimly-lit passage.

"Would you come with me?" he entreated. She did not answer; she shook herself free and ran into the kitchen, trembling with a vague fear.

One morning, earlier than his earliest hour of demanding shaving water, Tom rang the bell violently and asked the alarmed Polly what had become of Mr Roxdal.

"How should I know, sir?" she gasped. "Ain't he been in, sir?"

"Apparently not," Tom answered anxiously. "He never remains out. We have been here for weeks now, and I can't recall a single night he hasn't been home before twelve. I can't make it out." All inquiries proved futile. Mrs Seacon reminded him of the thick fog that had come on suddenly the night before.

"What fog?" asked Tom.

"Lord! didn't you notice it, sir?"

"No, I came in early, smoked, read, and went to bed about eleven. I never thought of looking out of the window."

"It began about ten," said Mrs Seacon, "and got thicker and thicker. I couldn't see the lights of the river from my bedroom. The poor gentleman has been and gone and walked into the water." She began to whimper.

"Nonsense, nonsense," said Tom, though his expression belied his words. "At the worst I should think he couldn't find his way home, and couldn't get a cab, so put up for the night at some hotel. I daresay it will be all right." He began to whistle as if in restored cheerfulness. At eight o'clock there came a letter for Roxdal, marked *Immediate*, but as he did not turn up for breakfast, Tom went round personally to the City and Suburban Bank. He waited half an hour there, but the manager did not make his appearance. Then he left the letter with the cashier and went away.

That afternoon it was all over London that the manager of the City and Suburban had disappeared, and that many thousands of pounds in gold and notes had disappeared with him.

Scotland Yard opened the letter marked *Immediate*, and noted that there had been a delay in its delivery, for the address had been obscure, and an official alteration had been made. It was written in a feminine hand and said: "On second thought I cannot accompany you. Do not try to see me again. Forget me. I shall never forget you."

There was no signature.

Clara Newell, distracted, disclaimed all knowledge of this letter. Polly deposed that the fugitive had proposed flight to her, and the routes to Africa and South America were especially watched.

Yet months passed without result. Tom Peters went about overwhelmed with grief and astonishment. The police took possession of all the missing man's effects.

Gradually the hue and cry dwindled, and died.

"At last we meet!" cried Tom Peters, his face lighting up in joy. "How are you, dear Miss Newell?"

Clara greeted him coldly. Her face had an abiding pallor now. Her lover's flight and shame had prostrated her for weeks. Her soul was the arena of contending instincts. Alone of all the world she still believed in Everard's innocence, felt that there was something more than met the eye, divined some devilish mystery behind it all. And yet that damning letter from the anonymous lady shook her sadly. Then, too, there was the deposition of Polly. When she heard Peters's voice accosting her, all her old repugnance resurged. It flashed upon her that this man – Roxdal's boon companion – must know far more than he had told to the police. She remembered how Everard had spoken of him, with what affection and confidence! Was it likely he was utterly ignorant of Everard's movements?

Mastering her repugnance, she held out her hand. It might be well to keep in touch with him; he was possibly the clue to the mystery. She noticed he was dressed a shade more trimly, and was smoking a meerschaum. He walked along at her side, making no offer to put his pipe out.

"You have not heard from Everard?" he asked. She flushed.

"Do you think I'm an accessory after the fact?" she cried.

"No, no," he said soothingly. "Pardon me, I was thinking he might have written – giving no exact address, of course. Men do sometimes dare to write thus to women. But, of course, he knows you too well – you would have told the police."

"Certainly," she exclaimed, indignantly. "Even if he is innocent he must face the charge."

"Do you still entertain the possibility of his innocence?"

"I do," she said boldly, and looked him full in the face. His eyelids drooped with a quiver. "Don't you?"

"I have hoped against hope," he replied, in a voice faltering with emotion. "Poor old Everard! But I am afraid there is no room for doubt. Oh, this wicked curse of money – tempting the noblest and the best of us."

The weeks rolled on. Gradually she found herself seeing more and more of Tom Peters, and gradually, strange to say, he grew less repulsive. From the talks they had together, she began to see that there was really no reason to put faith in Everard; his criminality, his faithlessness, were too flagrant. Gradually she grew ashamed of her early mistrust of Peters; remorse bred esteem, and esteem ultimately ripened into feelings so warm that when Tom gave freer vent to the love that had been visible to Clara from the first, she did not repulse him.

It is only in books that love lives forever. Clara, so her father thought, showed herself a sensible girl in plucking out an unworthy affection and casting it from her heart. He invited the new suitor to his house, and took to him at once. Roxdal's somewhat supercilious manner had always jarred upon the unsophisticated corn merchant. With Tom the old man got on much better. While evidently quite as well informed and cultured as his whilom friend, Tom knew how to impart his superior knowledge with the accent on the knowledge rather than on the superiority, while he had the air of gaining much information in return. Those who are most conscious of the defects in early education are most resentful of other people sharing their consciousness. Moreover, Tom's *bonhomie* was far more to the old fellow's liking than the studied politeness of his predecessor, so that on the whole Tom made more of a conquest of the father than of the daughter. Nevertheless, Clara was by no means unresponsive to Tom's affection, and when, after one of his visits to the house, the old man kissed her fondly and spoke of the happy turn things had taken, and how, for the second time in their lives, things had mended when they seemed at their blackest, her heart swelled with a gush of gratitude and joy, and she fell sobbing into her father's arms.

Tom calculated that he made a clear five hundred a year by occasional journalism, besides possessing some profitable investments which he had inherited from his mother, so that there was no reason for delaying the marriage. It was fixed for May-day, and the honeymoon was to be spent in Italy.

But Clara was not destined to happiness. From the moment she had promised herself to her first love's friend, old memories began to rise up and reproach her. Strange thoughts stirred in the depths of her soul, and in the silent watches of the night she seemed to hear Everard's voice, charged with grief and upbraiding. Her uneasiness increased as her wedding day drew near. One night, after a pleasant afternoon spent in being rowed by Tom among the upper reaches of the Thames, she retired full of vague forebodings. And she dreamed a terrible dream. The dripping figure of Everard stood by her bedside, staring at her with ghastly eyes. Had he been drowned on the passage to his land of exile? Frozen with horror, she put the question.

"I have never left England!" the vision answered.

Her tongue clove to the roof of her mouth.

"Never left England?" she repeated, in tones which did not seem to be hers.

The wraith's stony eyes stared on.

"Where have you been?" she asked in her dream.

"Very near you."

"There has been foul play then!" she shrieked.

The phantom shook its head in doleful assent.

"I knew it!" she shrieked. "Tom Peters – Tom Peters has done away with you. Is it not he? Speak!"

"Yes, it is he – Tom Peters – whom I loved more than all the world."

Even in the terrible oppression of the dream she could not resist saying, woman-like: "Did I not warn you against him?"

The phantom made no reply.

"But what was the motive?" she asked at length.

"Love of gold – and you. And you are giving yourself to him," it said sternly.

"No, no, Everard! I will not! I swear it! Forgive me!"

The spirit shook its head.

"You love him. Women are false – as false as men."

She strove to protest again, but her tongue refused to speak.

"If you marry him, I shall always be with you! Beware!"

The dripping figure vanished as suddenly as it came, and Clara awoke in a cold perspiration. Oh, it was horrible! The man she had learned to love was the murderer of the man she had learned to forget! How her original prejudice had been justified! Distracted, shaken to her depths, she would not take counsel even of her father, but informed the police of her suspicions. A raid was made on Tom's rooms, and lo! the stolen notes were found.

Tom was arrested. Attention was now concentrated on the corpses washed up by the river. It was not long before the body of Roxdal came to shore, the face distorted beyond recognition by long immersion, but the clothes patently his, a pocketbook in the breast-pocket removing the last doubt. Mrs Seacon and Polly and Clara Newell all identified the body. Both juries returned a verdict of murder against Tom Peters, the recital of Clara's dream producing a unique impression in the court and throughout the country. The theory of the prosecution was that Roxdal had brought home the money, whether to fly alone or to divide it, or even for some innocent purpose, as Clara believed; that Peters determined to have it all, that he had gone out for a walk with the deceased, and had pushed him into the river, and that he was further impelled to the crime by his love for Clara Newell, as was evident from his subsequent relations with her. The judge put on the black cap. Tom Peters was duly hanged by the neck till he was dead.

BRIEF RÉSUMÉ OF THE CULPRIT'S CONFESSION

When you all read this I shall be dead and laughing at you. I have been hanged for my own murder. I am Everard G. Roxdal. I am also Tom Peters. *We two were one!*

When I was a young man my moustache and beard wouldn't come. I bought false ones to improve my appearance. One day, after I had become manager of the City and Suburban Bank, I took off my beard and moustache at home, and then the thought crossed my mind that nobody would know me without them. I was another man. Instantly it flashed upon me that if I ran away from the Bank, that other man could be left in London, while the police were scouring the world for a non-existent fugitive.

But this was only the crude germ of the idea. Slowly I matured my plan. The man who was going to be left in London must be known to a circle of acquaintances beforehand. It would be easy enough to masquerade in the evenings in my beardless condition, with other disguises of dress and voice. But this was not brilliant enough. *I conceived the idea of living with him!*

We shared rooms at Mrs Seacon's. It was a great strain, but it was only for a few weeks. I had trick clothes in my bedroom like those of quick-change artists; in a moment I could pass from Roxdal to Peters and from Peters to Roxdal. Polly had to clean two pairs of boots each morning, cook two dinners, and so on. She and Mrs Seacon saw one or the other of us nearly every moment; it never dawned upon them that *they never saw both of us together!*

At meals I would not be interrupted, ate off two plates, and conversed with my friend in loud tones. At other times we dined at different hours. On Sundays one was supposed to be asleep when the other was in church. There is no landlady in the world to whom the idea would have occurred that one man was troubling himself to be two (and to pay for two, including washing).

I worked up the idea of Roxdal's flight, asked Polly to go with me, manufactured that feminine letter that arrived on the morning of my disappearance. As Tom Peters I mixed with a journalistic set. I had another room where I kept the gold and notes till I mistakenly thought the thing had blown over. Unfortunately, returning from the other room on the night of my disappearance with Roxdal's clothes in a bundle I intended to drop into the river, the bundle was stolen from me in the fog, and the man into whose possession it ultimately came appears to have committed suicide.

What, perhaps, ruined me was my desire to keep Clara's love, and to transfer it to the survivor. Everard told her I was the best of fellows. Once married to her, I would not have had anything to fear. Even if she had discovered the trick, a wife cannot give evidence against her husband, and often does not want to. I made none of the usual slips, but no man can guard against a girl's nightmare after a day up the river and a supper at the Star and Garter. I might have told the judge he was an ass, but then I should have had penal servitude for bank robbery, and that sentence would have been a great deal worse than death.

The only thing that puzzles me, though, is whether the law has committed murder or I have committed suicide.

Anna Katherine Green

The Doctor, His Wife and the Clock

Another writer – American this time – who was established before the Holmes era was Anna Katherine Green (1846–1935), later Mrs Rohlfs. Her The Leavenworth Case *(1878) was a huge success in its day, and brought fame and fortune to its quiet author, who went on writing mystery stories well into the next century, pioneering the idea of the female sleuth in her tales of Violet Strange.*

Her best-known detective, though, was Ebenezer Gryce, who features in The Doctor, His Wife and the Clock. *First published in 1895 as a self-contained volume, this novelette with its Greenawayesque title is perhaps Gryce's finest performance.*

I

On the 17th of July, 1851, a tragedy of no little interest occurred in one of the residences of the Colonnade in Lafayette Place.

Mr Hasbrouck, a well-known and highly respected citizen, was attacked in his room by an unknown assailant, and shot dead before assistance could reach him. His murderer escaped, and the problem offered to the police was, how to identify this person who, by some happy chance or by the exercise of the most remarkable forethought, had left no traces behind him, or any clue by which he could be followed.

The affair was given to a young man, named Ebenezer Gryce, to investigate, and the story, as he tells it, is this:

When, some time after midnight, I reached Lafayette Place, I found the block lighted from end to end. Groups of excited men and women peered from the open doorways, and mingled their shadows with those of the huge pillars which adorn the front of this picturesque block of dwellings.

The house in which the crime had been committed was near the center of the row, and, long before I reached it, I had learned from more than one source that the alarm was first given to the street by a woman's shriek, and secondly by the shouts of an old man-servant who had appeared, in a half-dressed condition, at the window of Mr Hasbrouck's room, crying, "Murder! murder!"

But when I had crossed the threshold, I was astonished at the paucity of the facts to be gleaned from the inmates themselves. The old servitor, who was the first to talk, had only this account of the crime to give.

The family, which consisted of Mr Hasbrouck, his wife, and three servants, had retired for the night at the usual hour and under the usual auspices. At eleven o'clock the lights were all extinguished, and the whole household asleep, with the possible exception of Mr Hasbrouck himself, who, being a man of large business responsibilities, was frequently troubled with insomnia.

Suddenly Mrs Hasbrouck woke with a start. Had she dreamed the words that were ringing in her ears, or had they been actually uttered in her hearing? They were short, sharp words, full of terror and menace, and she had nearly satisfied herself that she had imagined them, when there came, from somewhere near the door, a sound she neither understood nor could interpret, but which filled her with inexplicable terror, and made her afraid to breathe, or even to stretch forth her hand towards her husband, whom she supposed to be sleeping at her side. At length another strange sound, which she was sure was not due to her imagination, drove her to make an attempt to rouse him, when she was horrified to find that she was alone in the bed, and her husband nowhere within reach.

Filled now with something more than nervous apprehension, she flung herself to the floor, and tried to penetrate, with frenzied glances, the surrounding darkness. But the blinds and shutters both having been carefully closed by Mr Hasbrouck before retiring, she found this impossible, and she was about to sink in terror to the floor, when she heard a low gasp on the other side of the room, followed by the suppressed cry:

"God! what have I done!"

The voice was a strange one, but before the fear aroused by this fact could culminate in a shriek of dismay, she caught the sound of retreating footsteps, and, eagerly listening, she heard them descend the stairs and depart by the front door.

Had she known what had occurred – had there been no doubt in her mind as to what lay in the darkness on the other side of the room –

it is likely that, at the noise caused by the closing front door, she would have made at once for the balcony that opened out from the window before which she was standing, and taken one look at the flying figure below. But her uncertainty as to what lay hidden from her by the darkness chained her feet to the floor, and there is no knowing when she would have moved, if a carriage had not at that moment passed down Astor Place, bringing with it a sense of companionship which broke the spell that held her, and gave her strength to light the gas, which was in ready reach of her hand.

As the sudden blaze illuminated the room, revealing in a burst the old familiar walls and well-known pieces of furniture, she felt for a moment as if released from some heavy nightmare and restored to the common experiences of life. But in another instant her former dread returned, and she found herself quaking at the prospect of passing around the foot of the bed into that part of the room which was as yet hidden from her eyes.

But the desperation which comes with great crises finally drove her from her retreat; and, creeping slowly forward, she cast one glance at the floor before her, when she found her worst fears realized by the sight of the dead body of her husband lying prone before the open doorway, with a bullet-hole in his forehead.

Her first impulse was to shriek, but, by a powerful exercise of will, she checked herself, and, ringing frantically for the servants who slept on the top floor of the house, flew to the nearest window and endeavored to open it. But the shutters had been bolted so securely by Mr Hasbrouck, in his endeavor to shut out light and sound, that by the time she had succeeded in unfastening them, all trace of the flying murderer had vanished from the street.

Sick with grief and terror, she stepped back into the room just as the three frightened servants descended the stairs. As they appeared in the open doorway, she pointed at her husband's inanimate form, and then, as if suddenly realizing in its full force the calamity which had befallen her, she threw up her arms, and sank forward to the floor in a dead faint.

The two women rushed to her assistance, but the old butler, bounding over the bed, sprang to the window, and shrieked his alarm to the street.

In the interim that followed, Mrs Hasbrouck was revived, and the master's body laid decently on the bed; but no pursuit was made, nor any inquiries started likely to assist me in establishing the identity of the assailant.

Indeed, every one, both in the house and out, seemed dazed by the unexpected catastrophe, and as no one had any suspicions to offer as to the probable murderer, I had a difficult task before me.

I began, in the usual way, by inspecting the scene of the murder. I found nothing in the room, or in the condition of the body itself, which added an iota to the knowledge already obtained. That Mr Hasbrouck had been in bed; that he had risen upon hearing a noise; and that he had been shot before reaching the door, were self-evident facts. But there was nothing to guide me further. The very simplicity of the circumstances caused a dearth of clues, which made the difficulty of procedure as great as any I ever encountered.

My search through the hall and down the stairs elicited nothing; and an investigation of the bolts and bars by which the house was secured, assured me that the assassin had either entered by the front door, or had already been secreted in the house when it was locked up for the night.

"I shall have to trouble Mrs Hasbrouck for a short interview," I hereupon announced to the trembling old servitor, who had followed me like a dog about the house.

He made no demur, and in a few minutes I was ushered into the presence of the newly made widow, who sat quite alone, in a large chamber in the rear. As I crossed the threshold she looked up, and I encountered a good plain face, without the shadow of guile in it.

"Madame," said I, "I have not come to disturb you. I will ask two or three questions only, and then leave you to your grief. I am told that some words came from the assassin before he delivered his fatal shot. Did you hear these distinctly enough to tell me what they were?"

"I was sound asleep," said she, "and dreamt, as I thought, that a fierce, strange voice cried somewhere to someone: 'Ah! you did not expect me!' But I dare not say that these words were really uttered to my husband, for he was not the man to call forth hate, and only a man in the extremity of passion could address such an exclamation in such a tone as rings in my memory in connection with the fatal shot which woke me."

"But that shot was not the work of a friend," I argued. "If, as these words seem to prove, the assassin had some other motive than gain in his assault, then your husband had an enemy, though you never suspected it."

"Impossible!" was her steady reply, uttered in the most convincing tone. "The man who shot him was a common burglar, and, frightened at having been betrayed into murder, fled without looking for booty. I am sure I heard him cry out in terror and remorse: 'God! what have I done!'"

"Was that before you left the side of the bed?"

"Yes; I did not move from my place till I heard the front door close. I was paralyzed by my fear and dread."

"Are you in the habit of trusting to the security of a latchlock only in the fastening of your front door at night? I am told that the big key was not in the lock, and that the bolt at the bottom of the door was not drawn."

"The bolt at the bottom of the door is never drawn. Mr Hasbrouck was so good a man he never mistrusted any one. That is why the big lock was not fastened. The key, not working well, he took it some days ago to the locksmith, and when the latter failed to return it, he laughed, and said he thought no one would ever think of meddling with his front door."

"Is there more than one night-key to your house?" I now asked. She shook her head.

"And when did Mr Hasbrouck last use his?"

"To-night, when he came home from prayer-meeting," she answered, and burst into tears.

Her grief was so real and her loss so recent that I hesitated to afflict her by further questions. So returning to the scene of the tragedy, I stepped out upon the balcony which ran in front. Soft voices instantly struck my ears. The neighbors on either side were grouped in front of their own windows, and were exchanging the remarks natural under the circumstances. I paused, as in duty bound, and listened. But I heard nothing worth recording, and would have instantly re-entered the house if I had not been impressed by the appearance of a very graceful woman who stood at my right. She was clinging to her husband, who was gazing at one of the pillars before him in a strange, fixed way which astonished me till he attempted to move, and then I saw that he was blind. Instantly I remembered that there lived in this row a blind doctor, equally celebrated for his skill and for his uncommon personal attractions, and, greatly interested not only in his affliction, but in the sympathy evinced for him by his young and affectionate wife, I stood still till I heard her say in the soft and appealing tones of love:

"Come in, Constant; you have heavy duties for to-morrow, and you should get a few hours' rest, if possible."

He came from the shadow of the pillar, and for one minute I saw his face with the lamplight shining full upon it. It was as regular of feature as a sculptured Adonis, and it was as white.

"Sleep!" he repeated, in the measured tones of deep but suppressed feeling. "Sleep! with murder on the other side of the wall!" And he stretched out his hands in a dazed way that insensibly accentuated the horror I myself felt of the crime which had so lately taken place in the room behind me.

She, noting the movement, took one of the groping hands in her own and drew him gently towards her.

"This way," she urged; and, guiding him into the house, she closed the window and drew down the shades, making the street seem darker by the loss of her exquisite presence.

This may seem a digression, but I was at the time a young man of thirty, and much under the dominion of woman's beauty. I was therefore slow in leaving the balcony, and persistent in my wish to learn something of this remarkable couple before leaving Mr Hasbrouck's house.

The story told me was very simple. Dr Zabriskie had not been born blind, but had become so after a grievous illness which had stricken him down soon after he received his diploma. Instead of succumbing to an affliction which would have daunted most men, he expressed his intention of practicing his profession, and soon became so successful in it that he found no difficulty in establishing himself in one of the best-paying quarters of the city. Indeed, his intuition seemed to have developed in a remarkable degree after his loss of sight, and he seldom, if ever, made a mistake in diagnosis. Considering this fact, and the personal attractions which gave him distinction, it was no wonder that he soon became a popular physician whose presence was a benefaction and whose word a law.

He had been engaged to be married at the time of his illness, and, when he learned what was likely to be its results, had offered to release the young lady from all obligation to him. But she would not be released, and they were married. This had taken place some five years previous to Mr Hasbrouck's death, three of which had been spent by them in Lafayette Place.

So much for the beautiful woman next door.

There being absolutely no clue to the assailant of Mr Hasbrouck, I naturally looked forward to the inquest for some evidence upon which to work. But there seemed to be no underlying facts to this tragedy. The most careful study into the habits and conduct of the deceased brought nothing to light save his general beneficence and rectitude, nor was there in his history or in that of his wife any secret or hidden obligation calculated to provoke any such act of revenge as murder. Mrs Hasbrouck's surmise that the intruder was simply a burglar, and that she had rather imagined than heard the words that pointed to the shooting as a deed of vengeance, soon gained general credence. But, though the police worked long and arduously in this new direction, their efforts were without fruit, and the case bade fair to remain an unsolvable mystery.

But the deeper the mystery the more persistently does my mind cling to it, and some five months after the matter had been delegated to oblivion, I found myself starting suddenly from sleep, with these words ringing in my ears:

"Who uttered the scream that gave the first alarm of Mr Hasbrouck's violent death?"

I was in such a state of excitement that the perspiration stood out on my forehead. Mrs Hasbrouck's story of the occurrence returned to me, and I remembered as distinctly as if she were then speaking, that she had expressly stated that she did not scream when confronted by the sight of her husband's dead body. But some one had screamed, and that very loudly. Who was it, then? One of the maids, startled by the sudden summons from below, or some one else – some involuntary witness of the crime, whose testimony had been suppressed at the inquest, by fear or influence?

The possibility of having come upon a clue even at this late day, so fired my ambition, that I took the first opportunity of revisiting Lafayette Place. Choosing such persons as I thought most open to my questions, I learned that there were many who could testify to having heard a woman's shrill scream on that memorable night just prior to the alarm given by old Cyrus; but no one could tell from whose lips it had come. One fact, however, was immediately settled. It had not been the result of the servant-women's fears. Both of the girls were positive that they had uttered no sound, nor had they themselves heard any, till Cyrus rushed to the window with his wild cries. As the scream, by whomever given, was uttered before they descended the stairs, I was convinced by these assurances that it had issued from one of the front windows, and not from the rear of the house, where their own rooms lay. Could it be that it had sprung from the adjoining dwelling, and that – My thoughts went no further, but I made up my mind to visit the doctor's house at once.

It took some courage to do this, for the doctor's wife had attended the inquest, and her beauty, seen in broad daylight, had worn such an aspect of mingled sweetness and dignity, that I hesitated to encounter it under any circumstances likely to disturb its pure serenity. But a clue, once grasped, cannot be lightly set aside by a true detective, and it would have taken more than a woman's frown to stop me at this point. So I rang Dr Zabriskie's bell.

I am seventy years old now and am no longer daunted by the

charms of a beautiful woman, but I confess that when I found myself in the fine reception parlor on the first-floor, I experienced no little trepidation at the prospect of the interview that awaited me. But as soon as the fine commanding form of the doctor's wife crossed the threshold, I recovered my senses and surveyed her with as direct a gaze as my position allowed. For her aspect bespoke a degree of emotion that astonished me; and even before I spoke I perceived her to be trembling, though she was a woman of no little natural dignity and self-possession.

"I seem to know your face," she said, advancing courteously towards me, "but your name" – and here she glanced at the card she held in her hand – "is totally unfamiliar to me."

"I think you saw me some eighteen months ago," said I. "I am the detective who gave testimony at the inquest which was held over the remains of Mr Hasbrouck."

I had not meant to startle her, but at this introduction of myself I saw her naturally pale cheek turn paler, and her fine eyes, which had been fixed curiously upon me, gradually sink to the floor.

"Great heaven!" thought I, "what is this I have stumbled upon!"

"I do not understand what business you can have with me," she presently remarked, with a show of gentle indifference that did not in the least deceive me.

"I do not wonder," I rejoined. "The crime which took place next door is almost forgotten by the community, and even if it were not, I am sure you would find it difficult to conjecture the nature of the question I have to put to you."

"I am surprised," she began, rising in her involuntary emotion and thereby compelling me to rise also. "How can you have any question to ask me on this subject? Yet if you have," she continued, with a rapid change of manner that touched my heart in spite of myself, "I shall, of course, do my best to answer you."

There are women whose sweetest tones and most charming smiles only serve to awaken distrust in men of my calling; but Mrs Zabriskie was not of this number. Her face was beautiful, but it was also candid in expression, and beneath the agitation which palpably disturbed her, I was sure there lurked nothing either wicked or false. Yet I held fast by the clue which I had grasped, as it were, in the dark, and without knowing whither I was tending, much less whither I was leading her, I proceeded to say:

"The question which I presume to put to you as the next-door neighbor of Mr Hasbrouck, is this: Who was the woman who screamed out so loudly that the whole neighborhood heard her on the night of that gentleman's assassination?"

The gasp she gave answered my question in a way she little realized, and, struck as I was by the impalpable links that had led me to the threshold of this hitherto unsolvable mystery, I was about to press my advantage and ask another question, when she quickly started forward and laid her hand on my lips.

Astonished, I looked at her inquiringly, but her head was turned aside, and her eyes, fixed upon the door, showed the greatest anxiety. Instantly I realized what she feared. Her husband was entering the house, and she dreaded lest his ears should catch a word of our conversation.

Not knowing what was in her mind, and unable to realize the importance of the moment to her, I yet listened to the advance of her blind husband with an almost painful interest. Would he enter the room where we were, or would he pass immediately to his office in the rear? She seemed to wonder, too, and almost held her breath as he neared the door, paused, and stood in the open doorway, with his ear turned toward us.

As for myself, I remained perfectly still, gazing at his face in mingled surprise and apprehension. For besides its beauty, which was of a marked order, I have already observed, it had a touching expression which irresistibly aroused both pity and interest in the spectator. This may have been the result of his affliction, or it may have sprung from some deeper cause; but, whatever its source, this look in his face produced a strong impression upon me and interested me at once in his personality. Would he enter? Or would he pass on? Her look of silent appeal showed me in which direction her wishes lay, but while I answered her glance by complete silence, I was conscious in some indistinct way that the business I had undertaken would be better furthered by his entrance.

The blind have been often said to possess a sixth sense in place of the one they have lost. Though I am sure we made no noise, I soon perceived that he was aware of our presence. Stepping hastily forward he said, in the high and vibrating tone of restrained passion:

"Helen, are you here?"

For a moment I thought she did not mean to answer, but knowing doubtless from experience the impossibility of deceiving him, she answered with a cheerful assent, dropping her hand as she did so from before my lips.

He heard the slight rustle which accompanied the movement, and a look I found it hard to comprehend flashed over his features, altering his expression so completely that he seemed another man.

"You have some one with you," he declared, advancing another step, but with none of the uncertainty which usually accompanies the movements of the blind. "Some dear friend," he went on, with an almost sarcastic emphasis and a forced smile that had little of gaiety in it.

The agitated and distressed blush which answered him could have but one interpretation. He suspected that her hand had been clasped in mine, and she perceived his thought and knew that I perceived it also.

Drawing herself up, she moved towards him, saying in a sweet womanly tone that to me spoke volumes:

"It is no friend, Constant, not even an acquaintance. The person whom I now present to you is an agent from the police. He is here upon a trivial errand which will be soon finished, when I will join you in your office."

I knew she was but taking a choice between two evils. That she would have saved her husband the knowledge of a detective's presence in the house, if her self-respect would have allowed it, but neither she nor I anticipated the effect which this presentation produced upon him.

"A police officer," he repeated, staring with his sightless eyes, as if, in his eagerness to see, he half hoped his lost sense would return. "He can have no trivial errand here; he has been sent by God Himself to – "

"Let me speak for you," hastily interposed his wife, springing to his side and clasping his arm with a fervor that was equally expressive of appeal and command. Then turning to me, she explained: "Since Mr Hasbrouck's unaccountable death, my husband has been laboring under an hallucination which I have only to mention for you to recognize its perfect absurdity. He thinks – oh! do not look like that, Constant; you know it is an hallucination which must vanish the moment we drag it into broad daylight – that he – he, the best man in all the world, was himself the assailant of Mr Hasbrouck."

"Good God!"

"I say nothing of the impossibility of this being so," she went on in a fever of expostulation. "He is blind, and could not have delivered such a shot even if he had desired to; besides, he had no weapon. But the inconsistency of the thing speaks for itself, and should assure him that his mind is unbalanced and that he is merely suffering from a shock that was greater than we realized. He is a physician and has had many such instances in his own practise. Why, he was very much attached to Mr Hasbrouck! They were the best of friends, and though he insists that he killed him, he cannot give any reason for the deed."

At these words the doctor's face grew stern, and he spoke like an automaton repeating some fearful lesson.

"I killed him. I went to his room and deliberately shot him. I had nothing against him, and my remorse is extreme. Arrest me, and let me pay the penalty of my crime. It is the only way in which I can obtain peace."

Shocked beyond all power of self-control by this repetition of what she evidently considered the unhappy ravings of a madman, she let go his arm and turned upon me in frenzy.

"Convince him!" she cried. "Convince him by your questions that he never could have done this fearful thing."

I was laboring under great excitement myself, for I felt my youth against me in a matter of such tragic consequence. Besides, I agreed with her that he was in a distempered state of mind, and I hardly knew how to deal with one so fixed in his hallucination and with so much intelligence to support it. But the emergency was great, for he was holding out his wrists in the evident expectation of my taking him into instant custody; and the sight was killing his wife, who had sunk on the floor between us, in terror and anguish.

"You say you killed Mr Hasbrouck," I began. "Where did you get your pistol, and what did you do with it after you left his house?"

"My husband had no pistol; never had any pistol," put in Mrs Zabriskie, with vehement assertion. "If I had seen him with such a weapon – "

"I threw it away. When I left the house, I cast it as far from me as possible, for I was frightened at what I had done, horribly frightened."

"No pistol was ever found," I answered, with a smile, forgetting for the moment that he could not see. "If such an instrument had been found in the street after a murder of such consequence it certainly would have been brought to the police."

"You forget that a good pistol is valuable property," he went on stolidly. "Some one came along before the general alarm was given; and seeing such a treasure lying on the sidewalk, picked it up and carried it off. Not being honest, he preferred to keep it to drawing the attention of the police upon himself."

"Hum, perhaps," said I; "but where did you get it? Surely you can tell where you procured such a weapon, if, as your wife intimates, you did not own one."

"I bought it that self-same night of a friend; a friend whom I will not name, since he resides no longer in this country. I" – He paused; intense passion was in his face; he turned towards his wife, and a low cry escaped him, which made her look up in fear.

"I do not wish to go into any particulars," said he. "God forsook me, and I committed a horrible crime. When I am punished, perhaps peace will return to me and happiness to her. I would not wish her to suffer too long or too bitterly for my sin."

"Constant!" What love was in the cry! and what despair! It seemed to move him and turn his thoughts for a moment into a different channel.

"Poor child!" he murmured, stretching out his hands by an irresistible impulse towards her. But the change was but momentary, and he was soon again the stern and determined self-accuser. "Are you going to take me before a magistrate?" he asked. "If so, I have a few duties to perform which you are welcome to witness."

"I have no warrant," I said; "besides, I am scarcely the one to take such a responsibility upon myself. If, however, you persist in your declaration, I will communicate with my superiors, who will take such action as they think best."

"That will be still more satisfactory to me," said he; "for though I have many times contemplated giving myself up to the authorities, I have still much to do before I can leave my home and practice without injury to others. Good-day; when you want me, you will find me here."

He was gone, and the poor young wife was left crouching on the floor alone. Pitying her shame and terror, I ventured to remark that it was not an uncommon thing for a man to confess to a crime he had never committed, and assured her that the matter would be inquired into very carefully before any attempt was made upon his liberty.

She thanked me, and, slowly rising, tried to regain her equanimity; but the manner as well as the matter of her husband's self-condemnation was too overwhelming in its nature for her to recover readily from her emotions.

"I have long dreaded this," she acknowledged. "For months I have foreseen that he would make some rash communication or insane avowal. If I had dared, I would have consulted some physician about this hallucination of his; but he was so sane on other points that I hesitated to give my dreadful secret to the world. I kept hoping that time and his daily pursuits would have their effect and restore him to himself. But his illusion grows, and now I fear that nothing will ever convince him that he did not commit the deed of which he accuses himself. If he were not blind I would have more hope, but the blind have so much time for brooding."

"I think he had better be indulged in his fancies for the present," I ventured. "If he is laboring under an illusion it might be dangerous to cross him."

"If?" she echoed in an indescribable tone of amazement and dread. "Can you for a moment harbor the idea that he has spoken the truth?"

"Madame," I returned, with something of the cynicism of my later years, "what caused you to give such an unearthly scream just before this murder was made known to the neighborhood?"

She stared, paled, and finally began to tremble, not, as I now believe, at the insinuation latent in my words, but at the doubts which my question aroused in her own breast.

"Did I?" she asked; then with a great burst of candor, which seemed inseparable from her nature, she continued: "Why do I try to mislead you or deceive myself? I did give a shriek just before the alarm was raised next door; but it was not from any knowledge I had of a crime having been committed, but because I unexpectedly saw before me my husband whom I supposed to be on his way to Poughkeepsie. He was looking very pale and strange, and for a moment I thought I was beholding his ghost. But he soon explained his appearance by saying that he had fallen from the train and had been only saved by a miracle from being dismembered; and I was just bemoaning his mishap and trying to calm him and myself, when that terrible shout was heard next door of 'Murder! murder!' Coming so soon after the shock he had himself experienced, it quite unnerved him, and I think we can date his mental disturbance from that moment. For he began almost immediately to take a morbid interest in the affair next door, though it was weeks, if not months, before he let a word fall of the nature of those you have just heard. Indeed it was not till I repeated to him some of the expressions he was continually letting fall in his sleep, that he commenced to accuse himself of crime and talk of retribution."

"You say that your husband frightened you on that night by appearing suddenly at the door when you thought him on his way to Poughkeepsie. Is Dr Zabriskie in the habit of thus going and coming alone at an hour so late as this must have been?"

"You forget that to the blind, night is less full of perils than the day. Often and often has my husband found his way to his patients' houses alone after midnight; but on this especial evening he had Harry with him. Harry was his driver, and always accompanied him when he went any distance."

"Well, then," said I, "all we have to do is to summon Harry and hear what he has to say concerning this affair. He surely will know whether or not his master went into the house next door."

"Harry has left us," she said. "Dr Zabriskie has another driver now. Besides (I have nothing to conceal from you), Harry was not with him when he returned to the house that evening, or the doctor would not have been without his portmanteau till the next day. Something – I have never known what – caused them to separate, and that is why I have no answer to give the doctor when he accuses himself of committing a deed on that night which is wholly out of keeping with every other act of his life."

"And have you never questioned Harry why they separated and why he allowed his master to come home alone after the shock he had received at the station?"

"I did not know there was any reason for doing so till long after he left us."

"And when did he leave?"

"That I do not remember. A few weeks or possibly a few days after that dreadful night."

"And where is he now?"

"Ah, that I have not the least means of knowing. But," she suddenly cried, "what do you want of Harry? If he did not follow Dr Zabriskie to his own door, he could tell us nothing that would convince my husband that he is laboring under an illusion."

"But he might tell us something which would convince us that Dr Zabriskie was not himself after the accident, that he – "

"Hush!" came from her lips in imperious tones. "I will not believe that he shot Mr Hasbrouck, even if you prove him to have been insane at the time. How could he? My husband is blind. It would take a man of very keen sight to force himself into a house that was closed for the night, and kill a man in the dark at one shot."

"Rather," cried a voice from the doorway, "it is only a blind man who could do this. Those who trust to eyesight must be able to catch some glimpse of the mark they aim at, and this room, as I have been told, was without a glimmer of light. But the blind trust to sound, and as Mr Hasbrouck spoke – "

"Oh!" burst from the horrified wife, "is there no one to stop him when he speaks like that?"

II

When I related to my superiors the details of the foregoing interview, two of them coincided with the wife in thinking that Dr Zabriskie was in an irresponsible condition of mind which made any statement of his questionable. But the third seemed disposed to argue the matter, and, casting me an inquiring look, seemed to ask what my opinion was on the subject. Answering him as if he had spoken, I gave my conclusion as follows: That whether insane or not, Dr Zabriskie had fired the shot which terminated Mr Hasbrouck's life.

It was the inspector's own idea, but it was not shared in by the others, one of whom had known the doctor for years. Accordingly they compromised by postponing all opinion till they had themselves interrogated the doctor, and I was detailed to bring him before them the next afternoon.

He came without reluctance, his wife accompanying him. In the short time which elapsed between their leaving Lafayette Place and entering headquarters, I embraced the opportunity of observing them, and I found the study equally exciting and interesting. His face was calm but hopeless, and his eye, which should have shown a wild glimmer if there was truth in his wife's hypothesis, was dark and unfathomable, but neither frenzied nor uncertain. He spoke but once and listened to nothing, though now and then his wife moved as if to attract his attention, and once even stole her hand towards his, in the tender hope that he would feel its approach and accept her sympathy. But he was deaf as well as blind; and sat wrapped up in thoughts which she, I know, would have given worlds to penetrate.

Her countenance was not without its mystery also. She showed in every lineament passionate concern and misery, and a deep tenderness from which the element of fear was not absent. But she, as well as he, betrayed that some misunderstanding, deeper than any I had previously suspected, drew its intangible veil between them and made the near proximity in which they sat, at once a heart-piercing delight and unspeakable pain. What was this misunderstanding? and what was the character of the fear that modified her every look of love in his direction? Her perfect indifference to my presence proved that it was not connected with the position in which he had put himself towards the police by his voluntary confession of crime, nor could I thus interpret the expression of frantic question which now and then contracted her features, as she raised her eyes towards his sightless orbs, and strove to read, in his firm-set lips, the meaning of those assertions she could only ascribe to a loss of reason.

The stopping of the carriage seemed to awaken both from thoughts that separated rather than united them. He turned his face in her direction, and she, stretching forth her hand, prepared to lead him from the carriage, without any of that display of timidity which had been previously evident in her manner.

As his guide, she seemed to fear nothing; as his lover, everything.

"There is another and a deeper tragedy underlying the outward and obvious one," was my inward conclusion, as I followed them into the presence of the gentlemen awaiting them.

Dr Zabriskie's appearance was a shock to those who knew him; so was his manner, which was calm, straightforward, and quietly determined.

"I shot Mr Hasbrouck," was his steady affirmation, given without any show of frenzy or desperation. "If you ask me why I did it, I cannot answer; if you ask me how, I am ready to state all that I know concerning the matter."

"But, Dr Zabriskie," interposed his friend, "the why is the most important thing for us to consider just now. If you really desire to convince us that you committed the dreadful crime of killing a totally inoffensive man, you should give us some reason for an act so opposed to all your instincts and general conduct."

But the doctor continued unmoved:

"I had no reason for murdering Mr Hasbrouck. A hundred questions can elicit no other reply; you had better keep to the how."

A deep-drawn breath from the wife answered the looks of the three gentlemen to whom this suggestion was offered. "You see," that breath seemed to protest, "that he is not in his right mind."

I began to waver in my own opinion, and yet the intuition which has served me in cases as seemingly impenetrable as this, bade me beware of following the general judgement.

"Ask him to inform you how he got into the house," I whispered to Inspector D—, who sat nearest me.

Immediately the Inspector put the question I had suggested:

"By what means did you enter Mr Hasbrouck's house at so late an hour as this murder occurred?"

The blind doctor's head fell forward on his breast, and he hesitated for the first and only time.

"You will not believe me," said he; "but the door was ajar when I came to it. Such things make crime easy; it is the only excuse I have to offer for this dreadful deed."

The front door of a respectable citizen's house ajar at half-past eleven at night. It was a statement that fixed in all minds the conviction of the speaker's irresponsibility. Mrs Zabriskie's brow cleared, and her beauty became for a moment dazzling as she held out her hands in irrepressible relief towards those who were interrogating her husband. I alone kept my impassibility. A possible explanation of this crime had flashed like lightning across my mind; an explanation from which I inwardly recoiled, even while I was forced to consider it.

"Dr Zabriskie," remarked the inspector, who was most friendly to him, "such old servants as those kept by Mr Hasbrouck do not leave the front door ajar at twelve o'clock at night."

"Yet ajar it was," repeated the blind doctor, with quiet emphasis; "and finding it so, I went in. When I came out again, I closed it. Do you wish me to swear to what I say? If so, I am ready."

What could we reply? To see this splendid-looking man, hallowed by an affliction so great that in itself it called forth the compassion of the most indifferent, accusing himself of a cold-blooded crime, in tones that sounded dispassionate because of the will that forced their utterance, was too painful in itself for us to indulge in any unnecessary words. Compassion took the place of curiosity, and each and all of us turned involuntary looks of pity upon the young wife pressing so eagerly to his side.

"For a blind man," ventured one, "the assault was both deft and certain. Are you accustomed to Mr Hasbrouck's house, that you found your way with so little difficulty to his bedroom?"

"I am accustomed – " he began.

But here his wife broke in with irrepressible passion:

"He is not accustomed to that house. He has never been beyond the first door. Why, why do you question him? Do you not see – "

His hand was on her lips.

"Hush!" he commanded. "You know my skill in moving about a house; how I sometimes deceive those who do not know me into believing that I can see, by the readiness with which I avoid obstacles and find my way even in strange and untried scenes. Do not try to make them think I am not in my right mind, or you will drive me into the very condition you deprecate."

His face, rigid, cold and set, looked like that of a mask. Hers, drawn with horror and filled with question that was fast taking the form of doubt, bespoke an awful tragedy from which more than one of us recoiled.

"Can you shoot a man dead without seeing him?" asked the superintendent, with painful effort.

"Give me a pistol and I will show you," was the quick reply.

A low cry came from the wife. In a drawer near to every one of us there lay a pistol, but no one moved to take it out. There was a look in the doctor's eye which made us fear to trust him with a pistol just then.

"We will accept your assurance that you possess a skill beyond that of most men," returned the superintendent. And beckoning me forward, he whispered: "This is a case for the doctors and not for the police. Remove him quietly, and notify Dr Southyard of what I say."

But Dr Zabriskie, who seemed to have an almost supernatural acuteness of hearing, gave a violent start at this and spoke up for the first time with real passion in his voice:

"No, no, I pray you. I can bear anything but that. Remember, gentlemen, that I am blind; that I cannot see who is about me; that my life would be a torture if I felt myself surrounded by spies watching to catch some evidence of madness in me. Rather conviction at once, death, dishonor, and obloquy. These I have incurred. These I have brought upon myself by crime, but not this worse fate – oh! not this worse fate."

His passion was so intense and yet so confined within the bounds of decorum, that we felt strangely impressed by it. Only the wife stood transfixed, with the dread growing in her heart, till her white, waxen visage seemed even more terrible to contemplate than his passion-distorted one.

"It is not strange that my wife thinks me demented," the doctor continued, as if afraid of the silence that answered him. "But it is your business to discriminate, and you should know a sane man when you see him."

Inspector D— no longer hesitated.

"Very well," said he, "give us the least proof that your assertions are true, and we will lay your case before the prosecuting attorney."

"Proof? Is not a man's word – "

"No man's confession is worth much without some evidence to support it. In your case there is none. You cannot even produce the pistol with which you assert yourself to have committed the deed."

"True, true. I was frightened by what I had done, and the instinct of self-preservation led me to rid myself of the weapon in any way I could. But some one found this pistol; some one picked it up from the sidewalk of Lafayette Place on that fatal night. Advertise for it. Offer a reward. I will give you the money." Suddenly he appeared to realize how all this sounded. "Alas!" cried he, "I know the story seems improbable; all I say seems improbable; but it is not the probable things that happen in this life, but the improbable, as you should know, who every day dig deep into the heart of human affairs."

Were these the ravings of insanity? I began to understand the wife's terror.

"I bought the pistol," he went on, "of – alas! I cannot tell you his name. Everything is against me. I cannot adduce one proof; yet she, even she, is beginning to fear that my story is true. I know it by her silence, a silence that yawns between us like a deep and unfathomable gulf."

But at these words her voice rang out with passionate vehemence.

"No, no; it is false! I will never believe that your hands have been plunged in blood. You are my own pure-hearted Constant, cold, perhaps, and stern, but with no guilt upon your conscience, save in your own wild imagination."

"Helen, you are no friend to me," he declared, pushing her gently aside. "Believe me innocent, but say nothing to lead these others to doubt my word."

And she said no more, but her looks spoke volumes.

The result was that he was not detained, though he prayed for instant commitment. He seemed to dread his own home, and the surveillance to which he instinctively knew he would henceforth be subjected. To see him shrink from his wife's hand as she strove to lead him from the room was sufficiently painful; but the feeling thus aroused was nothing to that with which we observed the keen and agonized expectancy of his look as he turned and listened for the steps of the officer who followed him.

"I shall never again know whether or not I am alone," was his final observation as he left our presence.

I said nothing to my superiors of the thoughts I had had while listening to the above interrogatories. A theory had presented itself to my mind which explained in some measure the mysteries of the doctor's conduct, but I wished for time and opportunity to test its reasonableness before submitting it to their higher judgement. And these seemed likely to be given me, for the inspectors continued divided in their opinion of the blind physician's guilt, and the district-attorney, when told of the affair, pooh-poohed it without mercy, and declined to stir in the matter unless some tangible evidence were forthcoming to substantiate the poor doctor's self-accusations.

"If guilty, why does he shrink from giving his motives," said he, "and if so anxious to go to the gallows, why does he suppress the very facts calculated to send him there? He is as mad as a March hare, and it is to an asylum he should go and not to jail."

In this conclusion I failed to agree with him, and as time wore on my suspicions took shape and finally ended in a fixed conviction. Dr Zabriskie had committed the crime he avowed, but – let me proceed a little further with my story before I reveal what lies beyond that "but."

Notwithstanding Dr Zabriskie's almost frenzied appeal for solitude, a man had been placed in surveillance over him in the shape of a young doctor skilled in the diseases of the brain. This man communicated more or less with the police, and one morning I received from him the following extracts from the diary he had been ordered to keep:

"The doctor is settling into a deep melancholy from which he tries to rise at times, but with only indifferent success. Yesterday he rode around to all his patients for the purpose of withdrawing his services on the plea of illness. But he still keeps his office open, and to-day I had the opportunity of witnessing his reception and treatment of the many sufferers who came to him for aid. I think he was conscious of my presence, though an attempt had been made to conceal it. For the listening look never left his face from the moment he entered the room, and once he rose and passed quickly from wall to wall, groping with outstretched hands into every nook and corner, and barely escaping contact with the curtain behind which I was hidden. But if he suspected my presence, he showed no displeasure at it, wishing perhaps for a witness to his skill in the treatment of disease.

"And truly I never beheld a finer manifestation of practical insight in cases of a more or less baffling nature than I beheld in him to-day. He is certainly a most wonderful physician, and I feel bound to record that his mind is as clear for business as if no shadow had fallen upon it.

"Dr Zabriskie loves his wife, but in a way that tortures both himself and her. If she is gone from the house he is wretched, and yet when she returns he often forbears to speak to her, or if he does speak, it is with a constraint that hurts her more than his silence. I was present when she came in to-day. Her step, which had been eager on the stairway, flagged as she approached the room, and he naturally noted the change and gave his own interpretation to it. His face, which had been very pale, flushed suddenly, and a nervous trembling seized him, which he sought in vain to hide. But by the time her tall and beautiful figure stood in the doorway he was his usual self again in all but the expression of his eyes, which stared straight before him in agony of longing only to be observed in those who have once seen.

"'Where have you been, Helen?' he asked, as, contrary to his wont, he moved to meet her.

"'To my mother's, to Arnold & Constable's, and to the hospital, as you requested,' was her quick answer, made without faltering or embarrassment.

"He stepped still nearer and took her hand, and as he did so my physician's eye noted how his finger lay over her pulse in seeming unconsciousness.

"'Nowhere else?' he queried.

"She smiled the saddest kind of smile and shook her head; then, remembering that he could not see this movement, she cried in a wistful tone:

"'Nowhere else, Constant; I was too anxious to get back.'

"I expected him to drop her hand at this, but he did not; and his finger still rested on her pulse.

"'And whom did you see while you were gone?' he continued.

"She told him, naming over several names.

"'You must have enjoyed yourself,' was his cold comment, as he let go her hand and turned away. But his manner showed relief, and I could not but sympathize with the pitiable situation of a man who found himself forced to means like these for probing the heart of his young wife.

"Yet when I turned towards her I realized her position was but little happier than his. Tears are no strangers to her eyes, but those that welled up at this moment seemed to possess a bitterness that promised but little peace for her future. Yet she quickly dried them and busied herself with ministrations for his comfort.

"If I am any judge of woman, Helen Zabriskie is superior to most of her sex. That her husband mistrusts her is evident, but whether this is the result of the stand she has taken in his regard, or only a manifestation of dementia, I have as yet been unable to determine. I dread to leave them alone together, and yet when I presume to suggest that she should be on her guard in her interviews with him, she smiles very placidly and tells me that nothing would give her greater joy than to see him lift his hand against her, for that would argue that he is not accountable for his deeds or for his assertions.

"Yet it would be a grief to see her injured by this passionate and unhappy man.

"You have said that you wanted all the details I could give; so I feel bound to say that Dr Zabriskie tries to be considerate of his wife, though he often fails in the attempt. When she offers herself as his guide, or assists him with his mail, or performs any of the many acts of kindness by which she continually manifests her sense of his affliction, he thanks her with courtesy and often with kindness, yet I know she would willingly exchange all his set phrases for one fond embrace or impulsive smile of affection. That he is not in the full possession of his faculties would be too much to say, and yet upon what other hypothesis can we account for the inconsistencies of his conduct?

"I have before me two visions of mental suffering. At noon I passed the office door, and, looking within, saw the figure of Dr Zabriskie seated in his great chair, lost in thought or deep in those memories which make an abyss in one's consciousness. His hands, which were clenched, rested upon the arms of his chair, and in one of them I detected a woman's glove, which I had no difficulty in recognizing as one of the pair worn by his wife this morning. He held it as a tiger might hold his prey or as a miser his gold, but his set features and sightless eyes betrayed that a conflict of emotions was waging within him, among which tenderness had but little share.

"Though alive, as he usually is, to every sound, he was too absorbed at this moment to notice my presence, though I had taken no pains to approach quietly. I therefore stood for a full minute watching him, till an irresistible sense of shame of thus spying upon a blind man in his moments of secret anguish seized upon me and I turned away. But not before I saw his features relax in a storm of passionate feeling, as he rained kisses after kisses on the senseless kid he had so long held in his motionless grasp. Yet when an hour later he entered the dining-room on his wife's arm, there was nothing in his manner to show that he had in any way changed in his attitude towards her.

"The other picture was more tragic still. I have no business with Mrs Zabriskie's affairs; but as I passed upstairs to my room an hour ago, I caught a fleeting vision of her tall form, with the arms thrown up over her head in a paroxysm of feeling which made her as oblivious to my presence as her husband had been several hours before. Were the words that escaped her lips, 'Thank God we have no children!' or was this exclamation suggested to me by the passion and unrestrained impulse of her action?"

Side by side with these lines, I, Ebenezer Gryce, placed the following extracts from my own diary:

"Watched the Zabriskie mansion for five hours this morning, from the second story window of an adjoining hotel. Saw the doctor when he drove away on his round of visits, and saw him when he returned. A colored man accompanied him.

"To-day I followed Mrs Zabriskie. I had a motive for this, the nature of which I think it wisest not to divulge. She went first to a house in Washington Place, where I am told her mother lives. Here she stayed for some time, after which she drove down to Canal Street, where she did some shopping, and later stopped at the hospital, into which I took the liberty of following her. She seemed to know many there, and passed from cot to cot with a smile in which I alone discerned the sadness of a broken heart. When she left, I left also, without having learned anything beyond the fact that Mrs Zabriskie is one who does her duty in sorrow as in happiness. A rare and trustworthy woman I should say, and yet her husband does not trust her. Why?

"I have spent this day in accumulating details in regard to Dr and Mrs Zabriskie's life previous to the death of Mr Hasbrouck. I learned from sources it would be unwise to quote just here, that Mrs Zabriskie had not lacked enemies ready to charge her with coquetry; that while she had never sacrificed her dignity in public, more than one person had been heard to declare that Dr Zabriskie was fortunate in being blind, since the sight of his wife's beauty would have but poorly compensated him for the pain he would have suffered in seeing how that beauty was admired.

"That all gossip is more or less tinged with exaggeration I have no doubt, yet when a name is mentioned in connection with such stories, there is usually some truth at the bottom of them. And a name is mentioned in this case, though I do not think it worth my while to repeat it here; and loth as I am to recognize the fact, it is a name that carries with it doubts that might easily account for the husband's jealousy. True, I have found no one who dares to hint that she still continues to attract attention or to bestow smiles in any direction save where they legally belong. For since a certain memorable night which we all know, neither Dr Zabriskie nor his wife have been seen save in their own domestic circle, and it is not into such scenes that this serpent, of which I have spoken, ever intrudes, nor is it in places of sorrow or suffering that his smile shines, or his fascinations flourish.

"And so one portion of my theory is proved to be sound. Dr Zabriskie is jealous of his wife: whether with good cause or bad I am not prepared to decide; for her present attitude, clouded as it is by the tragedy in which she and her husband are both involved, must differ very much from that which she held when her life was unshadowed by doubt, and her admirers could be counted by the score.

"I have just found out where Harry is. As he is in service some miles up the river, I shall have to be absent from my post for several hours, but I consider the game well worth the candle.

"Light at last. I have seen Harry, and, by means known only to the police, have succeeded in making him talk. His story is substantially this: That on the night so often mentioned, he packed his master's portmanteau at eight o'clock and at ten called a carriage and rode with the doctor to the Twenty-ninth Street station. He was told to buy tickets for Poughkeepsie, where his master had been called in consultation, and, having done this, hurried back to join his master on the platform. They had walked together as far as the cars, and Dr Zabriskie was just stepping on to the train when a man pushed himself hurriedly between them and whispered something into his master's ear, which caused him to fall back and lose his footing. Dr Zabriskie's body slid half under the car, but he was withdrawn before any harm was done, though the cars gave a lurch at the moment which must have frightened him exceedingly, for his face was white when he rose to his feet, and when Harry offered to assist him again on to the train, he refused to go, and said he would return home and not attempt to ride to Poughkeepsie that night.

"The gentleman, whom Harry now saw to be Mr Stanton, an intimate friend of Dr Zabriskie, smiled very queerly at this, and taking the doctor's arm led him away to a carriage. Harry naturally followed them, but the doctor, hearing his steps, turned and bade him, in a very peremptory tone, to take the omnibus home, and then, as if on second thought, told him to go to Poughkeepsie in his stead and explain to the people there that he was too shaken up by his mis-step to do his duty, and that he would be with them next morning. This seemed strange to Harry, but he had no reasons for disobeying his master's orders, and so rode to Poughkeepsie. But the doctor did not follow him the next day; on the contrary, he telegraphed for him to return, and when he got back dismissed him with a month's wages. This ended Harry's connection with the Zabriskie family.

"A simple story bearing out what the wife has already told us; but it furnishes a link which may prove invaluable. Mr Stanton, whose first name is Theodore, knows the real reason why Dr Zabriskie returned home on the night of the seventeenth of July, 1851. Mr Stanton, consequently, I must see, and this shall be my business to-morrow.

"Checkmate! Theodore Stanton is not in this country. Though this points him out as the man from whom Dr Zabriskie bought the pistol, it does not facilitate my work, which is becoming more and more difficult.

"Mr Stanton's whereabouts are not even known to his most intimate friends. He sailed from this country most unexpectedly on the eighteenth of July a year ago, which was the day after the murder of Mr Hasbrouck. It looks like a flight, especially as he has failed to maintain open communication even with his relatives. Was he the man who shot Mr Hasbrouck? No; but he was the man who put the pistol in Dr Zabriskie's hand that night, and, whether he did this with purpose or not, was evidently so alarmed at the catastrophe which followed that he took the first outgoing steamer to Europe. So far, all is clear, but there are mysteries yet to be solved, which will require my utmost tact. What if I should seek out the gentleman with whose name that of Mrs Zabriskie has been linked, and see if I can in any way connect him with Mr Stanton or the events of that night?

"Eureka! I have discovered that Mr Stanton cherished a mortal hatred for the gentleman above mentioned. It was a covert feeling, but no less deadly on that account; and while it never led him into any extravagances, it was of force sufficient to account for many a secret misfortune which happened to that gentleman. Now, if I can prove he was the Mephistopheles who whispered insinuations into the ear of our blind Faust, I may strike a fact that will lead me out of this maze.

"But how can I approach secrets so delicate without compromising the woman I feel bound to respect, if only for the devoted love she manifests for her unhappy husband!

"I shall have to appeal to Joe Smithers. This is something which I always hate to do, but as long as he will take money, and as long as he is fertile in resources for obtaining the truth from people I am myself unable to reach, so long must I make use of his cupidity and his genius. He is an honorable fellow in one way, and never retails as gossip what he acquires for our use. How will he proceed in this case, and by what tactics will he gain the very delicate information which we need? I own that I am curious to see.

"I shall really have to put down at length the incidents of this night. I always knew that Joe Smithers was invaluable to the police, but I really did not know he possessed talents of so high an order. He wrote me this morning that he had succeeded in getting Mr T—'s promise to spend the evening with him, and advised me that if I desired to be present also, his own servant would not be at home, and that an opener of bottles would be required.

"As I was very anxious to see Mr T— with my own eyes, I accepted the invitation to play the spy upon a spy, and went at the proper hour to Mr Smithers' rooms, which are in the University Building. I found them picturesque in the extreme. Piles of books stacked here and there to the ceiling made nooks and corners which could be quite shut off by a couple of old pictures that were set into movable frames that swung out or in at the whim or convenience of the owner.

"As I liked the dark shadows cast by these pictures, I pulled them both out, and made such other arrangements as appeared likely to facilitate the purpose I had in view; then I sat down and waited for the two gentlemen who were expected to come in together.

"They arrived almost immediately, whereupon I rose and played my part with all necessary discretion. While ridding Mr T— of his overcoat, I stole a look at his face. It is not a handsome one, but it boasts of a gay, devil-may-care expression which doubtless makes it dangerous to many women, while his manners are especially attractive, and his voice the richest and most persuasive that I ever heard. I contrasted him, almost against my will, with Dr Zabriskie, and decided that with most women the former's undoubted fascinations of speech and bearing would outweigh the latter's great beauty and mental endowments; but I doubted if they would with her.

"The conversation which immediately began was brilliant but desultory, for Mr Smithers, with an airy lightness for which he is remarkable, introduced topic after topic, perhaps for the purpose of showing off Mr T—'s versatility, and perhaps for the deeper and more sinister purpose of shaking the kaleidoscope of talk so thoroughly that the real topic which we were met to discuss should not make an undue impression on the mind of his guest.

"Meanwhile one, two, three bottles passed, and I saw Joe Smithers' eye grow calmer and that of Mr T— more brilliant and more uncertain. As the last bottle showed signs of failing, Joe cast me a meaning glance, and the real business of the evening began.

"I shall not attempt to relate the half-dozen failures which Joe made in endeavoring to elicit the facts we were in search of, without arousing the suspicion of his visitor. I am only going to relate the successful attempt. They had been talking now for some two hours, and I, who had long before been waved from their immediate presence, was hiding my curiosity and growing excitement behind one of the pictures, when suddenly I heard Joe say:

"'He has the most remarkable memory I ever met. He can tell to a day when any notable event occurred.'

"'Pshaw!' answered his companion, who, by-the-bye was known to pride himself upon his own memory for dates. 'I can state where I went and what I did on every day in the year. That may not embrace what you call "notable events," but the memory required is all the more remarkable, is it not?'

"'Pooh!' was his friend's provoking reply, 'you are bluffing, Ben; I will never believe that."

"Mr T—, who had passed by this time into that state of intoxication which makes persistence in an assertion a duty as well as a pleasure, threw back his head and, as the wreaths of smoke rose in airy spirals from his lips, reiterated his statement, and offered to submit to any test of his vaunted powers which the other might dictate.

"'You have a diary' – began Joe.

"'Which is at home,' completed the other.

"'Will you allow me to refer to it to-morrow, if I am suspicious of the accuracy of your recollections?'

"'Undoubtedly,' returned the other.

"'Very well, then, I will wager you a cool fifty that you cannot tell where you were between the hours of ten and eleven on a certain night which I will name.'

"'Done!' cried the other, bringing out his pocket-book and laying it on the table before him.

"Joe followed his example and then summoned me.

"'Write a date down here,' he commanded, pushing a piece of paper towards me, with a look as keen as the flash of a blade. 'Any date, man,' he added, as I appeared to hesitate in the embarrassment I thought natural under the circumstances. 'Put down day, month, and year, only don't go too far back; no farther than two years.'

"Smiling with the air of a flunkey admitted to the sports of his superiors, I wrote a line and laid it before Mr Smithers, who at once pushed it with a careless gesture towards his companion. You can, of course, guess the date I made use of: July 17, 1851. Mr T—, who evidently looked upon this matter as mere play, flushed scarlet as he read these words, and for one instant looked as if he had rather flee our presence than answer Joe Smithers' nonchalant glance of inquiry.

"'I have given my word and will keep it,' he said at last, but with a look in my direction that sent me reluctantly back to my retreat. 'I don't suppose you want names,' he went on, 'that is if anything I have to tell is of a delicate nature?'

"'Oh, no,' answered the other, 'only facts and places.'

"'I don't think places are necessary either,' he returned. 'I will tell you what I did and that must serve you. I did not promise to give number and street.'

"'Well, well,' Joe exclaimed; 'earn your fifty, that is all. Show that you remember where you were on the night of' – and with an admirable show of indifference he pretended to consult the paper between them – 'the seventeenth of July, 1851, and I shall be satisfied.'

"'I was at the club for one thing,' said Mr T—; 'then I went to see a lady friend, where I stayed till eleven. She wore a blue muslin – What is that?'

"I had betrayed myself by a quick movement which sent a glass tumbler to the floor. Helen Zabriskie had worn a blue muslin on that same night. I had noted it when I stood on the balcony watching her and her husband.

"'That noise?' It was Joe who was speaking. 'You don't know Reuben as well as I do or you wouldn't ask. It is his practice, I am sorry to say, to accentuate his pleasure in draining my bottles by dropping a glass at every third one.'

"Mr T— went on.

"'She was a married woman and I thought she loved me; but – and this is the greatest proof I can offer you that I am giving you a true account of that night – she had not had the slightest idea of the extent of my passion, and only consented to see me at all because she thought, poor thing, that a word from her would set me straight, and rid her of attentions that were fast becoming obnoxious. A sorry figure for a fellow to cut who has not been without his triumphs; but you caught me on the most detestable date in my calendar, and – "

"There is where he stopped being interesting, so I will not waste time by quoting further. And now what reply shall I make when Joe Smithers asks me double his usual price, as he will be sure to do, next time? Has he not earned an advance? I really think so.

"I have spent the whole day in weaving together the facts I have gleaned, and the suspicions I have formed, into a consecutive whole likely to present my theory in a favorable light to my superiors. But just as I thought myself in shape to meet their inquiries, I received an immediate summons into their presence, where I was given a duty to perform of so extraordinary and unexpected a nature, that it effectually drove from my mind all my own plans for the elucidation of the Zabriskie mystery.

"This was nothing more nor less than to take charge of a party of people who were going to the Jersey heights for the purpose of testing Dr Zabriskie's skill with a pistol."

III

The cause of this sudden move was soon explained to me. Mrs Zabriskie, anxious to have an end put to the present condition of affairs, had begged for a more rigid examination into her husband's state. This being accorded, a strict and impartial inquiry had taken place, with a result not unlike that which followed the first one. Three out of his four interrogators judged him insane, and could not be moved from their opinion, though opposed by the verdict of the young expert who had been living in the house with him. Dr Zabriskie seemed to read their thoughts, and, showing extreme agitation, begged as before for an opportunity to prove his sanity by showing his skill in shooting. This time a disposition was evinced to grant his request, which Mrs Zabriskie no sooner perceived, than she added her supplications to his that the question might be thus settled.

A pistol was accordingly brought; but at sight of it her courage failed, and she changed her plea to an entreaty that the experiment should be postponed till the next day, and should then take place in the woods away from the sight and hearing of needless spectators.

Though it would have been much wiser to have ended the matter there and then, the superintendent was prevailed upon to listen to her entreaties, and thus it was that I came to be a spectator, if not a participator, in the final scene of this most somber drama.

There are some events which impress the human mind so deeply that their memory mingles with all after-experiences. Though I have made it a rule to forget as soon as possible the tragic episodes into which I am constantly plunged, there is one scene in my life which will not depart at my will; and that is, the sight which met my eyes from the bow of the small boat in which Dr Zabriskie and his wife were rowed over to Jersey on that memorable afternoon.

Though it was by no means late in the day, the sun was already sinking, and the bright red glare which filled the heavens and shone full upon the faces of the half-dozen persons before me added much to the tragic nature of the scene, though we were far from comprehending its full significance.

The doctor sat with his wife in the stern, and it was upon their faces my glance was fixed. The glare shone luridly on his sightless eyeballs, and as I noticed his unwinking lids I realized as never before what it was to be blind in the midst of sunshine. Her eyes, on the contrary, were lowered, but there was a look of hopeless misery in her colorless face which made her appearance infinitely pathetic, and I felt confident that if he could only have seen her, he would not have maintained the cold and unresponsive manner which chilled the words on her lips and made all advance on her part impossible.

On the seat in front of them sat the inspector and a doctor, and from some quarter, possibly from under the inspector's coat, there came the monotonous ticking of a small clock, which, I had been told, was to serve as a target for the blind man's aim.

This ticking was all I heard, though the noise and bustle of a great traffic were pressing upon us on every side. And I am sure it was all she heard, as, with hand pressed to her heart and eyes fixed on the opposite shore, she waited for the event which was to determine whether the man she loved was a criminal or only a being afflicted of God, and worthy of her unceasing care and devotion.

As the sun cast its last scarlet gleam over the water, the boat grounded, and it fell to my lot to assist Mrs Zabriskie up the bank. As I did so, I allowed myself to say: "I am your friend, Mrs Zabriskie," and was astonished to see her tremble, and turn towards me with a look like that of a frightened child.

But there was always this characteristic blending in her countenance of the childlike and the severe, such as may so often be seen in the faces of nuns, and beyond an added pang of pity for this beautiful but afflicted woman, I let the moment pass without giving it the weight it perhaps demanded.

"The doctor and his wife had a long talk last night," was whispered in my ear as we wound our way along into the woods. I turned, and perceived at my side the expert physician, portions of whose diary I have already quoted. He had come by another boat.

"But it did not seem to heal whatever breach lies between them," he proceeded. Then in a quick, curious tone, he asked: "Do you believe this attempt on his part is likely to prove anything but a farce?"

"I believe he will shatter the clock to pieces with his first shot," I answered, and could say no more, for we had already reached the ground which had been selected for this trial at arms, and the various members of the party were being placed in their several positions.

The doctor, to whom light and darkness were alike, stood with his face towards the western glow, and at his side were grouped the inspector and the two physicians. On the arm of one of the latter hung Dr Zabriskie's overcoat, which he had taken off as soon as he had reached the field.

Mrs Zabriskie stood at the other end of the opening, near a tall stump, upon which it had been decided that the clock should be placed when the moment came for the doctor to show his skill. She had been accorded the privilege of setting the clock on this stump, and I saw it shining in her hand as she paused for a moment to glance back at the circle of gentlemen who were awaiting her movements. The hands of the clock stood at five minutes to five, though I scarcely noted the fact at the time, for her eyes were on mine, and as she passed me she spoke:

"If he is not himself, he cannot be trusted. Watch him carefully, and see that he does no mischief to himself or others. Be at his right hand, and stop him if he does not handle his pistol properly."

I promised, and she passed on, setting the clock upon the stump and immediately drawing back to a suitable distance at the right, where she stood, wrapped in her long, dark cloak, quite alone. Her face shone ghastly white, even in its environment of snow-covered boughs which surrounded her, and, noting this, I wished the minutes fewer between the present moment and the hour of five, at which he was to draw the trigger.

"Dr Zabriskie," quoth the inspector, "we have endeavored to make this trial a perfectly fair one. You are to have one shot at a small clock which has been placed within a suitable distance, and which you are expected to hit, guided only by the sound which it will make in striking the hour of five. Are you satisfied with the arrangement?"

"Perfectly. Where is my wife?"

"On the other side of the field, some ten paces from the stump upon which the clock is fixed."

He bowed, and his face showed satisfaction.

"May I expect the clock to strike soon?"

"In less than five minutes," was the answer.

"Then let me have the pistol; I wish to become acquainted with its size and weight."

We glanced at each other, then across at her.

She made a gesture; it was one of acquiescence.

Immediately the inspector placed the weapon in the blind man's hand. It was at once apparent that the doctor understood the instrument, and my last doubt vanished as to the truth of all he had told us.

"Thank God I am blind this hour, and cannot see her," fell unconsciously from his lips; then, before the echo of these words had left my ears, he raised his voice and observed calmly enough, considering that he was about to prove himself a criminal in order to save himself from being thought a madman:

"Let no one move. I must have my ears free for catching the first stroke of the clock." And he raised the pistol before him.

There was a moment of torturing suspense and deep, unbroken silence. My eyes were on him, and so I did not watch the clock, but suddenly I was moved by some irresistible impulse to note how Mrs Zabriskie was bearing herself at this critical moment, and, casting a hurried glance in her direction, I perceived her tall figure swaying from side to side, as if under an intolerable strain of feeling. Her eyes were on the clock, the hands of which seemed to creep with snail-like pace along the dial, when unexpectedly, and a full minute before the minute-hand had reached the stroke of five, I caught a movement on her part, saw the flash of something round and white show for an instant against the darkness of her cloak, and was about to shriek warning to the doctor, when the shrill, quick stroke of a clock rang out on the frosty air, followed by the ping and flash of a pistol.

A sound of shattered glass, followed by a suppressed cry, told us that the bullet had struck the mark, but before we could move, or rid our eyes of the smoke which the wind had blown into our faces, there came another sound which made our hair stand on end, and sent the blood back in terror to our hearts. Another clock was striking, the clock which we now perceived was still standing upright on the stump where Mrs Zabriskie had placed it.

Whence came the clock, then, which had struck before the time, and had been shattered for its pains? One quick look told us. On the ground, ten paces at the right, lay Helen Zabriskie, a broken clock at her side, and in her breast a bullet which was fast sapping the life from her sweet eyes.

We had to tell him, there was such pleading in her looks; and never shall I forget the scream that rang from his lips as he realized the truth. Breaking from our midst, he rushed forward, and fell at her feet as if guided by some supernatural instinct.

"Helen!" he shrieked; "what is this? Were not my hands dyed deep enough in blood that you should make me answerable for your life also?"

Her eyes were closed, but she opened them. Looking long and steadily at his agonized face, she faltered forth:

"It is not you who have killed me; it is your crime. Had you been innocent of Mr Hasbrouck's death, your bullet would never have found my heart. Did you think I could survive the proof that you had killed that good man?"

"I – I did it unwittingly. I – "

"Hush!" she commanded, with an awful look, which, happily, he could not see. "I had another motive. I wished to prove to you, even at the cost of my life, that I loved you, had always loved you, and not – "

It was now his turn to silence her. His hand crept over her lips, and his despairing face turned itself blindly towards us.

"Go!" he cried; "leave us! Let me take a last farewell of my dying wife, without listeners or spectators."

Consulting the eye of the physician who stood beside me, and seeing no hope in it, I fell slowly back. The others followed, and the doctor was left alone with his wife. From the distant position we took, we saw her arms creep round his neck, saw her head fall confidingly on his breast, then silence settled upon them and upon all nature, the gathering twilight deepening, till the last glow disappeared from the heavens above and from the circle of leafless trees which enclosed this tragedy from the outside world.

But at last there came a stir, and Dr Zabriskie, rising before us, with the dead body of his wife held closely to his breast, confronted us with a countenance so rapturous that he looked like a man transfigured.

"I will carry her to the boat," said he. "Not another hand shall touch her. She was my true wife, my true wife!" And he towered into an attitude of such dignity and passion, that for a moment he took on heroic proportions and we forgot that he had just proved himself to have committed a cold-blooded and ghastly crime.

The stars were shining when we again took our seats in the boat; and if the scene of our crossing to Jersey was impressive, what shall be said of that of our return?

The doctor, as before, sat in the stern, an awesome figure, upon which the moon shone with a white radiance that seemed to lift his face out of the surrounding darkness and set it, like an image of frozen horror, before our eyes. Against his breast he held the form of his dead wife, and now and then I saw him stoop as if he were listening for some tokens of life at her set lips. Then he would lift himself again, with hopelessness stamped upon his features, only to lean forward in renewed hope that was again destined to disappointment.

The inspector and the accompanying physician had taken seats at the bow, and unto me had been assigned the special duty of watching over the doctor. This I did from a low seat in front of him. I was therefore so close that I heard his laboring breath, and though my heart was full of awe and compassion, I could not prevent myself from bending towards him and saying these words:

"Dr Zabriskie, the mystery of your crime is no longer a mystery to me. Listen and see if I do not understand your temptation, and how you, a conscientious and God-fearing man, came to slay your innocent neighbor.

"A friend of yours, or so he called himself, had for a long time filled your ears with tales tending to make you suspicious of your wife and jealous of a certain man whom I will not name. You knew that your friend had a grudge against this man, and so for many months turned a deaf ear to his insinuations. But finally some change which you detected in your wife's bearing or conversation roused your own suspicions, and you began to doubt if all was false that came to your ears, and to curse your blindness, which in a measure rendered you helpless. The jealous fever grew and had risen to a high point, when one night – a memorable night – this friend met you just as you were leaving town, and with cruel craft whispered in your ear that the man you hated was even then with your wife, and that if you would return at once to your home you would find him in her company.

"The demon that lurks at the heart of all men, good or bad, thereupon took complete possession of you, and you answered this false friend by saying that you would not return without a pistol. Whereupon he offered to take you to his house and give you his. You consented, and getting rid of your servant by sending him to Poughkeepsie with your excuses, you entered a coach with your friend.

"You say you bought the pistol, and perhaps you did, but, however that may be, you left his house with it in your pocket and, declining companionship, walked home, arriving at the Colonnade a little before midnight.

"Ordinarily you have no difficulty in recognizing your own doorstep. But, being in a heated frame of mind, you walked faster than usual and so passed your own house and stopped at that of Mr Hasbrouck's, one door beyond. As the entrances of these houses are all alike, there was but one way in which you could have made yourself sure that you had reached your own dwelling, and that was by feeling for the doctor's sign at the side of the door. But you never thought of that. Absorbed in dreams of vengeance, your sole impulse was to enter by the quickest means possible. Taking out your night-key, you thrust it into the lock. It fitted, but it took strength to turn it, so much strength that the key was bent and twisted by the effort. But this incident, which would have attracted your attention at another time, was lost upon you at this moment. An entrance had been effected, and you were in too excited a frame of mind to notice at what cost, or to detect the small differences apparent in the atmosphere and furnishings of the two houses – trifles which would have arrested your attention under other circumstances, and made you pause before the upper floor had been reached.

"It was while going up the stairs that you took out your pistol, so that by the time you arrived at the front-room door you held it ready cocked and drawn in your hand. For, being blind, you feared escape on the part of your victim, and so waited for nothing but the sound of a man's voice before firing. When, therefore, the unfortunate Mr Hasbrouck, roused by this sudden intrusion, advanced with an exclamation of astonishment, you pulled the trigger, killing him on the spot. It must have been immediately upon his fall that you recognized some word he uttered, or from some contact you may have had with your surroundings, that you were in the wrong house and had killed the wrong man; for you cried out, in evident remorse, 'God! what have I done!' and fled without approaching your victim.

"Descending the stairs, you rushed from the house, closing the front door behind you and regaining your own without being seen. But here you found yourself baffled in your attempted escape by two things. First, by the pistol you still held in your hand, and secondly, by the fact that the key upon which you depended for entering your own door was so twisted out of shape that you knew it would be useless for you to attempt to use it. What did you do in this emergency? You have already told us, though the story seemed so improbable at the time, you found nobody to believe it but myself. The pistol you flung far away from you down the pavement, from which, by one of those rare chances which sometimes happen in this world, it was presently picked up by some late passer-by of more or less doubtful character. The door offered less of an obstacle than you anticipated; for when you turned to it again you found it, if I am not greatly mistaken, ajar, left so, as we have reason to believe, by one who had gone out of it but a few minutes before in a state which left him but little master of his actions. It was this fact which provided you with an answer when you were asked how you succeeded in getting into Mr Hasbrouck's house after the family had retired for the night.

"Astonished at the coincidence, but hailing with gladness the deliverance which it offered, you went in and ascended at once into your wife's presence; and it was from her lips, and not from those of Mrs Hasbrouck, that the cry arose which startled the neighborhood and prepared men's minds for the tragic words which were shouted a moment later from the next house.

But she who uttered the scream knew of no tragedy save that which was taking place in her own breast. She had just repulsed a dastardly suitor, and, seeing you enter so unexpectedly in a state of unaccountable horror and agitation, was naturally stricken with dismay, and thought she saw your ghost, or, what was worse, a possible avenger; while you, having failed to kill the man you sought, and having killed a man you esteemed, let no surprise on her part lure you into any dangerous self-betrayal. You strove instead to soothe her, and even attempted to explain the excitement under which you labored, by an account of your narrow escape at the station, till the sudden alarm from next door distracted her attention, and sent both your thoughts and hers in a different direction. Not till conscience had fully awakened and the horror of your act had had time to tell upon your sensitive nature, did you breathe forth those vague confessions, which, not being supported by the only explanations which would have made them credible, led her, as well as the police, to consider you affected in your mind. Your pride as a man, and your consideration for her as a woman, kept you silent, but did not keep the worm from preying upon your heart.

"Am I not correct in my surmises, Dr Zabriskie, and is not this the true explanation of your crime?"

With a strange look, he lifted up his face.

"Hush!" said he; "you will awaken her. See how peacefully she sleeps! I should not like to have her awakened now, she is so tired, and I – I have not watched over her as I should."

Appalled at his gesture, his look, his tone, I drew back, and for a few minutes no sound was to be heard but the steady dip-dip of the oars and the lap-lap of the waters against the boat. Then there came a quick uprising, the swaying before me of something dark and tall and threatening, and before I could speak or move, or even stretch forth my hands to stay him, the seat before me was empty and darkness had filled the place where but an instant previous he had sat, a fearsome figure, erect and rigid as a sphinx.

What little moonlight there was only served to show us a few rising bubbles, marking the spot where the unfortunate man had sunk with his much-loved burden. We could not save him. As the widening circles fled farther and farther out, the tide drifted us away, and we lost the spot which had seen the termination of one of earth's saddest tragedies.

The bodies were never recovered. The police reserved to themselves the right of withholding from the public the real facts which made this catastrophe an awful remembrance to those who witnessed it. A verdict of accidental death by drowning answered all purposes, and saved the memory of the unfortunate pair from such calumny as might have otherwise assailed it. It was the least we could do for two beings whom circumstances had so greatly afflicted.

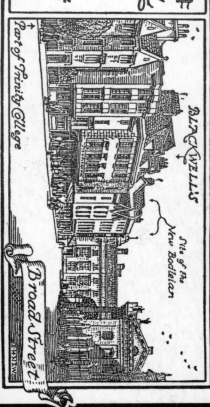

B•H•
BLACKWELL
Ltd
50 & 51
Broad Street
OXFORD

BLACKWELL'S

Site of the
New Bodleian

Part of Trinity College

Broad Street

Vintage edition bookmark
Originally designed and distributed between 1887–1918

Arthur Morrison

The Flitterbat Lancers

Of that crowd of detectives that sprang up after the success of Sherlock Holmes the most popular – and indeed one of the best – was Martin Hewitt, who also appeared in the pages of The Strand Magazine. *Where Holmes was eccentric, Hewitt is about as normal as a detective can be: plump, of medium height, with an amiable nature and no discernible oddities.*

His creator, Arthur Morrison (1863–1945), was a freelance journalist whose books, apart from the Hewitt titles, included A Child of the Jago *and* Tales of Mean Streets: *the latter a phrase that has rung down the ages of detective fiction! Morrison's collection of Oriental art was acquired after his death by the British Museum, and his* The Painters of Japan *remains a standard text on the subject.*

"The Flitterbat Lancers" is one of the best of the early Martin Hewitt stories and it is told, as they all were, by Hewitt's "Watson", the journalist Brett.

IT WAS LATE on a summer evening, two or three years back, that I drowsed in my armchair over a particularly solid and ponderous volume of essays on social economy. I was doing a good deal of reviewing at the time, and I remember well that this particular volume had a property of such exceeding toughness that I had already made three successive attacks on it, on as many successive evenings, each attack having been defeated in the end by sleep. The weather was hot, my chair was very comfortable, and the book had somewhere about its strings of polysyllables an essence as of laudanum. Still something had been done on each evening, and now on the fourth I strenuously endeavored to finish the book. I was just beginning to feel that the words before me were sliding about and losing their meanings, when a sudden crash and a jingle of broken glass behind me woke me with a start, and I threw the book down. A pane of glass in my window was smashed, and I hurried across and threw up the sash to see, if I could, whence the damage had come.

The building in which my chambers (and Martin Hewitt's office) were situated was accessible – or rather visible, for there was no entrance –

from the rear. There was, in fact, a small courtyard, reached by a passage from the street behind, and into this courtyard, my sitting-room window looked.

"Hullo, there!" I shouted. But there came no reply. Nor could I distinguish anybody in the courtyard. Some men had been at work during the day on a drainpipe, and I reflected that probably their litter had provided the stone with which my window had been smashed. As I looked, however, two men came hurrying from the passage into the court, and going straight into the deep shadow of one corner, presently appeared again in a less obscure part, hauling forth a third man, who must have already been there in hiding. The third man struggled fiercely, but without avail, and was dragged across toward the passage leading to the street beyond. But the most remarkable feature of the whole thing was the silence of all three men. No cry, no exclamation, escaped any of them. In perfect silence the two hauled the third across the courtyard, and in perfect silence he swung and struggled to resist and escape. The matter astonished me not a little, and the men were entering the passage before I found voice to shout at them. But they took no notice, and disappeared. Soon after I heard cab wheels in the street beyond, and had no doubt that the two men had carried off their prisoner.

I turned back into my room a little perplexed. It seemed probable that the man who had been borne off had broken my window. But why? I looked about on the floor, and presently found the missile. It was, as I had expected, a piece of broken concrete, but it was wrapped up in a worn piece of paper, which had partly opened out as it lay on my carpet, thus indicating that it had just been crumpled round the stone.

I disengaged the paper and spread it out. Then I saw it to be a rather hastily written piece of manuscript music, whereof I append a reduced facsimile:

This gave me no help. I turned the paper this way and that, but could make nothing of it. There was not a mark on it that I could discover, except the music and the scrawled title, *Flitterbat Lancers*, at the top. The paper was old, dirty, and cracked. What did it all mean? One might conceive of a person in certain circumstances sending a message – possibly an appeal for help – through a friend's window, wrapped round a stone, but this seemed to be nothing of that sort.

Once more I picked up the paper, and with an idea to hear what the *Flitterbat Lancers* sounded like, I turned to my little pianette and strummed over the notes, making my own time and changing it as seemed likely. But I could by no means extract from the notes anything resembling an air. I half thought of trying Martin Hewitt's office door, in case he might still be there and offer a guess at the meaning of my smashed window and the scrap of paper, when Hewitt himself came in. He had stayed late to examine a bundle of papers in connection with a case just placed in his hands, and now, having finished, came to find if I were disposed for an evening stroll before turning in. I handed him the paper and the piece of concrete, observing, "There's a little job for you, Hewitt, instead of the stroll." And I told him the complete history of my smashed window.

Hewitt listened attentively, and examined both the paper and the fragment of paving. "You say these people made absolutely no sound whatever?" he asked.

"None but that of scuffling, and even that they seemed to do quietly."

"Could you see whether or not the two men gagged the other, or placed their hands over his mouth?"

"No, they certainly didn't do that. It was dark, of course, but not so dark as to prevent my seeing generally what they were doing."

Hewitt stood for half a minute in thought, and then said, "There's something in this, Brett – what, I can't guess at the moment, but something deep, I fancy. Are you sure you won't come out now?"

I told Hewitt that I was sure, and that I should stick to my work.

"Very well," he said; "then perhaps you will lend me these articles?" holding up the paper and the stone.

"Delighted," I said. "If you get no more melody out of the clinker than I did out of the paper, you won't have a musical evening. Goodnight!"

Hewitt went away with the puzzle in his hand, and I turned once more to my social economy, and, thanks to the gentleman who smashed my window, conquered.

*   *   *

At this time my only regular daily work was on an evening paper so that I left home at a quarter to eight on the morning following the adventure of my broken window, in order, as usual, to be at the office at eight; consequently it was not until lunchtime that I had an opportunity of seeing Hewitt. I went to my own rooms first, however, and on the landing by my door I found the housekeeper in conversation with a shortish, sun-browned man, whose accent at once convinced me that he hailed from across the Atlantic. He had called, it appeared, three or four times during the morning to see me, getting more impatient each time. As he did not seem even to know my name, the housekeeper had not considered it expedient to give him any information about me, and he was growing irascible under the treatment. When I at last appeared, however, he left her and approached me eagerly.

"See here, sir," he said, "I've been stumpin' these here durn stairs o' yours half through the mornin'. I'm anxious to apologize, and fix up some damage."

He had followed me into my sitting-room, and was now standing with his back to the fireplace, a dripping umbrella in one hand, and the forefinger of the other held up shoulder-high and pointing, in the manner of a pistol, to my window, which, by the way, had been mended during the morning, in accordance with my instructions to the housekeeper.

"Sir," he continued, "last night I took the extreme liberty of smashin' your winder."

"Oh," I said, "that was you, was it?"

"It was, sir – me. For that I hev come humbly to apologize. I trust the draft has not discommoded you, sir. I regret the accident, and I wish to pay for the fixin' up and the general inconvenience." He placed a sovereign on the table. "I 'low you'll call that square now, sir, and fix things friendly and comfortable as between gentlemen, an' no ill will. Shake."

And he formally extended his hand.

I took it at once. "Certainly," I said. "As a matter of fact, you haven't inconvenienced me at all; indeed, there were some circumstances about the affair that rather interested me." And I pushed the sovereign toward him.

"Say now," he said, looking a trifle disappointed at my unwillingness to accept his money, "didn't I startle your nerves?"

"Not a bit," I answered, laughing. "In fact, you did me a service by preventing me going to sleep just when I shouldn't; so we'll say no more of that."

"Well – there was one other little thing," he pursued, looking at me rather sharply as he pocketed the sovereign. "There was a bit o' paper round that pebble that came in here. Didn't happen to notice that, did you?"

"Yes, I did. It was an old piece of manuscript music."

"That was it – exactly. Might you happen to have it handy now?"

"Well," I said, "as a matter of fact a friend of mine has it now. I tried playing it over once or twice, as a matter of curiosity, but I couldn't make anything of it, and so I handed it to him."

"Ah!" said my visitor, watching me narrowly, "that's a puzzler, that *Flitterbat Lancers* – a real puzzler. It whips 'em all. Ha, ha!" He laughed suddenly – a laugh that seemed a little artificial. "There's music fellers as 'lows to set right down and play off anything right away that can't make anything of the *Flitterbat Lancers*. That was two of 'em that was monkeyin' with me last night. They never could make anythin' of it at all, and I was tantalizing them with it all along till they got real mad, and reckoned to get it out o' my pocket and learn it at home. Ha, ha! So I got away for a bit, and just rolled it round a stone and heaved it through your winder before they could come up, your winder being the nearest one with a light in it. Ha, ha! I'll be considerable obliged if you'll get it from your friend right now. Is he stayin' hereabout?"

The story was so ridiculously lame that I determined to confront my visitor with Hewitt, and observe the result. If he had succeeded in making any sense of the *Flitterbat Lancers*, the scene might be amusing. So I answered at once, "Yes; his office is on the floor below; he will probably be in at about this time. Come down with me."

We went down, and found Hewitt in his outer office. "This gentleman," I told him with a solemn intonation, "has come to ask for his piece of manuscript music, the *Flitterbat Lancers*. He is particularly proud of it, because nobody who tries to play it can make any sort of tune out of it, and it was entirely because two dear friends of his were anxious to drag it out of his pocket and practice it over on the quiet that he flung it through my windowpane last night, wrapped round a piece of concrete."

The stranger glanced sharply at me, and I could see that my manner and tone rather disconcerted him. But Hewitt came forward at once. "Oh, yes," he said. "Just so – quite a natural sort of thing. As a matter of fact, I quite expected you. Your umbrella's wet – do you mind putting it in the stand? Thank you. Come into my private office."

We entered the inner room, and Hewitt, turning to the stranger, went on: "Yes, that is a very extraordinary piece of music, that *Flitterbat Lancers*. I have been having a little bit of practice with it myself, though I'm really nothing of a musician. I don't wonder you are anxious to keep it to yourself. Sit down."

The stranger, with a distrustful look at Hewitt, complied. At this moment, Hewitt's clerk, Kerrett, entered from the outer office with a slip of paper. Hewitt glanced at it, and crumpled it in his hand. "I am engaged just now," was his remark, and Kerrett vanished.

"And now," Hewitt said, as he sat down and suddenly turned to the stranger with an intent gaze, "and now, Mr Hooker, we'll talk of this music."

The stranger started and frowned. "You've the advantage of me, sir," he said; "you seem to know my name, but I don't know yours."

Hewitt smiled pleasantly. "My name," he said, "is Hewitt – Martin Hewitt, and it is my business to know a great many things. For instance, I know that you are Mr Reuben B. Hooker, of Robertsville, Ohio."

The visitor pushed his chair back, and stared. "Well – that gits me," he said. "You're a pretty smart chap, Mr Hewitt. I've heard your name before, of course. And – and so you've been a-studyin' the *Flitterbat Lancers*, have you?" This with a keen glance at Hewitt's face. "Well, s'pose you have. What's your idea?"

"Why," answered Hewitt, still keeping his steadfast gaze on Hooker's eyes, "I think it's pretty late in the century to be fishing about for the Wedlake jewels."

These words astonished me almost as much as they did Mr Hooker. The great Wedlake jewel robbery is, as many will remember, a traditional story of the 'sixties. I remembered no more of it at the time than probably most men do who have at some time or another read the *causes célèbres* of the century. Sir Francis Wedlake's country house had been robbed, and the whole of Lady Wedlake's magnificent collection of jewels stolen. A man named Shiels, a strolling musician, had been arrested and had been sentenced to a long term of penal servitude. Another man named Legg – one of the comparatively wealthy scoundrels who finance promising thefts or swindles and pocket the greater part of the proceeds – had also been punished, but only a very few of the trinkets, and those quite unimportant items, had been recovered. The great bulk of the booty was never brought to light. So much I remembered, and Hewitt's sudden mention of the Wedlake jewels in connection with my broken window, Mr Reuben B. Hooker, and the *Flitterbat Lancers*, astonished me not a little.

As for Hooker, he did his best to hide his perturbation, but with little success. "Wedlake jewels, eh?" he said; "and – and what's that to do with it, anyway."

"To do with it?" responded Hewitt, with an air of carelessness. "Well, well, I had my idea, nothing more. If the Wedlake jewels have nothing to do with it, we'll say no more about it, that's all. Here's your paper, Mr Hooker – only a little crumpled." He rose and placed the article in Mr Hooker's hand, with the manner of terminating the interview.

Hooker rose, with a bewildered look on his face, and turned toward the door. Then he stopped, looked at the floor, scratched his cheek, and finally sat down and put his hat on the ground. "Come," he said, "we'll play a square game. That paper *has* something to do with the Wedlake jewels, and, win or lose, I'll tell you all I know about it. You're a smart man and whatever I tell you, I guess it won't do me no harm; it ain't done me no good yet, anyway."

"Say what you please, of course," Hewitt answered, "but think first. You might tell me something you'd be sorry for afterward."

"Say, will you listen to what I say, and tell me if you think I've been swindled or not? My two hundred and fifty dollars is gone now, and I guess I won't go skirmishing after it anymore if you think it's no good. Will you do that much?"

"As I said before," Hewitt replied, "tell me what you please, and if I can help you I will. But remember, I don't ask for your secrets."

"That's all right, I guess, Mr Hewitt. Well, now, it was all like this." And Mr Reuben B. Hooker plunged into a detailed account of his adventures since his arrival in London.

Relieved of repetitions, and put as directly as possible, it was as follows: Mr Hooker was a wagon-builder, had made a good business from very humble beginnings, and intended to go on and make it still a better. Meantime, he had come over to Europe for a short holiday – a thing he had promised himself for years. He was wandering about the London streets on the second night after his arrival in the city, when he managed to get into conversation with two men at a bar. They were not very prepossessing men, though flashily dressed. Very soon they suggested a game of cards. But Reuben B. Hooker was not to be had in that way, and after a while, they parted. The two were amusing enough fellows in their way, and when Hooker saw them again the next night in the same bar, he made no difficulty in talking with them freely. After a succession of drinks, they told him that they had a speculation on hand – a speculation that meant thousands if it succeeded – and to carry out which they were only waiting for a paltry sum of £50. There was a house, they said, in which was hidden a great number of jewels of immense value, which had been deposited there by a man who was now dead. Exactly in what part of the house the jewels were to be found they did not know. There was a paper, they said, which was supposed to contain some information, but as yet they hadn't been quite able to make it out. But that would really matter very little if once they could get possession of the house. Then they would simply set to work and search from the topmost chimney to the lowermost brick, if necessary. The only present difficulty was that the house was occupied, and that the landlord wanted a large deposit of rent down before he would consent to turn out his present tenants and give them possession at a higher rental. This deposit would come to £50, and they hadn't the money. However, if any friend of theirs who meant business would put the necessary sum at their disposal, and keep his mouth shut, they would make him an equal partner in the proceeds with themselves; and as the value of the whole haul would probably be something not very far off £20,000, the speculation would bring a tremendous return to the man who was smart enough to put down his £50.

Hooker, very distrustful, skeptically demanded more detailed particulars of the scheme. But these two men (Luker and Birks were their names, he found, in course of talking) inflexibly refused to communicate.

"Is it likely," said Luker, "that we should give the 'ole thing away to anybody who might easily go with his fifty pounds and clear out the bloomin' show? Not much. We've told you what the game is, and if you'd like to take a flutter with your fifty, all right; you'll do as well as anybody, and we'll treat you square. If you don't – well, don't, that's all. We'll get the oof from somewhere – there's blokes as 'ud jump at the chance. Anyway, we ain't going to give the show away before you've done somethin' to prove you're on the job, straight. Put your money in, and you shall know as much as we do."

Then there were more drinks, and more discussion. Hooker was still reluctant, though tempted by the prospect, and growing more venturesome with each drink.

"Don't you see," said Birks, "that if we was a-tryin' to 'ave you we should out with a tale as long as yer arm, all complete, with the address of the 'ouse and all. Then I s'pose you'd lug out the pieces on the nail, without askin' a bloomin' question. As it is, the thing's so perfectly genuine that we'd rather lose the chance and wait for some other bloke to find the money than run a chance of givin' the thing away. It's a matter o' business, simple and plain, that's all. It's a question of either us trustin' you with a chance of collarin' twenty thousand pounds or you trustin' us with a paltry fifty. We don't lay out no 'igh moral sentiments, we only say the weight o' money is all on one side. Take it or leave it, that's all. 'Ave another Scotch?"

The talk went on and the drinks went on, and it all ended, at "chucking-out time," in Reuben B. Hooker handing over five £10 notes, with smiling, though slightly incoherent, assurances of his eternal friendship for Luker and Birks.

In the morning he awoke to the realization of a bad head, a bad tongue, and a bad opinion of his proceedings of the previous night. In his sober senses it seemed plain that he had been swindled. All day he cursed his fuddled foolishness, and at night he made for the bar that had been the scene of the transaction, with little hope of seeing either Luker or Birks, who had agreed to be there to meet him. There they were, however, and, rather to his surprise, they made no demand for more money. They asked him if he understood music, and showed him the worn old piece of paper containing the *Flitterbat Lancers*. The exact spot, they said, where the jewels were hidden was supposed to be indicated somehow on that piece of paper. Hooker did not understand music, and could find nothing on the paper that looked in the least like a direction to a hiding-place for jewels or anything else.

Luker and Birks then went into full particulars of their project. First, as to its history. The jewels were the famous Wedlake jewels, which had been taken from Sir Francis Wedlake's house in 1866 and never heard of again. A certain Jerry Shiels had been arrested in connection with the robbery, had been given a long sentence of penal servitude, and had died in jail. This Jerry Shiels was an extraordinarily clever criminal, and traveled about the country as a street musician. Although an expert burglar, he very rarely perpetrated robberies himself, but acted as a sort of traveling fence, receiving stolen property and transmitting it to London or out of the country. He also acted as the agent of a man named Legg, who had money, and who financed any likely looking project of a criminal nature that Shiels might arrange.

Jerry Shiels traveled with a "pardner" – a man who played the harp and acted as his assistant and messenger in affairs wherein Jerry was reluctant to appear personally. When Shiels was arrested, he had in his possession a quantity of printed and manuscript music, and after his first remand his "pardner," Jimmy Snape, applied for the music to be given up to him, in order, as he explained, that he might earn his living. No objection was raised to this, and Shiels was quite willing that Snape should have it, and so it was handed over. Now among the music was a small slip, headed *Flitterbat Lancers*, which Shiels had shown to Snape before the arrest. In case of Shiels being taken, Snape was to take this slip to Legg as fast as he could.

But as chance would have it, on that very day Legg himself was arrested, and soon after was sentenced also to a term of years. Snape hung about in London for a little while, and then emigrated. Before leaving, however, he gave the slip of music to Luker's father, a rag-shop keeper, to whom he owed money. He explained its history, and Luker senior made all sorts of fruitless efforts to get at the information concealed in the paper. He had held it to the fire to bring out concealed writing, had washed it, had held it to the light till his eyes ached, had gone over it with a magnifying glass – all in vain. He had got musicians to strum out the notes on all sorts of instruments – backwards, forwards, alternately, and in every other way he could think of. If at any time he fancied a resemblance in the resulting sound to some familiar song-tune, he got that song and studied all its words with loving care, upside-down, right-side up – every way. He took the words *Flitterbat Lancers* and transposed the letters in all directions, and did everything else he could think of. In the end he gave it up, and died. Now, lately, Luker junior had been impelled with a desire to see into the matter. He had repeated all the parental experiments, and more, with the same lack of success. He had taken his "pal" Birks into his confidence, and together they had tried other experiments till at last they began to believe that the message had probably been written in some sort of invisible ink which the subsequent washings had erased altogether. But he had done one other thing: he had found the house which Shiels had rented at the time of his arrest, and in which a good quantity of stolen property – not connected with the Wedlake case – was discovered. Here, he argued, if anywhere, Jerry Shiels had hidden the jewels. There was no other place where he could be found to have lived, or over which he had sufficient control to warrant his hiding valuables therein. Perhaps, once the house could be properly examined, something about it might give a clue as to what the message of the *Flitterbat Lancers* meant.

Hooker, of course, was anxious to know where the house in question stood, but this Luker and Birks would on no account inform him. "You've done your part," they said, "and now you leave us to do ours. There's a bit of a job about gettin' the tenants out. They won't go, and it'll take a bit of time before the landlord can make them. So you just hold your jaw and wait. When we're safe in the 'ouse, and there's no chance of anybody else pokin' in, then you can come and help find the stuff."

Hooker went home that night sober, but in much perplexity. The thing might be genuine, after all; indeed, there were many little things that made him think it was. But then, if it were, what guarantee had he that he would get his share, supposing the search turned out successful? None at all. But then it struck him for the first time that these jewels, though they may have lain untouched so long, were stolen property after all. The moral aspect of the affair began to trouble him a little, but the legal aspect troubled him more. That consideration, however, he decided to leave over for the present. He had no more than the word of Luker and Birks that the jewels (if they existed) *were* those of Lady Wedlake, and Luker and Birks themselves only professed to know from hearsay. At any rate, he made up his mind to have some guarantee for his money. In accordance with this resolve, he suggested, when he met the two men the next day, that he should take charge of the slip of music and make an independent study of it. This proposal, however, met with an instant veto.

Hooker resolved to make up a piece of paper, folded as like the slip of music as possible, and substitute one for the other at their next meeting. Then he would put the *Flitterbat Lancers* in some safe place, and face his fellow conspirators with a hand of cards equal to their own. He carried out his plan the next evening with perfect success, thanks to the contemptuous indifference with which Luker and Birks had begun to regard him. He got the slip in his pocket, and left the bar. He had not gone far, however, before Luker discovered the loss, and soon he became conscious of being followed. He looked for a cab, but he was in a dark street, and no cab was near. Luker and Birks turned the corner and began to run. He saw they must catch him. Everything now depended on his putting the *Flitterbat Lancers* out of their reach, but where he could himself recover it. He ran till he saw a narrow passageway on his right, and into this he darted. It led into a yard where stones were lying about, and in a large building before him he saw the window of a lighted room a couple of floors up. It was a desperate expedient, but there was no time for consideration. He wrapped a stone in the paper and flung it with all his force through the lighted window. Even as he did it he heard the feet of Luker and Birks as they hurried down the street. The rest of the adventure in the court I myself saw.

Luker and Birks kept Hooker in their lodgings all that night. They searched him unsuccessfully for the paper; they bullied, they swore, they cajoled, they entreated, they begged him to play the game square with his pals. Hooker merely replied that he had put the *Flitterbat Lancers* where they couldn't easily find it, and that he intended playing the game square as long as they did the same. In the end they released him, apparently with more respect than they had before entertained, advising him to get the paper into his possession as soon as he could.

"And now," said Mr Hooker, in conclusion of his narrative, "perhaps you'll give me a bit of advice. Am I playin' a fool-game running after these toughs, or ain't I?"

Hewitt shrugged his shoulders. "It all depends," he said, "on your friends Luker and Birks. They may want to swindle you, or they may not. I'm afraid they'd like to, at any rate. But perhaps you've got some little security in this piece of paper. One thing is plain: they certainly believe in the deposit of the jewels themselves, else they wouldn't have taken so much trouble to get the paper back."

"Then I guess I'll go on with the thing, if that's it."

"That depends, of course, on whether you care to take trouble to get possession of what, after all, is somebody else's lawful property."

Hooker looked a little uneasy. "Well," he said, "there's that, of course. I didn't know nothin' of that at first, and when I did I'd parted with my money and felt entitled to get something back for it. Anyway, the stuff ain't found yet. When it is, why then, you know, I might make a deal with the owner. But, say, how did you find out my name, and about this here affair being jined up with the Wedlake jewels?"

Hewitt smiled. "As to the name and address, you just think it over a little when you've gone away, and if you don't see how I did it, you're not so cute as I think you are. In regard to the jewels – well, I just read the message of the *Flitterbat Lancers*, that's all."

"You read it? Whew! And what does it say? How did you do it?" Hooker turned the paper over eagerly in his hands as he spoke.

"See, now," said Hewitt, "I won't tell you all that, but I'll tell you something, and it may help you to test the real knowledge of Luker and Birks. Part of the message is in these words, which you had better write down: *Over the coals the fifth dancer slides, says Jerry Shiels the horney.*"

"What?" Hooker exclaimed, "fifth dancer slides over the coals? That's mighty odd. What's it all about?"

"About the Wedlake jewels, as I said. Now you can go and make a bargain with Luker and Birks. The only other part of the message is an address, and that they already know, if they have been telling the truth about the house they intend taking. You can offer to tell them what I have told you of the message, after they have told you where the house is, and proved to you that they are taking the steps they talked of. If they won't agree to that, I think you had best treat them as common rogues and charge them with obtaining your money under false pretenses."

Nothing more would Hewitt say than that, despite Hooker's many questions; and when at last Hooker had gone, almost as troubled and perplexed as ever, my friend turned to me and said, "Now, Brett, if you haven't lunched and would like to see the end of this business, hurry!"

"The end of it?" I said. "Is it to end so soon? How?"

"Simply by a police raid on Jerry Shiels's old house with a search warrant. I communicated with the police this morning before I came here."

"Poor Hooker!" I said.

"Oh, I had told the police before I saw Hooker, or heard of him, of course. I just conveyed the message on the music slip – that was enough. But I'll tell you all about it when there's more time; I must be off now. With the information I have given him, Hooker and his friends may make an extra push and get into the house soon, but I couldn't resist the temptation to give the unfortunate Hooker some sort of sporting chance – though it's a poor one, I fear. Get your lunch as quickly as you can, and go at once to Colt Row, Bankside – Southwark way, you know. Probably we shall be there before you. If not, wait."

Colt Row was not difficult to find. It was one of those places that decay with an excess of respectability, like Drury Lane and Clare Market. Once, when Jacob's Island was still an island, a little farther down the river, Colt Row had evidently been an unsafe place for a person with valuables about him, and then it probably prospered, in its own way. Now it was quite respectable, but very dilapidated and dirty. Perhaps it was sixty yards long – perhaps a little more. It was certainly a very few yards wide, and the houses at each side had a patient and forlorn look of waiting for a metropolitan improvement to come along and carry them away to their rest.

I could see no sign of Hewitt, nor of the police, so I walked up and down the narrow pavement for a little while. As I did so, I became conscious of a face at the window of the least ruinous house in the row, a face that I fancied expressed particular interest in my movements. The house was an old gabled structure, faced with plaster. What had apparently once been a shopwindow on the ground floor was now shuttered up, and the face that watched me – an old woman's – looked out from the window above. I had noted these particulars with some curiosity, when, arriving again at the street corner, I observed Hewitt approaching, in company with a police inspector, and followed by two unmistakable plainclothesmen.

"Well," Hewitt said, "you're first here after all. Have you seen any more of our friend Hooker?"

"No, nothing."

"Very well – probably he'll be here before long, though."

The party turned into Colt Row, and the inspector, walking up to the door of the house with the shuttered bottom window, knocked sharply. There was no response, so he knocked again, equally in vain.

"All out," said the inspector.

"No," I said; "I saw a woman watching me from the window above not three minutes ago."

"Ho, ho!" the inspector replied. "That's so, eh? One of you – you, Johnson – step round to the back, will you?"

One of the plainclothesmen started off, and after waiting another minute or two the inspector began a thundering cannonade of knocks that brought every available head out of the window of every inhabited room in the Row. At this the woman opened the window, and began abusing the inspector with a shrillness and fluency that added a street-corner audience to that already congregated at the windows.

"Go away, you blaggards!" the lady said, "you ought to be 'orse-w'ipped, every one of ye! A-comin' 'ere a-tryin' to turn decent people out o' 'ouse and 'ome! Wait till my 'usband comes 'ome – 'e'll show yer, ye mutton-cadgin' scoundrels! Payin' our rent reg'lar, and good tenants as is always been – and I'm a respectable married woman, that's what I am, ye dirty great cow-ards!" – this last word with a low, tragic emphasis.

Hewitt remembered what Hooker had said about the present tenants refusing to quit the house on the landlord's notice. "She thinks we've come from the landlord to turn her out," he said to the inspector.

"We're not here from the landlord, you old fool!" the inspector said. "We don't want to turn you out. We're the police, with a search warrant, and you'd better let us in or you'll get into trouble."

"'Ark at 'im!" the woman screamed, pointing at the inspector. "'Ark at 'im! Thinks I was born yesterday, that feller! Go 'ome, ye dirty pie-stealer, go 'ome!"

The audience showed signs of becoming a small crowd, and the inspector's patience gave out. "Here, Bradley," he said, addressing the remaining plainclothesman, "give a hand with these shutters," and the two – both powerful men – seized the iron bar which held the shutters and began to pull. But the garrison was undaunted, and, seizing a broom, the woman began to belabour the invaders about the shoulders and head from above. But just at this moment, the woman, emitting a terrific shriek, was suddenly lifted from behind and vanished. Then the head of the plainclothesman who had gone round to the back appeared, with the calm announcement, "There's a winder open behind, sir. But I'll open the front door if you like."

In a minute the bolts were shot, and the front door swung back. The placid Johnson stood in the passage, and as we passed in he said, "I've locked 'er in the back room upstairs."

"It's the bottom staircase, of course," the inspector said; and we tramped down into the basement. A little way from the stairfoot Hewitt opened a cupboard door, which enclosed a receptacle for coals. "They still keep the coals here, you see," he said, striking a match and passing it to and fro near the sloping roof of the cupboard. It was of plaster, and covered the underside of the stairs.

"And now for the fifth dancer," he said, throwing the match away and making for the staircase again. "One, two, three, four, five," and he tapped the fifth stair from the bottom.

The stairs were uncarpeted, and Hewitt and the inspector began a careful examination of the one he had indicated. They tapped it in different places, and Hewitt passed his hands over the surfaces of both tread and riser. Presently, with his hand at the outer edge of the riser, Hewitt spoke. "Here it is, I think," he said; "it is the riser that slides."

He took out his pocketknife and scraped away the grease and paint from the edge of the old stair. Then a joint was plainly visible. For a long time the plank, grimed and set with age, refused to shift; but at last, by dint of patience and firm fingers, it moved, and was drawn clean out from the end.

Within, nothing was visible but grime, fluff, and small rubbish. The inspector passed his hand along the bottom angle. "Here's something," he said. It was the gold hook of an old-fashioned earring, broken off short.

Hewitt slapped his thigh. "Somebody's been here before us," he said, "and a good time back too, judging from the dust. That hook's a plain indication that jewelry was here once. There's plainly nothing more, except – except this piece of paper." Hewitt's eyes had detected – black with loose grime as it was – a small piece of paper lying at the bottom of the recess. He drew it out and shook off the dust. "Why, what's this?" he exclaimed. "More music!"

We went to the window, and there saw in Hewitt's hand a piece of written musical notation, thus:

Hewitt pulled out from his pocket a few pieces of paper. "Here is a copy I made this morning of the *Flitterbat Lancers*, and a note or two of my own as well," he said. He took a pencil, and, constantly referring to his own papers, marked a letter under each note on the last-found slip of music. When he had done this, the letters read:

You are a clever cove whoever you are but there was a cleverer says Jim Snape the horney's mate.

"You see?" Hewitt said, handing the inspector the paper. "Snape, the unconsidered messenger, finding Legg in prison, set to work and got the jewels for himself. The thing was a cryptogram, of course, of a very simple sort, though uncommon in design. Snape was a humorous soul, too, to leave this message here in the same cipher, on the chance of somebody else reading the *Flitterbat Lancers*."

"But," I asked, "why did he give that slip of music to Luker's father?"

"Well, he owed him money, and got out of it that way. Also, he avoided the appearance of 'flushness' that paying the debt might have given him, and got quietly out of the country with his spoils."

The shrieks upstairs had grown hoarser, but the broom continued vigorously. "Let that woman out," said the inspector, "and we'll go and report. Not much good looking for Snape now, I fancy. But there's some satisfaction in clearing up that old quarter-century mystery."

We left the place pursued by the execrations of the broom wielder, who bolted the door behind us, and from the window defied us to come back, and vowed she would have us all searched before a magistrate for what we had probably stolen. In the very next street we hove in sight of Reuben B. Hooker in the company of two swell-mob-looking fellows, who sheered off down a side turning in sight of our group. Hooker, too, looked rather shy at the sight of the inspector.

"The meaning of the thing was so very plain," Hewitt said to me afterwards, "that the duffers who had the *Flitterbat Lancers* in hand for so long never saw it at all. If Shiels had made an ordinary clumsy cryptogram, all letters and figures, they would have seen what it was at once, and at least would have tried to read it; but because it was put in the form of music, they tried everything else but the right way. It was a clever dodge of Shiels's, without a doubt. Very few people, police officers or not, turning over a heap of old music, would notice or feel suspicious of that little slip among the rest. But once one sees it is a cryptogram (and the absence of bar lines and of notes beyond the stave would suggest that) the reading is as easy as possible. For my part I tried it as a cryptogram at once. You know the plan – it has been described a hundred times. See here – look at this copy of the *Flitterbat Lancers*. Its only difficulty – and that is a small one – is that the words are not divided. Since there are positions for less than a dozen notes on the stave, and there are twenty-six letters to be indicated, it follows that crotchets, quavers, and semiquavers on the same line or space must mean different letters. The first step is obvious. We count the notes to ascertain which sign occurs most frequently, and we find that the crotchet in the top space is the sign required – it occurs no less than eleven times. Now the letter most frequently occurring in an ordinary sentence of English is *e*. Let us then suppose that this represents *e*. At once a coincidence strikes us. In ordinary musical notation in the treble clef the note occupying the top space would be E. Let us remember that presently. Now the most common word in the English language is *the*. We know the sign for *e*, the last letter of this word, so let us see if in more than one place that sign is preceded by two others identical in each case. If so, the probability is that the other two signs will represent *t* and *h*, and the whole word will be *the*. Now it happens in no less than four places the sign *e* is preceded by the same two other signs – once in the first line, twice in the second, and once in the fourth. No word of three letters ending in *e* would be in the least likely to occur four times in a short sentence except *the*. Then we will call it *the*, and note the signs preceding the *e*. They are a quaver under the bottom line for the *t*, and a crotchet on the first space for the *h*. We travel along the stave, and wherever these signs occur we mark them with *t* or *h*, as the case may be. But now we remember that *e*, the crotchet in the top space, is in its right place as a musical note, while the crotchet in the bottom space means *h*, which is no musical note at all. Considering this for a minute, we remember that among the notes which are expressed in ordinary music on the treble stave, without the use of ledger lines, *d e* and *f* are repeated at the lower and at the upper part of the stave. Therefore, anybody making a cryptogram of musical notes would probably use one set of these duplicate positions to indicate other letters, and as *h* is in the lower part of the stave, that is where the variation comes in. Let us experiment by assuming that all the crotchets above *f* in ordinary musical notation have their usual values, and let us set the letters over their respective notes. Now things begin to shape. Look toward the end of the second line: there is the word *the* and the letters *f f t h*, with another note between the two *f*s. Now that word can only possibly be *fifth*, so that now we have the sign for *i*. It is the crotchet on the bottom line. Let us go through and mark the *i*'s. And now observe. The first sign of the lot is *i*, and there is one other sign before the word *the*. The only words possible here beginning with *i*, and of two letters, are *it*, *if*, *is* and *in*. Now we have the signs for *t* and *f*, so we know that it isn't *it* or *if*. *Is* would be unlikely here, because there is a tendency, as you see, to regularity in these signs, and *t*, the next letter alphabetically to *s*, is at the bottom of the stave. Let us try *n*. At once we get the word *dance* at the beginning of line three. And now we have got enough to see the system of the thing. Make a stave and put G A B C and the higher D E F in their proper musical places. Then fill in the blank places with the next letters of the alphabet downward, *h i j*, and we find that *h* and *i* fall in the places we have already discovered for them as crotchets. Now take quavers, and go on with *k l m n o*, and so on as before, beginning on the A space. When you have filled the quavers, do the same with semiquavers – there are only six alphabetical letters left for this – *u v w x y z*. Now you will find that this exactly agrees with all we have ascertained already, and if you will use the other letters to fill up over the signs still unmarked you will get the whole message:

"*In the Colt Row ken over the coals the fifth dancer slides says Jerry Shiels the horney.*

"'Dancer,' as perhaps you didn't know, is thieves' slang for a stair, and 'horney' is the strolling musician's name for cornet player. Of course the thing took a little time to work out, chiefly because the sentence was short, and gave one few opportunities. But anybody with the key, using the cipher as a means of communication, would read it easily.

"As soon as I had read it, of course I guessed the purport of the *Flitterbat Lancers.* Jerry Shiels's name is well-known to anybody with half my knowledge of the criminal records of the century, and his connection with the missing Wedlake jewels, and his death in prison, came to my mind at once. Certainly here was something hidden, and as the Wedlake jewels seemed most likely, I made the shot in talking to Hooker."

"But you terribly astonished him by telling him his name and address. How was that?" I asked curiously.

Hewitt laughed aloud. "That," he said; "why, that was the thinnest trick of all. Why, the man had it engraved on the silver band of his umbrella handle. When he left his umbrella outside, Kerrett (I had indicated the umbrella to him by a sign) just copied the lettering on one of the ordinary visitors' forms, and brought it in. You will remember I treated it as an ordinary visitor's announcement." And Hewitt laughed again.

Fergus Hume

The Florentine Dante

1887 was the year that A Study in Scarlet *singularly failed to impress the reading public. What it was buying in huge quantities that year was* The Mystery of a Hansom Cab, *which became the best-selling mystery of the Victorian era. Its author Fergus Hume (1859–1932), though born in England, was a New Zealander, and little of his colossal output is read today. "The Florentine Dante", first published in the 1890s, is one of his relatively few short stories, and it features one of the lesser-known – and most delightful – sleuths who followed in the footsteps of Sherlock Holmes: the beautiful gipsy girl, Hagar.*

DURING A JUNE twilight Hagar Stanley, the gipsy girl, was summoned to the pawnshop by a sharp rapping, and on entering she found a young man waiting to pawn a book which he held in his hand. He was tall, slim, fair-haired and blue-eyed, with a clever and intellectual face, lighted by rather dreamy eyes. Quick at reading physiognomies, Hagar liked his appearance at first glance.

"I – I wish to get some money on this book," said the stranger in a hesitating manner, a flush invading his fair complexion. "Could you – that is, will you – " He paused in confusion, and held out the book, which Hagar took in silence.

It was an old and costly book, over which a bibliomaniac would have gloated.

The date was that of the fourteenth century, the printer a famous Florentine publisher of that epoch; and the author was none other than one Dante Alighieri, a poet not unknown to fame. In short, the volume was a second edition of *La Divina Commedia*, extremely rare, and worth much money. Hagar, who had learnt many things under the able tuition of Jacob Dix, from whom she inherited the shop, at once recognized the value of the book; but with keen business instinct she began promptly to disparage it.

"I don't care for old books," she said, offering it back to him. "Why not take it to a second-hand bookseller?"

"Because I don't want to part with it. At the present moment I need money, as you can see from my appearance. Let me have five pounds on the book until I can redeem it."

Hagar, who already had noted the haggard looks of this customer, and the threadbare quality of his apparel, laid down the Dante with a bang. "I can't give five pounds," she said, bluntly. "The book isn't worth it!"

"Shows how much you know of such things, my girl! It is a rare edition of a celebrated Italian poet, and it is worth over a hundred pounds."

"Really?" said Hagar dryly. "In that case, why not sell it?"

"Because I don't want to. Give me five pounds."

"No; four is all that I can advance."

"Four ten," pleaded the customer.

"Four," retorted the inexorable Hagar.

She pushed the book towards him with one finger. Seeing that he could get nothing more out of her, the young man sighed and relented. "Give me the four pounds," he said, gloomily.

"Name and address?" asked Hagar, making out the ticket.

"Eustace Lorn, 42, Castle Road," said the young man, giving an address near at hand.

"Four pounds," said Hagar, "there it is, in gold; your ticket also – No. 820. You can redeem the book whenever you like, on paying six per cent interest. Good night."

After the young man's departure, Hagar put away the Dante, and, as it was late, shut up the shop. Then she retired to the back-parlour to eat her supper – dry bread and cheese with cold water.

A week later, Lorn and his pawning of the book were recalled to her mind by a stranger who entered the shop shortly after midday. This man was short, stout, elderly and vulgar. He was much excited, and spoke badly, as Hagar noted when he laid a pawn-ticket, No. 820, on the counter.

"'Ere, girl," said he in rough tones, "gimme the book this ticket's for."

"You come from Mr Lorn?" asked Hagar, remembering the Dante.

"Yes; he wants that book. There's the brass. Sharp, now, young woman!"

Hagar made no move to get the volume, or even to take the money. Instead she asked a question. "Is Mr Lorn ill, that he

could not come himself?" she demanded, looking keenly at the
man's coarse face.

"No; but I've bought the pawn-ticket off him. 'Ere, gimme
the book!"

"I cannot at present," replied Hagar, who did not trust the looks
of this man.

"Dash yer imperance! Why not?"

"Because you did not pawn the Dante; and as it is a valuable
book, I might get into trouble if I gave it into other hands than
Mr Lorn's."

"Well, I'm blest! There's the ticket!"

"So I see; but how do I know the way you became possessed of
it?"

"Lorn gave it me," said the man, sulkily, "and I want the
Dante!"

"I'm sorry for that," retorted Hagar, certain now that all was not
right, "for no one but Mr Lorn shall get it. If he isn't ill, let him
come and receive it from me."

The man swore and completely lost his temper – a fact which did
not disturb Hagar in the least. "You may as well clear out," she said,
coldly. "I have said that you shan't have the book, so that closes the
question."

"I'll call in the police!"

"Do so; there's a station five minutes' walk from here."

Confounded by her coolness, the man snatched up the pawn-
ticket, and stamped out of the shop in a rage. Hagar took down the
Dante, looked at it carefully, and considered the position. Clearly
there was something wrong, and Eustace Lorn was in trouble, else
why should he send a stranger to redeem the book upon which he
set such store? In an ordinary case, Hagar might have received the
ticket and money without a qualm, so long as she was acting rightly
in a legal sense; but Eustace Lorn interested her strangely – why,
she could not guess – and she was anxious to guard his interest.
Moreover, the emissary possessed an untrustworthy face, and looked
a man capable, if not of crime, at least of treachery. How he had
obtained the ticket could only be explained by its owner; so, after
some cogitation, Hagar sent a message to Lorn. The gist of this was,
that he should come to the pawnshop after closing time.

"Who was that man you sent for your book?" she demanded, when
Lorn appeared.

"Jabez Treadle. I could not come myself, so I sent him with the
ticket. Why did you not give him the Dante?"

"Because I did not like his face, and I thought he might have stolen the ticket from you. Don't trust the man you sent here – Mr Treadle. See, here is your Dante, young man. Pay me the money, and take it away."

"I can't pay you the money, as I have none. I am as poor as Job, but hardly so patient."

"But you offered the money through that Treadle creature."

"Indeed no!" explained Lorn, frankly. "I gave him the ticket, and he wished to redeem the book with his own money."

"Did he really?" said Hagar, thoughtfully. "He does not look like a student – as you do. Why did he want this book?"

"To find out a secret."

"A secret contained in the Dante?"

"Yes. There is a secret in the book which means money."

"To you or Mr Treadle?" demanded Hagar.

Lorn shrugged his shoulders. "To either one of us who finds out the secret," he said, carelessly. "But indeed I don't think it will ever be discovered – at all events by me. Treadle may be more fortunate."

"If crafty ways can bring fortune, your man will succeed," said Hagar calmly. "He is a dangerous friend for you, that Treadle. There is evidently some story about this Dante of yours which he knows, and which he desires to turn to his own advantage. If the story means money, tell it to me, and I may be able to help you to the wealth. I am only a young girl, it is true, Mr Lorn; still, I am old in experience, and I may succeed where you fail."

"I doubt it," replied Lorn, gloomily. "Still, it is kind of you to take this interest in a stranger. I am much obliged to you, Miss – "

"Call me Hagar," she interrupted, hastily. "I am not used to fine titles."

"Well, then, Hagar," said he, with a kindly glance, "I'll tell you the story of my Uncle Ben and his strange will. My uncle, Benjamin Gurth, died six months ago at the age of fifty-eight. In his early days he had lived a roving life, and ten years ago he came home with a fortune from the West Indies."

"How much fortune?" demanded Hagar, always interested in financial matters.

"That is the odd part about it," continued Eustace. "Nobody ever knew the amount of his wealth, for he was a grumpy old curmudgeon, who confided in no one. He bought a little house and garden at Woking, and there lived for the ten years he was in England. His great luxury was books, and as he knew many languages – Italian among others – he collected quite a polyglot library."

"Where is it now?"

"It was sold after his death along with the house and land. A man in the City claimed the money and obtained it."

"A creditor. What about the fortune?"

"I'm telling you, Hagar, if you'll only listen," said Eustace, impatiently. "Well, Uncle Ben, as I have said, was a miser. He hoarded up all his moneys and kept them in the house, trusting neither banks nor investments. My mother was his sister, and very poor; but he never gave her a penny, and to me nothing but the Dante, which he presented in an unusual fit of generosity."

"But from what you said before," remarked Hagar, shrewdly, "it seemed to me that he had some motive in giving you the Dante."

"No doubt," assented Eustace, admiring her sharpness. "The secret of where his money is hidden is contained in that Dante."

"Then you may be sure, Mr Lorn, that he intended to make you his heir. But what has your friend Treadle to do with the matter?"

"Oh, Treadle is a grocer in Woking," responded Lorn. "He is greedy for money, and knowing that Uncle Ben was rich, he tried to get the cash left to him. He wheedled and flattered the old man; he made him presents, and always tried to set him against me as his only relative."

"Didn't I say the man was your enemy? Well, go on."

"There is little more to tell, Hagar. Uncle Ben hid his money away, and left a will which gives it all to the person who should find out where it was concealed. The testament said the secret was contained in the Dante. You may be sure that Treadle visited me at once and asked to see the book. I showed it to him, but neither of us could find any sign in its pages likely to lead us to discover the hidden treasure. The other day Treadle came to see the Dante again. I told him that I had pawned it, so he volunteered to redeem it if I gave him the ticket. I did so, and he called on you. The result you know."

"Yes; I refused to give it to him," said Hagar, "and I see now that I was quite right to do so, as the man is your enemy. Well, Mr Lorn, it seems from your story that a fortune is waiting for you, if you can find it."

"Very true; but I can't find it. There isn't a single sign in the Dante by which I can trace the hiding place."

"Do you know Italian?"

"Very well. Uncle Ben taught it to me."

"That's one point gained," said Hagar, placing the Dante on the table and lighting another candle. "The secret may be contained in the poem itself. However, we shall see. Is there any mark in the book – a marginal mark, I mean?"

"Not one. Look for yourself."

The two young heads were bent over the book in that dismal and tenebrous atmosphere. Eustace yielded in all things to Hagar. She turned over page after page of the old Florentine edition, but not one pencil or pen-mark marred its pure white surface from beginning to end. From *L'Inferno* to *Il Paradiso* no hint betrayed the secret of the hidden money. At the last page, Eustace, with a sigh, threw himself back in his chair.

"You see, Hagar, there is nothing. What are you frowning at?"

"I am not frowning, but thinking, young man," was her reply. "If the secret is in this book, there must be some trace of it. Now, nothing appears at present, but later on – "

"Later on?" asked Eustace.

"Invisible ink."

"Invisible ink!" he exclaimed. "I don't quite understand."

"My late master," said Hagar, "was accustomed to deal with thieves, rogues, and vagabonds. Naturally, he had many secrets, and sometimes, by force of circumstances, he had to trust these secrets to the mail. Naturally, also, he did not wish to risk discovery, so when he sent a letter, about stolen goods for instance, he always wrote it in lemon juice."

"In lemon juice! And what good was that?"

"It was good for invisible writing. When the letter was written, it looked like a blank page. No one, you understand, could read what was set out, for to the ordinary eye there was no writing at all."

"And to the cultured eye?" asked Eustace.

"It appeared the same – a blank sheet," retorted Hagar. "But then the cultured mind came in, young man. The person to whom the letter was sent warmed the seeming blank page over the fire, when at once the writing appeared, black and legible."

"The deuce!" Eustace jumped up in his excitement. "And you think – "

"I think that your late uncle may have adopted the same plan," interrupted Hagar, coolly, "but I am not sure. However, we shall soon see." She turned over a page or two of the Dante. "It is impossible to heat these over the fire," she added, "as the book is valuable, and we must not spoil it; but I know of a plan."

With a confident smile she left the room and returned with a flat iron, which she placed on the fire. While it was heating Eustace looked at this quick-witted woman with admiration.

"We will not begin at the beginning of the book," said Hagar, taking the iron off the fire, "but at the end."

"Why?" asked Eustace, who could see no good reason for this decision.

"Well," said Hagar, poising the heated iron over the book, "when I search for an article I find it always at the bottom of a heap of things I don't want. As we began with the first page of this book and found nothing, let us start this time from the end, and perhaps we shall learn your uncle's secret the sooner. It is only a whim of mine, but I should like to satisfy it by way of experiment."

Eustace nodded and laughed, while Hagar placed a sheet of brown paper over the last page of the Dante to preserve the book from being scorched. In a minute she lifted the iron and paper, but the page still showed no mark. With a cheerful air the girl shook her head, and repeated the operation on the second page from the end. This time, when she took away the brown paper, Eustace, who had been watching her actions with much interest, bent forward with an ejaculation of surprise. Hagar echoed it with one of delight; for there was a mark and date on the page, half-way down, as thus:

> Oh, abbondante grazia, ond' io presumi
> Ficcar lo viso per la luce eterna 27.12.38.
> Tanto, che le veduta vi consumi!

"There, Mr Lorn!" cried Hagar, joyously. "There is the secret! My fancy for beginning at the end was right. I was right also about the invisible ink."

"You are a wonder!" said Eustace, with sincere admiration. "But I am as much in the dark as ever. I see a marked line, and a date, the twenty-seventh of December, in the year, I presume, one thousand eight hundred and thirty-eight. We can't make any sense out of that simplicity."

"Don't be in a hurry," said Hagar, soothingly. "We have found out so much, we may learn more. First of all, please translate those three lines."

"Roughly," said Eustace, reading them, "they run thus: 'O abundant grace, with whom I tried to look through the eternal light so much that I lost my sight.'" He shrugged his shoulders. "I don't see how that transcendentalism can help us."

"What about the date?"

"One thousand eight hundred and thirty-eight," said Lorn, thoughtfully. "And this is eighteen ninety-six. Take one from the other, it leaves fifty-eight, the age at which, as I told you before, my uncle died. Evidently this is the date of his birth."

"A date of birth – a line of Dante!" muttered Hagar. "I must say that it is difficult to make sense out of it. Yet, in figures and letters, I am sure the place where the money is concealed is told."

"Well," remarked Eustace, giving up the solution of this problem in despair, "if you can make out the riddle it is more than I can."

"Patience, patience!" replied Hagar, with a nod. "Sooner or later we shall find out the meaning. Could you take me to see your uncle's house at Woking?"

"Oh, yes; it is not yet let, so we can easily go over it. But will you trouble about coming all that way with me?"

"Certainly! I am anxious to know the meaning of this line and date. There may be something about your uncle's house likely to give a clue to its reading. I shall keep the Dante, and puzzle over the riddle; you can call for me on Sunday, when the shop is closed, and we shall go to Woking together."

"O Hagar! How can I ever thank – "

"Thank me when you get the money, and rid yourself of Mr Treadle!" said Hagar, cutting him short. "Besides, I am only doing this to satisfy my own curiosity."

"You are an angel!"

"And you a fool, who talks nonsense!" said Hagar, sharply. "Here is your hat and cane. Good night."

"But may I say – "

"Nothing, nothing!" retorted Hagar, pushing him out of the door. "Good night."

Punctual to the appointed hour, Eustace appeared at the door of the pawnshop. Hagar was already waiting for him, with the Dante in her hand. She wore a black dress, a black cloak, and a hat of the same sombre hue – such clothes being the mourning she had worn, and was wearing, for Jacob Dix.

"Why are you taking the Dante?" asked Eustace, when they set out for Waterloo Station.

"It may be useful to read the riddle," said Hagar.

"Have you solved it?"

"I don't know; I am not sure," she said, meditatively. "I tried by counting the lines on that page up and down. You understand – twenty-seven, twelve, thirty-eight; but the lines gave me no clue."

"You didn't understand them?"

"Yes I did," replied Hagar, coolly. "I got a second-hand copy of a translation from the old bookseller in Carby's Crescent, and by counting the lines to correspond with those in the Florentine edition I arrived at the sense."

"And none of them point to the solution of the problem?"

"Not one. Then I tried by pages. I counted twenty-seven pages, but could find no clue; I reckoned twelve pages; also thirty-eight; still the same result. Then I took the twelfth, the twenty-seventh, and the thirty-eighth page by numbers, but found nothing. The riddle is hard to read."

"Impossible, I should say," said Eustace, in despair.

"No; I think I have found out the meaning."

"How? How? Tell me quick!"

"Not now. I found a word, but it seems nonsense, as I could not find it in the Italian dictionary which I borrowed."

"What is the word?"

"I'll tell you when I have seen the house."

In vain Eustace tried to move her from this determination. Hagar was stubborn when she took an idea into her strong brain; so she simply declined to explain until she arrived at Woking – at the house of Uncle Ben.

It was a bare little cottage, small and shabby, set at the end of a square of ground fenced in from the barren moor. Within the quadrangle there were fruit trees – cherry, apple, plum, and pear; also a large fig-tree in the centre of the unshaven lawn facing the house. All was desolate and neglected; the fruit trees were unpruned, the grass was growing in the paths, and the flowers were straggling here and there, rich masses of ragged colour. Desolate certainly, this deserted hermitage, but not lonely, for as Hagar and her companion turned in at the little gate a figure rose from a stooping position under an apple tree. It was that of a man with a spade in his hand, who had been digging for some time, as was testified by the heap of freshly turned earth at his feet.

"Mr Treadle!" cried Lorn, indignantly. "What are you doing here?"

"Lookin' fur the old un's cash!" retorted Mr Treadle, with a scowl directed equally at the young man and Hagar. "An' if I gets it I keeps it. Lord! To think as 'ow I pampered that old sinner with figs and such like – to say nothing of French brandy, which he drank by the quart!"

"You have no business here!"

"No more 'ave you!" snapped the irate grocer. "If I ain't, you ain't, fur till the 'ouse is let it's public property. I s'pose you've come 'ere with that Jezebel to look fur the money?"

Hagar, hearing herself called names, stepped promptly up to Mr Treadle, and boxed his red ears. "Now then," she said, when the grocer fell back in dismay at this onslaught, "perhaps you'll be civil! Mr Lorn, sit down on this seat, and I'll explain the riddle."

"The Dante!" cried Mr Treadle, recognizing the book which lay on Hagar's lap. "An' she'll explain the riddle – swindling me out of my rightful cash!"

"The cash belongs to Mr Lorn, as his uncle's heir!" said Hagar wrathfully. "Be quiet, sir, or you'll get another box on the ears!"

"Never mind him," said Eustace, impatiently. "Tell me the riddle."

"I don't know if I have guessed it correctly," answered Hagar, opening the book. "But I've tried by line and page and number, all of which revealed nothing. Now I try by letters, and you will see if the word they make is a proper Italian one."

She read out the marked line and the date. "'*Ficcar lo viso per la luce eterna*, 27th December, '38.' Now," said Hagar, slowly, "if you run all the figures together they stand as 271238."

"Yes, yes!" said Eustace, impatiently. "I see. Go on, please."

Hagar continued: "Take the second letter of the word *Ficcar*."

"*I*."

"Then the seventh letter from the beginning of the line."

Eustace counted. "*L*. I see," he went on, eagerly. "Then the first letter, *f*, the second again, *i*, the third and the eighth, *c* and *o*."

"Good!" said Hagar, writing these down. "Now, the whole make up the word *ilfico*. Is that an Italian word?"

"I'm not sure," said Eustace, thoughtfully. "*Ilfico*. No."

"Shows what eddication 'e's got!" growled Mr Treadle, who was leaning on his spade.

Eustace raised his eyes to dart a withering glance at the grocer, and in doing so his vision passed on to the tree looming up behind the man. At once the meaning of the word flashed on his brain.

"*Il fico!*" he cried, rising. "Two words instead of one! You have found it, Hagar! It means the fig-tree – the one yonder. I believe the money is buried under it."

Before he could advance a step Treadle had leaped forward, and was slashing away at the tangled grass round the fig-tree like a madman.

"If 'tis there, 'tis mine!" he shouted. "Don't you come nigh me, young Lorn, or I'll brain you with my spade! I fed up that old uncle of yours like a fighting cock, and now I'm going to have his cash to pay me!"

Eustace leaped forward in the like manner as Treadle had done, and would have wrenched the spade out of his grip, but that Hagar laid a detaining hand on his arm.

"Let him dig," she said, coolly. "The money is yours; I can prove it. He'll have the work and you the fortune."

At this moment, Treadle gave a shout of glee and with both arms wrenched a goodly-sized tin box out of the hole he had dug.

"Mine! Mine!" he cried, plumping this down on the grass. "This will pay for the dinners I gave him, the presents I made him. I've bin castin' my bread on the waters, and here it's back again."

He fell to forcing the lid of the box with the edge of the spade, all the time laughing and crying like one demented. Lorn and Hagar drew near, in the expectation of seeing a shower of gold pieces rain on the ground when the lid was opened. As Treadle gave a final wrench it flew wide, and they saw – an empty box.

"Why – what – " stammered Treadle, thunderstruck – "what does it mean?"

Eustace, equally taken aback, bent down and looked in. There was absolutely nothing in the box but a piece of folded paper. Unable to make a remark, he held it out to the amazed Hagar.

"This explains," said Hagar, running her eye over the writing. "It seems that this wealthy Uncle Ben was a pauper."

"A pauper!" cried Eustace.

"Listen!" said Hagar, and read out from the page:

When I returned to England I was thought wealthy, so that all my friends and relations fawned on me for the crumbs which fell from the rich man's table. But I had just enough money to rent the cottage for a term of years, and to purchase an annuity barely sufficient for the necessities of life. But, owing to the report of my wealth, the luxuries have been supplied by those who hoped for legacies. This is my legacy to one and all – these golden words, which I have proved true: It is better to be thought rich than to be rich.

The paper fell from the hand of Hagar, and Treadle, with a howl of rage, threw himself on the grass, loading the memory of the deceased with opprobrious names. Seeing that all was over, that the expected fortune had vanished into thin air, Hagar left the disappointed grocer weeping with rage over the deceptive tin box, and led Eustace away. He followed her as in a dream, and all the time during their sad journey back to town he spoke hardly a word. On arriving at the door of the pawnshop Hagar gave the copy of Dante to the young man. "I give this back to you," she said, pressing his hand. "Sell it, and with the proceeds build up your own fortune."

E. W. Hornung

Nine Points of the Law

E. W. Hornung (1866–1921) was the brother-in-law of Arthur Conan Doyle, and an excellent writer on his own account. Much of his early work was based upon his experiences in Australia, where he had been sent for health reasons at the age of eighteen, and his tales of convicts and bushwhackers are still among the best of their kind. His major creation, though, was Raffles, the gentleman-thief who can in some ways be regarded as the criminal counterpart of Sherlock Holmes. "There's no p'lice like Holmes" was Raffles backhanded compliment to his rival.

The Raffles stories are still immensely entertaining today, and Hornung's classic character has also inspired numerous film and TV versions. "Nine Points of the Law" is from the first series of Raffles adventures, and is one of the best.

"WELL," SAID RAFFLES, "what do you make of it?"

I read the advertisement once more before replying. It was in the last column of the *Daily Telegraph*, and it ran:

> TWO THOUSAND POUNDS REWARD. – The above sum may be earned by any one qualified to undertake delicate mission and prepared to run certain risk. – Apply by telegram, Security, London.

"I think," said I, "it's the most extraordinary advertisement that ever got into print!"

Raffles smiled.

"Not quite all that, Bunny; still, extraordinary enough, I grant you."

"Look at the figure!"

"It is certainly large."

"And the mission – and the risk!"

"Yes; the combination is frank, to say the least of it. But the really original point is requiring applications by telegram to a telegraphic address! There's something in the fellow who thought of that, and something in his game; with one word he chokes off the million who answer an advertisement every day – when they can raise the stamp. My answer cost me five bob; but then I prepaid another."

"You don't mean to say that you've applied?"

"Rather," said Raffles. "I want two thousand pounds as much as any man."

"Put your own name?"

"Well – no, Bunny, I didn't. In point of fact, I smell something interesting and illegal, and you know what a cautious chap I am. I signed myself Glasspool, care of Hickey, 38 Conduit Street; that's my tailor; and after sending the wire I went round and told him what to expect. He promised to send the reply along the moment it came. I shouldn't be surprised if that's it!"

And he was gone before a double knock on the outer door had done ringing through the rooms, to return next minute with an open telegram and a face full of news.

"What do you think?" said he. "Security's that fellow Addenbrooke, the police-court lawyer, and he wants to see me instanter!"

"Do you know him, then?"

"Merely by repute. I only hope he doesn't know me. He's the chap who got six weeks for sailing too close to the wind in the Sutton-Wilmer case; everybody wondered why he wasn't struck off the rolls. Instead of that he's got a first-rate practice on the seamy side, and every blackguard with half a case takes it straight to Bennett Addenbrooke. He's probably the one man who would have the cheek to put in an advertisement like that, and the one man who could do it without exciting suspicion. It's simply in his line; but you may be sure there's something shady at the bottom of it. The odd thing is that I have long made up my mind to go to Addenbrooke myself if accidents should happen."

"And you're going to him now?"

"This minute," said Raffles, brushing his hat; "and so are you."

"But I came in to drag you out to lunch."

"You shall lunch with me when we've seen this fellow. Come on, Bunny, and we'll choose your name on the way. Mine's Glasspool, and don't you forget it."

Mr Bennett Addenbrooke occupied substantial offices in Wellington Street, Strand, and was out when we arrived; but he had only just gone "over the way to the court;" and five minutes sufficed to produce a brisk, fresh-coloured, resolute-looking man, with a very confident, rather festive air, and black eyes that opened wide at the sight of Raffles.

"Mr – Glasspool?" exclaimed the lawyer.

"My name," said Raffles with dry effrontery.

"Not up at Lord's, however!" said the other slyly. "My dear sir, I have seen you take far too many wickets to make any mistake!"

For a single moment Raffles looked venomous; then he shrugged and smiled, and the smile grew into a little cynical chuckle.

"So you have bowled me out in my turn?" said he. "Well, I don't think there's anything to explain. I am harder up than I wished to admit under my own name, that's all, and I want that thousand pounds reward."

"Two thousand," said the solicitor. "And the man who is not above an alias happens to be just the sort of man I want; so don't let that worry you, my dear sir. The matter, however, is of a strictly private and confidential character." And he looked very hard at me.

"Quite so," said Raffles. "But there was something about a risk?"

"A certain risk is involved."

"Then surely three heads will be better than two. I said I wanted that thousand pounds; my friend here wants the other. We are both cursedly hard up, and we go into this thing together or not at all. Must you have his name too? – I should give him my real one, Bunny."

Mr Addenbrooke raised his eyebrows over the card I found for him; then he drummed upon it with his finger-nail, and his embarrassment expressed itself in a puzzled smile.

"The fact is I find myself in a difficulty," he confessed at last. "Yours is the first reply I have received; people who can afford to send long telegrams don't rush to the advertisements in the *Daily Telegraph*; but, on the other hand, I was not quite prepared to hear from men like yourselves. Candidly, and on consideration, I am not sure that you are the stamp of men for me – men who belong to good clubs! I rather intended to appeal to the – er – adventurous classes."

"We are adventurers," said Raffles gravely.

"But you respect the law?"

The black eyes gleamed shrewdly.

"We are not professional rogues, if that's what you mean," said Raffles, smiling. "But on our beam-ends we are; we would do a good deal for a thousand pounds apiece – eh, Bunny?"

"Anything," I murmured.

The solicitor rapped his desk.

"I'll tell you what I want you to do. You can but refuse. It's illegal, but it's illegality in a good cause; that's the risk, and my client is prepared to pay for it. He will pay for the attempt, in case of failure; the money is as good as yours once you consent to run the risk. My client is Sir Bernard Debenham, of Broom Hall, Esher."

"I know his son," I remarked.

Raffles knew him too, but said nothing, and his eye drooped disapproval in my direction. Bennett Addenbrooke turned to me.

"Then," said he, "you have the privilege of knowing one of the most complete young blackguards about town, and the *fons et origo* of the whole trouble. As you know the son, you may know the father too, at all events by reputation; and in that case I needn't tell you that he is a very peculiar man. He lives alone in a storehouse of treasures which no eyes but his ever behold. He is said to have the finest collection of pictures in the south of England, though nobody ever sees them to judge; pictures, fiddles, and furniture are his hobby, and he is undoubtedly very eccentric. Nor can one deny that there has been considerable eccentricity in his treatment of his son. For years Sir Bernard paid his debts, and the other day, without the slightest warning, not only refused to do so any more, but absolutely stopped the lad's allowance. Well, I'll tell you what has happened; but first of all you must know, or you may remember, that I appeared for young Debenham in a little scrape he got into a year or two ago. I got him off all right, and Sir Bernard paid me handsomely on the nail. And no more did I hear or see of either of them until one day last week."

The lawyer drew his chair nearer ours, and leant forward with a hand on either knee.

"On Tuesday of last week I had a telegram from Sir Bernard; I was to go to him at once. I found him waiting for me in the drive; without a word he led me to the picture-gallery, which was locked and darkened, drew up a blind, and stood simply pointing to an empty picture-frame. It was a long time before I could get a word out of him. Then at last he told me that that frame had contained one of the rarest and most valuable pictures in England – in the world – an original Velasquez. I have checked this," said the lawyer, "and it seems literally true; the picture was a portrait of the Infanta Maria Teresa, said to be one of the artist's greatest works, second only to another portrait of one of the Popes of Rome – so they told me at the National Gallery, where they had its history by heart. They say there that the picture is practically priceless. And young Debenham has sold it for five thousand pounds!"

"The deuce he has!" said Raffles.

I inquired who had bought it.

"A Queensland legislator of the name of Craggs – the Hon. John Montagu Craggs, M.L.C., to give him his full title. Not that we knew anything about him on Tuesday last; we didn't even know for certain that young Debenham had stolen the picture. But he had gone down for money on the Monday evening, had been refused, and it was plain enough that he had helped himself in this way; he had threatened revenge, and this was it. Indeed, when I hunted him up in town on the Tuesday night, he confessed as much in the most brazen manner imaginable. But he wouldn't tell me who was the purchaser, and finding out took the rest of the week; but I did find out, and a nice time I've had of it ever since! Backwards and forwards between Esher and the Metropole, where the Queenslander is staying, sometimes twice a day; threats, offers, prayers, entreaties, not one of them a bit of good!"

"But," said Raffles, "surely it's a clear case? The sale was illegal; you can pay him back his money and force him to give the picture up."

"Exactly; but not without an action and a public scandal, and that my client declines to face. He would rather lose even his picture than have the whole thing get into the papers; he has disowned his son, but he will not disgrace him; yet his picture he must have by hook or crook, and there's the rub! I am to get it back by fair means or foul. He gives me *carte blanche* in the matter, and, I verily believe, would throw in a blank cheque if asked. He offered one to the Queenslander, but Craggs simply tore it in two; the one old boy is as much a character as the other, and between the two of them I'm at my wit's end."

"So you put that advertisement in the paper?" said Raffles, in the dry tones he had adopted throughout the interview.

"As a last resort. I did."

"And you wish us to steal this picture?"

It was magnificently said; the lawyer flushed from his hair to his collar.

"I knew you were not the men!" he groaned. "I never thought of men of your stamp! But it's not stealing," he exclaimed heatedly; "it's recovering stolen property. Besides, Sir Bernard will pay him his five thousand as soon as he has the picture; and, you'll see, old Craggs will be just as loth to let it come out as Sir Bernard himself. No, no – it's an enterprise, an adventure, if you like – but not stealing."

"You yourself mentioned the law," murmured Raffles.

"And the risk," I added.

"We pay for that," he said once more.

"But not enough," said Raffles, shaking his head. "My good sir, consider what it means to us. You spoke of those clubs; we should not only get kicked out of them, but put in prison like common burglars! It's true we're hard up, but it simply isn't worth it at the price. Double your stakes, and I for one am your man."

Addenbrooke wavered.

"Do you think you could bring it off?"

"We could try."

"But you have no – "

"Experience? Well, hardly!"

"And you would really run the risk for four thousand pounds?"

Raffles looked at me. I nodded.

"We would," said he, "and blow the odds!"

"It's more than I can ask my client to pay," said Addenbrooke, growing firm.

"Then it's more than you can expect us to risk."

"You are in earnest?"

"God wot!"

"Say three thousand if you succeed!"

"Four is our figure, Mr Addenbrooke."

"Then I think it should be nothing if you fail."

"Double or quits?" cried Raffles. "Well, that's sporting. Done!"

Addenbrooke opened his lips, half rose, then sat back in his chair, and looked long and shrewdly at Raffles – never once at me.

"I know your bowling," said he reflectively. "I go up to Lords whenever I want an hour's real rest, and I've seen you bowl again and again – yes, and take the best wickets in England on a plumb pitch. I don't forget the last Gentlemen and Players; I was there. You're up to every trick – every one . . . I'm inclined to think that if anybody could bowl out this old Australian . . . Damme, I believe you're my very man!"

The bargain was clenched at the Café Royal, where Bennett Addenbrooke insisted on playing host at an extravagant luncheon. I remember that he took his whack of champagne with the nervous freedom of a man at high pressure, and have no doubt I kept him in countenance by an equal indulgence; but Raffles, ever an exemplar in such matters, was more abstemious even than his wont, and very poor company to boot. I can see him now, his eyes in his place – thinking – thinking. I can see the solicitor glancing from him to me in an apprehension of which I did my best to disabuse him by reassuring looks. At the close Raffles apologized for his pre-occupation, called for an ABC time-table, and announced his intention of catching the 3.02 to Esher.

"You must excuse me, Mr Addenbrooke," said he, "but I have my own idea, and for the moment I would much prefer to keep it to myself. It may end in fizzle, so I would rather not speak about it to either of you just yet. But speak to Sir Bernard I must, so will you write me one line to him on your card? Of course, if you wish, you must come down with me and hear what I say; but I really don't see much point in it."

And as usual Raffles had his way, though Bennett Addenbrooke showed some temper when he was gone, and I myself shared his annoyance to no small extent. I could only tell him that it was in the nature of Raffles to be self-willed and secretive, but that no man of my acquaintance had half his audacity and determination; that I for my part would trust him through and through and let him gang his own gait every time. More I dared not say, even to remove those chill misgivings with which I knew that the lawyer went his way.

That day I saw no more of Raffles, but a telegram reached me when I was dressing for dinner: "Be in your rooms to-morrow from noon and keep rest of day clear. – Raffles."

It had been sent off from Waterloo at 6.42.

So Raffles was back in town; at an earlier stage of our relations I should have hunted him up then and there, but now I knew better. His telegram meant that he had no desire for my society that night or the following forenoon; that when he wanted me I should see him soon enough.

And see him I did, towards one o'clock next day. I was watching for him from my window in Mount Street, when he drove up furiously in a hansom, and jumped out without a word to the man. I met him next minute at the lift gates, and he fairly pushed me back into my rooms.

"Five minutes, Bunny!" he cried. "Not a moment more."

And he tore off his coat before flinging himself into the nearest chair.

"I'm fairly on the rush," he panted; "having the very devil of a time! Not a word till I've told you all I've done. I settled my plan of campaign yesterday at lunch. The first thing was to get in with this man Craggs; you can't break into a place like the Metropole, it's got to be done from the inside. Problem one, how to get at the fellow. Only one sort of pretext would do – it must be something to do with this blessed picture, so that I might see where he'd got it and all that. Well, I couldn't go and ask to see it out of curiosity, and I couldn't go as a second representative of the old chap, and it was thinking how I could go that made me such a bear at lunch. But I saw my way before we got up. If I could only lay hold of a copy of the picture, I might ask leave to go and compare it with the original. So down I went to Esher to find out if there was a copy in existence, and was at Broom Hall for one hour and a half yesterday afternoon. There was no copy there, but they must exist, for Sir Bernard himself (there's 'copy' there!) has allowed a couple to be made since the picture has been in his possession. He hunted up the painters' addresses, and the rest of the evening I spent in hunting up the painters themselves; but their work had been done on commission; one copy had gone out of the country, and I'm still on the track of the other."

"Then you haven't seen Craggs yet?"

"Seen him and made friends with him, and if possible he's the funnier old cuss of the two; but you should study 'em both. I took the bull by the horns this morning, went in and lied like Ananias, and it was just as well I did – the old ruffian sails for Australia by to-morrow's boat. I told him a man wanted to sell me a copy of the celebrated Infanta Maria Teresa of Velasquez, that I'd been down to the supposed owner of the picture, only to find that he had just sold it to him. You should have seen his face when I told him that! He grinned all round his wicked old head. 'Did old Debenham admit the sale?' says he; and when I said he had he chuckled to himself for about five minutes. He was so pleased that he did just what I hoped he would do: he showed me the great picture – luckily it isn't by any means a large one – also the case he's got it in. It's an iron map-case in which he brought over the plans of his land in Brisbane; he wants to know who would suspect it of containing an Old Master too? But he's had it fitted with a new Chubb's lock, and I managed to take an interest in the key while he was gloating over the canvas. I had the wax in the palm of my hand, and I shall make my duplicate this afternoon."

Raffles looked at his watch and jumped up saying he had given me a minute too much.

"By the way," he added, "you've got to dine with him at the Metropole to-night!"

"I?"

"Yes; don't look so scared. Both of us are invited – I swore you were dining with me. I accepted for us both; but I shan't be there."

His clear eye was upon me, bright with meaning and with mischief. I implored him to tell me what his meaning was.

"You will dine in his private sitting-room," said Raffles; "it adjoins his bedroom. You must keep him sitting as long as possible, Bunny, and talking all the time!"

In a flash I saw his plan.

"You're going for the picture while we're at dinner?"

"I am."

"If he hears you!"

"He shan't."

"But if he does!"

And I fairly trembled at the thought.

"If he does," said Raffles, "there will be a collision, that's all. Revolvers would be out of place in the Metropole, but I shall certainly take a life-preserver."

"But it's ghastly!" I cried. "To sit and talk to an utter stranger and to know that you're at work in the next room!"

"Two thousand apiece," said Raffles quietly.

"Upon my soul I believe I shall give it away!"

"Not you, Bunny. I know you better than you know yourself."

He put on his coat and his hat.

"What time have I to be there?" I asked him, with a groan.

"Quarter to eight. There will be a telegram from me saying I can't turn up. He's a terror to talk, you'll have no difficulty to keep the ball rolling; but head him off his picture for all you're worth. If he offers to show it you, say you must go. He locked up the case elaborately this afternoon, and there's no earthly reason why he should unlock it again in this hemisphere."

"Where shall I find you when I get away?"

"I shall be down at Esher. I hope to catch the 9.55."

"But surely I can see you again this afternoon?" I cried in a ferment, for his hand was on the door. "I'm not half coached up yet! I know I shall make a mess of it!"

"Not you," he said again, "but I shall if I waste any more time. I've got a deuce of a lot of rushing about to do yet. You won't find me at my rooms. Why not come down to Esher yourself by the last train? That's it – down you come with the latest news! I'll tell old Debenham to expect you: he shall give us both a bed. By Jove! he won't be able to do us too well if he's got his picture."

"If!" I groaned as he nodded his adieu; and he left me limp with apprehension, sick with fear, in a perfectly pitiable condition of pure stage-fright.

For, after all, I had only to act my part; unless Raffles failed where he never did fail, unless Raffles the neat and noiseless was for once clumsy and inept, all I had to do was indeed to "smile and smile and be a villain." I practised that smile half the afternoon. I rehearsed putative parts in hypothetical conversations. I got up stories. I dipped in a book on Queensland at the club. And at last it was 7.45, and I was making my bow to a somewhat elderly man with a small bald head and a retreating brow.

"So you're Mr Raffles's friend?" said he, overhauling me rather rudely with his light small eyes. "Seen anything of him? Expected him early to show me something, but he's never come."

No more, evidently, had his telegram, and my troubles were beginning early. I said I had not seen Raffles since one o'clock, telling the truth with unction while I could; even as we spoke there came a knock at the door; it was the telegram at last, and, after reading it himself, the Queenslander handed it to me.

"Called out of town!" he grumbled. "Sudden illness of near relative! What near relatives has he got?"

I knew of none, and for an instant I quailed before the perils of invention; then I replied that I had never met any of his people, and again felt fortified by my veracity.

"Thought you were bosom pals?" said he, with (as I imagined) a gleam of suspicion in his crafty little eyes.

"Only in town," said I. "I've never been to his place."

"Well," he growled. "I suppose it can't be helped. Don't know why he couldn't come and have his dinner first. Like to see the death-bed I'd go to without my dinner; it's a full-skin billet, if you ask me. Well, must just dine without him, and he'll have to buy his pig in a poke after all. Mind touching that bell? Suppose you know what he came to see me about. Sorry I shan't see him again, for his own sake. I liked Raffles – took to him amazingly. He's a cynic. Like cynics. One myself. Rank bad form of his mother, or his aunt, and I hope she will kick the bucket."

I connect these specimens of his conversation, though they were doubtless detached at the time, and interspersed with remarks of mine here and there. They filled the interval until dinner was served, and they gave me an impression of the man which his every subsequent utterance confirmed. It was an impression which did away with all remorse for my treacherous presence at his table. He was that terrible type, the Silly Cynic, his aim a caustic commentary on all things and all men, his achievement mere vulgar irreverence and unintelligent scorn. Ill-bred and ill-informed, he had (on his own showing) fluked into fortune on a rise in land; yet cunning he possessed, as well as malice, and he chuckled till he choked over the misfortunes of less astute speculators in the same boom. Even now I cannot feel much compunction for my behaviour to the Hon. J. M. Craggs, M.L.C.

But never shall I forget the private agonies of the situation, the listening to my host with one ear and for Raffles with the other! Once I heard him – though the rooms were not divided by the old-fashioned folding-doors, and though the door that did divide them was not only shut but richly curtained, I could have sworn I heard him once. I spilt my wine and laughed at the top of my voice at some coarse sally of my host's. And I heard nothing more, though my ears were on the strain. But later, to my horror, when the waiter had finally withdrawn, Craggs himself sprang up and rushed to his bedroom without a word. I sat like stone till he returned.

"Thought I heard a door go," he said. "Must have been mistaken . . . imagination . . . gave me quite a turn. Raffles tell you priceless treasure I got in there?"

It was the picture at last; up to this point I had kept him to Queensland and the making of his pile. I tried to get him back there now, but in vain. He was reminded of his great ill-gotten possession. I said that Raffles had just mentioned it, and that set him off. With the confidential garrulity of a man who has dined too well, he plunged into his darling topic, and I looked past him at the clock. It was only a quarter to ten.

In common decency I could not go yet. So there I sat (we were still at port) and learnt what had originally fired my host's ambition to possess what he was pleased to call a "real, genuine, twin-screw, double-funnelled, copper-bottomed Old Master;" it was to "go one better" than some rival legislator of pictorial proclivities. But even an epitome of his monologue would be so much weariness; suffice it that it ended inevitably in the invitation I had dreaded all the evening.

"But you must see it. Next room. This way."

"Isn't it packed up?" I inquired hastily.

"Lock and key. That's all."

"Pray don't trouble," I urged.

"Trouble be hanged!" said he. "Come along."

And all at once I saw that to resist him further would be to heap suspicion upon myself against the moment of impending discovery. I therefore followed him into his bedroom without further protest, and suffered him first to show me the iron map-case which stood in one corner; he took a crafty pride in this receptacle, and I thought he would never cease descanting on its innocent appearance and its Chubb's lock. It seemed an interminable age before the key was in the latter. Then the ward clicked, and my pulse stood still.

"By Jove!" I cried next instant.

The canvas was in its place among the maps!

"Thought it would knock you," said Craggs, drawing it out and unrolling it for my benefit. "Grand thing, ain't it? Wouldn't think it had been painted two hundred and thirty years? It has, though, my word! Old Johnson's face will be a treat when he sees it; won't go bragging about his pictures much more. Why, this one's worth all the pictures in Colony o' Queensland put together. Worth fifty thousand pounds, my boy – and I got it for five!"

He dug me in the ribs, and seemed in the mood for further confidences. My appearance checked him, and he rubbed his hands.

"If you take it like that," he chuckled, "how will old Johnson take it? Go out and hang himself to his own picture-rods, I hope!"

Heaven knows what I contrived to say at last. Struck speechless first by my relief, I continued silent from a very different cause. A new tangle of emotions tied my tongue. Raffles had failed – could I not succeed? Was it too late? Was there no way?

"So long," he said, taking a last look at the canvas before he rolled it up – "so long till we get to Brisbane."

The flutter I was in as he closed the case!

"For the last time," he went on, as his keys jingled back into his pocket. "It goes straight into the strongroom on board."

For the last time! If I could but send him out to Australia with only its legitimate contents in his precious map-case! If I could but succeed where Raffles had failed!

We returned to the other room. I have no notion how long he talked, or what about. Whisky and soda-water became the order of the hour. I scarcely touched it, but he drank copiously, and before eleven I left him incoherent. And the last train for Esher was the 11.50 out of Waterloo.

I took a hansom to my rooms. I was back at the hotel in thirteen minutes. I walked upstairs. The corridor was empty; I stood an instant on the sitting-room threshold, heard a snore within, and admitted myself softly with my gentleman's own key, which it had been a very simple matter to take away with me.

Craggs never moved; he was stretched on the sofa fast asleep. But not fast enough for me. I saturated my handkerchief with the chloroform I had brought, and I laid it gently over his mouth. Two or three stertorous breaths, and the man a log.

I removed the handkerchief; I extracted the keys from his pocket. In less than five minutes I put them back, after winding the picture about my body beneath my Inverness cape. I took some whisky and soda-water before I went.

The train was easily caught – so easily that I trembled for ten minutes in my first-class smoking carriage, in terror of every footstep on the platform – in unreasonable terror till the end. Then at last I sat back and lit a cigarette, and the lights of Waterloo reeled out behind.

Some men were returning from the theatre. I can recall their conversation even now. They were disappointed with the piece they had seen. It was one of the later Savoy operas, and they spoke wistfully of the days of *Pinafore* and *Patience*. One of them hummed a stave, and there was an argument as to whether the air was out of *Patience* or the *Mikado*. They all got out at Surbiton, and I was alone with my triumph for a few intoxicating minutes. To think that I had succeeded where Raffles had failed! Of all our adventures this was the first in which I had played a commanding part; and, of them all, this was infinitely the least discreditable. It left me without a conscientious qualm; I had but robbed a robber, when all was said. And I had done it myself, single-handed – *ipse egomet!*

I pictured Raffles, his surprise, his delight. He would think a little more of me in future. And that future, it should be different. We had two thousand pounds apiece – surely enough to start afresh as honest men – and all through me.

In a glow I sprang out at Esher, and took the one belated cab that was waiting under the bridge. In a perfect fever I beheld Broom Hall, with the lower storey still lit up, and saw the front door open as I climbed the steps.

"Thought it was you," said Raffles cheerily. "It's all right. There's a bed for you. Sir Bernard's sitting up to shake your hand."

His good spirits disappointed me. But I knew the man: he was one of those who wear their brightest smile in the blackest hour. I knew him too well by this time to be deceived.

"I've got it!" I cried in his ear. "I've got it!"

"Got what?" he asked me, stepping back.

"The picture!"

"What?"

"The picture. He showed it me. You had to go without it; I saw that. So I determined to have it. And here it is."

"Let's see," said Raffles grimly.

I threw off my cape and unwound the canvas from about my body. While I was doing so an untidy old gentleman made his appearance in the hall, and stood looking on with raised eyebrows.

"Looks pretty fresh for an Old Master, doesn't she?" said Raffles. His tone was strange. I could only suppose that he was jealous of my success.

"So Craggs said. I hardly looked at it myself."

"Well, look now – look closely. By Jove, I must have faked her better than I thought!"

"It's a copy!" I cried.

"It's the copy," he answered. "It's the copy I've been tearing all over the country to procure. It's the copy I faked back and front, so that, on your own showing, it imposed upon Craggs, and might have made him happy for life. And you go and rob him of that!"

I could not speak.

"How did you manage it?" inquired Sir Bernard Debenham.

"Have you killed him?" asked Raffles sardonically.

I did not look at him; I turned to Sir Bernard Debenham, and to him I told my story, hoarsely, excitedly, for it was all that I could do to keep from breaking down. But as I spoke I became calmer, and I finished in mere bitterness, with the remark that another time Raffles might tell me what he meant to do.

"Another time!" he cried instantly. "My dear Bunny, you speak as though we were going to turn burglars for a living!"

"I trust you won't," said Sir Bernard, smiling, "for you are certainly two very daring young men. Let us hope our friend from Queensland will do as he said, and not open his map-case till he gets back there. He will find my cheque awaiting him, and I shall be very much surprised if he troubles any of us again."

Raffles and I did not speak till I was in the room which had been prepared for me. Nor was I anxious to do so then. But he followed me and took my hand.

"Bunny," said he, "don't you be hard on a fellow! I was in the deuce of a hurry, and didn't know that I should get what I wanted in time, and that's a fact. But it serves me right that you should have gone and undone one of the best things I ever did. As for your handiwork, old chap, you won't mind my saying that I didn't think you had it in you. In future – "

"Don't talk to me about the future!" I cried. "I hate the whole thing! I'm going to chuck it up!"

"So am I," said Raffles, "when I've made my pile."

Richard Harding Davis

In the Fog

Richard Harding Davis (1864–1916) was the son of Rebecca Harding Davis, one of the pioneers of the naturalistic novel in America, and he became one of the leading newspaper reporters of his generation, working for the Philadelphia Record *and achieving fame as its war correspondent.*

Davis also wrote a good deal of fiction which was also very popular in its time; "Ranson's Folly" is a classic tale of a frontier fort in the American West, and "Bar Sinister" is a dog story to rival one of Jack London's. "In the Fog", a rare venture into mystery fiction, with its intertwined plots and surprise ending has become something of a classic too. It was first published in 1901.

I

THE GRILL IS the club most difficult of access in the world. To be placed on its rolls distinguishes the new member as greatly as though he had received a vacant Garter or had been caricatured in "Vanity Fair."

Men who belong to the Grill Club never mention that fact. If you were to ask one of them which clubs he frequents, he will name all save that particular one. He is afraid if he told you he belonged to the Grill, that it would sound like boasting.

The Grill Club dates back to the days when Shakespeare's Theatre stood on the present site of the "Times" office. It has a golden Grill which Charles the Second presented to the Club, and the original manuscript of "Tom and Jerry in London," which was bequeathed to it by Pierce Egan himself. The members, when they write letters at the Club, still use sand to blot the ink.

The Grill enjoys the distinction of having blackballed, without political prejudice, a Prime Minister of each party. At the same sitting at which one of these fell, it elected, on account of his brogue and his bulls, Quiller, Q.C., who was then a penniless barrister.

When Paul Preval, the French artist who came to London by royal command to paint a portrait of the Prince of Wales, was made an honorary member – only foreigners may be honorary members – he said, as he signed his first wine-card, "I would rather see my name on that than on a picture in the Louvre."

At which Quiller remarked, "That is a devil of a compliment, because the only men who can read their names in the Louvre to-day have been dead fifty years."

On the night after the great fog of 1897 there were five members in the Club, four of them busy with supper and one reading in front of the fireplace. There is only one room to the Club, and one long table. At the far end of the room the fire of the grill glows red, and, when the fat falls, blazes into flame, and at the other there is a broad bow-window of diamond panes, which looks down upon the street. The four men at the table were strangers to each other, but as they picked at the grilled bones, and sipped their Scotch and soda, they conversed with such charming animation that a visitor to the Club, which does not tolerate visitors, would have counted them as friends of long acquaintance, certainly not as Englishmen who had met for the first time, and without the form of an introduction. But it is the etiquette and tradition of the Grill that whoever enters it must speak with whomever he finds there. It is to enforce this rule that there is but one long table, and whether there are twenty men at it or two, the waiters, supporting the rule, will place them side by side.

For this reason the four strangers at supper were seated together, with the candles grouped about them, and the long length of the table cutting a white path through the outer gloom.

"I repeat," said the gentleman with the black pearl stud, "that the days for romantic adventure and deeds of foolish daring have passed, and that the fault lies with ourselves. Voyages to the pole I do not catalogue as adventures. That African explorer, young Chetney, who turned up yesterday after he was supposed to have died in Uganda, did nothing adventurous. He made maps and explored the sources of rivers. He was in constant danger, but the presence of danger does not constitute adventure. Were that so, the chemist who studies high explosives, or who investigates deadly poisons, passes through adventures daily. No, "adventures are for the adventurous.' But one no longer ventures. The spirit of it has died of inertia. We are grown too practical, too just, above all, too sensible. In this room, for instance, members of this Club have, at the sword's point, disputed the proper scanning of one of Pope's couplets. Over so weighty a matter as spilled Burgundy on a gentleman's cuff, ten men fought across this table, each with his rapier in one hand and a candle in the other. All ten were wounded. The question of the spilled Burgundy concerned but two of them. The eight others engaged because they were men of "spirit." They were, indeed, the first gentlemen of the day. To-night, were you to spill Burgundy on my cuff, were you even to insult me grossly, these gentlemen would not consider it incumbent upon them to kill each other. They would separate us, and to-morrow morning appear as witnesses against us at Bow Street. We have here to-night, in the persons of Sir Andrew and myself, an illustration of how the ways have changed."

The men around the table turned and glanced toward the gentleman in front of the fireplace. He was an elderly and somewhat portly person, with a kindly, wrinkled countenance, which wore continually a smile of almost childish confidence and good-nature. It was a face which the illustrated prints had made intimately familiar. He held a book from him at arm's-length, as if to adjust his eyesight, and his brows were knit with interest.

"Now, were this the eighteenth century," continued the gentleman with the black pearl, "when Sir Andrew left the Club to-night I would have him bound and gagged and thrown into a sedan chair. The watch would not interfere, the passers-by would take to their heels, my hired bullies and ruffians would convey him to some lonely spot where we would guard him until morning. Nothing would come of it, except added reputation to myself as a gentleman of adventurous spirit, and possibly an essay in the 'Tatler,' with stars for names, entitled, let us say, 'The Budget and the Baronet.'"

"But to what end, sir?" inquired the youngest of the members. "And why Sir Andrew, of all persons – why should you select him for this adventure?"

The gentleman with the black pearl shrugged his shoulders.

"It would prevent him speaking in the House to-night. The Navy Increase Bill," he added, gloomily. "It is a Government measure, and Sir Andrew speaks for it. And so great is his influence and so large his following that if he does" – the gentleman laughed ruefully – "if he does, it will go through. Now, had I the spirit of our ancestors," he exclaimed, "I would bring chloroform from the nearest chemist's and drug him in that chair. I would tumble his unconscious form into a hansom-cab, and hold him prisoner until daylight. If I did, I would save the British taxpayer the cost of five more battleships, many millions of pounds."

The gentleman again turned, and surveyed the baronet with freshened interest. The honorary member of the Grill, whose accent already had betrayed him as an American, laughed softly.

"To look at him now," he said, "one would not guess he was deeply concerned with the affairs of state."

The others nodded silently.

"He has not lifted his eyes from that book since we first entered," added the youngest member. "He surely cannot mean to speak tonight."

"Oh, yes, he will speak," muttered the one with the black pearl, moodily. "During these last hours of the session the House sits late, but when the Navy bill comes up on its third reading he will be in his place – and he will pass it."

The fourth member, a stout and florid gentleman of a somewhat sporting appearance, in a short smoking-jacket and black tie, sighed enviously.

"Fancy one of us being as cool as that, if he knew he had to stand up within an hour and rattle off a speech in Parliament. I'd be in a devil of a funk myself. And yet he is as keen over that book he's reading as though he had nothing before him until bedtime."

"Yes, see how eager he is," whispered the youngest member. "He does not lift his eyes even now when he cuts the pages. It is probably an Admiralty Report, or some other weighty work of statistics which bears upon his speech."

The gentleman with the black pearl laughed morosely.

"The weighty work in which the eminent statesman is so deeply engrossed," he said, "is called 'The Great Rand Robbery.' It is a detective novel, for sale at all bookstalls."

The American raised his eyebrows in disbelief.

"'The Great Rand Robbery'?" he repeated, incredulously. "What an odd taste!"

"It is not a taste, it is his vice," returned the gentleman with the pearl stud. "It is his one dissipation. He is noted for it. You, as a stranger, could hardly be expected to know of this idiosyncrasy. Mr Gladstone sought relaxation in the Greek poets, Sir Andrew finds his in Gaboriau. Since I have been a member of Parliament, I have never seen him in the library without a shilling shocker in his hands. He brings them even into the sacred precincts of the House, and from the Government benches reads them concealed inside his hat. Once started on a tale of murder, robbery, and sudden death, nothing can tear him from it, not even the call of the division-bell, nor of hunger, nor the prayers of the party Whip. He gave up his country house because when he journeyed to it in the train he would become so absorbed in his detective-stories that he was invariably carried past his station." The member of Parliament twisted his pearl stud nervously, and bit at the edge of his mustache. "If it only were the first pages of 'The Rand Robbery' that he were reading," he murmured bitterly, "instead of the last! With such another book as that, I swear I could hold him here until morning. There would be no need of chloroform to keep him from the House."

The eyes of all were fastened upon Sir Andrew, and each saw, with fascination, that, with his forefinger, he was now separating the last two pages of the book. The member of Parliament struck the table, softly, with his open palm.

"I would give a hundred pounds," he whispered, "if I could place in his hands at this moment a new story of Sherlock Holmes – a thousand pounds," he added, wildly – "five thousand pounds!"

The American observed the speaker sharply, as though the words bore to him some special application, and then, at an idea which apparently had but just come to him, smiled, in great embarrassment.

Sir Andrew ceased reading, but, as though still under the influence of the book, sat looking, blankly, into the open fire. For a brief space, no one moved until the baronet withdrew his eyes and, with a sudden start of recollection, felt, anxiously, for his watch. He scanned its face eagerly, and scrambled to his feet.

The voice of the American instantly broke the silence in a high, nervous accent.

"And yet Sherlock Holmes himself," he cried, "could not decipher the mystery which to-night baffles the police of London."

At these unexpected words, which carried in them something of the tone of a challenge, the gentlemen about the table started as suddenly as though the American had fired a pistol in the air, and Sir Andrew halted, abruptly, and stood observing him with grave surprise.

The gentleman with the black pearl was the first to recover.

"Yes, yes," he said, eagerly, throwing himself across the table. "A mystery that baffles the police of London. I have heard nothing of it. Tell us at once, pray do – tell us at once."

The American flushed uncomfortably, and picked, uneasily, at the table-cloth.

"No one but the police has heard of it," he murmured, "and they only through me. It is a remarkable crime, to which, unfortunately, I am the only person who can bear witness. Because I am the only witness, I am, in spite of my immunity as a diplomat, detained in

London by the authorities of Scotland Yard. My name," he said, inclining his head, politely, "is Sears, Lieutenant Ripley Sears, of the United States Navy, at present Naval Attaché to the Court of Russia. Had I not been detained to-day by the police, I would have started this morning for Petersburg."

The gentleman with the black pearl interrupted with so pronounced an exclamation of excitement and delight that the American stammered and ceased speaking.

"Do you hear, Sir Andrew?" cried the member of Parliament, jubilantly. "An American diplomat halted by our police because he is the only witness of a most remarkable crime – *the* most remarkable crime, I believe you said, sir," he added, bending eagerly toward the naval officer, "which has occurred in London in many years."

The American moved his head in assent, and glanced at the two other members. They were looking, doubtfully, at him, and the face of each showed that he was greatly perplexed.

Sir Andrew advanced to within the light of the candles and drew a chair toward him.

"The crime must be exceptional, indeed," he said, "to justify the police in interfering with a representative of a friendly power. If I were not forced to leave at once, I should take the liberty of asking you to tell us the details."

The gentleman with the pearl pushed the chair toward Sir Andrew, and motioned him to be seated.

"You cannot leave us now," he exclaimed. "Mr Sears is just about to tell us of this remarkable crime."

He nodded, vigorously, at the naval officer and the American, after first glancing, doubtfully, toward the servants at the far end of the room, leaned forward across the table. The others drew their chairs nearer and bent toward him. The baronet glanced, irresolutely, at his watch, and, with an exclamation of annoyance, snapped down the lid. "They can wait," he muttered. He seated himself quickly, and nodded at Lieutenant Sears.

"If you will be so kind as to begin, sir," he said, impatiently.

"Of course," said the American, "you understand that I understand that I am speaking to gentlemen. The confidences of this Club are inviolate. Until the police give the facts to the public press, I must consider you my confederates. You have heard nothing, you know no one connected with this mystery. Even I must remain anonymous."

The gentlemen seated around him nodded gravely.

"Of course," the baronet assented, with eagerness, "of course."

"We will refer to it," said the gentleman with the black pearl, "as 'The Story of the Naval Attaché.'"

"I arrived in London two days ago," said the American, "and I engaged a room at the Bath Hotel. I know very few people in London, and even the members of our embassy were strangers to me. But in Hong Kong I had become great pals with an officer in your navy, who has since retired, and who is now living in a small house in Rutland Gardens, opposite the Knightsbridge Barracks. I telegraphed him that I was in London, and yesterday morning I received a most hearty invitation to dine with him the same evening at his house. He is a bachelor, so we dined alone and talked over all our old days on the Asiatic Station, and of the changes which had come to us since we had last met there. As I was leaving the next morning for my post at Petersburg, and had many letters to write, I told him, about ten o'clock, that I must get back to the hotel, and he sent out his servant to call a hansom.

"For the next quarter of an hour, as we sat talking, we could hear the cab-whistle sounding, violently, from the doorstep, but apparently with no result.

"'It cannot be that the cabmen are on strike,' my friend said, as he rose and walked to the window.

"He pulled back the curtains and at once called to me.

"'You have never seen a London fog, have you?' he asked. 'Well, come here. This is one of the best, or, rather, one of the worst, of them.' I joined him at the window, but I could see nothing. Had I not known that the house looked out upon the street I would have believed that I was facing a dead wall. I raised the sash and stretched out my head, but still I could see nothing. Even the light of the street-lamps, opposite, and in the upper windows of the barracks, had been smothered in the yellow mist. The lights of the room in which I stood penetrated the fog only to the distance of a few inches from my eyes.

"Below me the servant was still sounding his whistle, but I could afford to wait no longer, and told my friend that I would try and find the way to my hotel on foot. He objected, but the letters I had to write were for the Navy Department, and, besides, I had always heard that to be out in a London fog was the most wonderful experience, and I was curious to investigate one for myself.

"My friend went with me to his front door, and laid down a course for me to follow. I was first to walk straight across the street to the brick wall of the Knightsbridge Barracks. I was then to feel my way along the wall until I came to a row of houses set back from the sidewalk. They would bring me to a cross street. On the other side of this street was a row of shops which I was to follow until they joined the iron railings of Hyde Park. I was to keep to the railings until I reached the gates at Hyde Park Corner, where I was to lay a diagonal course across Piccadilly, and tack in toward the railings of Green Park. At the end of these railings, going east, I would find the Walsingham, and my own hotel.

"To a sailor the course did not seem difficult, so I bade my friend good-night and walked forward until my feet touched the paving. I continued upon it until I reached the curbing of the sidewalk. A few steps further, and my hands struck the wall of the barracks. I turned in the direction from which I had just come, and saw a square of faint light cut in the yellow fog. I shouted, 'All right,' and the voice of my friend answered, 'Good luck to you.' The light from his open door disappeared with a bang, and I was left alone in a dripping, yellow darkness. I have been in the Navy for ten years, but I have never known such a fog as that of last night, not even among the icebergs of Behring Sea. There one at least could see the light of the binnacle, but last night I could not even distinguish the hand by which I guided myself along the barrack-wall. At sea a fog is a natural phenomenon. It is as familiar as the rainbow which follows a storm, it is as proper that a fog should spread upon the waters as that steam shall rise from a kettle. But a fog which springs from the paved streets, that rolls between solid house-fronts, that forces cabs to move at half speed, that drowns policemen and extinguishes the electric lights of the music-hall, that to me is incomprehensible. It is as out of place as a tidal wave on Broadway.

"As I felt my way along the wall, I encountered other men who were coming from the opposite direction, and each time when we hailed each other I stepped away from the wall to make room for them to pass. But the third time I did this, when I reached out my hand, the wall had disappeared, and the further I moved to find it the further I seemed to be sinking into space. I had the unpleasant conviction that at any moment I might step over a precipice. Since I had set out, I had heard no traffic in the street, and now, although I listened some minutes, I could only distinguish the occasional footfalls of pedestrians. Several times I called aloud, and once a jocular gentleman answered me, but only to ask me where I thought he was, and then even he was swallowed up in the silence. Just above me I could make out a jet of gas which I guessed came from a street-lamp, and I moved over to that, and, while I tried to recover my bearings, kept my hand on the iron post. Except for this flicker of gas, no larger than the tip of my finger, I could distinguish nothing about me. For the rest, the mist hung between me and the world like a damp and heavy blanket.

"I could hear voices, but I could not tell from whence they came, and the scrape of a foot, moving cautiously, or a muffled cry as someone stumbled, were the only sounds that reached me.

"I decided that until someone took me in tow I had best remain where I was, and it must have been for ten minutes that I waited by the lamp, straining my ears and hailing distant footfalls. In a house near me some people were dancing to the music of a Hungarian band. I even fancied I could hear the windows shake to the rhythm of their feet, but I could not make out from which part of the compass the sounds came. And sometimes, as the music rose, it seemed close at my hand, and, again, to be floating high in the air above my head. Although I was surrounded by thousands of householders, I was as completely lost as though I had been set down by night in the Sahara Desert. There seemed to be no reason in waiting longer for an escort, so I again set out, and at once bumped against a low, iron fence. At first I believed this to be an area railing, but, on following it, I found that it stretched for a long distance, and that it was pierced at regular intervals with gates. I was standing, uncertainly, with my hand on one of these, when a square of light suddenly opened in the night, and in it I saw, as you see a picture thrown by a biograph in a darkened theatre, a young gentleman in evening dress, and, back of him, the lights of a hall. I guessed, from its elevation and distance from the sidewalk, that this light must come from the door of a house set back from the street, and I determined to approach it and ask the young man to tell me where I was. But, in fumbling with the lock of the gate, I instinctively bent my head, and when I raised it again the door had partly closed, leaving only a narrow shaft of light. Whether the young man had re-entered the house, or had left it I could not tell, but I hastened to open the gate, and as I stepped forward I found myself upon an asphalt walk. At the same instant there was the sound of quick steps upon the path, and someone rushed past me. I called to him, but he made no reply, and I heard the gate click and the footsteps hurrying away upon the sidewalk.

"Under other circumstances the young man's rudeness, and his recklessness in dashing so hurriedly through the mist, would have struck me as peculiar, but everything was so distorted by the fog that at the moment I did not consider it. The door was still as he had left it, partly open. I went up the path, and, after much fumbling, found the knob of the door-bell and gave it a sharp pull. The bell answered me from a great depth and distance, but no movement followed from inside the house, and, although I pulled the bell again and again, I could hear nothing save the dripping of the mist about me. I was anxious to be on my way, but unless I knew where I was going there was little chance of my making any speed, and I was determined that until I learned my bearings I would not venture back into the fog. So I pushed the door open and stepped into the house.

"I found myself in a long and narrow hall, upon which doors opened from either side. At the end of the hall was a staircase with a balustrade which ended in a sweeping curve. The balustrade was covered with heavy, Persian rugs, and the walls of the hall were also hung with them. The door on my left was closed, but the one nearer me on the right was open, and, as I stepped opposite to it, I saw that it was a sort of reception or waiting-room, and that it was empty. The door below it was also open, and, with the idea that I would surely find someone there, I walked on up the hall. I was in evening dress, and I felt I did not look like a burglar, so I had no great fear that, should I encounter one of the inmates of the house, he would shoot me on sight. The second door in the hall opened into a dining-room. This was also empty. One person had been dining at the table, but the cloth had not been cleared away, and a flickering candle showed half-filled wineglasses and the ashes of cigarettes. The greater part of the room was in complete darkness.

"By this time I had grown conscious of the fact that I was wandering about in a strange house, and that, apparently, I was alone in it. The silence of the place began to try my nerves, and in a sudden, unexplainable panic I started for the open street. But as I turned, I saw a man sitting on a bench, which the curve of the balustrade had hidden from me. His eyes were shut, and he was sleeping soundly.

"The moment before I had been bewildered because I could see no one, but at sight of this man I was much more bewildered.

"He was a very large man, a giant in height, with long, yellow hair, which hung below his shoulders. He was dressed in a red silk shirt, that was belted at the waist and hung outside black velvet trousers, which, in turn, were stuffed into high, black boots. I recognized the costume at once as that of a Russian servant, but what a Russian servant in his native livery could be doing in a private house in Knightsbridge was incomprehensible.

"I advanced and touched the man on the shoulder, and, after an effort, he awoke, and, on seeing me, sprang to his feet and began bowing rapidly, and making deprecatory gestures. I had picked up enough Russian in Petersburg to make out that the man was apologizing for having fallen asleep, and I also was able to explain to him that I desired to see his master.

"He nodded vigorously, and said, 'Will the Excellency come this way? The Princess is here.'

"I distinctly made out the word 'princess,' and I was a good deal embarrassed. I had thought it would be easy enough to explain my intrusion to a man, but how a woman would look at it was another matter, and as I followed him down the hall I was somewhat puzzled.

"As we advanced, he noticed that the front door was standing open, and with an exclamation of surprise, hastened toward it and closed it. Then he rapped twice on the door of what was apparently the drawing-room. There was no reply to his knock, and he tapped again, and then, timidly, and cringing subserviently, opened the door and stepped inside. He withdrew himself at once and stared stupidly at me, shaking his head.

"'She is not there,' he said. He stood for a moment, gazing blankly through the open door, and then hastened toward the dining-room. The solitary candle which still burned there seemed to assure him that the room also was empty. He came back and bowed me toward the drawing-room. 'She is above,' he said; 'I will inform the Princess of the Excellency's presence.'

"Before I could stop him, he had turned and was running up the staircase, leaving me alone at the open door of the drawing-room. I decided that the adventure had gone quite far enough, and if I had been able to explain to the Russian that I had lost my way in the fog, and only wanted to get back into the street again, I would have left the house on the instant.

"Of course, when I first rang the bell of the house I had no other expectation than that it would be answered by a parlor-maid who would direct me on my way. I certainly could not then foresee that I would disturb a Russian princess in her boudoir, or that I might be thrown out by her athletic bodyguard. Still, I thought I ought not now to leave the house without making some apology, and, if the worst should come, I could show my card. They could hardly believe that a member of an Embassy had any designs upon the hat-rack.

"The room in which I stood was dimly lighted, but I could see that, like the hall, it was hung with heavy, Persian rugs. The corners were filled with palms, and there was the unmistakable odor in the air of Russian cigarettes, and strange, dry scents that carried me back to the bazaars of Vladivostok. Near the front windows was a grand piano, and at the other end of the room a heavily carved screen of some black wood, picked out with ivory. The screen was overhung with a canopy of silken draperies, and formed a sort of alcove. In front of the alcove was spread the white skin of a polar bear, and set on that was one of those low, Turkish coffee-tables. It held a lighted spirit-lamp and two gold coffee-cups. I had heard no movement from above stairs, and it must have been fully three minutes that I stood waiting, noting these details of the room and wondering at the delay, and at the strange silence.

"And then, suddenly, as my eye grew more used to the half-light, I saw, projecting from behind the screen, as though it were stretched along the back of a divan, the hand of a man and the lower part of his arm. I was as startled as though I had come across a footprint on a deserted island. Evidently, the man had been sitting there since I had come into the room, even since I had entered the house, and he had heard the servant knocking upon the door. Why he had not declared himself I could not understand, but I supposed that, possibly, he was a guest, with no reason to interest himself in the Princess's other visitors, or, perhaps, for some reason, he did not wish to be observed. I could see nothing of him except his hand, but I had an unpleasant feeling that he had been peering at me through the carving in the screen, and that he still was doing so. I moved my feet noisily on the floor and said, tentatively, 'I beg your pardon.'

"There was no reply, and the hand did not stir. Apparently, the man was bent upon ignoring me, but, as all I wished was to apologize for my intrusion and to leave the house, I walked up to the alcove and peered around it. Inside the screen was a divan piled with cushions, and on the end of it nearer me the man was sitting. He was a young Englishman with light-yellow hair and a deeply bronzed face. He was seated with his arms stretched out along the back of the divan, and with his head resting against a cushion. His attitude was one of complete ease. But his mouth had fallen open, and his eyes were set with an expression of utter horror. At the first glance, I saw that he was quite dead.

"For a flash of time I was too startled to act, but in the same flash I was convinced that the man had met his death from no accident, that he had not died through any ordinary failure of the laws of nature. The expression on his face was much too terrible to be misinterpreted. It spoke as eloquently as words. It told me that before the end had come he had watched his death approach and threaten him.

"I was so sure he had been murdered that I instinctively looked on the floor for the weapon, and, at the same moment, out of concern for my own safety, quickly behind me; but the silence of the house continued unbroken.

"I have seen a great number of dead men; I was on the Asiatic Station during the Japanese-Chinese war. I was in Port Arthur after the massacre. So a dead man, for the single reason that he is dead, does not repel me, and, though I knew that there was no hope that this man was alive, still, for decency's sake, I felt his pulse, and, while I kept my ears alert for any sound from the floors above me, I pulled open his shirt and placed my hand upon his heart. My fingers instantly touched upon the opening of a wound, and as I withdrew them I found them wet with blood. He was in evening dress, and in the wide bosom of his shirt I found a narrow slit, so narrow that in the dim light it was scarcely discernible. The wound was no wider than the smallest blade of a pocket-knife, but when I stripped the shirt away from the chest and left it bare, I found that the weapon, narrow as it was, had been long enough to reach his heart. There is no need to tell you how I felt as I stood by the body of this boy, for he was hardly older than a boy, or of the thoughts that came into my head. I was bitterly sorry for this stranger, bitterly indignant at his murderer, and, at the same time, selfishly concerned for my own safety and for the notoriety which I saw was sure to follow. My instinct was to leave the body where it lay, and to hide myself in the fog, but I also felt that since a succession of accidents had made me the only witness to a crime, my duty was to make myself a good witness and to assist to establish the facts of this murder.

"That it might, possibly, be a suicide, and not a murder, did not disturb me for a moment. The fact that the weapon had disappeared, and the expression on the boy's face were enough to convince, at least me, that he had had no hand in his own death. I judged it, therefore, of the first importance to discover who was in the house, or, if they had escaped from it, who had been in the house before I entered it. I had seen one man leave it; but all I could tell of him was that he was a young man, that he was in evening dress, and that he had fled in such haste that he had not stopped to close the door behind him.

"The Russian servant I had found apparently asleep, and, unless he acted a part with supreme skill, he was a stupid and ignorant boor, and as innocent of the murder as myself. There was still the Russian princess whom he had expected to find, or had pretended to expect to find, in the same room with the murdered man. I judged that she must now be either upstairs with the servant, or that she had, without his knowledge, already fled from the house. When I recalled his apparently genuine surprise at not finding her in the drawing-room, this latter supposition seemed the more probable. Nevertheless, I decided that it was my duty to make a search, and after a second hurried look for the weapon among the cushions of the divan, and upon the floor, I cautiously crossed the hall and entered the dining-room.

"The single candle was still flickering in the draught, and showed only the white cloth. The rest of the room was draped in shadows. I picked up the candle, and, lifting it high above my head, moved around the corner of the table. Either my nerves were on such a stretch that no shock could strain them further, or my mind was inoculated to horrors, for I did not cry out at what I saw nor retreat from it. Immediately at my feet was the body of a beautiful woman, lying at full length upon the floor, her arms flung out on either side of her, and her white face and shoulders gleaming, dully, in the unsteady light of the candle. Around her throat was a great chain of diamonds, and the light played upon these and made them flash and blaze in tiny flames. But the woman who wore them was dead, and I was so certain as to how she had died that, without an instant's hesitation, I dropped on my knees beside her and placed my hands above her heart. My fingers again touched the thin slit of a wound. I had no doubt in my mind but that this was the Russian princess, and when I lowered the candle to her face I was assured that this was so. Her features showed the finest lines of both the Slav and the Jewess; the eyes were black, the hair blue-black and wonderfully heavy, and her skin, even in death, was rich in color. She was a surpassingly beautiful woman.

"I rose and tried to light another candle with the one I held, but I found that my hand was so unsteady that I could not keep the wicks together. It was my intention to again search for this strange dagger which had been used to kill both the English boy and the beautiful princess, but before I could light the second candle I heard footsteps descending the stairs, and the Russian servant appeared in the doorway.

"My face was in darkness, or I am sure that, at the sight of it, he would have taken alarm, for at that moment I was not sure but that this man himself was the murderer. His own face was plainly visible to me in the light from the hall, and I could see that it wore an expression of dull bewilderment. I stepped quickly toward him and took a firm hold upon his wrist.

"'She is not there,' he said. 'The Princess has gone. They have all gone.'

"'Who have gone?' I demanded. 'Who else has been here?'

"'The two Englishmen,' he said.

"'What two Englishmen?' I demanded. 'What are their names?'

"The man now saw by my manner that some question of great moment hung upon his answer, and he began to protest that he did not know the names of the visitors and that until that evening he had never seen them.

"I guessed that it was my tone which frightened him, so I took my hand off his wrist and spoke less eagerly.

"'How long have they been here?' I asked, 'and when did they go?'

"He pointed behind him toward the drawing-room.

"'One sat there with the Princess,' he said; 'the other came after I had placed the coffee in the drawing-room. The two Englishmen talked together, and the Princess returned here to the table. She sat there in that chair, and I brought her cognac and cigarettes. Then I sat outside upon the bench. It was a feast-day, and I had been drinking. Pardon, Excellency, but I fell asleep. When I woke, your Excellency was standing by me, but the Princess and the two Englishmen had gone. That is all I know.'

"I believed that the man was telling me the truth. His fright had passed, and he was now apparently puzzled, but not alarmed.

"'You must remember the names of the Englishmen,' I urged. "Try to think. When you announced them to the Princess what name did you give?'

"At this question he exclaimed, with pleasure, and, beckoning to me, ran hurriedly down the hall and into the drawing-room. In the corner furthest from the screen was the piano, and on it was a silver tray. He picked this up and, smiling with pride at his own intelligence, pointed at two cards that lay upon it. I took them up and read the names engraved upon them."

The American paused abruptly, and glanced at the faces about him. "I read the names," he repeated. He spoke with great reluctance.

"Continue!" cried the baronet, sharply.

"I read the names," said the American with evident distaste, "and the family name of each was the same. They were the names of two brothers. One is well known to you. It is that of the African explorer of whom this gentleman was just speaking. I mean the Earl of Chetney. The other was the name of his brother, Lord Arthur Chetney."

The men at the table fell back as though a trapdoor had fallen open at their feet.

"Lord Chetney?" they exclaimed, in chorus. They glanced at each other and back to the American, with every expression of concern and disbelief.

"It is impossible!" cried the Baronet. "Why, my dear sir, young Chetney only arrived from Africa yesterday. It was so stated in the evening papers."

The jaw of the American set in a resolute square, and he pressed his lips together.

"You are perfectly right, sir," he said, "Lord Chetney did arrive in London yesterday morning, and yesterday night I found his dead body."

The youngest member present was the first to recover. He seemed much less concerned over the identity of the murdered man than at the interruption of the narrative.

"Oh, please let him go on!" he cried. "What happened then? You say you found two visiting-cards. How do you know which card was that of the murdered man?"

The American, before he answered, waited until the chorus of exclamations had ceased. Then he continued as though he had not been interrupted.

"The instant I read the names upon the cards," he said, "I ran to the screen and, kneeling beside the dead man, began a search through his pockets. My hand at once fell upon a card-case, and I found on all the cards it contained the title of the Earl of Chetney. His watch and cigarette-case also bore his name. These evidences, and the fact of his bronzed skin, and that his cheek-bones were worn with fever, convinced me that the dead man was the African explorer, and the boy who had fled past me in the night was Arthur, his younger brother.

"I was so intent upon my search that I had forgotten the servant, and I was still on my knees when I heard a cry behind me. I turned, and saw the man gazing down at the body in abject horror.

"Before I could rise, he gave another cry of terror, and, flinging himself into the hall, raced toward the door to the street. I leaped after him, shouting to him to halt, but before I could reach the hall he had torn open the door, and I saw him spring out into the yellow fog. I cleared the steps in a jump and ran down the garden-walk but just as the gate clicked in front of me. I had it opened on the instant, and, following the sound of the man's footsteps, I raced after him across the open street. He, also, could hear me, and he instantly stopped running, and there was absolute silence. He was so near that I almost fancied I could hear him panting, and I held my own breath to listen. But I could distinguish nothing but the dripping of the mist about us, and from far off the music of the Hungarian band, which I had heard when I first lost myself.

"All I could see was the square of light from the door I had left open behind me, and a lamp in the hall beyond it flickering in the draught. But even as I watched it, the flame of the lamp was blown violently to and fro, and the door, caught in the same current of air, closed slowly. I knew if it shut I could not again enter the house, and I rushed madly toward it. I believe I even shouted out, as though it were something human which I could compel to obey me, and then I caught my foot against the curb and smashed into the sidewalk. When I rose to my feet I was dizzy and half stunned, and though I thought then that I was moving toward the door, I know now that I probably turned directly from it; for, as I groped about in the night, calling frantically for the police, my fingers touched nothing but the dripping fog, and the iron railings for which I sought seemed to have melted away. For many minutes I beat the mist with my arms like one at blind man's bluff, turning sharply in circles, cursing aloud at my stupidity and crying continually for help. At last a voice answered me from the fog, and I found myself held in the circle of a policeman's lantern.

"That is the end of my adventure. What I have to tell you now is what I learned from the police.

"At the station-house to which the man guided me I related what you have just heard. I told them that the house they must at once find was one set back from the street within a radius of two hundred yards from the Knightsbridge Barracks, that within fifty yards of it someone was giving a dance to the music of a Hungarian band, and that the railings before it were as high as a man's waist and filed to a point. With that to work upon, twenty men were at once ordered out into the fog to search for the house, and Inspector Lyle himself was despatched to the home of Lord Edam, Chetney's father, with a warrant for Lord Arthur's arrest. I was thanked and dismissed on my own recognizance.

"This morning, Inspector Lyle called on me, and from him I learned the police theory of the scene I had just described.

"Apparently, I had wandered very far in the fog, for up to noon to-day the house had not been found, nor had they been able to arrest Lord Arthur. He did not return to his father's house last night, and there is no trace of him; but from what the police knew of the past lives of the people I found in that lost house, they have evolved a theory, and their theory is that the murders were committed by Lord Arthur.

"The infatuation of his elder brother, Lord Chetney, for a Russian princess, so Inspector Lyle tells me, is well known to everyone. About two years ago the Princess Zichy, as she calls herself, and he were constantly together, and Chetney informed his friends that they were about to be married. The woman was notorious in two continents, and when Lord Edam heard of his son's infatuation he appealed to the police for her record.

"It is through his having applied to them that they know so much concerning her and her relations with the Chetneys. From the police Lord Edam learned that Madame Zichy had once been a spy in the employ of the Russian Third Section, but that lately she had been repudiated by her own government and was living by her wits, by blackmail, and by her beauty. Lord Edam laid this record before his son, but Chetney either knew it already or the woman persuaded him not to believe in it, and the father and son parted in great anger. Two days later the marquis altered his will, leaving all of his money to the younger brother, Arthur.

"The title and some of the landed property he could not keep from Chetney, but he swore if his son saw the woman again that the will should stand as it was, and he would be left without a penny.

"This was about eighteen months ago, when, apparently, Chetney tired of the Princess, and suddenly went off to shoot and explore in Central Africa. No word came from him, except that twice he was reported as having died of fever in the jungle, and finally two traders reached the coast who said they had seen his body. This was accepted by all as conclusive, and young Arthur was recognized as the heir to the Edam millions. On the strength of this supposition he at once began to borrow enormous sums from the money-lenders. This is of great importance, as the police believe it was these debts which drove him to the murder of his brother. Yesterday, as you know, Lord Chetney suddenly returned from the grave, and it was the fact that for two years he had been considered as dead which lent such importance to his return and which gave rise to those columns of detail concerning him which appeared in all the afternoon papers. But, obviously, during his absence he had not tired of the Princess Zichy, for we know that a few hours after he reached London he sought her out. His brother, who had also learned of his reappearance through the papers, probably suspected which would be the house he would first visit, and followed him there, arriving, so the Russian servant tells us, while the two were at coffee in the drawing-room. The Princess, then, we also learn from the servant, withdrew to the dining-room, leaving the brothers together. What happened one can only guess.

"Lord Arthur knew now that when it was discovered he was no longer the heir, the money-lenders would come down upon him. The police believe that he at once sought out his brother to beg for money to cover the post-obits, but that, considering the sum he needed was several hundreds of thousands of pounds, Chetney refused to give it him. No one knew that Arthur had gone to seek out his brother. They were alone. It is possible, then, that in a passion of disappointment, and crazed with the disgrace which he saw before him, young Arthur made himself the heir beyond further question. The death of his brother would have availed nothing if the woman remained alive. It is then possible that he crossed the hall, and, with the same weapon which made him Lord Edam's heir, destroyed the solitary witness to the murder. The only other person who could have seen it was sleeping in a drunken stupor, to which fact undoubtedly he owed his life. And yet," concluded the Naval Attaché, leaning forward and marking each word with his finger, "Lord Arthur blundered fatally. In his haste he left the door of the house open, so giving access to the first passer-by, and he forgot that when he entered it he had handed his card to the servant. That piece of paper may yet send him to the gallows. In the meantime, he has disappeared completely, and somewhere, in one of the millions of streets of this great capital, in a locked and empty house, lies the body of his brother, and of the woman his brother loved, undiscovered, unburied, and with their murder unavenged."

In the discussion which followed the conclusion of the story of the Naval Attaché, the gentleman with the pearl took no part. Instead, he arose, and, beckoning a servant to a far corner of the room, whispered earnestly to him until a sudden movement on the part of Sir Andrew caused him to return hurriedly to the table.

"There are several points in Mr Sears' story I want explained," he cried. "Be seated, Sir Andrew," he begged. "Let us have the opinion of an expert. I do not care what the police think, I want to know what you think."

But Sir Henry rose reluctantly from his chair.

"I should like nothing better than to discuss this," he said. "But it is most important that I proceed to the House. I should have been there some time ago." He turned toward the servant and directed him to call a hansom.

The gentleman with the pearl stud looked appealingly at the Naval Attaché. "There are surely many details that you have not told us," he urged. "Some you have forgotten."

The Baronet interrupted quickly.

"I trust not," he said, "for I could not possibly stop to hear them."

"The story is finished," declared the Naval Attaché; "until Lord Arthur is arrested or the bodies are found there is nothing more to tell of either Chetney or the Princess Zichy."

"Of Lord Chetney, perhaps not," interrupted the sporting-looking gentleman with the black tie, "but there'll always be something to tell of the Princess Zichy. I know enough stories about her to fill a book. She was a most remarkable woman." The speaker dropped the end of his cigar into his coffee-cup and, taking his case from his pocket, selected a fresh one. As he did so he laughed and held up the case that the others might see it. It was an ordinary cigar-case of well-worn pig-skin, with a silver clasp.

"The only time I ever met her," he said, "she tried to rob me of this."

The Baronet regarded him closely.

"She tried to rob you?" he repeated.

"Tried to rob me of this," continued the gentleman in the black tie, "and of the Czarina's diamonds." His tone was one of mingled admiration and injury.

"The Czarina's diamonds!" exclaimed the Baronet. He glanced quickly and suspiciously at the speaker, and then at the others about the table. But their faces gave evidence of no other emotion than that of ordinary interest.

"Yes, the Czarina's diamonds," repeated the man with the black tie. "It was a necklace of diamonds. I was told to take them to the Russian Ambassador in Paris, who was to deliver them at Moscow. I am a Queen's Messenger," he added.

"Oh, I see," exclaimed Sir Andrew, in a tone of relief. "And you say that this same Princess Zichy, one of the victims of this double murder, endeavored to rob you of – of – that cigar-case."

"And the Czarina's diamonds," answered the Queen's Messenger, imperturbably. "It's not much of a story, but it gives you an idea of the woman's character. The robbery took place between Paris and Marseilles."

The Baronet interrupted him with an abrupt movement. "No, no," he cried, shaking his head in protest. "Do not tempt me. I really cannot listen. I must be at the House in ten minutes."

"I am sorry," said the Queen's Messenger. He turned to those seated about him. "I wonder if the other gentlemen – " he inquired, tentatively. There was a chorus of polite murmurs, and the Queen's Messenger, bowing his head in acknowledgment, took a preparatory sip from his glass. At the same moment the servant to whom the man with the black pearl had spoken, slipped a piece of paper into his hand. He glanced at it, frowned, and threw it under the table.

The servant bowed to the Baronet.

"Your hansom is waiting, Sir Andrew," he said.

"The necklace was worth twenty thousand pounds," began the Queen's Messenger. "It was a present from the Queen of England to celebrate – " The Baronet gave an exclamation of angry annoyance.

"Upon my word, this is most provoking," he interrupted. "I really ought not to stay. But I certainly mean to hear this." He turned irritably to the servant. "Tell the hansom to wait," he commanded, and, with an air of a boy who is playing truant, slipped guiltily into his chair.

The gentleman with the black pearl smiled blandly, and rapped upon the table.

"Order, gentlemen," he said. "Order for the story of the Queen's Messenger and the Czarina's diamonds."

II

"The necklace was a present from the Queen of England to the Czarina of Russia," began the Queen's Messenger. "It was to celebrate the occasion of the Czar's coronation. Our Foreign Office knew that the Russian Ambassador in Paris was to proceed to Moscow for that ceremony, and I was directed to go to Paris and turn over the necklace to him. But when I reached Paris I found he had not expected me for a week later and was taking a few days' vacation at Nice. His people asked me to leave the necklace with them at the Embassy, but I had been charged to get a receipt for it from the Ambassador himself, so I started at once for Nice. The fact that Monte Carlo is not two thousand miles from Nice may have had something to do with making me carry out my instructions so carefully.

"Now, how the Princess Zichy came to find out about the necklace I don't know, but I can guess. As you have just heard, she was at one time a spy in the service of the Russian Government. And after they dismissed her she kept up her acquaintance with many of the Russian agents in London. It is probable that through one of them she learned that the necklace was to be sent to Moscow, and which one of the Queen's Messengers had been detailed to take it there. Still, I doubt if even that knowledge would have helped her if she had not also known something which I supposed no one else in the world knew but myself and one other man. And, curiously enough, the other man was a Queen's Messenger, too, and a friend of mine. You must know that up to the time of this robbery I had always concealed my despatches in a manner peculiarly my own. I got the idea from that play called 'A Scrap of Paper.' In it a man wants to hide a certain compromising document. He knows that all his rooms will be secretly searched for it, so he puts it in a torn envelope and sticks it up where anyone can see it on his mantel-shelf. The result is that the woman who is ransacking the house to find it looks in all the unlikely places, but passes over the scrap of paper that is just under her nose. Sometimes the papers and packages they give us to carry about Europe are of very great value, and sometimes they are special makes of cigarettes, and orders to court-dressmakers. Sometimes we know what we are carrying and sometimes we do not. If it is a large sum of money or a treaty, they generally tell us. But, as a rule, we have no knowledge of what the package contains; so, to be on the safe side, we naturally take just as great care of it as though we knew it held the terms of an ultimatum or the crown-jewels. As a rule, my confrères carry the official packages in a despatch-box, which is just as obvious as a lady's jewel-bag in the hands of her maid. Everyone knows they are carrying something of value. They put a premium on dishonesty. Well, after I saw the 'Scrap-of-Paper' play, I determined to put the government valuables in the most unlikely place that anyone would look for them. So I used to hide the documents they gave me inside my riding-boots, and small articles, such as money or jewels, I carried in an old cigar-case. After I took to using my case for that purpose I bought a new one, exactly like it, for my cigars. But, to avoid mistakes, I had my initials placed on both sides of the new one, and the moment I touched the case, even in the dark, I could tell which it was by the raised initials.

"No one knew of this except the Queen's Messenger of whom I spoke. We once left Paris together on the Orient Express. I was going to Constantinople and he was to stop off at Vienna. On the journey I told him of my peculiar way of hiding things and showed him my cigar-case. If I recollect rightly, on that trip it held the grand cross of St Michael and St George, which the Queen was sending to our Ambassador. The Messenger was very much entertained at my scheme, and some months later when he met the Princess he told her about it as an amusing story. Of course, he had no idea she was a Russian spy. He didn't know anything at all about her, except that she was a very attractive woman. It was indiscreet, but he could not possibly have guessed that she could ever make any use of what he told her.

"Later, after the robbery, I remembered that I had informed this young chap of my secret hiding-place, and when I saw him again I questioned him about it. He was greatly distressed, and said he had never seen the importance of the secret. He remembered he had told several people of it, and among others the Princess Zichy. In that way I found out that it was she who had robbed me, and I know that from the moment I left London she was following me, and that she knew then that the diamonds were concealed in my cigar-case.

"My train for Nice left Paris at ten in the morning. When I travel at night I generally tell the *chef de gare* that I am a Queen's Messenger, and he gives me a compartment to myself, but in the daytime I take whatever offers. On this morning I had found an empty compartment, and I had tipped the guard to keep everyone else out, not from any fear of losing the diamonds, but because I wanted to smoke. He had locked the door, and as the last bell had rung I supposed I was to travel alone, so I began to arrange my traps and make myself comfortable. The diamonds in the cigar-case were in the inside pocket of my waistcoat, and as they made a bulky package, I took them out, intending to put them in my hand-bag. It is a small satchel like a book-maker's, or those hand-bags that couriers carry. I wear it slung from a strap across my shoulders, and, no matter whether I am sitting or walking, it never leaves me.

"I took the cigar-case which held the necklace from my inside pocket and the case which held the cigars out of the satchel, and while I was searching through it for a box of matches I laid the two cases beside me on the seat.

"At that moment the train started, but at the same instant there was a rattle at the lock of the compartment, and a couple of porters lifted and shoved a woman through the door, and hurled her rugs and umbrellas in after her.

"Instinctively I reached for the diamonds. I shoved them quickly into the satchel and, pushing them far down to the bottom of the bag, snapped the spring-lock. Then I put the cigars in the pocket of my coat, but with the thought that now that I had a woman as a travelling companion I would probably not be allowed to enjoy them.

"One of her pieces of luggage had fallen at my feet, and a roll of rugs had landed at my side. I thought if I hid the fact that the lady was not welcome, and at once endeavored to be civil, she might permit me to smoke. So I picked her hand-bag off the floor and asked her where I might place it.

"As I spoke I looked at her for the first time, and saw that she was a most remarkably handsome woman.

"She smiled charmingly and begged me not to disturb myself. Then she arranged her own things about her, and, opening her dressing-bag, took out a gold cigarette-case.

"'Do you object to smoke?' she asked.

"I laughed and assured her I had been in great terror lest she might object to it herself.

"'If you like cigarettes,' she said, 'will you try some of these? They are rolled especially for my husband in Russia, and they are supposed to be very good.'

"I thanked her, and took one from her case, and I found it so much better than my own that I continued to smoke her cigarettes throughout the rest of the journey. I must say that we got on very well. I judged from the coronet on her cigarette-case, and from her manner, which was quite as well bred as that of any woman I ever met, that she was someone of importance, and though she seemed almost too good-looking to be respectable, I determined that she was some *grande dame* who was so assured of her position that she could afford to be unconventional. At first she read her novel, and then she made some comment on the scenery, and finally we began to discuss the current politics of the Continent. She talked of all the cities in Europe, and seemed to know everyone worth knowing. But she volunteered nothing about herself except that she frequently made use of the expression, 'When my husband was stationed at Vienna,' or 'When my husband was promoted to Rome.' Once she said to me, 'I have often seen you at Monte Carlo. I saw you when you won the pigeon-championship.' I told her that I was not a pigeon-shot, and she gave a little start of surprise. 'Oh, I beg your pardon,' she said; 'I thought you were Morton Hamilton, the English champion. As a matter of fact, I do look like Hamilton, but I know now that her object was to make me think that she had no idea as to who I really was. She needn't have acted at all, for I certainly had no suspicions of her, and was only too pleased to have so charming a companion.

"The one thing that should have made me suspicious was the fact that at every station she made some trivial excuse to get me out of the compartment. She pretended that her maid was travelling back of us in one of the second-class carriages, and kept saying she could not imagine why the woman did not come to look after her, and if the maid did not turn up at the next stop, would I be so very kind as to get out and bring her whatever it was she pretended she wanted.

"I had taken my dressing-case from the rack to get out a novel, and had left it on the seat opposite to mine, and at the end of the compartment farthest from her. And once when I came back from buying her a cup of chocolate, or from some other fool-errand, I found her standing at my end of the compartment with both hands on the dressing-bag. She looked at me without so much as winking an eye, and shoved the case carefully into a corner. 'Your bag slipped off on the floor,' she said. 'If you've got any bottles in it, you had better look and see that they're not broken.'

"And I give you my word, I was such an ass that I did open the case and looked all through it. She must have thought I *was* a Juggins. I get hot all over whenever I remember it. But, in spite of my dulness, and her cleverness, she couldn't gain anything by sending me away, because what she wanted was in the hand-bag, and every time she sent me away the hand-bag went with me.

"After the incident of the dressing-case her manner changed. Either in my absence she had had time to look through it, or, when I was examining it for broken bottles, she had seen everything it held.

"From that moment she must have been certain that the cigar-case, in which she knew I carried the diamonds, was in the bag that was fastened to my body, and from that time on she probably was plotting how to get it from me.

"Her anxiety became most apparent. She dropped the great-lady manner, and her charming condescension went with it. She ceased talking, and, when I spoke, answered me irritably, or at random. No doubt her mind was entirely occupied with her plan. The end of our journey was drawing rapidly nearer, and her time for action was being cut down with the speed of the express-train. Even I, unsuspicious as I was, noticed that something was very wrong with her. I really believe that before we reached Marseilles if I had not, through my own stupidity, given her the chance she wanted, she might have stuck a knife in me and rolled me out on the rails. But as it was, I only thought that the long journey had tired her. I suggested that it was a very trying trip, and asked her if she would allow me to offer her some of my cognac.

"She thanked me and said, 'No,' and then suddenly her eyes lighted, and she exclaimed, 'Yes, thank you, if you will be so kind.'

"My flask was in the hand-bag, and I placed it on my lap and, with my thumb, slipped back the catch. As I keep my tickets and railroad-guide in the bag, I am so constantly opening it that I never bother to lock it, and the fact that it is strapped to me has always been sufficient protection. But I can appreciate now what a satisfaction, and what a torment, too, it must have been to that woman when she saw that the bag opened without a key.

"While we were crossing the mountains I had felt rather chilly and had been wearing a light racing-coat. But after the lamps were lighted the compartment became very hot and stuffy, and I found the coat uncomfortable. So I stood up, and, after first slipping the strap of the bag over my head, I placed the bag in the seat next me and pulled off the racing-coat. I don't blame myself for being careless; the bag was still within reach of my hand, and nothing would have happened if at that exact moment the train had not stopped at Arles. It was the combination of my removing the bag and our entering the station at the same instant which gave the Princess Zichy the chance she wanted to rob me.

"I needn't say that she was clever enough to take it. The train ran into the station at full speed and came to a sudden stop. I had just thrown my coat into the rack, and had reached out my hand for the bag. In another instant I would have had the strap around my shoulder. But at that moment the Princess threw open the door of the compartment and beckoned wildly at the people on the platform. 'Natalie!' she called, 'Natalie! here I am. Come here! This way!' She turned upon me in the greatest excitement. 'My maid!' she cried. 'She is looking for me. She passed the window without seeing me. Go, please, and bring her back. She continued pointing out of the door and beckoning me with her other hand. There certainly was something about that woman's tone which made one jump. When she was giving orders you had no chance to think of anything else. So I rushed out on my errand of mercy, and then rushed back again to ask what the maid looked like.

"'In black,' she answered, rising and blocking the door of the compartment. 'All in black, with a bonnet!'

"The train waited three minutes at Arles, and in that time I suppose I must have rushed up to over twenty women and asked, 'Are you Natalie?' The only reason I wasn't punched with an umbrella or handed over to the police was that they probably thought I was crazy.

"When I jumped back into the compartment the Princess was seated where I had left her, but her eyes were burning with happiness. She placed her hand on my arm almost affectionately, and said, in a hysterical way, "You are very kind to me. I am sorry to have troubled you."

"I protested that every woman on the platform was dressed in black.

"'Indeed, I am so sorry," she said, laughing; and she continued to laugh until she began to breathe so quickly that I thought she was going to faint.

"I can see now that the last part of that journey must have been a terrible half-hour for her. She had the cigar-case safe enough, but she knew that she herself was not safe. She understood if I were to open my bag, even at the last minute, and miss the case, I would know positively that she had taken it. I had placed the diamonds in the bag at the very moment she entered the compartment, and no one but our two selves had occupied it since. She knew that when we reached Marseilles she would either be twenty thousand pounds richer than when she left Paris, or that she would go to jail. That was the situation as she must have read it, and I don't envy her her state of mind during that last half-hour. It must have been hell.

"I saw that something was wrong, and, in my innocence, I even wondered if possibly my cognac had not been a little too strong. For she suddenly developed into a most brilliant conversationalist, and applauded and laughed at everything I said, and fired off questions at me like a machine-gun, so that I had no time to think of anything but of what she was saying. Whenever I stirred, she stopped her chattering and leaned toward me, and watched me like a cat over a mouse-hole. I wondered how I could have considered her an agreeable travelling-companion. I thought I would have preferred to be locked in with a lunatic. I don't like to think how she would have acted if I had made a move to examine the bag, but as I had it safely strapped around me again, I did not open it, and I reached Marseilles alive. As we drew into the station she shook hands with me and grinned at me like a Cheshire cat.

"'I cannot tell you,' she said, 'how much I have to thank you for.' What do you think of that for impudence?

"I offered to put her in a carriage, but she said she must find Natalie, and that she hoped we would meet again at the hotel. So I drove off by myself, wondering who she was, and whether Natalie was not her keeper.

"I had to wait several hours for the train to Nice, and as I wanted to stroll around the city I thought I had better put the diamonds in the safe of the hotel. As soon as I reached my room I locked the door, placed the hand-bag on the table, and opened it. I felt among the things at the top of it, but failed to touch the cigar-case. I shoved my hand in deeper, and stirred the things about, but still I did not reach it. A cold wave swept down my spine, and a sort of emptiness came to the pit of my stomach. Then I turned red-hot, and the sweat sprung out all over me. I wet my lips with my tongue, and said to myself, 'Don't be an ass. Pull yourself together, pull yourself together. Take the things out, one at a time. It's there, of course, it's there. Don't be an ass.'

"So I put a brake on my nerves and began very carefully to pick out the things, one by one, but, after another second, I could not stand it, and I rushed across the room and threw out everything on the bed. But the diamonds were not among them. I pulled the things about and tore them open and shuffled and rearranged and sorted them, but it was no use. The cigar-case was gone. I threw everything in the dressing-case out on the floor, although I knew it was useless to look for it there. I knew that I had put it in the bag. I sat down and tried to think. I remembered I had put it in the satchel at Paris just as that woman had entered the compartment, and I had been alone with her ever since, so it was she who had robbed me. But how? It had never left my shoulder. And then I remembered that it had – that I had taken it off when I had changed my coat and for the few moments that I was searching for Natalie. I remembered that the woman had sent me on that goose-chase, and that at every other station she had tried to get rid of me on some fool-errand.

"I gave a roar like a mad bull, and I jumped down the stairs, six steps at a time.

"I demanded at the office if a distinguished lady of title, possibly a Russian, had just entered the hotel.

"As I expected, she had not. I sprang into a cab and inquired at two other hotels, and then I saw the folly of trying to catch her without outside help, and I ordered the fellow to gallop to the office of the Chief of Police. I told my story, and the ass in charge asked me to calm myself, and wanted to take notes. I told him this was no time for taking notes, but for doing something. He got wrathy at that, and I demanded to be taken at once to his Chief. The Chief, he said, was very busy, and could not see me. So I showed him my silver greyhound. In eleven years I had never used it but once before. I stated, in pretty vigorous language, that I was a Queen's Messenger, and that if the Chief of Police did not see me instantly he would lose his official head. At that the fellow jumped off his high horse and ran with me to his Chief – a smart young chap, a colonel in the army, and a very intelligent man.

"I explained that I had been robbed, in a French railway-carriage, of a diamond-necklace belonging to the Queen of England, which her Majesty was sending as a present to the Czarina of Russia. I pointed out to him that if he succeeded in capturing the thief he would be made for life, and would receive the gratitude of three great powers.

"He wasn't the sort that thinks second thoughts are best. He saw Russian and French decorations sprouting all over his chest, and he hit a bell, and pressed buttons, and yelled out orders like the captain of a penny-steamer in a fog. He sent her description to all the city-gates, and ordered all cabmen and railway-porters to search all trains leaving Marseilles. He ordered all passengers on outgoing vessels to be examined, and telegraphed the proprietors of every hotel and pension to send him a complete list of their guests within the hour. While I was standing there he must have given at least a hundred orders, and sent out enough commissaires, sergeants de ville, gendarmes, bicycle-police, and plain-clothes Johnnies to have captured the entire German army. When they had gone he assured me that the woman was as good as arrested already. Indeed, officially, she was arrested; for she had no more chance of escape from Marseilles than from the Château D'If.

"He told me to return to my hotel and possess my soul in peace. Within an hour he assured me he would acquaint me with her arrest.

"I thanked him, and complimented him on his energy, and left him. But I didn't share in his confidence. I felt that she was a very clever woman, and a match for any and all of us. It was all very well for him to be jubilant. He had not lost the diamonds, and had everything to gain if he found them; while I, even if he did recover the necklace, would only be where I was before I lost them, and if he did not recover it I was a ruined man. It was an awful facer for me. I had always prided myself on my record. In eleven years I had never mislaid an envelope, nor missed taking the first train. And now I had failed in the most important mission that had ever been intrusted to me. And it wasn't a thing that could be hushed up, either. It was too conspicuous, too spectacular. It was sure to invite the widest notoriety. I saw myself ridiculed all over the Continent, and perhaps dismissed, even suspected of having taken the thing myself.

"I was walking in front of a lighted café, and I felt so sick and miserable that I stopped for a pick-me-up. Then I considered that if I took one drink I would probably, in my present state of mind, not want to stop under twenty, and I decided I had better leave it alone. But my nerves were jumping like a frightened rabbit, and I felt I must have something to quiet them, or I would go crazy. I reached for my cigarette-case, but a cigarette seemed hardly adequate, so I put it back again and took out this cigar-case, in which I keep only the strongest and blackest cigars. I opened it and stuck in my fingers, but, instead of a cigar, they touched on a thin leather-envelope. My heart stood perfectly still. I did not dare to look, but I dug my finger-nails into the leather, and I felt layers of thin paper, then a layer of cotton, and then they scratched on the facets of the Czarina's diamonds!

"I stumbled as though I had been hit in the face, and fell back into one of the chairs on the sidewalk. I tore off the wrappings and spread out the diamonds on the café-table; I could not believe they were real. I twisted the necklace between my fingers and crushed it between my palms and tossed it up in the air. I believe I almost kissed it. The women in the café stood up on the chairs to see better, and laughed and screamed, and the people crowded so close around me that the waiters had to form a body-guard. The proprietor thought there was a fight, and called for the police. I was so happy I didn't care. I laughed, too, and gave the proprietor a five-pound note, and told him to stand everyone a drink. Then I tumbled into a fiacre and galloped off to my friend the Chief of Police. I felt very sorry for him. He had been so happy at the chance I had given him, and he was sure to be disappointed when he learned I had sent him off on a false alarm.

"But now that I had found the necklace, I did not want him to find the woman. Indeed, I was most anxious that she should get clear away, for, if she were caught, the truth would come out, and I was likely to get a sharp reprimand, and sure to be laughed at.

"I could see now how it had happened. In my haste to hide the diamonds when the woman was hustled into the carriage, I had shoved the cigars into the satchel, and the diamonds into the pocket of my coat. Now that I had the diamonds safe again, it seemed a very natural mistake. But I doubted if the Foreign Office would think so. I was afraid it might not appreciate the beautiful simplicity of my secret hiding-place. So, when I reached the police-station, and found that the woman was still at large, I was more than relieved.

"As I expected, the Chief was extremely chagrined when he learned of my mistake, and that there was nothing for him to do. But I was feeling so happy myself that I hated to have anyone else miserable, so I suggested that this attempt to steal the Czarina's necklace might be only the first of a series of such attempts by an unscrupulous gang, and that I might still be in danger.

"I winked at the Chief, and the Chief smiled at me, and we went to Nice together in a saloon-car with a guard of twelve carabineers and twelve plain-clothes men, and the Chief and I drank champagne all the way. We marched together up to the hotel where the Russian

Ambassador was stopping, closely surrounded by our escort of carabineers, and delivered the necklace with the most profound ceremony. The old Ambassador was immensely impressed, and when we hinted that already I had been made the object of an attack by robbers, he assured us that his Imperial Majesty would not prove ungrateful.

"I wrote a swingeing personal letter about the invaluable services of the Chief to the French Minister of Foreign Affairs, and they gave him enough Russian and French medals to satisfy even a French soldier. So, though he never caught the woman, he received his just reward."

The Queen's Messenger paused and surveyed the faces of those about him in some embarrassment.

"But the worst of it is," he added, "that the story must have got about; for, while the Princess obtained nothing from me but a cigar-case and five excellent cigars, a few weeks after the coronation the Czar sent me a gold cigar-case with his monogram in diamonds. And I don't know yet whether that was a coincidence, or whether the Czar wanted me to know that he knew that I had been carrying the Czarina's diamonds in my pigskin cigar-case. What do you fellows think?"

III

Sir Andrew rose, with disapproval written in every lineament.

"I thought your story would bear upon the murder," he said. "Had I imagined it would have nothing whatsoever to do with it, I would not have remained." He pushed back his chair and bowed, stiffly. "I wish you good night," he said.

There was a chorus of remonstrance, and, under cover of this and the Baronet's answering protests, a servant, for the second time, slipped a piece of paper into the hand of the gentleman with the pearl stud. He read the lines written upon it and tore it into tiny fragments.

The youngest member, who had remained an interested but silent listener to the tale of the Queen's Messenger, raised his hand, commandingly.

"Sir Andrew," he cried, "in justice to Lord Arthur Chetney, I must ask you to be seated. He has been accused in our hearing of a most serious crime, and I insist that you remain until you have heard me clear his character."

"You!" cried the Baronet.

"Yes," answered the young man, briskly. "I would have spoken sooner," he explained, "but that I thought this gentleman" – he inclined his head toward the Queen's Messenger – "was about to contribute some facts of which I was ignorant. He, however, has told us nothing, and so I will take up the tale at the point where Lieutenant Sears laid it down and give you those details of which Lieutenant Sears is ignorant. It seems strange to you that I should be able to add the sequel to this story. But the coincidence is easily explained. I am the junior member of the law firm of Chudleigh & Chudleigh. We have been solicitors for the Chetneys for the last two hundred years. Nothing, no matter how unimportant, which concerns Lord Edam and his two sons is unknown to us, and naturally we are acquainted with every detail of the terrible catastrophe of last night."

The Baronet, bewildered but eager, sank back into his chair.

"Will you be long, sir?" he demanded.

"I shall endeavor to be brief," said the young solicitor; "and," he added, in a tone which gave his words almost the weight of a threat, "I promise to be interesting."

"There is no need to promise that," said Sir Andrew, "I find it much too interesting as it is." He glanced ruefully at the clock and turned his eyes quickly from it.

"Tell the driver of that hansom," he called to the servant, "that I take him by the hour."

"For the last three days," began young Mr Chudleigh, "as you have probably read in the daily papers, the Marquis of Edam has been at the point of death, and his physicians have never left his house. Every hour he seemed to grow weaker; but although his bodily strength is apparently leaving him forever, his mind has remained clear and active. Late yesterday evening, word was received at our office that he wished my father to come at once to Chetney House and to bring with him certain papers. What these papers were is not essential; I mention them only to explain how it was that last night I happened to be at Lord Edam's bedside. I accompanied my father to Chetney House, but at the time we reached there Lord Edam was sleeping, and his physicians refused to have him awakened. My father urged that he should be allowed to receive Lord Edam's instructions concerning the documents, but the physicians would not disturb him, and we all gathered in the library to wait until he should awake of his own accord. It was about one o'clock in the morning, while we were still there, that Inspector Lyle and the officers from Scotland Yard came to arrest Lord Arthur on the charge of murdering his brother. You can

imagine our dismay and distress. Like everyone else, I had learned
from the afternoon papers that Lord Chetney was not dead, but that
he had returned to England, and, on arriving at Chetney House, I
had been told that Lord Arthur had gone to the Bath Hotel to look
for his brother and to inform him that if he wished to see their father
alive he must come to him at once. Although it was now past one
o'clock, Arthur had not returned. None of us knew where Madame
Zichy lived, so we could not go to recover Lord Chetney's body. We
spent a most miserable night, hastening to the window whenever a
cab came into the square, in the hope that it was Arthur returning,
and endeavoring to explain away the facts that pointed to him as the
murderer. I am a friend of Arthur's, I was with him at Harrow and
at Oxford, and I refused to believe for an instant that he was capable
of such a crime; but as a lawyer I could not help but see that the
circumstantial evidence was strongly against him.

"Toward early morning, Lord Edam awoke, and in so much better
a state of health that he refused to make the changes in the papers
which he had intended, declaring that he was no nearer death than
ourselves. Under other circumstances, this happy change in him
would have relieved us greatly, but none of us could think of anything
save the death of his elder son and of the charge which hung over
Arthur.

"As long as Inspector Lyle remained in the house, my father
decided that I, as one of the legal advisers of the family, should
also remain there. But there was little for either of us to do. Arthur
did not return, and nothing occurred until late this morning, when
Lyle received word that the Russian servant had been arrested. He
at once drove to Scotland Yard to question him. He came back to
us in an hour, and informed me that the servant had refused to tell
anything of what had happened the night before, or of himself, or
of the Princess Zichy. He would not even give them the address of
her house.

"'He is in abject terror,' Lyle said. 'I assured him that he was not
suspected of the crime, but he would tell me nothing.

"There were no other developments until two o'clock this afternoon, when word was brought to us that Arthur had been found, and
that he was lying in the accident-ward of St George's Hospital. Lyle
and I drove there together, and found him propped up in bed with
his head bound in a bandage. He had been brought to the hospital
the night before by the driver of a hansom that had run over him
in the fog. The cab-horse had kicked him on the head, and he had
been carried in unconscious. There was nothing on him to tell who

he was, and it was not until he came to his senses this afternoon that the hospital authorities had been able to send word to his people. Lyle at once informed him that he was under arrest, and with what he was charged, and though the Inspector warned him to say nothing which might be used against him, I, as his solicitor, instructed him to speak freely and to tell us all he knew of the occurrences of last night. It was evident to anyone that the fact of his brother's death was of much greater concern to him than that he was accused of his murder.

"'That', Arthur said, contemptuously, 'that is damned nonsense. It is monstrous and cruel. We parted better friends than we have been in years. I will tell you all that happened – not to clear myself, but to help you to find out the truth.' His story is as follows: Yesterday afternoon, owing to his constant attendance on his father, he did not look at the evening papers, and it was not until after dinner, when the butler brought him one and told him of its contents, that he learned that his brother was alive and at the Bath Hotel. He drove there at once, but was told that about eight o'clock his brother had gone out, but without giving any clew to his destination. As Chetney had not at once come to see his father, Arthur decided that he was still angry with him, and his mind, turning naturally to the cause of their quarrel, determined him to look for Chetney at the home of the Princess Zichy.

"Her house had been pointed out to him, and though he had never visited it, he had passed it many times and knew its exact location. He accordingly drove in that direction, as far as the fog would permit the hansom to go, and walked the rest of the way, reaching the house about nine o'clock. He rang, and was admitted by the Russian servant. The man took his card into the drawing-room, and at once his brother ran out and welcomed him. He was followed by the Princess Zichy, who also received Arthur most cordially.

"'You brothers will have much to talk about,' she said. 'I am going to the dinning-room. When you have finished, let me know.'

"As soon as she had left them, Arthur told his brother that their father was not expected to outlive the night, and that he must come to him at once.

"'This is not the moment to remember your quarrel,' Arthur said to him; 'you have come back from the dead only in time to make your peace with him before he dies.'

"Arthur says that at this Chetney was greatly moved.

"'You entirely misunderstand me, Arthur,' he returned. 'I did not know the governor was ill, or I would have gone to him the instant I arrived. My only reason for not doing so was because I thought he was still angry with me. I shall return with you immediately as soon as I have said good-by to the Princess. It is a final good-by. After to-night I shall never see her again.'

"'Do you mean that?' Arthur cried.

"'Yes,' Chetney answered. 'When I returned to London I had no intention of seeking her again, and I am here only through a mistake.' He then told Arthur that he had separated from the Princess even before he went to Central Africa, and that, moreover, while at Cairo on his way south, he had learned certain facts concerning her life there during the previous season, which made it impossible for him to ever wish to see her again. Their separation was final and complete.

"'She deceived me cruelly,' he said; 'I cannot tell you how cruelly. During the two years when I was trying to obtain my father's consent to our marriage she was in love with a Russian diplomat. During all that time he was secretly visiting her here in London, and her trip to Cairo was only an excuse to meet him there.'

"'Yet you are here with her to-night,' Arthur protested, 'only a few hours after your return.'

"'That is easily explained,' Chetney answered. 'As I finished dinner to-night at the hotel, I received a note from her from this address. In it she said she had just learned of my arrival, and begged me to come to her at once. She wrote that she was in great and present trouble, dying of an incurable illness, and without friends or money. She begged me, for the sake of old times, to come to her assistance. During the last two years in the jungle all my former feeling for Zichy has utterly passed away, but no one could have dismissed the appeal she made in that letter. So I came here, and found her, as you have seen her, quite as beautiful as she ever was, in very good health, and, from the look of the house, in no need of money.

"'I asked her what she meant by writing me that she was dying in a garret, and she laughed, and said she had done so because she was afraid, unless I thought she needed help, I would not try to see her. That was where we were when you arrived. And now,' Chetney added, 'I will say good-by to her, and you had better return home. No, you can trust me, I shall follow you at once. She has no influence over me now, but I believe, in spite of the way she has used me, that she is, after her queer fashion, still fond of me, and when she learns that this good-by is final there may be a scene, and it is not fair to her that you should be here. So, go home at once, and tell the governor that I am following you in ten minutes.'

"'That,' said Arthur, 'is the way we parted. I never left him on more friendly terms. I was happy to see him alive again, I was happy to think he had returned in time to make up his quarrel with my father, and I was happy that at last he was shut of that woman. I was never better pleased with him in my life.' He turned to Inspector Lyle, who was sitting at the foot of the bed, taking notes of all he told us.

"'Why, in the name of common-sense,' he cried, 'should I have chosen that moment, of all others, to send my brother back to the grave?' For a moment the Inspector did not answer him. I do not know if any of you gentlemen are acquainted with Inspector Lyle, but if you are not, I can assure you that he is a very remarkable man. Our firm often applies to him for aid, and he has never failed us; my father has the greatest possible respect for him. Where he has the advantage over the ordinary police-official is in the fact that he possesses imagination. He imagines himself to be the criminal, imagines how he would act under the same circumstances, and he imagines to such purpose that he generally finds the man he wants. I have often told Lyle that if he had not been a detective he would have made a great success as a poet or a playwright.

"When Arthur turned on him, Lyle hesitated for a moment, and then told him exactly what was the case against him.

"'Ever since your brother was reported as having died in Africa,' he said, 'your lordship has been collecting money on post-obits. Lord Chetney's arrival, last night, turned them into waste-paper. You were suddenly in debt for thousands of pounds – for much more than you could ever possibly pay. No one knew that you and your brother had met at Madame Zichy's. But you knew that your father was not expected to outlive the night, and that if your brother were dead also, you would be saved from complete ruin, and that you would become the Marquis of Edam.'

"'Oh, that is how you have worked it out, is it?' Arthur cried. 'And for me to become Lord Edam was it necessary that the woman should die, too?'

"'They will say,' Lyle answered, 'that she was a witness to the murder – that she would have told.'

"'Then why did I not kill the servant as well?' Arthur said.

"'He was asleep, and saw nothing.'

"'And you believe *that*?' Arthur demanded.

"'It is not a question of what I believe,' Lyle said, gravely. 'It is a question for your peers.'

"'The man is insolent!' Arthur cried. 'The thing is monstrous! Horrible!'

"Before we could stop him, he sprang out of his cot and began pulling on his clothes. When the nurses tried to hold him down, he fought with them.

"'Do you think you can keep me here,' he shouted, 'when they are plotting to hang me? I am going with you to that house!' he cried at Lyle. 'When you find those bodies I shall be beside you. It is my right. He is my brother. He has been murdered, and I can tell you who murdered him. That woman murdered him. She first ruined his life, and now she has killed him. For the last five years she has been plotting to make herself his wife, and last night, when he told her he had discovered the truth about the Russian, and that she would never see him again, she flew into a passion and stabbed him, and then, in terror of the gallows, killed herself. She murdered him, I tell you, and I promise you that we will find the knife she used near her – perhaps still in her hand. What will you say to that?'

"Lyle turned his head away and stared down at the floor. 'I might say,' he answered, 'that you placed it there.'

"Arthur gave a cry of anger and sprang at him, and then pitched forward into his arms. The blood was running from the cut under the bandage, and he had fainted. Lyle carried him back to the bed again, and we left him with the police and the doctors, and drove at once to the address he had given us. We found the house not three minutes' walk from St George's Hospital. It stands in Trevor Terrace, that little row of houses set back from Knightsbridge, with one end in Hill Street.

"As we left the hospital, Lyle had said to me, 'You must not blame me for treating him as I did. All is fair in this work, and if by angering that boy I could have made him commit himself, I was right in trying to do so; though, I assure you, no one would be better pleased than myself if I could prove his theory to be correct. But we cannot tell. Everything depends upon what we see for ourselves within the next few minutes.'

"When we reached the house, Lyle broke open the fastenings of one of the windows on the ground-floor, and, hidden by the trees in the garden, we scrambled in. We found ourselves in the reception-room, which was the first room on the right of the hall. The gas was still burning behind the colored glass and red, silk shades, and when the daylight streamed in after us it gave the hall a hideously dissipated look, like the foyer of a theatre at a matinée, or the entrance to an all-day gambling-hell. The house was oppressively silent, and, because we knew why it was so silent, we spoke in whispers. When Lyle turned the handle of the drawing-room door, I felt as though someone had put his hand upon my throat. But I followed, close at his shoulder, and saw, in the subdued light of many-tinted lamps, the body of Chetney at the foot of the divan, just as Lieutenant Sears had described it. In the drawing-room we found the body of the Princess Zichy, her arms thrown out, and the blood from her heart frozen in a tiny line across her bare shoulder. But neither of us, although we searched the floor on our hands and knees, could find the weapon which had killed her.

"'For Arthur's sake,' I said, 'I would have given a thousand pounds if we had found the knife in her hand, as he said we would.'

"'That we have not found it there,' Lyle answered, 'is to my mind the strongest proof that he is telling the truth, that he left the house before the murder took place. He is not a fool, and had he stabbed his brother and this woman, he would have seen that by placing the knife near her he could help to make it appear as if she had killed Chetney and then committed suicide. Besides, Lord Arthur insisted that the evidence in his behalf would be our finding the knife here. He would not have urged that if he knew we would *not* find it, if he knew he himself had carried it away. This is no suicide. A suicide does not rise and hide the weapon with which he kills himself, and then lie down again. No, this has been a double murder, and we must look outside of the house for the murderer.'

"While he was speaking, Lyle and I had been searching every corner, studying the details of each room. I was so afraid that, without telling me, he would make some deductions prejudicial to Arthur, that I never left his side. I was determined to see everything that he saw, and, if possible, to prevent his interpreting it in the wrong way. He finally finished his examination, and we sat down together in the drawing-room, and he took out his notebook and read aloud all that Mr Sears had told him of the murder and what we had just learned from Arthur. We compared the two accounts, word for word, and weighed statement with statement, but I could not determine, from anything Lyle said, which of the two versions he had decided to believe.

"'We are trying to build a house of blocks,' he exclaimed, 'with half of the blocks missing. We have been considering two theories,' he went on: 'one that Lord Arthur is responsible for both murders, and the other that the dead woman in there is responsible for one of them, and has committed suicide; but, until the Russian servant is ready to talk, I shall refuse to believe in the guilt of either.'

"'What can you prove by him?' I asked. 'He was drunk and asleep. He saw nothing.'

"Lyle hesitated, and then, as though he had made up his mind to be quite frank with me, spoke freely.

"'I do not know that he was either drunk or asleep,' he answered. 'Lieutenant Sears describes him as a stupid boor. I am not satisfied that he is not a clever actor. What was his position in this house? What was his real duty here? Suppose it was not to guard this woman, but to watch her. Let us imagine that it was not the woman he served, but a master, and see where that leads us. For this house has a master, a mysterious, absentee landlord, who lives in St Petersburg, the unknown Russian who came between Chetney and Zichy, and because of whom Chetney left her. He is the man who bought this house for Madame Zichy, who sent these rugs and curtains from St Petersburg to furnish it for her after his own tastes, and, I believe, it was he also who placed the Russian servant here, ostensibly to serve the Princess, but in reality to spy upon her. At Scotland Yard we do not know who this gentleman is; the Russian police confess to equal ignorance concerning him. When Lord Chetney went to Africa, Madame Zichy lived in St Petersburg; but there her receptions and dinners were so crowded with members of the nobility and of the army and diplomats, that, among so many visitors, the police could not learn which was the one for whom she most greatly cared.'

"Lyle pointed at the modern French paintings and the heavy, silk rugs which hung upon the walls.

"'The unknown is a man of taste and of some fortune,' he said, 'not the sort of man to send a stupid peasant to guard the woman he loves. So I am not content to believe, with Mr Sears, that the servant is a boor. I believe him, instead, to be a very clever ruffian. I believe him to be the protector of his master's honor, or, let us say, of his master's property, whether that property be silver plate or the woman his master loves. Last night, after Lord Arthur had gone away, the servant was left alone in this house with Lord Chetney and Madame Zichy. From where he sat in the hall, he could hear Lord Chetney bidding her farewell; for, if my idea of him is correct, he understands English quite as well as you or I. Let us imagine that he heard her entreating Chetney not to leave her, reminding him of his former wish to marry her, and let us suppose that he hears Chetney denounce her, and tell her that at Cairo he has learned of this Russian admirer – the servant's master. He hears the woman declare that she has had no admirer but himself, that this unknown Russian was, and is, nothing to her, that there is no man she loves but him, and that she cannot live, knowing that he is alive, without his love. Suppose Chetney believed her, suppose his former infatuation for her returned, and that, in a moment of weakness, he forgave her and took her in his arms. That is the moment the Russian master has feared. It is to guard against it that he has placed his watch-dog over the Princess, and how do we know but that, when the moment came, the watch-dog served his master, as he saw his duty, and killed them both? What do you think?' Lyle demanded. 'Would not that explain both murders?'

"I was only too willing to hear any theory which pointed to anyone else as the criminal than Arthur, but Lyle's explanation was too utterly fantastic. I told him that he certainly showed imagination, but that he could not hang a man for what he imagined he had done.

"'No,' Lyle answered, 'but I can frighten him by telling him what I think he has done, and now when I again question the Russian servant I will make it quite clear to him that I believe he is the murderer. I think that will open his mouth. A man will at least talk to defend himself. Come,' he said, 'we must return at once to Scotland Yard and see him. There is nothing more to do here.'

"He arose, and I followed him into the hall, and in another minute we would have been on our way to Scotland Yard. But just as he opened the street-door a postman halted at the gate of the garden, and began fumbling with the latch.

"Lyle stopped, with an exclamation of chagrin.

"'How stupid of me!' he exclaimed. He turned quickly and pointed to a narrow slit cut in the brass plate of the front door. 'The house has a private letter-box,' he said. 'and I had not thought to look in it! If we had gone out as we came in, by the window, I would never have seen it. The moment I entered the house I should have thought of securing the letters which came this morning. I have been grossly careless.' He stepped back into the hall and pulled at the lid of the letter-box, which hung on the inside of the door, but it was tightly locked. At the same moment the postman came up the steps holding a letter. Without a word, Lyle took it from his hand and began to examine it. It was addressed to the Princess Zichy, and on the back of the envelope was the name of a West End dressmaker.

"'That is of no use to me,' Lyle said. He took out his card and showed it to the postman. 'I am Inspector Lyle from Scotland Yard,' he said. 'The people in this house are under arrest. Everything it contains is now in my keeping. Did you deliver any other letters here this morning?'

"The man looked frightened, but answered, promptly, that he was now upon his third round. He had made one postal delivery at seven that morning and another at eleven.

"'How many letters did you leave here?' Lyle asked.

"'About six altogether,' the man answered.

"'Did you put them through the door into the letter-box?'

"The postman said, 'Yes, I always slip them into the box, and ring and go away. The servants collect them from the inside.'

"'Have you noticed if any of the letters you leave here bear a Russian postage-stamp?' Lyle asked.

"'The man answered, "Oh, yes, sir, a great many."

"'From the same person, would you say?'

"'The writing seems to be the same,' the man answered. 'They come regularly about once a week – one of those I delivered this morning had a Russian postmark.'

"'That will do,' said Lyle, eagerly. 'Thank you, thank you very much.'

"He ran back into the hall, and, pulling out his pen-knife, began to pick at the lock of the letter-box.

"'I have been supremely careless,' he said, in great excitement. 'Twice before when people I wanted had flown from a house I have been able to follow them by putting a guard over their mail-box. These letters, which arrive regularly every week from Russia in the same handwriting, they can come but from one person. At least, we shall now know the name of the master of this house. Undoubtedly, it is one of his letters that the man placed here this morning. We may make a most important discovery.'

"As he was talking he was picking at the lock with his knife, but he was so impatient to reach the letters that he pressed too heavily on the blade and it broke in his hand. I took a step backward and drove my heel into the lock, and burst it open. The lid flew back, and we pressed forward, and each ran his hand down into the letter-box. For a moment we were both too startled to move. The box was empty.

"I do not know how long we stood, staring stupidly at each other, but it was Lyle who was the first to recover. He seized me by the arm and pointed excitedly into the empty box.

"'Do you appreciate what that means?' he cried. 'It means that someone has been here ahead of us. Someone has entered this house not three hours before we came, since eleven o'clock this morning.'

"'It was the Russian servant!' I exclaimed.

"'The Russian servant has been under arrest at Scotland Yard,' Lyle cried. 'He could not have taken the letters. Lord Arthur has been in his cot at the hospital. That is his alibi. There is someone else, someone we do not suspect, and that someone is the murderer. He came back here either to obtain those letters because he knew they would convict him, or to remove something he had left here at the time of the murder, something incriminating – the weapon, perhaps, or some personal article; a cigarette-case, a handkerchief with his name upon it, or a pair of gloves. Whatever it was, it must have been damning evidence against him to have made him take so desperate a chance.'

"'How do we know,' I whispered, 'that he is not hidden here now?'

"'No, I'll swear he is not,' Lyle answered. 'I may have bungled in some things, but I have searched this house thoroughly. Nevertheless,' he added, 'we must go over it again, from the cellar to the roof. We have the real clew now, and we must forget the others and work only it.' As he spoke he began again to search the drawing-room, turning over even the books on the tables and the music on the piano.

"'Whoever the man is,' he said over his shoulder, 'we know that he has a key to the front door and a key to the letter-box. That shows us he is either an inmate of the house or that he comes here when he wishes. The Russian says that he was the only servant in the house. Certainly, we have found no evidence to show that any other servant slept here. There could be but one other person who would possess a key to the house and the letter-box – and he lives in St Petersburg. At the time of the murder he was two thousand miles away.' Lyle interrupted himself, suddenly, with a sharp cry, and turned upon me, with his eyes flashing. 'But was he?' he cried 'Was he? How do we know that last night he was not in London, in this very house when Zichy and Chetney met?'

"He stood, staring at me without seeing me, muttering, and arguing with himself.

"'Don't speak to me,' he cried, as I ventured to interrupt him. 'I can see it now. It is all plain. It was not the servant, but his master, the Russian himself, and it was he who came back for the letters! He came back for them because he knew they would convict him. We must find them. We must have those letters. If we find the one with the Russian postmark, we shall have found the murderer.' He spoke like a madman, and as he spoke he ran around the room, with one hand held out in front of him as you have seen a mind-reader at a theatre seeking for something hidden in the stalls. He pulled the old letters from the writing-desk, and ran them over as swiftly as a gambler deals out cards; he dropped on his knees before the fireplace and dragged out the dead coals with his bare fingers, and then, with a low, worried cry, like a hound on a scent, he ran back to the waste-paper basket and, lifting the papers from it, shook them out upon the floor. Instantly, he gave a shout of triumph, and, separating a number of torn pieces from the others, held them up before me.

"'Look!' he cried. 'Do you see? Here are five letters, torn across in two places. The Russian did not stop to read them, for, as you see, he has left them still sealed. I have been wrong. He did not return for the letters. He could not have known their value. He must have returned for some other reason, and, as he was leaving, saw the letter-box, and, taking out the letters, held them together – so – and tore them twice across, and then, as the fire had gone out, tossed them into this basket. Look!' he cried, 'here in the upper corner of this piece is a Russian stamp. This is his own letter – unopened!'

"We examined the Russian stamp and found it had been cancelled in St Petersburg four days ago. The back of the envelope bore the postmark of the branch-station in upper Sloane Street, and was dated this morning. The envelope was of official, blue paper; and we had no difficulty in finding the other two parts of it. We drew the torn pieces of the letter from them and joined them together, side by side. There were but two lines of writing, and this was the message: 'I leave Petersburg on the night-train, and I shall see you at Trevor Terrace, after dinner, Monday evening.'

"'That was last night!' Lyle cried. 'He arrived twelve hours ahead of his letter – but it came in time – it came in time to hang him!'"

The Baronet struck the table with his hand.

"The name!" he demanded. "How was it signed? What was the man's name?"

The young solicitor rose to his feet and, leaning forward, stretched out his arm. "There was no name," he cried. "The letter was signed with only two initials. But engraved at the top of the sheet was the man's address. That address was 'THE AMERICAN EMBASSY, ST PETERSBURG, BUREAU OF THE NAVAL ATTACHÉ,' and the initials," he shouted, his voice rising into an exultant and bitter cry, "were those of the gentleman who sits opposite who told us that he was the first to find the murdered bodies, the Naval Attaché to Russia, Lieutenant Sears!"

A strained and awful hush followed the solicitor's words, which seemed to vibrate like a twanging bowstring that had just hurled its bolt. Sir Andrew, pale and staring, drew away, with an exclamation of repulsion. His eyes were fastened upon the Naval Attaché with fascinated horror. But the American emitted a sigh of great content, and sank, comfortably, into the arms of his chair. He clapped his hands, softly, together.

"Capital!" he murmured. "I give you my word I never guessed what you were driving at. You fooled *me*, I'll be hanged if you didn't – you certainly fooled me."

The man with the pearl stud leaned forward, with a nervous gesture. "Hush! be careful!" he whispered. But at that instant, for the third time, a servant, hastening through the room, handed him a piece of paper which he scanned eagerly. The message on the paper read, "The light over the Commons is out. The House has risen."

The man with the black pearl gave a mighty shout, and tossed the paper from him upon the table.

"Hurrah!" he cried. "The House is up! We've won!" He caught up his glass, and slapped the Naval Attaché, violently, upon the shoulder. He nodded joyously at him, at the solicitor, and at the Queen's Messenger. "Gentlemen, to you!" he cried; "my thanks and my congratulations!" He drank deep from the glass, and breathed forth a long sigh of satisfaction and relief.

"But I say," protested the Queen's Messenger, shaking his finger, violently, at the solicitor, "that story won't do. You didn't play fair – and – and you talked so fast I couldn't make out what it was all about. I'll bet you that evidence wouldn't hold in a court of law – you couldn't hang a cat on such evidence. Your story is condemned tommy-rot. Now, my story might have happened, my story bore the mark – "

In the joy of creation, the story-tellers had forgotten their audience, until a sudden exclamation from Sir Andrew caused them to turn, guiltily, toward him. His face was knit with lines of anger, doubt, and amazement.

"What does this mean?" he cried. "Is this a jest, or are you mad? If you know this man is a murderer, why is he at large? Is this a game you have been playing? Explain yourselves at once. What does it mean?"

The American, with first a glance at the others, rose and bowed, courteously.

"I am not a murderer, Sir Andrew, believe me," he said; "you need not be alarmed. As a matter of fact, at this moment I am much more afraid of you than you could possibly be of me. I beg you, please, to be indulgent. I assure you, we meant no disrespect. We have been matching stories, that is all, pretending that we are people we are not, endeavoring to entertain you with better detective-tales than, for instance, the last one you read, 'The Great Rand Robbery.'"

The Baronet brushed his hand, nervously, across his forehead.

"Do you mean to tell me," he exclaimed, "that none of this has

happened? That Lord Chetney is not dead, that his solicitor did not
find a letter of yours, written from your post in Petersburg, and that
just now, when he charged you with murder, he was in jest?"

"I am really very sorry," said the American, "but you see, sir, he
could not have found a letter written by me in St Petersburg because
I have never been in Petersburg. Until this week, I have never been
outside of my own country. I am not a naval officer. I am a writer
of short stories. And to-night, when this gentleman told me that you
were fond of detective-stories, I thought it would be amusing to tell
you one of my own – one I had just mapped out this afternoon."

"But Lord Chetney *is* a real person," interrupted the Baronet, "and
he did go to Africa two years ago, and he was supposed to have died
there, and his brother, Lord Arthur, has been the heir. And yesterday
Chetney did return. I read it in the papers."

"So did I," assented the American, soothingly; "and it struck me as
being a very good plot for a story. I mean his unexpected return from
the dead, and the probable disappointment of the younger brother.
So I decided that the younger brother had better murder the older
one. The Princess Zichy I invented out of a clear sky. The fog I did
not have to invent. Since last night I know all that there is to know
about a London fog. I was lost in one for three hours."

The Baronet turned, grimly, upon the Queen's Messenger.

"But this gentleman," he protested, "he is not a writer of short
stories; he is a member of the Foreign Office. I have often seen
him in Whitehall, and, according to him, the Princess Zichy is
not an invention. He says she is very well known, that she tried to
rob him."

The servant of the Foreign Office looked, unhappily, at the Cabinet
Minister, and puffed, nervously, on his cigar.

"It's true, Sir Andrew, that I am a Queen's Messenger," he said,
appealingly, "and a Russian woman once did try to rob a Queen's
Messenger in a railway carriage – only it did not happen to me, but
to a pal of mine. The only Russian princess I ever knew called herself
Zabrisky. You may have seen her. She used to do a dive from the roof
of the Aquarium."

Sir Andrew, with a snort of indignation, fronted the young solicitor.

"And I suppose yours was a cock-and-bull story, too," he said. "Of
course, it must have been, since Lord Chetney is not dead. But don't
tell me," he protested, "that you are not Chudleigh's son either."

"I'm sorry," said the youngest member, smiling, in some embarrassment, "but my name is not Chudleigh. I assure you, though,

that I know the family very well, and that I am on very good terms
with them."

"You should be!" exclaimed the Baronet; "and, judging from the
liberties you take with the Chetneys, you had better be on very good
terms with them, too."

The young man leaned back and glanced toward the servants at
the far end of the room.

"It has been so long since I have been in the Club," he said, "that
I doubt if even the waiters remember me. Perhaps Joseph may," he
added. "Joseph!" he called, and at the word a servant stepped briskly
forward.

The young man pointed to the stuffed head of a great lion which
was suspended above the fireplace.

"Joseph," he said, "I want you to tell these gentlemen who shot
that lion. Who presented it to the Grill?"

Joseph, unused to acting as master of ceremonies to members of
the Club, shifted, nervously, from one foot to the other.

"Why, you – you did," he stammered.

"Of course I did!" exclaimed the young man. "I mean, what is the
name of the man who shot it? Tell the gentlemen who I am. They
wouldn't believe me."

"Who you are, my lord?" said Joseph. "You are Lord Edam's son,
the Earl of Chetney."

"You must admit," said Lord Chetney, when the noise had died
away, "that I couldn't remain dead while my little brother was
accused of murder. I had to do something. Family pride demanded
it. Now, Arthur, as the younger brother, can't afford to be squeamish,
but, personally, I should hate to have a brother of mine hanged for
murder."

"You certainly showed no scruples against hanging me," said the
American, "but, in the face of your evidence, I admit my guilt, and
I sentence myself to pay the full penalty of the law as we are made to
pay it in my own country. The order of this court is," he announced,
"that Joseph shall bring me a wine-card, and that I sign it for five
bottles of the Club's best champagne."

"Oh, no!" protested the man with the pearl stud, "it is not for
you to sign it. In my opinion, it is Sir Andrew who should pay the
costs. It is time you knew," he said, turning to that gentleman,
"that, unconsciously, you have been the victim of what I may call
a patriotic conspiracy. These stories have had a more serious purpose
than merely to amuse. They have been told with the worthy object
of detaining you from the House of Commons. I must explain to

you that, all through this evening, I have had a servant waiting in
Trafalgar Square with instructions to bring me word as soon as the
light over the House of Commons had ceased to burn. The light is
now out, and the object for which we plotted is attained."

The Baronet glanced, keenly, at the man with the black pearl, and
then, quickly, at his watch. The smile disappeared from his lips, and
his face was set in stern and forbidding lines.

"And may I know," he asked, icily, "what was the object of
your plot?"

"A most worthy one," the other retorted. "Our object was to keep
you from advocating the expenditure of many millions of the people's
money upon more battleships. In a word, we have been working
together to prevent you from passing the Navy Increase Bill."

Sir Andrew's face bloomed with brilliant color. His body shook
with suppressed emotion.

"My dear sir!" he cried, "you should spend more time at the House
and less at your Club. The Navy Bill was brought up on its third reading at eight o'clock this evening. I spoke for three hours in its favor.
My only reason for wishing to return again to the House to-night was
to sup on the terrace with my old friend, Admiral Simons; for my work
at the House was completed five hours ago, when the Navy Increase
Bill was passed by an overwhelming majority."

The Baronet rose and bowed. "I have to thank you, sir," he said,
"for a most interesting evening."

The American shoved the wine-card which Joseph had given him
toward the gentleman with the black pearl.

"You sign it," he said.

Arnold Bennett

The Fire of London

Another author not primarily associated with the detective story was Arnold Bennett (1867–1931), whose tales of the Five Towns – based on his native Staffordshire potteries – and other novels such as The Old Wives' Tale *are regarded as modern classics. Some of his early work did contain some mystery elements, however; they include* The Grand Babylon Hotel *(1902) and a story called "Murder!", which is often anthologized. The tale reprinted below is from a very rare book called* The Loot of Cities *(1904), which collected six stories about the millionaire detective Cecil Thorold, who has some very unorthodox methods . . .*

I

"YOU'RE WANTED on the telephone, sir."

Mr Bruce Bowring, managing director of the Consolidated Mining and Investment Corporation, Limited (capital two millions, in one-pound shares, which stood at twenty-seven-and-six), turned and gazed querulously across the electric-lit spaces of his superb private office at the confidential clerk who addressed him. Mr Bowring, in shirt-sleeves before a Florentine mirror, was brushing his hair with the solicitude of a mother who has failed to rear most of a large family.

"Who is it?" he asked, as if that demand for him were the last straw but one. "Nearly seven on Friday evening!" he added, martyrized.

"I think a friend, sir."

The middle-aged financier dropped his gold-mounted brush and, wading through the deep pile of the Oriental carpet, passed into the telephone-cabinet and shut the door.

"Hallo!" he accosted the transmitter, resolved not to be angry with it. "Hal*lo !* Are you there? Yes, I'm Bowring. Who are you?"

"*Nrrrr*," the faint, unhuman voice of the receiver whispered in his ear. "*Nrrrr. Cluck.* I'm a friend."

"What name?"

"No name. I thought you might like to know that a determined robbery is going to be attempted to-night at your house in Lowndes Square, a robbery of cash – and before nine o'clock. *Nrrrr*. I thought you might like to know."

"Ah!" said Mr Bowring to the transmitter.

The feeble exclamation was all he could achieve at first. In the confined, hot silence of the telephone-cabinet this message, coming to him mysteriously out of the vast unknown of London, struck him with a sudden sick fear that perhaps his wondrously organized scheme might yet miscarry, even at the final moment. Why that night of all nights? And why before nine o'clock? Could it be that the secret was out, then?

"Any further interesting details?" he inquired, bracing himself to an assumption of imperturbable and gay coolness.

But there was no answer. And when after some difficulty he got the exchange-girl to disclose the number which had rung him up, he found that his interlocutor had been using a public call-office in Oxford Street. He returned to his room, donned his frock-coat, took a large envelope from a locked drawer and put it in his pocket, and sat down to think a little.

At that time Mr Bruce Bowring was one of the most famous conjurers in the City. He had begun, ten years earlier, with nothing but a silk hat; and out of that empty hat had been produced, first the Hoop-La Limited, a South African gold-mine of numerous stamps and frequent dividends, then the Hoop-La No. 2 Limited, a mine with as many reincarnations as Buddha, and then a dazzling succession of mines and combination of mines. The more the hat emptied itself, the more it was full; and the emerging objects (which now included the house in Lowndes Square and a perfect dream of a place in Hampshire) grew constantly larger, and the conjurer more impressive and persuasive, and the audience more enthusiastic in its applause. At last, with a unique flourish, and a new turning-up of sleeves to prove that there was no deception, had come out of the hat the CMIC, a sort of incredibly enormous Union Jack, which enwrapped all the other objects in its splendid folds. The shares of the CMIC were affectionately known in the Kaffir circus as "Solids"; they yielded handsome though irregular dividends, earned chiefly by flotation and speculation; the circus believed in them. And in view of the annual meeting of shareholders to be held on the following

Tuesday afternoon (the conjurer in the chair and his hat on the table), the market price, after a period of depression, had stiffened.

Mr Bowring's meditations were soon interrupted by a telegram. He opened it and read: "*Cook drunk again. Will dine with you Devonshire, seven-thirty. Impossible here. Have arranged about luggage. – Marie.*" Marie was Mr Bowring's wife. He told himself that he felt greatly relieved by that telegram; he clutched at it; and his spirits seemed to rise. At any rate, since he would not now go near Lowndes Square, he could certainly laugh at the threatened robbery. He thought what a wonderful thing Providence was, after all.

"Just look at that," he said to his clerk, showing the telegram with a humorous affectation of dismay.

"Tut, tut," said the clerk, discreetly sympathetic towards his employer thus victimized by debauched cooks. "I suppose you're going down to Hampshire to-night as usual, sir?"

Mr Bowring replied that he was, and that everything appeared to be in order for the meeting, and that he should be back on Monday afternoon or at the latest very early on Tuesday.

Then, with a few parting instructions, and with that eagle glance round his own room and into circumjacent rooms which a truly efficient head of affairs never omits on leaving business for the week-end, Mr Bowring sedately, yet magnificently, departed from the noble registered offices of the CMIC.

"Why didn't Marie telephone instead of wiring?' he mused, as his pair of greys whirled him and his coachman and his footman off to the Devonshire.

II

The Devonshire Mansion, a bright edifice of eleven storeys in the Foster and Dicksee style, constructional ironwork by Homan, lifts by Waygood, decorations by Waring, and terra-cotta by the rood, is situate on the edge of Hyde Park. It is a composite building. Its foundations are firmly fixed in the Tube railway; above that comes the wine cellarage, then the vast laundry, and then (a row of windows scarcely level with the street) a sporting club, a billiard-room, a grillroom, and a cigarette-merchant whose name ends in "opoulos." On the first floor is the renowned Devonshire Mansion Restaurant. Always, in London, there is just one restaurant where, if you are an entirely correct person, "you can get a decent meal." The place changes from season to season, but there is never more than one of it at a time. That season it happened to be the Devonshire. (The chef of the Devonshire had invented tripe suppers, *tripes à la mode de Caen*, and these suppers – seven-and-six – had been the rage.) Consequently all entirely correct people fed as a matter of course at the Devonshire, since there was no other place fit to go to. The vogue of the restaurant favourably affected the vogue of the nine floors of furnished suites above the restaurant; they were always full; and the heavenward attics, where the servants took off their smart liveries and became human, held much wealth. The vogue of the restaurant also exercised a beneficial influence over the status of the Kitcat Club, which was a cock-and-hen club of the latest pattern and had its "house" on the third floor.

It was a little after half-past seven when Mr Bruce Bowring haughtily ascended the grand staircase of this resort of opulence, and paused for an instant near the immense fireplace at the summit (September was inclement, and a fire burned nicely) to inquire from the head-waiter whether Mrs Bowring had secured a table. But Marie had not arrived – Marie, who was never late! Uneasy and chagrined, he proceeded, under the escort of the head-waiter, to the glittering Salle Louis Quatorze and selected, because of his morning attire, a table half-hidden behind an onyx pillar. The great room was moderately full of fair women and possessive men, despite the month. Immediately afterwards a youngish couple (the man handsomer and better dressed than the woman) took the table on the other side of the pillar. Mr Bowring waited five minutes, then he ordered Sole Mornay and a bottle of Romanée-Conti, and then he waited another five minutes. He went somewhat in fear of his wife, and did not care to begin without her.

"Can't you read?" It was the youngish man at the next table speaking in a raised voice to a squinting lackey with a telegraph form in his hand. "'Solids! Solids,' my friend. 'Sell – Solids – to – any – amount – to-morrow – and – Monday.' Got it? Well, send it off at once."

"Quite clear, my lord," said the lackey, and fled. The youngish man gazed fixedly but absently at Mr Bowring and seemed to see through him to the tapestry behind. Mr Bowring, to his own keen annoyance, reddened. Partly to conceal the blush, and partly because it was a quarter to eight and there was the train to catch, he lowered his face, and began upon the sole. A few minutes later the lackey returned, gave some change to the youngish man, and surprised Mr Bowring by advancing towards him and handing him an envelope – an envelope which bore on its flap the legend "Kitcat Club." The note within was scribbled in pencil in his wife's handwriting, and ran: "*Just arrived. Delayed by luggage. I'm too nervous to face the restaurant, and am eating a chop here alone. The place is fortunately empty. Come and fetch me as soon as you're ready.*"

Mr Bowring sighed angrily. He hated his wife's club, and this succession of messages telephonic, telegraphic, and calligraphic was exasperating him.

"No answer!" he ejaculated, and then he beckoned the lackey closer. "Who's that gentleman at the next table with the lady?" he murmured.

"I'm not rightly sure, sir," was the whispered reply. "Some authorities say he's the strong man at the Hippodrome, while others affirm he's a sort of American millionaire."

"But you addressed him as 'my lord.'"

"Just then I thought he was the strong man, sir," said the lackey, retiring.

"My bill!" Mr Bowring demanded fiercely of the waiter, and at the same time the youngish gentleman and his companion rose and departed.

At the lift Mr Bowring found the squinting lackey in charge.

"You're the liftman, too?"

"To-night, sir, I am many things. The fact is, the regular liftman has got a couple of hours off – being the recent father of twins."

"Well – Kitcat Club."

The lift seemed to shoot far upwards, and Mr Bowring thought the lackey had mistaken the floor, but on gaining the corridor he saw across the portals in front of him the remembered gold sign, "Kitcat Club. Members only." He pushed the door open and went in.

III

Instead of the familiar vestibule of his wife's club, Mr Bowring discovered a small ante-chamber, and beyond, through a doorway half-screened by a *portière*, he had glimpses of a rich, rose-lit drawing-room. In the doorway, with one hand raised to the *portière*, stood the youngish man who had forced him to blush in the restaurant.

"I beg your pardon," said Mr Bowring, stiffly – "is this the Kitcat Club?"

The other man advanced to the outer door, his brilliant eyes fixed on Mr Bowring's; his arm crept round the cheek of the door and came back bearing the gold sign; then he shut the door and locked it. "No, this isn't the Kitcat Club at all," he replied. "It is my flat. Come and sit down. I was expecting you."

"I shall do nothing of the kind," said Mr Bowring disdainfully.

"But when I tell you that I know you are going to decamp to-night, Mr Bowring – "

The youngish man smiled affably.

"Decamp?" The spine of the financier suddenly grew flaccid.

"I used the word."

"Who the devil are you?" snapped the financier, forcing his spine to rigidity.

"I am the 'friend' on the telephone. I specially wanted you at the Devonshire to-night, and I thought that the fear of a robbery at Lowndes Square might make your arrival here more certain. I am he who devised the story of the inebriated cook and favoured you with a telegram signed 'Marie.' I am the humorist who pretended in a loud voice to send off telegraphic instructions to sell 'Solids,' in order to watch your demeanour under the test. I am the expert who forged your wife's handwriting in a note from the Kitcat. I am the patron of the cross-eyed menial who gave you the note and who afterwards raised you too high in the lift. I am the artificer of this gold sign, an exact duplicate of the genuine one two floors below, which induced you to visit me. The sign alone cost me nine-and-six; the servant's livery came to two pounds fifteen. But I never consider expense when, by dint of a generous outlay, I can avoid violence. I hate violence." He gently waved the sign to and fro.

"Then my wife – " Mr Bowring stammered in a panic rage.

"Is probably at Lowndes Square, wondering what on earth has happened to you."

Mr Bowring took breath, remembered that he was a great man, and steadied himself.

"You must be mad," he remarked quietly. "Open this door at once."

"Perhaps," the stranger judicially admitted. "Perhaps a sort of madness. But do come and sit down. We have no time to lose."

Mr Bowring gazed at that handsome face, with the fine nostrils, large mouth, and square clean chin, and the dark eyes, the black hair, and long, black moustache; and he noticed the long, thin hands. "Decadent!" he decided. Nevertheless, and though it was with the air of indulging the caprice of a lunatic, he did in fact obey the stranger's request.

It was a beautiful Chippendale drawing-room that he entered. Near the hearth, to which a morsel of fire gave cheerfulness, were two easy-chairs, and between them a small table. Behind was extended a fourfold draught-screen.

"I can give you just five minutes," said Mr Bowring, magisterially sitting down.

"They will suffice," the stranger responded, sitting down also. "You have in your pocket, Mr Bowring – probably your breast-pocket – fifty Bank of England notes for a thousand pounds each, and a number of smaller notes amounting to another ten thousand."

"Well?"

"I must demand from you the first-named fifty."

Mr Bowring, in the silence of the rose-lit drawing-room, thought of all the Devonshire Mansion, with its endless corridors and innumerable rooms, its acres of carpets, its forests of furniture, its gold and silver, and its jewels and its wines, its pretty women and possessive men – the whole humming microcosm founded on a unanimous pretence that the sacredness of property was a natural law. And he thought how disconcerting it was that he should be trapped there, helpless, in the very middle of the vast pretence, and forced to admit that the sacredness of property was a purely artificial convention.

"By what right do you make this demand?" he inquired, bravely sarcastic.

"By the right of my unique knowledge," said the stranger, with a bright smile. "Listen to what you and I alone know. You are at the end of the tether. The Consolidated is at the same spot. You have a past consisting chiefly of nineteen fraudulent flotations. You have paid dividends out of capital till there is no capital left. You have speculated and lost. You have cooked balance-sheets to a turn and ruined the eyesight of auditors with dust. You have lived like ten lords. Your houses are mortgaged. You own an unrivalled collection of unreceipted bills. You are worse than a common thief. (Excuse these personalities.)"

"My dear, good sir – " Mr Bowring interrupted, grandly.

"Permit me. What is more serious, your self-confidence has been gradually deserting you. At last, perceiving that some blundering person was bound soon to put his foot through the brittle shell of your ostentation and tread on nothing, and foreseeing for yourself an immediate future consisting chiefly of Holloway, you have by a supreme effort of your genius, borrowed £60,000 from a bank on CMIC scrip, for a week (eh?), and you have arranged, you and your wife, to – melt into thin air. You will affect to set out as usual for your country place in Hampshire, but it is Southampton that will see you to-night, and Havre will see you to-morrow. You may run over to Paris to change some notes, but by Monday you will be on your way to – frankly, I don't know where; perhaps Monte Video. Of course you take the risk of extradition, but the risk is preferable to the certainty that awaits you in England. I think you will elude extradition. If I thought otherwise, I should not have had you here to-night, because, once extradited, you might begin to amuse yourself by talking about me."

"So it's blackmail," said Mr Bowring, grim.

The dark eyes opposite to him sparkled gaily.

"It desolates me," the youngish man observed, "to have to commit you to the deep with only ten thousand. But, really, not less than fifty thousand will requite me for the brain-tissue which I have expended in the study of your interesting situation."

Mr Bowring consulted his watch.

"Come, now," he said, huskily; "I'll give you ten thousand. I flatter myself I can look facts in the face, and so I'll give you ten thousand."

"My friend," answered the spider, "you are a judge of character. Do you honestly think I don't mean precisely what I say – to sixpence? It is eight-thirty. You are, if I may be allowed the remark, running it rather fine."

"And suppose I refuse to part?" said Mr Bowring, after reflection. "What then?"

"I have confessed to you that I hate violence. You would therefore leave this room unmolested, but you wouldn't step off the island."

Mr Bowring scanned the agreeable features of the stranger. Then, while the lifts were ascending and descending, and the wine was sparkling, and the jewels flashing, and the gold chinking, and the pretty women being pretty, in all the four quarters of the Devonshire, Mr Bruce Bowring in the silent parlour counted out fifty notes on to the table. After all, it was a fortune, that little pile of white on the crimson polished wood.

"*Bon voyage!*" said the stranger. "Don't imagine that I am not full of sympathy for you. I am. You have only been unfortunate. *Bon voyage!*"

"No! By Heaven!" Mr Bowring almost shouted, rushing back from the door, and drawing a revolver from his hip pocket. "It's too much! I didn't mean to – but confound it! what's a revolver for?"

The youngish man jumped up quickly and put his hands on the notes.

"Violence is always foolish, Mr Bowring," he murmured.

"Will you give them up, or won't you?"

"I won't."

The stranger's fine eyes seemed to glint with joy in the drama.

"Then – "

The revolver was raised, but in the same instant a tiny hand snatched it from the hand of Mr Bowring, who turned and beheld by his side a woman. The huge screen sank slowly and noiselessly to the floor in the surprising manner peculiar to screens that have been overset.

Mr Bowring cursed. "An accomplice! I might have guessed!" he grumbled in final disgust.

He ran to the door, unlocked it, and was no more seen.

IV

The lady was aged twenty-seven or so; of medium height, and slim, with a plain, very intelligent and expressive face, lighted by courageous, grey eyes, and crowned with loose, abundant, fluffy hair. Perhaps it was the fluffy hair, perhaps it was the mouth that twitched as she dropped the revolver – who can say? – but the whole atmosphere of the rose-lit chamber was suddenly changed. The incalculable had invaded it.

"You seem surprised, Miss Fincastle," said the possessor of the bank-notes, laughing gaily.

"Surprised!" echoed the lady, controlling that mouth. "My dear Mr Thorold, when, strictly as a journalist, I accepted your invitation, I did not anticipate this sequel; frankly I did not."

She tried to speak coldly and evenly, on the assumption that a journalist has no sex during business hours. But just then she happened to be neither less nor more a woman than a woman always is.

"If I have had the misfortune to annoy you –!" Thorold threw up his arms in gallant despair.

"Annoy is not the word," said Miss Fincastle, nervously smiling. "May I sit down? Thanks. Let us recount. You arrive in England, from somewhere, as the son and heir of the late Ahasuerus Thorold, the New York operator, who died worth six million dollars. It becomes known that while in Algiers in the spring you stayed at the Hôtel St James, famous as the scene of what is called the 'Algiers Mystery,' familiar to English newspaper-readers since last April. The editor of my journal therefore instructs me to obtain an interview with

you. I do so. The first thing I discover is that, though an American,
you have no American accent. You explain this by saying that since
infancy you have always lived in Europe with your mother."

"But surely you do not doubt that I am Cecil Thorold!" said the
man. Their faces were approximate over the table.

"Of course not. I merely recount. To continue. I interview you
as to the Algerian mystery, and get some new items concerning it.
Then you regale me with tea and your opinions, and my questions
grow more personal. So it comes about that, strictly on behalf of my
paper, I inquire what your recreations are. And suddenly you answer:
'Ah! My recreations! Come to dinner to-night, quite informally, and I
will show you how I amuse myself!' I come. I dine. I am stuck behind
that screen and told to listen. And – and – the millionaire proves to
be nothing but a blackmailer."

"You must understand, my dear lady – "

"I understand everything, Mr Thorold, except your object in
admitting me to the scene."

"A whim!" cried Thorold vivaciously, "a freak of mine! Possibly
due to the eternal and universal desire of man to show off before
woman!"

The journalist tried to smile, but something in her face caused
Thorold to run to a chiffonnier.

"Drink this," he said, returning with a glass.

"I need nothing." The voice was a whisper.

"Oblige me."

Miss Fincastle drank and coughed.

"Why did you do it?" she asked sadly, looking at the notes.

"You don't mean to say," Thorold burst out, "that you are
feeling sorry for Mr Bruce Bowring? He has merely parted with
what he stole. And the people from whom he stole, stole. All the
activities which centre about the Stock Exchange are simply various
manifestations of one primeval instinct. Suppose I had not – had not
interfered. No one would have been a penny the better off except
Mr Bruce Bowring. Whereas – "

"You intend to restore this money to the Consolidated?" said Miss
Fincastle eagerly.

"Not quite! The Consolidated doesn't deserve it. You must not
regard its shareholders as a set of innocent shorn lambs. They knew
the game. They went in for what they could get. Besides, how could
I restore the money without giving myself away? I want the money
myself."

"But you are a millionaire."

"It is precisely because I am a millionaire that I want more. All millionaires are like that."

"I am sorry to find you a thief, Mr Thorold."

"A thief! No. I am only direct, I only avoid the middleman. At dinner, Miss Fincastle, you displayed somewhat advanced views about property, marriage, and the aristocracy of brains. You said that labels were for the stupid majority, and that the wise minority examined the ideas behind the labels. You label me a thief, but examine the idea, and you will perceive that you might as well call yourself a thief. Your newspaper every day suppresses the truth about the City, and it does so in order to live. In other words, it touches the pitch, it participates in the game. To-day it has a fifty-line advertisement of a false balance-sheet of the Consolidated, at two shillings a line. That five pounds, part of the loot of a great city, will help to pay for your account of our interview this afternoon."

"Our interview to-night," Miss Fincastle corrected him stiffly, "and all that I have seen and heard."

At these words she stood up, and as Cecil Thorold gazed at her his face changed.

"I shall begin to wish," he said slowly, "that I had deprived myself of the pleasure of your company this evening."

"You might have been a dead man had you done so," Miss Fincastle retorted, and observing his blank countenance she touched the revolver. "Have you forgotten already?" she asked tartly.

"Of course it wasn't loaded," he remarked. "Of course I had seen to that earlier in the day. I am not such a bungler – "

"Then I didn't save your life?"

"You force me to say that you did not, and to remind you that you gave me your word not to emerge from behind the screen. However, seeing the motive, I can only thank you for that lapse. The pity is that it hopelessly compromises you."

"Me?" exclaimed Miss Fincastle.

"You. Can't you see that you are in it, in this robbery, to give the thing a label. You were alone with the robber. You succoured the robber at a critical moment . . . 'Accomplice,' Mr Bowring himself said. My dear journalist, the episode of the revolver, empty though the revolver was, seals your lips."

Miss Fincastle laughed rather hysterically, leaning over the table with her hands on it.

"My dear millionaire," she said rapidly, "you don't know the new journalism to which I have the honour to belong. You would know it better had you lived more in New York. All I have to announce is that, compromised or not, a full account of this affair will appear in my paper tomorrow morning. No, I shall not inform the police. I am a journalist simply, but a journalist I *am*."

"And your promise, which you gave me before going behind the screen, your solemn promise that you would reveal nothing? I was loth to mention it."

"Some promises, Mr Thorold, it is a duty to break, and it is my duty to break this one. I should never have given it had I had the slightest idea of the nature of your recreations."

Thorold still smiled, though faintly.

"Really, you know," he murmured, "this is getting just a little serious."

"It is very serious," she stammered.

And then Thorold noticed that the new journalist was softly weeping.

V

The door opened.

"Miss Kitty Sartorius," said the erstwhile liftman, who was now in plain clothes and had mysteriously ceased to squint.

A beautiful girl, a girl who had remarkable loveliness and was aware of it (one of the prettiest women of the Devonshire), ran impulsively into the room and caught Miss Fincastle by the hand.

"My dearest Eve, you're crying. What's the matter?"

"Lecky," said Thorold aside to the servant. "I told you to admit no one."

The beautiful blonde turned sharply to Thorold.

"I told him I wished to enter," she said imperiously, half closing her eyes.

"Yes, sir," said Lecky. "That was it. The lady wished to enter."

Thorold bowed.

"It was sufficient," he said. "That will do, Lecky."

"Yes, sir."

"But I say, Lecky, when next you address me publicly, try to remember that I am not in the peerage."

The servant squinted.

"Certainly, sir." And he retired.

"Now we are alone," said Miss Sartorius. "Introduce us, Eve, and explain."

Miss Fincastle, having regained self-control, introduced her dear friend the radiant star of the Regency Theatre, and her acquaintance the millionaire.

"Eve didn't feel *quite* sure of you," the actress stated; "and so we arranged that if she wasn't up at my flat by nine o'clock, I was to come down and reconnoitre. What have you been doing to make Eve cry?"

"Unintentional, I assure you – " Thorold began.

"There's something between you two," said Kitty Sartorius sagaciously, in significant accents. "What is it?"

She sat down, touched her picture hat, smoothed her white gown, and tapped her foot. "What is it, now? Mr Thorold, I think *you* had better tell me."

Thorold raised his eyebrows and obediently commenced the narration, standing with his back to the fire.

"How perfectly splendid!" Kitty exclaimed. "I'm so glad you cornered Mr Bowring. I met him one night and I thought he was horrid. And these are the notes? Well, of all the –!"

Thorold proceeded with his story.

"Oh, but you can't do *that*, Eve!" said Kitty, suddenly serious. "You can't go and split! It would mean all sorts of bother; your wretched newspaper would be sure to keep you hanging about in London, and we shouldn't be able to start on our holiday to-morrow. Eve and I are starting on quite a long tour to-morrow, Mr Thorold; we begin with Ostend."

"Indeed!" said Thorold. "I, too, am going in that direction soon. Perhaps we may meet."

"I hope so," Kitty smiled, and then she looked at Eve Fincastle. "You really mustn't do *that*, Eve," she said.

"I must, I must!" Miss Fincastle insisted, clenching her hands.

"And she will," said Kitty tragically, after considering her friend's face. "She will, and our holiday's ruined. I see it – I see it plainly. She's in one of her stupid conscientious moods. She's fearfully advanced and careless and unconventional in theory, Eve is; but when it comes to practice –! Mr Thorold, you have just got everything into a dreadful knot. Why did you want those notes so very particularly?"

"I don't want them so very particularly."

"Well, anyhow, it's a most peculiar predicament. Mr Bowring doesn't count, and this Consolidated thingummy isn't any the worse off. Nobody suffers who oughtn't to suffer. It's your unlawful gain that's wrong. Why not pitch the wretched notes in the fire?" Kitty laughed at her own playful humour.

"Certainly," said Thorold. And with a quick movement he put the fifty trifles in the grate, where they made a bluish yellow flame.

Both the women screamed and sprang up.

"*Mr* Thorold!"

"Mr *Thorold!*" ("He's adorable!" Kitty breathed.)

"The incident, I venture to hope, is now closed," said Thorold calmly, but with his dark eyes sparkling. "I must thank you both for a very enjoyable evening. Some day, perhaps, I may have an opportunity of further explaining my philosophy to you."

Robert Barr

Lord Chizelrigg's Missing Fortune

Eugène Valmont was one of the first in a long line of comic French (or French-speaking) detectives, who with his conceited manner and somewhat outrageous exploits has become one of the best-remembered creations of the period – though it seems to be for just one story, "The Absent-Minded Coterie". The present tale, also from The Triumphs of Eugène Valmont *(1906), is equally good and much less well-known.*

Valmont's creator was Robert Barr (1850–1912), a Scot who also wrote under the name of Luke Sharp. His output was large and varied – it included adventure stories, westerns, science fiction and mainstream novels as well as a great deal of journalism – and he was also one of the earliest parodists of Sherlock Holmes.

ONE DAY MY servant brought into me a card on which was engraved "Lord Chizelrigg."

"Show his lordship in," I said, and there appeared a young man of perhaps twenty-four or twenty-five, well dressed, and of most charming manners, who, nevertheless, began his interview by asking a question such as had never before been addressed to me, and which, if put to a solicitor, or other professional man, would have been answered with some indignation. Indeed, I believe it is a written or unwritten law of the legal profession that the acceptance of such a proposal as Lord Chizelrigg made to me, would if proved, result in the disgrace and ruin of the lawyer.

"Monsieur Valmont," began Lord Chizelrigg, "do you ever take up cases on speculation?"

"On speculation, sir? I do not think I understand you."

His lordship blushed like a girl, and stammered slightly as he attempted an explanation.

"What I mean is, do you accept a case on a contingent fee? That is to say, monsieur – er – well, not to put too fine a point upon it, no results, no pay."

I replied somewhat severely:

"Such an offer has never been made to me, and I may say at once that I should be compelled to decline it were I favoured with the opportunity. In the cases submitted to me, I devote my time and attention to their solution. I try to deserve success, but I cannot command it, and as in the interim I must live, I am reluctantly compelled to make a charge for my time, at least. I believe the doctor sends in his bill, though the patient dies."

The young man laughed uneasily, and seemed almost too embarrassed to proceed, but finally he said:

"Your illustration strikes home with greater accuracy than probably you imagined when you uttered it. I have just paid my last penny to the physician who attended my late uncle, Lord Chizelrigg, who died six months ago. I am fully aware that the suggestion I made may seem like a reflection upon your skill, or rather, as implying a doubt regarding it. But I should be grieved, monsieur, if you fell into such an error. I could have come here and commissioned you to undertake some elucidation of the strange situation in which I find myself, and I make no doubt you would have accepted the task if your numerous engagements had permitted. Then, if you failed, I should have been unable to pay you, for I am practically bankrupt. My whole desire, therefore, was to make an honest beginning, and to let you know exactly how I stand. If you succeed, I shall be a rich man; if you do not succeed, I shall be what I am now, penniless. Have I made it plain now why I began with a question which you had every right to resent?"

"Perfectly plain, my lord, and your candour does you credit."

I was very much taken with the unassuming manners of the young man, and his evident desire to accept no service under false pretences. When I had finished my sentence the pauper nobleman rose to his feet, and bowed.

"I am very much your debtor, monsieur, for your courtesy in receiving me, and can only beg pardon for occupying your time on a futile quest. I wish you good-morning, monsieur."

"One moment, my lord," I rejoined, waving him to his chair again. "Although I am unprepared to accept a commission on the terms you suggest, I may, nevertheless, be able to offer a hint or two that will prove of service to you. I think I remember the announcement of Lord Chizelrigg's death. He was somewhat eccentric, was he not?"

"Eccentric?" said the young man, with a slight laugh, seating himself again – "well, *rather!*"

"I vaguely remember that he was accredited with the possession of something like twenty thousand acres of land?"

"Twenty-seven thousand, as a matter of fact," replied my visitor.

"Have you fallen heir to the lands as well as to the title?"

"Oh, yes; the estate was entailed. The old gentleman could not divert it from me if he would, and I rather suspect that fact must have been the cause of some worry to him."

"But surely, my lord, a man who owns, as one might say, a principality in this wealthy realm of England, cannot be penniless?"

Again the young man laughed.

"Well, no," he replied, thrusting his hand in his pocket and bringing to light a few brown coppers, and a white silver piece.

"I possess enough money to buy some food to-night, but not enough to dine at the Hotel Cecil. You see, it is like this. I belong to a somewhat ancient family, various members of whom went the pace, and mortgaged their acres up to the hilt. I could not raise a further penny on my estates were I to try my hardest, because at the time the money was lent, land was much more valuable than it is to-day. Agricultural depression, and all that sort of thing, have, if I may put it so, left me a good many thousands worse off than if I had no land at all. Besides this, during my late uncle's life, Parliament, on his behalf, intervened once or twice, allowing him in the first place to cut valuable timber, and in the second place to sell the pictures of Chizelrigg Chase at Christie's for figures which made one's mouth water."

"And what became of the money?" I asked, whereupon once more this genial nobleman laughed.

"That is exactly what I came up in the lift to learn if Monsieur Valmont could discover."

"My lord, you interest me," I said, quite truly, with an uneasy apprehension that I should take up his case after all, for I liked the young man already. His lack of pretence appealed to me, and that sympathy which is so universal among my countrymen enveloped him, as I may say, quite independent of my own will.

"My uncle," went on Lord Chizelrigg, "was somewhat of an anomaly in our family. He must have been a reversal to a very, very ancient type; a type of which we have no record. He was as miserly as his forefathers were prodigal. When he came into the title and estate some twenty years ago, he dismissed the whole retinue of servants, and, indeed, was defendant in several cases at law where retainers of our family brought suit against him for wrongful dismissal, or dismissal without a penny compensation in lieu of notice. I am pleased to say he lost all his cases, and when he pleaded poverty, got permission to sell a certain number of heirlooms, enabling him to make compensation, and giving him something on which to live. These heirlooms at auction sold so unexpectedly well, that my uncle acquired a taste, as it were, of what might be done. He could always prove that the rents went to the mortgagees, and that he had nothing on which to exist, so on several occasions he obtained permission from the courts to cut timber and sell pictures, until he denuded the estate and made an empty barn of the old manor house. He lived like any labourer, occupying himself sometimes as a carpenter, sometimes as a blacksmith; indeed, he made a blacksmith's shop of the library, one of the most noble rooms in Britain, containing thousands of valuable books which again and again he applied for permission to sell, but this privilege was never granted to him. I find on coming into the property that my uncle quite persistently evaded the law, and depleted this superb collection, book by book, surreptitiously through dealers in London. This, of course, would have got him into deep trouble if it had been discovered before his death, but now the valuable volumes are gone, and there is no redress. Many of them are doubtless in America, or in museums and collections of Europe."

"You wish me to trace them, perhaps?" I interpolated.

"Oh, no; they are past praying for. The old man made tens of thousands by the sale of the timber, and other of thousands by disposing of the pictures. The house is denuded of its fine old furniture, which was immensely valuable, and then the books, as I have said, must have brought in the revenue of a prince, if he got anything like their value, and you may be sure he was shrewd enough to know their worth. Since the last refusal of the courts to allow him further relief, as he termed it, which was some seven years ago, he had quite evidently been disposing of books and furniture by a private sale, in defiance of the law. At that time I was under age, but my guardians opposed his application to the courts, and demanded an account of the moneys already in his hands. The judges upheld the opposition of my guardians, and refused to allow a further spoliation of the estate, but they did not grant the accounting my guardians asked, because the proceeds of the former sales were entirely at the disposal of my uncle, and were sanctioned by the law to permit him to live as befitted his station. If he lived meagrely instead of lavishly, as my guardians contended, that, the judges said, was his affair, and there the matter ended.

"My uncle took a violent dislike to me on account of this opposition to his last application, although, of course, I had nothing whatever to do with the matter. He lived like a hermit, mostly in the library, and was waited upon by an old man and his wife, and these three were the only inhabitants of a mansion that could comfortably house a hundred. He visited nobody, and would allow no one to approach Chizelrigg Chase. In order that all who had the misfortune to have dealing with him should continue to endure trouble after his death, he left what might be called a will, but which rather may be termed a letter to me. Here is a copy of it.

MY DEAR TOM, You will find your fortune between a couple of sheets of paper in the library.
"'Your affectionate uncle,
"'REGINALD MORAN, EARL OF CHIZELRIGG.

"I should doubt if that were a legal will," said I.

"It doesn't need to be," replied the young man with a smile. "I am next-of-kin, and heir to everything he possessed, although, of course, he might have given his money elsewhere if he had chosen to do so. Why he did not bequeath it to some institution, I do not know. He knew no man personally except his own servants, whom he misused and starved, but, as he told them, he misused and starved himself, so they had no cause to grumble. He said he was treating them like one of the family. I suppose he thought it would cause me more worry and anxiety if he concealed the money and put me on the wrong scent, which I am convinced he has done, than to leave it openly to any person or charity."

"I need not ask if you have searched the library?"

"Searched it? Why, there never was such a search since the world began!"

"Possibly you put the task into incompetent hands?"

"You are hinting, Monsieur Valmont, that I engaged others until my money was gone, then came to you with a speculative proposal. Let me assure you such is not the case. Incompetent hands, I grant you, but the hands were my own. For the past six months I have lived practically as my uncle lived. I have rummaged that library from floor to ceiling. It was left in a frightful state, littered with old newspapers, accounts, and what-not. Then, of course, there were the books remaining in the library, still a formidable collection."

"Was your uncle a religious man?"

"I could not say. I surmise not. You see, I was unacquainted with him, and never saw him until after his death. I fancy he was not religious, otherwise he could not have acted as he did. Still, he proved himself a man of such twisted mentality that anything is possible."

"I knew a case once where an heir who expected a large sum of money was bequeathed a family Bible, which he threw into the fire, learning afterwards, to his dismay, that it contained many thousands of pounds in Bank of England notes, the object of the devisor being to induce the legatee to read the good Book or suffer through the neglect of it."

"I have searched the Scriptures," said the youthful Earl with a laugh, "but the benefit has been moral rather than material."

"Is there any chance that your uncle has deposited his wealth in a bank, and has written a cheque for the amount, leaving it between two leaves of a book?"

"Anything is possible, monsieur, but I think that highly improbable. I have gone through every tome, page by page, and I suspect very few of the volumes have been opened for the last twenty years."

"How much money do you estimate he accumulated?"

"He must have cleared more than a hundred thousand pounds, but speaking of banking it, I would like to say that my uncle evinced a deep distrust of banks, and never drew a cheque in his life so far as I am aware. All accounts were paid in gold by this old steward, who first brought the receipted bill in to my uncle, and then received the exact amount, after having left the room, and waited until he was rung for, so that he might not learn the repository from which my uncle drew his store. I believe if the money is ever found it will be in gold, and I am very sure that this will was written, if we may call it a will, to put us on the wrong scent."

"Have you had the library cleared out?"

"Oh, no, it is practically as my uncle left it. I realized that if I were to call in help, it would be well that the new-comer found it undisturbed."

"You were quite right, my lord. You say you examined all the papers?"

"Yes; so far as that is concerned, the room has been very fairly gone over, but nothing that was in it the day my uncle died has been removed, not even his anvil."

"His anvil?"

"Yes; I told you he made a blacksmith's shop, as well as bedroom, of the library. It is a huge room, with a great fire-place at one end which formed an excellent forge. He and the steward built the forge in the eastern fire-place, of brick and clay, with their own hands, and erected there a second-hand blacksmith's bellows."

"What work did he do at his forge?"

"Oh, anything that was required about the place. He seems to have been a very expert ironworker. He would never buy a new implement for the garden or the house so long as he could get one second-hand, and he never bought anything second-hand while at his forge he might repair what was already in use. He kept an old cob, on which he used to ride through the park, and he always put the shoes on this cob himself, the steward informs me, so he must have understood the use of blacksmith's tools. He made a carpenter's shop of the chief drawing-room and erected a bench there. I think a very useful mechanic was spoiled when my uncle became an earl."

"You have been living at the Chase since your uncle died?"

"If you call it living, yes. The old steward and his wife have been looking after me, as they looked after my uncle, and, seeing me day after day, coatless and covered with dust, I imagine they think me a second edition of the old man."

"Does the steward know the money is missing?"

"No; no one knows it but myself. This will was left on the anvil, in an envelope addressed to me."

"Your statement is exceedingly clear, Lord Chizelrigg, but I confess I don't see much daylight through it. Is there a pleasant country around Chizelrigg Chase?"

"Very; especially at this season of the year. In autumn and winter the house is a little draughty. It needs several thousand pounds to put it in repair."

"Draughts do not matter in the summer. I have been long enough in England not to share the fear of my countrymen for a *courant d'air*. Is there a spare bed in the manor house, or shall I take down a cot with me, or let us say a hammock?"

"Really," stammered the earl, blushing again, "you must not think I detailed all these circumstances in order to influence you to take up what may be a hopeless case. I, of course, am deeply interested, and, therefore, somewhat prone to be carried away when I begin a recital of my uncle's eccentricities. If I receive your permission, I will call on you again in a month or two. To tell you the truth, I borrowed a little money from the old steward, and visited London to see my legal advisers, hoping that in the circumstances I may get permission to sell something that will keep me from starvation. When I spoke of the house being denuded I meant relatively, of course. There are still a good many antiquities which would doubtless bring me in a comfortable sum of money. I have been borne up by the belief that I should find my uncle's gold. Lately, I have been beset by a suspicion that the old gentleman thought the library the only valuable asset left, and for this reason wrote his note, thinking I would be afraid to sell anything from that room. The old rascal must have made a pot of money out of those shelves. The catalogue shows that there was a copy of the first book printed in England by Caxton, and several priceless Shakespeares, as well as many other volumes that a collector would give a small fortune for. All these are gone. I think when I show this to be the case, the authorities cannot refuse me the right to sell something, and, if I get this permission, I shall at once call upon you."

"Nonsense, Lord Chizelrigg. Put your application in motion, if you like. Meanwhile I beg of you to look upon me as a more substantial banker than your old steward. Let us enjoy a good dinner together at the Cecil to-night, if you will do me the honour to be my guest. To-morrow we can leave for Chizelrigg Chase. How far is it?"

"About three hours," replied the young man, becoming as red as a new Queen Anne villa. "Really, Monsieur Valmont, you overwhelm me with your kindness, but nevertheless I accept your generous offer."

"Then that's settled. What's the name of the old steward?"

"Higgins."

"You are certain he has no knowledge of the hiding-place of this treasure?"

"Oh, quite sure. My uncle was not a man to make a confidant of any one, least of all an old babbler like Higgins."

"Well, I should like to be introduced to Higgins as a benighted foreigner. That will make him despise me and treat me like a child."

"Oh, I say," protested the earl, "I should have thought you'd lived long enough in England to have got out of the notion that we do not appreciate the foreigner. Indeed, we are the only nation in the world that extends a cordial welcome to him, rich or poor."

"*Certainement*, my lord, I should be deeply disappointed did you not take me at my proper valuation, but I cherish no delusions regarding the contempt with which Higgins will regard me. He will look upon me as a sort of simpleton to whom the Lord had been unkind by not making England my native land. Now, Higgins must be led to believe that I am in his own class; that is, a servant of yours. Higgins and I will gossip over the fire together, should these spring evenings prove chilly, and before two or three weeks are past I shall have learned a great deal about your uncle that you never dreamed of. Higgins will talk more freely with a fellow-servant than with his master, however much he may respect that master, and then, as I am a foreigner, he will babble down to my comprehension, and I shall get details that he never would think of giving to a fellow-countryman."

The young earl's modesty in such description of his home as he had given me, left me totally unprepared for the grandeur of the mansion, one corner of which he inhabited. It is such a place as you read of in romances of the Middle Ages; not a pinnacled or turreted French château of that period, but a beautiful and substantial stone manor house of a ruddy colour, whose warm hue seemed to add a softness to the severity of its architecture. It is built round an outer and an inner courtyard and could house a thousand, rather than the hundred with which its owner had accredited it. There are many stone-mullioned windows, and one at the end of the library might well have graced a cathedral. This superb residence occupies the centre of a heavily timbered park, and from the lodge at the gates we drove at least a mile and a half under the grandest avenue of old oaks I have ever seen. It seemed incredible that the owner of all this should actually lack the ready money to pay his fare to town!

Old Higgins met us at the station with a somewhat rickety cart, to which was attached the ancient cob that the late earl used to shoe. We entered a noble hall, which probably looked the larger because of the entire absence of any kind of furniture, unless two complete suits of venerable armour which stood on either hand might be considered as furnishing. I laughed aloud when the door was shut, and the sound echoed like the merriment of ghosts from the dim timbered roof above me.

"What are you laughing at?" asked the earl.

"I am laughing to see you put your modern tall hat on that mediaeval helmet."

"Oh, that's it! Well, put yours on the other. I mean no disrespect to the ancestor who wore this suit, but we are short of the harmless, necessary hat-rack, so I put my topper on the antique helmet, and thrust the umbrella (if I have one) in behind here, and down one of his legs. Since I came in possession, a very crafty-looking dealer from London visited me, and attempted to sound me regarding the sale of these suits of armour. I gathered he would give enough money to keep me in new suits, London made, for the rest of my life, but when I endeavoured to find out if he had had commercial dealings with my prophetic uncle, he became frightened and bolted. I imagine that if I had possessed presence of mind enough to have lured him into one of our most uncomfortable dungeons, I might have learned where some of the family treasures went to. Come up these stairs, Monsieur Valmont, and I will show you your room."

We had lunched on the train coming down, so after a wash in my own room I proceeded at once to inspect the library. It proved, indeed, a most noble apartment, and it had been scandalously used by the old reprobate, its late tenant. There were two huge fire-places, one in the middle of the north wall and the other at the eastern end. In the latter had been erected a rude brick forge, and beside the forge hung a great black bellows, smoky with usage. On a wooden block lay the anvil, and around it rested and rusted several hammers, large and small. At the western end was a glorious window filled with ancient stained glass, which, as I have said, might have adorned a cathedral. Extensive as the collection of books was, the great size of this chamber made it necessary that only the outside wall should be covered with book cases, and even these were divided by tall windows. The opposite wall was blank, with the exception of a picture here and there, and these pictures offered a further insult to the room, for they were cheap prints, mostly coloured lithographs that had appeared in Christmas numbers of London weekly journals, encased in poverty-stricken frames, hanging from nails ruthlessly driven in above them. The floor was covered with a litter of papers, in some places knee-deep, and in the corner farthest from the forge still stood the bed on which the ancient miser had died.

"Looks like a stable, doesn't it?" commented the earl, when I had finished my inspection. "I am sure the old boy simply filled it up with this rubbish to give me the trouble of examining it. Higgins tells me that up to within a month before he died the room was reasonably clear of all this muck. Of course, it had to be, or the place would have caught fire from the sparks of the forge. The old man made Higgins gather all the papers he could find anywhere about the place, ancient accounts, newspapers, and what not, even to the brown wrapping paper you see, in which parcels came, and commanded him to strew the floor with this litter, because, as he complained, Higgins's boots on the boards made too much noise, and Higgins, who is not in the least of an inquiring mind, accepted this explanation as entirely meeting the case."

Higgins proved to be a garrulous old fellow, who needed no urging to talk about the late earl; indeed, it was almost impossible to deflect his conversation into any other channel. Twenty years' intimacy with the eccentric nobleman had largely obliterated that sense of deference with which an English servant usually approaches his master. An English underling's idea of nobility is the man who never by any possibility works with his hands. The fact that Lord Chizelrigg had toiled at the carpenter's bench; had mixed cement in the drawing-room; had caused the anvil to ring out till midnight, aroused no admiration in Higgins's mind. In addition to this, the ancient nobleman had been penuriously strict in his examination of accounts, exacting the uttermost farthing, so the humble servitor regarded his memory with supreme contempt. I realized before the drive was finished from the station to Chizelrigg Chase that there was little use of introducing me to Higgins as a foreigner and a fellow-servant. I found myself completely unable to understand what the old fellow said. His dialect was as unknown to me as the Choctaw language would have been, and the young earl was compelled to act as interpreter on the occasions when we set this garrulous talking-machine going.

The new Earl of Chizelrigg, with the enthusiasm of a boy, proclaimed himself my pupil and assistant, and said he would do whatever he was told. His thorough and fruitless search of the library had convinced him that the old man was merely chaffing him, as he put it, by leaving such a letter as he had written. His lordship was certain that the money had been hidden somewhere else; probably buried under one of the trees in the park. Of course this was possible, and represented the usual method by which a stupid person conceals treasure, yet I did not think it probable. All conversations with Higgins showed the earl to have been an extremely suspicious man; suspicious of banks, suspicious even of Bank of England notes, suspicious of every person on earth, not omitting Higgins himself. Therefore, as I told his nephew, the miser would never allow the fortune out of his sight and immediate reach.

From the first the oddity of the forge and anvil being placed in his bedroom struck me as peculiar, and I said to the young man, –

"I'll stake my reputation that forge or anvil, or both, contain the secret. You see, the old gentleman worked sometimes till midnight, for Higgins could hear his hammering. If he used hard coal on the forge the fire would last through the night, and being in continual terror of thieves, as Higgins says, barricading the castle every evening before dark as if it were a fortress, he was bound to place the treasure in the most unlikely spot for a thief to get at it. Now, the coal fire smouldered all night long, and if the gold was in the forge underneath the embers, it would be extremely difficult to get at. A robber rummaging in the dark would burn his fingers in more senses than one. Then, as his lordship kept no less than four loaded revolvers under his pillow, all he had to do, if a thief entered his room was to allow the search to go on until the thief started at the forge, then doubtless, as he had the range with reasonable accuracy night or day, he might sit up in bed and blaze away with revolver after revolver. There were twenty-eight shots that could be fired in about double as many seconds, so you see the robber stood little chance in the face of such a fusillade. I propose that we dismantle the forge."

Lord Chizelrigg was much taken by my reasoning, and one morning early we cut down the big bellows, tore it open, found it empty, then took brick after brick from the forge with a crowbar, for the old man had builded better than he knew with Portland cement. In fact, when we cleared away the rubbish between the bricks and the core of the furnace we came upon one cube of cement which was as hard as granite. With the aid of Higgins, and a set of rollers and levers, we managed to get this block out into the park, and attempted to crush it with the sledge hammers belonging to the forge, in which we were entirely unsuccessful. The more it resisted our efforts, the more certain we became that the coins would be found within it. As this would not be treasure-trove in the sense that the Government might make a claim upon it, there was no particular necessity for secrecy, so we had up a man from the mines near by with drills and dynamite, who speedily shattered the block into a million pieces, more or less. Alas! there was no trace in its debris of "pay dirt," as the western miner puts it. While the dynamite expert was on the spot, we induced him to shatter the anvil as well as the block of cement, and then the workman, doubtless thinking the new earl was as insane as the old one had been, shouldered his tools, and went back to his mine.

The earl reverted to his former opinion that the gold was concealed in the park, while I held even more firmly to my own belief that the fortune rested in the library.

"It is obvious," I said to him, "that if the treasure is buried outside, some one must have dug the hole. A man so timorous and so reticent as your uncle would allow no one to do this but himself. Higgins maintained the other evening that all picks and spades were safely locked up by himself each night in the tool-house. The mansion itself was barricaded with such exceeding care that it would have been difficult for your uncle to get outside even if he wished to do so. Then such a man as your uncle is described to have been would continually desire ocular demonstration that his savings were intact, which would be practically impossible if the gold had found a grave in the park. I propose now that we abandon violence and dynamite, and proceed to an intellectual search of the library."

"Very well," replied the young earl, "but as I have already searched the library very thoroughly, your use of the word 'intellectual,' Monsieur Valmont, is not in accord with your customary politeness. However, I am with you. 'Tis for you to command, and me to obey."

"Pardon me, my lord!" I said, "I used the word 'intellectual' in contradistinction to the word 'dynamite.' It had no reference to your former search. I merely propose that we now abandon the use of chemical reaction, and employ the much greater force of mental activity. Did you notice any writing on the margins of the newspapers you examined?"

"No, I did not."

"Is it possible that there may have been some communication on the white border of a newspaper?"

"It is, of course, possible."

"Then will you set yourself to the task of glancing over the margin of every newspaper, piling them away in another room when your scrutiny of each is complete? Do not destroy anything, but we must clear out the library completely. I am interested in the accounts, and will examine them."

It was exasperatingly tedious work, but after several days my assistant reported every margin scanned without result, while I had collected each bill and memorandum, classifying them according to date. I could not get rid of a suspicion that the contrary old beast had written instructions for the finding of the treasure on the back of some account, or on the fly-leaf of a book, and as I looked at the thousands of volumes still left in the library, the prospect of such a patient and minute search appalled me. But I remembered Edison's words to the effect that if a thing exists, search, exhaustive enough, will find it. From the mass of accounts I selected several; the rest I placed in another room, alongside the heap of the earl's newspapers.

"Now," said I to my helper, "if it please you, we will have Higgins in, as I wish some explanation of these accounts."

"Perhaps I can assist you," suggested his lordship, drawing up a chair opposite the table on which I had spread the statements. "I have lived here for six months, and know as much about things as Higgins does. He is so difficult to stop when once he begins to talk. What is the first account you wish further to light upon?"

"To go back thirteen years I find that your uncle bought a second-hand safe in Sheffield. Here is the bill. I consider it necessary to find that safe."

"Pray forgive me, Monsieur Valmont," cried the young man,

springing to his feet and laughing; "so heavy an article as a safe should not slip readily from a man's memory, but it did from mine. The safe is empty, and I gave no more thought to it."

Saying this the earl went to one of the bookcases that stood against the wall, pulled it round as if it were a door, books and all, and displayed the front of an iron safe, the door of which he also drew open, exhibiting the usual empty interior of such a receptacle.

"I came on this," he said, "when I took down all these volumes. It appears that there was once a secret door leading from the library into an outside room, which has long since disappeared; the walls are very thick. My uncle doubtless caused this door to be taken off its hinges, and the safe placed in the aperture, the rest of which he then bricked up."

"Quite so," said I, endeavouring to conceal my disappointment. "As this strong box was bought second-hand and not made to order, I suppose there can be no secret crannies in it?"

"It looks like a common or garden safe," reported my assistant, "but we'll have it out if you say so."

"Not just now," I replied; "we've had enough of dynamiting to make us feel like housebreakers already."

"I agree with you. What's the next item on the programme?"

"Your uncle's mania for buying things at second-hand was broken in three instances so far as I have been able to learn from a scrutiny of these accounts. About four years ago he purchased a new book from Denny and Co., the well-known booksellers of the Strand. Denny and Co. deal only in new books. Is there any comparatively new volume in the library?"

"Not one."

"Are you sure of that?"

"Oh, quite; I searched all the literature in the house. What is the name of the volume he bought?"

"That I cannot decipher. The initial letter looks like 'M,' but the rest is a mere wavy line. I see, however, that it cost twelve-and-sixpence, while the cost of carriage by parcel post was sixpence, which shows it weighed something under four pounds. This, with the price of the book, induces me to think that it was a scientific work, printed on heavy paper and illustrated."

"I know nothing of it," said the earl.

"The third account is for wall paper; twenty-seven rolls of an expensive wall paper, and twenty-seven rolls of a cheap paper, the latter being just half the price of the former. This wall paper seems to have been supplied by a tradesman in the station road in the village of Chizelrigg."

"There's your wall paper," cried the youth, waving his hand; "he was going to paper the whole house, Higgins told me, but got tired after he had finished the library, which took him nearly a year to accomplish, for he worked at it very intermittently, mixing the paste in the boudoir, a pailful at a time as he needed it. It was a scandalous thing to do, for underneath the paper is the most exquisite oak panelling, very plain, but very rich in colour."

I rose and examined the paper on the wall. It was dark brown, and answered the description of the expensive paper on the bill.

"What became of the cheap paper?" I asked.

"I don't know."

"I think," said I, "we are on the track of the mystery. I believe that paper covers a sliding panel or concealed door."

"It is very likely," replied the earl. "I intended to have the paper off, but I had no money to pay a workman, and I am not so industrious as was my uncle. What is your remaining account?"

"The last also pertains to paper, but comes from a firm in Budge Row, London, E.C. He has had, it seems, a thousand sheets of it, and it appears to have been frightfully expensive. This bill is also illegible, but I take it a thousand sheets were supplied, although of course it may have been a thousand quires, which would be a little more reasonable for the price charged, or a thousand reams, which would be exceedingly cheap."

"I don't know anything about that. Let's turn on Higgins."

Higgins knew nothing of this last order of paper either. The wall paper mystery he at once cleared up. Apparently the old earl had discovered by experiment that the heavy, expensive wall paper would not stick to the glossy panelling, so he had purchased a cheaper paper, and had pasted that on first. Higgins said he had gone all over the panelling with a yellowish-white paper, and after that was dry, he pasted over it the more expensive rolls.

"But," I objected, "the two papers were bought and delivered at the same time; therefore, he could not have found by experiment that the heavy paper would not stick."

"I don't think there is much in that," commented the earl; "the heavy paper may have been bought first, and found to be unsuitable, and then the coarse, cheap paper bought afterwards. The bill merely shows that the account was sent in on that date. Indeed, as the village of Chizelrigg is but a few miles away, it would have been quite possible for my uncle to have bought the heavy paper in the morning, tried it, and in the afternoon sent for the commoner lot; but in any case, the bill would not have been presented until months after the order, and the two purchases were thus lumped together."

I was forced to confess that this seemed reasonable.

Now, about the book ordered from Denny's. Did Higgins remember anything regarding it? It came four years ago.

Ah, yes, Higgins did; he remembered it very well indeed. He had come in one morning with the earl's tea, and the old man was sitting up in bed reading this volume with such interest that he was unaware of Higgins's knock, and Higgins himself, being a little hard of hearing, took for granted the command to enter. The earl hastily thrust the book under the pillow, alongside the revolvers, and rated Higgins in a most cruel way for entering the room before getting permission to do so. He had never seen the earl so angry before, and he laid it all to this book. It was after the book had come that the forge had been erected and the anvil bought. Higgins never saw the book again, but one morning, six months before the earl died, Higgins, in raking out the cinders of the forge, found what he supposed was a portion of the book's cover. He believed his master had burnt the volume.

Having dismissed Higgins, I said to the earl:

"The first thing to be done is to enclose this bill to Denny and Co., booksellers, Strand. Tell them you have lost the volume, and ask them to send another. There is likely some one in the shop who can decipher the illegible writing. I am certain the book will give us a clue. Now, I shall write to Braun and Sons, Budge Row. This is evidently a French company; in fact, the name as connected with paper-making runs in my mind, although I cannot at this moment place it. I shall ask them the use of this paper that they furnished to the late earl."

This was done accordingly, and now, as we thought, until the answers came, we were two men out of work. Yet the next morning, I am pleased to say, and I have always rather plumed myself on the fact, I solved the mystery before replies were received from London. Of course, both the book and the answer of the paper agents, by putting two and two together, would have given us the key.

After breakfast, I strolled somewhat aimlessly into the library, whose floor was now strewn merely with brown wrapping paper, bits of string, and all that. As I shuffled among this with my feet, as if tossing aside dead autumn leaves in a forest path, my attention was suddenly drawn to several squares of paper, unwrinkled, and never used for wrapping. These sheets seemed to me strangely familiar. I picked one of them up, and at once the significance of the name Braun and Sons occurred to me. They are paper makers in France, who produce a smooth, very tough sheet, which, dear as it is, proves infinitely cheap compared with the fine vellum it deposed in a certain branch of industry. In Paris, years before, these sheets had given me the knowledge of how a gang of thieves disposed of their gold without melting it. The paper was used instead of vellum in the rougher processes of manufacturing gold leaf. It stood the constant beating of the hammer nearly as well as the vellum, and here at once there flashed on me the secret of the old man's midnight anvil work. He was transforming his sovereigns into gold-leaf, which must have been of a rude, thick kind, because to produce the gold-leaf of commerce he still needed the vellum as well as a "crutch" and other machinery, of which we had found no trace.

"My lord," I called to my assistant; he was at the other end of the room; "I wish to test a theory on the anvil of your own fresh common sense."

"Hammer away," replied the earl, approaching me with his usual good-natured, jocular expression.

"I eliminate the safe from our investigations because it was purchased thirteen years ago, but the buying of the book, of wall covering, of this tough paper from France, all group themselves into a set of incidents occurring within the same month as the purchase of the anvil and the building of the forge; therefore, I think they are related to one another. Here are some sheets of paper he got from Budge Row. Have you ever seen anything like it? Try to tear this sample."

"It's reasonably tough," admitted his lordship, fruitlessly endeavouring to grip it apart.

"Yes. It was made in France, and is used in gold beating. Your uncle beat his sovereigns into gold-leaf. You will find that the book from Denny's is a volume on gold beating, and now as I remember that scribbled word which I could not make out, I think the title of the volume is 'Metallurgy.' It contains, no doubt, a chapter on the manufacture of gold-leaf."

"I believe you," said the earl; "but I don't see that the discovery sets us any further forward. We're now looking for gold-leaf instead of sovereigns."

"Let's examine this wall paper," said I.

I placed my knife under a corner of it at the floor, and quite easily ripped off a large section. As Higgins had said, the brown paper was on top, and the coarse, light-coloured paper underneath. But even that came away from the oak panelling as easily as though it hung there from habit, and not because of paste.

"Feel the weight of that," I cried, handing him the sheet I had torn from the wall.

"By Jove!" said the earl, in a voice almost of awe.

I took it from him, and laid it, face downwards, on the wooden table, threw a little water on the back, and with a knife scraped away the porous white paper. Instantly there gleamed up at us the baleful yellow of the gold. I shrugged my shoulders and spread out my hands. The Earl of Chizelrigg laughed aloud and very heartily.

"You see how it is," I cried. "The old man first covered the entire wall with this whitish paper. He heated his sovereigns at the forge and beat them out on the anvil, then completed the process rudely between the sheets of this paper from France. Probably he pasted the gold to the wall as soon as he shut himself in for the night, and covered it over with the more expensive paper before Higgins entered in the morning."

We found afterwards, however, that he had actually fastened the thick sheets of gold to the wall with carpet tacks.

His lordship netted a trifle over a hundred and twenty-three thousand pounds through my discovery, and I am pleased to pay tribute to the young man's generosity by saying that his voluntary settlement made my bank account swell stout as a City alderman.

O. Henry

A Retrieved Information

"O. Henry" was the pseudonym of William Stanley Porter (1862–1910) and one of the most famous names of American popular literature. He specialized in the short story form – usually with a twist in the tail – and in his large output of more than 600 stories many were concerned with crime and mystery. The author had had some experience in this area, having spent several years in the Ohio State Penitentiary for embezzlement.

"A Retrieved Information" introduces the safecracker Jimmy Valentine, who achieved even greater fame when the story was adapted into a successful play: a small masterpiece of American literature, with a memorable detective – and a twist in the tail.

A GUARD CAME to the prison shoe-shop, where Jimmy Valentine was assiduously stitching uppers, and escorted him to the front office. There the warden handed Jimmy his pardon, which had been signed that morning by the governor. Jimmy took it in a tired kind of way. He had served nearly ten months of a four-year sentence. He had expected to stay only about three months, at the longest. When a man with as many friends on the outside as Jimmy Valentine had is received in the "stir" it is hardly worth while to cut his hair.

"Now, Valentine," said the warden, "you'll go out in the morning. Brace up, and make a man of yourself. You're not a bad fellow at heart. Stop cracking safes, and live straight."

"Me?" said Jimmy, in surprise. "Why, I never cracked a safe in my life."

"Oh, no," laughed the warden. "Of course not. Let's see, now. How was it you happened to get sent up on that Springfield job? Was it because you wouldn't prove an alibi for fear of compromising somebody in extremely high-toned society? Or was it simply a case of a mean old jury that had it in for you? It's always one or the other with you innocent victims."

"Me?" said Jimmy, still blankly virtuous. "Why, warden, I never was in Springfield in my life!"

"Take him back, Cronin," smiled the warden, "and fix him up with outgoing clothes. Unlock him at seven in the morning, and let him come to the bull-pen. Better think over my advice, Valentine."

At a quarter past seven on the next morning Jimmy stood in the warden's outer office. He had on a suit of the villainously fitting, ready-made clothes and a pair of the stiff, squeaky shoes that the state furnishes to its discharged compulsory guests.

The clerk handed him a railroad ticket and the five-dollar bill with which the law expected him to rehabilitate himself into good citizenship and prosperity. The warden gave him a cigar, and shook hands. Valentine, 9762, was chronicled on the books "Pardoned by Governor," and Mr James Valentine walked out into the sunshine.

Disregarding the song of the birds, the waving green trees, and the smell of the flowers, Jimmy headed straight for a restaurant. There he tasted the first sweet joys of liberty in the shape of a broiled chicken and a bottle of white wine – followed by a cigar a grade better than the one the warden had given him. From there he proceeded leisurely to the depot. He tossed a quarter into the hat of a blind man sitting by the door, and boarded his train. Three hours set him down in a little town near the state line. He went to the café of one Mike Dolan and shook hands with Mike, who was alone behind the bar.

"Sorry we couldn't make it sooner, Jimmy, me boy," said Mike. "But we had that protest from Springfield to buck against, and the governor nearly balked. Feeling all right?"

"Fine," said Jimmy. "Got my key?"

He got his key and went upstairs, unlocking the door of a room at the rear. Everything was just as he had left it. There on the floor was still Ben Price's collar-button that had been torn from that eminent detective's shirt-band when they had overpowered Jimmy to arrest him.

Pulling out from the wall a folding-bed, Jimmy slid back a panel in the wall and dragged out a dust-covered suitcase. He opened this and gazed fondly at the finest set of burglar's tools in the East. It was a complete set, made of specially tempered steel, the latest designs in drills, punches, braces and bits, jimmies, clamps, and augers, with two or three novelties invented by Jimmy himself, in which he took pride. Over nine hundred dollars they had cost him to have made at—, a place where they make such things for the profession.

In half an hour Jimmy went downstairs and through the café. He was now dressed in tasteful and well-fitting clothes, and carried his dusted and cleaned suitcase in his hand.

"Got anything on?" asked Mike Dolan, genially.

"Me?" said Jimmy, in a puzzled tone. "I don't understand. I'm representing the New York Amalgamated Short Snap Biscuit Cracker and Frazzled Wheat Company."

This statement delighted Mike to such an extent that Jimmy had to take a seltzer-and-milk on the spot. He never touched "hard" drinks.

A week after the release of Valentine, 9762, there was a neat job of safe-burglary done in Richmond, Indiana, with no clue to the author. A scant eight hundred dollars was all that was secured. Two weeks after that a patented, improved, burglar-proof safe in Logansport was opened like a cheese to the tune of fifteen hundred dollars, currency; securities and silver untouched. That began to interest the rogue-catchers. Then an old-fashioned bank-safe in Jefferson City became active and threw out of its crater an eruption of bank-notes amounting to five thousand dollars. The losses were now high enough to bring the matter up into Ben Price's class of work. By comparing notes, a remarkable similarity in the methods of the burglaries was noticed. Ben Price investigated the scenes of the robberies, and was heard to remark:

"That's Dandy Jim Valentine's autograph. He's resumed business. Look at that combination knob – jerked out as easy as pulling up a radish in wet weather. He's got the only clamps that can do it. And look how clean those tumblers were punched out! Jimmy never has to drill but one hole. Yes, I guess I want Mr Valentine. He'll do his bit next time without any short-time or clemency foolishness."

Ben Price knew Jimmy's habits. He had learned them while working up the Springfield case. Long jumps, quick get-aways, no confederates, and a taste for good society – these ways had helped Mr Valentine to become noted as a successful dodger of retribution. It was given out that Ben Price had taken up the trail of the elusive cracksman, and other people with burglar-proof safes felt more at ease.

One afternoon Jimmy Valentine and his suitcase climbed out of the mail-hack in Elmore, a little town five miles off the railroad down in the black-jack country of Arkansas. Jimmy, looking like an athletic young senior just home from college, went down the board sidewalk toward the hotel.

A young lady crossed the street, passed him at the corner and entered a door over which was the sign "The Elmore Bank." Jimmy

Valentine looked into her eyes, forgot what he was, and became another man. She lowered her eyes and colored slightly. Young men of Jimmy's style and looks were scarce in Elmore.

Jimmy collared a boy that was loafing on the steps of the bank as if he were one of the stock-holders, and began to ask him questions about the town, feeding him dimes at intervals. By and by the young lady came out, looking royally unconscious of the young man with the suitcase, and went her way.

"Isn't that young lady Miss Polly Simpson?" asked Jimmy, with specious guile.

"Naw," said the boy. "She's Annabel Adams. Her pa owns this bank. What'd you come to Elmore for? Is that a gold watch-chain? I'm going to get a bulldog. Got any more dimes?"

Jimmy went to the Planters' Hotel, registered as Ralph D. Spencer, and engaged a room. He leaned on the desk and declared his platform to the clerk. He said he had come to Elmore to look for a location to go into business. How was the shoe business, now, in the town? He had thought of the shoe business. Was there an opening?

The clerk was impressed by the clothes and manner of Jimmy. He, himself, was something of a pattern of fashion to the thinly gilded youth of Elmore, but he now perceived his shortcomings. While trying to figure out Jimmy's manner of tying his four-in-hand he cordially gave information.

Yes, there ought to be a good opening in the shoe line. There wasn't an exclusive shoe-store in the place. The dry-goods and general stores handled them. Business in all lines was fairly good. Hoped Mr Spencer would decide to locate in Elmore. He would find it a pleasant town to live in, and the people very sociable.

Mr Spencer thought he would stop over in the town a few days and look over the situation. No, the clerk needn't call the boy. He would carry up his suitcase, himself; it was rather heavy.

Mr Ralph Spencer, the phoenix that arose from Jimmy Valentine's ashes – ashes left by the flame of a sudden and alternative attack of love – remained in Elmore, and prospered. He opened a shoe-store and secured a good run of trade.

Socially he was also a success, and made many friends. And he accomplished the wish of his heart. He met Miss Annabel Adams, and became more and more captivated by her charms.

At the end of a year the situation of Mr Ralph Spencer was this: he had won the respect of the community, his shoe-store was flourishing, and he and Annabel were engaged to be married in two weeks. Mr Adams, the typical, plodding, country banker, approved

of Spencer. Annabel's pride in him almost equalled her affection. He
was as much at home in the family of Mr Adams and that of Annabel's
married sister as if he were already a member.

One day Jimmy sat down in his room and wrote this letter, which
he mailed to the safe address of one of his old friends in St Louis:

Dear Old Pal,

I want you to be at Sullivan's place, in Little Rock, next
Wednesday night at nine o'clock. I want you to wind up some
little matters for me. And, also, I want to make you a present
of my kit of tools. I know you'll be glad to get them – you
couldn't duplicate the lot for a thousand dollars. Say, Billy,
I've quit the old business – a year ago. I've got a nice store.
I'm making an honest living, and I'm going to marry the finest
girl on earth two weeks from now. It's the only life, Billy – the
straight one. I wouldn't touch a dollar of another man's money
now for a million. After I get married I'm going to sell out and
go West, where there won't be so much danger of having old
scores brought up against me. I tell you, Billy, she's an angel.
She believes in me; and I wouldn't do another crooked thing for
the whole world. Be sure to be at Sully's, for I must see you. I'll
bring along the tools with me.

Your old friend,
Jimmy

On the Monday night after Jimmy wrote this letter, Ben Price
jogged unobtrusively into Elmore in a livery buggy. He lounged
about town in his quiet way until he found out what he wanted to
know. From the drug-store across the street from Spencer's shoe-store
he got a good look at Ralph D. Spencer.

"Going to marry the banker's daughter are you, Jimmy?" said Ben
to himself, softly. "Well, I don't know!"

The next morning Jimmy took breakfast at the Adamses. He was
going to Little Rock that day to order his wedding-suit and buy
something nice for Annabel. That would be the first time he had
left town since he came to Elmore. It had been more than a year now
since those last professional "jobs," and he thought he could safely
venture out.

After breakfast quite a family party went down town together –
Mr Adams, Annabel, Jimmy, and Annabel's married sister with her
two little girls, aged five and nine. They came by the hotel where
Jimmy still boarded, and he ran up to his room and brought along

his suitcase. Then they went on to the bank. There stood Jimmy's horse and buggy and Dolph Gibson, who was going to drive him over to the railroad station.

All went inside the high, carved oak railings into the banking-room – Jimmy included, for Mr Adams's future son-in-law was welcome anywhere. The clerks were pleased to be greeted by the good-looking, agreeable young man who was going to marry Miss Annabel. Jimmy set his suitcase down. Annabel, whose heart was bubbling with happiness and lively youth, put on Jimmy's hat and picked up the suitcase. "Wouldn't I make a nice drummer?" said Annabel. "My! Ralph, how heavy it is. Feels like it was full of gold bricks."

"Lot of nickel-plated shoe-horns in there," said Jimmy, coolly, "that I'm going to return. Thought I'd save express charges by taking them up. I'm getting awfully economical."

The Elmore Bank had just put in a new safe and vault. Mr Adams was very proud of it, and insisted on an inspection by every one. The vault was a small one, but it had a new patented door. It fastened with three solid steel bolts thrown simultaneously with a single handle, and had a time-lock. Mr Adams beamingly explained its workings to Mr Spencer, who showed a courteous but not too intelligent interest. The two children, May and Agatha, were delighted by the shining metal and funny clock and knobs.

While they were thus engaged Ben Price sauntered in and leaned on his elbow, looking casually inside between the railings. He told the teller that he didn't want anything; he was just waiting for a man he knew.

Suddenly there was a scream or two from the women, and a commotion. Unperceived by the elders, May, the nine-year-old girl, in a spirit of play, had shut Agatha in the vault. She had then shot the bolts and turned the knob of the combination as she had seen Mr Adams do.

The old banker sprang to the handle and tugged at it for a moment. "The door can't be opened," he groaned. "The clock hasn't been wound nor the combination set."

Agatha's mother screamed again, hysterically.

"Hush!" said Mr Adams, raising his trembling hand. "All be quiet for a moment, Agatha!" he called as loudly as he could: "Listen to me." During the following silence they could just hear the faint sound of the child wildly shrieking in the dark vault in a panic of terror.

"My precious darling!" wailed the mother. "She will die of fright! Open the door! Oh, break it open! Can't you men do something?"

"There isn't a man nearer than Little Rock who can open that door," said Mr Adams, in a shaky voice. "My God! Spencer, what shall we do? That child – she can't stand it long in there. There isn't enough air, and, besides, she'll go into convulsions from fright."

Agatha's mother, frantic now, beat the door of the vault with her hands. Somebody wildly suggested dynamite. Annabel turned to Jimmy, her large eyes full of anguish, but not yet despairing. To a woman nothing seems quite impossible to the powers of the man she worships.

"Can't you do something, Ralph – *try*, won't you?"

He looked at her with a queer, soft smile on his lips and in his keen eyes.

"Annabel," he said, "give me that rose you are wearing, will you?"

Hardly believing that she heard him aright, she unpinned the bud from the bosom of her dress, and placed it in his hand. Jimmy stuffed it into his vest-pocket, threw off his coat and pulled up his shirt-sleeves. With that act Ralph D. Spencer passed away and Jimmy Valentine took his place.

"Get away from the door, all of you," he commanded, shortly.

He set his suitcase on the table, and opened it out flat. From that time on he seemed to be unconscious of the presence of any one else. He laid out the shining, queer implements swiftly and orderly, whistling softly to himself as he always did when at work. In a deep silence and immovable, the others watched him as if under a spell.

In a minute Jimmy's pet drill was biting smoothly into the steel door. In ten minutes – breaking his own burglarious record – he threw back the bolts and opened the door.

Agatha, almost collapsed, but safe, was gathered into her mother's arms.

Jimmy Valentine put on his coat, and walked outside the railings toward the front door. As he went he thought he heard a far-away voice that he once knew call "Ralph!" But he never hesitated.

At the door a big man stood somewhat in his way.

"Hello, Ben!" said Jimmy, still with his strange smile. "Got around at last, have you? Well, let's go. I don't know that it makes much difference, now."

And then Ben Price acted rather strangely.

"Guess you're mistaken, Mr Spencer," he said. "Don't believe I recognize you. Your buggy's waiting for you, ain't it?"

And Ben Price turned and strolled down the street.

Edgar Wallace

The Four Just Men

An illegitimate child raised amongst the ten other children of a Billingsgate fish porter, Edgar Wallace (1875–1932) escaped from his humble origins by joining the army and serving in South Africa, where he began writing poetry and then journalism, and started to make a name for himself. He wanted fortune as well as fame, and since no publisher would take on the book with which he planned to launch his best-selling career he published it himself, in 1905, with a massive promotion and a prize of £500 for anyone who could solve the puzzle he had set. This was The Four Just Men, *which is still his most famous work as well as being one of his best. Its publication was initially a disaster, however, for several correct solutions were forthcoming and Wallace had to pay for all of them out of his own pocket.*

He went on to produce more mysteries and eventually found the fortune he sought – though he was adept at squandering money as quickly as he made it. His rate of production was phenomenal too, and by the 1920s he was writing dozens of books and plays each year, often working on several simultaneously. Nowadays the name of Edgar Wallace tends to be associated with these hasty thrillers, although there are signs that his better work is gaining the recognition it deserves; his tales of Mr J. G. Reeder have always been well-regarded by mystery aficionados, and he himself felt that his first four books were his best work.

The Four Just Men *was the first, and one of the delights of a collection such as this is that there is room to include the whole of it: something to get one's teeth into, for it remains an exciting thriller and an ingenious locked-room puzzle. No prizes are offered for guessing the solution before the end, however.*

PROLOGUE: THERY'S TRADE

IF YOU LEAVE the Plaza del Mina, go down the narrow street, where, from ten till four, the big flag of the United States Consulate hangs lazily; through the square on which the Hotel de la France fronts, round by the Church of Our Lady, and along the clean, narrow thoroughfare that is the High Street of Cadiz, you will come to the Café of the Nations.

At five o'clock there will be few people in the broad, pillared saloon, and usually the little round tables that obstruct the sidewalk before its doors are untenanted.

In the late summer (in the year of the famine) four men sat about one table and talked business.

Leon Gonsalez was one, Poiccart was another, George Manfred was a notable third, and one, Thery, or Saimont, was the fourth. Of this quartet, only Thery requires no introduction to the student of contemporary history. In the Bureau of Public Affairs you will find his record. As Thery, alias Saimont, he is registered.

You may, if you are inquisitive, and have the necessary permission, inspect his photograph taken in eighteen positions – with his hands across his broad chest, full faced, with a three-days' growth of beard, profile, with – but why enumerate the whole eighteen?

There are also photographs of his ears – and very ugly, bat-shaped ears they are – and a long and comprehensive story of his life.

Signor Paolo Mantegazza, Director of the National Museum of Anthropology, Florence, has done Thery the honour of including him in his admirable work (see chapter on "Intellectual Value of a Face"); hence I say that to all students of criminology and physiognomy, Thery must need no introduction.

He sat at a little table, this man, obviously ill at ease, pinching his fat cheeks, smoothing his shaggy eyebrows, fingering the white scar on his unshaven chin, doing all the things that the lower classes do when they suddenly find themselves placed on terms of equality with their betters.

For although Gonsalez, with the light blue eyes and the restless hands, and Poiccart, heavy, saturnine, and suspicious, and George Manfred, with his grey-shot beard and single eyeglass, were less famous in the criminal world, each was a great man, as you shall learn.

Manfred laid down the *Heraldo di Madrid*, removed his eyeglass, rubbed it with a spotless handkerchief, and laughed quietly.

"These Russians are droll," he commented.

Poiccart frowned and reached for the newspaper. "Who is it – this time?"

"A governor of one of the Southern Provinces."

"Killed?"

Manfred's moustache curled in scornful derision.

"Bah! Who ever killed a man with a bomb! Yes, yes; I know it has been done – but so clumsy, so primitive, so very much like undermining a city wall that it may fall and slay – amongst others – your enemy."

Poiccart was reading the telegram deliberately and without haste, after his fashion.

"The Prince was severely injured and the would-be assassin lost an arm," he read, and pursed his lips disapprovingly. The hands of Gonsalez, never still, opened and shut nervously, which was Leon's sign of perturbation.

"Our friend here" – Manfred jerked his head in the direction of Gonsalez and laughed – "our friend has a conscience and – "

"Only once," interrupted Leon quickly, "and not by my wish you remember, Manfred; you remember, Poiccart" – he did not address Thery – "I advised against it. You remember?" He seemed anxious to exculpate himself from the unspoken charge. "It was a miserable little thing, and I was in Madrid," he went on breathlessly, "and they came to me, some men from a factory at Barcelona. They said what they were going to do, and I was horror-stricken at their ignorance of the elements of the laws of chemistry. I wrote down the ingredients and the proportions, and begged them, yes, almost on my knees, to use some other method. 'My children,' I said, 'you are playing with something that even chemists are afraid to handle. If the owner of the factory is a bad man, by all means exterminate him, shoot him, wait on him after he has dined and is slow and dull, and present a petition with the right hand and – with the left hand – so'"

Leon twisted his knuckles down and struck forward and upward at an imaginary oppressor. "But they would listen to nothing I had to say."

Manfred stirred the glass of creamy liquid that stood at his elbow and nodded his head with an amused twinkle in his grey eyes.

"I remember – several people died, and the principal witness at the trial of the expert in explosives was the man for whom the bomb was intended."

Thery cleared his throat as if to speak, and the three looked at him curiously. There was some resentment in Thery's voice.

"I do not profess to be a great man like you, señors. Half the time I don't understand what you are talking about – you speak of governments and kings and constitutions and causes. If a man does *me* an injury I smash his head" – he hesitated – "I do not know how to say it . . . but I mean . . . well, you kill people without hating them, men who have not hurt you. Now, that is not my way . . ." He hesitated again, tried to collect his thoughts, looked intently at the middle of the roadway, shook his head, and relapsed into silence.

The others looked at him, then at one another, and each man smiled. Manfred took a bulky case from his pocket, extracted an untidy cigarette, re-rolled it deftly and struck a government match on the sole of his boot.

"Your-way-my-dear-Thery" – he puffed – "is a fool's way. You kill for benefit; we kill for justice, which lifts us out of the ruck of professional slayers. When we see an unjust man oppressing his fellows; when we see an evil thing done against the good God" – Thery crossed himself – "and against man – and know that by the laws of man this evildoer may escape punishment – we punish."

"Listen," interrupted the taciturn Poiccart: "once there was a girl, young and beautiful, up there" – he waved his hand northward with unerring instinct – "and a priest – a priest, you understand – and the parents winked at it because it is often done . . . but the girl was filled with loathing and shame, and would not go a second time, so he trapped her and kept her in a house, and then when the bloom was off turned her out, and I found her. She was nothing to me, but I said, 'Here is a wrong that the law cannot adequately right.' So one night I called on the priest with my hat over my eyes and said that I wanted him to come to a dying traveller. He would not have come then, but I told him that the dying man was rich and was a great person. He mounted the horse I had brought, and we rode to a little house on the mountain . . . I locked the door and he turned round – so! Trapped, and he knew it. 'What are you going to do?' he said with a gasping noise. 'I am going to kill you, señor,' I said, and he believed me. I told him the story of the girl . . . He screamed when I moved towards him, but he might as well have saved his breath. 'Let me see a priest,' he begged; and I handed him – a mirror."

Poiccart stopped to sip his coffee.

"They found him on the road next day without a mark to show how he died," he said simply.

"How?" They bent forward eagerly, but Poiccart permitted himself to smile grimly, and made no response.

They bent his brows and looked suspiciously from one to the other.

"If you kill as you say you can, why have you sent for me? I was happy in Jerez working at the wine factory . . . there is a girl there . . . they call her Juan Samarez." He mopped his forehead and looked quickly from one to the other. "When I received your message I thought I should like to kill you – whoever you were –

you understand I am happy . . . and there is the girl – and the old life I have forgotten – ".

Manfred arrested the incoherent protests.

"Listen," said he imperiously; "it is not for you to inquire the wherefore and the why; we know who you are and what you are; we know more of you even than the police know, for we could send you to the garotte."

Poiccart nodded his head in affirmation, and Gonsalez looked at Thery curiously, like the student of human nature that he was.

"We want a fourth man," went on Manfred, "for something we wish to do; we would have wished to have had one animated by no other desire than to see justice done. Failing that, we must have a criminal, a murderer if you like."

Thery opened and shut his mouth as if about to speak.

"One whom we can at a word send to his death if he fails us; you are the man; you will run no risk; you will be well rewarded; you may not be asked to slay. Listen," went on Manfred, seeing that Thery had opened his mouth to speak. "Do you know England? I see that you do not. You know Gibraltar? Well, this is the same people. It is a country up there" – Manfred's expressive hands waved north – "a curious, dull country, with curious, dull people. There is a man, a member of the Government, and there are men whom the Government have never heard of. You remember one Garcia, Manuel Garcia, leader in the Carlist movement; he is in England; it is the only country where he is safe; from England he directs the movement here, the great movement. You know of what I speak?"

Thery nodded.

"This year as well as last there has been a famine, men have been dying about the church doors, starving in the public squares; they have watched corrupt Government succeed corrupt Government; they have seen millions flow from the public treasury into the pockets of politicians. This year something will happen; the old regime must go. The Government know this; they know where the danger lies, they know their salvation can only come if Garcia is delivered into their hands before the organization for revolt is complete. But Garcia is safe for the present and would be safe for all time were it not for a member of the English Government, who is about to introduce and pass into law a Bill. When that is passed, Garcia is as good as dead. You must help us to prevent that from ever becoming law; that is why we have sent for you."

Thery looked bewildered. "But how?" he stammered.

Manfred drew a paper from his pocket and handed it to Thery.

"This, I think," he said, speaking deliberately, "is an exact copy of the police description of yourself." Thery nodded. Manfred leant over and, pointing to a word that occurred half way down the sheet, "Is that your trade?" he asked.

Thery looked puzzled. "Yes," he replied.

"Do you really know anything about that trade?" asked Manfred earnestly; and the other two men leant forward to catch the reply.

"I know," said Thery slowly, "everything there is to be known: had it not been for a – mistake I might have earned great money."

Manfred heaved a sigh of relief and nodded to his two companions.

"Then," said he briskly, "the English Minister is a dead man."

I   A NEWSPAPER STORY

On the fourteenth day of August, 19—, a tiny paragraph appeared at the foot of an unimportant page in London's most sober journal to the effect that the Secretary of State for Foreign Affairs had been much annoyed by the receipt of a number of threatening letters, and was prepared to pay a reward of fifty pounds to any person who would give such information as would lead to the apprehension and conviction of the person or persons, etc. The few people who read London's most sober journal thought, in their ponderous Athenæum Club way, that it was a remarkable thing that a Minister of State should be annoyed at anything; more remarkable that he should advertise his annoyance, and most remarkable of all that he could imagine for one minute that the offer of a reward would put a stop to the annoyance.

News editors of less sober but larger circulated newspapers, wearily scanning the dull columns of *Old Sobriety*, read the paragraph with a newly acquired interest.

"Hullo, what's this?" asked Smiles of the *Comet*, and cut out the paragraph with huge shears, pasted it upon a sheet of copy-paper and headed it:

Who is Sir Philip's Correspondent?

As an afterthought – the *Comet* being in Opposition – he prefixed an introductory paragraph, humorously suggesting that the letters were from an intelligent electorate grown tired of the shilly-shallying methods of the Government.

The news editor of the *Evening World* – a white-haired gentleman of deliberate movement – read the paragraph twice, cut it out carefully, read it again and, placing it under a paperweight, very soon forgot all about it.

The news editor of the *Megaphone*, which is a very bright newspaper indeed, cut the paragraph as he read it, rang a bell, called a reporter, all in a breath, so to speak, and issued a few terse instructions.

"Go down to Portland Place, try to see Sir Philip Ramon, secure the story of that paragraph – why he is threatened, what he is threatened with; get a copy of one of the letters if you can. If you cannot see Ramon, get hold of a secretary."

And the obedient reporter went forth.

He returned in an hour in that state of mysterious agitation peculiar to the reporter who has got a "beat". The news editor duly reported to the Editor-in-Chief, and that great man said, "That's very good, that's very good indeed" – which was praise of the highest order.

What was "very good indeed" about the reporter's story may be gathered from the half-column that appeared in the *Megaphone* on the following day:

CABINET MINISTER IN DANGER
THREATS TO MURDER THE FOREIGN SECRETARY
'THE FOUR JUST MEN'
PLOT TO ARREST THE PASSAGE OF THE
ALIENS EXTRADITION BILL
EXTRAORDINARY REVELATIONS

Considerable comment was excited by the appearance in the news columns of yesterday's *National Journal* of the following paragraph:

The Secretary of State for Foreign Affairs (Sir Philip Ramon) has during the past few weeks been the recipient of threatening letters, all apparently emanating from one source and written by one person. These letters are of such a character that they cannot be ignored by his Majesty's Secretary of State for Foreign Affairs, who hereby offers a reward of Fifty pounds (£50) to any person or persons, other than the actual writer, who will lay such information as will lead to the apprehension and conviction of the author of these anonymous letters.

So unusual was such an announcement, remembering that anonymous and threatening letters are usually to be found daily in the letter-bags of every statesman and diplomat, that the *Daily Megaphone* immediately instituted inquiries as to the cause for this unusual departure.

A representative of this newspaper called at the residence of Sir Philip Ramon, who very courteously consented to be seen.

"It is quite an unusual step to take," said the great Foreign Secretary, in answer to our representative's question, "but it has been taken with the full concurrence of my colleagues of the Cabinet. We have reasons to believe there is something behind the threats, and I might say that the matter has been in the hands of the police for some weeks past.

"Here is one of the letters," and Sir Philip produced a sheet of foreign notepaper from a portfolio, and was good enough to allow our representative to make a copy.

It was undated, and beyond the fact that the handwriting was of the flourishing effeminate variety that is characteristic of the Latin races, it was written in good English.

It ran :

Your Excellency,

The Bill that you are about to pass into law is an unjust one . . . It is calculated to hand over to a corrupt and vengeful Government men who now in England find an asylum from the persecutions of despots and tyrants. We know that in England opinion is divided upon the merits of your Bill, and that upon your strength, and your strength alone, depends the passing into law of the Aliens Political Offences Bill.

Therefore it grieves us to warn you that unless your Government withdraws this Bill, it will be necessary to remove you, and not alone you, but any other person who undertakes to carry into law this unjust measure.

(Signed) FOUR JUST MEN.

"The Bill referred to," Sir Philip resumed, "is of course the Aliens Extradition (Political Offences) Bill, which, had it not been for the tactics of the Opposition, might have passed quietly into law last session."

Sir Philip went on to explain that the Bill was called into being by the insecurity of the succession in Spain.

"It is imperative that neither England nor any other country should harbour propagandists who, from the security of these, or other shores, should set Europe ablaze. Coincident with the passage of this measure similar Acts or proclamations have been made in every country in Europe. In fact, they are all in existence, having been arranged to come into law simultaneously with ours, last session."

"Why do you attach importance to these letters?" asked the *Daily Megaphone* representative.

"Because we are assured, both by our own police and the continental police, that the writers are men who are in deadly earnest. The 'FOUR JUST MEN', as they sign themselves, are known collectively in almost every country under the sun. Who they are individually we should all very much like to know. Rightly or wrongly, they consider that justice as meted out here on earth is inadequate, and have set themselves about correcting the law. They were the people who assassinated General Trelovitch, the leader of the Servian Regicides: they hanged the French Army Contractor, Conrad, in the Place de la Concorde – with a hundred policemen within call. They shot Hermon le Blois, the poet-philosopher, in his study for corrupting the youth of the world with his reasoning."

The Foreign Secretary then handed to our representative a list of the crimes committed by this extraordinary quartet.

Our readers will recollect the circumstance of each murder, and it will be remembered that until today – so closely have the police of the various nationalities kept the secret of the Four Men – no one crime has been connected with the other; and certainly none of the circumstances which, had they been published, would have assuredly revealed the existence of this band, have been given to the public before today.

The *Daily Megaphone* is able to publish a full list of sixteen murders committed by the four men.

"Two years ago, after the shooting of le Blois, by some hitch in their almost perfect arrangements, one of the four was recognized by a detective as having been seen leaving le Blois's house on the Avenue Kléber, and he was shadowed for three days, in the hope that the four might be captured together. In the end he discovered he was being watched, and made a bolt for liberty. He was driven to bay in a café in Bordeaux – they had followed him from Paris: and before he was killed he shot a sergeant de ville and two other policemen. He was photographed, and the print was circulated throughout Europe, but who he was or what he was, even what nationality he was, is a mystery to this day."

"But the four are still in existence?"

Sir Philip shrugged his shoulders. "They have either recruited another, or they are working shorthanded," he said.

In conclusion the Foreign Secretary said:

"I am making this public through the Press, in order that the danger which threatens, not necessarily myself, but any public man who runs counter to the wishes of this sinister force, should be recognized. My second reason is that the public may in its knowledge assist those responsible for the maintenance of law and order in the execution of their office, and by their vigilance prevent the committal of further unlawful acts."

Inquiries subsequently made at Scotland Yard elicited no further information on the subject beyond the fact that the Criminal Investigation Department was in communication with the chiefs of the continental police.

The following is a complete list of the murders committed by the Four Just Men, together with such particulars as the police have been able to secure regarding the cause for the crimes. We are indebted to the Foreign Office for permission to reproduce the list.

London, October 7, 1899. – Thomas Cutler, master tailor, found dead under suspicious circumstances. Coroner's jury returned a verdict of "Wilful murder against some person or persons unknown."

(Cause of murder ascertained by police: Cutler, who was a man of some substance, and whose real name was Bentvitch, was a sweater of a particularly offensive type. Three convictions under the Factory Act. Believed by the police there was a further and more intimate cause for the murder not unconnected with Cutler's treatment of women employees.)

Liege, February 28, 1900. – Jacques Ellerman, prefect: shot dead returning from the Opera House. Ellerman was a notorious evil liver, and upon investigating his affairs after his death it was found that he had embezzled nearly a quarter of a million francs of the public funds.

Seattle (Kentucky), October, 1900. – Judge Anderson. Found dead in his room, strangled. Anderson had thrice been tried for his life on charges of murder. He was the leader of the Anderson faction in the Anderson-Hara feud. Had killed in all seven of the Hara clan, was three times indicted and three times released on a verdict of Not Guilty. It will be remembered that on the last occasion, when charged with the treacherous murder of the Editor of the *Seattle Star*, he shook hands with the packed jury and congratulated them.

New York, October 30, 1900. – Patrick Welch, a notorious grafter and stealer of public moneys. Sometime City Treasurer;

moving spirit in the infamous Street Paving Syndicate; exposed by the *New York Journal*. Welch was found hanging in a little wood on Long Island. Believed at the time to have been suicide.

Paris, March 4, 1901. – Madame Despard. Asphyxiated. This also was regarded as suicide till certain information came to hands of French police. Of Madame Despard nothing good can be said. She was a notorious "dealer in souls".

Paris, March 4, 1902 (exactly a year later). – Monsieur Gabriel Lanfin, Minister of Communication. Found shot in his brougham in the Bois de Boulogne. His coachman was arrested but eventually discharged. The man swore he heard no shot or cry from his master. It was raining at the time, and there were few pedestrians in the Bois.

(Here followed ten other cases, all on a par with those quoted above, including the cases of Trelovitch and le Blois.)

It was undoubtedly a great story.

The Editor-in-Chief, seated in his office, read it over again and said, "Very good indeed."

The reporter – whose name was Smith – read it over and grew pleasantly warm at the consequences of his achievement.

The Foreign Secretary read it in bed as he sipped his morning tea, and frowningly wondered if he had said too much.

The chief of the French police read it – translated and telegraphed – in *Le Temps*, and furiously cursed the talkative Englishman who was upsetting his plans.

In Madrid, at the Café de la Paix, in the Place of the Sun, Manfred, cynical, smiling, and sarcastic, read extracts to three men – two pleasantly amused, the other heavy-jowled and pasty of face, with the fear of death in his eyes.

II THE FAITHFUL COMMONS

Somebody – was it Mr Gladstone? – placed it on record that there is nothing quite so dangerous, quite so ferocious, quite so terrifying as a mad sheep. Similarly, as we know, there is no person quite so indiscreet, quite so foolishly talkative, quite so amazingly gauche, as the diplomat who for some reason or other has run off the rails.

There comes a moment to the man who has trained himself to

guard his tongue in the Councils of Nations, who has been schooled to walk warily amongst pitfalls digged cunningly by friendly Powers, when the practice and precept of many years are forgotten, and he behaves humanly. Why this should be has never been discovered by ordinary people, although the psychological minority who can generally explain the mental processes of their fellows, have doubtless very adequate and convincing reasons for these acts of disbalancement.

Sir Philip Ramon was a man of peculiar temperament. I doubt whether anything in the wide world would have arrested his purpose once his mind had been made up. He was a man of strong character, a firm, square-jawed, big-mouthed man, with that shade of blue in his eyes that one looks for in peculiarly heartless criminals, and particularly famous generals. And yet Sir Philip Ramon feared, as few men imagined he feared, the consequence of the task he had set himself.

There are thousands of men who are physically heroes and morally poltroons, men who would laugh at death – and live in terror of personal embarrassments. Coroner's courts listen daily to the tale of such men's lives – and deaths.

The Foreign Secretary reversed these qualities. Good animal men would unhesitatingly describe the Minister as a coward, for he feared pain and he feared death.

"If this thing is worrying you so much," the Premier said kindly – it was at the Cabinet Council two days following the publication of the *Megaphone*'s story – "why don't you drop the Bill? After all, there are matters of greater importance to occupy the time of the House, and we are getting near the end of the session."

An approving murmur went round the table.

"We have every excuse for dropping it. There must be a horrible slaughtering of the innocents – Braithewaite's Unemployed Bill must go; and what the country will say to that, Heaven only knows."

"No, no!" The Foreign Secretary brought his fist down on the table with a crash. "It shall go through; of that I am determined. We are breaking faith with the Cortes, we are breaking faith with France, we are breaking faith with every country in the Union. I have promised the passage of this measure – and we must go through with it, even though there are a thousand 'Just Men', and a thousand threats."

The Premier shrugged his shoulders.

"Forgive me for saying so, Ramon," said Bolton, the Solicitor, "but I can't help feeling you were rather indiscreet to give particulars to the Press as you did. Yes, I know we were agreed that you should have a free hand to deal with the matter as you wished, but somehow I did not think you would have been quite so – what shall I say? – candid."

"My discretion in the matter, Sir George, is not a subject that I care to discuss," replied Ramon stiffly.

Later, as he walked across Palace Yard with the youthful-looking Chancellor, Mr Solicitor-General, smarting under the rebuff, said, *à propos* of nothing, "Silly old ass." And the youthful guardian of Britain's finances smiled.

"If the truth be told," he said, "Ramon is in a most awful funk. The story of the Four Just Men is in all the clubs, and a man I met at the Carlton at lunch has rather convinced me that there is really something to be feared. He was quite serious about it – he's just returned from South America and has seen some of the work done by these men."

"What was that?"

"A president or something of one of these rotten little republics . . . about eight months ago – you'll see it in the list . . . They hanged him . . . most extraordinary thing in the world. They took him out of bed in the middle of the night, gagged him, blindfolded him, carried him to the public jail, gained admission, and hanged him on the public gallows – and escaped!"

Mr Solicitor saw the difficulties of such proceedings, and was about to ask for further information when an under-secretary buttonholed the Chancellor and bore him off. "Absurd," muttered Mr Solicitor crossly.

There were cheers for the Secretary for Foreign Affairs as his brougham swept through the crowd that lined the approaches to the House. He was in no wise exalted, for popularity was not a possession he craved. He knew instinctively that the cheers were called forth by the public's appreciation of his peril; and the knowledge chilled and irritated him. He would have liked to think that the people scoffed at the existence of this mysterious four – it would have given him some peace of mind had he been able to think 'the people have rejected the idea'.

For although popularity or unpopularity was outside his scheme of essentials, yet he had an unswerving faith in the brute instincts of the mob. He was surrounded in the lobby of the House with a crowd of eager men of his party, some quizzical, some anxious, all clamouring for the latest information – all slightly in fear of the acid-tongued Minister.

"Look here, Sir Philip" – it was the stout, tactless member for West Brondesbury – "what is all this we hear about threatenin' letters?

Surely you're not goin' to take notice of things of that sort – why, I get two or three every day of my life."

The Minister strode impatiently away from the group, but Tester – the member – caught his arm.

"Look here – " he began.

"Go to the devil," said the Foreign Secretary plainly, and walked quickly to his room.

"Beastly temper that man's got, to be sure," said the honourable member despairingly. "Fact is, old Ramon's in a blue funk. The idea of making a song about threatenin' letters! Why, I get – "

A group of men in the members' smokeroom discussed the question of the Just Four in a perfectly unoriginal way.

"It's too ridiculous for words," said one oracularly. "Here are four men, a mythical four, arrayed against all the forces and established agencies of the most civilized nation on earth."

"Except Germany," interrupted Scott, MP, wisely.

"Oh, leave Germany out of it for goodness' sake," begged the first speaker tartly. "I do wish, Scott, we could discuss a subject in which the superiority of German institutions could not be introduced."

"Impossible," said the cheerful Scott, flinging loose the reins of his hobby horse: "remember that in steel and iron alone the production per head of the employee has increased 43 per cent, that her shipping – "

"Do you think Ramon will withdraw the bill?" asked the senior member for Aldgate East, disentangling his attention from the babble of statistics.

"Ramon? Not he – he'd sooner die."

"It's a most unusual circumstance," said Aldgate East; and three boroughs, a London suburb, and a midland town nodded and "thought it was".

"In the old days, when old Bascoe was a young member" – Aldgate East indicated an aged senator bent and white of beard and hair, who was walking painfully toward a seat – "in the old days – "

"Thought old Bascoe had paired?" remarked an irrelevant listener.

"In the old days," continued the member for the East End, "before the Fenian trouble – "

"– talk of civilization," went on the enthusiastic Scott. "Rheinbaken said last month in the Lower House, 'Germany had reached that point where –'"

"If I were Ramon," resumed Aldgate East profoundly, "I know

exactly what I should do. I should go to the police and say 'Look here –'"

A bell rang furiously and continuously, and the members went scampering along the corridor. "Division – 'vision."

Clause Nine of the Medway Improvement Bill having been satisfactorily settled and the words "Or as may hereafter be determined" added by a triumphant majority of twenty-four, the faithful Commons returned to the interrupted discussion.

"What I say, and what I've always said about a man in the Cabinet," maintained an important individual, "is that he must, if he is a true statesman, drop all consideration for his own personal feelings."

"Hear!" applauded somebody.

"His own personal feelings," repeated the orator. "He must put his duty to the state before all other – er – considerations. You remember what I said to Barrington the other night when we were talking out the Estimates? I said, 'The right honourable gentleman has not, cannot have, allowed for the strong and almost unanimous desires of the great body of the electorate. The action of a Minister of the Crown must primarily be governed by the intelligent judgement of the great body of the electorate, whose fine feelings' – no – 'whose higher instincts' – no – that wasn't it – at any rate I made it very clear what the duty of a Minister was," concluded the oracle lamely.

"Now I –" commenced Aldgate East, when an attendant approached with a tray on which lay a greenish-grey envelope.

"Has any gentleman dropped this?" he inquired, and, picking up the letter, the member fumbled for his eyeglasses.

"To the Members of the House of Commons," he read, and looked over his pince-nez at the circle of men about him.

"Company prospectus," said the stout member for West Brondesbury, who had joined the party; "I get hundreds. Only the other day – "

"Too thin for a prospectus," said Aldgate East, weighing the letter in his hand.

"Patent medicine, then," persisted the light of Brondesbury. "I get one every morning – 'Don't burn the candle at both ends', and all that sort of rot. Last week a feller sent me – "

"Open it," someone suggested, and the member obeyed. He read a few lines and turned red.

"Well, I'm damned!" he gasped, and read aloud:

CITIZENS,

The Government is about to pass into law a measure which will place in the hands of the most evil Government of modern times men who are patriots and who are destined to be the saviours of their countries. We have informed the Minister in charge of this measure, the title of which appears in the margin, that unless he withdraws this Bill we will surely slay him.

We are loath to take this extreme step, knowing that otherwise he is an honest and brave gentleman, and it is with a desire to avoid fulfilling our promise that we ask the members of the Mother of Parliaments to use their every influence to force the withdrawal of this Bill.

Were we common murderers or clumsy anarchists we could with ease wreak a blind and indiscriminate vengeance on the members of this assembly, and in proof thereof, and as an earnest that our threat is no idle one, we beg you to search beneath the table near the recess in this room. There you will find a machine sufficiently charged to destroy the greater portion of this building.

(*Signed*) FOUR JUST MEN

Postscript. – We have not placed either detonator or fuse in the machine, which may therefore be handled with impunity.

As the reading of the letter proceeded the faces of the listeners grew pallid.

There was something very convincing about the tone of the letter, and instinctively all eyes sought the table near the recess.

Yes, there was something, a square black something, and the crowd of legislators shrank back. For a moment they stood spellbound – and then there was a mad rush for the door.

"Was it a hoax?" asked the Prime Minister anxiously, but the hastily summoned expert from Scotland Yard shook his head.

"Just as the letter described it," he said gravely, "even to the absence of fuses."

"Was it really – "

"Enough to wreck the House, sir," was the reply.

The Premier, with a troubled face, paced the floor of his private room.

He stopped once to look moodily through the window that gave a view of a crowded terrace and a mass of excited politicians gesticulating and evidently all speaking at once.

"Very, very serious – very, very serious," he muttered. Then aloud, "We said so much we might as well continue. Give the newspapers as full an account of this afternoon's happenings as they think necessary

– give them the text of the letter." He pushed a button and his Secretary entered noiselessly.

"Write to the Commissioner telling him to offer a reward of a thousand pounds for the arrest of the man who left this thing and a free pardon and the reward to any accomplice."

The Secretary withdrew and the Scotland Yard expert waited.

"Have your people found how the machine was introduced?"

"No, sir; the police have all been relieved and been subjected to separate interrogation. They remember seeing no stranger either entering or leaving the House."

The Premier pursed his lips in thought.

"Thank you," he said simply, and the expert withdrew.

On the terrace Aldgate East and the oratorical member divided honours.

"I must have been standing quite close to it," said the latter impressively; "'pon my word it makes me go cold all over to think about it. You remember, Mellin? I was saying about the duty of the Ministry – "

"I asked the waiter," said the member for Aldgate to an interested circle, "when he brought the letter: 'Where did you find it?' 'On the floor, sir!' he said. 'I thought it was a medicine advertisement; I wasn't going to open it, only somebody – "

"It was me," claimed the stout gentleman from Brondesbury proudly; "you remember I was saying – "

"I knew it was somebody," continued Aldgate East graciously. "I opened it and read the first few lines. 'Bless my soul,' I said – "

"You said, 'Well, I'm damned,'" corrected Brondesbury.

"Well, I know it was something very much to the point," admitted Aldgate East. "I read it – and, you'll quite understand, I couldn't grasp its significance, so to speak. Well – "

The three stalls reserved at the Star Music Hall in Oxford Street were occupied one by one. At half past seven prompt came Manfred, dressed quietly; at eight came Poiccart, a fairly prosperous middle-aged gentleman; at half past eight came Gonsalez, asking in perfect English for a programme. He seated himself between the two others.

When pit and gallery were roaring themselves hoarse over a patriotic song, Manfred smilingly turned to Leon, and said:

"I saw it in the evening papers."

Leon nodded quickly.

"There was nearly trouble," he said quietly. "As I went in

somebody said, 'I thought Bascoe had paired,' and one of them almost came up to me and spoke."

III   ONE THOUSAND POUNDS REWARD

To say that England was stirred to its depths – to quote more than one leading article on the subject – by the extraordinary occurrence in the House of Commons, would be stating the matter exactly.

The first intimation of the existence of the Four Just Men had been received with pardonable derision, particularly by those newspapers that were behindhand with the first news.

Only the *Daily Megaphone* had truly and earnestly recognized how real was the danger which threatened the Minister in charge of the obnoxious Act. Now, however, even the most scornful could not ignore the significance of the communication that had so mysteriously found its way into the very heart of Britain's most jealously guarded institution. The story of the Bomb Outrage filled the pages of every newspaper throughout the country, and the latest daring venture of the Four was placarded the length and breadth of the Isles.

Stories, mostly apocryphal, of the men who were responsible for the newest sensation made their appearance from day to day, and there was no other topic in the mouths of men wherever they met but the strange quartet – who seemed to hold the lives of the mighty in the hollows of their hands.

Never since the days of the Fenian outrages had the mind of the public been so filled with apprehension as it was during the two days following the appearance in the Commons of the "blank bomb", as one journal felicitously described it.

Perhaps in exactly the same kind of apprehension, since there was a general belief, which grew out of the trend of the letters, that the Four menaced none other than one man.

The first intimation of their intentions had excited widespread interest. But the fact that the threat had been launched from a small French town, and that in consequence the danger was very remote, had somehow robbed the threat of some of its force. Such was the vague reasoning of an ungeographical people that did not realize that Dax is no farther from London than Aberdeen.

But here was the Hidden Terror in the Metropolis itself. Why, argued London, with suspicious sidelong glances, every man we rub elbows with may be one of the Four, and we none the wiser.

Heavy, black-looking posters stared down from blank walls, and filled the breadth of every police noticeboard.

£1000 REWARD

Whereas, on August 18, at about 4.30 o'clock in the afternoon, an infernal machine was deposited in the Members' Smoke-Room by some person or persons unknown.

AND WHEREAS there is reason to believe that the person or persons implicated in the disposal of the aforesaid machine are members of an organized body of criminals known as The Four Just Men, against whom warrants have been issued on charges of wilful murder in London, Paris, New York, New Orleans, Seattle (USA), Barcelona, Tomsk, Belgrade, Christiania, Capetown and Caracas.

Now, THEREFORE, the above reward will be paid by his Majesty's Government to any person or persons who shall lay such information as shall lead to the apprehension of any of or the whole of the persons styling themselves The Four Just Men and identical with the band before mentioned.

AND, FURTHERMORE, a free pardon and the reward will be paid to any member of the band for such information, providing the person laying such information has neither committed nor has been an accessory before or after the act of any of the following murders.

(*Signed*) RYDAY MONTGOMERY,

His Majesty's Secretary of State for Home Affairs.

J. B. CALFORT, Commissioner of Police.

[Here followed a list of the sixteen crimes alleged against the four men.]

GOD SAVE THE KING

All day long little knots of people gathered before the broadsheets, digesting the magnificent offer.

It was an unusual hue and cry, differing from those with which Londoners were best acquainted. For there was no appended description of the men wanted; no portraits by which they might be identified, no stereotyped "when last seen was wearing a dark blue serge suit, cloth cap, check tie", on which the searcher might base his scrutiny of the passer-by.

It was a search for four men whom no person had ever consciously seen, a hunt for a will-o'-the-wisp, a groping in the dark after indefinite shadows.

Detective Superintendent Falmouth, who was a very plain-spoken man (he once brusquely explained to a Royal Personage that he hadn't got eyes in the back of his head), told the Assistant Commissioner exactly what he thought about it.

"You can't catch men when you haven't got the slightest idea who or what you're looking for. For the sake of argument, they might be women for all we know – they might be chinamen or niggers; they might be tall or short; they might – why, we don't even know their nationality! They've committed crimes in almost every country in the world. They're not French because they killed a man in Paris, or Yankee because they strangled Judge Anderson."

"The writing," said the Commissioner, referring to a bunch of letters he held in his hand.

"Latin; but that may be a fake. And suppose it isn't? There's no difference between the handwriting of a Frenchman, Spaniard, Portuguese, Italian, South American, or Creole – and, as I say, it might be a fake, and probably is."

"What have you done?" asked the Commissioner.

"We've pulled in all the suspicious characters we know. We've cleaned out Little Italy, combed Bloomsbury, been through Soho, and searched all the colonies. We raided a place at Nunhead last night – a lot of Armenians live down there, but – "

The detective's face bore a hopeless look.

"As likely as not," he went on, "we should find them at one of the swagger hotels – that's if they were fools enough to bunch together; but you may be sure they're living apart, and meeting at some unlikely spot once or twice a day."

He paused, and tapped his fingers absently on the big desk at which he and his superior sat.

"We've had de Courville over," he resumed. "He saw the Soho crowd, and what is more important, saw his own man who lives amongst them – and it's none of them, I'll swear – or at least he swears, and I'm prepared to accept his word."

The Commissioner shook his head pathetically.

"They're in an awful stew in Downing Street," he said. "They do not know exactly what is going to happen next."

Mr Falmouth rose to his feet with a sigh and fingered the brim of his hat.

"Nice time ahead of us – I don't think," he remarked paradoxically.

"What are the people thinking about it?" asked the Commissioner.

"You've seen the papers?"

Mr Commissioner's shrug was uncomplimentary to British journalism.

"The papers! Who in Heaven's name is going to take the slightest notice of what is in the papers!" he said petulantly.

"I am, for one," replied the calm detective; "newspapers are more often than not led by the public; and it seems to me the idea of running a newspaper in a nutshell is to write so that the public will say, 'That's smart – it's what I've said all along.'"

"But the public themselves – have you had an opportunity of gathering their idea?"

Superintendent Falmouth nodded.

"I was talking in the Park to a man only this evening – a master-man by the look of him, and presumably intelligent. 'What's your idea of this Four Just Men business?' I asked. 'It's very queer,' he said: 'do you think there's anything in it?' – and that," concluded the disgusted police officer, "is all the public thinks about it."

But if there was sorrow at Scotland Yard, Fleet Street itself was all a-twitter with pleasurable excitement. Here was great news indeed: news that might be heralded across double columns, blared forth in headlines, shouted by placards, illustrated, diagramized, and illuminated by statistics.

"Is it the Mafia?" asked the *Comet* noisily, and went on to prove that it was.

The *Evening World*, with its editorial mind lingering lovingly in the 'sixties, mildly suggested a vendetta, and instanced "The Corsican Brothers".

The *Megaphone* stuck to the story of the Four Just Men, and printed pages of details concerning their nefarious acts. It disinterred from dusty files, continental and American, the full circumstances of each murder; it gave the portraits and careers of the men who were slain, and, whilst in no way palliating the offence of the Four, yet set forth justly and dispassionately the lives of the victims, showing the sort of men they were.

It accepted warily the reams of contributions that flowed into the office; for a newspaper that has received the stigma "yellow" exercises more caution than its more sober competitors. In newspaper-land a dull lie is seldom detected, but an interesting exaggeration drives an unimaginative rival to hysterical denunciations.

And reams of Four Men anecdotes did flow in. For suddenly, as if by magic, every outside contributor, every literary gentleman who made a speciality of personal notes, every kind of man who wrote, discovered that he had known the Four intimately all his life.

"When I was in Italy . . ." wrote the author of *Come Again* (Hackworth Press, 6s.: "slightly soiled", Farringdon Book Mart, 2d.) "I remember I heard a curious story about these Men of Blood . . ."

Or –

"No spot in London is more likely to prove the hiding-place of the Four Villains than Tidal Basin," wrote another gentleman, who stuck *Collins* in the north-east corner of his manuscript. "Tidal Basin in the reign of Charles II was known as . . ."

"Who's Collins?" asked the super-chief of the *Megaphone* of his hard-worked editor.

"A liner," described the editor wearily, thereby revealing that even the newer journalism had not driven the promiscuous contributor from his hard-fought field; "he does police-courts, fires, inquests, and things. Lately he's taken to literature and writes Picturesque-Bits-of-Old-London and Famous Tombstones-of-Hornsey epics . . ."

Throughout the offices of the newspapers the same thing was happening. Every cable that arrived, every piece of information that reached the sub-editor's basket was coloured with the impending tragedy uppermost in men's minds. Even the police-court reports contained some allusion to the Four. It was the overnight drunk and disorderly's justification for his indiscretion.

"The lad has always been honest," said the peccant errand boy's tearful mother; "it's reading these horrible stories about the Four Foreigners that's made him turn out like this"; and the magistrate took a lenient view of the offence.

To all outward showing, Sir Philip Ramon, the man mostly interested in the development of the plot, was the least concerned.

He refused to be interviewed any further; he declined to discuss the possibilities of assassination, even with the Premier, and his answer to letters of appreciation that came to him from all parts of the country was an announcement in the *Morning Post* asking his correspondents to be good enough to refrain from persecuting him with picture postcards, which found no other repository than his wastepaper basket.

He had thought of adding an announcement of his intention of carrying the Bill through Parliament at whatever cost, and was only deterred by the fear of theatricality.

To Falmouth, upon whom had naturally devolved the duty of protecting the Foreign Secretary from harm, Sir Philip was unusually gracious, and incidentally permitted that astute officer to get a glimpse of the terror in which a threatened man lives.

"Do you think there's any danger, Superintendent?" he asked, not once but a score of times; and the officer, stout defender of an infallible police force, was very reassuring.

"For," as he argued to himself, "what is the use of frightening a man who is half scared of death already? If nothing happens, he will see I have spoken the truth, and if – if – well, he won't be able to call me a liar."

Sir Philip was a constant source of interest to the detective, who must have shown his thoughts once or twice. For the Foreign Secretary, who was a remarkably shrewd man, intercepting a curious glance of the police officer, said sharply, "You wonder why I still go on with the Bill knowing the danger? Well, it will surprise you to learn that I do *not* know the danger, nor can I imagine it! I have never been conscious of physical pain in my life, and in spite of the fact that I have a weak heart, I have never had so much as a single ache. What death will be, what pangs or peace it may bring, I have no conception. I argue with Epictetus that the fear of death is by way of being an impertinent assumption of a knowledge of the hereafter, and that we have no reason to believe it is any worse condition than our present. I am not afraid to die – but I am afraid of dying."

"Quite so, sir," murmured the sympathetic but wholly uncomprehending detective, who had no mind for nice distinctions.

"But," resumed the Minister – he was sitting in his study in Portland Place – "if I cannot imagine the exact process of dissolution, I can imagine and have experienced the result of breaking faith with the chancellories, and I have certainly no intention of laying up a store of future embarrassments for fear of something that may after all be comparatively trifling."

Which piece of reasoning will be sufficient to indicate what the Opposition of the hour was pleased to term "the tortuous mind of the right honourable gentleman".

And Superintendent Falmouth, listening with every indication of attention, yawned inwardly and wondered who Epictetus was.

"I have taken all possible precautions, sir," said the detective in the pause that followed the recital of this creed. "I hope you won't mind for a week or two being followed about by some of my men. I want you to allow two or three officers to remain in the house whilst you are here, and of course there will be quite a number on duty at the Foreign Office."

Sir Philip expressed his approval, and later, when he and the detective drove down to the House in a closed brougham, he understood why cyclists rode before and on either side of the carriage, and why two cabs followed the brougham into Palace Yard.

At Notice Time, with a House sparsely filled, Sir Philip rose in his place and gave notice that he would move the second reading of the Aliens Extradition (Political Offences) Bill, on Tuesday week, or, to be exact, in ten days.

That evening Manfred met Gonsalez in North Tower Gardens and remarked on the fairy-like splendour of the Crystal Palace grounds by night.

A Guards' band was playing the overture to *Tannhäuser*, and the men talked music.

Then –

"What of Thery?" asked Manfred.

"Poiccart has him today; he is showing him the sights." They both laughed.

"And you?" asked Gonsalez.

"I have had an interesting day; I met that delightfully naïve detective in Green Park, who asked me what I thought of ourselves!"

Gonsalez commented on the movement in G minor, and Manfred nodded his head, keeping time with the music.

"Are we prepared?" asked Leon quietly.

Manfred still nodded and softly whistled the number. He stopped with the final crash of the band, and joined in the applause that greeted the musicians.

"I have taken a place," he said, clapping his hands. "We had better come together."

"Is everything there?"

Manfred looked at his companion with a twinkle in his eye.

"Almost everything."

The band broke into the National Anthem, and the two men rose and uncovered.

The throng about the bandstand melted away in the gloom, and Manfred and his companion turned to go.

Thousands of fairy lamps gleamed in the grounds, and there was a strong smell of gas in the air.

"Not that way this time?" questioned, rather than asserted, Gonsalez.

"Most certainly not that way," replied Manfred decidedly.

IV PREPARATIONS

When an advertisement appeared in the *Newspaper Proprietor* announcing
that there was –

> FOR SALE: An old-established zinco-engraver's business with a
> splendid new plant and a stock of chemicals.

everybody in the printing world said "That's Etherington's." To the
uninitiated a photo-engraver's is a place of buzzing saws, and lead
shavings, and noisy lathes, and big bright arc lamps.

To the initiated a photo-engraver's is a place where works of art are
reproduced by photography on zinc plates, and consequently used for
printing purposes.

To the very knowing people of the printing world, Etherington's
was the worst of its kind, producing the least presentable of pictures
at a price slightly above the average.

Etherington's had been in the market (by order of the trustees) for
three months, but partly owing to its remoteness from Fleet Street (it
was in Carnaby Street), and partly to the dilapidated condition of the
machinery (which shows that even an official receiver has no moral
sense when he starts advertising), there had been no bids.

Manfred, who interviewed the trustee in Carey Street, learnt that
the business could be either leased or purchased; that immediate
possession in either circumstances was to be had: that there were
premises at the top of the house which had served as a dwelling-place
to generations of caretakers, and that a banker's reference was all that
was necessary in the way of guarantee.

"Rather a crank," said the trustee at a meeting of creditors, "thinks
that he is going to make a fortune turning out photogravures of
Murillo at a price within reach of the inartistic. He tells me that
he is forming a small company to carry on the business, and that so
soon as it is formed he will buy the plant outright."

And sure enough that very day Thomas Brown, merchant; Arthur
W. Knight, gentleman; James Selkirk, artist; Andrew Cohen, financial agent; and James Leech, artist, wrote to the Registrar of Joint
Stock Companies, asking to be formed into a company, limited by
shares, with the object of carrying on business as photo-engravers,
with which object they had severally subscribed for the shares set
against their names.

(In parenthesis, Manfred was a great artist.)

And five days before the second reading of the Aliens Extradition Act, the company had entered into occupation of their new premises in preparation to starting business.

"Years ago, when I first came to London," said Manfred, "I learned the easiest way to conceal one's identity was to disguise oneself as a public enemy. There's a wealth of respectability behind the word 'limited', and the pomp and circumstance of a company directorship diverts suspicion, even as it attracts attention."

Gonsalez printed a neat notice to the effect that the Fine Arts Reproduction Syndicate would commence business on October 1, and a further neat label that "no hands were wanted", and a further terse announcement that travellers and others could only be seen by appointment, and that all letters must be addressed to the Manager.

It was a plain-fronted shop, with a deep basement crowded with the dilapidated plant left by the liquidated engraver. The ground floor had been used as offices, and neglected furniture and grimy files predominated.

There were pigeonholes filled with old plates, pigeonholes filled with dusty invoices, pigeonholes in which all the debris that is accumulated in an office by a clerk with salary in arrear was deposited.

The first floor had been a workshop, the second had been a store, and the third and most interesting floor of all was that on which were the huge cameras and the powerful arc lamps that were so necessary an adjunct to the business.

In the rear of the house on this floor were the three small rooms that had served the purpose of the bygone caretaker.

In one of these, two days after the occupation, sat the four men of Cadiz.

Autumn had come early in the year, a cold driving rain was falling outside, and the fire that burnt in the Georgian grate gave the chamber an air of comfort.

This room alone had been cleared of litter, the best furniture of the establishment had been introduced, and on the ink-stained writing-table that filled the centre of the apartment stood the remains of a fairly luxurious lunch.

Gonsalez was reading a small red book, and it may be remarked that he wore gold-rimmed spectacles; Poiccart was sketching at a corner of the table, and Manfred was smoking a long thin cigar and studying a manufacturing chemist's price list. Thery (or as some prefer to call him Saimont) alone did nothing, sitting, a brooding heap before the fire, twiddling his fingers, and staring absently at the leaping little flames in the grate.

Conversation was carried on spasmodically, as between men whose minds were occupied by different thoughts. Thery concentrated the attentions of the three by speaking to the point. Turning from his study of the fire with a sudden impulse he asked:

"How much longer am I to be kept here?"

Poiccart looked up from his drawing and remarked:

"That is the third time he has asked today."

"Speak Spanish!" cried Thery passionately. "I am tired of this new language. I cannot understand it, any more than I can understand you."

"You will wait till it is finished," said Manfred, in the staccato patois of Andalusia; "we have told you that."

Thery growled and turned his face to the grate.

"I am tired of this life," he said sullenly. "I want to walk about without a guard – I want to go back to Jerez, where I was a free man. I am sorry I came away."

"So am I," said Manfred quietly; "not very sorry though – I hope for your sake I shall not be."

"Who are you?" burst forth Thery, after a momentary silence. "What are you? Why do you wish to kill? Are you anarchists? What money do you make out of this? I want to know."

Neither Poiccart nor Gonsalez nor Manfred showed any resentment at the peremptory demand of their recruit. Gonsalez's clean-shaven, sharp-pointed face twitched with pleasurable excitement, and his cold blue eyes narrowed.

"Perfect! perfect!" he murmured, watching the other man's face: "pointed nose, small forehead and – *articulorum se ipsos torquentium sonus; gemitus, mugitusque parum explanatis* – "

The physiognomist might have continued Seneca's picture of the Angry Man, but Thery sprang to his feet and glowered at the three.

"Who are you?" he asked slowly. "How do I know that you are not to get money for this? I want to know why you keep me a prisoner, why you will not let me see the newspapers, why you never allow me to walk alone in the street, or speak to somebody who knows my language? You are not from Spain, nor you, nor you – your Spanish is – yes, but you are not of the country I know. You want me to kill – but you will not say how – "

Manfred rose and laid his hand on the other's shoulder.

"Señor," he said – and there was nothing but kindness in his eyes – "restrain your impatience, I beg of you. I again assure you that we do not kill for gain. These two gentlemen whom you see have each fortunes exceeding six million pesetas, and I am even richer; we kill and we will kill because we are each sufferers through acts of injustice, for which the law gave us no remedy. If – if – " he hesitated, still keeping his grey eyes fixed unflinchingly on the Spaniard. Then he resumed gently: "If we kill you it will be the first act of the kind."

Thery was on his feet, white and snarling, with his back to the wall; a wolf at bay, looking from one to the other with fierce suspicion.

"Me – me!" he breathed, "kill me?"

Neither of the three men moved save Manfred, who dropped his outstretched hand to his side.

"Yes, you." He nodded as he spoke. "It would be new work for us, for we have never slain except for justice – and to kill you would be an unjust thing."

Poiccart looked at Thery pityingly.

"That is why we chose you," said Poiccart, "because there was always a fear of betrayal, and we thought – it had better be you."

"Understand," resumed Manfred calmly, "that not a hair of your head will be harmed if you are faithful – that you will receive a reward that will enable you to live – remember the girl at Jerez."

Thery sat down again with a shrug of indifference but his hands were trembling as he struck a match to light his cigarette.

"We will give you more freedom – you shall go out every day. In a few days we shall all return to Spain. They called you the silent man in the prison at Granada – we shall believe that you will remain so."

After this the conversation became Greek to the Spaniard, for the men spoke in English.

"He gives very little trouble," said Gonsalez. "Now that we have dressed him like an Englishman, he does not attract attention. He doesn't like shaving every day; but it is necessary, and luckily he is fair. I do not allow him to speak in the street, and this tries his temper somewhat."

Manfred turned the talk into a more serious channel.

"I shall send two more warnings, and one of those must be delivered in his very stronghold. He is a brave man."

"What of Garcia?" asked Poiccart.

Manfred laughed.

"I saw him on Sunday night – a fine old man, fiery, and oratorical. I sat at the back of a little hall whilst he pleaded eloquently in French for the rights of man. He was a Jean-Jacques Rousseau, a Mirabeau, a broad-viewed Bright, and the audience was mostly composed of

Cockney youths, who had come that they might boast they had stood in the temple of Anarchism."

Poiccart tapped the table impatiently.

"Why is it, George, that an element of bathos comes into all these things?"

Manfred laughed.

"You remember Anderson? When we had gagged him and bound him to the chair, and had told him why he had to die – when there were only the pleading eyes of the condemned, and the half-dark room with a flickering lamp, and you and Leon and poor Clarice masked and silent, and I had just sentenced him to death – you remember how there crept into the room the scent of frying onions from the kitchen below."

"I, too, remember," said Leon, "the case of the regicide."

Poiccart made a motion of agreement.

"You mean the corsets," he said, and the two nodded and laughed.

"There will always be bathos," said Manfred; "poor Garcia with a nation's destinies in his hand, an amusement for shop-girls – tragedy and the scent of onions – a rapier thrust and the whalebone of corsets – it is inseparable."

And all the time Thery smoked cigarettes, looking into the fire with his head on his hands.

"Going back to this matter we have on our hands," said Gonsalez. "I suppose that there is nothing more to be done till – the day?"

"Nothing."

"And after?"

"There are our fine art reproductions."

"And after," persisted Poiccart.

"There is a case in Holland, Hermannus van der Byl, to wit; but it will be simple, and there will be no necessity to warn."

Poiccart's face was grave.

"I am glad you have suggested van der Byl, he should have been dealt with before – Hook of Holland or Flushing?"

"If we have time, the Hook by all means."

"And Thery?"

"I will see to him," said Gonsalez easily; "we will go overland to Jerez – where the girl is," he added laughingly.

The object of their discussion finished his tenth cigarette and sat up in his chair with a grunt.

"I forgot to tell you," Leon went on, "that today, when we were taking our exercise walk, Thery was considerably interested in the posters he saw everywhere, and was particularly curious to know why so many people were reading them. I had to find a lie on the spur of the minute, and I hate lying" – Gonsalez was perfectly sincere. "I invented a story about racing or lotteries or something of the sort, and he was satisfied."

Thery had caught his name in spite of its anglicized pronunciation, and looked inquiry.

"We will leave you to amuse our friend," said Manfred rising. "Poiccart and I have a few experiments to make."

The two left the room, traversed the narrow passage, and paused before a small door at the end. A larger door on the right, padlocked and barred, led to the studio. Drawing a small key from his pocket, Manfred opened the door, and, stepping into the room, switched on a light that shone dimly through a dust-covered bulb. There had been some attempt at restoring order from the chaos. Two shelves had been cleared of rubbish, and on these stood rows of bright little phials, each bearing a number. A rough table had been pushed against the wall beneath the shelves, and on the green baize with which the table was covered was a litter of graduated measures, test tubes, condensers, delicate scales, and two queer-shaped glass machines, not unlike gas generators.

Poiccart pulled a chair to the table, and gingerly lifted a metal cup that stood in a dish of water. Manfred, looking over his shoulder, remarked on the consistency of the liquid that half filled the vessel, and Poiccart bent his head, acknowledging the remark as though it were a compliment.

"Yes," he said, satisfied, "it is a complete success, the formula is quite right. Some day we may want to use this."

He replaced the cup in its bath, and reaching beneath the table, produced from a pail a handful of ice-dust, with which he carefully surrounded the receptacle.

"I regard that as the *multum in parvo* of explosives," he said, and took down a small phial from the shelf, lifted the stopper with the crook of his little finger, and poured a few drops of a whitish liquid into the metal cup.

"That neutralizes the elements," said Poiccart, and gave a sigh of relief. "I am not a nervous man, but the present is the first comfortable moment I have had for two days."

"It makes an abominable smell," said Manfred, with his handkerchief to his nose.

A thin smoke was rising from the cup.

"I never notice those things," Poiccart replied, dipping a thin glass rod into the mess. He lifted the rod, and watched reddish drops dripping from the end.

"That's all right," he said.

"And it is an explosive no more?" asked Manfred.

"It is as harmless as a cup of chocolate."

Poiccart wiped the rod on a rag, replaced the phial, and turned to his companion.

"And now?" he asked.

Manfred made no answer, but unlocked an old-fashioned safe that stood in the corner of the room. From this he removed a box of polished wood. He opened the box and disclosed the contents.

"If Thery is the good workman he says he is, here is the bait that shall lure Sir Philip Ramon to his death," he said.

Poiccart looked. "Very ingenious," was his only comment. Then – "Does Thery know, quite know, the stir it has created?"

Manfred closed the lid and replaced the box before he replied.

"Does Thery know that he is the fourth Just Man?" he asked; then slowly, "I think not – and it is as well as he does not know; a thousand pounds is roughly thirty-three thousand pesetas, and there is the free pardon – and the girl at Jerez," he added thoughtfully.

A brilliant idea came to Smith, the reporter, and he carried it to the chief.

"Not bad," said the editor, which meant that the idea was really very good – "not bad at all."

"It occurred to me," said the gratified reporter, "that one or two of the four might be foreigners who don't understand a word of English."

"Quite so," said the chief; "thank you for the suggestion. I'll have it done tonight."

Which dialogue accounts for the fact that the next morning the *Megaphone* appeared with the police notice in French, Italian, German – and Spanish.

V   THE OUTRAGE AT THE "MEGAPHONE"

The editor of the *Megaphone*, returning from dinner, met the super-chief on the stairs. The super-chief, boyish of face, withdrew his mind from the mental contemplation of a new project (Megaphone House is the home of new projects) and inquired after the Four Just Men.

"The excitement is keeping up," replied the editor. "People are talking of nothing else but the coming debate on the Extradition Bill, and the Government is taking every precaution against an attack upon Ramon."

"What is the feeling?"

The editor shrugged his shoulders.

"Nobody really believes that anything will happen in spite of the bomb."

The super-chief thought for a moment, and then quickly:

"What do *you* think?"

The editor laughed.

"I think the threat will never be fulfilled; for once the Four have struck against a snag. If they hadn't warned Ramon they might have done something, but forewarned – "

"We shall see," said the super-chief, and went home.

The editor wondered, as he climbed the stairs, how much longer the Four would fill the contents bill of his newspaper, and rather hoped that they would make their attempt, even though they met with a failure, which he regarded as inevitable.

His room was locked and in darkness, and he fumbled in his pocket for the key, found it, turned the lock, opened the door and entered.

"I wonder," he mused, reaching out his hand and pressing down the switch of the light . . .

There was a blinding flash, a quick splutter of flame, and the room was in darkness again.

Startled, he retreated to the corridor and called for a light.

"Send for the electrician," he roared; "one of these damned fuses has gone!"

A lamp revealed the room to be filled with a pungent smoke; the electrician discovered that every globe had been carefully removed from its socket and placed on the table.

From one of the brackets suspended a curly length of thin wire which ended in a small black box, and it was from this that thick fumes were issuing.

"Open the windows," directed the editor; and a bucket of water having been brought, the little box was dropped carefully into it.

Then it was that the editor discovered the letter – the greenish-grey letter that lay upon his desk. He took it up, turned it over, opened it, and noticed that the gum on the flap was still wet.

Honoured Sir (ran the note), *when you turned on your light this evening you probably imagined for an instant that you were a victim of one of those "outrages" to which you are fond of referring. We owe you an apology for any annoyance we may have caused you. The removal of your lamp and the substitution of a "plug" connecting a small charge of magnesium powder is the cause of your discomfiture. We ask you to believe that it would have been as simple to have connected a charge of nitroglycerine, and thus have made you your own executioner. We have arranged this as evidence of our inflexible intention to carry out our promise in respect of the Aliens Extradition Act. There is no power on earth that can save Sir Philip Ramon from destruction, and we ask you, as the directing force of a great medium, to throw your weight into the scale in the cause of justice, to call upon your Government to withdraw an unjust measure, and save not only the lives of many inoffensive persons who have found an asylum in your country, but also the life of a Minister of the Crown whose only fault in our eyes is his zealousness in an unrighteous cause.*

(Signed) THE FOUR JUST MEN

"Whew!" whistled the editor, wiping his forehead and eyeing the sodden box floating serenely at the top of the bucket.

"Anything wrong, sir?" asked the electrician daringly.

"Nothing," was the sharp reply. "Finish your work, refix these globes, and go."

The electrician, ill-satisfied and curious, looked at the floating box and the broken length of wire.

"Curious-looking thing, sir," he said. "If you ask me – "

"I don't ask you anything; finish your work," the great journalist interrupted.

"Beg pardon, I'm sure," said the apologetic artisan.

Half an hour later the editor of the *Megaphone* sat discussing the situation with Welby.

Welby, who is the greatest foreign editor in London, grinned amiably and drawled his astonishment.

"I have always believed that these chaps meant business," he said cheerfully, "and what is more, I feel pretty certain that they will keep their promise. When I was in Genoa" – Welby got much of his information first-hand – "when I was in Genoa – or was it Sofia? – I met a man who told me about the Trelovitch affair. He was one of the men who assassinated the King of Servia, you remember. Well, one night he left his quarters to visit a theatre – the same night he was found dead in the public square with a sword thrust through his heart. There were two extraordinary things about it." The foreign editor ticked them off on his fingers. "First, the General was a noted swordsman, and there was every evidence that he had not been killed in cold blood, but had been killed in a duel; the second was that he wore corsets, as many of these Germanized officers do, and one of his assailants had discovered this fact, probably by a sword thrust, and had made him discard them; at any rate when he was found this frippery was discovered close by his body."

"Was it known at the time that it was the work of the Four?" asked the editor.

Welby shook his head.

"Even I had never heard of them before," he said resentfully. Then asked, "What have you done about your little scare?"

"I've seen the hall porters and the messengers, and every man on duty at the time, but the coming and the going of our mysterious friend – I don't suppose there was more than one – is unexplained. It really is a remarkable thing. Do you know, Welby, it gives me quite an uncanny feeling; the gum on the envelope was still wet; the letter must have been written on the premises and sealed down within a few seconds of my entering the room."

"Were the windows open?"

"No; all three were shut and fastened, and it would have been impossible to enter the room that way."

The detective who came to receive a report of the circumstances endorsed this opinion.

"The man who wrote this letter must have left your room not longer than a minute before you arrived," he concluded, and took charge of the letter.

Being a young and enthusiastic detective, before finishing his investigations he made a most minute search of the room, turning up carpets, tapping walls, inspecting cupboards, and taking laborious and unnecessary measurements with a foot-rule.

"There are a lot of our chaps who sneer at detective stories," he explained to the amused editor, "but I have read almost everything that has been written by Gaboriau and Conan Doyle, and I believe in taking notice of little things. There wasn't any cigar ash or anything of that sort left behind, was there?" he asked wistfully.

"I'm afraid not," said the editor gravely.

"Pity," said the detective, and wrapping up the "infernal machine" and its appurtenances, he took his departure.

Afterwards the editor informed Welby that the disciple of Holmes had spent half an hour with a magnifying glass examining the floor.

"He found half a sovereign that I lost weeks ago, so it's really an ill wind – "

All that evening nobody but Welby and the chief knew what had happened in the editor's room. There was some rumour in the sub-editor's department that a small accident had occurred in the sanctum.

"Chief busted a fuse in his room and got a devil of a fright," said the man who attended to the Shipping List.

"Dear me," said the weather expert, looking up from his chart, "do you know something like that happened to me: the other night – "

The chief had directed a few firm words to the detective before his departure.

"Only you and myself know anything about this occurrence," said the editor, "so if it gets out I shall know it comes from Scotland Yard."

"You may be sure nothing will come from us," was the detective's reply: "we've got into too much hot water already."

"That's good," said the editor, and "that's good" sounded like a threat.

So that Welby and the chief kept the matter a secret till half an hour before the paper went to press.

This may seem to the layman an extraordinary circumstance, but experience has shown most men who control newspapers that news has an unlucky knack of leaking out before it appears in type.

Wicked compositors – and even compositors can be wicked – have been known to screw up copies of important and exclusive news, and throw them out of a convenient window so that they have fallen close to a patient man standing in the street below and have been immediately hurried off to the office of a rival newspaper and sold for more than their weight in gold. Such cases have been known.

But at half past eleven the buzzing hive of Megaphone House began to hum, for then it was that the sub-editors learnt for the first time of the "outrage".

It was a great story – yet another *Megaphone* scoop, headlined half down the page with THE "JUST FOUR" AGAIN – OUTRAGE AT THE OFFICE OF THE *Megaphone* – DEVILISH INGENUITY – *Another Threatening Letter – The Four Will Keep Their Promise – Remarkable Document – Will the Police save Sir Philip Ramon?*

"A very good story," said the chief complacently, reading the proofs.

He was preparing to leave, and was speaking to Welby by the door.

"Not bad," said the discriminating Welby. "What I think – hullo!"

The last was addressed to a messenger who appeared with a stranger.

"Gentleman wants to speak to somebody, sir – bit excited, so I brought him up; he's a foreigner, and I can't understand him, so I brought him to you" – this to Welby.

"What do you want?" asked the chief in French.

The man shook his head, and said a few words in a strange tongue.

"Ah!" said Welby, "Spanish – what do you wish?" he said in that language.

"Is this the office of that paper?" The man produced a grimy copy of the *Megaphone*.

"Yes."

"Can I speak to the editor?"

The chief looked suspicious.

"I am the editor," he said.

The man looked over his shoulder, then leant forward.

"I am one of The Four Just Men," he said hesitatingly. Welby took a step towards him and scrutinized him closely.

"What is your name?" he asked quickly.

"Miguel Thery of Jerez," replied the man.

It was half past ten when, returning from a concert, the cab that bore Poiccart and Manfred westward passed through Hanover Square and turned off to Oxford Street.

"You ask to see the editor," Manfred was explaining; "they take you up to the offices; you explain your business to somebody; they are very sorry, but they cannot help you; they are very polite, but not to the extent of seeing you off the premises, so, wandering about seeking your way out, you come to the editor's room, and, knowing that he is out, slip in, make your arrangements, walk out, locking the door after you if nobody is about, addressing a few farewell words to an imaginary occupant, if you are seen, and *voilà!*"

Poiccart bit the end of his cigar.

"Use for your envelope a gum that will not dry under an hour and you heighten the mystery," he said quietly, and Manfred was amused.

"The envelope-just-fastened is an irresistible attraction to an English detective."

The cab speeding along Oxford Street turned into Edgware Road, when Manfred put up his hand and pushed open the trap in the roof.

"We'll get down here," he called, and the driver pulled up to the sidewalk.

"I thought you said Pembridge Gardens?" he remarked as Manfred paid him.

"So I did," said Manfred; "goodnight."

They waited chatting on the edge of the pavement until the cab had disappeared from view, then turned back to the Marble Arch, crossed to Park Lane, walked down that plutocratic thoroughfare and round into Piccadilly. Near the Circus they found a restaurant with a long bar and many small alcoves, where men sat around marble tables, drinking, smoking, and talking. In one of these, alone, sat Gonsalez, smoking a long cigarette and wearing on his clean-shaven mobile face a look of meditative content.

Neither of the men evinced the slightest sign of surprise at meeting him – yet Manfred's heart missed a beat, and into the pallid cheeks of Poiccart crept two bright red spots.

They seated themselves, a waiter came and they gave their orders, and when he had gone Manfred asked in a low tone, "Where is Thery?"

Leon gave the slightest shrug.

"Thery has made his escape," he answered calmly.

For a minute neither man spoke, and Leon continued:

"This morning, before you left, you gave him a bundle of newspapers?"

Manfred nodded.

"They were English newspapers," he said. "Thery does not know a word of English. There were pictures in them – I gave them to amuse him."

"You gave him, amongst others, the *Megaphone*?"

"Yes – ha!" Manfred remembered.

"The offer of a reward was in it – and the free pardon – printed in Spanish."

Manfred was gazing into vacancy.

"I remember," he said slowly. "I read it afterwards."

"It was very ingenious," remarked Poiccart commendingly.

"I noticed he was rather excited, but I accounted for this by the fact that we had told him last night of the method we intended adopting for the removal of Ramon and the part he was to play."

Leon changed the topic to allow the waiter to serve the refreshments that had been ordered.

"It is preposterous," he went on without changing his key, "that a horse on which so much money has been placed should not have been sent to England at least a month in advance."

"The idea of a bad Channel-crossing leading to the scratching of the favourite of a big race is unheard of," added Manfred severely.

The waiter left them.

"We went for a walk this afternoon," resumed Leon, "and were passing along Regent Street, he stopping every few seconds to look in the shops, when suddenly – we had been staring at the window of a photographer's – I missed him. There were hundreds of people in the street – but no Thery . . . I have been seeking him ever since."

Leon sipped his drink and looked at his watch.

The other two men did nothing, said nothing.

A careful observer might have noticed that both Manfred's and Poiccart's hands strayed to the top button of their coats.

"Perhaps not so bad as that," smiled Gonsalez.

Manfred broke the silence of the two.

"I take all blame," he commenced, but Poiccart stopped him with a gesture.

"If there is any blame, I alone am blameless," he said with a short laugh. "No, George, it is too late to talk of blame. We underrated the cunning of m'sieur, the enterprise of the English newspapers and – and – "

"The girl at Jerez," concluded Leon.

Five minutes passed in silence, each man thinking rapidly.

"I have a car not far from here," said Leon at length. "You had told me you would be at this place by eleven o'clock; we have the naphtha launch at Burnham-on-Crouch – we could be in France by daybreak."

Manfred looked at him. "What do you think yourself?" he asked.

"I say stay and finish the work," said Leon.

"And I," said Poiccart quietly but decisively.

Manfred called the waiter.

"Have you the last editions of the evening papers?"

The waiter thought he could get them, and returned with two.

Manfred scanned the pages carefully, then threw them aside.

"Nothing in these," he said. "If Thery has gone to the police we must hide and use some other method to that agreed upon, or we could strike now. After all, Thery has told us all we want to know, but – "

"That would be unfair to Ramon." Poiccart finished the sentence in such a tone as summarily ended that possibility. "He has still two days, and must receive yet another, and last, warning."

"Then we must find Thery."

It was Manfred who spoke, and he rose, followed by Poiccart and Gonsalez.

"If They has not gone to the police – where would he go?"

The tone of Leon's question suggested the answer.

"To the office of the newspaper that published the Spanish advertisement," was Manfred's reply, and instinctively the three men knew that this was the correct solution.

"Your motor-car will be useful," said Manfred, and all three left the bar.

In the editor's room Thery faced the two journalists.

"Thery?" repeated Welby; "I do not know that name. Where do you come from? What is your address?"

"I come from Jerez in Andalusia, from the wine farm of Sienor."

"Not that," interrupted Welby; "where do you come from now – what part of London?"

Thery raised his hands despairingly.

"How should I know? There are houses and streets and people – and it is in London, and I was to kill a man, a Minister, because he had made a wicked law – they did not tell me – "

"They – who?" asked the editor eagerly.

"The other three."

"But their names?"

Thery shot a suspicious glance at his questioner.

"There is a reward," he said sullenly, "and a pardon. I want these before I tell – "

The editor stepped to his desk.

"If you are one of the Four you shall have your reward – you shall have some of it now." He pressed a button and a messenger came to the door.

"Go to the composing room and tell the printer not to allow his men to leave until I give orders."

Below, in the basement, the machines were thundering as they flung out the first numbers of the morning news.

"Now" – the editor turned to Thery, who had stood, uneasily shifting from foot to foot whilst the order was being given – "now, tell me all you know."

Thery did not answer; his eyes were fixed on the floor.

"There is a reward and a pardon," he muttered doggedly.

"Hasten!" cried Welby. "You will receive your reward and the pardon also. Tell us, who are the Four Just Men? Who are the other three? Where are they to be found?"

"Here," said a clear voice behind him; and he turned as a stranger, closing the door as he entered, stood facing the three men – a stranger in evening dress, masked from brow to chin.

There was a revolver in the hand that hung at his side.

"I am one," repeated the stranger calmly; "there are two others waiting outside the building."

"How did you get here – what do you want?" demanded the editor, and stretched his hand to an open drawer in his desk.

"Take your hand away" – and the thin barrel of the revolver rose with a jerk. "How I came here your doorkeeper will explain, when he recovers consciousness. Why I am here is because I wish to save my life – not an unreasonable wish. If Thery speaks I may be a dead man – I am about to prevent him speaking. I have no quarrel with either of you gentlemen, but if you hinder me I shall kill you," he said simply. He spoke all the while in English, and Thery, with wide-stretched eyes and distended nostrils, shrank back against the wall, breathing quickly.

"You," said the masked man, turning to the terror-stricken informer and speaking in Spanish, "would have betrayed your comrades – you would have thwarted a great purpose, therefore it is just that you should die."

He raised the revolver to the level of Thery's breast, and Thery fell on his knees, mouthing the prayer he could not articulate.

"By God – no!" cried the editor, and sprang forward.

The revolver turned on him.

"Sir," said the unknown – and his voice sank almost to a whisper – "for God's sake do not force me to kill you."

"You shall not commit a cold-blooded murder," cried the editor in a white heat of anger, and moved forward, but Welby held him back. "What is the use?" said Welby in an undertone; "he means it – we can do nothing."

"You can do something," said the stranger, and his revolver dropped to his side.

Before the editor could answer there was a knock at the door.

"Say you are busy"; and the revolver covered Thery, who was a whimpering, huddled heap by the wall.

"Go away," shouted the editor, "I am busy."

"The printers are waiting," said the voice of the messenger.

"Now," asked the chief, as the footsteps of the boy died away; "what can we do?"

"You can save this man's life."

"How?"

"Give me your word of honour that you will allow us both to depart, and will neither raise an alarm nor leave this room for a quarter of an hour."

The editor hesitated.

"How do I know that the murder you contemplate will not be committed as soon as you get clear?"

The other laughed under his mask.

"How do I know that as soon as I have left the room you will not raise an alarm?"

"I should have given my word, sir," said the editor stiffly.

"And I mine," was the quiet response; "And my word has never been broken."

In the editor's mind a struggle was going on; here in his hand was the greatest story of the century; another minute and he would have extracted from Thery the secret of the Four.

Even now a bold dash might save everything – and the printers were waiting . . . but the hand that held the revolver was the hand of a resolute man, and the chief yielded.

"I agree, but under protest," he said. "I warn you that your arrest and punishment is inevitable."

"I regret," said the masked man with a slight bow, "that I cannot agree with you – nothing is inevitable save death. Come, Thery," he said, speaking in Spanish. "On my word as a Caballero I will not harm you."

Thery hesitated, then slunk forward with his head bowed and his eyes fixed on the floor.

The masked man opened the door an inch, listened, and in the moment came the inspiration of the editor's life.

"Look here," he said quickly, the man giving place to the journalist, "when you get home will you write us an article about yourselves? You needn't give us any embarrassing particulars, you know – something about your aspirations, your *raison d'être*."

"Sir," said the masked man – and there was a note of admiration in his voice – "I recognize in you an artist. The article will be delivered tomorrow"; and opening the door the two men stepped into the darkened corridor.

VI   THE CLUES

Blood-red placards, hoarse newsboys, overwhelming headlines, and column after column of leaded type told the world next day how near the Four had been to capture. Men in the train leant forward, their newspapers on their knees, and explained what they would have done had they been in the editor of the *Megaphone*'s position. People stopped talking about wars and famines and droughts and street accidents and parliaments and ordinary everyday murders and the German Emperor, in order to concentrate their minds upon the topic of the hour. Would the Four Just Men carry out their promise and slay the Secretary for Foreign Affairs on the morrow?

Nothing else was spoken about. Here was a murder threatened a month ago, and, unless something unforeseen happened, to be committed tomorrow.

No wonder that the London Press devoted the greater part of its space to discussing the coming of Thery and his recapture.

". . . It is not so easy to understand," said the *Telegram*, "why, having the miscreants in their hands, certain journalists connected with a sensational and halfpenny contemporary allowed them to go free to work their evil designs upon a great statesman whose unparalleled . . . We say *if*, for unfortunately in these days of cheap journalism every story emanating from the sanctum sanctorum of sensation-loving sheets is not to be accepted on its pretensions; so if, as it stated, these desperadoes really did visit the office of a contemporary last night . . ."

At noonday Scotland Yard circulated broadcast a hastily printed sheet:

£1000 REWARD

WANTED, on suspicion of being connected with a criminal organization known as the Four Just Men, MIGUEL THERY, *alias* SAIMONT, *alias* LE CHICO, late of Jerez, Spain, a Spaniard speaking no English. Height 5 feet 8 inches. Eyes brown, hair black, slight black moustache, face broad. Scars: white scar on cheek, old knife wound on body. Figure, thick-set.

The above reward will be paid to any person or persons who shall give such information as shall lead to the identification of the said Thery with the band known as the Four Just Men and his apprehension.

From which may be gathered that, acting on the information furnished by the editor and his assistant at two o'clock in the morning, the Direct Spanish Cable had been kept busy; important personages had been roused from their beds in Madrid, and the history of Thery as recorded in the Bureau had been reconstructed from pigeon-hole records for the enlightenment of an energetic Commissioner of Police.

Sir Philip Ramon, sitting writing in his study at Portland Place, found a difficulty in keeping his mind upon the letter that lay before him.

It was a letter addressed to his agent at Branfell, the huge estate over which he, in the years he was out of office, played squire.

Neither wife nor chick nor child had Sir Philip. ". . . If by any chance these men succeed in carrying out their purpose I have made ample provision not only for yourself but for all who have rendered me faithful service," he wrote – from which may be gathered the tenor of his letter.

During these past few weeks, Sir Philip's feelings towards the possible outcome of his action had undergone a change.

The irritation of a constant espionage, friendly on the one hand, menacing on the other, had engendered so bitter a feeling of resentment, that in this newer emotion all personal fear had been swallowed up. His mind was filled with one unswerving determination, to carry through the measure he had in hand, to thwart the Four Just Men, and to vindicate the integrity of a Minister of the Crown. "It would be absurd," he wrote in the course of an article entitled *Individuality in its Relation to the Public Service*, and which was published some months later in the *Quarterly Review* – "it would be monstrous to suppose that incidental criticism from a wholly unauthoritative source should affect or in any way influence a member of the Government in his conception of the legislation necessary for the millions of people entrusted to his care. He is the instrument, duly appointed, to put into tangible form the wishes and desires of those who naturally look to him not only to furnish means and methods for the betterment of their conditions, or the amelioration of irksome restrictions upon international commercial relations, but to find them protection from risks extraneous of purely commercial liabilities . . . in such a case a Minister of the Crown with a due appreciation of his responsibilities ceases to exist as a man and becomes merely an unhuman automaton."

Sir Philip Ramon was a man with very few friends. He had none of the qualities that go to the making of a popular man. He was an honest man, a conscientious man, a strong man. He was the cold-blooded, cynical creature that a life devoid of love had left him. He had no enthusiasm – and inspired none. Satisfied that a certain procedure was less wrong than any other, he adopted it. Satisfied that a measure was for the immediate or ultimate good of his fellows, he carried that measure through to the bitter end. It may be said of him that he had no ambitions – only aims. He was the most dangerous man in the Cabinet, which he dominated in his masterful way, for he knew not the meaning of the blessed word "compromise".

If he held views on any subject under the sun, those views were to be the views of his colleagues.

Four times in the short history of the administration had *Rumoured Resignation of a Cabinet Minister* filled the placards of the newspapers, and each time the Minister whose resignation was ultimately recorded was the man whose views had clashed with the Foreign Secretary. In small things, as in great, he had his way.

His official residence he absolutely refused to occupy, and No 44 Downing Street was converted into half office, half palace. Portland Place was his home, and from there he drove every morning, passing the Horse Guards clock as it finished the last stroke of ten.

A private telephone wire connected his study in Portland Place with the official residence, and but for this Sir Philip had cut himself adrift from the house in Downing Street, to occupy which had been the ambition of the great men of his party.

Now, however, with the approach of the day on which every effort would be taxed, the police insisted upon his taking up his quarters in Downing Street.

Here, they said, the task of protecting the Minister would be simplified. No 44 Downing Street they knew. The approaches could be better guarded, and, moreover, the drive – that dangerous drive! – between Portland Place and the Foreign Office would be obviated.

It took a considerable amount of pressure and pleading to induce Sir Philip to take even this step, and it was only when it was pointed out that the surveillance to which he was being subjected would not be so apparent to himself that he yielded.

"You don't like to find my men outside your door with your shaving water," said Superintendent Falmouth bluntly. "You objected to one of my men being in your bathroom when you went in the other morning, and you complained about a plain-clothes officer driving on your box – well, Sir Philip, in Downing Street I promise that you shan't even see them."

This clinched the argument.

It was just before leaving Portland Place to take up his new quarters that he sat writing to his agent whilst the detective waited outside the door.

The telephone at Sir Philip's elbow buzzed – he hated bells – and the voice of his private secretary asked with some anxiety how long he would be.

"We have got sixty men on duty at 44," said the secretary, zealous and young, "and today and tomorrow we shall – " And Sir Philip listened with growing impatience to the recital.

"I wonder you have not got an iron safe to lock me in," he said petulantly, and closed the conversation.

There was a knock at the door and Falmouth put his head inside.

"I don't want to hurry you, sir," he said, "but – "

So the Foreign Secretary drove off to Downing Street in something remarkably like a temper.

For he was not used to being hurried, or taken charge of, or ordered hither and thither. It irritated him further to see the now familiar cyclists on either side of the carriage, to recognize at every few yards an obvious policeman in mufti admiring the view from the sidewalk, and when he came to Downing Street and found it barred to all carriages but his own, and an enormous crowd of morbid sightseers gathered to cheer his ingress, he felt as he had never felt before in his life – humiliated.

He found his secretary waiting in his private office with the rough draft of the speech that was to introduce the second reading of the Extradition Bill.

"We are pretty sure to meet with a great deal of opposition," informed the secretary, "but Mainland has sent out three-line whips, and expects to get a majority of thirty-six – at the very least."

Ramon read over the notes and found them refreshing. They brought back the old feeling of security and importance. After all, he was a great Minister of State. Of course the threats were too absurd – the police were to blame for making so much fuss; and of course the Press – yes, that was it – a newspaper sensation.

There was something buoyant, something almost genial in his air, when he turned with a half smile to his secretary.

"Well, what about my unknown friends – what do the blackguards call themselves? – the Four Just Men?"

Even as he spoke he was acting a part; he had not forgotten their title, it was with him day and night.

The secretary hesitated; between his chief and himself the Four Just Men had been a tabooed subject.

"They – oh, we've heard nothing more than you have read," he said lamely; "we know now who Thery is, but we can't place his three companions."

The Minister pursed his lips.

"They give me till tomorrow night to recant," he said.

"You have heard from them again?"

"The briefest of notes," said Sir Philip lightly.

"And otherwise?"

Sir Philip frowned. "They will keep their promise," he said shortly, for the "otherwise" of his secretary had sent a coldness into his heart that he could not quite understand.

In the top room in the workshop at Carnaby Street, Thery, subdued, sullen, fearful, sat facing the three.

"I want you to quite understand," said Manfred, "that we bear you no ill-will for what you have done. I think, and Señor Poiccart thinks, that Señor Gonsalez did right to spare your life and bring you back to us."

Thery dropped his eyes before the half-quizzical smile of the speaker.

"Tomorrow night you will do as you agreed to do – if the necessity still exists. Then you will go – " he paused.

"Where?" demanded Thery in sudden rage. "Where in the name of Heaven? I have told them my name, they will know who I am – they will find that by writing to the police. Where am I to go?"

He sprang to his feet, glowering on the three men, his hands trembling with rage, his great frame shaking with the intensity of his anger.

"You betrayed yourself," said Manfred quietly; "that is your punishment. But we will find a place for you, a new Spain under other skies – and the girl at Jerez shall be there waiting for you."

Thery looked from one to the other suspiciously. Were they laughing at him?

There was no smile on their faces; Gonsalez alone looked at him with keen, inquisitive eyes, as though he saw some hidden meaning in the speech.

"Will you swear that?" asked Thery hoarsely, "will you swear that by the – "

"I promise that – if you wish it I will swear it," said Manfred. "And now," he went on, his voice changing, "you know what is expected of you tomorrow night – what you have to do?"

Thery nodded.

"There must be no hitch – no bungling; you and I and Poiccart and Gonsalez will kill this unjust man in a way that the world will never guess – such an execution as shall appal mankind. A swift death, a sure death, a death that will creep through cracks, that will pass by

the guards unnoticed. Why, there never has been such a thing done
– such – " he stopped dead with flushed cheeks and kindling eyes, and
met the gaze of his two companions. Poiccart impassive, sphinxlike,
Leon interested and analytic. Manfred's face went a duller red.

"I am sorry," he said almost humbly; "for the moment I had
forgotten the cause, and the end, in the strangeness – of the means."

He raised his hand deprecatingly.

"It is understandable," said Poiccart gravely, and Leon pressed
Manfred's arm.

The three stood in embarrassed silence for a moment, then
Manfred laughed.

"To work!" he said, and led the way to the improvised laboratory.

Inside Thery took off his coat. Here was his province, and from
being the cowed dependant he took charge of the party, directing
them, instructing, commanding, until he had the men of whom, a
few minutes before, he had stood in terror running from studio to
laboratory, from floor to floor.

There was much to be done, much testing, much calculating, many
little sums to be worked out on paper, for in the killing of Sir Philip
Ramon all the resources of modern science were to be pressed into
the service of the Four.

"I am going to survey the land," said Manfred suddenly, and
disappearing into the studio returned with a pair of step-ladders.
These he straddled in the dark passage, and mounting quickly pushed
up a trapdoor that led to the flat roof of the building.

He pulled himself up carefully, crawled along the leaden surface, and raising himself cautiously looked over the low parapet.

He was in the centre of a half mile circle of uneven roofs. Beyond
the circumference of his horizon London loomed murkily through
smoke and mist. Below was a busy street. He took a hasty survey of
the roof with its chimney stacks, its unornamental telegraph pole, its
leaden floor and rusty guttering; then, through a pair of field-glasses,
made a long, careful survey southward. He crawled slowly back to
the trapdoor, raised it, and let himself down very gingerly till his feet
touched the top of the ladder. Then he descended rapidly, closing the
door after him.

"Well?" asked Thery with something of triumph in his voice.

"I see you have labelled it," said Manfred.

"It is better so – since we shall work in the dark," said Thery.

"Did you see then –?" began Poiccart.

Manfred nodded.

"Very indistinctly – one could just see the Houses of Parliament dimly, and Downing Street is a jumble of roofs."

Thery had turned to the work that was engaging his attention. Whatever was his trade he was a deft workman. Somehow he felt that he must do his best for these men. He had been made forcibly aware of their superiority in the last days, he had now an ambition to assert his own skill, his individuality, and to earn commendation from these men who had made him feel his littleness.

Manfred and the others stood aside and watched him in silence. Leon, with a perplexed frown, kept his eyes fixed on the workman's face. For Leon Gonsalez, scientist, physiognomist (his translation of the *Theologi Physiognomia Humana* of Lequetius is regarded today as the finest), was endeavouring to reconcile the criminal with the artisan.

After a while Thery finished.

"All is now ready," he said with a grin of satisfaction: "let me find your Minister of State, give me a minute's speech with him, and the next minute he dies."

His face, repulsive in repose, was now demoniacal. He was like some great bull from his own country made more terrible with the snuffle of blood in his nostrils.

In strange contrast were the faces of his employers. Not a muscle of either face stirred. There was neither exultation nor remorse in their expressions – only a curious something that creeps into the set face of the judge as he pronounces the dread sentence of the law. Thery saw that something, and it froze him to his very marrow.

He threw up his hands as if to ward them off.

"Stop! stop!" he shouted; "don't look like that, in the name of God – don't, don't!" He covered his face with shaking hands.

"Like what, Thery?" asked Leon softly.

Thery shook his head.

"I cannot say – like the judge at Granada when he says – when he says, 'Let the thing be done!'"

"If we look so," said Manfred harshly, "it is because we are judges – and not alone judges but executioners of our judgement."

"I thought you would have been pleased," whimpered Thery.

"You have done well," said Manfred gravely.

"Bueno, bueno!" echoed the others.

"Pray God that we are successful," added Manfred solemnly, and Thery stared at this strange man in amazement.

*   *   *

Superintendent Falmouth reported to the Commissioner that after-noon that all arrangements were now complete for the protection of the threatened Minister.

"I've filled up 44 Downing Street," he said; "there's practically a man in every room. I've got four of our best men on the roof, men in the basement, men in the kitchens."

"What about the servants?" asked the Commissioner.

"Sir Philip has brought up his own people from the country, and now there isn't a person in the house from the private secretary to the doorkeeper whose name and history I do not know from A to Z."

The Commissioner breathed an anxious sigh.

"I shall be very glad when tomorrow is over," he said. "What are the final arrangements?"

"There has been no change, sir, since we fixed things up the morning Sir Philip came over. He remains at 44 all day tomorrow until half past eight, goes over to the House at nine to move the reading of the Bill, returns at eleven."

"I have given orders for the traffic to be diverted along the Embankment between a quarter to nine and a quarter after, and the same at eleven," said the Commissioner. "Four closed carriages will drive from Downing Street to the House, Sir Philip will drive down in a car immediately afterwards."

There was a rap at the door – the conversation took place in the Commissioner's office – and a police officer entered. He bore a card in his hand, which he laid upon the table.

"Señor Jose di Silva," read the Commissioner, "the Spanish Chief of Police," he explained to the Superintendent. "Show him in, please."

Señor di Silva, a lithe little man, with a pronounced nose and a beard, greeted the Englishmen with the exaggerated politeness that is peculiar to Spanish official circles.

"I am sorry to bring you over," said Mr Commissioner, after he had shaken hands with the visitor and had introduced him to Falmouth; "we thought you might be able to help us in our search for Thery."

"Luckily I was in Paris," said the Spaniard; "yes, I know Thery, and I am astounded to find him in such distinguished company. Do I know the Four?" – his shoulders went up to his ears – "who does? I know of them – there was a case at Malaga, you know? . . . Thery is not a good criminal. I was astonished to learn that he had joined the band."

"By the way," said the chief, picking up a copy of the police notice that lay on his desk, and running his eye over it, "your people omitted to say – although it really isn't of very great importance – what is Thery's trade?"

The Spanish policeman knitted his brow.

"Thery's trade! Let me remember." He thought for a moment. "Thery's trade? I don't think I know; yet I have an idea that it is something to do with rubber. His first crime was stealing rubber; but if you want to know for certain – "

The Commissioner laughed.

"It really isn't at all important," he said lightly.

VII   THE MESSENGER OF THE FOUR

There was yet another missive to be handed to the doomed Minister. In the last he had received there had occurred the sentence: *One more warning you shall receive, and so that we may be assured it shall not go astray, our next and last message shall be delivered into your hands by one of us in person.*

This passage afforded the police more comfort than had any episode since the beginning of the scare. They placed a curious faith in the honesty of the Four Men; they recognized that these were not ordinary criminals and that their pledge was inviolable. Indeed, had they thought otherwise the elaborate precautions that they were taking to ensure the safety of Sir Philip would not have been made. The honesty of the Four was their most terrible characteristic.

In this instance it served to raise a faint hope that the men who were setting at defiance the establishment of the law would overreach themselves. The letter conveying this message was the one to which Sir Philip had referred so airily in his conversation with his secretary. It had come by post, bearing the date mark, *Balham, 12.15.*

"The question is, shall we keep you absolutely surrounded, so that these men cannot by any possible chance carry out their threat?" asked Superintendent Falmouth in some perplexity, "or shall we apparently relax our vigilance in order to lure one of the Four to his destruction?"

The question was directed to Sir Philip Ramon as he sat huddled up in the capacious depths of his office chair.

"You want to use me as a bait?" he asked sharply.

The detective expostulated.

"Not exactly that, sir; we want to give these men a chance – "

"I understand perfectly," said the Minister, with some show of irritation.

The detective resumed:

"We know now how the infernal machine was smuggled into the House; on the day on which the outrage was committed an old member, Mr Bascoe, the member for North Torrington, was seen to enter the House."

"Well?" asked Sir Philip in surprise.

"Mr Bascoe was never within a hundred miles of the House of Commons on that date," said the detective quietly. "We might never have found it out, for his name did not appear in the division list. We've been working quietly on that House of Commons affair ever since, and it was only a couple of days ago that we made the discovery."

Sir Philip sprang from his chair and nervously paced the floor of his room.

"Then they are evidently well acquainted with the conditions of life in England," he asserted rather than asked.

"Evidently; they've got the lay of the land, and that is one of the dangers of the situation."

"But," frowned the other, "you have told me there were no dangers, no real dangers."

"There is this danger, sir," replied the detective, eyeing the Minister steadily, and dropping his voice as he spoke, "men who are capable of making such disguise are really outside the ordinary run of criminals. I don't know what their game is, but whatever it is, they are playing it thoroughly. One of them is evidently an artist at that sort of thing, and he's the man I'm afraid of – today."

Sir Philip's head tossed impatiently.

"I am tired of all this, tired of it" – and he thrashed the edge of his desk with an open palm – "detectives and disguises and masked murderers until the atmosphere is, for all the world, like that of a melodrama."

"You must have patience for a day or two," said the plain-spoken officer.

The Four Just Men were on the nerves of more people than the Foreign Minister.

"And we have not decided what is to be our plan for this evening," he added.

"Do as you like," said Sir Philip shortly, and then: "Am I to be allowed to go to the House tonight?"

"No; that is not part of the programme," replied the detective.

Sir Philip stood for a moment in thought.

"These arrangements; they are kept secret, I suppose?"

"Absolutely."

"Who knows of them?"

"Yourself, the Commissioner, your secretary, and myself."

"And no one else?"

"No one; there is no danger likely to arise from that source. If upon the secrecy of your movements your safety depended it would be plain sailing."

"Have these arrangements been committed to writing?" asked Sir Philip.

"No, sir; nothing has been written; our plans have been settled upon and communicated verbally; even the Prime Minister does not know."

Sir Philip breathed a sigh of relief.

"That is all to the good," he said, as the detective rose to go.

"I must see the Commissioner. I shall be away for less than half an hour; in the meantime I suggest that you do not leave your room," he said.

Sir Philip followed him out to the ante-room, in which sat Hamilton, the secretary.

"I have had an uncomfortable feeling," said Falmouth, as one of his men approached with a long coat, which he proceeded to help the detective into, "a sort of instinctive feeling this last day or two, that I have been watched and followed, so that I am using a car to convey me from place to place: they can't follow that, without attracting some notice." He dipped his hand into the pocket and brought out a pair of motoring goggles. He laughed somewhat shamefacedly as he adjusted them. "This is the only disguise I ever adopt, and I might say, Sir Philip," he added with some regret, "that this is the first time during my twenty-five years of service that I have ever played the fool like a stage detective."

After Falmouth's departure the Foreign Minister returned to his desk.

He hated being alone: it frightened him. That there were two score detectives within call did not dispel the feeling of loneliness. The terror of the Four was ever with him, and this had so worked upon his nerves that the slightest noise irritated him. He played with the pen-holder that lay on the desk. He scribbled inconsequently on the blotting-pad before him, and was annoyed to find that the scribbling had taken the form of numbers of figure 4.

Was the Bill worth it? Was the sacrifice called for? Was the measure of such importance as to justify the risk? These things he asked himself again and again, and then immediately, What sacrifice? What risk?

"I am taking the consequence too much for granted," he muttered, throwing aside the pen, and half turning from the writing-table. "There is no certainty that they will keep their words; bah! it is impossible that they should – "

There was a knock at the door.

"Hullo, Superintendent," said the Foreign Minister as the knocker entered. "Back again already!"

The detective, vigorously brushing the dust from his moustache with a handkerchief, drew an official-looking blue envelope from his pocket.

"I thought I had better leave this in your care," he said, dropping his voice; "it occurred to me just after I had left; accidents happen, you know."

The Minister took the document.

"What is it?" he asked.

"It is something which would mean absolute disaster for me if by chance it was found in my possession," said the detective, turning to go.

"What am I to do with it?"

"You would greatly oblige me by putting it in your desk until I return"; and the detective stepped into the ante-room, closed the door behind him and, acknowledging the salute of the plain-clothes officer who guarded the outer door, passed to the motor-car that awaited him.

Sir Philip looked at the envelope with a puzzled frown.

It bore the superscription *Confidential* and the address, *Department A, CID, Scotland Yard.*

"Some confidential report," thought Sir Philip, and an angry doubt as to the possibility of it containing particulars of the police arrangements for his safety filled his mind. He had hit by accident upon the truth had he but known. The envelope contained those particulars.

He placed the letter in a drawer of his desk and drew some papers towards him.

They were copies of the Bill for the passage of which he was daring so much.

It was not a long document. The clauses were few in number, the objects, briefly described in the preamble, were tersely defined. There was no fear of this Bill failing to pass on the morrow. The Government's majority was assured. Men had been brought back to town, stragglers had been whipped in, prayers and threats alike had assisted in concentrating the rapidly dwindling strength of the administration on this one effort of legislation; and what the frantic entreaties of the Whips had failed to secure, curiosity had accomplished, for members of both parties were hurrying to town to be present at a scene which might perhaps be history, and, as many feared, tragedy.

As Sir Philip conned the paper he mechanically formed in his mind the line of attack – for, tragedy or no, the Bill struck at too many interests in the House to allow of its passage without a stormy debate. He was a master of dialectics, a brilliant casuist, a coiner of phrases that stuck and stung. There was nothing for him to fear in the debate. If only – It hurt him to think of the Four Just Men. Not so much because they threatened his life – he had gone past that – but the mere thought that there had come a new factor into his calculations, a new and terrifying force, that could not be argued down or brushed aside with an acid jest, nor intrigued against, nor adjusted by any parliamentary method. He did not think of compromise. The possibility of making terms with his enemy never once entered his head.

"I'll go through with it!" he cried, not once but a score of times; "I'll go through with it!" and now, as the moment grew nearer to hand, his determination to try conclusions with this new world-force grew stronger than ever.

The telephone at his elbow purred – he was sitting at his desk with his head on his hands – and he took the receiver. The voice of his house steward reminded him that he had arranged to give instructions for the closing of the house in Portland Place.

For two or three days, or until this terror had subsided, he intended his house should be empty. He would not risk the lives of his servants. If the Four intended to carry out their plan they would run no risks of failure, and if the method they employed were a bomb, then, to make assurance doubly sure, an explosion at Downing Street might well synchronize with an outrage at Portland Place.

He had finished his talk, and was replacing the receiver when a knock at the door heralded the entry of the detective.

He looked anxiously at the Minister.

"Nobody been, sir?" he asked.

Sir Philip smiled.

"If by that you mean have the Four delivered their ultimatum in person, I can comfort your mind – they have not."

The detective's face was evidence of his relief.

"Thank Heaven!" he said fervently. "I had an awful dread that whilst I was away something would happen. But I have news for you, sir."

"Indeed!"

"Yes, sir, the Commissioner has received a long cable from America. Since the two murders in that country one of Pinkerton's men has been engaged in collecting data. For years he has been piecing together the scrappy evidence he has been able to secure, and this is his cablegram." The detective drew a paper from his pocket and, spreading it on the desk, read:

> *Pinkerton, Chicago, to Commissioner of Police,*
> *Scotland Yard, London.*
>
> *Warn Ramon that the Four do not go outside their promise. If they have threatened to kill in a certain manner at a certain time they will be punctual. We have proof of this characteristic. After Anderson's death small memorandum book was discovered outside window of room evidently dropped. Book was empty save for three pages, which were filled with neatly written memoranda headed "Six methods of execution". It was initialled "C." (third letter in alphabet). Warn Ramon against following: drinking coffee in any form, opening letters or parcels, using soap that has not been manufactured under eye of trustworthy agent, sitting in any room other than that occupied day and night by police officer. Examine his bedroom; see if there is any method by which heavy gases can be introduced. We are sending two men by "Lucania" to watch.*

The detective finished reading. "Watch" was not the last word in the original message, as he knew. There had been an ominous postscript, *Afraid they will arrive too late.*

"Then you think –?" asked the statesman.

"That your danger lies in doing one of the things that Pinkerton warns us against," replied the detective. "There is no fear that the American police are talking idly. They have based their warning on some sure knowledge, and that is why I regard their cable as important."

There was a sharp rap on the panel of the door, and without waiting for invitation the private secretary walked into the room, excitedly waving a newspaper.

"Look at this!" he cried, "read this! The Four have admitted their failure."

"What!" shouted the detective, reaching for the journal.

"What does this mean?" asked Sir Philip sharply.

"Only this, sir: these beggars, it appears, have actually written an article on their 'mission'."

"In what newspaper?"

"The *Megaphone*. It seems when they recaptured Thery the editor asked the masked man to write him an article about himself, and they've done it; and it's here, and they've admitted defeat, and – and – "

The detective had seized the paper and broke in upon the incoherent secretary's speech.

"*The Creed of the Four Just Men*," he read. "Where is their confession of failure?"

"Half way down the column – I have marked the passage – here"; and the young man pointed with a trembling finger to a paragraph.

"'We leave nothing to chance,'" read the detective, "'if the slightest hitch occurs, if the least detail of our plan miscarries, we acknowledge defeat. So assured are we that our presence on earth is necessary for the carrying out of a great plan, so certain are we that we are the indispensable instruments of a divine providence, that we dare not, for the sake of our very cause, accept unnecessary risks. It is essential therefore that the various preliminaries to every execution should be carried out to the full. As an example, it will be necessary for us to deliver our final warning to Sir Philip Ramon; and to add point to this warning, it is, by our code, essential that that should be handed to the Minister by one of us in person. All arrangements have been made to carry this portion of our programme into effect. But such are the extraordinary exigencies of our system that unless this warning can be handed to Sir Philip in accordance with our promise, and before eight o'clock this evening, our arrangements fall to the ground, and the execution we have planned must be forgone.'"

The detective stopped reading, with disappointment visible on every line of his face.

"I thought, sir, by the way you were carrying on that you had discovered something new. I've read all this, a copy of the article was sent to the Yard as soon as it was received."

The secretary thumped the desk impatiently.

"But don't you see!" he cried, "don't you understand that there is no longer any need to guard Sir Philip, that there is no reason to use him as a bait, or, in fact, to do anything if we are to believe these men – look at the time – "

The detective's hand flew to his pocket; he drew out his watch, looked at the dial, and whistled.

"Half past eight, by God!" he muttered in astonishment, and the three stood in surprised silence.

Sir Philip broke the silence.

"Is it a ruse to take us off our guard?" he said hoarsely.

"I don't think so," replied the detective slowly, "I feel sure that it is not; nor shall I relax my watch – but I am a believer in the honesty of these men – I don't know why I should say this, for I have been dealing with criminals for the past twenty-five years, and never once have I put an ounce of faith in the word of the best of 'em, but somehow I can't disbelieve these men. If they have failed to deliver their message they will not trouble us again."

Ramon paced his room with quick, nervous steps.

"I wish I could believe that," he muttered; "I wish I had your faith."

A tap on the door panel.

"An urgent telegram for Sir Philip," said a grey-haired attendant.

The Minister stretched out his hand, but the detective was before him.

"Remember Pinkerton's wire, sir," he said, and ripped open the brown envelope.

Just received a telegram handed in at Charing Cross 7.52. Begins: We have delivered our last message to the Foreign Secretary, signed Four. Ends. Is this true? Editor, Megaphone.

"What does this mean?" asked Falmouth in bewilderment when he had finished reading.

"It means, my dear Mr Falmouth," replied Sir Philip testily, "that your noble Four are liars and braggarts as well as murderers; and it means at the same time, I hope, an end to your ridiculous faith in their honesty."

The detective made no answer, but his face was clouded and he bit his lips in perplexity.

"Nobody came after I left?" he asked.

"Nobody."

"You have seen no person besides your secretary and myself?"

"Absolutely nobody has spoken to me, or approached within a dozen yards of me," Ramon answered shortly.

Falmouth shook his head despairingly.

"Well – I – where are we?" he asked, speaking more to himself than to anybody in the room, and moved towards the door.

Then it was that Sir Philip remembered the package left in his charge.

"You had better take your precious documents," he said, opening his drawer and throwing the package left in his charge on to the table.

The detective looked puzzled.

"What is this?" he asked, picking up the envelope.

"I'm afraid the shock of finding yourself deceived in your estimate of my persecutors has dazed you," said Sir Philip, and added pointedly, "I must ask the Commissioner to send an officer who has a better appreciation of the criminal mind, and a less childlike faith in the honour of murderers."

"As to that, sir," said Falmouth, unmoved by the outburst, "you must do as you think best. I have discharged my duty to my own satisfaction; and I have no more critical taskmaster than myself. But what I am more anxious to hear is exactly what you mean by saying that I handed any papers into your care."

The Foreign Secretary glared across the table at the imperturbable police officer.

"I am referring, sir," he said harshly, "to the packet which you returned to leave in my charge."

The detective stared.

"I – did – not – return," he said in a strained voice. "I have left no papers in your hands." He picked up the package from the table, tore it open, and disclosed yet another envelope. As he caught sight of the grey-green cover he gave a sharp cry.

"This is the message of the Four," said Falmouth.

The Foreign Secretary staggered back a pace, white to the lips.

"And the man who delivered it?" he gasped.

"Was one of the Four Just Men," said the detective grimly. "They have kept their promise."

He took a quick step to the door, passed through into the ante-room and beckoned the plain-clothes officer who stood on guard at the outer door.

"Do you remember my going out?" he asked.

"Yes, sir – both times."

"Both times, eh!" said Falmouth bitterly, "and how did I look the second time?"

His subordinate was bewildered at the form the question took.

"As usual, sir," he stammered.

"How was I dressed?"

The constable considered.

"In your long dust-coat."

"I wore my goggles, I suppose?"

"Yes, sir."

"I thought so," muttered Falmouth savagely, and raced down the broad marble stairs that led to the entrance-hall. There were four men on duty who saluted him as he approached.

"Do you remember my going out?" he asked of the sergeant in charge.

"Yes, sir – both times," the officer replied.

"Damn your 'both' times'!" snapped Falmouth; "how long had I been gone the first time before I returned?"

"Five minutes, sir," was the astonished officer's reply.

"They just gave themselves time to do it," muttered Falmouth, and then aloud, "Did I return in my car?"

"Yes, sir."

"Ah!" – hope sprang into the detective's breast – "did you notice the number?" he asked, almost fearful to hear the reply.

"Yes!"

The detective could have hugged the stolid officer.

"Good – what was it?"

"A17164."

The detective made a rapid note of the number.

"Jackson," he called, and one of the men in mufti stepped forward and saluted.

"Go to the Yard; find out the registered owner of this car. When you have found this go to the owner; ask him to explain his movements; if necessary, take him into custody."

Falmouth retraced his steps to Sir Philip's study. He found the statesman still agitatedly walking up and down the room, the secretary nervously drumming his fingers on the table, and the letter still unopened.

"As I thought," explained Falmouth, "the man you saw was one of the Four impersonating me. He chose his time admirably: my own men were deceived. They managed to get a car exactly similar in build and colour to mine, and, watching their opportunity, they drove to Downing Street a few minutes after I had left. There is one last chance of our catching him – luckily the sergeant on duty noticed the number of the car, and we might be able to trace him through that – hullo." An attendant stood at the door.

Would the Superintendent see Detective Jackson?

Falmouth found him waiting in the hall below.

"I beg your pardon, sir," said Jackson, saluting, "but is there not some mistake in this number?"

"Why?" asked the detective sharply.

"Because," said the man, "A17164 is the number of your own car."

VIII   THE POCKET-BOOK

The final warning was brief and to the point:

> *We allow you until tomorrow evening to reconsider your position in the matter of the Aliens Extradition Bill. If by six o'clock no announcement is made in the afternoon newspapers of your withdrawing this measure we shall have no other course to pursue but to fulfil our promise. You will die at eight in the evening. We append for your enlightenment a concise table of the secret police arrangements made for your safety tomorrow. Farewell.*
>
> (*Signed*) FOUR JUST MEN

Sir Philip read this over without a tremor. He read too the slip of paper on which was written, in the strange foreign hand, the details that the police had not dared to put into writing.

"There is a leakage somewhere," he said, and the two anxious watchers saw that the face of their charge was grey and drawn.

"These details were known only to four," said the detective quietly, "and I'll stake my life that it was neither the Commissioner nor myself."

"Nor I!" said the private secretary emphatically.

Sir Philip shrugged his shoulders with a weary laugh.

"What does it matter? – they know," he exclaimed; "by what uncanny method they learnt the secret I neither know nor care. The question is, can I be adequately protected tomorrow night at eight o'clock?"

Falmouth shut his teeth.

"Either you'll come out of it alive or, by the Lord, they'll kill two," he said, and there was a gleam in his eye that spoke for his determination.

The news that yet another letter had reached the great statesman was on the streets at ten o'clock that night. It circulated through the clubs and theatres, and between the acts grave-faced men stood in the vestibules discussing Ramon's danger. The House of Commons was seething with excitement. In the hope that the Minister would come down, a strong House had gathered, but the members were disappointed, for it was evident soon after the dinner recess that Sir Philip had no intention of showing himself that night.

"Might I ask the right honourable the Prime Minister whether

it is the intention of His Majesty's Government to proceed with
the Aliens Extradition (Political Offences) Bill," asked the Radical
Member for West Deptford, "and whether he has not considered, in
view of the extraordinary conditions that this Bill has called into life,
the advisability of postponing the introduction of this measure?"

The question was greeted with a chorus of "hear-hears", and the
Prime Minister rose slowly and turned an amused glance in the
direction of the questioner.

"I know of no circumstance that is likely to prevent my right
honourable friend, who is unfortunately not in his place tonight,
from moving the second reading of the Bill tomorrow," he said, and
sat down.

"What the devil was he grinning at?" grumbled West Deptford
to a neighbour.

"He's deuced uncomfortable, is JK," said the other wisely, "deuced
uncomfortable; a man in the Cabinet was telling me today that old
JK has been feeling deuced uncomfortable. 'You mark my words,'
he said, 'this Four Just Men business is making the Premier deuced
uncomfortable,'" and the hon. member subsided to allow West
Deptford to digest his neighbour's profundities.

"I've done my best to persuade Ramon to drop the Bill," the
Premier was saying, "but he is adamant, and – the pitiable thing
is that he believes in his heart of hearts that these fellows intend
keeping faith."

"It is monstrous," said the Colonial Secretary hotly; "it is inconceivable that such a state of affairs can last. Why, it strikes at the
root of everything, it unbalances every adjustment of civilization."

"It is a poetical idea," said the phlegmatic Premier, "and the
standpoint of the Four is quite a logical one. Think of the enormous
power for good or evil often vested in one man: a capitalist controlling
the markets of the world, a speculator cornering cotton or wheat
whilst mills stand idle and people starve, tyrants and despots with
the destinies of nations between their thumb and finger – and then
think of the four men, known to none; vague, shadowy figures stalking
tragically through the world, condemning and executing the capitalist, the corner maker, the tyrant – evil forces all, and all beyond reach
of the law. We have said of these people, such of us as are touched
with mysticism, that God would judge them. Here are men arrogating
to themselves the divine right of superior judgement. If we catch
them they will end their lives unpicturesquely, in a matter-of-fact,
commonplace manner in a little shed in Pentonville Gaol, and the
world will never realize how great are the artists who perish."

"But Ramon?"

The Premier smiled.

"Here, I think, these men have just overreached themselves. Had they been content to slay first and explain their mission afterwards I have little doubt that Ramon would have died. But they have warned and warned and exposed their hand a dozen times over. I know nothing of the arrangements that are being made by the police, but I should imagine that by tomorrow night it will be as difficult to get within a dozen yards of Ramon as it would be for a Siberian prisoner to dine with the Czar."

"Is there no possibility of Ramon withdrawing the Bill?" asked the Colonies.

The Premier shook his head.

"Absolutely none," he said.

The rising of a member of the Opposition front bench at that moment to move an amendment to a clause under discussion cut short the conversation.

The House rapidly emptied when it became generally known that Ramon did not intend appearing, and the members gathered in the smoking-room and lobby – to speculate upon the matter which was uppermost in their minds.

In the vicinity of Palace Yard a great crowd had gathered, as in London crowds will gather, on the off-chance of catching a glimpse of the man whose name was in every mouth. Street vendors sold his portrait, frowsy men purveying the real life and adventures of the Four Just Men did a roaring trade, and itinerant street singers, introducing extemporized verses into their repertoire, declaimed the courage of that statesman bold, who dared for to resist the threats of coward alien and deadly anarchist.

There was praise in these poor lyrics for Sir Philip, who was trying to prevent the foreigner from taking the bread out of the mouths of honest working men.

The humour of which appealed greatly to Manfred, who, with Poiccart, had driven to the Westminster end of the Embankment; having dismissed their cab, they were walking to Whitehall.

"I think the verse about the 'deadly foreign anarchist' taking the bread out of the mouth of the home-made variety is distinctly good," chuckled Manfred.

Both men were in evening dress, and Poiccart wore in his button-hole the silken button of a Chevalier of the Légion d'Honneur.

Manfred continued:

"I doubt whether London has had such a sensation since – when?"

Poiccart's grim smile caught the other's eye and he smiled in sympathy.

"Well?"

"I asked the same question of the maître d'hôtel," he said slowly, like a man loath to share a joke; "*he* compared the agitation to the atrocious East-End murders."

Manfred stopped dead and looked with horror on his companion.

"Great heavens!" he exclaimed in distress, "it never occurred to me that we should be compared with – him!"

They resumed their walk.

"It is part of the eternal bathos," said Poiccart serenely; "even De Quincey taught the English nothing. The God of Justice has but one interpreter here, and he lives in a public-house in Lancashire, and is an expert and dexterous disciple of the lamented Marwood, whose system he has improved upon."

They were traversing that portion of Whitehall from which Scotland Yard runs.

A man, slouching along with bent head and his hands thrust deep into the pockets of his tattered coat, gave them a swift sidelong glance, stopped when they had passed, and looked after them. Then he turned and quickened his shuffle on their trail. A press of people and a seeming ceaseless string of traffic at the corner of Cockspur Street brought Manfred and Poiccart to a standstill, waiting for an opportunity to cross the road. They were subjected to a little jostling as the knot of waiting people thickened, but eventually they crossed and walked towards St Martin's Lane.

The comparison which Poiccart had quoted still rankled with Manfred.

"There will be people at His Majesty's tonight," he said, "applauding Brutus as he asks, 'What villain touched his body and not for justice?' You will not find a serious student of history, or any commonplace man of intelligence, for the matter of that, who, if you asked, Would it not have been God's blessing for the world if Bonaparte had been assassinated on his return from Egypt? would not answer without hesitation, Yes. But we – we are murderers!"

"They would not have erected a statue of Napoleon's assassin," said Poiccart easily, "any more than they have enshrined Felton, who slew a profligate and debauched Minister of Charles I. Posterity may do us justice," he spoke half mockingly; "for myself I am satisfied with the approval of my conscience."

He threw away the cigar he was smoking, and put his hand to

the inside pocket of his coat to find another. He withdrew his hand without the cigar and whistled a passing cab.

Manfred looked at him in surprise.

"What is the matter? I thought you said you would walk?"

Nevertheless he entered the hansom and Poiccart followed, giving his direction through the trap, "Baker Street Station."

The cab was rattling through Shaftesbury Avenue before Poiccart gave an explanation.

"I have been robbed," he said, sinking his voice, "my watch has gone, but that does not matter; the pocketbook with the notes I made for the guidance of Thery has gone – and that matters a great deal."

"It may have been a common thief," said Manfred: "he took the watch."

Poiccart was feeling his pockets rapidly.

"Nothing else has gone," he said; "it may have been as you say, a pickpocket, who will be content with the watch and will drop the notebook down the nearest drain; but it may be a police agent."

"Was there anything in it to identify you?" asked Manfred, in a troubled tone.

"Nothing," was the prompt reply; "but unless the police are blind they would understand the calculations and the plans. It may not come to their hands at all, but if it does and the thief can recognize us we are in a fix."

The cab drew up at the down station at Baker Street, and the two men alighted.

"I shall go east," said Poiccart, "we will meet in the morning. By that time I shall have learnt whether the book has reached Scotland Yard. Goodnight."

And with no other farewell than this the two men parted.

If Billy Marks had not had a drop of drink he would have been perfectly satisfied with his night's work. Filled, however, with that false liquid confidence that leads so many good men astray, Billy thought it would be a sin to neglect the opportunities that the gods had shown him. The excitement engendered by the threats of the Four Just Men had brought all suburban London to Westminster, and on the Surrey side of the bridge Billy found hundreds of patient suburbanites waiting for conveyance to Streatham, Camberwell, Clapham, and Greenwich.

So, the night being comparatively young, Billy decided to work the trams.

He touched a purse from a stout old lady in black, a Waterbury watch from a gentleman in a top hat, a small hand mirror from a dainty bag, and decided to conclude his operations with the exploration of a superior young lady's pocket.

Billy's search was successful. A purse and a lace handkerchief rewarded him, and he made arrangements for a modest retirement. Then it was that a gentle voice breathed into his ear. "Hullo, Billy!"

He knew the voice, and felt momentarily unwell.

"Hullo, Mister Howard," he exclaimed with feigned joy; "'ow are you, sir? Fancy meetin' you!"

"Where are you going, Billy?" asked the welcome Mr Howard, taking Billy's arm affectionately.

"'Ome," said the virtuous Billy.

"Home it is," said Mr Howard, leading the unwilling Billy from the crowd; "home, sweet home, it is, Billy." He called another young man, with whom he seemed to be acquainted: "Go on that car, Porter, and see who has lost anything. If you can find anyone bring them along"; and the other young man obeyed.

"And now," said Mr Howard, still holding Billy's arm affectionately, "tell me how the world has been using you."

"Look 'ere, Mr Howard," said Billy earnestly, "what's the game? where are you takin' me?"

"The game is the old game," said Mr Howard sadly – "the same old game, Bill, and I'm taking you to the same old sweet spot."

"You've made a mistake this time, guv'nor'" cried Bill fiercely, and there was a slight clink.

"Permit me, Billy," said Mr Howard, stooping quickly and picking up the purse Billy had dropped.

At the police station the sergeant behind the charge desk pretended to be greatly overjoyed at Billy's arrival, and the gaoler, who put Billy into a steel-barred dock, and passed his hands through cunning pockets, greeted him as a friend.

"Gold watch, half a chain, gold, three purses, two handkerchiefs, and a red moroccer pocketbook," reported the gaoler.

The sergeant nodded approvingly.

"Quite a good day's work, William," he said.

"What shall I get this time?" inquired the prisoner, and Mr Howard, a plain-clothes officer engaged in filling in particulars of the charge, opined nine moons.

"Go on!" exclaimed Mr Billy Marks in consternation.

"Fact," said the sergeant; "you're a rogue and a vagabond, Billy, you're a petty larcenist, and you're for the sessions this time – Number Eight."

This latter was addressed to the gaoler, who bore Billy off to the cells protesting vigorously against a police force that could only tumble to poor blokes, and couldn't get a touch on sanguinary murderers like the Four Just Men.

"What do we pay rates and taxes for?" indignantly demanded Billy through the grating of his cell.

"Fat lot you'll ever pay, Billy," said the gaoler, putting the double lock on the door.

In the charge office Mr Howard and the sergeant were examining the stolen property, and three owners, discovered by PC Porter, were laying claim to their own.

"That disposes of all the articles except the gold watch and the pocketbook," said the sergeant after the claimants had gone, "gold watch, Elgin half-hunter No 5029020, pocketbook containing no papers, no card, no address, and only three pages of writing. What this means I don't know." The sergeant handed the book to Howard. The page that puzzled the policeman contained simply a list of streets. Against each street was scrawled a cabalistic character.

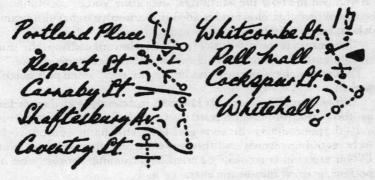

"Looks like the diary of a paperchase," said Mr Howard. "What is on the other pages?"

They turned the leaf. This was filled with figures.

"H'm," said the disappointed sergeant, and again turned overleaf. The contents of this page was understandable and readable although evidently written in a hurry as though it had been taken down at dictation.

"The chap who wrote this must have had a train to catch," said the facetious Mr Howard, pointing to the abbreviations:

Will not leave D.S., except for Hs. Will drive to Hs in M.C. (4 dummy brghms first), 8.30. At 2 600 p arve traf divtd Embank. 80 spls. inside

D.S. One each rm, three each cor, six basmt, six rf. All drs wide opn allow each off see another, all spls will carry revr. Nobody except F and H to approach R. In Hse strange gal filled with spl, all press vouched for. 200 spl. in cor. If nec battalion guards at disposal.

The policeman read this over slowly.

"Now what the devil does that mean?" asked the sergeant helplessly.

It was at that precise moment that Constable Howard earned his promotion.

"Let me have that book for ten minutes," he said excitedly. The sergeant handed the book over with wondering stare.

"I think I can find an owner for this," said Howard, his hand trembling as he took the book, and ramming his hat on his head he ran out into the street.

He did not stop running until he reached the main road, and finding a cab he sprang in with a hurried order to the driver.

"Whitehall, and drive like blazes," he called, and in a few minutes he was explaining his errand to the inspector in charge of the cordon that guarded the entrance of Downing Street.

"Constable Howard, 946 L. reserve," he introduced himself. "I've a very important message for Superintendent Falmouth."

That officer, looking tired and beaten, listened to the policeman's story.

"It looks to me," went on Howard breathlessly, "as though this has something to do with your case, sir. D.S. is Downing Street, and – " He produced the book and Falmouth snatched at it.

He read a few words and then gave a triumphant cry.

"Our secret instructions," he cried, and catching the constable by the arm he drew him to the entrance hall.

"Is my car outside?" he asked, and in response to a whistle a car drew up. "Jump in, Howard," said the detective, and the car slipped into Whitehall.

"Who is the thief?" asked the senior.

"Billy Marks, sir," replied Howard; "you may not know him, but down at Lambeth he is a well-known character."

"Oh, yes," Falmouth hastened to correct, "I know Billy very well indeed – we'll see what he has to say."

The car drew up at the police station and the two men jumped out.

The sergeant rose to his feet as he recognized the famous Falmouth, and saluted.

"I want to see the prisoner Marks," said Falmouth shortly, and Billy, roused from his sleep, came blinking into the charge office.

"Now, Billy," said the detective, "I've got a few words to say to you."

"Why, it's Mr Falmouth," said the astonished Billy, and something like fear shaded his face. "I wasn't in that 'Oxton affair, s'help me."

"Make your mind easy, Billy; I don't want you for anything, and if you'll answer my questions truthfully, you may get off the present charge and get a reward into the bargain."

Billy was suspicious.

"I'm not going to give anybody away if that's what you mean," he said sullenly.

"Nor that either," said the detective impatiently. "I want to know where you found this pocketbook," and he held it up.

Billy grinned.

"Found it lyin' on the pavement," he lied.

"I want the truth," thundered Falmouth.

"Well," said Billy sulkily, "I pinched it."

"From whom?"

"I didn't stop to ask him his name," was the impudent reply.

The detective breathed deeply.

"Now, look here," he said, lowering his voice, "you've heard about the Four Just Men?"

Billy nodded, opening his eyes in amazement at the question.

"Well," exclaimed Falmouth impressively, "the man to whom this pocketbook belongs is one of them."

"What!" cried Billy.

"For his capture there is a reward of a thousand pounds offered. If your description leads to his arrest that thousand is yours."

Marks stood paralysed at the thought.

"A thousand – a thousand?" he muttered in a dazed fashion, "and I might just as easily have caught him."

"Come, come!" cried the detective sharply, "you may catch him yet – tell us what he looked like."

Billy knitted his brows in thought.

"He looked like a gentleman," he said, trying to recall from the chaos of his mind a picture of his victim; "he had a white weskit, a white shirt, nice patent shoes – "

"But his face – his face!" demanded the detective.

"His face?" cried Billy indignantly, "how do I know what it

looked like? I don't look a chap in the face when I'm pinching his watch, do I?"

IX THE CUPIDITY OF MARKS

"You cursed dolt, you infernal fool!" stormed the detective, catching Billy by the collar and shaking him like a rat. "Do you mean to tell me that you had one of the Four Just Men in your hand, and did not even take the trouble to look at him?"

Billy wrenched himself free.

"You leave me alone!" he said defiantly. "How was I to know it was one of the Four Just Men, and how do you know it was?" he added with a cunning twist of his face. Billy's mind was beginning to work rapidly. He saw in this staggering statement of the detective a chance of making capital out of the position which to within a few minutes he had regarded as singularly unfortunate.

"I did get a bit of a glance at 'em," he said, "they – "

"Them – they?" said the detective quickly. "How many were there?"

"Never mind," said Billy sulkily. He felt the strength of his position.

"Billy," said the detective earnestly, "I mean business; if you know anything you've got to tell us."

"Ho!" cried the prisoner in defiance. "Got to, 'ave I? Well, I know the lor as well as you – you can't make a chap speak if he don't want. You can't – "

The detective signalled the other police officers to retire, and when they were out of earshot he dropped his voice and said:

"Harry Moss came out last week."

Billy flushed and lowered his eyes.

"I don't know no Harry Moss," he muttered doggedly.

"Harry Moss came out last week," continued the detective shortly, "after doing three years for robbery with violence – three years and ten lashes."

"I don't know anything about it," said Marks in the same tone.

"He got clean away and the police had no clues," the detective went on remorselessly, "and they might not have caught him to this day, only – only 'from information received' they took him one night out of his bed in Leman Street."

Billy licked his dry lips, but did not speak.

"Harry Moss would like to know who he owes his three stretch to –
and the ten. Men who've had the cat have a long memory, Billy."

"That's not playing the game, Mr Falmouth," cried Billy thickly.
"I – I was a bit hard up, an' Harry Moss wasn't a pal of mine – and
the p'lice wanted to find out – "

"And the police want to find out now," said Falmouth.

Billy Marks made no reply for a moment.

"I'll tell you all there is to be told," he said at last, and cleared
his throat. The detective stopped him.

"Not here," he said. Then turning to the officer in charge:

"Sergeant, you may release this man on bail – I will stand sponsor."
The humorous side of this appealed to Billy at least, for he grinned
sheepishly and recovered his former spirits.

"First time I've been bailed out by the p'lice," he remarked
facetiously.

The motor-car bore the detective and his charge to Scotland Yard,
and in Superintendent Falmouth's office Billy prepared to unburden
himself.

"Before you begin," said the officer, "I want to warn you that you
must be as brief as possible. Every minute is precious."

So Billy told his story. In spite of the warning there were embel-
lishments, to which the detective was forced to listen impatiently.

At last the pickpocket reached the point.

"There was two of 'em, one a tall chap and one not so tall. I
heard one say 'My dear George' – the little one said that, the one
I took the ticker from and the pocketbook. Was there anything in
the notebook?" Billy asked suddenly.

"Go on," said the detective.

"Well," resumed Billy, "I follered 'em up to the end of the street,
and they was waitin' to cross towards Charing Cross Road when I
lifted the clock, you understand?"

"What time was this?"

"'Arf past ten – or it might've been eleven."

"And you did not see their faces?"

The thief shook his head emphatically.

"If I never get up from where I'm sittin' I didn't, Mr Falmouth,"
he said earnestly.

The detective rose with a sigh.

"I'm afraid you're not much use to me, Billy," he said ruefully.
"Did you notice whether they wore beards, or were they clean-
shaven, or – "

Billy shook his head mournfully.

"I could easily tell you a lie, Mr Falmouth," he said frankly, "and I could easily pitch a tale that would take you in, but I'm playin' it square with you."

The detective recognized the sincerity of the man and nodded.

"You've done your best, Billy," he said, and then: "I'll tell you what I'm going to do. You are the only man in the world who has ever seen one of the Four Just Men – and lived to tell the story. Now, although you cannot remember his face, perhaps if you met him again in the street you would know him – there may be some little trick of walking, some habit of holding the hands that you cannot recall now, but if you saw again you would recognize. I shall therefore take upon myself the responsibility of releasing you from custody until the day after tomorrow. I want you to find this man you robbed. Here is a sovereign; go home, get a little sleep, turn out as early as you can and go west." The detective went to his desk, and wrote a dozen words on a card. "Take this: if you see the man or his companion, follow them, show this card to the first policeman you meet, point out the man, and you'll go to bed a thousand pounds richer than when you woke."

Billy took the card.

"If you want me at any time you will find somebody here who will know where I am. Goodnight," and Billy passed into the street, his brain in a whirl, and a warrant written on a visiting card in his waistcoat pocket.

The morning that was to witness great events broke bright and clear over London. Manfred, who, contrary to his usual custom, had spent the night at the workshop in Carnaby Street, watched the dawn from the flat roof of the building.

He lay face downwards, a rug spread beneath him, his head resting on his hands. Dawn with its white, pitiless light, showed his strong face, seamed and haggard. The white streaks in his trim beard were accentuated in the light of morning. He looked tired and disheartened, so unlike his usual self that Gonsalez, who crept up through the trap just before the sun rose, was as near alarmed as it was possible for that phlegmatic man to be. He touched him on the arm and Manfred started.

"What is the matter?" asked Leon softly.

Manfred's smile and shake of head did not reassure the questioner.

"Is it Poiccart and the thief?"

"Yes," nodded Manfred. Then speaking aloud, he asked: "Have you ever felt over any of our cases as you feel in this?"

They spoke in such low tones as almost to approach whispering. Gonsalez stared ahead thoughtfully.

"Yes," he admitted, "once – the woman at Warsaw. You remember how easy it all seemed, and how circumstance after circumstance thwarted us ... till I began to feel, as I feel now, that we should fail."

"No, no, no!" said Manfred fiercely. "There must be no talk of failure, Leon, no thought of it."

He crawled to the trapdoor and lowered himself into the corridor, and Gonsalez followed.

"They?" he asked.

"Asleep."

They were entering the studio, and Manfred had his hand on the door handle when a footstep sounded on the bottom floor.

"Who's there?" cried Manfred, and a soft whistle from below sent him flying downstairs.

"Poiccart!" he cried.

Poiccart it was, unshaven, dusty, weary.

"Well?" Manfred's ejaculation was almost brutal in its bluntness.

"Let us go upstairs," said Poiccart shortly. The three men ascended the dusty stairway, not a word being spoken until they had reached the small living-room.

Then Poiccart spoke:

"The very stars in their courses are fighting against us," he said, throwing himself into the only comfortable chair in the room, and flinging his hat into a corner. "The man who stole my pocketbook has been arrested by the police. He is a well-known criminal of a sneak-thief order, and unfortunately he had been under observation during the evening. The pocketbook was found in his possession, and all might have been well, but an unusually smart police officer associated the contents with us.

"After I had left you I went home and changed, then made my way to Downing Street. I was one of the curious crowd that stood watching the guarded entrance. I knew that Falmouth was there, and I knew, too, if there was any discovery made it would be communicated immediately to Downing Street. Somehow I felt sure the man was an ordinary thief, and that if we had anything to fear it was from a chance arrest. Whilst I was waiting a cab dashed up, and out an excited man jumped. He was obviously a policeman, and I had just time to engage a hansom when Falmouth and the new arrival came flying out. I followed them in the cab as fast as possible without exciting the suspicion of the driver. Of course, they out-distanced us, but their destination was evident. I dismissed the cab at the corner of the street in which the police station is situated, and walked down and found, as I had expected, the car drawn up at the door.

"I managed to get a fleeting glance at the charge room – I was afraid that any interrogation there might be would have been conducted in the cell, but by the greatest of good luck they had chosen the charge room. I saw Falmouth, and the policeman, and the prisoner. The latter, a mean-faced, long-jawed man with shifty eyes – no, no, Leon, don't question me about the physiognomy of the man – my view was for photographic purposes – I wanted to remember him.

"In that second I could see the detective's anger, the thief's defiance, and I knew that the man was saying that he could not recognize us."

"Ha!" It was Manfred's sigh of relief that put a period to Poiccart's speech.

"But I wanted to make sure," resumed the latter. "I walked back the way I had come. Suddenly I heard the hum of the car behind me, and it passed me with another passenger. I guessed that they were taking the man back to Scotland Yard.

"I was content to walk back; I was curious to know what the police intended doing with their new recruit. Taking up a station that gave me a view of the entrance of the street, I waited. After a while the man came out alone. His step was light and buoyant. A glimpse I got of his face showed me a strange blending of bewilderment and gratification. He turned on to the Embankment, and I followed close behind."

"There was a danger that he was being shadowed by the police, too," said Gonsalez.

"Of that I was well satisfied," Poiccart rejoined. "I took a very careful survey before I acted. Apparently the police were content to let him roam free. When he was abreast of the Temple steps he stopped and looked undecidedly left and right, as though he were not quite certain as to what he should do next. At that moment I came abreast of him, passed him, and then turned back, fumbling in my pockets.

"'Can you oblige me with a match?' I asked.

"He was most affable; produced a box of matches and invited me to help myself.

"I took a match, struck it, and lit my cigar, holding the match so that he could see my face."

"That was wise," said Manfred gravely.

"It showed his face too, and out of the corner of my eye I watched him searching every feature. But there was no sign of recognition and I began a conversation. We lingered where we had met for a while and then by mutual consent we walked in the direction of Blackfriars, crossed the bridge, chatting on inconsequent subjects, the poor, the weather, the newspapers. On the other side of the bridge is a coffee-stall. I determined to make my next move. I invited him to take a cup of coffee, and when the cups were placed before us, I put down a sovereign. The stall-keeper shook his head, said he could not change it. 'Hasn't your friend any small change?' he asked.

"It was here that the vanity of the little thief told me what I wanted to know. He drew from his pocket, with a nonchalant air – a sovereign. 'This is all that I have got,' he drawled. I found some coppers – I had to think quickly. He had told the police something, something worth paying for – what was it? It could not have been a description of ourselves, for if he had recognized us then, he would have known me when I struck the match and when I stood there, as I did, in the full glare of the light of the coffee-stall. And then a cold fear came to me. Perhaps he had recognized me, and with a thief's cunning was holding me in conversation until he could get assistance to take me."

Poiccart paused for a moment, and drew a small phial from his pocket; this he placed carefully on the table.

"He was as near to death then as ever he has been in his life," he said quietly, "but somehow the suspicion wore away. In our walk we had passed three policemen – there was an opportunity if he had wanted it.

"He drank his coffee and said, 'I must be going home.'

"'Indeed!' I said. 'I suppose I really ought to go home too – I have a lot of work to do tomorrow.' He leered at me. 'So have I,' he said with a grin, 'but whether I can do it or not I don't know.'

"We had left the coffee-stall, and now stopped beneath a lamp that stood at the corner of the street.

"I knew that I had only a few seconds to secure the information I wanted – so I played bold and led directly to the subject. 'What of these Four Just Men?' I asked, just as he was about to slouch away. He turned back instantly. 'What about them?' he asked quickly. I led him on from that by gentle stages to the identity of the Four. He was eager to talk about them, anxious to know what I thought, but most concerned of all about the reward. He was engrossed in the subject, and then suddenly he leant forward, and, tapping me on the chest, with a grimy forefinger, he commenced to state a hypothetical case."

Poiccart stopped to laugh – his laugh ended in a sleepy yawn.

"You know the sort of questions," said he, "and you know how very naïve the illiterate are when they are seeking to disguise their identities by elaborate hypotheses. Well, that is the story. He – Marks is his name – thinks he may be able to recognize one of us by some extraordinary trick of memory. To enable him to do this, he has been granted freedom – tomorrow he would search London, he said."

"A full day's work," laughed Manfred.

"Indeed," agreed Poiccart soberly, "but hear the sequel. We parted, and I walked westward perfectly satisfied of our security. I made for Covent Garden Market, because this is one of the places in London where a man may be seen at four o'clock in the morning without exciting suspicion.

"I had strolled through the market, idly watching the busy scene, when, for some cause that I cannot explain, I turned suddenly on my heel and came face to face with Marks! He grinned sheepishly, and recognized me with a nod of his head.

"He did not wait for me to ask him his business, but started in to explain his presence.

"I accepted his explanation easily, and for the second time that night invited him to coffee. He hesitated at first, then accepted. When the coffee was brought, he pulled it to him as far from my reach as possible, and then I knew that Mr Marks had placed me at fault, that I had underrated his intelligence, that all the time he had been unburdening himself he had recognized me. He had put me off my guard."

"But why –?" began Manfred.

"That is what I thought," the other answered. "Why did he not have me arrested?" He turned to Leon, who had been a silent listener. "Tell us, Leon, why?"

"The explanation is simple," said Gonsalez quietly: "why did not Thery betray us? – cupidity, the second most potent force of civilization. He has some doubt of the reward. He may fear the honesty of the police – most criminals do so; he may want witnesses." Leon walked to the wall, where his coat hung. He buttoned it thoughtfully, ran his hand over his smooth chin, then pocketed the little phial that stood on the table.

"You have slipped him, I suppose?" he asked.

Poiccart nodded.

"He lives –?"

"At 700 Red Cross Street, in the Borough – it is a common lodging-house."

Leon took a pencil from the table and rapidly sketched a head upon the edge of a newspaper.

"Like this?" he asked.

Poiccart examined the portrait.

"Yes," he said in surprise; "have you seen him?"

"No," said Leon carelessly, "but such a man would have such a head."

He paused on the threshold.

"I think it is necessary." There was a question in his assertion. It was addressed rather to Manfred, who stood with his folded arms and knit brow staring at the floor.

For answer Manfred extended his clenched fist.

Leon saw the down-turned thumb, and left the room.

Billy Marks was in a quandary. By the most innocent device in the world his prey had managed to slip through his fingers. When Poiccart, stopping at the polished doors of the best hotel in London, whither they had strolled, casually remarked that he would not be a moment and disappeared into the hotel, Billy was nonplussed. This was a contingency for which he was not prepared. He had followed the suspect from Blackfriars; he was almost sure that this was the man he had robbed. He might, had he wished, have called upon the first constable he met to take the man into custody; but the suspicion of the thief, the fear that he might be asked to share the reward with the man who assisted him restrained him. And besides, it might not be the man at all, argued Billy, and yet –

Poiccart was a chemist, a man who found joy in unhealthy precipitates, who mixed evil-smelling drugs and distilled, filtered, carbonated, oxydized, and did all manner of things in glass tubes, to the vegetable, animal, and mineral products of the earth.

Billy had left Scotland Yard to look for a man with a discoloured hand. Here again, he might, had he been less fearful of treachery, have placed in the hands of the police a very valuable mark of identification.

It seems a very lame excuse to urge on Billy's behalf that this cupidity alone stayed his hand when he came face to face with the man he was searching for. And yet it was so. Then again there was a sum in simple proportion to be worked out. If one Just Man was worth a thousand pounds, what was the commercial value of four? Billy was a thief with a business head. There were no waste products in his day's labour. He was not a conservative scoundrel who stuck to one branch of his profession. He would pinch a watch, or snatch a till, or pass snide florins with equal readiness. He was a butterfly of crime, flitting from one illicit flower to another, and not above figuring as the X of "information received".

So that when Poiccart disappeared within the magnificent portals of the Royal Hotel in Northumberland Avenue, Billy was hipped. He realized in a flash that his captive had gone whither he could not follow without exposing his hand; that the chances were he had gone for ever. He looked up and down the street; there was no policeman in sight. In the vestibule, a porter in shirt sleeves was polishing brasses. It was still very early; the streets were deserted, and Billy, after a few moments' hesitation, took a course that he would not have dared at a more conventional hour.

He pushed open the swing doors and passed into the vestibule. The porter turned on him as he entered and favoured him with a suspicious frown.

"What do you want?" asked he, eyeing the tattered coat of the visitor in some disfavour.

"Look 'ere, old feller," began Billy, in his most conciliatory tone.

Just then the porter's strong right arm caught him by the coat collar, and Billy found himself stumbling into the street.

"Outside – you," said the porter firmly.

It needed this rebuff to engender in Marks the necessary self-assurance to carry him through.

Straightening his ruffled clothing, he pulled Falmouth's card from his pocket and returned to the charge with dignity.

"I am a p'lice officer," he said, adopting the opening that he knew so well, "and if you interfere with me, look out, young feller!"

The porter took the card and scrutinized it.

"What do you want?" he asked in more civil tones. He would have added 'sir', but somehow it stuck in his throat. If the man is a detective, he argued to himself, he is very well disguised.

"I want that gentleman that came in before me," said Billy.

The porter scratched his head.

"What is the number of his room?" he asked.

"Never mind about the number of his room," said Billy rapidly. "Is there any back way to this hotel – any way a man can get out of it? I mean, besides through the front entrance?"

"Half a dozen," replied the porter.

Billy groaned.

"Take me round to one of them, will you?" he asked. And the porter led the way.

One of the tradesmen's entrances was from a small back street; and here it was that a street scavenger gave the information that Marks had feared. Five minutes before a man answering to the description had walked out, turned towards the Strand and, picking up a cab in the sight of the street cleaner, had driven off.

Baffled, and with the added bitterness that had he played boldly he might have secured at any rate a share of a thousand pounds, Billy walked slowly to the Embankment, cursing the folly that had induced him to throw away the fortune that was in his hands. With hands thrust deep into his pockets, he tramped the weary length of the Embankment, going over again and again the incidents of the night and each time muttering a lurid condemnation of his error. It must have been an hour after he had lost Poiccart that it occurred to him all was not lost. He had the man's description, he had looked at his face, he knew him feature by feature. That was something, at any rate. Nay, it occurred to him that if the man was arrested through his description he would still be entitled to the reward – or a part of it. He dared not see Falmouth and tell him that he had been in company with the man all night without effecting his arrest. Falmouth would never believe him, and, indeed, it was curious that he should have met him.

This fact struck Billy for the first time. By what strange chance had he met this man? Was it possible – the idea frightened Marks – that the man he had robbed had recognized him, and that he had deliberately sought him out with murderous intent?

A cold perspiration broke upon the narrow forehead of the thief. These men were murderers, cruel, relentless murderers: suppose –?

He turned from the contemplation of the unpleasant possibilities to meet a man who was crossing the road towards him. He eyed the stranger doubtingly. The newcomer was a young-looking man, clean-shaven, with sharp features and restless blue eyes. As he came closer, Marks noted that first appearance had been deceptive; the man was not so young as he looked. He might have been forty, thought Marks. He approached, looked hard at Billy, then beckoned him to stop, for Billy was walking away.

"Is your name Marks?" asked the stranger authoritatively.

"Yes, sir," replied the thief.

"Have you seen Mr Falmouth?"

"Not since last night," replied Marks in surprise.

"Then you are to come at once to him."

"Where is he?"

"At Kensington Police Station – there has been an arrest, and he wants you to identify the man."

Billy's heart sank.

"Do I get any of the reward?" he demanded, "that is if I recognize 'im?"

The other nodded and Billy's hopes rose.

"You must follow me," said the newcomer, "Mr Falmouth does not wish us to be seen together. Take a first-class ticket to Kensington and get into the next carriage to mine – come."

He turned and crossed the road toward Charing Cross, and Billy followed at a distance.

He found the stranger pacing the platform and gave no sign of recognition. A train pulled into the station and Marks followed his conductor through a crowd of workmen the train had discharged. He entered an empty first-class carriage, and Marks, obeying instructions, took possession of the adjoining compartment, and found himself the solitary occupant.

Between Charing Cross and Westminster Marks had time to review his position. Between the last station and St James's Park, he invented his excuses to the detective; between the Park and Victoria he had completed his justification for a share of the reward. Then as the train moved into the tunnel for its five minutes' run to Sloane Square, Billy noticed a draught, and turned his head to see the stranger standing on the footboard of the swaying carriage, holding the half-opened door.

Marks was startled.

"Pull up the window on your side," ordered the man, and Billy, hypnotized by the authoritative voice, obeyed. At that moment he heard the tinkle of broken glass.

He turned with an angry snarl.

"What's the game?" he demanded.

For answer the stranger swung himself clear of the door and, closing it softly, disappeared.

"What's his game?" repeated Marks drowsily. Looking down he saw a broken phial at his feet, by the phial lay a shining sovereign. He stared stupidly at it for a moment, then, just before the train ran into Victoria Station, he stooped to pick it up . . .

X   THREE WHO DIED

A passenger leisurely selecting his compartment during the wait at
Kensington opened a carriage door and staggered back coughing.
A solicitous porter and an alarmed station official ran forward and
pulled open the door, and the sickly odour of almonds pervaded the
station.

A little knot of passengers gathered and peered over one another's
shoulders, whilst the station inspector investigated. By and by came
a doctor, and a stretcher, and a policeman from the street without.

Together they lifted the huddled form of a dead man from the
carriage and laid it on the platform.

"Did you find anything?" asked the policeman.

"A sovereign and a broken bottle," was the reply.

The policeman fumbled in the dead man's pockets.

"I don't suppose he'll have any papers to show who he is," he
said with knowledge. "Here's a first-class ticket – it must be a case
of suicide. Here's a card – "

He turned it over and read it, and his face underwent a change.

He gave a few hurried instructions, then made his way to the
nearest telegraph office.

Superintendent Falmouth, who had snatched a few hours' sleep
at the Downing Street house, rose with a troubled mind and an
uneasy feeling that in spite of all his precautions the day would
end disastrously. He was hardly dressed before the arrival of the
Assistant Commissioner was announced.

"I have your report, Falmouth," was the official's greeting; "you
did perfectly right to release Marks – have you had news of him this
morning?"

"No."

"H'm," said the Commissioner thoughtfully. "I wonder whether – "
He did not finish his sentence. "Has it occurred to you that the Four
may have realized their danger?"

The detective's face showed surprise.

"Why, of course, sir."

"Have you considered what their probable line of action will
be?"

"N – no – unless it takes the form of an attempt to get out of the
country."

"Has it struck you that whilst this man Marks is looking for them,
they are probably seeking him?"

"Bill is smart," said the detective uneasily.

"So are they," said the Commissioner with an emphatic nod. "My advice is, get in touch with Marks and put two of your best men to watch him."

"That shall be done at once," replied Falmouth; "I am afraid that it is a precaution that should have been taken before."

"I am going to see Sir Philip," the Commissioner went on, and he added with a dubious smile, "I shall be obliged to frighten him a little."

"What is the idea?"

"We wish him to drop this Bill. Have you seen the morning papers?"

"No, sir."

"They are unanimous that the Bill should be abandoned – they say because it is not sufficiently important to warrant the risk, that the country itself is divided on its merit; but as a matter of fact they are afraid of the consequence; and upon my soul I'm a little afraid too."

He mounted the stairs, and was challenged at the landing by one of his subordinates.

This was a system introduced after the episode of the disguised "detective". The Foreign Minister was now in a state of siege. Nobody had to be trusted, a password had been initiated, and every precaution taken to ensure against a repetition of the previous mistake.

His hand was raised to knock upon the panel of the study, when he felt his arm gripped. He turned to see Falmouth with white face and startled eyes.

"They've finished Billy," said the detective breathlessly. "He has just been found in a railway carriage at Kensington."

The Commissioner whistled.

"How was it done?" he asked.

Falmouth was the picture of haggard despair.

"Prussic acid gas," he said bitterly; "they are scientific. Look you, sir, persuade this man to drop his damned Bill."

He pointed to the door of Sir Philip's room. "We shall never save him. I have got the feeling in my bones that he is a doomed man."

"Nonsense!" the Commissioner answered sharply. "You are growing nervous – you haven't had enough sleep, Falmouth. That isn't spoken like your real self – we *must* save him."

He turned from the study and beckoned one of the officers who guarded the landing.

"Sergeant, tell Inspector Collins to send an emergency call

throughout the area for reserves to gather immediately. I will put such a cordon round Ramon today," he went on addressing Falmouth, "that no man shall reach him without the fear of being crushed to death."

And within an hour there was witnessed in London a scene that has no parallel in the history of the Metropolis. From every district there came a small army of policemen. They arrived by train, by tramway car, by motorbus, by every vehicle and method of traction that could be requisitioned or seized. They streamed from the stations, they poured through the thoroughfares, till London stood aghast at the realization of the strength of her civic defences.

Whitehall was soon packed from end to end; St James's Park was black with them. Automatically Whitehall, Charles Street, Birdcage Walk, and the eastern end of the Mall were barred to all traffic by solid phalanxes of mounted constables. St George's Street was in the hands of the force, the roof of every house was occupied by a uniformed man. Not a house or room that overlooked in the slightest degree the Foreign Secretary's residence but was subjected to a rigorous search. It was as though martial law had been proclaimed, and indeed two regiments of Guards were under arms the whole of the day ready for any emergency. In Sir Philip's room the Commissioner, backed by Falmouth, made his last appeal to the stubborn man whose life was threatened.

"I tell you, sir," said the Commissioner earnestly, "we can do no more than we have done, and I am still afraid. These men affect me as would something supernatural. I have a horrible dread that for all our precautions we have left something out of our reckoning; that we are leaving unguarded some avenue which by their devilish ingenuity they may utilize. The death of this man Marks has unnerved me – the Four are ubiquitous as well as omnipotent. I beg of you, sir, for God's sake, think well before you finally reject their terms. Is the passage of this Bill so absolutely necessary?" – he paused – "is it worth your life?" he asked with blunt directness; and the crudity of the question made Sir Philip wince.

He waited some time before he replied, and when he spoke his voice was low and firm.

"I shall not withdraw," he said slowly, with a dull, dogged evenness of tone. "I shall not withdraw in any circumstance.

"I have gone too far," he went on, raising his hand to check Falmouth's appeal. "I have got beyond fear, I have even got beyond resentment; it is now to me a question of justice. Am I right in introducing a law that will remove from this country colonies of dangerously intelligent criminals, who, whilst enjoying immunity from arrest, urge ignorant men forward to commit acts of violence and treason? If I am right, the Four Just Men are wrong. Or are they right: is this measure and unjust thing, an act of tyranny, a piece of barbarism dropped into the very centre of twentieth-century thought, an anachronism? If these men are right, then I am wrong. So it has come to this, that I have to satisfy my mind as to the standard of right and wrong that I must accept – and I accept my own."

He met the wondering gaze of the officers with a calm, unflinching countenance.

"You were wise to take the precautions you have," he resumed quietly. "I have been foolish to chafe under your protective care."

"We must take even further precautions," the Commissioner interrupted; "between six and half past eight o'clock tonight we wish you to remain in your study, and under no circumstance to open the door to a single person – even to myself or Mr Falmouth. During that time you must keep your door locked." He hesitated. "If you would rather have one of us with you – "

"No, no," was the Minister's quick reply; "after the impersonation of yesterday I would rather be alone."

The Commissioner nodded. "This room is anarchist-proof," he said, waving his hand round the apartment. "During the night we have made a thorough inspection, examined the floors, the wall, the ceiling, and fixed steel shields to the shutters."

He looked round the chamber with the scrutiny of a man to whom every visible object was familiar.

Then he noticed something new had been introduced. On the table stood a blue china bowl full of roses.

"This is new," he said, bending his head to catch the fragrance of the beautiful flowers.

"Yes," was Ramon's careless reply, "they were sent from my house in Hereford this morning."

The Commissioner plucked a leaf from one of the blooms and rolled it between his fingers. "They look so real," he said paradoxically, "that they might even be artificial."

As he spoke he was conscious that he associated the roses in some way with – what?

He passed slowly down the noble marble stairway – a policeman stood on every other step – and gave his views to Falmouth.

"You cannot blame the old man for his decision; in fact, I admire him today more than I have ever done before. But" – there was a sudden solemnity in his voice – "I am afraid – I am afraid."

Falmouth said nothing.

"The notebook tells nothing," the Commissioner continued, "save the route that Sir Philip might have taken had he been anxious to arrive at 44 Downing Street by back streets. The futility of the plan is almost alarming, for there is so much evidence of a strong subtle mind behind the seeming innocence of this list of streets that I am confident that we have not got hold of the true inwardness of its meaning."

He passed into the streets and threaded his way between crowds of policemen. The extraordinary character of the precautions taken by the police had the natural result of keeping the general public ignorant of all that was happening in Downing Street. Reporters were prohibited within the magic circle, and newspapers, and particularly the evening newspapers, had to depend upon such information as was grudgingly offered by Scotland Yard. This was scanty, while their clues and theories, which were many, were various and wonderful.

The *Megaphone*, the newspaper that regarded itself as being the most directly interested in the doings of the Four Just Men, strained every nerve to obtain news of the latest developments. With the coming of the fatal day, excitement had reached an extraordinary pitch; every fresh edition of the evening newspapers was absorbed as soon as it reached the streets. There was little material to satisfy the appetite of a sensation-loving public, but such as there was, was given. Pictures of 44 Downing Street, portraits of the Minister, plans of the vicinity of the Foreign Office, with diagrams illustrating existing police precautions, stood out from columns of letterpress dealing, not for the first but for the dozenth time, with the careers of the Four as revealed by their crimes.

And with curiosity at its height, and all London, all England, the whole of the civilized world, talking of one thing and one thing only there came like a bombshell the news of Marks' death.

Variously described as one of the detectives engaged in the case, as a foreign police officer, as Falmouth himself, the death of Marks grew from "Suicide in a Railway Carriage" to its real importance. Within an hour the story of tragedy, inaccurate in detail, true in substance, filled the columns of the Press. Mystery on mystery! Who was this ill-dressed man, what part was he playing in the great game, how came he by his death? asked the world instantly; and little by little, pieced together by ubiquitous newsmen, the story was made known. On top of this news came the great police march on Whitehall. Here was evidence of the serious view the authorities were taking.

"From my vantage place," wrote Smith in the *Megaphone*, "I could see the length of Whitehall. It was the most wonderful spectacle that London has ever witnessed. I saw nothing but a great sea of black helmets reaching from one end of the broad thoroughfare to the other. Police! the whole vicinity was black with police; they thronged side streets, they crowded into the Park, they formed not a cordon, but a mass through which it was impossible to penetrate."

For the Commissioners of Police were leaving nothing to chance. If they were satisfied that cunning could be matched by cunning, craft by craft, stealth by counter-stealth, they would have been content to defend their charge on conventional lines. But they were outmanœuvred. The stake was too high to depend upon strategy – this was a case that demanded brute force. It is difficult, writing so long after the event, to realize how the terror of the Four had so firmly fastened upon the finest police organization in the world, to appreciate the panic that had come upon a body renowned for its clear-headedness.

The crowd that blocked the approaches to Whitehall soon began to grow as the news of Billy's death circulated, and soon after two o'clock that afternoon, by order of the Commissioner, Westminster Bridge was closed to all traffic, vehicular or passenger. The section of the Embankment that runs between Westminster and Hungerford Bridge was next swept by the police and cleared of curious pedestrians; Northumberland Avenue was barred, and before three o'clock there was no space within five hundred yards of the official residence of Sir Philip Ramon that was not held by a representative of the law. Members of Parliament on their way to the House were escorted by mounted men, and, taking on a reflected glory, were cheered by the crowd. All that afternoon a hundred thousand people waited patiently, seeing nothing, save, towering above the heads of a host of constabulary, the spires and towers of the Mother of Parliaments, or the blank faces of the buildings – in Trafalgar Square, along the Mall as far as the police would allow them, at the lower end of Victoria Street, eight deep along the Albert Embankment, growing in volume every hour. London waited, waited in patience, orderly, content to stare steadfastly at nothing, deriving no satisfaction for their weariness but the sense of being as near as it was humanly possible to be to the scene of a tragedy. A stranger arriving in London, bewildered by this gathering, asked for the cause. A man standing on the outskirts of the Embankment throng pointed across the river with the stem of his pipe.

"We're waiting for a man to be murdered," he said simply, as one who describes a familiar function.

About the edge of these throngs newspaper boys drove a steady trade. From hand to hand the pink sheets were passed over the heads of the crowd. Every half hour brought a new edition, a new theory, a new description of the scene in which they themselves were playing an ineffectual if picturesque part. The clearing of the Thames Embankment produced an edition; the closing of Westminster Bridge brought another; the arrest of a foolish Socialist who sought to harangue the crowd in Trafalgar Square was worthy of another. Every incident of the day was faithfully recorded and industriously devoured.

All that afternoon they waited, telling and retelling the story of the Four, theorizing, speculating, judging. And they spoke of the culmination as one speaks of a promised spectacle, watching the slow-moving hands of Big Ben ticking off the laggard minutes. "Only two more hours to wait," they said at six o'clock, and that sentence, or rather the tone of pleasurable anticipation in which it was said, indicated the spirit of the mob. For a mob is a cruel thing, heartless and unpitying.

Seven o'clock boomed forth, and the angry hum of talk ceased. London watched in silence, and with a quicker beating heart, the last hour crawl round the great clock's dial.

There had been a slight alteration in the arrangements at Downing Street, and it was after seven o'clock before Sir Philip, opening the door of his study, in which he had sat alone, beckoned the Commissioner and Falmouth to approach. They walked towards him, stopping a few feet from where he stood.

The Minister was pale, and there were lines on his face that had not been there before. But the hand that held the printed paper was steady and his face was sphinxlike.

"I am about to lock my door," he said calmly. "I presume that the arrangements we have agreed upon will be carried out?"

"Yes, sir," answered the Commissioner quietly.

Sir Philip was about to speak, but he checked himself.

After a moment he spoke again.

"I have been a just man according to my lights," he said half to himself. "Whatever happens I am satisfied that I am doing the right thing — What is that?"

Through the corridor there came a faint roar.

"The people — they are cheering you," said Falmouth, who just before had made a tour of inspection.

The Minister's lip curled in disdain and the familiar acid crept into his voice.

"They will be terribly disappointed if nothing happens," he said bitterly. "The people! God save me from the people, their sympathy, their applause, their insufferable pity."

He turned and pushed open the door of his study, slowly closed the heavy portal, and the two men heard the snick of the lock as he turned the key.

Falmouth looked at his watch.

"Forty minutes," was his laconic comment.

In the dark stood the Four Men.

"It is nearly time," said the voice of Manfred, and Thery shuffled forward and groped on the floor for something.

"Let me strike a match," he grumbled in Spanish.

"No!"

It was Poiccart's sharp voice that arrested him; it was Gonsalez who stooped quickly and passed sensitive fingers over the floor.

He found one wire and placed it in Thery's hand, then he reached up and found the other, and Thery deftly tied them together.

"Is it not time?" asked Thery, short of breath from his exertions.

"Wait."

Manfred was examining the illuminated dial of his watch. In silence they waited.

"It is time," said Manfred solemnly, and Thery stretched out his hand.

Stretched out his hand – and groaned and collapsed.

The three heard the groan, felt rather than saw the swaying figure of the man, and heard the thud of him as he struck the floor.

"What has happened?" whispered a tremulous voice; it was Gonsalez.

Manfred was at Thery's side fumbling at his shirt.

"They has bungled and paid the consequence," he said in a hushed voice.

"But Ramon – "

"We shall see, we shall see," said Manfred, still with his fingers over the heart of the fallen man.

That forty minutes was the longest that Falmouth ever remembered spending. He had tried to pass it pleasantly by recounting some of the famous criminal cases in which he had played a leading role. But he found his tongue wandering after his mind. He grew incoherent, almost hysterical. The word had been passed round that there was to be no talking in tones above a whisper, and absolute silence reigned, save an occasional sibilant murmur as a necessary question was asked or answered.

Policemen were established in every room, on the roof, in the basement, in every corridor, and each man was armed. Falmouth looked round. He sat in the secretary's office, having arranged for Hamilton to be at the House. Every door stood wide open, wedged back, so that no group of policemen should be out of sight of another.

"I cannot think what can happen," he whispered for the twentieth time to his superior. "It is impossible for those fellows to keep their promise – absolutely impossible."

"The question, to my mind, is whether they will keep their other promise," was the Commissioner's reply, "whether having found that they have failed they will give up their attempt. One thing is certain," he proceeded, "if Ramon comes out of this alive, his rotten Bill will pass without opposition."

He looked at his watch. To be exact, he had held his watch in his hand since Sir Philip had entered his room.

"It wants five minutes." He sighed anxiously.

He walked softly to the door of Sir Philip's room and listened.

"I can hear nothing," he said.

The next five minutes passed more slowly than any of the preceding.

"It is just on the hour," said Falmouth in a strained voice. "We have – "

The distant chime of Big Ben boomed once.

"The hour!" he whispered, and both men listened.

"Two," muttered Falmouth, counting the strokes.

"Three."

"Four."

"Five – what's that?" he muttered quickly.

"I heard nothing – yes, I heard something." He sprang to the door and bent his head to the level of the keyhole. "What is that? What – "

Then from the room came a quick, sharp cry of pain, a crash – and silence.

"Quick – this way, men!" shouted Falmouth, and threw his weight against the door.

It did not yield a fraction of an inch.

"Together!"

Three burly constables flung themselves against the panels, and the door smashed open.

Falmouth and the Commissioner ran into the room.

"My God!" cried Falmouth in horror.

Sprawled across the table at which he had been sitting was the figure of the Foreign Secretary.

The paraphernalia that littered his table had been thrown to the floor as in a struggle.

The Commissioner stepped to the fallen man and raised him. One look at the face was sufficient.

"Dead!" he whispered hoarsely. He looked around – save for the police and the dead man the room was empty.

XI   A NEWSPAPER CUTTING

The court was again crowded today in anticipation of the evidence of the Assistant Commissioner of Police and Sir Francis Katling, the famous surgeon.

Before the proceedings recommenced the Coroner remarked that he had received a great number of letters from all kinds of people containing theories, some of them peculiarly fantastic, as to the cause of Sir Philip Ramon's death.

"The police inform me that they are eager to receive suggestions," said the Coroner, "and will welcome any view however bizarre."

The Assistant Commissioner of Police was the first witness called, and gave in detail the story of the events that had led up to the finding of the late Secretary's dead body. He then went on to describe the appearance of the room. Heavy bookcases filled two sides of the room, the third or south-west was pierced with three windows, the fourth was occupied by a case containing maps arranged on the roller principle.

Were the windows fastened? – Yes.

And adequately protected? – Yes; by wooden folding shutters sheathed with steel.

Was there any indication that these had been tampered with? – None whatever.

Did you institute a search of the room? – Yes; a minute search.

By the Foreman of the Jury: Immediately? – Yes: after the body was removed every article of furniture was taken out of the room, the carpets were taken up, and the walls and ceilings stripped.

And nothing was found? – Nothing.

Is there a fireplace in the room? – Yes.

Was there any possibility of any person effecting an entrance by that method? – Absolutely none.

You have seen the newspapers? – Yes; some of them.

You have seen the suggestion put forward that the deceased was slain by the introduction of a deadly gas? – Yes.

Was that possible? – I hardly think so.

By the Foreman: Did you find any means by which such a gas could be introduced? – (The witness hesitated.) None, except an old disused gaspipe that had an opening above the desk. (Sensation.)

Was there any indication of the presence of such a gas? – Absolutely none.

No smell? – None whatever.

But there are gases which are at once deadly and scentless – carbon dioxide, for example? – Yes; there are.

By the Foreman: Did you test the atmosphere for the presence of such a gas? – No; but I entered the room before it would have had time to dissipate; I should have noticed it.

Was the room disarranged in any way? – Except for the table there was no disarrangement.

Did you find the contents of the table disturbed? – Yes.

Will you describe exactly the appearance of the table? – One or two heavy articles of table furniture, such as the silver candlesticks, etc., alone remained in their positions. On the floor were a number of papers, the inkstand, a pen, and (here the witness drew a notecase from his pocket and extracted a small black shrivelled object) a smashed flower bowl and a number of roses.

Did you find anything in the dead man's hand? – Yes, I found this.

The detective held up a withered rosebud, and a thrill of horror ran through the court.

That is a rose? – Yes.

The Coroner consulted the Commissioner's written report.

Did you notice anything peculiar about the hand? – Yes, where the flower had been there was a round black stain. (Sensation.)

Can you account for that? – No.

By the Foreman: What steps did you take when you discovered this? – I had the flowers carefully collected and as much of the water as was possible absorbed by clean blotting-paper: these were sent to the Home Office for analysis.

Do you know the result of that analysis? – So far as I know, it has revealed nothing.

Did the analysis include leaves from the rose you have in your possession? – Yes.

The Assistant Commissioner then went on to give details of the police arrangements for the day. It was impossible, he emphatically stated, for any person to have entered or left 44 Downing Street without being observed. Immediately after the murder the police on duty were ordered to stand fast. Most of the men, said the witness, were on duty for twenty-six hours at a stretch.

At this stage there was revealed the most sensational feature of the inquiry. It came with dramatic suddenness, and was the result of a question put by the Coroner, who constantly referred to the Commissioner's signed statement that lay before him.

You know of a man called Thery? – Yes.

He was one of a band calling themselves "The Four Just Men"? – I believe so.

A reward was offered for his apprehension? – Yes.

He was suspected of complicity in the plot to murder Sir Philip Ramon? – Yes.

Has he been found? – Yes.

This monosyllabic reply drew a spontaneous cry of surprise from the crowded court.

When was he found? – This morning.

Where? – On Romney Marshes.

Was he dead? – Yes. (Sensation.)

Was there anything peculiar about the body? (The whole court waited for the answer with bated breath.) – Yes; on his right palm was a stain similar to that found on the hand of Sir Philip Ramon!

A shiver ran through the crowd of listeners.

Was a rose found in his hand also? – No.

By the Foreman: Was there any indication how Thery came to where he was found? – None.

The witness added that no papers or documents of any kind were found upon the man.

Sir Francis Katling was the next witness.

He was sworn and was accorded permission to give his evidence from the solicitor's table, on which he had spread the voluminous notes of his observations. For half an hour he devoted himself to a purely technicai record of his examinations. There were three possible causes of death. It might have been natural: the man's weak heart was sufficient to cause such; it might have been by asphyxiation; it might have been the result of a blow that by some extraordinary means left no contusion.

There were no traces of poison? – None.

You have heard the evidence of the last witness? – Yes.

And that portion of the evidence that dealt with a black stain? – Yes.

Did you examine that stain? – Yes.

Have you formed any theories regarding it? – Yes; it seems to me as if it were formed by an acid.

Carbolic acid, for instance? – Yes; but there was no indication of any of the acids of commerce.

You saw the man Thery's hand? – Yes.

Was the stain of a similar character? – Yes, but larger and more irregular.

Were there any signs of acid? – None.

By the Foreman: You have seen many of the fantastic theories put forward by the Press and public? – Yes; I have paid careful attention to them.

And you see nothing in them that would lead you to believe that the deceased met his end by the method suggested? – No.

Gas? – Impossible; it must have been immediately detected.

The introduction into the room of some subtle poison that would asphyxiate and leave no trace? – Such a drug is unknown to medical science.

You have seen the rose found in Sir Philip's hand? – Yes.

How do you account for that? – I cannot account for it.

Nor for the stain? – No.

By the Foreman: You have formed no definite opinion regarding the cause of death? – No; I merely submit one of the three suggestions I have offered.

Are you a believer in hypnotism? – Yes, to a certain extent.

In hypnotic suggestion? – Again, to a certain extent.

Is it possible that the suggestion of death coming at a certain hour so persistently threatened might have led to death? – I do not quite understand you.

Is it possible that the deceased is a victim to hypnotic suggestion? – I do not believe it possible.

By the Foreman: You speak of a blow leaving no contusion. In your experience have you ever seen such a case? – Yes; twice.

But a blow sufficient to cause death? – Yes.

Without leaving a bruise or any mark whatever? – Yes; I saw a case in Japan where a man by exerting a peculiar pressure on the throat produced instant death.

Is that ordinary? – No; it is very unordinary; sufficiently so to create a considerable stir in medical circles. The case was recorded in the *British Medical Journal* in 1896.

And there was no contusion or bruise? – Absolutely none whatever.

The famous surgeon then read a long extract from the *British Medical Journal* bearing out this statement.

Would you say that the deceased died in this way? – It is possible.

By the Foreman: Do you advance that as a serious possibility? – Yes.

With a few more questions of a technical character the examination closed.

As the great surgeon left the box there was a hum of conversation, and keen disappointment was felt on all sides. It had been hoped that the evidence of the medical expert would have thrown light into dark places, but it left the mystery of Sir Philip Ramon's death as far from explanation as ever.

Superintendent Falmouth was the next witness called.

The detective, who gave his evidence in clear tones, was evidently speaking under stress of very great emotion. He seemed to appreciate very keenly the failure of the police to safeguard the life of the dead Minister. It is an open secret that immediately after the tragedy both the officer and the Assistant Commissioner tendered their resignations, which, at the express instruction of the Prime Minister, were not accepted.

Mr Falmouth repeated a great deal of the evidence already given by the Commissioner, and told the story of how he had stood on duty outside the Foreign Secretary's door at the moment of the tragedy. As he detailed the events of that evening a deathly silence came upon the court.

You say you heard a noise proceeding from the study? – Yes.

What sort of a noise? – Well, it is hard to describe what I heard; it was one of those indefinite noises that sounded like a chair being pulled across a soft surface.

Would it be a noise like the sliding of a door or panel? – Yes. (Sensation.)

That is the noise as you described it in your report? – Yes.

Was any panel discovered? – No.

Or any sliding door? – No.

Would it have been possible for a person to have secreted himself in any of the bureaux or bookcases? – No; these were examined.

What happened next? – I heard a click and a cry from Sir Philip, and endeavoured to burst open the door.

By the Foreman: It was locked? – Yes.

And Sir Philip was alone? – Yes; it was by his wish: a wish expressed earlier in the day.

After the tragedy did you make a systematic search both inside and outside the house? – Yes.

Did you make any discovery? – None, except that I made a discovery curious in itself, but having no possible bearing on the case now.

What was this? – Well, it was the presence on the window-sill of the room of two dead sparrows.

Were these examined? – Yes; but the surgeon who dissected them gave the opinion that they died from exposure and had fallen from the parapet above.

Was there any trace of poison in these birds? – None that could be discovered.

At this point Sir Francis Katling was recalled. He had seen the birds. He could find no trace of poison.

Granted the possibility of such a gas as we have already spoken of – a deadly gas with the property of rapid dissipation – might not the escape of a minute quantity of such a fume bring about the death of these birds? – Yes, if they were resting on the window-sill.

By the Foreman: Do you connect these birds with the tragedy? – I do not, replied the witness emphatically.

Superintendent Falmouth resumed his evidence.

Were there any other curious features that struck you? – None.

The Coroner proceeded to question the witness concerning the relations of Marks with the police.

Was the stain found on Sir Philip's hand, and on the hand of the man Thery, found also on Marks? – No.

It was as the court was dispersing, and little groups of men stood discussing the most extraordinary verdict ever given by a coroner's jury, "Death from some unknown cause, and wilful murder against some person or persons unknown", that the Coroner himself met on the threshold of the court a familiar face.

"Hullo, Carson!" he said in surprise, "you here too; I should have thought that your bankrupts kept you busy – even on a day like this – extraordinary case."

"Extraordinary," agreed the other.

"Were you there all the time?"

"Yes," replied the spectator.

"Did you notice what a bright foreman we had?"

"Yes; I think he would make a smarter lawyer than a company promoter."

"You know him, then?"

"Yes," yawned the Official Receiver; "poor devil, he thought he was going to set the Thames on fire, floated a company to reproduce photogravures and things – took Etherington's off our hands, but it's back again."

"Has he failed?" asked the Coroner in surprise.

"Not exactly failed. He's just given it up, says the climate doesn't suit him – what is his name again?"

"Manfred," said the Coroner.

XII   CONCLUSION

Falmouth sat on the opposite side of the Chief Commissioner's desk, his hands clasped before him. On the blotting-pad lay a thin sheet of grey notepaper.

The Commissioner picked it up again and re-read it.

> When you receive this [it ran] we who for want of a better title call ourselves The Four Just Men will be scattered throughout Europe, and there is little likelihood of your ever tracing us. In no spirit of boastfulness we say: We have accomplished that which we set ourselves to accomplish. In no sense of hypocrisy we repeat our regret that such a step as we took was necessary.
>
> Sir Philip Ramon's death would appear to have been an accident. This much we confess. They bungled – and paid the penalty. We depended too much upon his technical knowledge. Perhaps by diligent search you will solve the mystery of Sir Philip Ramon's death – when such a search is rewarded you will realize the truth of this statement. Farewell.

"It tells us nothing," said the Commissioner.

Falmouth shook his head despairingly.

"Search!" he said bitterly; "we have searched the house in Downing Street from end to end – where else can we search?"

"Is there no paper amongst Sir Philip's documents that might conceivably put you on the track?"

"None that we have seen."

The chief bit the end of his pen thoughtfully.

"Has his country house been examined?"

Falmouth frowned.

"I didn't think that necessary."

"Nor Portland Place?"

"No: it was locked up at the time of the murder."

The Commissioner rose.

"Try Portland Place," he advised. "At present it is in the hands of Sir Philip's executors."

The detective hailed a hansom, and in a quarter of an hour found himself knocking upon the gloomy portals of the late Foreign Secretary's town house. A grave manservant opened the door; it was Sir Philip's butler, a man known to Falmouth, who greeted him with a nod.

"I want to make a search of the house, Perks," he said. "Has anything been touched?"

The man shook his head.

"No, Mr Falmouth," he replied, "everything is just as Sir Philip left it. The lawyer gentlemen have not even made an inventory."

Falmouth walked through the chilly hall to the comfortable little room set apart for the butler.

"I should like to start with the study," he said.

"I'm afraid there will be a difficulty, then, sir," said Perks respectfully.

"Why?" demanded Falmouth sharply.

"It is the only room in the house for which we have no key. Sir Philip had a special lock for his study and carried the key with him. You see, being a Cabinet Minister, and a very careful man, he was very particular about people entering his study."

Falmouth thought.

A number of Sir Philip's private keys were deposited at Scotland Yard.

He scribbled a brief note to his chief and sent a footman by cab to the Yard.

Whilst he was waiting he sounded the butler.

"Where were you when the murder was committed, Perks?" he asked.

"In the country: Sir Philip sent away all the servants, you will remember."

"And the house?"

"Was empty – absolutely empty."

"Was there any evidence on your return that any person had effected an entrance?"

"None, sir; it would be next to impossible to burgle this house. There are alarm wires fixed communicating with the police station, and the windows are automatically locked."

"There were no marks on the doors or windows that would lead you to believe that an entrance had been attempted?"

The butler shook his head emphatically.

"None; in the course of my daily duty I make a very careful inspection of the paintwork, and I should have noticed any marks of the kind."

In half an hour the footman, accompanied by a detective, returned, and Falmouth took from the plain-clothed officer a small bunch of keys.

The butler led the way to the first floor.

He indicated the study, a massive oaken door, fitted with a microscopic lock.

Very carefully Falmouth made his selection of keys. Twice he tried unsuccessfully, but at the third attempt the lock turned with a click, and the door opened noiselessly.

He stood for a moment at the entrance, for the room was in darkness.

"I forgot," said Perks, "the shutters are closed – shall I open them?"

"If you please," said the detective.

In a few minutes the room was flooded with light.

It was a plainly furnished apartment, rather similar in appearance to that in which the Foreign Secretary met his end. It smelt mustily of old leather, and the walls of the room were covered with bookshelves. In the centre stood a big mahogany writing-table, with bundles of papers neatly arranged.

Falmouth took a rapid and careful survey of this desk. It was thick with accumulated dust. At one end, within reach of the vacant chair stood an ordinary table telephone.

"No bells," said Falmouth.

"No," replied the butler. "Sir Philip disliked bells – there is a 'buzzer'."

Falmouth remembered.

"Of course," he said quickly. "I remember – hullo!"

He bent forward eagerly.

"Why, what has happened to the telephone?"

He might well ask, for its steel was warped and twisted. Beneath where the vulcanite receiver stood was a tiny heap of black ash, and of the flexible cord that connected it with the outside world nothing remained but a twisted piece of discoloured wire.

The table on which it stood was blistered as with some great heat.

The detective drew a long breath.

He turned to his subordinate.

"Run across to Miller's in Regent Street – the electrician – and ask Mr Miller to come here at once."

He was still standing gazing at the telephone when the electrician arrived.

"Mr Miller," said Falmouth slowly, "what has happened to this telephone?"

The electrician adjusted his pince-nez and inspected the ruin.

"H'm," he said, "it rather looks as though some linesman had been criminally careless."

"Linesman? What do you mean?" demanded Falmouth.

"I mean the workmen engaged to fix telephone wires." He made another inspection.

"Cannot you see?"

He pointed to the battered instrument.

"I see that the machine is entirely ruined – but why?"

The electrician stooped and picked up the scorched wire from the ground.

"What I mean is this," he said. "Somebody has attached a wire carrying a high voltage – probably an electric-lighting wire – to this telephone line: and if anybody had happened to have been at – " He stopped suddenly, and his face went white.

"Good God!" he whispered, "Sir Philip Ramon was electrocuted!"

For a while not one of the party spoke. Then Falmouth's hand darted into his pocket and he drew out the little notebook which Billy Marks had stolen.

"That is the solution," he cried; "here is the direction the wires took – but how is it that the telephone at Downing Street was not destroyed in a similar manner?"

The electrician, white and shaking, shook his head impatiently.

"I have given up trying to account for the vagaries of electricity," he said; "besides, the current, the full force of the current, might have been diverted – a short circuit might have been effected – anything might have happened."

"Wait!" said Falmouth eagerly. "Suppose the man making the

connection had bungled – had taken the full force of the current himself – would that have brought about this result?"

"It might – "

"'Thery bungled – and paid the penalty,'" quoted Falmouth slowly. "Ramon got a slight shock – sufficient to frighten him – he had a weak heart – the burn on his hand, the dead sparrows! By Heaven! it's as clear as daylight!"

Later, a strong force of police raided the house in Carnaby Street, but they found nothing – except a half smoked cigarette bearing the name of a London tobacconist, and the counterfoil of a passage ticket to New York.

It was marked *per RMS "Lucania"*, and was for three first-class passengers.

When the *Lucania* arrived at New York she was searched from stem to stern, but the Four Just Men were not discovered.

It was Gonsalez who had placed the "clue" for the police to find.

Maurice Leblanc

The Mysterious Railway-Passenger

If Raffles was the English rogue par excellence, Arsène Lupin was the French one. Created by Maurice Leblanc (1864–1941), Lupin is firmly in the tradition of audacious French rascals that derives from the real (?) exploits of Vidocq. Leblanc had worked for some years as a playwright and novelist without causing much of a stir until the first appearance of Arsène Lupin, after which his reputation soared, ultimately securing him membership of the French Legion of Honour.

The fast-paced adventures of Lupin began with purely criminal exploits – he was even pitted against "Holmlock Shears" in a couple of stories, and of course won – but later Lupin turned detective, as had Vidocq before him. "The Mysterious Railway-Passenger", translated by Alexander Teixeira de Mattos, comes from the first collection of Lupin stories, The Seven of Hearts.

I HAD SENT MY motor-car to Rouen, by road, on the previous day. I was to meet it by train and go on to some friends who have a house on the Seine.

A few minutes before we left Paris, my compartment was invaded by seven gentlemen, five of whom were smoking. Short though the journey by the fast train is, I did not relish the prospect of taking it in such company, the more so as the old-fashioned carriage had no corridor. I therefore collected my overcoat, my newspapers and my railway-guide and sought refuge in one of the neighbouring compartments.

It was occupied by a lady. At the sight of me, she made a movement of vexation which did not escape my notice and leant towards a gentleman standing on the footboard: her husband, no doubt, who had come to see her off. The gentleman took stock of me and the examination seemed to conclude to my advantage, for he whispered to his wife and smiled, giving her the look with which we reassure a frightened child. She smiled, in her turn, and cast a friendly glance in my direction, as though she suddenly realized that I was one of those decent men with whom a woman can remain locked up for an hour or two, in a little box six feet square, without having anything to fear.

Her husband said to her:

"You mustn't mind, darling, but I have an important appointment and I can't wait."

He kissed her affectionately and went away. His wife blew him some discreet little kisses through the window and waved her handkerchief.

Then the guard's whistle sounded and the train started.

At that moment and in spite of the warning shouts of the railway-officials, the door opened and a man burst into our carriage. My travelling-companion, who was standing up and arranging her things in the rack, uttered a cry of terror and dropped down upon the seat.

I am no coward, far from it, but I confess that these sudden incursions at the last minute are always annoying. They seem so ambiguous, so unnatural. There must be something behind them, else . . .

The appearance and bearing of the newcomer, however, were such as to correct the bad impression produced by the manner of his entrance. He was neatly, almost smartly dressed; his tie was in good taste, his gloves clean; he had a powerful face . . . But, speaking of his face, where on earth had I seen it before? For I had seen it: of that there was no doubt. Or, at least to be accurate, I found within myself that sort of recollection which is left by the sight of an oft-seen portrait of which one has never beheld the original. And at the same time, I felt the uselessness of any effort of memory that I might exert, so inconsistent and vague was that recollection.

But, when my eyes reverted to the lady, I sat astounded at the pallor and disorder of her features. She was staring at her neighbour – he was seated on the same side of the carriage – with an expression of genuine affright; and I saw one of her hands steal trembling towards a little wrist-bag that lay on the cushion a few inches from her lap. She ended by taking hold of it and nervously drawing it to her.

Our eyes met and I read in hers so great an amount of uneasiness and anxiety that I could not help saying:

"I hope you are not unwell, madame? . . . Shall I open the window?"

She made no reply, but, with a timid gesture, called my attention to the man. I smiled as her husband had done, shrugged my shoulders, and explained to her by signs that she had no cause for alarm, that I was there and that, besides, the gentleman seemed quite harmless.

Just then, he turned towards us, and after contemplating us, one after the other, from head to foot, huddled himself into his corner and made no further movement.

A silence ensued; but the lady, as though summoning all her energies to perform an act of despair, said to me, in a hardly intelligible tone:

"You know he is in our train?"

"Who?"

"Why, he . . . he himself . . . I assure you."

"Whom do you mean?"

"Arsène Lupin!"

She had not removed her eyes from the passenger; and it was at him rather than at me that she flung the syllables of that dread name.

He pulled his hat down upon his nose. Was this to conceal his agitation, or was he merely preparing to go to sleep?

I objected:

"Arsène Lupin was sentenced yesterday, in his absence, to twenty years' penal servitude. It is not likely that he would commit the imprudence of showing himself in public today. Besides, the newspapers have discovered that he has been spending the winter in Turkey, ever since his famous escape from the Santé."

"He is in this train," repeated the lady, with the more and more marked intention of being overheard by our companion. "My husband is a deputy prison governor, and the station inspector himself told us that they were looking for Arsène Lupin."

"That is no reason why . . ."

"He was seen at the booking-office. He took a ticket for Rouen."

"It would have been easy to lay hands upon him."

"He disappeared. The ticket collector at the door of the waiting-room did not see him; but they thought that he must have gone round by the suburban platforms and stepped into the express that leaves ten minutes after us."

"In that case, they will have caught him there."

"And supposing that, at the last moment, he jumped out of the express and entered this, our own train . . . as he probably . . . as he most certainly did?"

"In that case, they will catch him here. For the porters and the police cannot have failed to see him going from one train to the other and, when we reach Rouen, they will nab him finely."

"Him? Never! He will find some means of escaping again."

"In that case, I wish him a good journey."

"But think of all that he may do in the meantime!"

"What?"

"How can I tell? One must be prepared for anything."

She was greatly agitated; and, in point of fact, the situation, to a certain degree, warranted her nervous state of excitement. Almost in spite of myself, I said:

"There are such things as curious coincidences, it is true . . . But calm yourself. Admitting that Arsène Lupin is in one of these carriages, he is sure to keep quiet and, rather than bring fresh trouble upon himself, he will have no other idea than to avoid the danger that threatens him."

My words failed to reassure her. However, she said no more, fearing, no doubt, lest I should think her troublesome.

As for myself, I opened my newspapers and read the reports of Arsène Lupin's trial. They contained nothing that was not already known and they interested me but slightly. Moreover, I was tired, I had had a poor night, I felt my eyelids growing heavy and my head began to nod.

"But, surely, sir, you are not going to sleep!"

The lady snatched my paper from my hands and looked at me with indignation.

"Certainly not," I replied. "I have no wish to."

"It would be most imprudent," she said.

"Most," I repeated.

And I struggled hard, fixing my eyes on the landscape, on the clouds that streaked the sky, and soon all this became confused in space, the picture of the excited lady and the drowsy man was obliterated from my mind and I was filled with a great, deep silence of sleep.

It was soon made agreeable by light and incoherent dreams, in which a being who played the part and bore the name of Arsène Lupin occupied a certain place. He turned and shifted on the horizon, his back laden with valuables, clambering over walls and stripping country houses of their contents.

But the outline of this being, who had ceased to be Arsène Lupin, grew more distinct. He came towards me, grew bigger and bigger, leapt into the carriage with incredible agility and fell full upon my chest.

A sharp pain . . . a piercing scream . . . I awoke. The man, my fellow-traveller, with one knee on my chest, was clutching my throat.

I saw this very dimly, for my eyes were shot with blood. I also saw the lady, in a corner, writhing in a violent fit of hysterics. I did not even attempt to resist. I should not have had the strength for it, had I wished to: my temples were throbbing, I choked . . . my throat rattled . . . Another minute . . . and I should have been suffocated.

The man must have felt this. He loosened his grip. Without leaving hold of me, with his right hand he stretched a rope, in which he had prepared a slip-knot, and, with a quick turn, tied my wrists together. In a moment, I was bound, gagged, rendered motionless and helpless.

And he performed this task in the most natural manner in the world, with an ease that revealed the knowledge of a master, of an expert in theft and crime. Not a word, not a fevered movement. Sheer coolness and audacity. And there was I on the seat, tied up like a mummy, I, Arsène Lupin!

It was really ridiculous. And, notwithstanding the seriousness of the circumstances, I could not but appreciate and almost enjoy the irony of the situation. Arsène Lupin "done" like a novice! Stripped like a first-comer − for of course the scoundrel relieved me of my pocket-book and purse! Arsène Lupin victimized in his turn, duped, defeated! What an adventure!

There remained the lady. He took no notice of her at all. He contented himself with picking up the wrist-bag that lay on the floor and extracting the jewels, the purse, the gold and silver knick-knacks which it contained. The lady opened her eyes, shuddered with fright, took off her rings and handed them to the man, as though she wished to spare him any superfluous exertion. He took the rings and looked at her: she fainted away.

Then, calm and silent as before, without troubling about us further, he resumed his seat, lit a cigarette, and abandoned himself to a careful scrutiny of the treasures which he had captured, the inspection of which seemed to satisfy him completely.

I was much less satisfied. I am not speaking of the twelve thousand francs of which I had been unduly plundered: this was a loss which I accepted only for the time; I had no doubt that those twelve thousand francs would return to my possession after a short interval, together with the exceedingly important papers which my pocket-book contained: plans, estimates, specifications, addresses, lists of correspondents, letters of a compromising character. But, for the moment, a more immediate and serious care was worrying me: what was to happen next?

As may be readily imagined, the excitement caused by my passing through the Gare Saint-Lazare had not escaped me. As I was going to stay with friends who knew me by the name of Guillaume Berlat and to whom my resemblance to Arsène Lupin was the occasion of many a friendly jest, I had not been able to disguise myself after my wont and my presence had been discovered. Moreover, a man, doubtless Arsène Lupin, had been seen to rush from the express into the other train. Hence it was inevitable and fated that the commissary of police at Rouen, warned by telegram, would await the arrival of the train, assisted by a respectable number of constables, question any suspicious passengers and proceed to make a minute inspection of the carriages.

All this I had foreseen and had not felt greatly excited about it; for I was certain that the Rouen police would display no greater perspicacity than the Paris police and that I should have been able to pass unperceived: was it not sufficient for me, at the wicket, carelessly to show my deputy's card, thanks to which I had already inspired the ticket-collector at Saint-Lazare with every confidence? But how things had changed since then! I was no longer free. It was impossible to attempt one of my usual moves. In one of the carriages the commissary would discover the Sieur Arsène Lupin, whom a propitious fate was sending to him bound hand and foot, gentle as a lamb, packed up complete. He had only to accept delivery, just as you receive a parcel addressed to you at a railway station, a hamper of game or a basket of vegetables and fruit.

And to avoid this annoying catastrophe what could I do, entangled as I was in my bonds?

The train was speeding towards Rouen, the next and only stopping place; it rushed through Vernon, through Saint-Pierre . . .

I was puzzled also by another problem, in which I was not so directly interested, but the solution of which aroused my professional curiosity. What were my fellow-traveller's intentions?

If I had been alone, he would have had ample time to alight quite calmly at Rouen. But the lady? As soon as the carriage door was opened, the lady, meek and quiet as she sat at present, would scream and throw herself about and cry for assistance!

Hence my astonishment. Why did he not reduce her to the same state of helplessness as myself, which would have given him time to disappear before his two-fold misdemeanour was discovered?

He was still smoking, his eyes fixed on the view outside, which a hesitating rain was beginning to streak with long, slanting lines.

Once, however, he turned round, took up my railway guide and consulted it.

As for the lady, she made every effort to continue fainting, so as to quiet her enemy. But a fit of coughing, produced by the smoke, gave the lie to her pretended swoon.

Myself, I was very uncomfortable and had pains all over my body. And I thought . . . I planned . . .

Pont-de-l'Arche . . . Oissell . . . The train was hurrying on, glad drunk with speed . . . Saint-Etienne . . .

At that moment, the man rose and took two steps towards us, to which the lady hastened to reply with a new scream and a genuine fainting fit.

But what could his object be? He lowered the window on our side. The rain was now falling in torrents and he made a movement of annoyance at having neither umbrella nor overcoat. He looked up at the rack: the lady's *en-tout-cas* was there; he took it. He also took my overcoat and put it on.

We were crossing the Seine. He turned up his trousers and then, leaning out of the window, raised the outer latch.

Did he mean to fling himself on the permanent way? At the rate at which we were going, it would have been certain death. We plunged into the tunnel through the Côte Sainte-Catherine. The man opened the door and, with one foot, felt for the step. What madness! The darkness, the smoke, the din all combined to lend a fantastic appearance to any such attempt. But, suddenly, the train slowed up, the Westinghouse brakes counteracted the movement of the wheels. In a minute, the pace from fast became normal and decreased still more. Without a doubt, there was a gang at work repairing this part of the tunnel; this would necessitate a slower passage of the trains, for some days perhaps; and the man knew it.

He had only, therefore, to put his other foot on the step, climb down to the footboard and walk quietly away, not without first closing the door and throwing back the latch.

He had scarcely disappeared when the smoke showed whiter in the daylight. We emerged into a valley. One more tunnel and we should be at Rouen.

The lady at once recovered her wits and her first care was to bewail the loss of her jewels. I gave her a beseeching glance. She understood and relieved me of the gag which was stifling me. She wanted also to unfasten my bonds, but I stopped her:

"No, no: the police must see everything as it was. I want them to be fully informed as regards that blackguard's actions."

"Shall I pull the alarm signal?"

"Too late: you should have thought of that while he was attacking me."

"But he would have killed me! Ah, sir, didn't I tell you that he was travelling by this train? I knew him at once, by his portrait. And now he's taken my jewels."

"They'll catch him, have no fear."

"Catch Arsène Lupin! Never."

"It all depends on you, madame. Listen. When we arrive, be at the window, call out, make a noise. The police and porters will come up. Tell them what you have seen, in a few words: the assault of which I was the victim and the flight of Arsène Lupin. Give his description: a soft hat, an umbrella – yours – a grey frock overcoat . . ."

"Yours," she said.

"Mine? No, his own. I didn't have one."

"I thought that he had none either when he got in."

"He must have had . . . unless it was a coat which some one had left behind in the rack. In any case, he had it when he got out and that is the essential thing . . . A grey frock overcoat, remember . . . Oh, I was forgetting . . . tell them your name to start with. Your husband's position will stimulate their zeal."

We were arriving. She was already leaning out of the window. I resumed, in a louder, almost imperious voice, so that my words should sink into her brain:

"Give my name also, Guillaume Berlat. If necessary, say you know me . . . That will save time . . . we must hurry on the preliminary inquiries . . . the important thing is to catch Arsène Lupin . . . with your jewels . . . You quite understand, don't you? Guillaume Berlat, a friend of your husband's."

"Quite . . . Guillaume Berlat."

She was already calling out and gesticulating. Before the train had come to a standstill, a gentleman climbed in, followed by a number of other men. The critical hour was at hand.

Breathlessly, the lady exclaimed:

"Arsène Lupin . . . he attacked us . . . he has stolen my jewels . . . I am Madame Renaud . . . my husband is a deputy prison governor . . . Ah, here is my brother Georges Andelle, manager of the Crédit Rouennais . . . What I want to say is . . ."

She kissed a young man who had just come up and who exchanged greetings with the commissary of police. She continued, weeping:

"Yes, Arsène Lupin . . . He flew at this gentleman's throat in his sleep . . . Monsieur Berlat, a friend of my husband's."

"But where is Arsène Lupin?"

"He jumped out of the train in the tunnel, after we had crossed the Seine."

"Are you sure it was he?"

"Certain; I recognized him at once. Besides, he was seen at the Gare Saint-Lazare. He was wearing a soft hat . . ."

"No, a hard felt hat, like this," said the commissary, pointing to my hat.

"A soft hat, I assure you," repeated Madame Renaud, "and a grey frock overcoat."

"Yes," muttered the commissary, "the telegram mentions a grey frock overcoat with a black velvet collar."

"A black velvet collar, that's it!" exclaimed Madame Renaud, triumphantly.

I breathed again. What a good, excellent friend I had found in her!

Meanwhile, the policeman had released me from my bonds. I bit my lips violently till the blood flowed. Bent in two, with my handkerchief to my mouth, as seems proper to a man who has long been sitting in a constrained position and who bears on his face the blood-stained marks of the gag, I said to the commissary, in a feeble voice:

"Sir, it was Arsène Lupin, there is no doubt of it . . . You can catch him, if you hurry . . . I think I may be of some use to you . . ."

The coach, which was needed for the inspection by the police, was slipped. The remainder of the train went on to Le Havre. We were taken to the station master's office through a crowd of onlookers who filled the platform.

Just then, I felt a hesitation. I must make some excuse to absent myself, find my motor-car and be off. It was dangerous to wait. If anything happened, if a telegram came from Paris, I was lost.

Yes, but what about my robber? Left to my own resources, in a district with which I was not very familiar, I could never hope to come up with him.

"Bah!" I said to myself. "Let us risk it and stay. It's a difficult hand to win, but a very amusing one to play. And the stakes are worth the trouble."

And, as we were being asked provisionally to repeat our depositions, I exclaimed:

"Mr Commissary, Arsène Lupin is at this moment getting a start on us. My motor is waiting for me in the station yard. If you will do me the pleasure to accept a seat in it, we will try . . ."

The commissary gave a knowing smile:

"It's not a bad idea . . . such a good idea, in fact, that it's already being carried out."

"Oh?"

"Yes, two of my officers started on bicycles . . . some time ago."

"But where to?"

"To the entrance of the tunnel. There they will pick up the clues and the evidence and follow the track of Arsène Lupin."

I could not help shrugging my shoulders:

"Your two officers will pick up no clues and no evidence."

"Really!"

"Arsène Lupin will have arranged that no one should see him leave the tunnel. He will have taken the nearest road and, from there . . ."

"From there made for Rouen, where we shall catch him."

"He will not go to Rouen."

"In that case, he will remain in the neighbourhood, where we shall be even more certain . . ."

"He will not remain in the neighbourhood."

"Oh? Then where will he hide himself?"

I took out my watch:

"At the present moment Arsène Lupin is hanging about the station at Darnétal. At ten-fifty, that is to say, in twenty-two minutes from now, he will take the train which leaves Rouen, from the Gare du Nord, for Amiens."

"Do you think so? And how do you know?"

"Oh, it's very simple. In the carriage, Arsène Lupin consulted my railway guide. What for? To see if there was another line near the place where he disappeared, a station on that line and a train which stopped at that station. I have just looked at the guide myself and learnt what I wanted to know."

"Upon my word, sir," said the commissary, "you possess marvellous powers of deduction. What an expert you must be!"

Dragged on by my conviction, I had blundered into displaying too much cleverness. He looked at me in astonishment and I saw that a suspicion flickered through his mind. Only just, it is true, for the photographs dispatched in every direction were so unlike, represented an Arsène Lupin so different from the one that stood before him, that he could not possibly recognize the original in me. Nevertheless, he was troubled, restless, perplexed.

There was a moment of silence. A certain ambiguity and doubt seemed to interrupt our words. A shudder of anxiety passed through me. Was luck about to turn against me? Mastering myself, I began to laugh:

"Ah, well, there's nothing to sharpen one's wits like the loss of a pocket-book and the desire to find it again. And it seems to me, that, if you will give me two of your men, the three of us might, perhaps . . ."

"Oh, please, Mr Commissary," exclaimed Madame Renaud, "do what Monsieur Berlat suggests."

My kind friend's intervention turned the scale. Uttered by her, the wife of an influential person, the name of Berlat became mine in reality and conferred upon me an identity which no suspicion could touch. The commissary rose:

"Believe me, Monsieur Berlat, I shall be only too pleased to see you succeed. I am as anxious as yourself to have Arsène Lupin arrested."

He escorted me to my car. He introduced two of his men to me: Honoré Massol and Gaston Delivet. They took their seats. I placed myself at the wheel. My chauffeur started the engine. A few seconds later we had left the station. I was saved.

I confess that, as we dashed in my powerful 35-hp Moreau-Lepton along the boulevards that skirt the old Norman city, I was not without a certain sense of pride. The engine hummed harmoniously. The trees sped behind us to right and left. And now, free and out of danger, I had nothing to do but to settle my little private affairs, with the co-operation of those two worthy representatives of the law. Arsène Lupin was going in search of Arsène Lupin.

Ye humble mainstays of the social order of things, Gaston Delivet and Honoré Massol, how precious was your assistance to me! Where should I have been without you? But for you, at how many cross-roads should I have taken the wrong turning! But for you, Arsène Lupin would have gone astray and the other escaped!

But all was not over yet. Far from it. I had first to capture the fellow and next to take possession, myself, of the papers of which he had robbed me. At no cost must my two satellites be allowed to catch a sight of those documents, much less lay hands upon them. To make use of them and yet act independently of them was what I wanted to do; and it was no easy matter.

We reached Darnétal three minutes after the train had left. I had the consolation of learning that a man in a grey frock overcoat with a black velvet collar had got into a second-class carriage, with a ticket for Amiens. There was no doubt about it: my first appearance as a detective was a promising one.

Delivet said:

"The train is an express and does not stop before Montérolier-Buchy, in nineteen minutes from now. If we are not there before Arsène Lupin, he can go on towards Amiens, branch off to Clères, and, from there, make for Dieppe or Paris."

"How far is Montérolier?"

"Fourteen and a half miles."

"Fourteen and a half miles in nineteen minutes . . . We shall be there before him."

It was a stirring race. Never had my trusty Moreau-Lepton responded to my impatience with greater ardour and regularity. It seemed to me as though I communicated my wishes to her directly, without the intermediary of levers or handles. She shared my desires. She approved of my determination. She understood my animosity against that blackguard Arsène Lupin. The scoundrel! The sneak! Should I get the better of him? Or would he once more baffle authority, that authority of which I was the embodiment?

"Right!" cried Delivet . . . "Left! . . . Straight ahead! . . ."

We skimmed the ground. The milestones looked like little timid animals that fled at our approach.

And suddenly, at the turn of a road, a cloud of smoke, the north express!

For half a mile, it was a struggle, side by side, an unequal struggle, of which the issue was certain. We beat the train by twenty lengths.

In three seconds we were on the platform, in front of the second class. The doors were flung open. A few people stepped out. My thief was not among them. We examined the carriages. No Arsène Lupin.

"By jove!" I exclaimed. "He must have recognized me in the motor, while we were going alongside, and jumped out!"

The guard of the train confirmed my supposition. He had seen a man scrambling down the embankment, at two hundred yards from the station.

"There he is! . . . Look! . . . At the level crossing!"

I darted in pursuit, followed by my two satellites, or rather by one of them, for the other, Massol, turned out to be an uncommonly fast sprinter, gifted with both speed and staying power. In a few seconds, the distance between him and the fugitive was greatly diminished. The man saw him, jumped a hedge and scampered off towards a slope, which he climbed. We saw him further still, entering a little wood.

When we reached the wood, we found Massol waiting for us. He had thought it wiser not to go on, lest he should lose us.

"You were quite right, my dear fellow," I said. "After a run like this, our friend must be exhausted. We've got him."

I examined the skirts of the wood, while thinking how I could best proceed alone to arrest the fugitive, in order myself to effect certain recoveries which the law, no doubt, would only have allowed after a number of disagreeable inquiries. Then I returned to my companions.

"Look here, it's quite easy. You, Massol, take up your position on the left: you, Delivet, on the right. From there, you can watch the whole rear of the wood and he can't leave it, unseen by you, except by this hollow way, where I shall stand. If he does not come out, I'll go in and force him back towards one or the other. You have nothing to do, therefore, but wait. Oh, I was forgetting: in case of alarm, I'll fire a shot."

Massol and Delivet moved off, each to his own side. As soon as they were out of sight, I made my way into the wood, with infinite precautions, so as to be neither seen nor heard. It consisted of close thickets, contrived for the shooting, and intersected by very narrow paths, in which it was only possible to walk by stooping, as though in a leafy tunnel.

One of these ended in a glade where the damp grass showed the marks of footsteps. I followed them, taking care to steal through the undergrowth. They led me to the bottom of a little mound, crowned by a rickety lath-and-plaster hovel.

"He must be there," I thought. "He has chosen a good post of observation."

I crawled close up to the building. A slight sound warned me of his presence and, in fact, I caught sight of him through an opening, with his back turned towards me.

Two bounds brought me upon him. He tried to point the revolver which he held in his hand. I did not give him time, but pulled him to the ground, in such a way that his two arms were twisted and caught under him, while I held him pinned down with my knee upon his chest.

"Listen to me, old chap," I whispered in his ear. "I am Arsène Lupin. You've got to give me back my pocket-book and the lady's wrist-bag, this minute and without fuss . . . in return for which I'll save you from the clutches of the police and enrol you among my pals. Which is it to be: yes or no?"

"Yes," he muttered.

"That's right. Your plan of this morning was cleverly thought out. We shall be good friends."

I got up. He fumbled in his pocket, fetched out a great knife, and tried to strike me with it.

"You ass!" I cried.

With one hand I parried the attack. With the other, I caught him a violent blow on the carotid artery, the blow which is known as the "carotid hook". He fell back stunned.

In my pocket-book, I found my papers and bank notes. I took his own out of curiosity. On an envelope addressed to him I read his name: Pierre Onfrey.

I gave a start. Pierre Onfrey, the perpetrator of the murder in the Rue Lafontaine at Auteuil! Pierre Onfrey, the man who had cut the throats of Madame Delbois and her two daughters! I bent over him. Yes, that was the face which, in the railway carriage, had aroused in me the memory of features which I had seen before.

But time was passing. I placed two hundred-franc notes in an envelope, with a visiting-card bearing these words: "Arsène Lupin to his worthy assistants, Honoré Massol and Gaston Delivet, with his best thanks."

I laid this where it could be seen, in the middle of the room. Beside it I placed Madame Renaud's wrist-bag. Why should it not be restored to the kind friend who had rescued me? I confess, however that I took from it everything that seemed in any way interesting, leaving only a tortoise-shell comb, a stick of lip salve, and an empty purse. Business is business, when all is said and done! And, besides, her husband followed such a disreputable occupation! . . .

There remained the man. He was beginning to move. What was I to do? I was not qualified either to save or to condemn him.

I took away his weapons and fired my revolver in the air:

"That will bring the two others," I thought. "He must find a way out of his difficulties. Let fate take its course."

And I went down the hollow way at a run.

Twenty minutes later, a cross-road, which I had noticed during our pursuit, brought me back to my car.

At four o'clock I telegraphed to my friends from Rouen that an unexpected incident compelled me to put off my visit. Between ourselves, I greatly fear that, in view of what they must now have learnt, I shall be obliged to postpone it indefinitely. It will be a cruel disappointment for them!

At six o'clock, I returned to Paris by L'Isle-Adam, Enghien and the Porte Bineau.

I gathered from the evening papers that the police had at last succeeded in capturing Pierre Onfrey.

The next morning – why should we despise the advantages of intelligent advertisement? – the *Echo de France* contained the following sensational paragraph:

Yesterday, near Buchy, after a number of incidents, Arsène Lupin effected the arrest of Pierre Onfrey. The Auteuil murderer had robbed a lady of the name of Renaud, the wife of the deputy prison governor, in the train between Paris and Le Havre. Arsène Lupin has restored to Madame Renaud the wrist-bag which contained her jewels and has generously rewarded the two detectives who assisted him in the matter of this dramatic arrest.

Victor L. Whitechurch

The Affair of the Corridor Express

The real specialist in railway mysteries was Canon Victor L. Whitechurch (1869–1933), whose Thrilling Stories of the Railway *(1912) is a* Queen's Quorum *choice and in its original edition an extremely rare book. Other railway stories followed and later, towards the end of the author's life, a succession of full-length detective novels too.*

A country canon for many years and, we may imagine, a suitably eccentric one, Whitechurch was later appointed honorary canon at Christ Church College, Oxford. "The Affair of the Corridor Express" is a pleasant example of this curious subgenre, so different from Leblanc's railway story, and it features the detective Thorpe Hazell (special interests: vegetarianism, exercise and railways), who was first featured in the pages of The Royal Magazine.

THORPE HAZELL STOOD in his study in his London flat. On the opposite wall he had pinned a bit of paper, about an inch square, at the height of his eye, and was now going through the most extraordinary contortions.

With his eyes fixed on the paper he was craning his neck as far as it would reach and twisting his head about in all directions. This necessitated a fearful rolling of the eyes in order to keep them on the paper, and was supposed to be a means of strengthening the muscles of the eye for angular sight.

Presently there came a tap at the door.

"Come in!" cried Hazell, still whirling his head round.

"A gentleman wishes to see you at once, sir!" said the servant, handing him a card.

Hazell paused in his exercises, took it from the tray, and read:

"Mr F. W. Wingrave, M.A., B.Sc."

"Oh, show him in," said Hazell, rather impatiently, for he

hated to be interrupted when he was doing his "eye gymnastics."

There entered a young man of about five-and-twenty, with a look of keen anxiety on his face.

"You are Mr Thorpe Hazell?" he asked.

"I am."

"You will have seen my name on my card – I am one of the masters at Shillington School – I had heard your name, and they told me at the station that it might be well to consult you – I hope you don't mind – I know you're not an ordinary detective, but – "

"Sit down, Mr Wingrave," said Hazell, interrupting his nervous flow of language. "You look quite ill and tired."

"I have just been through a very trying experience," replied Wingrave, sinking into a seat. "A boy I was in charge of has just mysteriously disappeared, and I want you to find him for me, and I want to ask your opinion. They say you know all about railways, but – "

"Now, look here, my dear sir, you just have some hot toast and water before you say another word. I conclude you want to consult me on some railway matter. I'll do what I can, but I won't hear you till you've had some refreshment. Perhaps you prefer whiskey – though I don't advise it."

Wingrave, however, chose the whiskey, and Hazell poured him out some, adding soda-water.

"Thank you," he said. "I hope you'll be able to give me advice. I am afraid the poor boy must be killed; the whole thing is a mystery, and I – "

"Stop a bit, Mr Wingrave. I must ask you to tell me the story from the very beginning. That's the best way."

"Quite right. The worry of it has made me incoherent, I fear. But I'll try and do what you propose. First of all, do you know the name of Carr-Mathers?"

"Yes, I think so. Very rich is he not?"

"A millionaire. He has only one child, a boy of about ten, whose mother died at his birth. He is a small boy for his age, and idolized by his father. About three months ago this young Horace Carr-Mathers was sent to our school – Cragsbury House, just outside Shillington. It is not a very large school, but exceedingly select, and the headmaster, Dr Spring, is well known in high-class circles. I may tell you that we have the sons of some of the leading nobility preparing for the public schools. You will readily understand that in such an establishment as ours the most scrupulous care is exercised over the boys, not only

as regards their moral and intellectual training, but also to guard
against any outside influences."

"Kidnapping, for example," interposed Hazell.

"Exactly. There have been such cases known, and Dr Spring has
a very high reputation to maintain. The slightest rumour against
the school would go ill with him – and with all of us masters.

"Well, this morning the headmaster received a telegram about
Horace Carr-Mathers, requesting that he should be sent up to
town."

"Do you know the exact wording?" asked Hazell.

"I have it with me," replied Wingrave, drawing it from his
pocket.

Hazell took it from him, and read as follows:

*Please grant Horace leave of absence for two days. Send him to
London by 5.45 express from Shillington, in first-class carriage, giving
guard instructions to look after him. We will meet train in town. –
Carr-Mathers.*

"Um," grunted Hazell, as he handed it back. "Well, he can afford
long telegrams."

"Oh, he's always wiring about something or other," replied
Wingrave; "he seldom writes a letter. Well, when the doctor received
this he called me into his study.

"'I suppose I must let the boy go,' he said, 'but I'm not at all
inclined to allow him to travel by himself. If anything should happen
to him his father would hold us responsible as well as the railway
company. So you had better take him up to town, Mr Wingrave.'

"'Yes, sir.'

"'You need do no more than deliver him to his father. If
Mr Carr-Mathers is not at the terminus to meet him, take him
with you in a cab to his house in Portland Place. You'll probably
be able to catch the last train home, but, if not, you can get a bed
at an hotel.'

"'Very good, sir.'

"So, shortly after half-past five, I found myself standing on the
platform at Shillington, waiting for the London express."

"Now, stop a moment," interrupted Hazell, sipping a glass of filtered water which he had poured out for himself. "I want to get a clear
notion of this journey of yours from the beginning, for, I presume, you
will shortly be telling me that something strange happened during it.
Was there anything to be noticed before the train started?"

"Nothing at the time. But I remembered afterwards that two men seemed to be watching me rather closely when I took the tickets, and I heard one of them say 'Confound,' beneath his breath. But my suspicions were not aroused at the moment."

"I see. If there is anything in this it was probably because he was disconcerted when he saw you were going to travel with the boy. Did these two men get into the train?"

"I'm coming to that. The train was in sharp to time, and we took our seats in a first-class compartment."

"Please describe the exact position."

"Our carriage was the third from the front. It was a corridor train, with access from carriage to carriage all the way through. Horace and myself were in a compartment alone. I had bought him some illustrated papers for the journey, and for some time he sat quietly enough, looking through them. After a bit he grew fidgety, as you know boys will."

"Wait a minute. I want to know if the corridor of your carriage was on the left or on the right – supposing you to be seated facing the engine?"

"On the left."

"Very well, go on."

"The door leading into the corridor stood open. It was still daylight, but dusk was setting in fast – I should say it was about half-past six, or a little more. Horace had been looking out of the window on the right side of the train when I drew his attention to Rutherham Castle, which we were passing. It stands, as you know, on the left side of the line. In order to get a better view of it he went out into the corridor and stood there. I retained my seat on the right side of the compartment, glancing at him from time to time. He seemed interested in the corridor itself, looking about him, and once or twice shutting and opening the door of our compartment. I can see now that I ought to have kept a sharper eye on him, but I never dreamed that any accident could happen. I was reading a paper myself, and became rather interested in a paragraph. It may have been seven or eight minutes before I looked up. When I did so, Horace had disappeared.

"I didn't think anything of it at first, but only concluded that he had taken a walk along the corridor."

"You don't know which way he went?" inquired Hazell.

"No. I couldn't say. I waited a minute or two, and then rose and looked out into the corridor. There was no one there. Still my suspicions were not aroused. It was possible that he had gone to the lavatory. So I sat down again, and waited. Then I began to get a little anxious, and determined to have a look for him. I walked to either end of the corridor, and searched the lavatories, but they were both empty. Then I looked in all the other compartments of the carriage, and asked their occupants if they had seen him go by, but none of them had noticed him."

"Do you remember how these compartments were occupied?"

"Yes. In the first, which was reserved for ladies, there were five ladies. The next was a smoker with three gentlemen in it. Ours came next. Then, going towards the front of the train, were the two men I had noticed at Shillington; the last compartment had a gentleman and lady and their three children."

"Ah! how about those two men – what were they doing?"

"One of them was reading a book, and the other appeared to be asleep."

"Tell me. Was the door leading to the corridor from their compartment shut?"

"Yes, it was."

"Go on."

"Well, I was in a most terrible fright, and I went back to my compartment and pulled the electric communicator. In a few seconds the front guard came along the corridor and asked me what I wanted. I told him I had lost my charge. He suggested that the boy had walked through to another carriage, and I asked him if he would mind my making a thorough search of the train with him. To this he readily agreed. We went back to the first carriage and began to do so. We examined every compartment from end to end of the train; we looked under every seat, in spite of the protestations of some of the passengers; we searched all the lavatories – every corner of the train – and we found absolutely no trace of Horace Carr-Mathers. No one had seen the boy anywhere."

"Had the train stopped?"

"Not for a second. It was going at full speed all the time. It only slowed down after we had finished the search – but it never quite stopped."

"Ah! We'll come to that presently. I want to ask you some questions first. Was it still daylight?"

"Dusk, but quite light enough to see plainly – besides which, the train lamps were lit."

"Exactly. Those two men, now, in the next compartment to yours – tell me precisely what happened when you visited them the second time with the guard."

"They asked a lot of questions – like many of the other passengers – and seemed very surprised."

"You looked underneath their seats?"

"Certainly."

"On the luggage-racks? A small boy like that could be rolled up in a rug and put on the rack."

"We examined every rack on the train."

Thorpe Hazell lit a cigarette and smoked furiously, motioning to his companion to keep quiet. He was thinking out the situation. Suddenly he said:

"How about the window in those two men's compartment?"

"It was shut – I particularly noticed it."

"You are *quite sure* you searched the whole of the train?"

"Absolutely certain; so was the guard."

"Ah!" remarked Hazell, "even guards are mistaken sometimes. It – er – was only the inside of the train you searched, eh?"

"Of course."

"Very well," replied Hazell, "now, before we go any further, I want to ask you this. Would it have been to anyone's interest to have murdered the boy?"

"I don't think so – from what I know. I don't see how it could be."

"Very well. We will take it as a pure case of kidnapping, and presume that he is alive and well. This ought to console you to begin with."

"Do you think you can help me?"

"I don't know yet. But go on and tell me all that happened."

"Well, after we had searched the train I was at my wits' end – and so was the guard. We both agreed, however, that nothing more could be done till we reached London. Somehow, my strongest suspicions concerning those two men were aroused, and I travelled in their compartment for the rest of the journey."

"Oh! Did anything happen?"

"Nothing. They both wished me good-night, hoped I'd find the boy, got out, and drove off in a hansom."

"And then?"

"I looked about for Mr Carr-Mathers, but he was nowhere to be seen. Then I saw an inspector, and put the case before him. He promised to make inquiries and to have the line searched on the part where I missed Horace. I took a hansom to Portland Place, only to discover that Mr Carr-Mathers is on the Continent and not expected home for a week. Then I came on to you – the inspector had advised me to do so. And that's the whole story. It's a terrible thing for me, Mr Hazell. What do you think of it?"

"Well," replied Hazell, "of course it's very clear that there is a distinct plot. Someone sent that telegram, knowing Mr Carr-Mathers' proclivities. The object was to kidnap the boy. It sounds absurd to talk of brigands and ransoms in this country, but the thing is done over and over again for all that. It is obvious that the boy was expected to travel alone, and that the train was the place chosen for the kidnapping. Hence the elaborate directions. I think you were quite right in suspecting those two men, and it might have been better if you had followed them up without coming to me."

"But they went off alone!"

"Exactly. It's my belief they had originally intended doing so after disposing of Horace, and that they carried out their original intentions."

"But what became of the boy? – how did they – "

"Stop a bit. I'm not at all clear in my own mind. But you mentioned that while you were concluding your search with the guard the train slackened speed?"

"Yes. It almost came to a stop – and then went very slowly for a minute or so. I asked the guard why, but I didn't understand his reply."

"What was it?"

"He said it was a P.W. operation."

Hazell laughed.

"P.W. stands for permanent way," he explained, "I know exactly what you mean now. There is a big job going on near Longmoor – they are raising the level of the line, and the up-trains are running on temporary rails. So they have to proceed very slowly. Now it was after this that you went back to the two men whom you suspected?"

"Yes."

"Very well. Now let me think the thing over. Have some more whiskey? You might also like to glance at the contents of my book-case. If you know anything of first editions and bindings they will interest you."

Wingrave, it is to be feared, paid but small heed to the books, but watched Hazell anxiously as the latter smoked cigarette after cigarette, his brows knit in deep thought. After a bit he said slowly:

"You will understand that I am going to work upon the theory that the boy has been kidnapped and that the original intention has been carried out, in spite of the accident of your presence in the train. How the boy was disposed of meanwhile is what baffles me; but that is a detail – though it will be interesting to know how it was done. Now, I don't want to raise any false hopes, because I may very likely be wrong, but we are going to take action upon a very feasible assumption, and if I am at all correct, I hope to put you definitely on the track. Mind, I don't promise to do so, and, at best, I don't promise to do *more* than put you on a track. Let me see – it's just after nine. We have plenty of time. We'll drive first to Scotland Yard, for it will be as well to have a detective with us."

He filled a flask with milk, put some plasmon biscuits and a banana into a sandwich case, and then ordered his servant to hail a cab.

An hour later, Hazell, Wingrave, and a man from Scotland Yard were closeted together in one of the private offices of the Mid-Eastern Railway with one of the chief officials of the line. The latter was listening attentively to Hazell.

"But I can't understand the boy not being anywhere in the train, Mr Hazell," he said.

"I can – partly," replied Hazell, "but first let me see if my theory is correct."

"By all means. There's a down-train in a few minutes. I'll go with you, for the matter is very interesting. Come along, gentlemen."

He walked forward to the engine and gave a few instructions to the driver, and then they took their seats in the train. After a run of half an hour or so they passed a station.

"That's Longmoor," said the official, "now we shall soon be on the spot. It's about a mile down that the line is being raised."

Hazell put his head out of the window. Presently an ominous red light showed itself. The train came almost to a stop, and then proceeded slowly, the man who had shown the red light changing it to green. They could see him as they passed, standing close to a little temporary hut. It was his duty to warn all approaching drivers, and for this purpose he was stationed some three hundred yards in front of the bit of line that was being operated upon. Very soon they were passing this bit. Naphtha lamps shed a weird light over a busy scene, for the work was being continued night and day. A score or so of sturdy navvies were shovelling and picking along the track.

Once more into the darkness. On the other side of the scene of operations, at the same distance, was another little hut, with a guardian for the up-train. Instead of increasing the speed in passing this hut, which would have been usual, the driver brought the train almost to a standstill. As he did so the four men got out of the carriage, jumping from the footboard to the ground. On went the train, leaving them on the left side of the down track, just opposite the little hut. They could see the man standing outside, his back partly turned to them. There was a fire in a brazier close by that dimly outlined his figure.

He started suddenly, as they crossed the line towards him.

"What are you doing here?" he cried. "You've no business here – you're trespassing."

He was a big, strong-looking man, and he backed a little towards his hut as he spoke.

"I am Mr Mills, the assistant-superintendent of the line," replied the official, coming forward.

"Beg pardon, sir; but how was I to know that?" growled the man.

"Quite right. It's your duty to warn off strangers. How long have you been stationed here?"

"I came on at five o'clock; I'm regular nightwatchman, sir."

"Ah! Pretty comfortable, eh?"

"Yes, thank you, sir," replied the man, wondering why the question was asked, but thinking, not unnaturally, that the assistant-superintendent had come down with a party of engineers to inspect things.

"Got the hut to yourself?"

"Yes, sir."

"Without another word, Mr Mills walked to the door of the hut. The man, his face suddenly growing pale, moved, and stood with his back to it.

"It's – it's private, sir!" he growled.

Hazell laughed.

"All right, my man," he said. "I was right, I think – hullo! – look out! Don't let him go!"

For the man had made a quick rush forward. But the Scotland Yard officer and Hazell were on him in a moment, and a few seconds later the handcuffs clicked on his wrists. Then they flung the door open, and there, lying in the corner, gagged and bound, was Horace Carr-Mathers.

An exclamation of joy broke forth from Wingrave, as he opened his knife to cut the cords. But Hazell stopped him.

"Just half a moment," he said: "I want to see how they've tied him up."

"A peculiar method had been adopted in doing this. His wrists were fastened behind his back, a stout cord was round his body just under the armpits, and another cord above the knees. These were connected by a slack bit of rope.

"All right!" went on Hazell; "let's get the poor lad out of his troubles – there, that's better. How do you feel, my boy?"

"Awfully stiff!" said Horace, "but I'm not hurt. I say, sir," he continued to Wingrave, "how did you know I was here. I *am* glad you've come."

"The question is how did you *get* here?" replied Wingrave. "Mr Hazell, here, seemed to know where you were, but it's a puzzle to me at present."

"If you'd come half an hour later you wouldn't have found him," growled the man who was handcuffed. "I ain't so much to blame as them as employed me."

"Oh, is that how the land lies?" exclaimed Hazell. "I see. You shall tell us presently, my boy, how it happened. Meanwhile, Mr Mills, I think we can prepare a little trap – eh?"

In five minutes all was arranged. A couple of the navvies were brought up from the line, one stationed outside to guard against trains, and with certain other instructions, the other being inside the hut with the rest of them. A third navvy was also dispatched for the police.

"How are they coming?" asked Hazell of the handcuffed man.

"They were going to take a train down from London to Rockhampstead on the East-Northern, and drive over. It's about ten miles off."

"Good! they ought soon to be here," replied Hazell, as he munched some biscuits and washed them down with a draught of milk, after which he astonished them all by solemnly going through one of his "digestive exercises."

A little later they heard the sound of wheels on a road beside the line. Then the man on watch said, in gruff tones:

"The boy's inside!"

But they found more than the boy inside, and an hour later all three conspirators were safely lodged in Longmoor gaol.

"Oh, it was awfully nasty, I can tell you," said Horace Carr-Mathers, as he explained matters afterwards. "I went into the corridor, you know, and was looking about at things, when all of a sudden I felt my coat-collar grasped behind, and a hand was laid over my mouth. I tried to kick and shout, but it was no go. They got me into the compartment, stuffed a handkerchief into my mouth, and tied it in. It was just beastly. Then they bound me hand and foot, and opened the window on the right-hand side – opposite the corridor. I was in a funk, for I thought they were going to throw me out, but one of them told me to keep my pecker up, as they weren't going to hurt me. Then they let me down out of the window by that slack rope, and made it fast to the handle of the door outside. It was pretty bad. There was I, hanging from the door-handle in a sort of doubled-up position, my back resting on the foot-board of the carriage, and the train rushing along like mad. I felt sick and awful, and I had to shut my eyes. I seemed to hang there for ages."

"I told you you only examined the *inside* of the train," said Thorpe Hazell to Wingrave. "I had my suspicions that he was somewhere on the outside all the time, but I was puzzled to know where. It was a clever trick."

"Well," went on the boy, "I heard the window open above me after a bit. I looked up and saw one of the men taking the rope off the handle. The train was just beginning to slow down. Then he hung out of the window, dangling me with one hand. It was horrible. I was hanging below the footboard now. Then the train came almost to a stop, and someone caught me round the waist. I lost my senses for a minute or two, and then I found myself lying in the hut."

"Well, Mr Hazell," said the assistant-superintendent," you were perfectly right, and we all owe you a debt of gratitude."

"Oh!" said Hazell, "it was only a guess at the best. I presumed it was simply kidnapping, and the problem to be solved was how and where the boy was got off the train without injury. It was obvious that he had been disposed of before the train reached London. There was only one other inference. The man on duty was evidently the confederate, for, if not, his presence would have stopped the whole plan of action. I'm very glad to have been of any use. There are interesting points about the case, and it has been a pleasure to me to undertake it."

A little while afterwards Mr Carr-Mathers himself called on Hazell to thank him.

"I should like," he said, "to express my deep gratitude substantially; but I understand you are not an ordinary detective. But is there any way in which I can serve you, Mr Hazell?"

"Yes – two ways."

"Please name them."

"I should be sorry for Mr Wingrave to get into trouble through this affair – or Dr Spring either."

"I understand you, Mr Hazell. They were both to blame, in a way. But I will see that Dr Spring's reputation does not suffer, and that Wingrave comes out of it harmlessly."

"Thank you very much."

"You said there was a second way in which I could serve you."

"So there is. At Dunn's sale last month you were the purchaser of two first editions of 'The New Bath Guide.' If you cared to dispose of one, I – "

"Say no more, Mr Hazell. I shall be glad to give you one for your collection."

Hazell stiffened.

"You misunderstand me!" he exclaimed icily. "I was about to add that if you cared to dispose of a copy I would write you out a cheque."

"Oh, certainly," replied Mr Carr-Mathers with a smile, "I shall be extremely pleased."

Whereupon the transaction was concluded.

Jacques Futrelle

The Diamond Master

*One of the greatest detectives of the post-Holmes era was Professor S. F. X.
Van Dusen, "The Thinking Machine", the creation of the American journalist
and author Jacques Futrelle (1875–1912). The Professor's greatest triumph
was related in "The Problem of Cell 13", which has been called "the most
popular story in mystery literature". Certainly, it has appeared in far too many
anthologies to need another airing in this one.*

*Instead, since we have more space at our disposal, here is a complete short
novel by Futrelle, and the one which undoubtedly contains his best work apart
from the "Thinking Machine" tales.* The Diamond Master *is an unusual
and intriguing puzzle with a dash of science fiction too.*

Jacques Futrelle was lost with the Titanic. *One can only wonder what
other innovations he might have brought to the mystery story had
he survived.*

I THE FIRST DIAMOND

THERE WERE THIRTY or forty personally addressed letters, the daily
heritage of the head of a great business establishment; and a plain,
yellow-wrapped package about the size of a cigarette-box, some three
inches long, two inches wide and one inch deep. It was neatly tied
with thin scarlet twine, and innocent of markings except for the
superscription in a precise, copperplate hand, and the smudge of the
postmark across the ten-cent stamp in the upper right-hand corner.
The imprint of the cancellation, faintly decipherable, showed that
the package had been mailed at the Madison Square substation at
half-past seven o'clock of the previous evening.

Mr Henry Latham, president and active head of the H. Latham
Company, manufacturing jewelers in Fifth Avenue, found the letters
and the package on his desk when he entered his private office a few

minutes past nine o'clock. The simple fact that the package bore no
return address or identifying mark of any sort caused him to pick it
up and examine it, after which he shook it inquiringly. Then, with
kindling curiosity, he snipped the scarlet thread with a pair of silver
scissors, and unfolded the wrappings. Inside was a glazed paper box,
such as jewelers use, but still there was no mark, no printing, either
on top or bottom.

The cover of the box came off in Mr Latham's hand, disclosing a
bed of white cotton. He removed the downy upper layer, and there
– there, nestling against the snowy background, blazed a single
splendid diamond, of six, perhaps seven, carats. Myriad colours
played in its blue-white depths, sparkling, flashing, dazzling in the
subdued light. Mr Latham drew one long quick breath, and walked
over to the window to examine the stone in the full glare of day.

A minute or more passed, a minute of wonder, admiration,
allurement, but at last he ventured to lift the diamond from the
box. It was perfect, so far as he could see; perfect in cutting and
colour and depth, prismatic, radiant, bewilderingly gorgeous. Its
value? Even he could not offer an opinion – only the appraisement of
his expert would be worth listening to on that point. But one thing he
knew instantly – in the million-dollar stock of precious stones stored
away in the vaults of the H. Latham Company, there was not one
to compare with this.

At length, as he stared at it fascinated, he remembered that he
didn't know its owner, and for the second time he examined the
wrappings, the box inside and out, and finally he lifted out the
lower layer of cotton, seeking a fugitive card or mark of some sort.
Surely the owner of so valuable a stone would not be so careless as
to send it this way, through the mail – unregistered – without some
method of identification! Another sharp scrutiny of box and cotton
and wrappings left him in deep perplexity.

Then another idea came. One of the letters, of course! The owner
of the diamond had sent it this way, perhaps to be set, and had sent
instructions under another cover. An absurd, even a reckless thing
to do, but –! And Mr Latham attacked the heap of letters neatly
stacked up in front of him. There were thirty-six of them, but not
one even remotely hinted at diamonds. In order to be perfectly sure,
Mr Latham went through his mail a second time. Perhaps the letter
of instructions had come addressed to the company, and had gone
to the secretary, Mr Flitcroft.

He arose to summon Mr Flitcroft from an adjoining room, then
changed his mind long enough carefully to replace the diamond in

the box and thrust the box into a pigeonhole of his desk. Then he called Mr Flitcroft in.

"Have you gone through your morning mail?" Mr Latham inquired of the secretary.

"Yes," he replied. "I have just finished."

"Did you happen to come across a letter bearing on – that is, was there a letter to-day, or has there been a letter of instructions as to a single large diamond which was to come, or had come, by mail?"

"No, nothing," replied Mr Flitcroft promptly. "The only letter received to-day which referred to diamonds was a notification of a shipment from South Africa."

Mr Latham thoughtfully drummed on his desk.

"Well, I'm expecting some such letter," he explained. "When it comes please call my attention to it. Send my stenographer in."

Mr Flitcroft nodded and withdrew; and for an hour or more Mr Latham was engrossed in the routine of correspondence. There was only an occasional glance at the box in the pigeonhole, and momentary fits of abstraction, to indicate an unabated interest and growing curiosity in the diamond. The last letter was finished, and the stenographer arose to leave.

"Please ask Mr Czenki to come here," Mr Latham directed.

And after a while Mr Czenki appeared. He was a spare little man, with beady black eyes, bushy brows, and a sinister scar extending from the point of his chin across the right jaw. Mr Czenki drew a salary of twenty-five thousand dollars a year from the H. Latham Company, and was worth twice that much. He was the diamond expert of the firm; and for five or six years his had been the final word as to quality and value. He had been a labourer in the South African diamond fields – the scar was an assagai thrust – about the time Cecil Rhodes' grip was first felt there; later he was employed as an expert by Barney Barnato at Kimberley, and finally he went to London with Adolph Zeidt. Mr Latham nodded as he entered, and took the box from the pigeonhole.

"Here's something I'd like you to look at," he remarked.

Mr Czenki removed the cover and turned the glittering stone out into his hand. For a minute or more he stood still, examining it, as he turned and twisted it in his fingers, then walked over to a window, adjusted a magnifying glass in his left eye and continued the scrutiny. Mr Latham swung around in his chair and stared at him intently.

"It's the most perfect blue-white I've ever seen," the expert announced at last. "I dare say it's the most perfect in the world."

Mr Latham arose suddenly and strode over to Mr Czenki, who was twisting the jewel in his fingers, singling out, dissecting, studying the colourful flashes, measuring the facets with practiced eyes, weighing it on his finger-tips, seeking a possible flaw.

"The cutting is very fine," the expert went on. "Of course I would have to use instruments to tell me if it is mathematically correct; and the weight, I imagine, is – is about six carats, perhaps a fraction more."

"What's it worth?" asked Mr Latham. "Approximately, I mean?"

"We know the colour is perfect," explained Mr Czenki precisely. "If, in addition, the cutting is perfect, and the depth is right, and the weight is six carats or a fraction more, it's worth – in other words, if that is the most perfect specimen in existence, as it seems to be, it's worth whatever you might choose to demand for it – twenty, twenty-five, thirty thousand dollars. With this colour, and assuming it to be six carats, even if *badly* cut, it would be worth ten or twelve thousand."

Mr Latham mopped his brow. And this had come by mail, unregistered!

"It would not be possible to say where – where such a stone came from – what country," Mr Latham inquired curiously. "What's your opinion?"

The expert shook his head. "If I had to guess I should say Brazil, of course," he replied; "but that would be merely because the most perfect blue-white diamonds come from Brazil. They are found all over the world – in Africa, Russia, India, China, even in the United States. The simple fact that this colour is perfect makes conjecture useless."

Mr Latham lapsed into silence, and for a time paced back and forth across his office; Mr Czenki stood waiting.

"Please get the exact weight," Mr Latham requested abruptly. "Also test the cutting. It came into my possession in rather an – an unusual manner, and I'm curious."

The expert went out. An hour later he returned and placed the white, glazed box on the desk before Mr Latham.

"The weight is six and three-sixteenths carats," he stated. "The depth is absolutely perfect, according to the diameter of the girdle. The *bezel* facets are mathematically correct to the minutest fraction – thirty-three, including the table. The facets on the *collet* side are equally exact – twenty-five including the *collet*, or fifty-eight facets in all. As I said, the colour is flawless. In other words," he continued without hesitation, "I should say, speaking as an expert, that it is the most perfect diamond existing in the world to-day."

Mr Latham had been staring at him mutely, and he still sat silent for an instant after Mr Czenki had finished.

"And its value?" he asked at last.

"Its value!" Mr Czenki repeated musingly. "You know, Mr Latham," he went on suddenly, "there are a hundred experts, commissioned by royalty, scouring the diamond markets of the world for such stones as this. So, if you are looking for a sale and a price, by all means offer it abroad first." He lifted the sparkling, iridescent jewel from the box again, and gazed at it reflectively. "There is not one stone belonging to the British crown, for instance, which would in any way compare with this."

"Not even the Koh-i-noor?" Mr Latham demanded, surprised.

Mr Czenki shook his head.

"Not even the Koh-i-noor. It is larger, that's all – a fraction more than one hundred and six carats, but it has neither the colouring nor the cutting of this." There was a pause. "Would it be impertinent if I ask who owns this?"

"I don't know," replied Mr Latham slowly. "I don't know; but it isn't ours. Perhaps later I'll be able to – "

"I beg your pardon," the expert interrupted courteously, and there was a slight expression of surprise on his thin scarred face. "Is that all?"

Mr Latham nodded absently and Mr Czenki left the room.

II   TWEEDLEDUM AND TWEEDLEDEE

A little while later, when Mr Latham started out to luncheon, he thrust the white glazed box into an inside pocket. It had occurred to him that Schultze – Gustave Schultze, the greatest importer of precious stones in America – was usually at the club where he had luncheon, and –

He found Mr Schultze, a huge blond German, sitting at a table in an alcove, alone, gazing out upon Fifth Avenue in deep abstraction, with perplexed wrinkles about his blue eyes. The German glanced around at Latham quickly as he proceeded to draw out a chair on the opposite side of the table.

"Sid down, Laadham, sid down," he invited explosively. "I haf yust send der vaiter to der delephone to ask – "

There was a restrained note of excitement in the German's voice, but at the moment it was utterly lost upon Mr Latham.

"Schultze, you've probably imported more diamonds in the last ten years than any other half-dozen men in the United States," he interrupted. "I have something here I want you to see. Perhaps, at some time, it may have passed through your hands."

He placed the glazed box on the table. For an instant the German stared at it with amazed eyes, then one fat hand darted toward it, and he spilled the diamond out on the napkin in his plate. Then he sat gazing as if fascinated by the lambent, darting flashes deep from the blue-white heart.

"*Mein Gott*, Laadham!" he exclaimed, and with fingers which shook a little he lifted the stone and squinted through it toward the light, with critical eyes. Mr Latham was leaning forward on the table, waiting, watching, listening.

"Well?" he queried impatiently, at last.

"Laadham, id is der miracle!" Mr Schultze explained solemnly, with his characteristic, whimsical philosophy. "I haf der dupligade of id, Laadham – der dwin, der liddle brudder. Zee here!"

From an inner pocket he produced a glazed white box, identical with that which Mr Latham had just set down, then carefully laid the cover aside.

"Look, Laadham, look!"

Mr Latham looked – and gasped! Here was the counterpart of the mysterious diamond which still lay in Mr Schultze's outstretched palm.

"Dey are dwins, Laadham," remarked the German quaintly, finally. "Id came by der mail in dis morning – yust like das, wrapped in paper, but mit no marks, no name, no noddings. Id yust came!"

With his right hand Mr Latham lifted the duplicate diamond from its cotton bed, and with his left took the other from the German's hand. Then, side by side, he examined them; colour, cutting, diameter, depth, all seemed to be the same.

"Dwins, I dell you," repeated Mr Schultze stolidly. "Dweedledum und Dweedledee, born of der same mudder und fadder. Laadham, id iss der miracle! Dey are der most beaudiful der world in – yust der pair of dem."

"Have you made," Mr Latham began, and there was an odd, uncertain note in his voice – "Have you made an expert examination?"

"I haf. I measure him, der deepness, der cudding, der facets, und id iss perfect. Und I take my own judgement of a diamond, Laadham, before any man der vorld in but Czenki."

"And the weight?"

"Prezizely six und d'ree-sixdeendh carads. Dere iss nod more as a difference of a d'irty-second bedween dem."

Mr Latham regarded the importer steadily, the while he fought back an absurd, nervous thrill in his voice.

"There isn't that much, Schultze. Their weight is exactly the same."

For a long time the two men sat staring at each other unseeingly. Finally the German, with a prodigious Teutonic sigh, replaced the diamond from Mr Latham's right hand in one of the glazed boxes and carefully stowed it away in a cavernous pocket; Mr Latham mechanically disposed of the other in the same manner.

"Whose are they?" he demanded at length. "Why are they sent to us like this, with no name, no letter of explanation? Until I saw the stone you have I had believed this other had been sent to me by some careless fool for setting, perhaps, and that a letter would follow it. I merely brought it here on the chance that it was one of your importations and that you could identify it. But since you have received one under circumstances which seem to be identical, now – " He paused helplessly. "What does it mean?"

Mr Schultze shrugged his huge shoulders and thoughtfully flicked the ashes from his cigar into the consommé.

"You know, Laadham," he said slowly, "dey don't pick up diamonds like dose on der streed gorners. I didn't believe dere vas a stone of so bigness in der Unided States whose owner I didn't know id vas. Dose dat are here I haf bring in myself, mostly – dose I did nod I haf kept drack of. I don'd know, Laadham, I don'd know. Der longer I lif der more I don'd know."

The two men completed a scant luncheon in silence.

"Obviously," remarked Mr Latham as he laid his napkin aside, "the diamonds were sent to us by the same person; obviously they were sent to us with a purpose; obviously we will, in time, hear from the person who sent them; obviously they were intended to be perfectly matched; so let's see if they are. Come to my office and let Czenki examine the one you have." He hesitated an instant. "Suppose you let me take it. We'll try a little experiment."

He carefully placed the jewel which the German handed to him, in an outside pocket, and together they went to his office. Mr Czenki appeared, in answer to a summons, and Mr Latham gave him the German's box.

"That's the diamond you examined for me this morning, isn't it?" he inquired.

Mr Czenki turned it out into his hand and scrutinized it perfunctorily.

"Yes," he replied after a moment.

"Are you quite certain?" Mr Latham insisted.

Something in the tone caused Mr Czenki to raise his beady black eyes questioningly for an instant, after which he walked over to a window and adjusted his magnifying glass again. For a moment or more he stood there, then:

"It's the same stone," he announced positively.

"Id *iss* der miracle, Laadham, when Czenki make der misdake!" the German exploded suddenly. "Show him der odder von."

Mr Czenki glanced from one to the other with a quick, inquisitive glance; then, without a word, Mr Latham produced the second box and opened it. The expert stared incredulously at the two perfect stones and finally, placing them side by side on a sheet of paper, returned to the window and sat down. Mr Latham and Mr Schultze stood beside him, looking on curiously as he turned and twisted the jewels under his powerful glass.

"As a matter of fact," asked Mr Latham pointedly at last, "you would not venture to say which of those stones it was you examined this morning, would you?"

"No," responded Mr Czenki curtly, "not without weighing them."

"And if the weight is identical?"

"No," said Mr Czenki again. " If the weight is the same there is not the minutest fraction of a difference between them."

III   THURSDAY AT THREE

Mr Latham ran through his afternoon mail with feverish haste and found – nothing; Mr Schultze achieved the same result more ponderously. On the following morning the mail still brought nothing. About eleven o'clock Mr Latham's desk telephone rang.

"Come to my office," requested Mr Schultze, in guttural excitement. "*Mein Gott*, Laadham, der – come to my offiz, Laadham, und bring der diamond!"

Mr Latham went. Including himself, there were the heads of the five greatest jewel establishments in America, representing, perhaps,

one-tenth of the diamond trade of the country, in Mr Schultze's office.
He found the other four gathered around a small table, and on this
table – Mr Latham gasped as he looked – lay four replicas of the
mysterious diamond in his pocket.

"Pud id down here, Laadham," directed Mr Schultze. "Dey're all
dwins alike – Dweedledums and Dweedledeeses."

Mr Latham silently placed the fifth diamond on the table, and
for a minute or more the five men stood still and gazed, first at the
diamonds, then at one another, and then again at the diamonds.
Mr Solomon, the crisply spoken head of Solomon, Berger and
Company, broke the silence.

"These all came yesterday morning by mail, one to each of us, just
as the one came to you," he informed Mr Latham. "Mr Harris here,
of Harris and Blacklock, learned that I had received such a stone,
and brought the one he had received for comparison. We made some
inquiries together and found that a duplicate had been received by
Mr Stoddard, of Hale-Stoddard-Higginson. The three of us came
here to see if Mr Schultze could give us any information, and he
telephoned for you."

Mr Latham listened blankly.

"It's positively beyond belief," he burst out. "What – what does
it mean?"

"Id means," the German importer answered philosophically, "dat
if diamonds like dese keep popping up like dis, dat in anoder d'ree
months dey vill nod be vorth more as five cents a bucketful."

The truth of the observation came to the four others simultaneously. Hitherto there had been only the sense of wonder and
admiration; now came the definite knowledge that diamonds,
even of such great size and beauty as these, would grow cheap
if they were to be picked out of the void; and realization of this
astonishing possibility brought five shrewd business brains to a
unit of investigation. First it was necessary to find how many
other jewelers had received duplicates; then it was necessary to
find whence they came. A plan was adopted, and an investigation
ordered to begin at once.

"Dere iss someding back of id, of course," declared Mr Schultze.
"*Vas iss?* Dey are not being send for our healdh!"

During the next six days half a score of private detectives
were at work on the mystery, with the slender clues at hand.
They scanned hotel registers, quizzed paper-box manufacturers,
pestered stamp clerks, bedevilled postal officials, and the sum
total of their knowledge was negative, save in the fact that they

established beyond question that only these five men had received the diamonds.

And meanwhile the heads of the five greatest jewel houses in New York were assiduous in their search for that copperplate superscription in their daily mail. On the morning of the eighth day it came. Mr Latham was nervously shuffling his unopened personal correspondence when he came upon it – a formal white square envelope, directed by that same copperplate hand which had directed the boxes. He dropped into his chair, and opened the envelope with eager fingers. Inside was this letter:

My Dear Sir,

One week ago I took the liberty of sending to you, and to each of four other leading jewelers of this city whose names you know, a single large diamond of rare cutting and colour. Please accept this as a gift from me, and be good enough to convey my compliments to the other four gentlemen, and assure them that theirs, too, were gifts.

Believe me, I had no intention of making a mystery of this. It was necessary definitely to attract your attention, and I could conceive of no more certain way than in this manner. In return for the value of the jewels I shall ask that you and the four others concerned give me an audience in your office on Thursday afternoon next at three o'clock; that you make known this request to the others; and that three experts whose judgement you will all accept shall meet with us.

I believe you will appreciate the necessity of secrecy in this matter, for the present at least. Respectfully,

E. VAN CORTLANDT WYNNE

They were on hand promptly, all of them – Mr Latham, Mr Schultze, Mr Solomon, Mr Stoddard and Mr Harris. The experts agreed upon were the unemotional Mr Czenki, Mr Cawthorne, an Englishman in the employ of Solomon, Berger and Company, and Mr Schultze, who gravely admitted that he was the first expert in the land, after Mr Czenki, and whose opinion of himself was unanimously accepted by the others. The meeting place was the directors' room of the H. Latham Company.

At one minute to three o'clock a clerk entered with a card, and handed it to Mr Latham.

"'Mr E. van Cortlandt Wynne,'" Mr Latham read aloud, and every man in the room moved a little in his chair. Then: "Show him in here, please."

"Now, gendlemens," observed Mr Schultze sententiously, "ve shall zee vat ve shall zee."

The clerk went out and a moment later Mr Wynne appeared. He was tall and rather slender, alert of eyes, graceful of person; perfectly self-possessed and sure of himself, yet without one trace of egotism in manner or appearance – a fair type of the brisk, courteous young business man of New York. He wore a tweed suit, and in his left hand carried a small sole-leather grip. For an instant he stood, framed by the doorway, meeting the sharp scrutiny of the assembled jewelers with a frank smile. For a little time no one spoke – merely gazed – and finally:

"Mr Latham?" queried Mr Wynne, looking from one to the other.

Mr Latham came to his feet with a sudden realization of his responsibilities as a temporary host, and introductions followed. Mr Wynne passed along one side of the table, shaking hands with each man in turn until he came to Mr Czenki. Mr Latham introduced them.

"Mr Czenki," repeated Mr Wynne, and he allowed his eyes to rest frankly upon the expert for a moment. "Your name has been repeated to me so often that I almost feel as if I knew you."

Mr Czenki bowed without speaking.

"I am assuming that this is the Mr Czenki who was associated with Mr Barnato and Mr Zeidt?" the young man went on.

"That is correct, yes," replied the expert.

"And I believe, too, that you once did some special work for Professor Henri Moissan in Paris?"

Mr Czenki's black eyes seemed to be searching the other's face for an instant, and then he nodded affirmatively.

"I made some tests for him, yes," he volunteered.

Mr Wynne passed on along the other side of the long table, and stopped at the end. Mr Latham was at his right, Mr Schultze at his left, and Mr Czenki sat at the far end, facing him. The small sole-leather grip was on the floor at Mr Wynne's feet. For a moment he permitted himself to enjoy the varying expressions of interest on the faces around the table.

"Gentlemen," he began, then, "you all, probably, have seen my letter to Mr Latham, or at least you are aware of its contents, so you understand that the diamonds which were mailed to you are your property. I am not an eleemosynary institution for the relief of diamond merchants," and he smiled a little, "for the gifts are preliminary to a plain business proposition – a method of concentrating your attention, and, in themselves, part payment, if I may say it, for any worry or inconvenience which followed upon their appearance. There are only five of them in the world, they are precisely alike, and they are yours. I beg of you to accept them with my compliments."

Mr Schultze tilted his chair back a little, the better to study the young man's countenance.

"I am going to make some remarkable statements," the young man continued, "but each of those statements is capable of demonstration here and now. Don't hesitate to interrupt if there is a question in your mind, because everything I shall say is vital to each of you as bearing on the utter destruction of the world's traffic in diamonds. It is coming, gentlemen, it is coming, just as inevitably as that night follows day, unless you stop it. You *can* stop it by concerted action, in a manner which I shall explain later."

He paused and glanced along the table. Only the face of Mr Czenki was impassive.

"Since the opening of the fields in South Africa," Mr Wynne resumed quietly, "something like five hundred million dollars' worth of diamonds have been found there; and we'll say arbitrarily that all the other diamond fields of the world, including Brazil and Australia, have produced another five hundred million dollars' worth – in other words, since about 1868 a billion dollars' worth of diamonds has been placed upon the market. Gentlemen, that represents millions and millions of carats – forty, fifty, sixty million carats in the rough, say. Please bear those figures in mind a moment.

"Now, suddenly, and as yet secretly, the diamond output of the world has been increased fiftyfold – that is, gentlemen, within the year I can place *another* billion dollars' worth of diamonds, at the prices that hold now, in the open market; and within still another year I can place still another billion in the market; and on and on indefinitely. To put it differently, I have found the unlimited supply."

"*Mein Gott*, vere *iss* id?" demanded the German breathlessly.

Heedless of the question, Mr Wynne leaned forward on the table, and gazed with half-closed eyes into the faces before him. Incredulity was the predominant expression, and coupled with that was amazement. Mr Harris, with quite another emotion displaying itself on his face, pushed back his chair as if to rise; a slight wrinkle in his brow was all the evidence of interest displayed by Mr Czenki.

"I am not crazy, gentlemen," Mr Wynne went on after a moment, and the perfectly normal voice seemed to reassure Mr Harris, for he sat still. "The diamonds are now in existence, untold millions of dollars' worth of them – but there is the tedious work of cutting. They're in existence, packed away as you pack potatoes – I thrust my two hands into a bag and bring them out full of stones as perfect as the ones I sent you."

He straightened up again and the deep earnestness of his face relaxed a little.

"I believe you said, Mr Wynne, that you could prove any assertion you might make, here and now?" suggested Mr Latham coldly. "It occurs to me that such extraordinary statements as these demand immediate proof."

Mr Wynne turned and smiled at him.

"You are quite right" he agreed; and then, to all of them: "It's hardly necessary to dwell upon the value of coloured diamonds – the rarest and most precious of all – the perfect rose-colour, the perfect blue and the perfect green." He drew a small, glazed white box from his pocket and opened it. "Please be good enough to look at this, Mr Czenki."

He spun a rosily glittering object, some three-quarters of an inch in diameter, along the table toward Mr Czenki. It flamed and flashed as it rolled, with that deep iridescent blaze which left no doubt of what it was. Every man at the table arose and crowded about Mr Czenki, who held a flamelike sphere in his outstretched palm for their inspection. There was a tense, breathless instant.

"It's a diamond!" remarked Mr Czenki, as if he himself had doubted it. "A deep rose-colour, cut as a perfect sphere."

"It's worth half a million dollars if it's worth a cent!" exclaimed Mr Solomon almost fiercely.

"And this, please."

Mr Wynne, from the other end of the table, spun another glittering sphere toward them – this as brilliantly, softly green as the verdure of early spring, prismatic, gleaming, radiant. Mr Czenki's beady eyes snapped as he caught it and held it out for the others to see, and some strange emotion within caused him to close his teeth savagely.

"And this!" said Mr Wynne again.

And a third sphere rolled along the table. This was blue – elusively blue as a moonlit sky. Its rounded sides caught the light from the windows and sparkled it back.

And now the three jewels lay side by side in Mr Czenki's open hand, the while the five greatest diamond merchants of the United States glutted their eyes upon them. Mr Latham's face went deathly white from sheer excitement, the German's violently red from the same emotion, and the others – there was amazement, admiration, awe in them. Mr Czenki's countenance was again impassive.

IV   THE UNLIMITED SUPPLY

"If you will all be seated again, please?" requested Mr Wynne, who still stood, cool and self-certain, at the end of the table.

The sound of his voice brought a returning calm to the others, and they resumed their seats – all save Mr Cawthorne, who walked over to a window with the three spheres in his hand and stood there examining them under his glass.

"You gentlemen know, of course, the natural shape of the diamond in the rough?" Mr Wynne resumed questioningly. "Here are a dozen specimens which may interest you – the octahedron, the rhombic dodecahedron, the triakisoctahedron and the hexakisoctahedron." He spread them along the table with a sweeping gesture of his hand, colourless, inert pebbles, ranging in size from a pea to a peanut. "And now, you ask, where do they come from?"

The others nodded unanimously.

"I'll have to state a fact that you all know, as part answer to that question," replied Mr Wynne. "A perfect diamond is a perfect diamond, no matter where it comes from – Africa, Brazil, India, or New Jersey. There is not the slightest variation in value if the stone is perfect. That being true, it is a matter of no concern to you, as dealers, where these come from – sufficient it is that they are here, and, being here, they bring home to you the necessity of concerted action to uphold the diamond as a thing of value."

"You said der vorld's oudpud had been increased fiftyfold?" suggested Mr Schultze. "Do ve understand you prove him by dese?"

The young man smiled slightly and drew a leather packet from an inner pocket. He stripped it of several rubber bands, and then turned to Mr Czenki again.

"Mr Czenki, I have been told that a few years ago you had an opportunity of examining the Koh-i-noor. Is that correct?"

"Yes."

"I believe the Koh-i-noor was temporarily removed from its setting, and that you were one of three experts to whom was intrusted the task of selecting four stones of the identical coloring to be set alongside it?"

"That is correct," Mr Czenki agreed.

"You held the Koh-i-noor in your hand, and you would be able to identify it?"

"*I* would be able to identify it," said Mr Cawthorne positively.

He had turned at the window quickly; it was the first time he had spoken. Mr Wynne walked around the table to Mr Czenki, and Mr Cawthorne approached them.

"Suppose, then, you gentlemen examine this together," suggested Mr Wynne.

He lifted a great glittering jewel from the leather packet and held it aloft that all might see. Then he carefully placed it on the table in front of the experts; the others came to their feet and stood gazing as if fascinated.

"By Jove!" exclaimed Mr Cawthorne.

For a minute or more the two experts studied the huge diamond – one hundred and six carats and a fraction – beneath their glasses, and finally Mr Cawthorne picked it up and led the way toward the window. Mr Czenki and the German followed him.

"Gentlemen," and Mr Cawthorne now turned sharply to face the others, "this *is* the Koh-i-noor! Mr Wynne didn't mention it, but I was one of the three experts who had opportunity to examine the Koh-i-noor. This *is* the Koh-i-noor!"

Startled, questioning eyes were turned upon Mr Wynne; he was smiling. There was a question in his face as he regarded Mr Czenki.

"It is either the Koh-i-noor or an exact duplicate," said Mr Czenki.

"It *is* the Koh-i-noor," repeated Mr Cawthorne doggedly.

"Id seems to me," interposed Mr Schultze, "dat if der Koh-i-noor vas missing somebody would haf heard, ain'd id? I haf nod heard. Mr Czenki made a misdake der oder day – maybe you make id to-day?"

"You *have* made a mistake, I assure you, Mr Cawthorne," remarked Mr Wynne quietly. "You identify that as the Koh-i-noor, of course, by a slight inaccuracy in one of the facets adjoining the *collet*. That inaccuracy is known to every diamond expert – the mistake you make is a compliment to that as a replica."

He resumed his position at the end of the table, and Mr Schultze sat beside him. Amazement was a thing of the past, as far as he was concerned. Mr Czenki dropped into his chair again.

"And now, Mr Czenki, speaking as an expert, what would you say was the most perfect diamond in the world?" asked Mr Wynne.

"The five blue-white stones you mailed to these gentlemen," replied the expert without hesitation.

"Perhaps I should have specified the most perfect diamond known to the world at large," Mr Wynne added smilingly.

"The Regent."

Again Mr Cawthorne looked around, with bewilderment in his eyes. The others nodded their approval of Mr Czenki's opinion.

"The Regent, yes," Mr Wynne agreed; "one hundred and thirty-six and three-quarter carats, cut as a brilliant, worn by Napoleon in his sword-hilt, now in the Louvre at Paris, the property of the French Government – valued at two and a half million dollars." His hand disappeared into the leather packet again; poised on his finger-tips, when he withdrew them, was another huge jewel. He dropped it into Mr Schultze's hand. "There is further proof that the diamond output has increased fiftyfold."

Mr Schultze seemed dazed as he turned and twisted the diamond in his hand. After a moment he passed it on down the table without a word.

"A duplicate also," and Mr Wynne glanced at Mr Cawthorne. "It is reasonably certain that you would have heard of that if it had disappeared from the Louvre." He turned to Mr Schultze again. "I may add that this fiftyfold increase in output is not confined to small stones," he went on tauntingly. "They are of all sizes and values. For instance?"

He lifted still another jewel from the packet and held it aloft for an instant.

"The Orloff!" gasped Mr Solomon.

"No," the young man corrected; "this, too, is a duplicate. The original is in the Russian sceptre. This is a replica – colour, weight and cutting being identical – one hundred and ninety-three carats, nearly as large as a pigeon's egg."

Again Mr Wynne glanced along the table. Suddenly the frank amazement had vanished from the faces of these men, and he found only the tense interest of an audience watching a clever juggler. For a time Mr Schultze studied the Orloff duplicate, then passed it along to the experts.

"Der gread Cullinan diamond weighs only two or d'ree pounds," he questioned in a tone of deep resignation. "Maybe you haf *him* in der backage, alretty?"

"Not yet," replied Mr Wynne, "but I may possibly get that on my next trip out. Who knows?"

There was a long, tense silence. Mechanically Mr Czenki placed the three spheres and the replicas in an orderly little row on the table in front of him and the uncut stones beside them – six, seven, eight million dollars' worth of diamonds.

"Gentlemen, are you convinced?" demanded Mr Wynne suddenly. "Is there one lingering doubt in any mind here as to the tremendous find which makes the production of all those possible?"

"Id iss der miracle, Mr Vynne," admitted the German gravely, after a little pause. "Dere iss someding before us as nefer vas in der vorld. I am gonvinced!"

"Up to this moment, gentlemen, the De Beers Syndicate has controlled the diamond market," Mr Wynne announced, "but now, from this moment, I control it. I hold it there, in the palm of my hand, with the unlimited supply back of me. I am offering you an opportunity to prevent the annihilation of the market. It rests with you. If I turn loose a billion dollars' worth of diamonds within the year you are ruined – all of you. You *know* that – it's hardly necessary to tell you. And, gentlemen, I don't care to do it."

"What is your proposition?" queried Mr Latham quietly. His face was ghastly white; haggard lines, limned by amazement and realization, were marked clearly on it. "What is your proposition?" he repeated.

"Wait a minute," interposed Mr Solomon protestingly, and he turned to the young man. "The Syndicate controls the market by force of a reserve stock of ten or fifteen million dollars. Do we understand that you have more than these ready for market now?"

Mr Wynne stooped and lifted the small sole-leather grip which had been unheeded on the floor. He unfastened the catch and turned the bag upside down upon the table. When he raised it again the assembled jewelers gazed upon a spectacle unknown and undreamed of in the history of the world – a great, glittering heap of diamonds, flashing, colorful, prismatic, radiant, bedazzling. They rattled like pebbles upon the mahogany table as they slipped and slid one against another, and then, at rest, resolved themselves into a steady, multi-colored blaze which was almost blinding.

"Now, gentlemen, on the table before you there are about thirty million dollars' worth of diamonds," Mr Wynne announced calmly. "They are all perfect, every one of them; and they're mine. I know where they come from; you can't find out. It's none of your business. Are you satisfied *now*?"

Mr Latham looked, looked until his eyes seemed bursting from his head, and then, with an inarticulate little cry, fell forward on the table with his face on his arms. The German importer came to his feet with one vast Teutonic oath, then sat down again; Mr Solomon plunged his hand into the blazing heap and laughed senselessly. The others were silent, stunned, overcome. Mr Wynne walked around the table and replaced the spheres and replicas in his pocket, after which he resumed his former position.

"I have stated my case, gentlemen," he continued quietly, very quietly. "Now for my proposition. Briefly it is this: For a consideration I will destroy the unlimited supply. I will bind myself to secrecy, as you must; I will guarantee that no stone from the same source is ever offered in the market or privately, when you gentlemen," and his manner was emphatically deliberate, "purchase from me at one-half the carat price you now pay *one hundred million dollars' worth of diamonds!*"

He paused. There was not a sound; no one moved.

"You may put them on the market as you may agree, slowly, thus preventing any material fluctuation in value," he went on. "How to hold this tremendous reserve secretly and still permit the operation of the other diamond mines of the world is the great problem you will have to face."

He leaned over, picked up a handful from the heap and replaced them in the leather bag. The others he swept off into it, then snapped the lock.

"I will give you one week to decide what you will do," he said in conclusion. "If you accept the proposition, then six weeks from next Thursday at three o'clock I shall expect a cash payment of ten million dollars for a portion of the stones now cut and ready; within a year all the diamonds will have been delivered and the transaction must be closed." He hesitated an instant. "I'm sorry, gentlemen, if the terms seem hard, but I think, after consideration, you will agree that I have done you a favour by coming to you instead of going into the market and destroying it. I will call next Thursday at three for your answer. That is all. Good day!"

The door opened and closed behind him. A minute, two minutes, three minutes passed and no one spoke. At last the German came to his feet slowly with a sigh.

"Anyhow, gendlemens," he remarked, "dat young man has a hell of a lod of diamonds, ain'd id?"

V THE ASTUTE MR BIRNES

It was a few minutes past four o'clock when Mr Wynne strode through the immense retail sales department of the H. Latham

Company, and a uniformed page held open the front door for him to pass out. Once on the sidewalk the self-styled diamond master of the world paused long enough to pull on his gloves, carelessly chucking the small sole-leather grip with its twenty-odd million dollars' worth of precious stones under one arm; then he turned up Fifth Avenue toward Thirty-fourth Street. A sneak thief brushed past him, appraised him with one furtive glance, then went his way, seeking quarry more promising.

Simultaneously with Mr Wynne's appearance three men whose watchful eyes had been fastened on the doorway of the H. Latham Company for something more than an hour stirred. One of them – Frank Claflin – was directly across the street, strolling along idly, the most purposeless of all in the hurrying, well-dressed throng; another – Steve Birnes, chief of the Birnes Detective Agency – appeared from the hallway of a building adjoining the H. Latham Company, and moved along behind Mr Wynne, some thirty feet in the rear; the third – Jerry Malone – was half a block away, up Fifth Avenue, coming slowly toward them.

Mr Birnes adjusted his pace to that of Mr Wynne, step for step, and then, seeming assured of his safety from any chance glance, ostentatiously mopped his face with a handkerchief, flirting it a little to the left as he replaced it in his pocket. Claflin, across the street, understood from that that he was to go on up Fifth Avenue to Thirty-fourth Street, the next intersection, and turn west to board any crosstown car which Mr Wynne might possibly take; and a cabby who had been sitting motionless on his box down the street, understood from it that he was to move slowly along behind Mr Birnes, and be prepared for an emergency.

Half-way between Thirty-third and Thirty-fourth Streets, Jerry Malone approached and passed Mr Wynne without so much as a glance at him, and went on toward his chief.

"Drop in behind here," Mr Birnes remarked crisply to Malone, without looking around. "I'll walk on ahead and turn east in Thirty-fourth Street to nail him if he swings a car. Claflin's got him going west."

Mr Wynne was perhaps some twenty feet from the corner of Thirty-fourth Street and Fifth Avenue when Mr Birnes passed him. His glance lingered on the broad back of the chief reflectively as he swung by and turned into the cross street, after a quick, business-like glance at an approaching car. Then Mr Wynne smiled. He paused on the edge of the curb long enough for an automobile to pass, then went on across Thirty-fourth Street to the uptown side and, turning flatly, looked Mr Birnes over pensively, after which he leaned up against an electric-light pole and scribbled something on an envelope.

A closed cab came wriggling and squirming up Fifth Avenue. As it reached the middle of Thirty-fourth Street Mr Wynne raised his hand, and the cab drew up beside him. He said something to the driver, opened the door and stepped in. Mr Birnes smiled confidently. So that was it, eh? He, too, crossed Thirty-fourth Street and lifted his hand. The cab which had been drifting along behind him immediately came up.

"Now, Jimmy, get on the job," instructed Mr Birnes, as he stepped in. "Keep that chap in sight and when he stops you stop."

Mr Wynne's cab jogged along comfortably up the avenue, twisting and winding a path between the other vehicles, the while Mr Birnes regarded it with thoughtful gaze. Its number dangled on a white board in the rear; Mr Birnes just happened to note it.

"Grand Central Station, I'll bet a hat," he mused.

But the closed cab didn't turn into Forty-second Street; it went past, then on past Delmonico's, past the Cathedral, past the Plaza, at Fifty-ninth Street, and still on uptown. It was not hurrying – it merely moved steadily; but once free of the snarl which culminates at the Fifty-ninth Street entrance to Central Park, its speed was increased a little. Past Sixty-fourth Street, Sixty-fifth, Sixty-sixth, and at Sixty-seventh it slowed up and halted at the sidewalk on the far side.

"Stop in front of a door, Jimmy," directed the detective hastily.

Jimmy obeyed gracefully, and Mr Birnes stepped out, hardly half a block behind the closed cab. He went through an elaborate pretense of paying Jimmy, the while he regarded Mr Wynne, who had also alighted and was paying the driver. The small sole-leather grip was on the ground between his feet as he ransacked his pocketbook. A settlement was reached, the cabby nodded, touched his horse with his whip and continued to jog on up Fifth Avenue.

"Now, he didn't order that chap to come back or he wouldn't have paid him," the detective reasoned. "Therefore he's close to where he is going."

But Mr Wynne seemed in no hurry; instead he stood still for a minute gazing after the retreating vehicle, which fact made it necessary for Mr Birnes to start a dispute with Jimmy as to just how much the fare should be. They played the scene admirably; had Mr Wynne been listening he might even have heard a part of the vigorous argument. Whether he listened or not he turned and gazed straight at Mr Birnes until, finally, the detective recognized the necessity of getting out of sight.

With a final explosion he handed a bill to Jimmy and turned to go up the steps of the house. He had no business there, but he must do something.

Jimmy turned the cab short and went rattling away down Fifth Avenue to await orders in the lee of a corner a block or so away. And, meanwhile, as Mr Wynne still stood on the corner, Mr Birnes had to go on up the steps. But as he placed his foot on the third step he knew – though he had not looked, apparently, yet he knew – that Mr Wynne had raised his hand, and that in that hand was a small white envelope. And further, he knew that Mr Wynne was gazing directly at him.

Now that was odd. Slowly it began to dawn upon the detective that Mr Wynne was trying to attract his attention. If he heeded the signal – evidently it was intended as such – it would be a confession that he was following Mr Wynne, and realizing this he took two more steps up. Mr Wynne waved the envelope again, after which he folded it across twice and thrust it into a crevice of a water-plug beside him. Then he turned east along Sixty-seventh Street and disappeared.

The detective had seen the performance, all of it, and he was perplexed. It was wholly unprecedented. However, the first thing to do now was to keep Mr Wynne in sight, so he came down the steps and walked rapidly on to Sixty-seventh Street, pausing to peer around the corner before he turned. Mr Wynne was idling along, half a block away, without the slightest apparent interest in what was happening behind. Inevitably Mr Birnes' eyes were drawn to the water-plug across the street. A tag end of white paper gleamed tantalizingly. Now what the deuce did it mean?

Being only human, Mr Birnes went across the street and got the paper. It was an envelope. As he unfolded it and gazed at the address, written in pencil, his mouth opened in undignified astonishment. It was addressed to him – Steven Birnes, Chief of the Birnes Detective Agency. Mr Wynne had still not looked back, so the detective trailed along behind, opening the envelope as he walked. A note inside ran briefly:

> *My address is No. – East Thirty-seventh Street. If it is necessary for you to see me please call there about six o'clock this afternoon.*
>   E. van Cortlandt Wynne.

Now here was, perhaps, as savory a kettle of fish as Mr Birnes had ever stumbled upon. It is difficult to imagine a more embarrassing situation for the professional sleuth than to find himself suddenly taken into the confidence of the person he is shadowing. But *was* he being taken into Mr Wynne's confidence? Ah! That was the question! Admitting that Mr Wynne knew who he was, and admitting that he knew he was being followed, was not this apparent frankness an attempt to throw him off the scent? He would see, would Mr Birnes.

He quickened his pace a little, then slowed up instantly, because Mr Wynne had stopped on the corner of Madison Avenue, and as a downtown car came rushing along he stepped out to board it. Mr Birnes scuttled across the street, and by a dexterous jump swung on the car as it fled past. Mr Wynne had gone forward and was taking a seat; Mr Birnes remained on the back platform, sheltered by the accommodating bulk of a fat man, and flattered himself that Mr Wynne had not seen him. By peering over a huge shoulder the detective was still able to watch Mr Wynne.

He saw him pay his fare, and then he saw him place the small sole-leather grip on his knees and unfasten the catch. Not knowing what was in that grip Mr Birnes was curious to see what came out of it. Nothing came out of it – it was empty! There was no question of this, for Mr Wynne opened it wide and turned it upside down to shake it out. It didn't mean anything in particular to Mr Birnes, the fact that the grip was empty, so he didn't get excited about it.

Mr Wynne left the car at Thirty-fourth Street, the south end of the Park Avenue tunnel, by the front door, and the detective stepped off the rear end. Mr Wynne brushed past him as he went up the stairs, and as he did so he smiled a little – a very little. He walked on up Park Avenue to Thirty-seventh Street, turned in there and entered a house about the middle of the block, with a latch-key. The detective glanced at the number of the house, and felt aggrieved – it was the number that was written in the note! And Mr Wynne had entered with a key! Which meant, in all probability, that he *did* live there, as he had said!

But why did he take that useless cab ride up Fifth Avenue? If he had no objection to any one knowing his address, why did he go so far out of his way? Mr Birnes couldn't say. As he pondered these questions he saw a maid-servant come out of a house adjoining that which Mr Wynne had entered, and he went up boldly to question her.

Did a Mr Wynne live next door? Yes. How long had he lived there? Five or six months. Did he own the house? No. The people who owned the house had gone to Europe for a year and had rented it furnished. No, Mr Wynne didn't have a family. He lived there alone, except for two servants, a cook and a housemaid. She had never noticed anything unusual about Mr Wynne, or the servants, or the house. Yes, he went out every day, downtown to business. No, she didn't know what his business was, but she had an idea that he was a broker. That was all.

From a near-by telephone booth the detective detailed Claflin and Malone, who had returned to the office, to keep a sharp watch on the house, after which he walked on to Fifth Avenue, and down Fifth Avenue to the establishment of the H. Latham Company. Mr Latham would see him – yes. In fact, Mr Latham, harried by the events of the past two hours, bewildered by a hundred-million-dollar diamond deal which had been thrust down his throat gracefully, but none the less certainly, and ridden by the keenest curiosity, was delighted to see Mr Birnes.

"I've got his home address all right," Mr Birnes boasted, in the beginning. Of course it was against the ethics of the profession to tell *how* he got it.

"Progress already," commented Mr Latham with keen interest. "That's good."

Then the detective detailed the information he had received from the maid, adding thereto divers and sundry conclusions of his own.

Mr Latham marvelled exceedingly.

"He tried to shake us all right when he went out," Mr Birnes went on to explain, "but the trap was set and there was no escape."

With certain minor omissions he told of the cab ride to Sixty-seventh Street, the trip across to a downtown car, and, as a matter of convincing circumstantial detail, added the incident of the empty gripsack.

"Empty?" repeated Mr Latham, startled. "Empty, did you say?"

"Empty as a bass drum," the detective assured him complacently. "He turned it upside down and shook it."

"Then what became of them?" demanded Mr Latham.

"Became of what?"

"The diamonds, man – what became of the diamonds?"

"You didn't mention any diamonds to me except those five the other day," the detective reminded him coldly. "Your instructions were to find out all about this man – who he is, what he does, where he goes, and the rest. This is my preliminary report. You didn't mention diamonds."

"I didn't know he would have them," Mr Latham exploded irascibly. "That empty gripsack, man – when he left here he carried millions – I mean a great quantity of diamonds in it."

"A great quantity of – " the detective began; and then he sat up straight in his chair and stared at Mr Latham in bewilderment.

"If the gripsack was empty when he was on the car," Mr Latham rushed on excitedly, "then don't you see that he got rid of the diamonds somehow from the time he left here until you saw that the gripsack *was* empty? How did he get rid of them? Where does he keep them? And where does he get them?"

Mr Birnes closed his teeth grimly and his eyes snapped. *Now* he knew why Mr Wynne had taken that useless cab ride up Fifth Avenue. It was to enable him to get rid of the diamonds! There was an accomplice – in detective parlance the second person is always an accomplice – in that closed cab! It had all been prearranged; Mr Wynne had deliberately made a monkey of him – Steven Birnes! Reluctantly the detective permitted himself to remember that he didn't know whether there was anybody in that cab or not when Mr Wynne entered it, and – and –! Then he remembered that he did know one thing – *the number of the cab!*

He arose abruptly, with the light of a great determination in his face.

"Whose diamonds were they?" he demanded.

"They were his, as far as we know," replied Mr Latham.

"How much were they worth?"

Mr Latham looked him over thoughtfully.

"I am not at liberty to tell you that, Mr Birnes," he said at last. "There are a great number of them, and they are worth – they are worth a large sum of money. And they are all unset. That's enough for you to know, I think."

It seemed to be quite enough for Mr Birnes to know.

"It may be that I will have something further to report this evening," he told Mr Latham. "If not, I'll see you to-morrow, here."

He went out. Ten minutes later he was talking to a friend in police headquarters, over the telephone. The records there showed that the license for the particular cab he had followed had been issued to one William Johns. He was usually to be found around the cabstand in Madison Square, and lived in Charlton Street.

VI   THE MYSTERIOUS WOMAN

Mr Birnes' busy heels fairly spurned the pavements of Fifth Avenue as he started towards Madison Square. Here was a long line of cabs drawn up beside the curb, some twenty or thirty in all. The fifth from the end bore the number he sought – Mr Birnes chuckled; and there, alongside it, stood William Johns, swapping Billingsgate with the driver of a hansom, the while he kept one eye open for a prospective fare. It was too easy! Mr Birnes paused long enough to congratulate himself upon his marvellous acumen, and then he approached the driver.

"You are William Johns?" he accused him sharply.

"That's me, Cap," the cabby answered readily.

"A few minutes past four o'clock this afternoon you went up Fifth Avenue, and stopped at the corner of Thirty-fourth Street to pick up a fare – a young man."

"Yep."

"You drove him to the corner of Sixty-seventh Street and Fifth Avenue," the detective went on just to forestall possible denials. "He got out there, paid you, and you went on up Fifth Avenue."

"Far be it from me to deceive you, Cap," responded the cabby with irritating levity. "I done that same."

"Who was that man?" demanded Mr Birnes coldly.

"Search me! I never seen him before."

The detective regarded the cabby with accusing eyes. Then, quite casually, he flipped open his coat and Johns caught a glimpse of a silver shield. It might only have been accident, of course, still –

"Now, Johns, who was the man in the cab when you stopped to pick up the second man at Thirty-fourth Street?"

"Wrong, Cap," and the cabby grinned. "There wasn't any man."

"Don't attempt to deny –"

"No man, Cap. It was a woman."

"A woman!" the detective repeated. "A woman!"

"Sure thing – a woman, a regular woman. And, Cap, she was a pippin, a peachorino, a beauty bright," he added gratuitously.

Mr Birnes stared thoughtfully across the street for a little while. So there was a woman in it! Mr Wynne had transferred the contents of the gripsack to her, in a cab, on a crowded thoroughfare, right under his nose!

"I was a little farther down the line there," Johns went on to explain. "About a quarter of four o'clock, I guess, she came along. She got in, after telling me to drive slowly up Fifth Avenue so I would pass Thirty-fourth Street five minutes or so after four o'clock. If a young man with a gripsack hailed me at the corner I was to stop and let him get in; then I was to go on up Fifth Avenue. If I wasn't stopped I was to drive on to Thirty-fifth Street, cut across to Madison Avenue, down to Thirty-third Street, then back to Fifth Avenue and past Thirty-fourth Street again, going uptown. The guy with the gripsack caught us first crack out of the box."

"And then?" demanded the detective eagerly.

"I went on up Fifth Avenue, according to sailing orders, and the guy inside stopped me at Sixty-seventh Street. He got out and gimme a five-spot, telling me to go a few blocks, then turn and bring the lady back to the Sixth Avenue 'L' at Fifty-eighth Street. I done it. That's all. She went up the steps, and that's the last I seen of her."

"Did she carry a small gripsack?"

"Yep. It would hold about as much as a high hat."

Explicit as the information was it led nowhere, apparently. Mr Birnes readily understood this much, yet there was a chance – a bare chance – that he might trace the girl on the "L," in which case – anyway, it was worth trying.

"What did she look like? How was she dressed?" he asked.

"She had on one of them blue tailor-made things with a lid to match, and a long feather in it," the cabby answered obligingly. "She was pretty as a – as a – she was a beaut, Cap, sort of skinny, and had all sorts of hair on her head – brownish, goldish sort of hair. She was about twenty-two or three, maybe, and – and – Cap, she was the goods, that's all."

In the course of a day a thousand women, more or less, answering that description in a general sort of way, ride back and forth on the elevated trains. Mr Birnes sighed as he remembered this; still it might produce results. Then came another idea.

"Did you happen to look in the cab after the young woman left it?" he inquired.

"No."

"Had any fares since?"

"No."

Mr Birnes opened the door of the closed cab and glanced in. Perhaps there might be a stray glove, a handkerchief, some more definite clue than this vague description. He scrutinized the inside of the vehicle carefully; there was nothing. Yes, by Jingo, here *was* something – a white streak under the edge of the cushion on the seat! Mr Birnes' hopeful fingers fished it out. It was a white envelope, sealed and – *and addressed to him!*

If you are as clever as I imagine you are, you will find this. My address

*is No.— East Thirty-seventh Street. I shall be pleased to see you if you
will call.*

E. van CORTLANDT WYNNE.

It was most disconcerting, really.

VII   A WINGED MESSENGER

A snow-white pigeon dropped down out of an azure sky and settled
on a topmost girder of the great Singer Building. For a time it rested
there, with folded pinions, in a din of clanging hammers; and a
workman far out on a delicately balanced beam of steel paused in
his labors to regard the bird with friendly eyes. The pigeon returned
the gaze unafraid.

"Well, old chap, if I had as little trouble getting up here and down
again as you do I wouldn't mind the job," the workman remarked
cheerfully.

The pigeon cooed an answer. The steel worker extended a caressing
hand, whereupon the bird rose swiftly, surely, with white wings
widely stretched, circled once over the vast steel structure, then
darted away to the north. The workman watched the snow-white
speck until it was lost against the blue sky, then returned to
his labors.

Some ten minutes later Mr E. van Cortlandt Wynne, sitting at
a desk in his Thirty-seventh Street house, was aroused from his
meditations by the gentle tinkle of a bell. He glanced up, arose,
and went up the three flights of stairs to the roof. Half a dozen birds
rose and fluttered around him as he opened the trap; one door in
their cote at the rear of the building was closed. Mr Wynne opened
this door, reached in and detached a strip of tissue paper from the
leg of a snow-white pigeon. He unfolded it eagerly; on it was written:
Safe. I love you. D.

VIII   SOME CONJECTURES

Mr Gustave Schultze dropped in to see Mr Latham after luncheon,
and listened with puckered brows to a recital of the substance of the
detective's preliminary report, made the afternoon before.

"Mr Birnes left here rather abruptly," Mr Latham explained in
conclusion, "saying he would see me again, either last night or to-day.

He has not appeared yet, and it may be that when he comes he will be able to add materially to what we now know."

The huge German sat for a time with vacant eyes.

"Der gread question, Laadham," he observed at last, gravely, "iss vere does Vynne ged dem."

"I know that – I know it," said Mr Latham impatiently. "That is the very question we are trying to solve."

"Und if ve don'd solve him, Laadham, ve'll haf to do vatever as he says," Mr Schultze continued slowly. "Und ve *may* haf to do vatever as he says, anyhow."

"Put one hundred million dollars into diamonds in one year – just the five of us?" demanded the other. "It's preposterous."

"Id *iss* brebosterous," the German agreed readily; "but das iss no argument." He was silent for a little while. "Vere does he ged dem? Vere does he ged dem?" he repeated thoughtfully. "Do you believe, Laadham, it vould be bossible to smuggle in dwenty, d'irty, ein hundred million dollars of diamonds?"

"Certainly not," was the reply.

"Den, if dey were *nod* smuggled in, dey are somewhere on der records of der Custom House, ain'd id?"

Mr Latham snapped his fingers with a sudden realization of this possibility.

"Schultze, I believe that is our clue!" he exclaimed keenly. "Certainly they would have been listed by the customs department; and come to think of it, the tariff on them would have been enormous, so enormous that – that – " and he lost the hopeful tone – "so enormous that we must have heard of it when it became a matter of public record."

"*Yah*," Mr Schultze agreed. "Diamonds like dose dupligates of der Koh-i-noor, der Orloff und der Regent could never haf passed through der Custom House, Laadham, mitoud attracting attention, so?"

Mr Latham acquiesced by a nod of his head; Mr Schultze sat regarding him through half-closed eyelids.

"Und if dey are *nod* on der Custom House records," he continued slowly, "und dey are *nod* smuggled in, den, Laadham, *den – Mein Gott*, man, don'd you zee?"

"See what?"

"Den dey are produced in dis country!"

For a minute or two Mr Latham sat perfectly still, gazing into the other's eyes. First he was startled, then this gave way to incredulity, and at last he shook his head.

"No," he said flatly. "No."

"Laadham, ve Amerigans produce anyding," the German went on patiently. "In eighdeen hundred und forty-eight ve didn't know California vas full of gold; und so late as eighdeen hundred und ninedy-four ve didn't know der Klondike vas full of gold. Der greadest diamond fields ve know now are in Africa, bud in eighdeen hundred und sixty-six ve didn't know id! Dere iss no reason ve should *nod* produce diamonds."

"But look here, Schultze," Mr Latham expostulated, "it's – it's unheard of."

"So vas der Mizzizzippi River until id vas discovered," the German argued complacently. "You are a diamond dealer, Laadham, bud you don'd know much aboud dem from where dey come at. Iss Czenki here? Send for him. He knows more aboud diamonds as any man vat ever lived."

Mr Latham sent an office boy for Czenki, who a few minutes later appeared with an inquiry in his beady black eyes and a nod of recognition for Mr Schultze.

"Sid down, Mr Czenki," the German invited. "Sid down und draw a long breath, und den dell Mr Laadham here someding aboud diamonds."

"What is it, please?" Mr Czenki asked of Mr Latham.

"Mr Czenki, have you any very definite idea as to where those diamonds came from?" asked Mr Latham.

"No," was the unhesitating response.

"Is it possible that they might have been found in the – in the United States?" Mr Latham went on.

"Certainly. They might have been found anywhere."

"As a matter of fact, were any diamonds *ever* found in the United States?"

"Yes, frequently. One very large diamond was found in 1855 at Manchester, across the James River from Richmond, Virginia. It weighed twenty-four carats when cut, and is the largest, I believe, ever found in this country."

Mr Latham seemed surprised.

"Why, you astonish me," he remarked.

"Vait a minute und he'll astonish you some more," Mr Schultze put in confidently. "Vere else in der United States haf diamonds been found, Czenki?"

"In California, in North Carolina, and in Hall County, Georgia," replied the expert readily. "There is good ground for the belief that the stone found at Richmond had been washed down from the mountains farther in the interior, and, if this is true, there is a substantial basis for the scientific hypothesis that diamond fields lie somewhere in the Appalachian Range, because the diamonds found in both North Carolina and Georgia were adjacent to these mountains." He paused a moment. "This is all a matter of record."

His employer was leaning forward in his chair, gripping the arms fiercely as he stared at him.

"Do you believe it possible, Mr Czenki," he asked deliberately, "that Mr Wynne has found these diamond fields?"

The expert shrugged his slender shoulders.

"It is possible, of course," he replied. "From time to time great sums of money have been spent in searching for them, so – " He waved his hand and was silent.

"Zo you zee, Laadham," Mr Schultze interpolated, "ve don'd know anyding much. Ve *know* der African fields, und der Australian fields, und der Brazilian fields, und der fields in India, bud ve *don'd* know if new fields haf been found. By der time you haf lived so long as me you won't know any more as I do."

There was a silence for a long time. Mr Czenki sat with impassive face, and his hands at rest on the arms of the chair. At last he spoke:

"If you'll pardon me, Mr Latham, I may suggest another possibility."

"*Vas iss?*" demanded Mr Schultze quickly.

"Did you ever hear of the French scientist, Charles Friedel?" Mr Czenki asked, addressing Mr Latham.

"Never, no."

"Well, this idea has occurred to me. Some years ago he discovered two or three small diamonds in a meteor. We may safely assume, from the fact that there were diamonds in one meteor, that there may be diamonds in other meteors, therefore – "

The German importer anticipated his line of thought, and arose with a guttural burst of Teutonic expletives.

"Therefore," the expert went on steadily," "is it not possible that Mr Wynne has stumbled upon a huge deposit of diamonds in some meteoric substance some place in this country? A meteor may have fallen anywhere, of course, and it may have been only two months ago, or it may have been two thousand years ago. It may even be buried in his cellar."

The huge German nodded his head vigorously, with sparkling eyes.

"It seems extremely probable that if diamond fields had been discovered in the Appalachian Range," Mr Czenki went on, "it would have become public in spite of every effort to prevent it; whereas, it is possible that a meteor containing diamonds might have been hidden away easily; and, also, the production of diamonds from such a source in this country would not make it necessary for the diamonds to pass through the Custom House. Is it clear, sir?"

"Why, it's absurd, fantastic, chimerical!" Mr Latham burst out irritably. "It's ridiculous to consider such a thing."

"I beg your pardon," Mr Czenki apologized. "It is only a conjecture, of course. I may add that I don't believe that three stones of the size of the replicas which Mr Wynne produced here could have been found anywhere in the world and brought in here – smuggled in or in the usual way – and the secret held against the thousands of men who daily watch the diamond fields and market. It would not be difficult, however, if one man alone knew the source of the stones, to keep it from the world at large. I beg your pardon," he added.

He arose as if to go. Mr Schultze brought a heavy hand down on the slim shoulder of the expert, and turned to Mr Latham.

"Laadham, you are listening to der man who knows more as all of us pud in a crowd," he declared. "*Mein Gott*, I do believe he's right!"

Mr Latham was a cold, unimaginative man of business; he hadn't even believed in fairies when he was a boy. This was child-talk; he permitted himself to express his opinion by a jerk of his head, and was silent. Diamonds like those out of meteors! Bosh!

IX   AND MORE DIAMONDS!

There was a rap on the door, and a clerk thrust his head in.

"Mr Birnes to see you, sir," he announced.

"Show him in," directed Mr Latham. "Sit down, both of you, and let's see what he has to say."

There was an odd expression of hope deferred on the detective's face when he entered. He glanced inquiringly at Mr Schultze and Mr Czenki, whereupon Mr Latham introduced them.

"You may talk freely," he added. "We are all interested alike."

The detective crossed his legs and balanced his hat carefully on one knee, the while he favored Mr Czenki with a sharp scrutiny.

There was that in the thin, scarred face and in the beady black eyes which inevitably drew the attention of a stranger, and half a dozen times as he talked Mr Birnes glanced at the expert.

He retold the story of the cab ride up Fifth Avenue, and the car trip back downtown – omitting embarrassing details such as the finding of two notes addressed to himself – dwelt a moment upon the empty gripsack which Mr Wynne carried on the car, and then:

"When you told me, Mr Latham, that the gripsack had contained diamonds when Mr Wynne left here I knew instantly how he got rid of them. He transferred them to some person in the cab, in accordance with a carefully prearranged plan. That person was a woman!"

"A woman?" Mr Latham repeated, as if startled.

"Dere iss alvays wimmins in id," remarked Mr Schultze philosophically. "Go on."

Mr Birnes was not at all backward about detailing the persistence and skill it had required on his part to establish this fact; and he went on at length to acquaint them with the search that had been made by a dozen of his men to find a trace of the woman from the time she climbed the elevated stairs at Fifty-eighth Street. He admitted that the quest for her had thus far been fruitless, assuring them at the same time that it would go steadily on, for the present at least.

"And now, Mr Latham," he went on, and inadvertently he glanced at Mr Czenki, " I have been hampered, of course, by the fact that you have not taken me completely into your confidence in this matter. I mean," he added hastily, "that beyond a mere hint of their value I know nothing whatever about the diamonds which Mr Wynne had in the gripsack. I gathered, however, that they were worth a large sum of money – perhaps, even a million dollars?"

"Yah, a million dollars ad leasd," remarked Mr Schultze grimly.

"Thank you," and the detective smiled shrewdly. "Your instructions were to find where he got them. If there had been a theft of a million dollars' worth of diamonds anywhere in this world, I would have known it; so I took steps to examine the Custom House records of this and other cities to see if there had been an unusual shipment to Mr Wynne, or to any one else outside of the diamond dealers, thinking this might give me a clue."

"And what was the result?" demanded Mr Latham quickly.

"My agents have covered all the Atlantic ports and they did not come in through the Custom House," replied Mr Birnes. "I have not heard from the western agents as yet, but my opinion is – is that they were perhaps smuggled in. Smuggling after all, is simple with the thousands of miles of unguarded coasts of this country. I don't know this, of course; I advance it merely as a possibility."

Mr Latham turned to Mr Schultze and Mr Czenki with a triumphant smile. Diamonds in meteors! Tommyrot!

"Of course," the detective resumed, "the whole investigation centres about this man Wynne. He has been under the eyes of my agents as no other man ever was, and in spite of this has been able to keep in correspondence with his accomplices. And, gentlemen, he has done it not through the mails, not over the telephone, not by telegraph, and yet he has done it."

"By wireless, perhaps?" suggested Mr Czenki. It was the first time he had spoken, and the detective took occasion then and there to stare at him frankly.

"And not by wireless," he said at last. "He sends and receives messages from the roof of his house in Thirty-seventh Street by homing pigeons!"

"Some more fandastics, eh, Laadham?" Mr Schultze taunted. "Some more chimericals?"

"I demonstrated this much by the close watch I have kept of Mr Wynne," the detective went on, there being no response to his questioning look at Mr Schultze. "One of my agents, stationed on the roof of the house adjoining Mr Wynne's" (it was the maid-servant next door) "has, on at least one occasion, seen him remove a tissue-paper strip from a carrier pigeon's leg and read what was written on it, after which he kissed it, gentlemen, kissed it; then he destroyed it. What did it mean? It means that that particular message was from the girl to whom he transferred the diamonds in the cab, and that he is madly in love with her."

"Oh, dese wimmins! I dell you!" commented Mr Schultze.

There was a little pause, then Mr Birnes continued impressively:

"This correspondence is of no consequence in itself, of course. But it gives us this: Carrier pigeons will only fly home, so if Mr Wynne received a message by pigeon it means that at some time, within a week say, he has shipped that pigeon and perhaps others from the house in Thirty-seventh Street to that person who sent him the message. If he sends messages to that person it means that he has received a pigeon or pigeons from that person within a week. And how were these pigeons shipped? In all probability, by express. So, gentlemen, you see there ought to be a record in the express offices, which would give us the home town, even the name and address, of the person who now has the diamonds in his or her keeping. Is that clear to all of you?"

"It is perfectly clear," commented Mr Latham admiringly, while the German nodded his head in approval.

"And if that is the clue we are working on at the moment," the detective added. "Three of my men are now searching the records of all the express companies in the city – and there are a great many – for the pigeon shipments. If, as seems probable, this clue develops, it may be that we can place our hands on the diamonds within a few days."

"I don'd d'ink I vould yust blace my hands on dem," Mr Schultze advised. "Dey are his diamonds, you know, und your hands might ged in drouble."

"I mean figuratively, of course," the detective amended.

He stopped and drummed on his stiff hat with his fingers. Again he glanced at the impassive face of Mr Czenki with keen, questioning eyes; and for one bare instant it seemed as if he were trying to bring his memory to his aid.

"I've found out all about this man Wynne," he supplemented after a moment, "but nothing in his record seems to have any bearing on this case. He is an orphan. His mother was a Van Cortlandt of old Dutch stock, and his father was a merchant downtown. He left a few thousands to the son, and the son is now in business for himself with an office in lower Broad Street. He is an importer of brown sugar."

"Brown sugar?" queried Mr Czenki quickly, and the thin, scarred face reflected for a second some subtle emotion within him. "Brown sugar!" he repeated.

"Yes," drawled the detective, with an unpleasant stare, "brown sugar. He imports it from Cuba and Porto Rico and Brazil by the shipload, I understand, and makes a good thing of it."

A quick pallor overspread Mr Czenki's countenance, and he arose with his fingers working nervously. His beady eyes were glittering; his lips were pressed together until they were bloodless.

"*Vas iss?*" demanded Mr Schultze curiously.

"My God, gentlemen, don't you see?" the expert burst out violently. "Don't you see what this man has done? He has – he has – "

Suddenly, by a supreme effort, he regained control of himself, and resumed his seat.

"He has – what?" asked Mr Latham.

For half a minute Czenki stared at his employer; then his face grew impassive again.

"I beg your pardon," he said quietly. "Mr Wynne is a heavy importer of sugar from Brazil. Isn't it possible that those *are* Brazilian diamonds? That new workings have been discovered somewhere in the interior? That he has smuggled them in concealed in the sugar-bags, right into New York, under the noses of the customs officials? I beg your pardon," he concluded.

Late in the afternoon of the following day a drunken man, unshaven, unkempt, unclean and clothed in rags, lurched into a small pawnshop in the lower Bowery and planked down on the dirty counter a handful of inert, colourless pebbles, ranging in size from a pea to a peanut.

"Say, Jew, is them real diamonds?" he demanded thickly.

The man in charge glanced at them and nearly fainted. Ten minutes later Red Haney, knight of the road, was placed under arrest as a suspicious character. Uncut diamonds, valued roughly at fifty thousand dollars, were found in his possession.

"Where did you get them?" demanded the amazed police.

"Found 'em."

"*Where* did you find them?"

"None o' your business."

And that was all they were able to get out of him at the moment.

X THE BIG GAME

When the police of Mulberry Street find themselves face to face with some problem other than the trivial, every-day theft, burglary or murder, as the case may be, they are wont to rise up and run around in a circle. The case of Red Haney and the diamonds, blared to the world at large in the newspapers of Sunday morning, immediately precipitated a circular parade, while Haney, the objective centre, snored along peacefully in a drunken stupor.

The statement of the case in the public press was altogether negative. There had been no report of the theft of fifty thousand dollars' worth of uncut diamonds in any city of the United States; in fact, diamonds, as a commodity in crime, had not figured in police records for several weeks – not even an actress had mislaid a priceless necklace. The newspapers were unanimously certain that stones of such value could not rightfully belong to a man of Haney's type, therefore, to whom *did* they belong?

Four men, at least, of the thousands who read the detailed account of the affair Sunday morning, immediately made it a matter of personal interest to themselves. One of these was Mr Latham, another was Mr Schultze, and a third was Mr Birnes. The fourth was Mr E. van Cortlandt Wynne. In the seclusion of his home in Thirty-seventh Street, Mr Wynne read the story with puckered brows, then re-read it, after which he paced back and forth across his room in troubled thought for an hour or more. An oppressive sense of uneasiness was coming over him; and it was reflected in eyes grown sombre.

After a time, with sudden determination, the young man dropped into a chair at his desk, and wrote in duplicate, on a narrow strip of tough tissue-paper, just one line:

Are you safe? Is all well? Answer quick.
                                    W.

Then he mounted to the roof. As he flung open the trap a man on the top of the house next door darted behind a chimney. Mr Wynne saw him clearly – it was Frank Claflin – but he seemed to consider the matter of no consequence, for he paid not the slightest attention. Instead he went straight to a cage beside the pigeon-cote, wherein a dozen or more birds were imprisoned, removed one of them, attached a strip of the tissue-paper to its leg, and allowed it to rise from his out-stretched hand.

The pigeon darted away at an angle, up, up, until it grew indistinct against the void, then swung widely in a semicircle, hovered uncertainly for an instant, and flashed off to the west, straight as an arrow flies. Mr Wynne watched it thoughtfully until it had disappeared; and Claflin's interest was so intense that he forgot the necessity of screening himself, the result being that when he turned again toward Mr Wynne he found that young man gazing at him.

Mr Wynne even nodded in a friendly sort of way as he attached the second strip of tissue to the leg of another bird. This rose, as the other had done, and sped away toward the west.

"It may be worth your while to know, Mr Claflin," Mr Wynne remarked easily to the detective on the other house, "that if you ever put your foot on this roof to intercept any message which may come to me I shall shoot you."

Then he turned and went down the stairs again, closing and locking the trap in the roof behind him. He should get an answer to those questions in two hours, three hours at the most. If there was no answer within that time he would despatch more birds, and *then*, if no answer came, then – *then* – Mr Wynne sat down and carefully perused the newspaper story again.

At just about that moment the attention of one John Sutton, another of the watchful Mr Birnes' men, on duty in Thirty-seventh Street, was attracted to a woman who had turned in from Park Avenue, and was coming rapidly toward him, on the opposite side of the street. She was young, with the elasticity of perfect health in her step; and closely veiled. She wore a blue tailor-made gown, with hat to match; and recalcitrant strands of hair gleamed a golden brown.

"By George!" exclaimed the detective. "It's her!"

By which he meant that the mysterious young woman of the cab, whose description had been drilled into him by Mr Birnes, had at last reappeared. He lounged along the street, watching her with keen interest, fixing her every detail in his mind. She did not hesitate, she glanced neither to right nor left, but went straight to the house occupied by Mr Wynne, and rang the bell. A moment later the door was opened, and she disappeared inside. The detective mopped his face with tremulous joy.

"Doris!" exclaimed Mr Wynne, as the veiled girl entered the room where he sat. "Doris, my dear girl, what *are* you doing here?"

He arose and went toward her. She tore off the heavy veil impatiently, and lifted her moist eyes to his. There was suffering in them, uneasiness – and more than that.

"Have you heard from him – out there?" she demanded.

"Not to-day, no," he responded. "*Why* did you come here?"

"Gene, I can't stand it," she burst out passionately. "I'm worried to death. I can't hear a word, and – I'm worried to death."

Mr Wynne wondered if she, too, had seen the morning papers. He stared at her gravely for an instant, then turned, crumpled up the section of newspaper with its glaring head-lines, and dropped it into a waste-basket.

"I'm sorry," he said gently.

"I telephoned twice yesterday," she rushed on quickly, pleadingly, "and once last night and again this morning. There was no – no answer. Gene, I couldn't stand it. I had to come."

"It's only that he didn't happen to be within hearing of the telephone bell," he assured her. But her steadfast, accusing eyes read more than that in his face, and her hands trembled on his arm.

"I'm afraid, Gene, I'm afraid," she declared desperately. "Suppose – suppose something *has* happened?"

"It's absurd," and he attempted to laugh off her uneasiness. "Why, nothing could have happened."

"All those millions of dollars' worth of diamonds, Gene," she reminded him, "and he is – I shouldn't have left him alone."

"Why, my dear Doris," and Mr Wynne gathered the slender, trembling figure in his arms protectingly, "not one living soul, except you and I, knows that they are there. There's no incentive to robbery, my dear – a poor, shabby little cottage like that. There is not the slightest danger."

"There is always danger, Gene," she contradicted. "It makes me shudder just to think of it. He is so old and so feeble, simple as a child, and utterly helpless if anything should happen. Then, when I didn't hear from him after trying so many times over the telephone – I'm afraid, Gene, I'm afraid," she concluded desperately.

The long-pent-up tears came, and she buried her face on his shoulder. He stood silent, with narrowed, thoughtful eyes.

This, and the thing in the newspaper there! And evidently she had not seen that! It was not wise that she should see it just yet.

"That day I took the horrid things from you in the cab I was awfully frightened," she continued sobbingly. "I felt that every one I passed knew I had them; and you can't imagine what a relief it was when I took them back out there and left them. And now when I think that something may have happened to *him!*" She paused, then raised her tear-dimmed eyes to his face. "He is all I have in the world now, Gene, except you. Already the hateful things have cost the lives of my father and my brother, and now if he – Or you – Oh, my God, it would kill me! I hate them, hate them!"

She was shaken by a paroxysm of sobs. Mr Wynne led her to a chair, and she dropped into it wearily, with her face in her hands.

"Nothing can have happened, Doris," he repeated gently. "I sent a message out there in duplicate only a few minutes ago. In a couple of hours, now, we shall be getting an answer. Now, don't begin to cry," he added helplessly.

"And if you don't get an answer?" she insisted.

"I shall get an answer," he declared positively. There was a long pause. "And when I get that answer, Doris," he resumed, again becoming very grave, "you will see how unwise, how dangerous even, it was for you to come here this way. I know it's hard, dear," he supplemented apologetically, "but it was only for the week, you know; and now I don't see how you can go away from here again."

"Go away?" she repeated wonderingly. "Why shouldn't I go away? I was very careful to veil myself when I came – no one saw me enter, I am sure. Why can't I go away again?"

Mr Wynne paced the length of the room twice, with troubled brow.

"You don't understand, dear," he said quietly, as he paused before her. "From the moment I left Mr Latham's office last Thursday I have been under constant surveillance. I'm followed wherever I go – to my office, to luncheon, to the theatre, everywhere; and day and night, day and night, there are two men watching this house, and two other men watching at my office. They tamper with my correspondence, trace my telephone calls, question my servants, quiz my clerks. You don't understand, dear," he said again.

"But why should they do all this?" she asked curiously. "Why should they – "

"I had expected it all, of course," he interrupted, "and it doesn't disturb me in the least. I planned for months to anticipate every emergency; I know every detective who is watching me by name and by sight; and all my plans have gone perfectly until now. This is why it was necessary for you and I not to meet; why it was as necessary for me to keep away from out there as it was for you to keep away from here; why we could not afford to take chances by an interchange of letters or by telephone calls. When I left you in the cab I knew you would get away safely, because they did not know you were there, in the first place; and then it was the beginning of the chase and I forced them to centre their attention on me. But now it is different. Come here to the window a minute."

He led her across the room unresistingly. On the opposite side of the street, staring at the house, was a man.

"That man is a private detective," Mr Wynne informed her. "His name is Sutton, and he is only one of thirty or forty whose sole business in life, right now, is to watch me, to keep track of and follow any person who comes here. He saw you enter, and you couldn't escape him going out. There's another on the roof of the house next door. His name is Claflin. These men, or others from the same agency, are here all the time. There are two more at my office downtown; still others are searching customs records, examining the books of the express companies, probing into my private affairs. And they're all in the employ of the men with whom I am dealing. Do you understand now?"

"I didn't dream of such a thing," the girl faltered slowly. "I knew, of course, that – Gene, I shouldn't have come if – if only I could have heard from him."

"My dear girl, it's a big game we are playing – a hundred-million-dollar game! And we shall win it, unless – we *shall* win it, in spite of them. Naturally the diamond dealers don't want to be compelled to put up one hundred million dollars. They reason that if the stones

I showed them came from new fields, and the supply is unlimited, as I told them, that the diamond market is on the verge of collapse, anyway; and as they look at it they are compelled to know where they came from. As a matter of fact, if they did know, or if the public got one inkling of the truth, the diamond market would be wrecked, and all the diamond dealers in the world working together couldn't prevent it. If they succeed in doing this thing they feel they must do, they will only bring disaster upon themselves. It would do no good to tell them so; I merely laid my plans and am letting them alone. So you see, my dear, it is a big game – a big game!"

XI   THE SILENT BELL

He stood looking at her with earnest, thoughtful eyes. Suddenly the woman-soul within her awoke in a surging, inexplicable wave of emotion which almost overcame her; and after it came something of realization of the great fight he was making for her – for her, and the aged, feeble grandfather waiting patiently out there. He loved her, this master among men, and she sighed contentedly. For the moment the maddening anxiety that brought her here was forgotten; there was only the ineffable sweetness of seeing him again. She extended her hands to him impulsively, and he kissed them both.

"The difficulty of you leaving here," he went on after a little, "is that you would be followed, and within two hours these men would know all about you – where you are stopping, how long you have been there; they would know of your daily telephone messages to your grandfather, and then, inevitably, they would appear out there, and learn all the rest of it. It doesn't matter how closely they keep watch of me. My plans are all made, I know I am watched, and make no mistakes. But you!"

"So I should not have come?" she questioned. "I'm sorry."

"I understand your anxiety, of course," he assured her, and he was smiling a little, "but the worst never happens – so for the present we will not worry. In an hour or more, now, I imagine we shall receive a pigeon-o-gram which will show that all is well. And then I shall have to plan for you to get away somehow."

She leaned toward him a little and again he gathered her in his arms. The red lips were mutely raised, and he kissed her reverently.

"It's all for you and it will all be right," he assured her.

"Gene, dear Gene!"

He pressed a button on the wall and a maid appeared.

"You will have to wait for a couple of hours or so, at least, so if you would like to take off your things?" he suggested with grave courtesy. "I dare say the suite just above is habitable, and the maid is at your service."

The girl regarded him pensively for a moment, then turning ran swiftly up the stairs. The maid started to follow more staidly.

"Just a moment," said Mr Wynne crisply, in an undertone. "Miss Kellner is not to be allowed to use the telephone under any circumstances. You understand?" She nodded silently, and went up the stairs.

An hour passed. From the swivel chair at his desk Mr Wynne had twice seen Sutton stroll past on the opposite side of the street; and then Claflin had lounged along. Suddenly he arose and went to the window, throwing back the curtains. Sutton was leaning against an electric-light pole, half a block away; Claflin was half a block off in the other direction, in casual conversation with a policeman. Mr Wynne looked them over thoughtfully. Curiously enough he was wondering just how he would fare in a physical contest with either, or both.

He turned away from the window at last and glanced at his watch impatiently. One hour and forty minutes! In another half an hour the little bell over his desk should ring. That would mean that a pigeon had arrived from – from out there, and that the automatic door had closed upon it as it entered the cote. But if it didn't come – if it didn't come! Then what? There was only one conclusion to be drawn, and he shuddered a little when he thought of it. There could only remain this single possibility when he considered the sinister things that had happened – the failure of the girl to get an answer by telephone, and the unexpected appearance of Red Haney with the uncut diamonds. It might be necessary for him to go out there, and how could he do it? How, without leaving an open trail behind him? How, without inviting defeat in the fight he was making?

His meditations were interrupted by the appearance of Miss Kellner. She had crept down the stairs noiselessly, and stood beside him before he was aware of her presence. Her eyes sought his countenance questioningly, and the deadly pallor of her face frightened him. She crept into his arms and nestled there silently with dry, staring eyes. He stroked the golden-brown hair with an utter sense of helplessness.

"Nothing yet," he said finally, and there was a thin assumption

of cheeriness in his tone. "It may be another hour, but it will come
– it will come."

"But if it doesn't, Gene?" she queried insistently. Always her mind
went back to that possibility.

"We shall cross no bridges until we reach them," he replied. "There
is always a chance that the pigeons might have gone astray, for they
have this single disadvantage against the incalculable advantage of
offering no clue to any one as to where they go; and it is impossible
to follow them. If nothing comes within half an hour now I shall
send two more."

"And then, if nothing comes?"

"Then, my dear, then we shall begin to worry."

Half an hour passed; the little bell was silent; Claflin and
Sutton were still visible from the window. Miss Kellner's eyes
were immovably fixed on Mr Wynne's face, and he repressed his
gnawing anxiety with an effort. Finally he wrote again on the tissue
slips – three of them this time – and together they climbed to the
roof, attached the messages, and watched the birds disappear.

Another hour – two hours – two hours and a half passed. Suddenly
the girl arose with pallid face and colorless lips.

"I can't stand it, Gene, I can't!" she exclaimed hysterically. "I
must know. The telephone?"

"No," he commanded harshly, and he, too, arose. "No."

"I will!" she flashed.

She darted out of the room and along the hall. He followed her
with grim determination in his face. She seized the receiver from the
hook and held it to her ear.

"Hello!" called Central.

"Give me long distance – Coaldale, Number – "

"No," commanded Mr Wynne, and he placed one hand over the
transmitter tightly. "Doris, you must not!"

"I will!" she flamed. "Let me alone!"

"You'll ruin everything," he pleaded earnestly. "Don't you know
that they get every number I call? Don't you know that within fifteen
minutes they will have that number, and their men will start for
there?"

She faced him with blazing eyes.

"I don't care," she said deliberately, and the white face was
relieved by an angry flush. "I will know what has happened out
there! I must! Gene, don't you see that I'm frantic with anxiety?
The money means nothing to me. I want to know if he is safe."

His hand was still gripped over the transmitter. Suddenly she turned and tugged at it fiercely. Her sharp little nails bit into the flesh of his fingers. In a last desperate effort she placed the receiver to her lips.

"Give me long distance, Coaldale Number – "

With a quick movement he snapped the connecting wire from the instrument, and the receiver was free in her hand.

"Doris, you are mad!" he protested. "Wait a minute, my dear girl – just a minute."

"I don't care! I *will* know!"

Mr Wynne turned and picked up a heavy cane from the hall-stand, and brought it down on the transmitter with all his strength. The delicate mechanism jangled and tingled, then the front fell off at their feet. The diaphragm dropped and rolled away.

"Doris, you must not!" he commanded again gravely. "We will find another way, dear."

"How dare you?" she demanded violently. "It was cowardly."

"You don't understand – "

"I understand it all," she broke in. "I understand that this might lead to the failure of the thing you are trying to do. But I don't care. I understand that already I have lost my father and my brother in this; that my grandmother and my mother were nearly starved to death while it was all being planned; all for these hideous diamonds. Diamonds! Diamonds! Diamonds! I've heard nothing all my life but that. As a child it was dinned into me, and now I am sick and weary of it all. I know – I *know* something has happened to him now. I hate them! I hate them!"

She stopped, glared at him with scornful eyes for an instant, then ran up the stairs again. Mr Wynne touched a button in the wall, and the maid appeared.

"Go lock the back door, and bring me the key," he commanded.

The maid went away, and a moment later returned to hand him the key. He still stood in the hall, waiting.

After a little there came a rush of skirts, and Miss Kellner ran down the steps, dressed for the street.

"Doris," he pleaded, "you must not go out now. Wait just a moment – we'll find a way, and then I'll go with you."

She tried to pass him, but his outstretched arms made her a prisoner.

"Do I understand that you refuse to let me go?" she asked tensely.

"Not like this," he replied. "If you'll give me just a little while then perhaps – perhaps I may go with you. Even if something had happened there you could do nothing alone. I, too, am afraid now. Just half an hour – fifteen minutes! Perhaps I may be able to find a plan."

Suddenly she sank down on the stairs, with her face in her hands. He caressed her hair tenderly, then raised her to her feet.

"Suppose you step into the back parlor here," he requested. "Just give me fifteen minutes. Then, unless I can find a way for us to go together safely, we will throw everything aside and go anyway. Forgive me, dear."

She submitted quietly to be led along the hall. He opened the door into a room and stood aside for her to pass.

"Gene, Gene!" she exclaimed.

Her soft arms found their way about his neck, and she drew his face down and kissed him; then, without a word, she entered the room and he closed the door. A minute passed – two, four, five – and Mr Wynne stood as she left him, then he opened the front door and stepped out.

Frank Claflin was just starting toward the house from the corner with deliberate pace when he glanced up and saw Mr Wynne signalling for him to approach. Could it be possible? He had had no orders about talking to this man, but – Perhaps he was going to give it up! And with this idea he accelerated his pace and crossed the street.

"Oh, Mr Claflin, will you step in just a moment, please?" requested Mr Wynne courteously.

"Why?" demanded the detective suspiciously.

"There's a matter I want to discuss with you," responded Mr Wynne. "It may be that we can reach some sort of – of an agreement about this, and if you don't mind – "

Claflin went up the steps, Mr Wynne ushered him in and closed the door behind him.

Three minutes later Mr Wynne appeared on the steps again and beckoned to Sutton, who had witnessed the incident just preceding, and was positively being eaten by curiosity.

"This is Mr Sutton, isn't it?" inquired Mr Wynne.

"Yes, that's me."

"Well, Mr Claflin and I are discussing this matter, and my proposition to him was such that he felt it must be made in your presence. Would you mind stepping inside for a moment?"

"You and the girl decided to give it up?" queried Mr Sutton triumphantly.

"We are just discussing the matter now," was the answer.

Sutton went up the steps and disappeared inside.

And about four minutes after that Mr Wynne stood in the hallway, puffing a little as he re-adjusted his necktie. He picked up his hat, drew on his gloves and then rapped on the door of the back parlor. Miss Kellner appeared.

"We will go now," said Mr Wynne quietly.

"But is it safe, Gene?" she asked quickly.

"Perfectly safe, yes. There's no danger of being followed if we go immediately."

She gazed at him wonderingly, then followed him to the door. He opened it and she passed out, glancing around curiously. For one instant he paused, and there came a clatter and clamor from somewhere in the rear of the house. He closed the door with a grim smile.

"Which are the detectives?" asked Miss Kellner, in an awed whisper.

"I don't see them around just now," he replied. "We can get a cab at the corner."

XII   THE THIRD DEGREE

Some years ago a famous head of the police department clearly demonstrated the superiority of a knock-out blow, frequently administered, as against moral suasion, and from that moment the "third degree" became an institution. Whatever sort of criticism may be made of the "third degree," it is, nevertheless, amazingly effective, and beyond that, affords infinite satisfaction to the administrator. There is a certain vicious delight in brutally smashing a sullen, helpless prisoner in the face; and the "third degree" is not officially in existence.

Red Haney was submitted to the "third degree." His argument that he found the diamonds, and that having found them they were his until the proper owner appeared, was futile. Ten minutes after having passed into a room where sat Chief Arkwright, of the Mulberry Street force, and three of his men, and Steven Birnes, of the Birnes Detective Agency, Haney remembered that he hadn't found the diamonds at all – somebody had given them to him.

"Who gave them to you?" demanded the chief.

"I don't know the guy's name, Boss," Haney replied humbly.

"This is to remind you of it."

Haney found himself sprawling on the floor, and looked up, with a pleading, piteous expression. His eyes were still red and bleary, his motley face shot with purple, and the fumes of the liquor still clouded his brain. The chief stood above him with clenched fist.

"On the level, Boss, I don't know," he whined.

"Get up!" commanded the chief. Haney struggled to his feet and dropped into his chair. "What does he look like – this man who gave them to you? Where did you meet him? *Why* did he give them to you?"

"Now, Boss, I'm goin' to give you the straight goods," Haney pleaded. "Don't hit me any more an' I'll tell you all I know about it."

The chief sat down again with scowling face. Haney drew a long breath of relief.

"He's a little, skinny feller, Boss," the prisoner went on to explain, the while he thoughtfully caressed his jaw. "I meets him out here in a little town called Willow Creek, me havin' swung off a freight there to git somethin' to eat. He's just got a couple o' handouts an' he passes one to me, an' we gits to talkin'. He gits to tellin' me somethin' about a nutty old gazabo who lives in the next town, which he had just left. This old bazoo, he says, has a hatful o' diamonds up there, but they ain't polished or nothin', an' he's there by hisself, an' is old an' simple, an' it's findin' money, he says, to go over an' take 'em away from him. He reckoned there must 'a' been a thousan' dollars' worth altogether.

"Well, he puts the proposition to me," Haney continued circumstantially, "an' I falls for it. We're to go over, an' I'm to pipe it all off to see it's all right, then I'm to sort o' hang aroun' an' keep watch while he goes in an' gives the old nut a gentle tap on the coco, an' cops the sparks. That's what we done. I goes up an' takes a few looks aroun', then I whistles an' he appears from the back, an' goes up to the kitchen for a hand-out. The old guy opens the door, an' he goes in. About a minute later he comes out an' gives me a handful o' little rocks – them I had – an' we go away. He catches a freight goin' west, an' I swings one for Jersey City."

"When was this?" demanded Chief Arkwright.

"What's to-day?" asked Haney in turn.

"This is Sunday morning."

"Well, it was yesterday mornin' sometime, Saturday. When I gits to Jersey I takes one o' the little rocks an' goes into a place an' shows it to the bar-keep. He gives me a lot o' booze for it, an' I guess I gits considerable lit up, an' he also gives me some money to pay ferry fare, an' the next thing I knows I'm nabbed over in the hock-shop. I guess I *was* lit up good, 'cause if I'd 'a' been right I wouldn't 'a' went to the hock-shop an' got pinched."

He glanced around at the five other men in the room, and he read belief in each face, whereupon he drew a breath of relief.

"What town was it?" asked the chief.

"Little place named Coaldale."

"Coaldale," the chief repeated thoughtfully. "Where is that?"

"About forty or fifty miles out'n Jersey," said Haney.

"I know the place," remarked Mr Birnes.

"You are sure, Haney?" said the chief after a pause. "You are sure you don't know this other man's name?"

"I don't know it, Boss."

"Who was the man you robbed?"

"I don't know."

The chief arose quickly, and the prisoner cringed in his seat.

"I don't know," he went on protestingly. "Don't hit me again."

But the chief had no such intention; it was merely to walk back and forth across the room.

"What kind of a man was he – a tramp?"

Haney faltered and thoughtfully pulled his under-lip. The cunning brain behind the bleary eyes was working now.

"I wouldn't call him a tramp," he said evasively. "He had on collar an' cuffs an' good clothes, an' talked sort o' easy."

"Little, skinny man you said. What colour was his hair?"

The chief turned in his tracks and regarded Haney with keen, inquiring eyes. The prisoner withstood the scrutiny bravely.

"Sort o' blackish, brownish hair."

"Black, you mean?"

"Well, yes – black."

"And his eyes?"

"Black eyes – little an' round like gimlet holes."

"Heavy eyebrows, I suppose?"

"Yes," Haney agreed readily. "They sort o' stick out."

"And his nose? Big or little? Heavy or thin?"

Haney considered that thoughtfully for a moment before he answered. Then:

"Sort o' medium nose, Boss, with a point on it."

"And a thin face, naturally. How much did he weigh?"

"Oh, he was a little feller – skinny, you know. I reckon he didn't weigh no more'n a hundred an' twenty-five or thirty."

Some germ had been born in the fertile mind of Mr Birnes; now it burst into maturity. He leaned forward in his chair and stared coldly at Haney.

"Perhaps," he suggested slowly, "perhaps he had a scar on his face?"

Haney returned the gaze dully for an instant, then suddenly he nodded his head.

"Yes, a scar," he said.

"From here?" Mr Birnes placed one finger on the point of his chin and drew it across his right jaw.

"Yes, a scar – that's it," the prisoner acquiesced, "from his chin almost around to his ear."

Mr Birnes came to his feet, while the official police stared. The chief sat down again and crossed his fat legs.

"Why, what do *you* know, Birnes?" he queried.

"I know the *man*, Chief," the detective burst out confidently. "I'd gamble my head on it. I knew it! I knew it!" he told himself. Again he faced the tramp: "Haney, do you know how much the diamonds you had were worth?"

"Must 'a' been three or four hundred dollars."

"Something like fifty thousand dollars," Mr Birnes informed him impressively; "and if you got fifty thousand dollars for your share the other man got a million."

Haney only stared.

XIII   MR CZENKI APPEARS

Half an hour later Mr Birnes, Chief Arkwright and Detective Sergeant Connelly were on a train, bound for Coaldale. Mr Birnes had left them for a moment at the ferry and rushed into a telephone booth. When he came out he was exuberantly triumphant.

"It's my man, all right," he assured the chief. "He had been missing since Friday night, and no one knows his whereabouts. It's my man."

It was an hour's ride to Coaldale, a sprawling, straggly village with only four or five houses in sight from the station. When the three men left the train there, Mr Birnes walked over and spoke to the agent, a thin, cadaverous, tobacco-chewing specimen of his species.

"We are looking for an old gentleman who lives out here somewhere," he explained. "He probably lives alone, and we've been told that he has a little cottage somewhere over this way."

He waved his hand vaguely to the right, in accordance with

the directions of Red Haney. The station agent scratched his stubbly chin, and spat with great accuracy through a knot-hole ten feet away.

"'Spect you mean old man Kellner," he replied obligingly. "He lives by hisself part of the time; then again sometimes his granddarter lives with him."

Granddaughter! Mr Birnes almost jumped.

"A granddaughter, yes," he said with a forced calm. "Rather a pretty girl, twenty-two or three years old? Sometimes she dresses in blue?"

"Yes," the agent agreed. "'Spect them's them. Follow the road there till you come to Widow Gardiner's hog-lot, then turn to your left, and it's about a quarter of a mile on. The only house up that way – you can't miss it."

The agent stood squinting at them, with friendly inquiry radiating from his parchment-like countenance, and Mr Birnes took an opportunity to ask some other questions:

"By the way, what sort of an old man is this Mr Kellner? What does he do? Is he wealthy?"

A pleasant grin overspread his informant's face; one finger was raised to his head and twirled significantly.

"'Spect he's crazy," he went on to explain. "Don't do nothing, so far as nobody knows – lives like a hermit, stays in the house all the time, and has long whiskers. Don't know whether he's rich or not, but 'spect he ain't, becuz no man with money'd live like he does." He thrust a long forefinger into Mr Birnes' face. "And stingy! He's so stingy he won't let nobody come in the house – scared they'll wear the furniture out looking at it."

"How long has he lived here?"

"There ain't nobody in this town old enough to say. Why, mister, I'll bet that old man's a thousand years old. Wait'll you see him."

That was all. They went on as indicated.

"The very type of man who would scrimp and starve to put all his money in something like diamonds," mused Chief Arkwright. "The usual rich old miser who winds up by being murdered."

They passed the "Widow Gardiner's hog-lot" and came into a pleasant country road, which, turning, brought them to a shabby little cottage, embowered in trees. Through the foliage, farther on, they caught the amber gleam of a languid river; and around their feet, as they entered the yard, scores of pigeons fluttered.

"Carriers!" ejaculated Mr Birnes, as if startled.

With a strange feeling of elation the detective led the way up the steps to the veranda, and knocked. There was no answer. He glanced at the chief significantly, and tried the door. It was locked.

"Try the back door," directed Chief Arkwright tersely. "If that's locked we'll go in anyway."

They passed around the house to the rear, and Mr Birnes laid one hand upon the door-knob. He turned it and the door swung inward. Again he glanced at Chief Arkwright. The chief nodded, and led the way into the house. They stood in a kitchen, clean as to floors and tables, but now in the utmost disorder. They spent only a moment here, then passed into the narrow hall, along this to a door that stood open, and then – then Chief Arkwright paused, staring downward, and respectfully lifted his hat.

"Always the same," he remarked enigmatically.

Mr Birnes thrust himself forward and through the door. On the floor, with white face turned upward, and fixed, staring eyes, lay an old man. His venerable gray hair, long and unkempt, fell back from a brow of noble proportions, the wide, high brow of the student; and a great, snow-white beard rippled down over his breast. Save for the glassiness of the eyes the face was placid in death, even as it must have been in life.

Mutely Mr Birnes examined the body. A blow in the back of the head – that was all. Then he glanced around the room inquiringly. Everything was in order, except – except here lay an overturned cigar-box. He picked it up; two uncut diamonds were on the floor beneath it. The rough, inert pebbles silently attested the obvious manner of death which simultaneously forced itself upon the three men – the cowardly blow of an assassin, a dying struggle, perhaps, for the contents of the box, and this – the end!

From outside came sharply in the silence the rattle of wheels on the gravel of the road, and a vehicle stopped in front of the door.

"Sh-h-h-h!" warned the chief.

Some one came along the walk, up the steps and rapped briskly on the door; the detectives waited motionless, silent. The knob rattled under impatient fingers, then the footsteps passed along the veranda quickly, and were lost, as if some one had stepped off at the end intending to come to the back door, which was open. A moment later they heard steps in the kitchen, then in the narrow hall approaching, and the doorway of the room where they stood framed the figure of a man. It was Mr Czenki.

"There's your man, Chief," remarked Mr Birnes quietly.

The diamond expert permitted his gaze to wander from one to another of the three men, and then the beady black eyes came to rest on the silent, outstretched figure of the old man. He started forward impulsively; the grip of Detective-Sergeant Connelly on his arm stopped him.

"You're my prisoner!"

"Yes, I understand," said Mr Czenki impatiently. He didn't even look up; he was still gazing at the figure on the floor.

"Well, what have you got to say for yourself?" demanded Chief Arkwright coldly.

Mr Czenki met the accusing stare of the chief squarely for an instant, then the keen eyes shifted to the slightly flushed face of Mr Birnes and lingered there interrogatively.

"I have nothing whatever to say," he replied at last, and he drew one hand slowly across his thin, scarred face. "Yes, I understand," he repeated absently. "I have nothing to say."

XIV   CAUGHT IN THE NET

Doris looked down in great, dry-eyed horror upon the body of this withered old man whom she had loved, and the thin thread of life within her all but snapped. It had come; the premonition of disaster had been fulfilled; the last of her blood had been sacrificed to the mercilessly glittering diamonds – father, brother, and now him! Mr Wynne's face went white, and his teeth closed fiercely; he had loved this old man, too; then the shock passed, and he turned anxiously to Doris to receive the limp, inert figure in his arms. She had fainted.

"Well, what do *you* know about it?" inquired Chief Arkwright abruptly.

Mr Wynne was himself again instantly – the calm, self-certain, perfectly poised young man of affairs. He glanced at the chief, then shot a quick, inquiring look at Mr Czenki. Almost imperceptibly the diamond expert shook his head. Then Mr Wynne's eyes turned upon Mr Birnes. There had been triumph in the detective's face until that moment, but, under the steady, meaning glare which was directed at him, triumph faded to a sort of wonder, followed by a vague sense of uneasiness, and he read a command in the fixed eyes – a command to silence. Curiously enough it reminded him that he was in the employ of Mr Latham, and that there were certain business secrets to be protected. He regarded the coroner's physician, hastily summoned for a perfunctory examination.

"Well?" demanded the chief again.

"Nothing – of this," replied Mr Wynne. "I think, Doctor," and he addressed the physician, "that she needs you more than he does. We know only too well what's the matter with him."

The physician arose obediently. Mr Wynne gathered up the slender, still figure in his arms, and bore it away to another room. The doctor bent over Doris, and tested the fluttering heart.

"Only shock," he said finally, when he looked up. "She'll come around all right in a little while."

"Thank God!" the young man breathed softly.

He stooped and pressed reverent lips to the marble-white brow, then straightened up and, after one long, lingering look at her, turned quickly and left the room.

"I have no statement to make," Mr Czenki was saying, in that level, unemotional way of his, when Mr Wynne re-entered the room where lay the dead.

"We are to assume that you are guilty, then?" demanded Chief Arkwright with cold finality.

"I have nothing to say," replied the expert. His gaze met that of Mr Wynne for a moment, then settled on the venerable face of the old man.

"Guilty?" interposed Mr Wynne quickly. "Guilty of what?"

Chief Arkwright, without speaking, waved his hand toward the body on the floor. There was a flash of amazement in the young man's face, a subtle bewilderment; the diamond expert's countenance was expressionless.

"You don't deny that you killed him?" persisted the chief accusingly.

"I have nothing to say," said the expert again.

"And you don't deny that you were Red Haney's accomplice?"

"I have nothing to say," was the monotonous answer.

The chief shrugged his shoulders impatiently. Some illuminating thought shone for an instant in Mr Wynne's clear eyes, and he nodded as if a question in his mind had been answered.

"Perhaps, Chief, there may be some mistake?" he protested half-heartedly. "Perhaps this gentleman – what motive would – "

"There's motive enough," interrupted the chief brusquely. "We have this man's description straight from his accomplice, Red Haney, even to the scar on his face – " He paused abruptly, and regarded Mr Wynne through half-closed lids. "By the way," he continued deliberately, "who are *you*? What do *you* know about it?"

"My name is Wynne – E. van Cortlandt Wynne," was the ready response. "I am directly interested in this case through a long-standing friendship for Mr Kellner here, and through the additional fact that his granddaughter in the adjoining room is soon to become my wife." There was a little pause. "I may add that I live in New York, and that Miss Kellner has been stopping there for several days. She has been accustomed to hearing from her grandfather at least once a day by telephone, but she was unable to get an answer either yesterday or to-day, so she came to my home, and together we came out here."

Mr Birnes looked up quickly. It had suddenly occurred to him to wonder as to the whereabouts of Claflin and Sutton, who had been on watch at the Thirty-seventh Street house. The young man interpreted the expression of his face aright, and favoured him with a meaning glance.

"We came alone," he supplemented.

Mr Birnes silently pondered it.

"All that being true," Chief Arkwright suggested tentatively, "perhaps you can give us some information as to the diamonds that were stolen? How much were they worth? How many were there?" He held up the uncut stones that had been found on the floor.

"I don't know the exact number," was the reply. "Their value, I should say, was about sixty thousand dollars. Except for this little house, and the grounds adjoining, practically all of Mr Kellner's money was invested in diamonds. Those you have there are part of an accumulation of many years, imported in the rough, one or two at a time."

Mr Czenki was gazing abstractedly out of a window, but the expression on his lean face indicated the keenest interest, and – and something else: apprehension, maybe. The chief stared straight into the young man's eyes for an instant, and then:

"And Mr Kellner's family?" he inquired.

"There is no one, except his granddaughter, Doris."

Some change, sudden as it was pronounced, came over the chief, and his whole attitude altered. He dropped into a chair near the door.

"Have a seat, Mr Wynne," he invited courteously, "and let's understand this thing clearly. Over there, please," and he indicated a chair partly facing that in which Mr Czenki sat.

Mr Wynne sat down.

"Now you don't seem to believe," the chief went on pleasantly, "that Czenki here killed Mr Kellner?"

"Well, no," the young man admitted.

Mr Czenki glanced at him quickly, warningly. The chief was not looking, but he knew the glance had passed.

"And *why* don't you believe it?" he continued.

"In the first place," Mr Wynne began without hesitation, "the diamonds were worth only about sixty thousand dollars, and Mr Czenki here draws a salary of twenty-five thousand dollars a year. The proportion is wrong, you see. Again, Mr Czenki is a man of unquestioned integrity. As diamond expert of the Henry Latham Company he handles millions of dollars' worth of precious stones each year, and has practically unlimited opportunities for theft, without murder, if he were seeking to steal. He has been with that company for several years, and that fact alone is certainly to his credit."

"Very good," commented the chief ambiguously. He paused an instant to study this little man with an interest aroused by the sum of his salary. "And what of Haney's description? His accusation?" he asked.

"Haney might have lied, you know," retorted Mr Wynne. "Men in his position have been known to lie."

"I understood you to say," the chief resumed, heedless of the note of irony in the other's voice, "that you and Miss Kellner are to be married?"

"Yes."

"And that she is the only heir of her grandfather?"

"Yes."

"Therefore, at his death, the diamonds would become her property?"

For one instant Mr Wynne seemed startled, and turned his clear eyes full upon his interrogator, seeking the hidden meaning.

"Yes, but – " he began slowly.

"That's true, isn't it?" demanded the chief, with quick violence.

"Yes, that's true," Mr Wynne admitted calmly.

"Therefore, indirectly, it would have been to *your* advantage if Mr Kellner had died or had been killed?"

"In that the diamonds would have come to my intended wife, yes," was the reply.

Mr Czenki clasped and unclasped his thin hands nervously. His face was again expressionless, and the beady eyes were fastened immovably on Chief Arkwright's. Mr Birnes was frankly amazed at this unexpected turn of the affair. Suddenly Chief Arkwright brought his hand down on the arm of his chair with a bang.

"Suppose, for the moment, that Red Haney lied, and that

Mr Czenki is *not* the murderer, then – As a matter of fact *your* salary *isn't* twenty-five thousand a year, is it?"

He was on his feet now, with blazing eyes, and one hand was thrust accusingly into Mr Wynne's face. It was simulation; Mr Birnes understood it; a police method of exhausting possibilities. There was not the slightest movement by Mr Wynne to indicate uneasiness at the charge, not a tremor in his voice when he spoke again.

"I understand perfectly, Chief," he remarked coldly. "Just what was the time of the crime, may I ask?"

"Answer my question," insisted the Chief thunderously.

"Now look here, Chief," Mr Wynne went on frigidly, "I am not a child to be frightened into making any absurd statements. I do *not* draw a salary of twenty-five thousand a year, no. I am in business for myself, and make more than that. You may satisfy yourself by examining the books in my office if you like. By intimation, at least, you are accusing me of murder. Now answer me a question, please. What was the time of the crime?"

XV THE TRUTH IN PART

The chief dropped back into his chair with the utmost complacency. This was not the kind of man with whom mere bluster counted.

"Haney says Saturday morning," he answered. "The coroner's physician agrees with that."

"Yesterday morning," Mr Wynne mused; then, after a moment: "I think, Chief, you know Mr Birnes here? And that you would accept a statement of his as correct?"

"Yes," the chief agreed with a glance at Mr Birnes.

"Mr Birnes, where was I all day Saturday?" Mr Wynne queried, without so much as looking around at him.

"You were in your house from eleven o'clock Friday night until fifteen minutes of nine o'clock Saturday morning," was the response. "You left there at that time, and took the surface car at Thirty-fourth Street to your office. You left your office at five minutes of one, took luncheon alone at the Savarin, and returned to your office at two o'clock. You remained there until five, or a few minutes past, then returned home. At night you – "

"Is that sufficient?" interrupted Mr Wynne. "Does that constitute an alibi?"

Chief Arkwright seemed to be puzzled. He glanced from Mr Birnes to Mr Wynne, then back again.

"Yes," he admitted; "but how do you know all this, Birnes?"

"Mr Birnes and the men of his agency have favored me with the most persistent attentions during the last few days," Mr Wynne continued promptly. "He has had two men constantly on watch at my office, day and night, and two others constantly on watch at my home, day and night. There are two there now – one in a rear room of the basement, and another in the pantry, with the doors locked on the outside. Their names are Claflin and Sutton!"

So, that was it! It came home to Mr Birnes suddenly. Claflin and Sutton had been tricked into the house on some pretext, and locked in! Confound their stupidity!

"Why are they locked up?" demanded the chief, with kindling interest. "Why have you been watched?"

"I think, perhaps, Mr Birnes will agree with me when I say that that has nothing whatever to do with this crime," replied Mr Wynne easily.

"That's for me to decide," declared the chief bluntly.

There was a long pause. Mr Czenki was leaning forward in his chair, gripping the arms fiercely, with his lips pressed into a thin line. It was only by a supreme effort that he held himself in control; and the lean, scarred face was working strangely.

"Well, if you insist on knowing," observed Mr Wynne slowly, "I suppose I'll have to tell all of it. In the first place – "

"*Don't!*" It came finally, the one word, from Mr Czenki's half-closed lips, a smothered explosion which drew every eye upon him.

Mr Wynne turned slightly in his chair and regarded the diamond expert with an expression of astonishment on his face. The beady black eyes were all aglitter with the effort of repression, and some intangible message flashed in them.

"In the first place," resumed Mr Wynne, as if there had been no interruption, "Mr Kellner here – "

"Don't!" the expert burst out again desperately. "Don't! It means ruin – absolute ruin!"

"Mr Kellner had those diamonds – about sixty thousand dollars' worth of them," Mr Wynne continued distinctly. "Mr Kellner decided to sell some diamonds. One of the quickest and most satisfactory methods of selling rough gems, such as those you have in your hand, Chief, is to offer them directly to the men who deal in them. I went to Mr Henry Latham, and other jewellers of New York, on behalf of Mr Kellner, and offered them a quantity of diamonds. It may be that they regarded the quantity I offered as unusual; that I don't know, but I would venture the conjecture that they did."

He paused a moment. Mr Czenki's face, again grown expression-less, was turned toward the light of the window; Chief Arkwright was studying it shrewdly.

"Diamond merchants, of course, have to be careful," the young man went on smoothly. "They can't afford to buy whatever is offered by people whom they don't know. They had reason, too, to believe that I was not acting for myself alone. What was more natural, therefore, than that they should have called in Mr Birnes, and the men of his agency, to find out about me, and, if possible, to find out whom I represented, so they might locate the supply? I wouldn't tell them, because it was not desirable that they should deal directly with Mr Kellner, who was old and childish, and lacking, perhaps, in appreciation of the real value of diamonds.

"The result of all this was that the diamond dealers placed me under strict surveillance. My house was watched; my office was watched. My mail, going and coming, was subjected to scrutiny; my telephone calls were traced; telegrams opened and read. I had anticipated all this, of course, and was in communication with Mr Kellner here only by carrier-pigeons." He glanced meaningly at Mr Birnes, who was utterly absorbed in the recital. "Those carrier-pigeons were not exchanged by express, because the records would have furnished a clue to Mr Birnes' men; I personally took them back and forth in a suitcase before I approached Mr Latham with the original proposition."

He was giving categorical answers to a few of the multitude of questions to which Mr Birnes had been seeking answers. The tense expression about Mr Czenki's eyes was dissipated, and he sighed a little.

"I saw the Red Haney affair in the newspapers this morning, as you will know," he continued after a moment. "It was desirable that I should come here with Miss Kellner, but it was not desirable, even under those circumstances, that I should permit myself to be followed. That's how it happens that Mr Claflin and Mr Sutton are now locked up in my house." Again there was a pause. "Mr Birnes, I know, will be glad to confirm my statement of the case in so far as his instructions from Mr Latham and the other gentlemen interested bear on it?"

Chief Arkwright glanced at the detective inquiringly.

"That's right," Mr Birnes admitted with an uncertain nod – "that is, so far as my instructions go. I understood, though, that the diamonds were worth more than sixty thousand dollars; in fact, that there might have been a million dollars' worth of them."

"A million dollars!" repeated Chief Arkwright in amazement. "A million dollars!" he repeated. He turned fiercely upon Mr Wynne. "What about that?" he demanded.

"I'm sure I don't know what Mr Birnes *understood*," replied the young man, with marked emphasis. "But it's preposterous on the face of it, isn't it? Would a man with a million dollars' worth of diamonds live in a hovel like this?"

The chief considered the matter reflectively for a minute or more, the while his keen eyes alternately searched the faces of Mr Wynne and Mr Czenki.

"It would depend on the man, of course," he said at last. And then some new idea was born within him. "Your direct connection with the crime seems to be disproved, Mr Wynne," he remarked slowly; "and if we admit *his* innocence," he jerked a thumb at the expert, "there remains yet another view-point. Do you see it?"

The young man turned upon him quickly.

"Does it occur to you that every argument I advanced to furnish you with a motive for the crime might be applied with equal weight against – against Miss Kellner?"

"Doris!" flamed Mr Wynne. For the first time his perfect self-possession deserted him, and he came to his feet with gripping hands. "Why – why –! What are you talking about?"

"Sit down," advised the chief quietly.

Mr Czenki glanced at them once uneasily, then resumed his fixed stare out of the window.

"Sit down," said the chief again.

Mr Wynne glared at him for an instant, then dropped back into his chair. His hands were clenched desperately, and a slight flush in his clean-cut face showed the fight he was making to restrain himself.

"All the property this old man owned, including the diamonds, would become her property in the event of his death – or murder," the chief added mercilessly. "That's true, isn't it?"

"But when she entered this room her every act testified to her innocence," Mr Wynne burst out passionately.

The chief shrugged his shoulders.

"She has been living at a little hotel in Irving Place," the young man rushed on. "The people there can satisfy you as to her whereabouts on Saturday?"

Again the chief shrugged his shoulders.

"And remember, please, that the best answer to all that is that Haney had the diamonds!"

"It doesn't necessarily follow, Mr Wynne," said the other steadily, "that she committed the crime with her own hands. It comes down simply to this: If there were *only* sixty thousand dollars' worth of diamonds then the one motive which Czenki might have had is eliminated; because Haney had practically fifty thousand dollars' worth of them, and here are some others. There would have been no share for your expert here. And again, if there were only sixty thousand dollars' worth of the diamonds you or Miss Kellner would have been the only persons to benefit by this death."

"But Haney had those!" protested Mr Wynne.

"Just what I'm saying," agreed the other complacently. "Therefore there *were* more than sixty thousand dollars' worth. However we look at it, whoever may have been Haney's accomplice, that point seems settled."

"Or else Haney lied," declared Mr Wynne flatly. "If Haney came here alone, killed this old man and stole the diamonds there would be none of these questions, would there?"

Mr Birnes, who had listened silently, arose suddenly and left the room. Mr Wynne's last suggestion awakened a new train of thought in the police official's mind, and he considered it silently for a moment. Finally he shook his head.

"The fact remains," he said, as if reassuring himself, "that Haney described an accomplice, that that description fits Czenki perfectly, that Czenki has refused to defend himself or even make a denial; that he has drawn suspicion upon himself by everything he has done and said since he has been here, even by the strange manner of his appearance at this house. Therefore, there were more diamonds, and he got his share of them."

"Hello!" came in Mr Birnes' voice from the hall. "Give me 21845 River, New York . . . Yes . . . Is Mr Latham there? . . . Yes, Mr Henry Latham . . .

Again Mr Wynne's self-possession forsook him, and he came to his feet, evidently with the intention of interrupting that conversation. He started forward, with gritting teeth, and simultaneously Chief Arkwright, Detective-Sergeant Connelly and Mr Czenki laid restraining hands upon him. Something in the expert's grip on his wrist caused him to stop, and cease a futile struggle; then came a singular expression of resignation about the mouth and he sat down again.

"Hello! This Mr Latham? . . . This is detective Birnes. . . . I've been able to locate some diamonds, but it's necessary to know something of the quantity of those you mentioned. You remember Mr Schultze said something about . . . Yes. . . . Yes.

. . . Oh, there *were*? . . . Unexpected developments, yes. . . . I'll call and see you to-night about eight. . . . Yes. . . . Good-by!"

Mr Birnes re-entered the room, his face aglow with triumph. Mr Wynne glanced almost hopelessly at Mr Czenki, then turned again to the detective.

"I should say there *were* more than sixty thousand dollars' worth of them," Mr Birnes blurted. "There were at least a million dollars' worth. Mr Schultze intimated as much to me; now Mr Latham confirms it."

Chief Arkwright turned and glared scowlingly upon the diamond expert. The beady black eyes were aglint with some emotion which he failed to read.

"Where are they, Czenki?" demanded the chief harshly.

"I have nothing to say," replied Mr Czenki softly.

"So your disappearance Friday night, and your absence all day yesterday did have to do with this old man's death?" said the chief, directly accusing him.

"I have nothing to say," murmured Mr Czenki.

"That settles it, gentlemen," declared the chief with an air of finality. "Czenki, I charge you with the murder of Mr Kellner here. Anything you may say will be used against you. Come along, now; don't make any trouble."

XVI   MR CZENKI EXPLAINS

Fairly drunk with excitement, his lean face, usually expressionless, now flushed and working strangely, and his beady black eyes aglitter, Mr Czenki reeled into the study where Mr Latham and Mr Schultze sat awaiting Mr Birnes. He raised one hand, enjoining silence, closed the door, locked it and placed the key in his pocket, after which he turned upon Mr Latham.

"He *makes* them, man! He *makes them*!" he burst out between gritting teeth. "Don't you understand? *He makes them*!"

Mr Latham, astonished and a little startled, came to his feet; the phlegmatic German sat still, staring at the expert without comprehension. Mr Czenki's thin fist was clenched under his employer's nose, and the jeweler drew back a little, vaguely alarmed.

"I don't understand what – " he began.

"The diamonds!" Mr Czenki interrupted, and the long-pent-up excitement within him burst into a flame of impatience. "The diamonds! He makes them! Don't you see? Diamonds! He *manufactures* them!"

"*Gott in Himmel!*" exclaimed Mr Schultze, and it was anything but an irreverent ejaculation. He arose. "Der miracle has come to pass! Ve might haf known! Ve might haf known!"

"Millions and millions of dollars' worth of them, even *billions*, for all we know," the expert rushed on in incoherent violence. "A sum greater than all the combined wealth of the world in the hands of one man! Think of it!" Mr Latham only gazed at him blankly, and he turned instinctively to the one who understood – Mr Schultze. "Think of the mind that achieved it, man!"

He collapsed into a chair and sat looking at the floor, his fingers writhing within one another, muttering to himself. Mr Latham was a cold, sane, unimaginative man of business. As yet the full import of it all hadn't reached him. He stared dumbly, first at Mr Czenki, then at Mr Schultze. There was not even incredulity in the look, only faint amazement that two such well-balanced men should have gone mad at once. At last the German importer turned upon him flatly.

"Why don'd you ged egzited aboud id, Laadham?" he demanded. "He iss all righd, nod crazy," he added with whimsical assurance. "He is delling you dat dose diamonds are *made* – made like doughnuds, mitoud der hole; manufactured, pud togedher. Don'd you ged id?"

He ran off into guttural German expletives; and slowly, slowly the idea began to dawn upon Mr Latham. The diamonds Mr Wynne had shown were not real, then; they were artificial! It was some sort of a swindle! Of course! But the experts had agreed that they were diamonds – real diamonds! Perhaps they had been deceived, or – by George! Did these two men mean to say that they were real diamonds, but that they were *manufactured*? Mr Latham's tidy little imagination balked at that. Absurd! Whoever heard of a diamond as big as the Koh-i-noor, or the Regent, or the Orloff being made? They were crazy – the pair of them!

"Do I understand," he demanded in a tone of deliberate annoyance, "that you, Czenki, and you, Schultze, expect me to believe that those diamonds we saw were not natural, but *were* real diamonds turned out by machinery in a – in a diamond factory? Is that what you are driving at?"

"*Das iss!*" declared the German bluntly. "Id vas coming in dime, Laadham, id vas coming, of course. Und I haf always noticed dat whatever iss coming does come."

"Made, made – made as you make marbles," Mr Czenki repeated

monotonously. "Yes, it had to come, but – but imagine the insuperable difficulties that one brain had to surmount!" He passed a thin
hand across his flushed brow, and was thoughtfully silent.

"I don't believe it," asserted Mr Latham tartly. "It's impossible!
I don't believe it!" And sat down.

"Id don'd madder much whedher you belief id or nod," remarked
the German in a tone of resignation. "If id iss, id iss. Und all dose
diamonds in your place und mine are nod worth much more by der
bushel as potatoes."

Mr Latham turned away from him, half angrily, and glared at the
expert, who was still regarding the floor.

"What do you know about this, anyway, Czenki?" he demanded.
"How do you *know* he makes them? Have you *seen* him make
them?"

Thus directly addressed Mr Czenki looked up, and the living flame
of wonder within his eyes flickered and died. In silence, for a minute
or more, he studied the unconcealed skepticism in his employer's
face, and then asked slowly:

"Do you know what diamonds are, Mr Latham?"

"There is some theory that they are pure carbon, crystallized."

"They are that," declared the expert impatiently. "You know that
diamonds have been made?"

"Oh, I've read something about it, yes; but what I – "

"Every school-boy knows how to make a diamond, Mr Latham. If
pure carbon is heated to approximately five thousand degrees Fahrenheit, and simultaneously subjected to a pressure of approximately
six thousand tons to the square inch, it becomes a diamond. And
there's no theory about that – that's a fact! The difficulty has always
been to apply the knowledge we have in a commercially practicable
way – in other words, to isolate a carbon that is absolutely pure, and
invent a method of applying the heat and pressure simultaneously.
It has been done, Mr Latham; *it has been done!* Don't you understand
what it means to – "

With an effort he repressed the returning excitement which found
vent in a rising voice and quick, nervous gestures of the hands. After
a moment he went on:

"Half a score of scientists have made diamonds, minute particles
no larger than the point of a pin. Professor Henri Moissan, of Paris,
went further, and by the use of an electric furnace produced diamonds
as large as a pinhead. You may remember that when I first met
Mr Wynne he inquired if I had not done some special work for
Professor Moissan. I had; I tested the diamonds he made – *and*

they were diamonds! I dare say the suggestion Mr Wynne conveyed to me by that question – that is, the suggestion of manufactured diamonds – had been carefully planned, for he is a wonderful young man, Mr Wynne – a wonderful young man." He paused a moment. "We know that he had millions and millions of dollars' worth of them – we know because we saw them – and who can tell how many billions more there are? The one man holds in his hand the power to overturn the money values of the earth!"

"But how do you know he makes them?" demanded Mr Latham, returning to the main question.

"He suggested it by his question," Mr Czenki went on. "That suggestion lingered in my mind. When the detective, Mr Birnes, reported that Mr Wynne was an importer of brown sugar I was on the point of advancing a theory then that the diamonds were manufactured, because of all known substances burnt brown sugar is richest in carbon. But you, Mr Latham, had discredited a previous suggestion of mine, and I – I – well, I didn't suggest it. Instead, that night I personally began an investigation to see what disposition was made of the sugar. I found that the ships discharged their cargoes in Hoboken, that the sugar was there loaded on barges, and those barges hauled up a small stream to the little town of Coaldale, all consigned to a Mr Hugo Kellner.

"It took Friday, all day Saturday, and a great part of to-day to learn all this. This afternoon I went to see Mr Kellner. I found him murdered." He stated it merely as an inconvenient incident. "In the room with the body were Mr Birnes, Chief Arkwright of the New York police, and another New York detective. I had glanced at the story of Red Haney and the diamonds in the morning papers, and from what I knew, and from Mr Birnes' presence, I surmised something of the truth. I was instantly placed under arrest for murder – the murder of this man I had never seen – the *real* diamond master, the man who achieved it all."

He was silent a moment, as if from infinite weariness.

". . . Mr Wynne came, and a Miss Kellner, granddaughter of the dead man. . . . He saw me, and understood . . . between us we contrived that I should be taken away as the murderer, and so prevent an immediate search of the house. . . . I made no denial. . . . I permitted myself to be taken . . . some mistake as to identity. . . . I proved an alibi by the shipping men in Hoboken . . . the diamonds are there, untold millions of dollars' worth of them . . . the diamond master is dead!"

Mr Latham had been listening, as if dazed, to the hurried, somewhat disconnected, narrative; Mr Schultze, keener to comprehend all that the story meant, was silent for a moment.

"Den if all dose men know all he has told us, Laadham," he remarked finally, "our diamonds are nod worth any more as potatoes *alretty*."

"But they *don't* know," Mr Czenki burst out fiercely. "Don't you understand? Haney, or somebody, killed Mr Kellner and stole some uncut diamonds – you must have seen the newspaper account of it to-day. The New York police traced Haney's course to Coaldale and to that house. But all *they* know is that sixty thousand dollars' worth of uncut stones were stolen. There was not even a suggestion to them of the millions and millions of dollars' worth that were manufactured. Don't you understand? I permitted myself to be accused and arrested, knowing I could establish an alibi, in order to lead them away from there and gain time, at least, to give Mr Wynne an opportunity of hiding the other diamonds, if they were there. He understood what I was trying to do, and fell in with the plan. He knew that *I* knew the diamonds were made. Mr Birnes doesn't know; *no* one knows but you and me and Mr Wynne, and perhaps the girl! But, don't you see, if you don't accept the proposition he made the diamond market of the world is ruined? You are ruined!"

"But how do you know they are *made*?" insisted Mr Latham doggedly. "You've never seen them made, have you?"

"*Mein Gott*, Laadham, how do you know when you haf der boil on der pack of your neck? You can'd zee him, ain'd id?" Mr Schultze turned to Mr Czenki. "Der dhree of us vill go und zee Mr Vynne. Id iss der miracle! Vass iss, iss, und id don'd do any good to say id ain'd."

XVII   THE GREAT CUBE

A cube of solid, polished steel, some twenty feet square, set on a spreading base of concrete, and divided perpendicularly down the middle into Titanic halves, these being snugly fitted one to the other by a series of triangular corrugations, a variation of the familiar tongue and groove. Interlacing the ponderous mass, from corner to corner, were huge steel bolts, and the hulking heads of more bolts, some forty on each of the four sides, showed that the whole might be split into halves at will, and readily made whole again, one enormous side sliding back and forth on a short track.

In the two undivided faces of the cube, relatively squaring the centre, were four borings somewhat smaller in diameter than an ordinary pencil, and extending through; and directly in the centre was focused a network of insulated wires which dropped down out of the gloom overhead. In the other two sides of the great cube, just where the dividing lines of the halves came, were the funnel-like mouths of a two-inch boring. This, too, extended straight through.

Directly opposite each of the two mouths, a dozen feet away, was mounted a peculiarly-constructed heavy gun of the naval type. In a general sort of way these were not unlike twelve-inch ordnance, but the breech was much larger in proportion, the barrel longer, and the bore only two instead of twelve inches. The mountings were high, and the adjustment so delicate that, looking into the open breech of one gun, the bore through the twenty-foot cube and through the barrel of the gun on the other side seemed to be continuous.

"This is the diamond-making machine, gentlemen," said Mr Wynne, and he indicated to Mr Latham, Mr Schultze and Mr Czenki the cube and the two guns. "It is perfectly simple in construction, has enormous powers of resistance, as you may guess, and is as delicately fitted as a watch, being regulated by electric power. This cube is the solution of the high-pressure, high-temperature problem, which was only one of the many seemingly insuperable difficulties to be overcome. When the bolts are withdrawn one half slides back; when the bolts are in position it is as solid as if it were in one piece, and perfectly able to withstand a force greater than the ingenuity of man has ever before been able to contrive. This force is a combination of a heat one-half that of the sun on its surface, and a head-on impact of two one-hundred-pound projectiles fired less than forty feet apart with an enormous charge of cordite, and possessing an initial velocity greater than was ever recorded in gunnery.

"This vast force centres in a sort of furnace in the middle of the cube. The furnace is round, about three feet long and three feet in diameter, built of half-a-dozen fire-resisting substances in layers, perforated for electric wires, with an opening through it lengthwise of the exact size of the borings in the guns and in the cube. It fits snugly into a receptacle cut out for it in the centre of the cube, and is intended to protect the steel of the cube proper from the intense heat. This heat reaches the furnace by electric wires which enter the cube from the sides, as you see, being brought here by a conduit along the riverbed from a large power-plant five miles away. Twenty-eight large wires are necessary to bring it; I own the power-plant, ostensibly for the operation of a small sugar refinery. I may add that the furnace is a variation of the principle employed by Professor Moissan, in Paris." He turned to Mr Czenki. "You may remember having heard me mention him?"

"I remember," the expert acquiesced grimly.

"Now, pure carbon is vaporized, as you perhaps know, at a fraction less than five thousand degrees Fahrenheit," Mr Wynne continued. "A carbon not merely chemically pure but *absolutely* pure, in highly compressed discs, is packed in the furnace, the furnace placed within the cube, the ends of the two-inch opening in the furnace being blocked to prevent expansion, the cube closed, the bolts fastened, and heat applied, for several minutes – a heat, gentlemen, of five thousand two hundred and eighty degrees Fahrenheit. The heat of the sun is only about ten thousand degrees. And then the pressure of about seven thousand tons to the square inch is added by means of the two guns. In other words, gentlemen, pure carbon, vaporized, is caught between two projectiles which enter the cube simultaneously from opposite sides, being fired by electricity. The impact is so terrific that what had been two feet of compressed carbon is instantly condensed into an irregular disc, one inch or an inch and a half thick. *And that disc, gentlemen, is a diamond!*

"The violence of the operation, coupled with the intense heat, fuses everything – furnace, projectiles, electric wires, fire-brick, even asbestos, into a single mass. The cube is opened, and this mass, white-hot, is dropped into cold water. This increases the pressure until the mass is cool. Then it is broken away, and in the centre is a diamond – as big as a biscuit, gentlemen! Four small bores lead from the two-inch bore through the cube, and permit the escape of air as the projectiles enter. There is no rebound because the elastic quality of the carbon is crushed out of existence – driven, I may say, into the diamond itself. Of course the furnace, the two projectiles and the connecting electric wires are all destroyed at each charge, which brings the total cost of the operation to a little more than eight hundred dollars, including nearly three tons of brown sugar. The diamond resulting is worth at least a million when broken up for cutting, sometimes even two millions. That is all, I think."

There was a long, awed silence. Mr Latham, leaning against the giant cube, stared thoughtfully at his toes; Mr Schultze was peering curiously about him, thence off into the gloom; Mr Czenki still had a question.

"I understand that all the diamonds were made in that disc-like shape," he remarked at last. "Then the uncut stones that were stolen were – "

"They were natural stones," interrupted Mr Wynne, "imported for purposes of study and experiment. I told Chief Arkwright the truth, but not all of it. In the last twenty years Mr Kellner had destroyed some twenty thousand dollars' worth of diamonds in this way. I may add that while Mr Kellner had succeeded in making diamonds of large size he had never made a perfect one until eight years ago. But meanwhile the expenses of the work, as you will understand, were enormous, so during the past eight years about a million dollars' worth of diamonds have been sold, one or two at a time, to meet this expense."

He paused a moment, then resumed musingly:

"All this, you understand, is not the work of a day. Mr Kellner was nearly eighty-one years old, and it was fifty-eight years ago that he began work here. The cubes there were made and placed in position thirty years ago; the guns have been there for twenty-eight years – so long, in fact, that recollection of them has passed from the minds of the men who made them. And, until four years ago, he was assisted by his son, Miss Kellner's father, and her brother. There was some explosion in this chamber where we stand which killed them both, and since then he has worked alone. His son – Miss Kellner's father – was the inventor of the machine which has enabled us to cut all the stones I showed you. I mailed the application for patent on this machine to Washington three days ago. It is as intricate as a linotype and delicate as a chronometer, but it does the work of fifty expert handcutters. Until patent papers are granted I must ask that I be allowed to protect that."

Mr Latham turned upon him quickly.

"But you've explained all this to us fully," he exclaimed sharply, indicating the cube and the guns. "We *could* duplicate that if we liked."

"Yes, you could, Mr Latham," replied Mr Wynne slowly, "but you can't duplicate the brain that isolated absolutely pure carbon from the charred residue of brown sugar. That brain was Mr Kellner's; the secret died with him!"

Again there was a long silence, broken at last by Mr Schultze:

"Dat means no more diamonds can be made undil some one else can make der pure carbon, ain'd id? Yah! Und dat brings us down to der question, How many diamonds are made alretty?"

"The diamonds I showed you gentlemen were all that have been cut thus far," replied Mr Wynne. "Less than twenty of the discs were used in making them. There are now some five hundred more of those discs in existence – roughly a billion dollars' worth – so you see I am prepared to hold you to my proposition that you buy one hundred million dollars' worth of them at one-half the carat price you now pay in the open market."

Mr Latham passed one hand across a brow bedewed with perspiration, and stared helplessly at the German.

"The work of cutting could go on steadily here, under the direction of Mr Czenki," Mr Wynne resumed after a moment. "The secrecy of this place has not been violated for forty years. We are now one hundred and seventy feet below ground level, in a gallery of the abandoned coal mine which gave Coaldale its name, reached underground from the cellar in the cottage. Roofs and walls of the entire place are shored up to ensure safety, and heavy felts made this chamber sound-proof, smothering even the detonation of the guns. Mr Czenki is the man to do the work. Mr Kellner, for ten years, held him to be the first expert in the world, and it would be carrying out his wishes if Mr Czenki would agree. If *he* does not *I* shall undertake it, *and flood the market!*" His voice hardened a little. "And, gentlemen, call off your detectives. The secret now is more yours than mine. It destroys *you* if it becomes known, not *me!* The New York police have turned this end of the investigation over to the local police, and they are fools; all the forms have been complied with, so this place is safe. Now call off your men! On the day the last diamond is delivered to you, and the payment of one hundred million dollars is completed, everything here will be destroyed. That's all!"

"One hundred million dollars!" repeated Mr Latham. "Even if we accept the proposition, Schultze, how can we raise that enormous sum within a year, and preserve the secret?"

"Id ain'd a question of *can*, Laadham – id's a question of *musd*," was the reply. He thoughtfully regarded Mr Wynne. "Id's only Sunday nighd, yed; we haf undil Thursday to answer, you remember." He turned to Mr Latham, with a recurrence of whimsical philosophy. "Think of id, Laadham, der alchemisds tried for dhree thousand years to make a piece of gold so big as a needle-point und didn'd; und he made diamonds so big as your fist mit a liddle cordide und some elecdricity! *Mein Gott*, man! Think of id!"

The jewellers accepted Mr Wynne's proposition. Mr Wynne bowed his thanks, and handed to Mr Czenki a scientific periodical opened at a page which bore a head-line:

Newly Discovered Property of Radium. Diamonds, Rubies,
Emeralds and Sapphires. Changed in Color by Exposure of One
Month to Radium.

For the fourth time Red Haney underwent the "third degree." It
culminated in a full confession of the murder of Mr Kellner. There
had been no accomplice.

"Yer see, Chief," he explained apologetically, "you an' that other
guy" (meaning Mr Birnes) "was so dead set on sayin' there was
somebody else in it, an' was so ready wit' yer descriptions, that it
looked good to me, an' I said 'Sure,' but *I* done it."

Ellis Parker Butler

The Hard-Boiled Egg

The humour of bygone times does not always travel well, but the stories of Ellis Parker Butler (1869–1937) still amuse. His short story "Pigs is Pigs" occasionally crops up in collections of humorous writing, and his only detective collection, Philo Gubb, Correspondence School Detective, *is a delightful book that surely deserves reprinting. Gubb is a small-town paperhanger and Sherlock Holmes fan who is learning to become a detective by mail: how he fares we see in "The Hard-Boiled Egg", the first Gubb story.*

WALKING CLOSE ALONG the wall, to avoid the creaking floor boards, Philo Gubb, paper-hanger and student of the Rising Sun Detective Agency's Correspondence School of Detecting, tiptoed to the door of the bedroom he shared with the mysterious Mr Critz. In appearance Mr Gubb was tall and gaunt, reminding one of a modern Don Quixote or a human flamingo; by nature Mr Gubb was the gentlest and most simple-minded of men. Now, bending his long, angular body almost double, he placed his eye to a crack in the door panel and stared into the room. Within, just out of the limited area of Mr Gubb's vision, Roscoe Critz paused in his work and listened carefully. He heard the sharp whistle of Mr Gubb's breath as it cut against the sharp edge of the crack in the panel, and he knew he was being spied upon. He placed his chubby hands on his knees and smiled at the door, while a red flush of triumph spread over his face.

Through the crack in the door Mr Gubb could see the top of the washstand beside which Mr Critz was sitting, but he could not see Mr Critz. As he stared, however, he saw a plump hand appear and pick up, one by one, the articles lying on the washstand. They were: First, seven or eight half shells of English walnuts; second, a rubber shoe heel out of which a piece had been cut; third, a small rubber ball no larger than a pea; fourth, a paper-bound book; and lastly, a large and glittering brick of yellow gold. As the hand withdrew the golden brick, Mr Gubb pressed his face closer against the door in his effort to see more, and suddenly the door flew open and Mr Gubb sprawled on his hands and knees on the worn carpet of the bedroom.

"There, now!" said Mr Critz. "There, now! Serves you right. Hope you hurt chuself!"

Mr Gubb arose slowly, like a giraffe, and brushed his knees.

"Why?" he asked.

"Snoopin' an' sneakin' like that!" said Mr Critz crossly. "Scarin' me to fits, a'most. How'd I know who 't was? If you want to come in, why don't you come right in, 'stead of snoopin' an' sneakin' an' fallin' in that way?"

As he talked, Mr Critz replaced the shells and the rubber heel and the rubber pea and the gold-brick on the washstand. He was a plump little man with a shiny bald head and a white goatee. As he talked, he bent his head down, so that he might look above the glasses of his spectacles; and in spite of his pretended anger he looked like nothing so much as a kindly, benevolent old gentleman – the sort of old gentleman that keeps a small store in a small village and sells writing-paper that smells of soap, and candy sticks out of a glass jar with a glass cover.

"How'd I know but what you was a detective?" he asked, in a gentler tone.

"I am," said Mr Gubb soberly, seating himself on one of the two beds. "I'm putty near a deteckative, as you might say."

"Ding it all!" said Mr Critz. "Now I got to go and hunt another room. I can't room with no detective."

"Well, now, Mr Critz," said Mr Gubb, "I don't want you should feel that way."

"Knowin' you are a detective makes me all nervous," complained Mr Critz; "and a man in my business has to have a steady hand, don't he?"

"You ain't told me what your business is," said Mr Gubb.

"You need n't pretend you don't know," said Mr Critz. "Any detective that saw that stuff on the washstand would know."

"Well, of course," said Mr Gubb, "I ain't a full deteckative yet. You can't look for me to guess things as quick as a full deteckative would. Of course that brick sort of looks like a gold-brick – "

"It *is* a gold-brick," said Mr Critz.

"Yes," said Mr Gubb. "But – I don't mean no offense, Mr Critz – from the way you look – I sort of thought – well, that it was a gold-brick you'd bought."

Mr Critz turned very red.

"Well, what if I did buy it?" he said. "That ain't any reason I can't sell it, is it? Just because a man buys eggs once – or twice – ain't any reason he should n't go into the business of egg-selling, is it? Just because I've bought one or two gold-bricks in my day ain't any reason I should n't go to sellin' 'em, is it?"

Mr Gubb stared at Mr Critz with unconcealed surprise.

"You ain't, – you ain't a con' man, are you, Mr Critz?" he asked.

"If I ain't yet, that's no sign I ain't goin' to be," said Mr Critz firmly. "One man has as good a right to try his hand at it as another, especially when a man has had my experience in it. Mr Gubb, there ain't hardly a con' game I ain't been conned with. I been confidenced long enough; from now on I'm goin' to confidence other folks. That's what I'm goin' to do; and I won't be bothered by no detective livin' in the same room with me. Detectives and con' men don't mix noways! No, sir!"

"Well, sir," said Mr Gubb, "I can see the sense of that. But you don't need to move right away. I don't aim to start in deteckating in earnest for a couple of months yet. I got a couple of jobs of paper-hanging and decorating to finish up, and I can't start in sleuthing until I get my star, anyway. And I don't get my star until I get one more lesson, and learn it, and send in the examination paper, and five dollars extra for the diploma. Then I'm goin' at it as a reg'lar business. It's a good business. Every day there's more crooks – excuse me, I did n't mean to say that."

"That's all right," said Mr Critz kindly. "Call a spade a spade. If I ain't a crook yet, I hope to be soon."

"I did n't know how you'd feel about it," explained Mr Gubb. "Tactfulness is strongly advised into the lessons of the Rising Sun Deteckative Agency Correspondence School of Deteckating – "

"Slocum, Ohio?" asked Mr Critz quickly. "You did n't see the ad. in the 'Hearthstone and Farmside,' did you?"

"Yes, Slocum, Ohio," said Mr Gubb, "and that is the paper I saw the ad. into; 'Big Money in Deteckating. Be a Sleuth. We can make you the equal of Sherlock Holmes in twelve lessons.' Why?"

"Well, sir," said Mr Critz, "that's funny. That ad. was right atop of the one I saw, and I studied quite considerable before I could make up my mind whether 't would be best for me to be a detective and go out and get square with the fellers that sold me gold-bricks and things by putting them in jail, or to even things up by sending for this book that was advertised right under the 'Rising Sun Correspondence School.' How come I settled to do as I done was that I had a sort of stock to start with, with a fust-class gold-brick, and some green goods

I'd bought; and this book only cost a quatter of a dollar. And she's a hummer for a quatter of a dollar! A hummer!"

He pulled the paper-covered book from his pocket and handed it to Mr Gubb. The title of the book was "The Complete Con' Man, by the King of the Grafters. Price 25 cents."

"That there book," said Mr Critz proudly, as if he himself had written it, "tells everything a man need to know to work every con' game there is. Once I get it by heart, I won't be afraid to try any of them. Of course, I got to start in small. I can't hope to pull off a wire-tapping game right at the start, because that has to have a gang. You don't know anybody you could recommend for a gang, do you?"

"Not right offhand," said Mr Gubb thoughtfully.

"If you was n't goin' into the detective business," said Mr Critz, "you'd be just the feller for me. You look sort of honest and not as if you was too bright, and that counts a lot. Even in this here simple little shell game I got to have a podner. I got to have a podner I can trust, so I can let him look like he was winnin' money off of me. You see," he explained, moving to the washstand, "this shell game is easy enough when you know how. I put three shells down like this, on a stand, and I put the little rubber pea on the stand, and then I take up the three shells like this, two in one hand and one in the other, and I wave 'em around over the pea, and maybe push the pea around a little, and I say, 'Come on! Come on! The hand is quicker than the eye!' And all of a suddent I put the shells down, and you think the pea is under one of them, like that – "

"I don't think the pea is under one of 'em," said Mr Gubb. "I seen it roll onto the floor."

"It did roll onto the floor that time," said Mr Critz apologetically. "It most generally does for me, yet. I ain't got it down to perfection yet. This is the way it ought to work – oh, pshaw! there she goes onto the floor again! Went under the bed that time. Here she is! Now, the way she ought to work is – there she goes again!"

"You got to practice that game a lot before you try it onto folks in public, Mr Critz," said Mr Gubb seriously.

"Don't I know that?" said Mr Critz rather impatiently. "Same as you've got to practice snoopin', Mr Gubb. Maybe you thought I did n't know you was snoopin' after me wherever I went last night."

"Did you?" asked Mr Gubb, with surprise plainly written on his face.

"I seen you every moment from nine p.m. till eleven!" said Mr Critz. "I did n't like it, neither."

"I did n't think to annoy you," apologized Mr Gubb. "I was practicin' Lesson Four. You was n't supposed to know I was there at all."

"Well, I don't like it," said Mr Critz. "'T was all right last night, for I did n't have nothin' important on hand, but if I'd been workin' up a con' game, the feller I was after would have thought it mighty strange to see a man follerin' me everywhere like that. If you went about it quiet and unobtrusive, I would n't mind; but if I'd had a customer on hand and he'd seen you it would make him nervous. He'd think there was a – a crazy man follerin' us."

"I was just practicin'," apologized Mr Gubb. "It won't be so bad when I get the hang of it. We all got to be beginners sometime."

"I guess so," said Mr Critz, rearranging the shells and the little rubber pea. "Well, I put the pea down like this, and I dare you to bet which shell she's goin' to be under, and you don't bet, see? So I put the shells down, and you're willin' to bet you see me put the first shell over the pea like this. So you keep your eye on that shell, and I move the shells around like this – "

"She's under the same shell," said Mr Gubb.

"Well, yes, she is," said Mr Critz placidly, "but she had n't ought to be. By rights she ought to sort of ooze out from under whilst I'm movin' the shells around, and I'd ought to sort of catch her in between my fingers and hold her there so you don't see her. Then when you say which shell she's under, she ain't under any shell; she's between my fingers. So when you put down your money I tell you to pick up that shell and there ain't anything under it. And before you can pick up the other shells I pick one up, and let the pea fall on the stand like it had been under that shell all the time. That's the game, only up to now I ain't got the hang of it. She won't ooze out from under, and she won't stick between my fingers, and when she does stick, she won't drop at the right time."

"Except for that, you've got her all right, have you?" asked Mr Gubb.

"Except for that," said Mr Critz; "and I'd have that, only my fingers are stubby."

"What was it you thought of having me do if I was n't a deteckative?" asked Mr Gubb.

"The work you'd have to do would be capping work," said Mr Critz. "Capper – that's the professional name for it. You'd guess which shell the ball was under – "

"That would be easy, the way you do it now," said Mr Gubb.

"I told you I'd got to learn it better, did n't I?" asked Mr Critz impatiently. "You'd be capper, and you'd guess which shell the pea was under. No matter which you guessed, I'd leave it under that one, so'd you'd win, and you'd win ten dollars every time you bet – but not for keeps. That's why I've got to have an honest capper."

"I can see that," said Mr Gubb; "but what's the use lettin' me win it if I've got to bring it back?"

"That starts the boobs bettin'," said Mr Critz.

"The boobs see how you look to be winnin', and they want to win too. But they don't. When they bet, I win."

"That ain't a square game," said Mr Gubb seriously, "is it?"

"A crook ain't expected to be square," said Mr Critz. "It stands to reason, if a crook wants to be a crook, he's got to be crooked, ain't he?"

"Yes, of course," said Mr Gubb. "I had n't looked at it that way."

"As far as I can see," said Mr Critz, "the more I know how a detective acts, the better off I'll be when I start in doin' real business. Ain't that so? I guess, till I get the hang of things better, I'll stay right here."

"I'm glad to hear you say so, Mr Critz," said Mr Gubb with relief. "I like you, and I like your looks, and there's no tellin' who I might get for a roommate next time. I might get some one that was n't honest."

So it was agreed, and Mr Critz stood over the washstand and manipulated the little rubber pea and the three shells, while Mr Gubb sat on the edge of the bed and studied Lesson Eleven of the "Rising Sun Detective Agency's Correspondence School of Detecting."

When, presently, Mr Critz learned to work the little pea neatly, he urged Mr Gubb to take the part of capper, and each time Mr Gubb won he gave him a five-dollar bill. Then Mr Gubb posed as a "boob" and Mr Critz won all the money back again, beaming over his spectacle rims, and chuckling again and again until he burst into a fit of coughing that made him red in the face, and did not cease until he had taken a big drink of water out of the wash-pitcher. Never had he seemed more like a kindly old gentleman from behind the candy counter of a small village. He hung over the washstand, manipulating the little rubber pea as if fascinated.

"Ain't it curyus how a feller catches onto a thing like that all to once?" he said after a while. "If it had n't been that I was so anxious, I might have fooled with that for weeks and weeks and not got anywheres with it. I do wisht you could be my capper a while anyway, until I could get one."

"I need all my time to study," said Mr Gubb. "It ain't easy to learn deteckating by mail."

"Pshaw, now!" said Mr Critz. "I'm real sorry! Maybe if I was to pay you for your time and trouble five dollars a night? How say?"

Mr Gubb considered. "Well, I dunno!" he said slowly. "I sort of hate to take money for doin' a favor like that."

"Now, there ain't no need to feel that way," said Mr Critz. "Your time's wuth somethin' to me – it's wuth a lot to me to get the hang of this gold-brick game. Once I get the hang of it, it won't be no trouble for me to sell gold-bricks like this one for all the way from a thousand dollars up. I paid fifteen hundred for this one myself, and got it cheap. That's a good profit, for this brick ain't wuth a cent over one hundred dollars, and I know, for I took it to the bank after I bought it, and that's what they was willin' to pay me for it. So it's easy wuth a few dollars for me to have help whilst I'm learnin'. I can easy afford to pay you a few dollars, and to pay a friend of yours the same."

"Well, now," said Mr Gubb, "I don't know but what I might as well make a little that way as any other. I got a friend – " He stopped short. "You don't aim to *sell* the gold-brick to him, do you?"

Mr Critz's eyes opened wide behind their spectacles.

"Land's sakes, no!" he said.

"Well, I got a friend may be willing to help out," said Mr Gubb. "What'd he have to do?"

"You or him," said Mr Critz, "would be the 'come-on,' and pretend to buy the brick. And you or him would pretend to help me to sell it. Maybe you better have the brick, because you can look stupid, and the feller that's got the brick has got to look that."

"I can look anyway a'most," said Mr Gubb with pride.

"Do tell!" said Mr Critz, and so it was arranged that the first rehearsal of the gold-brick game should take place the next evening, but as Mr Gubb turned away Mr Critz deftly slipped something into the student detective's coat pocket.

It was toward noon the next day that Mr Critz, peering over his spectacles and avoiding as best he could the pails of paste, entered the parlor of the vacant house where Mr Gubb was at work.

"I just come around," said Mr Critz, rather reluctantly, "to say you better not say nothing to your friend. I guess that deal's off."

"Pshaw, now!" said Mr Gubb. "You don't mean so!"

I don't mean nothing in the way of aspersions, you mind," said Mr Critz with reluctance, "but I guess we better call it off. Of course, so far as I know, you are all right – "

"I don't know what you're gettin' at," said Mr Gubb. "Why don't you say it?"

"Well, I been buncoed so often," said Mr Critz. "Seem's like any one can get money from me any time and any way, and I got to thinkin' it over. I don't know anything about you, do I? And here I am, going to give you a gold-brick that cost me fifteen hundred dollars, and let you go out and wait until I come for it with your friend, and – well, what's to stop you from just goin' away with that brick and never comin' back?"

Mr Gubb looked at Mr Critz blankly.

"I've went and told my friend," he said. "He's all ready to start in."

"I hate it, to have to say it," said Mr Critz, "but when I come to count over them bills I lent you to cap the shell game with, there was a five-dollar one short."

"I know," said Gubb, turning red. "And if you go over there to my coat, you'll find it in my pocket, all ready to hand back to you. I don't know how I come to keep it in my pocket. Must ha' missed it, when I handed you back the rest."

"Well, I had a notion it was that way," said Mr Critz kindly. "You look like you was honest, Mr Gubb. But a thousand-dollar gold-brick, that any bank will pay a hundred dollars for – I got to get out of this way of trustin' everybody – "

Mr Critz was evidently distressed.

"If't was anybody else but you," he said with an effort, "I'd make him put up a hundred dollars to cover the cost of a brick like that whilst he had it. There! I've said it, and I guess you're mad!"

"I ain't mad," protested Mr Gubb, "'long as you're goin' to pay me and Pete, and it's business; I ain't so set against puttin' up what the brick is worth."

Mr Critz heaved a deep sigh of relief.

"You don't know how good that makes me feel," he said. "I was almost losin' what faith in mankind I had left."

Mr Gubb ate his frugal evening meals at the Pie Wagon, on Willow Street, just off Main, where, by day, Pie-Wagon Pete dispensed light viands; and Pie-Wagon Pete was the friend he had invited to share Mr Critz's generosity. The seal of secrecy had been put on Pie-Wagon Pete's lips before Mr Gubb offered him the opportunity to accept or decline; and when Mr Gubb stopped for his evening meal, Pie-Wagon Pete – now off duty – was waiting for him. The story of Mr Critz and his amateur con' business had amused Pie-Wagon Pete. He could hardly believe such utter innocence existed. Perhaps he did not believe it existed, for he had come from the city, and he had had shady companions before he landed in Riverbank. He was a sharp-eyed, red-headed fellow, with a hard fist, and a scar across his face, and when Mr Gubb had told him of Mr Critz and his affairs, he had seen an opportunity to shear a country lamb.

"How goes it for to-night, Philo?" he asked Mr Gubb, taking the stool next to Mr Gubb, while the night man drew a cup of coffee.

"Quite well," said Mr Gubb. "Everything is arranged satisfactory. I'm to be on the old houseboat by the wharf-house on the levee at nine, with *it*." He glanced at the night man's back and lowered his voice. "And Mr Critz will bring you there."

"Nine, eh?" said Pie-Wagon. "I meet him at your room, do I?"

"You meet him at the Riverbank Hotel at eight-forty-five," said Mr Gubb. "Like it was the real thing. I'm goin' over to my room now, and give him the money – "

"What money?" asked Pie-Wagon Pete quickly.

"Well, you see," said Mr Gubb, "he sort of hated to trust the – trust *it* out of his hands without a deposit. It's the only one he has. So I thought I'd put up a hundred dollars. He's all right – "

"Oh, sure!" said Pie-Wagon. "A hundred dollars, eh?"

He looked at Mr Gubb, who was eating a piece of apple pie hand-to-mouth fashion, and studied him in a new light.

"One hundred dollars, eh?" he repeated thoughtfully. "You give him a hundred-dollar deposit now and he meets you at nine, and me at eight-forty-five, and the train leaves for Chicago at eight-forty-three, halfway between the house-boat and the hotel! Say, Gubby, what does this old guy look like?"

Mr Gubb, albeit with a tongue unused to description, delineated Mr Critz as best he could, and as he proceeded, Pie-Wagon Pete became interested.

"Pinkish, and bald? Top of his head like a hard-boiled egg? He ain't got a scar across his face? The dickens he has! Short and plump, and a reg'lar old nice grandpa? Blue eyes? Say, did he have a coughin' spell and choke red in the face? Well, sir, for a brand-new detective, you've done well. Listen, Jim: Gubby's got the Hard-Boiled Egg!"

The night man almost dropped his cup of coffee.

"Go 'way!" he said. "Old Hard-Boiled? Himself?"

"That's right! And caught him with the goods. Say, listen, Gubby!"

For five minutes Pie-Wagon Pete talked, while Mr Gubb sat with his mouth wide open.

"See?" said Pie-Wagon at last. "And don't you mention me at all. Don't mention no one. Just say to the Chief: 'And havin' trailed him this far, Mr Wittaker, and arranged to have him took with the goods, it's up to you?' See? And as soon as you say that, have him send a couple of bulls with you, and if they can do it, they'll nab Old Hard-Boiled just as he takes your cash. And Old Sleuth and Sherlock Holmes won't be in it with you when tomorrow mornin's papers come out. Get it?"

Mr Gubb got it. When he entered his bedroom, Mr Critz was waiting for him. It was slightly after eight o'clock; perhaps eight-fifteen. Mr Critz had what appeared to be the gold-brick neatly wrapped in newspaper, and he looked up with his kindly blue eyes. He had been reading the "Complete Con' Man," and had pushed his spectacles up on his forehead as Mr Gubb entered.

"I done that brick up for you," he said, indicating it with his hand, "so 's it would n't glitter whilst you was goin' through the street. If word got passed around there was a gold-brick in town, folks might sort of get suspicious-like. Nice night for goin' out, ain't it? Got a letter from my wife this aft'noon," he chuckled. "She says she hopes I'm doin' well. Sally'd have a fit if she knew what business I was goin' into. Well, time's gettin' along – "

"I brung the money," said Mr Gubb, drawing it from his pocket.

"Don't seem hardly necess'ry, does it?" said Mr Critz mildly. "But I s'pose it's just as well. Thankee, Mister Gubb. I'll just pile into my coat – "

Mr Gubb had picked up the gold-brick, and now he let it fall. Once more the door flew open, but this time it opened for three stalwart policemen, whose revolvers pointed unwaveringly at Mr Critz. The plump little man gave one glance, and put up his hands.

"All right, boys, you've got me," he said in quite another voice, and allowed them to seize his arms. He paid no attention to the police, but at Mr Gubb, who was tearing the wrapper from what proved to be but a common vitrified paving-brick, he looked long and hard.

"Say," said Mr Critz to Mr Gubb, "I'm the goat. You stung *me* all right. You worked me to a finish. I thought I knew all of you from Burns down, but you're a new one to me. Who are you, anyway?"

Mr Gubb looked up.

"Me?" he said with pride. "Why – why – I'm Gubb, the foremost deteckative of Riverbank, Iowa."

Jack London

The Master of Mystery

*Like Edgar Wallace an illegitimate child from an impoverished background,
Jack London (1876–1910) turned to writing as an escape from a life of
back-breaking toil and hardship, and his self-education programme took him
to the works of Darwin, Marx and Nietzsche. It resulted in a curious blend
of socialist idealism and a worship of raw, primitive power. Books like* White
Fang, The Call of the Wild *and* The Iron Heel *brought him massive
popularity, and his name is still associated with tales of action and adventure.
His few forays into the field of crime and mystery are intriguing: "The Minions
of Midas" was admired by Borges, for instance, while the story below is certainly
the most unusual mystery in the present collection.*

THERE WAS COMPLAINT in the village. The women chattered
together with shrill, high-pitched voices. The men were glum and
doubtful of aspect, and the very dogs wandered dubiously about,
alarmed in vague ways by the unrest of the camp and ready to take
to the woods on the first outbreak of trouble. The air was filled with
suspicion. No man was sure of his neighbor, and each was conscious
that he stood in like unsureness with his fellows. Even the children
were oppressed and solemn, and little Di Ya, the cause of it all, had
been soundly thrashed, first by Hooniah, his mother, and then by his
father, Bawn, and was now whimpering and looking pessimistically
out upon the world from the shelter of the big overturned canoe on
the beach.

And to make the matter worse Scundoo, the shaman, was in
disgrace and his known magic could not be called upon to seek out
the evildoer. Forsooth, a month gone, he had promised a fair south
wind so that the tribe might journey to the *potlatch* at Tonkin, where
Taku Jim was giving away the savings of twenty years; and when the
day came, lo, a grievous north wind blew, and of the first three canoes
to venture forth, one was swamped in the big seas, and two were

pounded to pieces on the rocks, and a child was drowned. He had pulled the string of the wrong bag, he explained – a mistake. But the people refused to listen; the offerings of meat and fish and fur ceased to come to his door; and he sulked within – so they thought – fasting in bitter penance; in reality, eating generously from his well-stored cache and meditating upon the fickleness of the mob.

The blankets of Hooniah were missing. They were good blankets, of most marvelous thickness and warmth, and her pride in them was greatened in that they had been come by so cheaply. Ty-Kwan, of the next village but one, was a fool to have so easily parted with them. But then, she did not know they were the blankets of the murdered Englishman, because of whose take-off the United States cutter nosed along the coast for a time, while its launches puffed and snorted among the secret inlets. And not knowing that Ty-Kwan had disposed of them in haste so that his own people might not have to render account to the Government, Hooniah's pride was unshaken. And because the women envied her, her pride was without end and boundless, till it filled the village and spilled over along the Alaskan shore from Dutch Harbor to St Mary's. Her totem had become justly celebrated, and her name known on the lips of men wherever men fished and feasted, what of the blankets and their marvelous thickness and warmth. It was a most mysterious happening, the manner of their going.

"I but stretched them up in the sun by the sidewall of the house," Hooniah disclaimed for the thousandth time to her Thlinket sisters. "I but stretched them up and turned my back; for Di Ya, dough-thief and eater of raw flour that he is, with head into the big iron pot, overturned and stuck there, his legs waving like the branches of a forest tree in the wind. And I did but drag him out and twice knock his head against the door for riper understanding, and behold, the blankets were not!"

"The blankets were not!" the women repeated in awed whispers.

"A great loss," one added. A second, "Never were there such blankets." And a third, "We be sorry, Hooniah, for thy loss." Yet each woman was glad in her heart that the odious, dissension-breeding blankets were gone.

"I but stretched them up in the sun," Hooniah began again.

"Yea, yea," Bawn spoke up, wearied. "But there were no gossips in the village from other places. Wherefore it be plain that some of our own tribespeople have laid unlawful hand upon the blankets."

"How can that be, O Bawn?" the women chorused indignantly. "Who should there be?"

"Then has there been witchcraft," Bawn continued stolidly enough, though he stole a sly glance at their faces.

"*Witchcraft!*" And at the dread word their voices hushed and they looked fearfully at each other.

"Ay," Hooniah affirmed, the latent malignancy of her nature flashing into a moment's exultation. "And word has been sent to Klok-No-Ton, and strong paddles. Truly shall he be here with the afternoon tide."

The little groups broke up and fear descended upon the village. Of all misfortune, witchcraft was the most appalling. With the intangible and unseen things only the shamans could cope, and neither man, woman, nor child could know until the moment of ordeal whether devils possessed their souls or not. And of all shamans Klok-No-Ton, who dwelt in the next village, was the most terrible. None found more evil spirits than he, none visited his victims with more frightful tortures. Even had he found, once, a devil residing within the body of a three-months babe – a most obstinate devil which could only be driven out when the babe had lain for a week on thorns and briers. The body was thrown into the sea after that, but the waves tossed it back again and again as a curse upon the village, nor did it finally go away till two strong men were staked out at low tide and drowned.

And Hooniah had sent for this Klok-No-Ton. Better had it been if Scundoo, their own shaman, were undisgraced. For he had ever a gentler way, and he had been known to drive forth two devils from a man who afterward begat seven healthy children. But Klok-No-Ton! They shuddered with dire foreboding at thought of him, and each one felt himself the center of accusing eyes, and looked accusingly upon his fellows – each one and all, save Sime, and Sime was a scoffer whose evil end was destined with a certitude his success could not shake.

"Hoh! Hoh!" he laughed. "Devils and Klok-No-Ton! – than whom no greater devil can be found in Thlinket Land."

"Thou fool! Even now he cometh with witcheries and sorceries; so beware thy tongue, lest evil befall thee and thy days be short in the land!"

So spoke La-lah, otherwise the Cheater, and Sime laughed scornfully.

"I am Sime, unused to fear, unafraid of the dark. I am a strong man, as my father before me, and my head is clear. Nor you nor I have seen with our eyes the unseen evil things – "

"But Scundoo hath," La-lah made answer. "And likewise Klok-No-Ton. This we know."

"How dost thou know, son of a fool?" Sime thundered, the choleric blood darkening his thick bull neck.

"By the word of their mouths — even so."

Sime snorted. "A shaman is only a man. May not his words be crooked, even as thine and mine? Bah! Bah! And once more, bah! And this for thy shamans and thy shamans' devils! and this! and this!"

And Sime snapped his fingers to right and left.

When Klok-No-Ton arrived on the afternoon tide, Sime's defiant laugh was unabated; nor did he forebear to make a joke when the shaman tripped on the sand in the landing. Klok-No-Ton looked at him sourly, and without greeting stalked straight through their midst to the house of Scundoo.

Of the meeting with Scundoo none of the tribespeople might know, for they clustered reverently in the distance and spoke in whispers while the masters of mystery were together.

"Greeting, O Scundoo!" Klok-No-Ton rumbled, wavering perceptibly from doubt of his reception.

He was a giant in stature and towered massively above little Scundoo, whose thin voice floated upward like the faint far rasping of a cricket.

"Greeting, Klok-No-Ton," Scundoo returned. "The day is fair with thy coming."

"Yet it would seem . . ." Klok-No-Ton hesitated.

"Yea, yea," the little shaman put in impatiently, "that I have fallen on ill days, else would I not stand in gratitude to you in that you do my work."

"It grieves me, friend Scundoo . . ."

"Nay, I am made glad, Klok-No-Ton."

"But will I give thee half of that which be given me."

"Not so, good Klok-No-Ton," murmured Scundoo, with a deprecatory wave of the hand. "It is I who am thy slave, and my days shall be filled with desire to befriend thee."

"As I — "

"As thou now befriendest me."

"That being so, it is then a bad business, these blankets of the woman Hooniah?"

The big shaman blundered tentatively in his quest, and Scundoo smiled a wan, gray smile, for he was used to reading men, and all men seemed very small to him.

"Ever hast thou dealt in strong medicine," he said. "Doubtless the evildoer will be briefly known to thee."

"Ay, briefly known when I set eyes upon him." Again Klok-No-Ton hesitated. "Have there been gossips from other places?" he asked.

Scundoo shook his head. "Behold! Is this not a most excellent mucluc?"

He held up the foot-covering of sealskin and walrus hide, and his visitor examined it with interest.

"It did come to me by a close-driven bargain."

Klok-No-Ton nodded attentively.

"I got it from the man La-lah. He is a remarkable man, and often have I thought . . ."

"So?" Klok-No-Ton ventured impatiently.

"Often have I thought," Scundoo concluded, his voice falling as he came to a full pause. "It is a fair day, and thy medicine be strong, Klok-No-Ton."

Klok-No-Ton's face brightened. "Thou art a great man, Scundoo, a shaman of shamans. I go now. I shall remember thee always. And the man La-lah, as you say, is remarkable."

Scundoo smiled yet more wan and gray, closed the door on the heels of his departing visitor, and barred and double-barred it.

Sime was mending his canoe when Klok-No-Ton came down the beach, and he broke off from his work only long enough to load his rifle ostentatiously and place it near him.

The shaman noted the action and called out: "Let all the people come together on this spot! It is the word of Klok-No-Ton, devil-seeker and driver of devils!"

He had been minded to assemble them at Hooniah's house, but it was necessary that all should be present, and he was doubtful of Sime's obedience and did not wish trouble. Sime was a good man to let alone, his judgement ran, and a bad one for the health of any shaman.

"Let the woman Hooniah be brought," Klok-No-Ton commanded, glaring ferociously about the circle and sending chills up and down the spines of those he looked upon.

Hooniah waddled forward, head bent and gaze averted.

"Where be thy blankets?"

"I but stretched them up in the sun, and behold, they were not!" she whined.

"So?"

"It was because of Di Ya."

"So?"

"Him have I beaten sore, and he shall yet be beaten, for that he brought trouble upon us who be poor people."

"The blankets!" Klok-No-Ton bellowed hoarsely, foreseeing her desire to lower the price to be paid. "The blankets, woman! Thy wealth is known."

"I but stretched them up in the sun," she sniffled, "and we be poor people and have nothing."

He stiffened suddenly, with a hideous distortion of the face, and Hooniah shrank back. But so swiftly did he spring forward, with inturned eye-balls and loosened jaw, that she stumbled and fell groveling at his feet. He waved his arms about, wildly flagellating the air, his body writhing and twisting in torment. An epilepsy seemed to come upon him. A white froth flecked his lips, and his body was convulsed with shiverings and tremblings.

The women broke into a wailing chant, swaying backward and forward in abandonment, while one by one the men succumbed to the excitement. Only Sime remained. He, perched upon his canoe, looked on in mockery; yet the ancestors whose seed he bore pressed heavily upon him, and he swore his strongest oaths that his courage might be cheered. Klok-No-Ton was horrible to behold. He had cast off his blanket and torn his clothes from him, so that he was quite naked, save for a girdle of eagle-claws about his thighs. Shrieking and yelling, his long black hair flying like a blot of night, he leaped frantically about the circle. A certain rude rhythm characterized his frenzy, and when all were under its sway, swinging their bodies in accord with his and venting their cries in unison, he sat bolt upright, with arm outstretched and long, talon-like finger extended. A low moaning, as of the dead, greeted this, and the people cowered with shaking knees as the dread finger passed them slowly by. For death went with it, and life remained with those who watched it go; and being rejected, they watched with eager intentness.

Finally, with a tremendous cry, the fateful finger rested upon La-lah. He shook like an aspen, seeing himself already dead, his household goods divided, and his widow married to his brother. He strove to speak, to deny, but his tongue clove to his mouth and his throat was sanded with an intolerable thirst. Klok-No-Ton seemed half to swoon away, now that his work was done; but he waited with closed eyes, listening for the great blood-cry to go up – the great blood-cry, familiar to his ear from a thousand conjurations, when the tribespeople flung themselves like wolves upon the trembling victim. But there was only silence, then a low tittering from nowhere in particular which spread and spread until a vast laughter welled up to the sky.

"Wherefore?" he cried.

"Na! Na!" the people laughed. "Thy medicine be ill, O Klok-No-Ton!"

"It be known to all," La-lah stuttered. "For eight weary months have I been gone afar with the Siwash sealers, and but this day am I come back to find the blankets of Hooniah gone ere I came!"

"It be true!" they cried with one accord. "The blankets of Hooniah were gone ere he came!"

"And thou shalt be paid nothing for thy medicine which is of no avail," announced Hooniah, on her feet once more and smarting from a sense of ridiculousness.

But Klok-No-Ton saw only the face of Scundoo and its wan, gray smile, heard only the faint far cricket's rasping. "I got it from the man La-lah, and often have I thought," and, "It is a fair day and thy medicine be strong."

He brushed by Hooniah, and the circle instinctively gave way for him to pass. Sime flung a jeer from the top of the canoe, the women snickered in his face, cries of derision rose in his wake, but he took no notice, pressing onward to the house of Scundoo. He hammered on the door, beat it with his fists, and howled vile imprecations. Yet there was no response, save that in the lulls Scundoo's voice rose eerily in incantation. Klok-No-Ton raged about like a madman, but when he attempted to break in the door with a huge stone, murmurs arose from the men and women. And he, Klok-No-Ton, knew that he stood shorn of his strength and authority before an alien people. He saw a man stoop for a stone, and a second, and a bodily fear ran through him.

"Harm not Scundoo, who is a master!" a woman cried out.

"Better you return to your own village," a man advised menacingly.

Klok-No-Ton turned on his heel and went down among them to the beach, a bitter rage at his heart, and in his head a just apprehension for his defenseless back. But no stones were cast. The children swarmed mockingly about his feet, and the air was wild with laughter and derision, but that was all. Yet he did not breathe freely until his canoe was well out upon the water, when he rose up and laid a futile curse upon the village and its people, not forgetting to specify Scundoo who had made a mock of him.

Ashore there was a clamor for Scundoo and the whole population crowded his door, entreating and imploring in confused babel till he came forth and raised his hand.

"In that ye are my children I pardon freely," he said. "But never

again. For the last time thy foolishness goes unpunished. That which
ye wish shall be granted, and it be already known to me. This night,
when the moon has gone behind the world to look upon the mighty
dead, let all the people gather in the blackness before the house of
Hooniah. Then shall the evildoer stand forth and take his merited
reward. I have spoken."

"It shall be death!" Bawn vociferated, "for that it hath brought
worry upon us, and shame."

"So be it," Scundoo replied, and shut his door.

"Now shall all be made clear and plain, and content rest upon us
once again," La-lah declaimed oracularly.

"Because of Scundoo, the little man," Sime sneered.

"Because of the medicine of Scundoo, the little man," La-lah
corrected.

"Children of foolishness, these Thlinket people!" Sime smote his
thigh a resounding blow. "It passeth understanding that grown
women and strong men should get down in the dirt to dream-things
and wonder tales."

"I am a traveled man," La-lah answered. "I have journeyed on the
deep seas and seen signs and wonders, and I know that these things
be so. I am La-lah – "

"The Cheater – "

"So called, but the Far-Journeyer right-named."

"I am not so great a traveler – " Sime began.

"Then hold thy tongue," Bawn cut in, and they separated in
anger.

When the last silver moonlight had vanished beyond the world,
Scundoo came among the people huddled about the house of
Hooniah. He walked with a quick, alert step, and those who saw
him in the light of Hooniah's slush-lamp noticed that he came
empty-handed, without rattles, masks, or shaman's paraphernalia,
save for a great sleepy raven carried under one arm.

"Is there wood gathered for a fire, so that all may see when the
work be done?" he demanded.

"Yea," Bawn answered. "There be wood in plenty."

"Then let all listen, for my words be few. With me have I brought
Jelchs, the Raven, diviner of mystery and seer of things. Him, in his
blackness, shall I place under the big black pot of Hooniah, in the
blackest corner of her house. The slush-lamp shall cease to burn,
and all remain in outer darkness. It is very simple. One by one shall
ye go into the house, lay hand upon the pot for the space of one long

intake of the breath, and withdraw again. Doubtless Jelchs will make
outcry when the hand of the evildoer is nigh him. Or who knows but
otherwise he may manifest his wisdom. Are ye ready?"

"We be ready," came the multivoiced response.

"Then will I call the name aloud, each in his turn and hers, till all
are called."

La-lah was first chosen, and he passed in at once. Every ear
strained, and through the silence they could hear his footsteps
creaking across the rickety floor. But that was all. Jelchs made no
outcry, gave no sign. Bawn was next chosen, for it well might be that
a man should steal his own blankets with intent to cast shame upon
his neighbors. Hooniah followed, and other women and children, but
without result.

"Sime!" Scundoo called out.

"Sime!" he repeated.

But Sime did not stir.

"Art thou afraid of the dark?" La-lah, his own integrity being
proved, demanded fiercely.

Sime chuckled. "I laugh at it all, for it is a great foolishness. Yet will
I go in, not in belief in wonders, but in token that I am unafraid."

And he passed in boldly, and came out still mocking.

"Some day shalt thou die with great suddenness," La-lah whispered, righteously indignant.

"I doubt not," the scoffer answered airily. "Few men of us die in
our beds, what with the shamans and the deep sea."

When half the villagers had safely undergone the ordeal, the
excitement, because of its repression, became painfully intense.
When two-thirds had gone through, a young woman, close on her
first child-bed, broke down, and in nervous shrieks and laughter gave
form to her terror.

Finally the turn came for the last of all to go in – and nothing
had yet happened. And Di Ya was the last of all. It must surely be
he. Hooniah let out a lament to the stars, while the rest drew back
from the luckless lad. He was half dead from fright, and his legs gave
under him so that he staggered on the threshold and nearly fell.
Scundoo shoved him inside and closed the door. A long time went
by, during which could be heard only the boy's weeping. Then, very
slowly, came the creak of his steps to the far corner, a pause, and the
creaking of his return. The door opened and he came forth. Nothing
had happened and he was the last.

"Let the fire be lighted," Scundoo commanded.

"Surely the thing has failed," Hooniah whispered hoarsely.

"Yea," Bawn answered complacently. "Scundoo groweth old, and we stand in need of a new shaman."

Sime threw his chest out arrogantly and strutted up to the little shaman. "Hoh! Hoh! As I said, nothing has come of it!"

"So it would seem, so it would seem," Scundoo answered meekly. "And it would seem strange to those unskilled in the affairs of mystery."

"As thou?" Sime queried.

"Mayhap even as I." Scundoo spoke quite softly, his eyelids drooping, slowly drooping, down, down, till his eyes were all but hidden. "So I am minded of another test. *Let every man, woman, and child, now and at once, hold their hands up above their heads!*"

So unexpected was the order, and so imperatively was it given, that it was obeyed without question. Every hand was in the air.

"Let each look on the other's hands, and let all look," Scundoo commanded, "so that – "

But a noise of laughter, which was more of wrath, drowned his voice. All eyes had come to rest upon Sime. Every hand but his was black with soot, and his was guiltless of the smirch of Hooniah's pot.

A stone hurtled through the air and struck him on the cheek.

"It is a lie!" he yelled. "A lie! I know naught of Hooniah's blankets!"

A second stone gashed his brow, a third whistled past his head, the great blood-cry went up, and everywhere were people groping for missiles.

"Where hast thou hidden them?" Scundoo's shrill, sharp voice cut through the tumult like a knife.

"In the large skin-bale in my house, the one slung by the ridge-pole," came the answer. "But it was a joke – "

Scundoo nodded his head, and the air went thick with flying stones. Sime's wife was crying, but his little boy, with shrieks and laughter, was flinging stones with the rest.

Hooniah came waddling back with the precious blankets. Scundoo stopped her.

"We be poor people and have little," she whimpered. "So be not hard upon us, O Scundoo."

The people ceased from the quivering stone pile they had builded, and looked on.

"Nay, it was never my way, good Hooniah," Scundoo made answer, reaching for the blankets. "In token that I am not hard, these only shall I take. Am I not wise, my children?"

"Thou art indeed wise, O Scundoo!" they cried in one voice.

And Scundoo, the Master of Mystery, went away into the darkness, the blankets around him and Jelchs nodding sleepily under his arm.

Arthur B. Reeve

"Spontaneous Combustion"

Craig Kennedy was one of the first of the scientific detectives and was sometimes referred to as "the American Sherlock Holmes". For a while Kennedy was the most popular sleuth in the USA, and was the first American detective to win wide popularity in Britain too. Much of the science in the stories has dated rather badly, and the character has suffered accordingly: a pity, since the stories are well-paced and very readable. The phenomenon of spontaneous combustion has lately been the subject of renewed study, and the story reprinted below is an intriguing one.

The author of the Kennedy stories, Arthur B. Reeve (1880–1936), trained as a lawyer before turning to journalism and fiction. His interest in detection led him to set up his own collection of data, samples etc., which resulted in the creation, at the government's invitation, of the world's first scientific crime laboratory during the First World War.

KENNEDY AND I had risen early, for we were hustling to get off for a week-end at Atlantic City. Kennedy was tugging at the straps of his grip and remonstrating with it under his breath, when the door opened and a messenger-boy stuck his head in.

"Does Mr Kennedy live here?" he asked.

Craig impatiently seized the pencil, signed his name in the book, and tore open a night letter. From the prolonged silence that followed I felt a sense of misgiving. I, at least, had set my heart on the Atlantic City outing, but with the appearance of the messenger-boy I intuitively felt that the board walk would not see us that week.

"I'm afraid the Atlantic City trip is off, Walter," remarked Craig seriously. "You remember Tom Langley in our class at the university? Well, read that."

I laid down my safety razor and took the message. Tom had not spared words, and I could see at a glance at the mere length of the thing that it must be important. It was from Camp Hang-out in the Adirondacks.

"Dear old K.," it began, regardless of expense, "can you arrange to come up here by next train after you receive this? Uncle Lewis is dead. Most mysterious. Last night after we retired noticed peculiar odour about house. Didn't pay much attention. This morning found him lying on floor of living-room, head and chest literally burned to ashes, but lower part of body and arms untouched. Room shows no evidence of fire, but full of sort of oily soot. Otherwise nothing unusual. On table near body siphon of seltzer, bottle of imported gin, limes, and glass for rickeys. Have removed body, but am keeping room exactly as found until you arrive. Bring Jameson. Wire if you cannot come, but make every effort and spare no expense. Anxiously, Tom Langley."

Craig was impatiently looking at his watch as I hastily ran through the letter.

"Hurry, Walter," he exclaimed. "We can just catch the Empire State. Never mind shaving – we'll have a stop-over at Utica to wait for the Montreal express. Here, put the rest of your things in your grip. We'll get something to eat on the train – I hope. I'll wire we're coming. Don't forget to latch the door."

Kennedy was already half-way to the elevator, and I followed ruefully, still thinking of the ocean and the piers, the bands and the roller chairs.

It was a good ten-hour journey up to the little station nearest Camp Hang-out, and at least a two-hour ride after that. We had plenty of time to reflect over what this death might mean to Tom and his sister and to speculate on the manner of it. Tom and Grace Langley were relatives by marriage of Lewis Langley, who, after the death of his wife, had made them his protégés. Lewis Langley was principally noted, as far as I could recall, for being a member of some of the fastest clubs of both New York and London. Neither Kennedy nor myself had shared in the world's opinion of him, for we knew how good he had been to Tom at college, and, from Tom, how good he had been to Grace. In fact, he had made Tom assume the Langley name, and in every way had treated the brother and sister as if they had been his own children.

Tom met us with a smart trap at the station, a sufficient indication, if we had not already known, of the "roughing it" at such a luxurious Adirondack "camp" as Camp Hang-out. He was unaffectedly glad to see us, and it was not difficult to read in his face the worry which the affair had already given him.

"Tom, I'm awfully sorry to – " began Craig when, warned by Langley's look at the curious crowd that always gathers at the railroad station at train time, he cut it short. We stood silent a moment while Tom was arranging the trap for us.

As we swung around the bend in the road that cut off the little station and its crowd of lookers-on, Kennedy was the first to speak. "Tom," he said, "first of all, let me ask that when we get to the camp we are to be simply two old classmates whom you had asked to spend a few days before the tragedy occurred. Anything will do. There may be nothing at all in your evident suspicions, and then again there may. At any rate, play the game safely – don't arouse any feeling which might cause unpleasantness later in case you are mistaken."

"I quite agree with you," answered Tom. "You wired, from Albany, I think, to keep the facts out of the papers as much as possible. I'm afraid it is too late for that. Of course the thing became vaguely known in Saranac, although the county officers have been very considerate to us, and this morning a New York *Record* correspondent was over and talked with us. I couldn't refuse – that would have put a very bad face on it."

"Too bad," I exclaimed. "I had hoped, at least, to be able to keep the report down to a few lines in the *Star*. But the *Record* will have such a yellow story about it that I'll simply have to do something to counteract the effect."

"Yes," assented Craig. "But – wait. Let's see the *Record* story first. The office doesn't know you're up here. You can hold up the *Star* and give us time to look things over, perhaps get on to the real story and set things right. Anyhow, the news is out. That's certain. We must work quickly. Tell me, Tom, who are at the camp – any one except relatives?"

"No," he replied, guardedly measuring his words. "Uncle Lewis had invited his brother James and his niece and nephew, Isabelle and James, junior – we call him Junior. Then there are Grace and myself and a distant relative, Harrington Brown, and – oh, of course, uncle's physician, Doctor Putnam."

"Who is Harrington Brown?" asked Craig.

"He's on the other side of the Langley family, on Uncle Lewis's mother's side. I think, or at least Grace thinks, that he is quite in love with Isabelle. Harrington Brown would be quite a catch. Of course he isn't wealthy, but his family is mighty well connected. Oh, Craig," sighed Langley, "I wish he hadn't done it – Uncle Lewis, I mean. Why did he invite his brother up here now when he needed to recover from the swift pace of last winter in New York? You know –

or you don't know, I suppose, but you'll know it now – when he and Uncle Jim got together there was nothing but one drink after another. Doctor Putnam was quite disgusted – at least he professed to be – but, Craig," – he lowered his voice to a whisper, as if the very forest had ears – "they're all alike – they've been just waiting for Uncle Lewis to drink himself to death. Oh," he added bitterly, "there's no love lost between me and the relatives on that score, I can assure you."

"How did you find him that morning?" asked Kennedy, as if to turn off this unlocking of family secrets to strangers.

"That's the worst part of the whole affair," replied Tom, and even in the dusk I could see the lines of his face tighten. "You know Uncle Lewis was a hard drinker, but he never seemed to show it much. We had been out on the lake in the motor-boat fishing all the afternoon and – well, I must admit both my uncles had had frequent recourse to 'pocket pistols,' and I remember they referred to it each time as 'bait.' Then after supper nothing would do but fizzes and rickeys. I was disgusted, and after reading a bit went to bed. Harrington and my uncles sat up with Doctor Putnam – according to Uncle Jim – for a couple of hours longer. Then Harrington, Doctor Putnam, and Uncle Jim went to bed, leaving Uncle Lewis still drinking.

"I remember waking in the night, and the house seemed saturated with a peculiar odour. I never smelt anything like it in my life. So I got up and slipped into my bathrobe. I met Grace in the hall. She was sniffing.

" 'Don't you smell something burning?' she asked.

"I said I did, and started downstairs to investigate. Everything was dark, but that smell was all over the house. I looked in each room downstairs as I went, but could see nothing. The kitchen and dining-room were all right. I glanced into the living-room, but, while the smell was more noticeable there, I could see no evidence of a fire except the dying embers on the hearth. It had been coolish that night, and we had had a few logs blazing. I didn't examine the room – there seemed no reason for it. We went back to our rooms, and in the morning they found the gruesome object I had missed in the darkness and shadows of the living-room."

Kennedy was intently listening. "Who found him?" he asked.

"Harrington," replied Tom. "He roused us. Harrington's theory is that uncle set himself on fire with a spark from his cigar – a charred cigar-butt was found on the floor."

We found Tom's relatives a saddened, silent party in the face of the tragedy. Kennedy and I apologized very profusely for our intrusion, but Tom quickly interrupted, as we had agreed, and explained that he had insisted on our coming, as old friends on whom he felt he could rely, especially to set the matter right in the newspapers.

I think Craig noticed keenly in the family group a certain reticence – I might almost have called it suspicion. They did not seem to know just whether to take it as an accident or as something worse, and each seemed to entertain a reserve toward the rest which was very uncomfortable.

Mr Langley's attorney in New York had been notified, but apparently was out of town, for he had not been heard from. They seemed rather anxious to get word from him.

Dinner over, the family group separated, leaving Tom an opportunity to take us into the gruesome living-room. Of course the remains had been removed, but otherwise the room was exactly as it had been when Harrington discovered the tragedy. I did not see the body, which was lying in an anteroom; but Kennedy did, and spent some time in there.

After he rejoined us, Kennedy next examined the fireplace. It was full of ashes from the logs which had been lighted on that fatal night. He noted attentively the distance of Lewis Langley's chair from the fireplace, and remarked that the varnish on the chair was not even blistered.

Before the chair, on the floor where the body had been found, he pointed out to us the peculiar ash-marks for some space around, but it really seemed to me as if something else interested him more than these ash-marks.

We had been engaged perhaps half an hour in viewing the room. At last Craig suddenly stopped.

"Tom," he said, "I think I'll wait till daylight before I go any further. I can't tell with certainty under these lights, though perhaps they show me some things the sunlight wouldn't show. We'd better leave everything just as it is until morning."

So we locked the room again and went into a sort of library across the hall.

We were sitting in silence, each occupied with his own thoughts on the mystery, when the telephone rang. It proved to be a long-distance call from New York for Tom himself. His uncle's attorney had received the news at his home out on Long Island and had hurried to the city to take charge of the estate. But that was not the news that caused the grave look on Tom's face as he nervously rejoined us.

"That was uncle's lawyer, Mr Clark, of Clark & Burdick," he said. "He has opened uncle's personal safe in the offices of the Langley estate – you remember them, Craig – where all the property of the

Langley heirs is administered by the trustees. He says he can't find the will, though he knows there was a will, and that it was placed in that safe some time ago. There is no duplicate.

The full purport of this information at once flashed on me, and I was on the point of blurting out my sympathy, when I saw by the look which Craig and Tom exchanged that they had already realized it and understood each other. Without the will the blood-relatives would inherit all of Lewis Langley's interest in the old Langley estate. Tom and his sister would be penniless.

It was late, yet we sat for nearly an hour longer, and I don't think we exchanged a half-dozen sentences in all that time. Craig seemed absorbed in thought. At length, as the great hall-clock sounded midnight, we rose as if by common consent.

"Tom," said Craig, and I could feel the sympathy that welled up in his voice – " Tom, old man, I'll get at the bottom of this mystery if human intelligence can do it."

"I know you will, Craig," responded Tom, grasping each of us by the hand. "That's why I so much wanted you fellows to come up here."

Early in the morning Kennedy aroused me. "Now, Walter. I'm going to ask you to come down into the living-room with me. and we'll take a look at it in the daytime."

I hurried into my clothes, and together we quietly went down. Starting with the exact spot where the unfortunate man had been discovered, Kennedy began a minute examination of the floor, using his pocket-lens. Every few moments he would stop to examine a spot on the rug or on the hardwood floor more intently. Several times I saw him scrape up something with the blade of his knife and carefully preserve the scrapings, each in a separate piece of paper.

Sitting idly by, I could not for the life of me see just what good it did for me to be there, and I said as much. Kennedy laughed quietly.

"You're a material witness, Walter," he replied. "Perhaps I shall need you some day to testify that I actually found these spots in this room."

Just then Tom stuck his head in. "Can I help?" he asked. "Why didn't you tell me you were going at it so early?"

"No, thanks," answered Craig, rising from the floor. "I was just making a careful examination of the room before any one was up so that nobody would think I was too interested. I've finished. But you can help me after all. Do you think you could describe exactly how every one was dressed that night?"

"Why, I can try. Let me see. To begin with, uncle had on a

shooting-jacket – that was pretty well burnt, as you know. Why, in fact, we all had our shooting-jackets on. The ladies were in white."

Craig pondered a little, but did not seem disposed to pursue the subject further, until Tom volunteered the information that since the tragedy none of them had been wearing their shooting-jackets.

"We've all been wearing city clothes," he remarked.

"Could you get your Uncle James and your Cousin Junior to go with you for an hour or two this morning on the lake, or on a tramp in the woods?" asked Craig after a moment's thought.

"Really, Craig," responded Tom doubtfully, "I ought to go to Saranac to complete the arrangements for taking Uncle Lewis's body to New York."

"Very well, persuade them to go with you. Anything, so long as you keep me from interruption for an hour or two."

They agreed on doing that, and, as by that time most of the family were up, we went in to breakfast, another silent and suspicious meal.

After breakfast Kennedy tactfully withdrew from the family, and I did the same. We wandered off in the direction of the stables, and there fell to admiring some of the horses. The groom, who seemed to be a sensible and pleasant sort of fellow, was quite ready to talk, and soon he and Craig were deep in discussing the game of the north country.

"Many rabbits about here?" asked Kennedy at length, when they had exhausted the larger game.

"Oh yes. I saw one this morning, sir," replied the groom.

"Indeed?" said Kennedy. "Do you suppose you could catch a couple for me?"

"Guess I could, sir – alive, you mean?"

"Oh yes, alive – I don't want you to violate the game laws. This is the close season, isn't it?"

"Yes, sir, but then it's all right, sir, here on the estate."

"Bring them to me this afternoon, or – no, keep them here in the stable in a cage and let me know when you have them. If anybody asks you about them, say they belong to Mr Tom."

Craig handed a small Treasury note to the groom, who took it with a grin and touched his hat.

"Thanks," he said. "I'll let you know when I have the bunnies."

As we walked slowly back from the stables we caught sight of Tom down at the boathouse just putting off in the motor-boat with his uncle and cousin. Craig waved to him, and he walked up to meet us.

"While you're in Saranac," said Craig, "buy me a dozen or so of test-tubes. Only, don't let any one here at the house know you are buying them. They might ask questions."

While they were gone Kennedy stole into James Langley's room, and after a few minutes returned to our room with the hunting-jacket. He carefully examined it with his pocket-lens. Then he filled a drinking-glass with warm boiled water and added a few pinches of table salt. With a piece of sterilized gauze from Doctor Putnam's medicine-chest he carefully washed a few portions of the coat and set aside the glass with the gauze soaking in it. Then he returned the coat to the closet where he had found it. Next, as silently, he stole into Junior's room and repeated the process with his hunting-jacket, using another glass and piece of gauze.

"While I am out of the room, Walter," he said, "I want you to take these two glasses, cover them, and number them, and on a slip of paper, which you must retain, place the names of the owners of the respective coats. I don't like this part of it – I hate to play spy, and would much rather come out in the open, but there is nothing else to do, and it is much better for all concerned that I should play the game secretly just now. There may be no cause for suspicion at all. In that case I'd never forgive myself for starting a family row. And then again – but we shall see."

After I had numbered and recorded the glasses Kennedy returned, and we went downstairs again.

"Curious about the will, isn't it?" I remarked, as we stood on the wide verandah a moment.

"Yes," he replied. "It may be necessary to go back to New York to delve into that part of it before we get through, but I hope not. We'll wait."

At this point the groom interrupted us to say that he had caught the rabbits. Kennedy at once hurried to the stable. There he rolled up his sleeves, pricked a vein in his arm, and injected a small quantity of his own blood into one of the rabbits. The other he did not touch.

It was late in the afternoon when Tom returned from town with his uncle and cousin. He seemed even more agitated than usual. Without a word he hurried up from the landing and sought us out.

"What do you think of that?" he cried, opening a copy of the *Record* and laying it flat on the library table.

There on the front page was Lewis Langley's picture with a huge scare-head:

MYSTERIOUS CASE OF SPONTANEOUS COMBUSTION

"It's all out," groaned Tom, as we bent over to read the account. "And such a story!"

Under the date of the day previous, a Saranac dispatch ran:

Lewis Langley, well known as sporting man and club member in New York, and eldest son of the late Lewis Langley, the banker, was discovered dead under the most mysterious circumstances this morning at Camp Hang-out, twelve miles from this town.

The death of "Old Krook" in Dickens's *Bleak House* or of the victim in one of Marryat's most thrilling tales was not more gruesome than this actual fact. It is without doubt a case of spontaneous human combustion, such as is recorded beyond dispute in medical and medico-legal text-books of the past two centuries. Scientists in this city consulted for the *Record* agree that, while rare, spontaneous human combustion is an established fact, and that everything in this curious case goes to show that another has been added to the already well-authenticated list of cases recorded in America and Europe. The family refuse to be interviewed, which seems to indicate that the rumours in medical circles in Saranac have a solid basis of fact.

Then followed a circumstantial account of the life of Langley and the events leading up to the discovery of the body – fairly accurate in itself, but highly coloured.

"The *Record* man must have made good use of his time here," I commented, as I finished reading the dispatch. "And – well, they must have done some hard work in New York to get this story up so completely – see, after the dispatch follow a lot of interviews, and here is a short article on spontaneous combustion itself."

Harrington and the rest of the family had just come in.

"What's this we hear about the *Record* having an article?" Harrington asked. "Read it aloud, Professor, so we can all hear it."

"'Spontaneous human combustion, or *catacausis ebriosus*,'" began Craig, "'is one of the baffling human scientific mysteries. Indeed, there can be no doubt but that individuals have in some strange and inexplicable manner caught fire and been partially or almost wholly consumed.

"'Some have attributed it to gases in the body, such as carburetted hydrogen. Once it was noted at the Hôtel Dieu in Paris that a body on being dissected gave forth a gas which was inflammable and burned with a bluish flame. Others have attributed the combustion to alcohol. A toper several years ago in Brooklyn and New York used to make money by blowing his breath through a wire gauze and lighting it. Whatever the cause, medical literature records seventy-six cases of catacausis in two hundred years.

"'The combustion seems to be sudden and is apparently confined to the cavities – the abdomen, chest, and head. Victims of ordinary fire accidents rush hither and thither frantically, succumb from exhaustion, their limbs are burned, and their clothing is all destroyed. But in catacausis they are stricken down without warning, the limbs are rarely burned, and only the clothing in contact with the head and chest is consumed. The residue is like a distillation of animal tissue, grey and dark, with an overpowering fetid odour. They are said to burn with a flickering stifled blue flame, and water, far from arresting the combustion, seems to add to it. Gin is particularly rich in inflammable, empyreumatic oils, as they are called, and in most cases it is recorded that the catacausis took place among gin-drinkers, old and obese.

"'Within the past few years cases are on record which seem to establish catacausis beyond doubt. In one case the heat was so great as to explode a pistol in the pocket of the victim. In another, a woman, the victim's husband was asphyxiated by the smoke. The woman weighed one hundred and eighty pounds in life, but the ashes weighed only twelve pounds. In all these cases the proof of spontaneous combustion seems conclusive.'"

As Craig finished reading, we looked blankly, horrified, at one another. It was too dreadful to realize.

"What do you think of it, Professor?" asked James Langley at length. "I've read somewhere of such cases, but to think of its actually happening – and to my own brother. Do you really think Lewis could have met his death in this terrible manner?"

Kennedy made no reply. Harrington seemed absorbed in thought. A shudder passed over us as we thought about it. But, gruesome as it was, it was evident that the publication of the story in the *Record* had relieved the feelings of the family group in one respect – it at least seemed to offer an explanation. It was noticeable that the suspicious air with which every one had regarded every one else was considerably dispelled.

Tom said nothing until the others had withdrawn. "Kennedy," he burst out then, "do you believe that such combustion is absolutely *spontaneous*? Don't you believe that something else is necessary to start it?"

"I'd rather not express an opinion just yet, Tom," answered Craig carefully. "Now, if you can get Harrington and Doctor Putnam away from the house for a short time, as you did with your uncle and cousin this morning, I may be able to tell you something about this case soon."

Again Kennedy stole into another bedroom, and returned to our room with a hunting-jacket. Just as he had done before, he carefully washed portions of it with the gauze soaked in the salt solution and quickly returned the coat, repeating the process with Doctor Putnam's coat and, last, that of Tom himself. Finally he turned his back while I sealed the glasses and marked and recorded them on my slip.

The next day was spent mainly in preparations for the journey to New York with the body of Lewis Langley. Kennedy was very busy on what seemed to me to be preparations for some mysterious chemical experiments. I found myself fully occupied in keeping special correspondents from all over the country at bay.

That evening after dinner we were all sitting in the open summerhouse over the boathouse. Smudges of green pine were burning and smoking on little artificial islands of stone near the lake shore, lighting up the trees on every side with a red glare. Tom and his sister were seated with Kennedy and myself on one side, while some distance from us Harrington was engaged in earnest conversation with Isabelle. The other members of the family were further removed. That seemed typical to me of the way the family group split up.

"Mr Kennedy," remarked Grace in a thoughtful, low tone, "what do you make of that *Record* article?"

"Very clever, no doubt," replied Craig.

"But don't you think it strange about the will?"

"Hush," whispered Tom, for Isabelle and Harrington had ceased talking and might perhaps be listening.

Just then one of the servants came up with a telegram.

Tom hastily opened it and read the message eagerly in the corner of the summer-house nearest one of the glowing smudges. I felt instinctively that it was from his lawyer. He turned and beckoned to Kennedy and myself.

"What do you think of that?" he whispered hoarsely.

We bent over and in the flickering light read the message:

New York papers full of spontaneous combustion story. Record *had exclusive story yesterday, but all papers to-day feature even more. Is it true? Please wire additional details at once. Also immediate instructions regarding loss of will. Has been abstracted from safe. Could Lewis Langley have taken it himself? Unless new facts soon must make loss public or issue statement Lewis Langley intestate.*

DANIEL CLARK

Tom looked blankly at Kennedy, and then at his sister, who was sitting alone. I thought I could read what was passing in his mind. With all his faults Lewis Langley had been a good foster-parent to his adopted children. But it was all over now if the will was lost.

"What can I do?" asked Tom hopelessly. "I have nothing to reply to him."

"But I have," quietly returned Kennedy, deliberately folding up the message and handing it back. "Tell them all to be in the library in fifteen minutes. This message hurries me a bit, but I am prepared. You will have something to wire Mr Clark after that." Then he strode off toward the house, leaving us to gather the group together in considerable bewilderment.

A quarter of an hour later we had all assembled in the library, across the hall from the room in which Lewis Langley had been found. As usual Kennedy began by leaping straight into the middle of his subject.

"Early in the eighteenth century," he commenced slowly, "a woman was found burned to death. There were no clues, and the scientists of that time suggested spontaneous combustion. This explanation was accepted. The theory always has been that the process of respiration by which the tissues of the body are used up and got rid of gives the body a temperature, and it has seemed that it may be possible, by preventing the escape of this heat, to set fire to the body."

We were leaning forward expectantly, horrified by the thought that perhaps, after all, the *Record* was correct.

"Now," resumed Kennedy, his tone changing, "suppose we try a little experiment – one that was tried very convincingly by the immortal Liebig. Here is a sponge. I am going to soak it in gin from this bottle, the same that Mr Langley was drinking from on the night of the – er – the tragedy."

Kennedy took the saturated sponge and placed it in an agate-iron pan from the kitchen. Then he lighted it. The bluish flame shot upward, and in tense silence we watched it burn lower and lower, till all the alcohol was consumed. Then he picked up the sponge and passed it around. It was dry, but the sponge itself had not been singed.

"We now know," he continued, "that from the nature of combustion it is impossible for the human body to undergo spontaneous ignition or combustion in the way the scientific experts of the past century believed. Swathe the body in the thickest of non-conductors of heat, and what happens? A profuse perspiration exudes, and before such an ignition could possibly take place all the moisture of the body would have to be evaporated. As seventy-five per cent or more of the body is water, it is evident that enormous heat would be necessary – moisture is the great safeguard. The experiment which I have shown you could be duplicated with specimens of human organs preserved for years in alcohol in museums. They would burn just as this sponge – the specimen itself would be very nearly uninjured by the burning of the alcohol."

"Then, Professor Kennedy, you maintain that my brother did not meet his death by such an accident?" asked James Langley.

"Exactly that, sir," replied Craig. "One of the most important aspects of the historic faith in this phenomenon is that of its skilful employment in explaining away what would otherwise appear to be convincing circumstantial evidence in cases of accusations of murder."

"Then how do you explain Mr Langley's death?" demanded Harrington. "My theory of a spark from a cigar may be true, after all."

"I am coming to that in a moment," answered Kennedy quietly. "My first suspicion was aroused by what not even Doctor Putnam seems to have noticed. The skull of Mr Langley, charred and consumed as it was, seemed to show marks of violence. It might have been from a fracture of the skull, or it might have been an accident to his remains as they were being removed to the anteroom. Again, his tongue seemed as though it was protruding. That might have been natural suffocation, or it might have been from forcible strangulation. So far I had nothing but conjecture to work on. But in looking over the living-room I found near the table, on the hardwood floor, a spot – just one little round spot. Now, deductions from spots, even if we know them to be blood, must be made very carefully. I did not know this to be a blood-spot, and so was very careful at first.

"Let us assume it was a blood-spot, however. What did it show? It was just a little regular round spot, quite thick. Now, drops of blood falling only a few inches usually make a round spot with a smooth border. Still the surface on which the drop falls is quite as much a factor as the height from which it falls. If the surface is rough the border may be irregular. But this was a smooth surface and not absorbent. The thickness of a dried blood-spot on a non-absorbent surface varies inversely as to the height from which it has fallen. This was a thick spot. Now if it had fallen, say, six feet, the height of Mr Langley, the spot would have been thin – some secondary spatters might have been seen, or at least an irregular edge around the spot. Therefore, if it was a blood-spot, it had fallen only one or two feet. I ascertained next that the lower part of the body showed no wounds or bruises whatever.

"Tracks of blood such as are left by dragging a bleeding body differ very greatly from tracks of arterial blood which are left when the victim has strength to move himself. Continuing my speculations, supposing it to be a blood-spot, what did it indicate? Clearly that Mr Langley was struck by somebody on the head with a heavy instrument, perhaps in another part of the room, that he was choked, that as the drops of blood oozed from the wound on his head, he was dragged across the floor in the direction of the fireplace – "

"But, Professor Kennedy," interrupted Doctor Putnam, "have you proved that the spot was a blood-spot? Might it not have been a paint-spot or something of that sort?"

Kennedy had apparently been waiting for just such a question.

"Ordinarily, water has no effect on paint," he answered. "I found that the spot could be washed off with water. That is not all. I have a test for blood that is so delicately sensitive that the blood of an Egyptian mummy thousands of years old will respond to it. It was discovered by a German scientist, Doctor Uhlenhuth, and was recently applied in England in connection with the Clapham murder. The suspected murderer declared that stains on his clothes were only spatters of paint, but the test proved them to be spatters of blood. Walter, bring in the cage with the rabbits."

I opened the door and took the cage from the groom, who had brought it up from the stable and stood waiting with it some distance away.

"This test is very simple, Doctor Putnam," continued Craig, as I placed the cage on the table and Kennedy unwrapped the sterilized test-tubes. "A rabbit is inoculated with human blood, and after a time the serum that is taken from the rabbit supplies the material for the test.

"I will insert this needle in one of these rabbits which has been so inoculated and will draw off some of the serum, which I place in this test-tube to the right. The other rabbit has not been inoculated. I draw off some of its serum and place that tube here on the left – we will call that our 'control tube.' It will check the results of our tests.

"Wrapped up in this paper I have the scrapings of the spot which I found on the floor – just a few grains of dark, dried powder. To show how sensitive the test is, I will take only one of the smallest of these minute scrapings. I dissolve it in this third tube with distilled water. I will even divide it in half, and place the other half in this fourth tube.

"Next I add some of the serum of the uninoculated rabbit to the half in this tube. You observe, nothing happens. I add a little of the serum of the inoculated rabbit to the other half in this other tube. Observe how delicate the test is – "

Kennedy was leaning forward, almost oblivious of the rest of us in the room, talking almost as if to himself. We, too, had riveted our eyes on the tubes.

As he added the serum from the inoculated rabbit, a cloudy milky ring formed almost immediately in the hitherto colourless, very dilute blood-solution.

"That," concluded Craig, triumphantly holding the tube aloft – "that conclusively proves that the little round spot on the hardwood floor was not paint, was not anything in this wide world but blood."

No one in the room said a word, but I knew there must have been some one there who thought volumes in the few minutes that elapsed.

"Having found one blood-spot, I began to look about for more, but was able to find only two or three traces where spots seemed to have been. The fact is that the blood-spots had been apparently carefully wiped up. That is an easy matter. Hot water and salt, or hot water alone, or even cold water, will make quite short work of fresh blood-spots – at least to all outward appearances. But nothing but a most thorough cleaning can conceal them from the Uhlenhuth test, even when they are apparently wiped out. It is a case of Lady Macbeth over again, crying in the face of modern science, 'Out, out, damned spot.'

"I was able with sufficient definiteness to trace roughly a course of blood-spots from the fireplace to a point near the door of the living-room. But beyond the door, in the hall, nothing."

"Still," interrupted Harrington, "to get back to the facts in the case. They are perfectly in accord either with my theory of the cigar or the *Record*'s of spontaneous combustion. How do you account for the facts?"

"I suppose you refer to the charred head, the burned neck, the upper chest cavity, while the arms and legs were untouched?"

"Yes, and then the body was found in the midst of combustible furniture that was not touched. It seems to me that even the spontaneous-combustion theory has considerable support in spite of this very interesting circumstantial evidence about blood-spots. Next to my own theory, the combustion theory seems most in harmony with the facts."

"If you will go over in your mind all the points proved to have been discovered – not the added points in the *Record* story – I think you will agree with me that mine is a more logical interpretation than spontaneous combustion," reasoned Craig. "Hear me out and you will see that the facts are more in harmony with my less fanciful explanation. No, some one struck Lewis Langley down either in passion or in cold blood, and then, seeing what he had done, made a desperate effort to destroy the evidence of violence. Consider my next discovery."

Kennedy placed the five glasses, which I had carefully sealed and labelled, on the table before us.

"The next step," he said, "was to find out whether any articles of clothing in the house showed marks that might be suspected of being blood-spots. And here I must beg the pardon of all in the room for intruding in their private wardrobes. But in this crisis it was absolutely necessary, and under such circumstances I never let ceremony stand before justice.

"In these five glasses on the table I have the washings of spots from the clothing worn by Tom, Mr James Langley, Junior, Harrington Brown, and Doctor Putnam. I am not going to tell you which is which – indeed, I merely have them marked, and I do not know them myself. But Mr Jameson has the marks with the names opposite on a piece of paper in his pocket. I am simply going to proceed with the tests to see if any of the stains on the coats were of blood."

Just then Doctor Putnam interposed. "One question, Professor Kennedy. It is a comparatively easy thing to recognize a blood-stain, but it is difficult, usually impossible, to tell whether the blood is that of a man or of an animal. I recall that we were all in our hunting-jackets that day, had been all day. Now, in the morning there had been an operation on one of the horses at the stable, and I assisted the veterinary from town. I may have got a spot or two of blood on my coat from that operation. Do I understand that this test would show that?"

"No," replied Craig, "this test would not show that. Other tests would, but not this. But if the spot of human blood were less than the size of a pinhead, it would show – it would show if the spot contained even so little as one twenty-thousandth of a gram of albumin. Blood from a horse, a deer, a sheep, a pig, a dog, could be obtained, but when the test was applied the liquid in which they were diluted would remain clear. No white precipitin, as it is called, would form. But let human blood, ever so diluted, be added to the serum of the inoculated rabbit, and the test is absolute."

A deathlike silence seemed to pervade the room. Kennedy slowly and deliberately began to test the contents of the glasses. Dropping into each, as he broke the seal, some of the serum of the inoculated rabbit, he waited a moment to see if any change occurred.

It was thrilling. I think no one could have gone through that fifteen minutes without having it indelibly impressed on his memory. I recall thinking as Kennedy took each glass, "Which is it to be, guilt or innocence, life or death?" Could it be possible that a man's life might hang on such a slender thread? I knew Kennedy was too accurate and serious to deceive us. It was not only possible, it was actually a fact.

The first glass showed no reaction. Some one had been vindicated.

The second was neutral likewise – another person in the room had been proved innocent.

The third – no change. Science had released a third.

The fourth –

Almost it seemed as if the record in my pocket burned – spontaneously – so intense was my feeling. There in the glass was that fatal, tell-tale white precipitate.

"My God, it's the milk ring!" whispered Tom, close to my ear.

Hastily Kennedy dropped the serum into the fifth. It remained as clear as crystal.

My hand trembled as it touched the envelope containing my record of the names.

"The person who wore the coat with that blood-stain on it," declared Kennedy solemnly, "was the person who struck Lewis Langley down, who choked him and then dragged his scarcely dead body across the floor and obliterated the marks of violence in the blazing log fire. Jameson, whose name is opposite the sign on this glass?"

I could scarcely tear the seal to look at the paper in the envelope. At last I unfolded it, and my eye fell on the name opposite the fatal sign. But my mouth was dry, and my tongue refused to move. It was too much like reading a death-sentence. With my finger on the name I faltered an instant.

Tom leaned over my shoulder and read it to himself. "For Heaven's sake, Jameson," he cried, "let the ladies retire before you read the name."

"It's not necessary," said a thick voice. "We quarrelled over the estate. My share's mortgaged up to the limit, and Lewis refused to lend me more even until I could get Isabelle happily married. Now Lewis's goes to an outsider – Harrington, boy, take care of Isabelle, fortune or no fortune. Good – "

Some one seized James Langley's arm as he pressed an automatic revolver to his temple. He reeled like a drunken man and dropped the gun on the floor with an oath.

"Beaten again," he muttered. "Forgot to move the ratchet from 'safety' to 'fire.'"

Like a madman he wrenched himself loose from us, sprang through the door, and darted upstairs. "I'll show you some combustion!" he shouted back fiercely.

Kennedy was after him like a flash. "The will!" he cried.

We literally tore the door off its hinges and burst into James Langley's room. He was bending eagerly over the fireplace. Kennedy made a flying leap at him. Just enough of the will was left unburned to be admitted to probate.

R. Austin Freeman

A Wastrel's Romance

If Craig Kennedy was the first notable scientific detective, Dr Thorndike was and remains the greatest – indeed, he has been described as "the only convincing scientific investigator of detective fiction". The style of his creator, R. Austin Freeman (1862–1943), is leisurely in pace and painstaking in its attention to detail, though even as stern a critic as Raymond Chandler found in it "an even suspense that is quite unexpected".

The early stories of Dr Thorndike are still readable and entertaining, but Freeman took things a stage further with his invention of the "inverted" detective story, where the details of the crime and the identity of the criminal are known from the outset, and the fascination is not in the revelation of the solution but in watching the detective solve it, stage by stage. This was an important step in the development of the pure crime novel, and it is one of these longer, "inverted" Thorndike tales that is included here. It was first collected in the book which launched this new form, The Singing Bone *(1912).*

I THE SPINSTERS' GUEST

THE LINGERING SUMMER twilight was fast merging into night as a solitary cyclist, whose evening-dress suit was thinly disguised by an overcoat, rode slowly along a pleasant country road. From time to time he had been overtaken and passed by a carriage, a car or a closed cab from the adjacent town, and from the festive garb of the occupants he had made shrewd guesses at their destination. His own objective was a large house, standing in somewhat extensive grounds just off the road, and the peculiar circumstances that surrounded his visit to it caused him to ride more and more slowly as he approached his goal.

Willowdale – such was the name of the house – was, to-night, witnessing a temporary revival of its past glories. For many months it had been empty and a notice-board by the gate-keeper's lodge had silently announced its forlorn state; but, to-night, its rooms, their bare walls clothed in flags and draperies, their floors waxed or carpeted, would once more echo the sound of music and cheerful voices and vibrate to the tread of many feet. For on this night the spinsters of Raynesford were giving a dance; and chief amongst the spinsters was Miss Halliwell, the owner of Willowdale.

It was a great occasion. The house was large and imposing; the spinsters were many and their purses were long. The guests were numerous and distinguished, and included no less a person than Mrs Jehu B. Chater. This was the crowning triumph of the function, for the beautiful American widow was the lion (or should we say lioness?) of the season. Her wealth was, if not beyond the dreams of avarice, at least beyond the powers of common British arithmetic, and her diamonds were, at once, the glory and the terror of her hostesses.

All these attractions notwithstanding, the cyclist approached the vicinity of Willowdale with a slowness almost hinting at reluctance; and when, at length, a curve of the road brought the gates into view, he dismounted and halted irresolutely. He was about to do a rather risky thing, and, though by no means a man of weak nerve, he hesitated to make the plunge.

The fact is, he had not been invited.

Why, then, was he going? And how was he to gain admittance? To which questions the answer involves a painful explanation.

Augustus Bailey lived by his wits. That is the common phrase, and a stupid phrase it is. For do we not all live by our wits, if we have any? And does it need any specially brilliant wits to be a common rogue? However, such as his wits were, Augustus Bailey lived by them, and he had not hitherto made a fortune.

The present venture arose out of a conversation overheard at a restaurant table and an invitation-card carelessly laid down and adroitly covered with the menu. Augustus had accepted the invitation that he had not received (on a sheet of Hotel Cecil notepaper that he had among his collection of stationery) in the name of Geoffrey Harrington-Baillie; and the question that exercised his mind at the moment was, would he or would he not be spotted? He had trusted to the number of guests and the probable inexperience of the hostesses. He knew that the cards need not be shown, though there was the awkward ceremony of announcement.

But perhaps it wouldn't get as far as that. Probably not, if his acceptance had been detected as emanating from an uninvited stranger.

He walked slowly towards the gates with growing discomfort. Added to his nervousness as to the present were certain twinges of reminiscence. He had once held a commission in a line regiment – not for long, indeed; his "wits" had been too much for his brother officers – but there had been a time when he would have come to such a gathering as this an invited guest. Now, a common thief, he was sneaking in under a false name, with a fair prospect of being ignominiously thrown out by the servants.

As he stood hesitating, the sound of hoofs on the road was followed by the aggressive bellow of a motor-horn. The modest twinkle of carriage lamps appeared round the curve and then the glare of acetylene headlights. A man came out of the lodge and drew open the gates; and Mr Bailey, taking his courage in both hands, boldly trundled his machine up the drive.

Half-way up – it was quite a steep incline – the car whizzed by; a large Napier filled with a bevy of young men who economized space by sitting on the backs of the seats and on one another's knees. Bailey looked at them and decided that this was his chance, and, pushing forward, he saw his bicycle safely bestowed in the empty coach-house and then hurried on to the cloak-room. The young men had arrived there before him, and, as he entered, were gaily peeling off their overcoats and flinging them down on a table. Bailey followed their example, and, in his eagerness to enter the reception-room with the crowd, let his attention wander from the business of the moment, and, as he pocketed the ticket and hurried away, he failed to notice that the bewildered attendant had put his hat with another man's coat and affixed his duplicate to them both.

"Major Podbury, Captain Barker-Jones, Captain Sparker, Mr Watson, Mr Goldsmith, Mr Smart, *Mr Harrington-Baillie!*"

As Augustus swaggered up the room, hugging the party of officers and quaking inwardly, he was conscious that his hostesses glanced from one man to another with more than common interest.

But at that moment the footman's voice rang out, sonorous and clear –

"Mrs Chater, Colonel Crumpler!" and, as all eyes were turned towards the new arrivals, Augustus made his bow and passed into the throng. His little game of bluff had "come off," after all.

He withdrew modestly into the more crowded portion of the room, and there took up a position where he would be shielded from the gaze of his hostesses. Presently, he reflected, they would forget him, if they had really thought about him at all, and then he would see what could be done in the way of business. He was still rather shaky, and wondered how soon it would be decent to steady his nerves with a "refresher." Meanwhile he kept a sharp look-out over the shoulders of neighbouring guests, until a movement in the crowd of guests disclosed Mrs Chater shaking hands with the presiding spinster. Then Augustus got a most uncommon surprise.

He knew her at the first glance. He had a good memory for faces, and Mrs Chater's face was one to remember. Well did he recall the frank and lovely American girl with whom he had danced at the regimental ball years ago. That was in the old days when he was a subaltern, and before that little affair of the pricked court-cards that brought his military career to an end. They had taken a mutual liking, he remembered, that sweet-faced Yankee maid and he; had danced many dances and had sat out others, to talk mystical nonsense which, in their innocence, they had believed to be philosophy. He had never seen her since. She had come into his life and gone out of it again, and he had forgotten her name, if he had ever known it. But here she was, middle-aged now, it was true, but still beautiful and a great personage withal. And, ye gods! what diamonds! And here was he, too, a common rogue, lurking in the crowd that he might, perchance, snatch a pendant or "pinch" a loose brooch.

Perhaps she might recognize him. Why not? He had recognized her. But that would never do. And thus reflecting, Mr Bailey slipped out to stroll on the lawn and smoke a cigarette. Another man, somewhat older than himself, was pacing to and fro thoughtfully, glancing from time to time through the open windows into the brilliantly-lighted rooms. When they had passed once or twice, the stranger halted and addressed him.

"This is the best place on a night like this," he remarked; "it's getting hot inside already. But perhaps you're keen on dancing."

"Not so keen as I used to be," replied Bailey; and then, observing the hungry look that the other man was bestowing on his cigarette, he produced his case and offered it.

"Thanks awfully!" exclaimed the stranger, pouncing with avidity on the open case. "Good Samaritan, by Jove. Left my case in my overcoat. Hadn't the cheek to ask, though I was starving for a smoke." He inhaled luxuriously, and, blowing out a cloud of smoke, resumed: "These chits seem to be running the show pretty well, hm? Wouldn't take it for an empty house to look at it, would you?"

"I have hardly seen it," said Bailey; "only just come, you know."

"We'll have a look round, if you like," said the genial stranger, "when we've finished our smoke, that is. Have a drink too; may cool us a bit. Know many people here?"

"Not a soul," replied Bailey. "My hostess doesn't seem to have turned up."

"Well, that's easily remedied," said the stranger. "My daughter's one of the spinsters – Granby, my name; when we've had a drink, I'll make her find you a partner – that is, if you care for the light fantastic."

"I should like a dance or two," said Bailey, "though I'm getting a bit past it now, I suppose. Still, it doesn't do to chuck up the sponge prematurely."

"Certainly not," Granby agreed jovially; "a man's as young as he feels. Well, come and have a drink and then we'll hunt up my little girl." The two men flung away the stumps of their cigarettes and headed for the refreshments.

The spinsters' champagne was light, but it was well enough if taken in sufficient quantity; a point to which Augustus – and Granby too – paid judicious attention; and when he had supplemented the wine with a few sandwiches, Mr Bailey felt in notably better spirits. For, to tell the truth, his diet, of late, had been somewhat meagre. Miss Granby, when found, proved to be a blonde and guileless "flapper" of some seventeen summers, childishly eager to play her part of hostess with due dignity; and presently Bailey found himself gyrating through the eddying crowd in company with a comely matron of thirty or thereabouts.

The sensations that this novel experience aroused rather took him by surprise. For years past he had been living a precarious life of mean and sordid shifts that oscillated between mere shabby trickery and downright crime; now conducting a paltry swindle just inside the pale of the law, and now, when hard pressed, descending to actual theft; consorting with shady characters, swindlers and knaves and scurvy rogues like himself; gambling, borrowing, cadging and, if need be, stealing, and always slinking abroad with an apprehensive eye upon "the man in blue."

And now, amidst the half-forgotten surroundings, once so familiar; the gaily-decorated rooms, the rhythmic music, the twinkle of jewels, the murmur of gliding feet and the rustle of costly gowns, the moving vision of honest gentlemen and fair ladies; the shameful years seemed to drop away and leave him to take up the thread of his life where it had snapped so disastrously. After all, these were his own people.

The seedy knaves in whose steps he had walked of late were but aliens met by the way.

He surrendered his partner, in due course, with regret – which was mutual – to an inarticulate subaltern, and was meditating another pilgrimage to the refreshment-room, when he felt a light touch upon his arm. He turned swiftly. A touch on the arm meant more to him than to some men. But it was no wooden-faced plainclothes man that he confronted; it was only a lady. In short, it was Mrs Chater, smiling nervously and a little abashed by her own boldness.

"I expect you've forgotten me," she began apologetically, but Augustus interrupted her with an eager disclaimer.

"Of course I haven't," he said; "though I have forgotten your name, but I remember that Portsmouth dance as well as if it were yesterday; at least one incident in it – the only one that was worth remembering. I've often hoped that I might meet you again, and now, at last, it has happened."

"It's nice of you to remember," she rejoined. "I've often and often thought of that evening and all the wonderful things that we talked about. You were a nice boy then; I wonder what you are like now. Dear, dear, what a long time ago it is!"

"Yes," Augustus agreed gravely, "it *is* a long time. I know it by myself; but when I look at you, it seems as if it could only have been last season."

"Oh, fie!" she exclaimed. "You are not simple as you used to be. You didn't flatter then; but perhaps there wasn't the need." She spoke with gentle reproach, but her pretty face flushed with pleasure nevertheless, and there was a certain wistfulness in the tone of her concluding sentence.

"I wasn't flattering," Augustus replied, quite sincerely; "I knew you directly you entered the room and marvelled that Time had been so gentle with you. He hasn't been as kind to me."

"No. You have got a few grey hairs, I see, but after all, what are grey hairs to a man? Just the badges of rank, like the crown on your collar or the lace on your cuffs, to mark the steps of your promotion – for I guess you'll be a colonel by now."

"No," Augustus answered quickly, with a faint flush. "I left the army some years ago."

"My! what a pity!" exclaimed Mrs Chater. "You must tell me all about it – but not now. My partner will be looking for me. We will sit out a dance and have a real gossip. But I've forgotten your name – never could recall it, in fact, though that didn't prevent me from remembering you; but, as our dear W. S. remarks, 'What's in a name?'"

"Ah, indeed," said Mr Harrington-Baillie; and apropos of that sentiment, he added: "mine is Rowland – Captain Rowland. You may remember it now."

Mrs Chater did not, however, and said so. "Will number six do?" she asked, opening her programme; and, when Augustus had assented, she entered his provisional name, remarking complacently: "We'll sit out and have a right-down good talk, and you shall tell me all about yourself and if you still think the same about free-will and personal responsibility. You had very lofty ideals, I remember, in those days, and I hope you have still. But one's ideals get rubbed down rather faint in the friction of life. Don't you think so?"

"Yes, I am afraid you're right," Augustus assented gloomily. "The wear and tear of life soon fetches the gilt off the gingerbread. Middle age is apt to find us a bit patchy, not to say naked."

"Oh, don't be pessimistic," said Mrs Chater; "that is the attitude of the disappointed idealist, and I am sure you have no reason, really, to be disappointed in yourself. But I must run away now. Think over all the things you have to tell me, and don't forget that it is number six." With a bright smile and a friendly nod she sailed away, a vision of glittering splendour, compared with which Solomon in all his glory was a mere matter of commonplace bullion.

The interview, evidently friendly and familiar, between the unknown guest and the famous American widow had by no means passed unnoticed; and in other circumstances, Bailey might have endeavoured to profit by the reflected glory that enveloped him. But he was not in search of notoriety; and the same evasive instinct that had led him to sink Mr Harrington-Baillie in Captain Rowland, now advised him to withdraw his dual personality from the vulgar gaze. He had come here on very definite business. For the hundredth time he was "stony-broke," and it was the hope of picking up some "unconsidered trifles" that had brought him. But, somehow, the atmosphere of the place had proved unfavourable. Either opportunities were lacking or he failed to seize them. In any case, the game pocket that formed an unconventional feature of his dress-coat was still empty, and it looked as if a pleasant evening and a good supper were all that he was likely to get. Nevertheless, be his conduct never so blameless, the fact remained that he was an uninvited guest, liable at any moment to be ejected as an impostor, and his recognition by the widow had not rendered this possibility any the more remote.

He strayed out on to the lawn, whence the grounds fell away on all sides. But there were other guests there, cooling themselves after the last dance, and the light from the rooms streamed through the windows, illuminating their figures, and among them, that of the too-companionable Granby. Augustus quickly drew away from the lighted area, and, chancing upon a narrow path, strolled away along it in the direction of a copse or shrubbery that he saw ahead. Presently he came to an ivy-covered arch, lighted by one or two fairy lamps, and, passing through this, he entered a winding path, bordered by trees and shrubs and but faintly lighted by an occasional coloured lamp suspended from a branch.

Already he was quite clear of the crowd; indeed, the deserted condition of the pleasant retreat rather surprised him, until he reflected that to couples desiring seclusion there were whole ranges of untenanted rooms and galleries available in the empty house.

The path sloped gently downwards for some distance; then came a long flight of rustic steps and, at the bottom, a seat between two trees. In front of the seat the path extended in a straight line, forming a narrow terrace; on the right the ground sloped up steeply towards the lawn; on the left it fell away still more steeply towards the encompassing wall of the grounds; and on both sides it was covered with trees and shrubs.

Bailey sat down on the seat to think over the account of himself that he should present to Mrs Chater. It was a comfortable seat, built into the trunk of an elm, which formed one end and part of the back. He leaned against the tree, and, taking out his silver case, selected a cigarette. But it remained unlighted between his fingers as he sat and meditated upon his unsatisfactory past and the melancholy tale of what might have been. Fresh from the atmosphere of refined opulence that pervaded the dancing-rooms, the throng of well-groomed men and dainty women, his mind travelled back to his sordid little flat in Bermondsey, encompassed by poverty and squalor, jostled by lofty factories, grimy with the smoke of the river and the reek from the great chimneys. It was a hideous contrast. Verily the way of the transgressor was not strewn with flowers.

At that point in his meditations he caught the sound of voices and footsteps on the path above and rose to walk on along the path. He did not wish to be seen wandering alone in the shrubbery. But now a woman's laugh sounded from somewhere down the path. There were people approaching that way too. He put the cigarette back in the case and stepped round behind the seat, intending to retreat in that direction, but here the path ended, and beyond was nothing but a rugged slope down to the wall thickly covered with bushes. And while he was hesitating, the sound of feet descending the steps and the rustle of a woman's dress left him to choose between staying where he was or coming out to confront the new-comers. He chose the former, drawing up close behind the tree to wait until they should have passed on.

But they were not going to pass on. One of them – a woman – sat down on the seat, and then a familiar voice smote on his ear.

"I guess I'll rest here quietly for a while; this tooth of mine is aching terribly; and, see here, I want you to go and fetch me something. Take this ticket to the cloak-room and tell the woman to give you my little velvet bag. You'll find in it a bottle of chloroform and a packet of cotton-wool."

"But I can't leave you here all alone, Mrs Chater," her partner expostulated.

"I'm not hankering for society just now," said Mrs Chater. "I want that chloroform. Just you hustle off and fetch it, like a good boy. Here's the ticket."

The young officer's footsteps retreated rapidly, and the voices of the couple advancing along the path grew louder. Bailey, cursing the chance that had placed him in his ridiculous and uncomfortable position, heard them approach and pass on up the steps; and then all was silent, save for an occasional moan from Mrs Chater and the measured creaking of the seat as she rocked uneasily to and fro. But the young man was uncommonly prompt in the discharge of his mission, and in a very few minutes Bailey heard him approaching at a run along the path above and then bounding down the steps.

"Now I call that real good of you," said the widow gratefully. "You must have run like the wind. Cut the string of the packet and then leave me to wrestle with this tooth."

"But I can't leave you here all – "

"Yes, you can," interrupted Mrs Chater. "There won't be anyone about – the next dance is a waltz. Besides, you must go and find your partner."

"Well, if you'd really rather be alone," the subaltern began; but Mrs Chater interrupted him.

"Of course I would, when I'm fixing up my teeth. Now go along, and a thousand thanks for your kindness."

With mumbled protestations the young officer slowly retired, and Bailey heard his reluctant feet ascending the steps. Then a deep silence fell on the place in which the rustle of paper and the squeak of a withdrawn cork seemed loud and palpable. Bailey had turned with his face towards the tree, against which he leaned with his lips parted scarcely daring to breathe. He cursed himself again and again for having thus entrapped himself for no tangible reason, and longed to get away. But there was no escape now without betraying himself. He must wait for the woman to go.

Suddenly, beyond the edge of the tree, a hand appeared holding an open packet of cotton-wool. It laid the wool down on the seat, and, pinching off a fragment, rolled it into a tiny ball. The fingers of the hand were encircled by rings, its wrist enclosed by a broad bracelet; and from rings and bracelet the light of the solitary fairy-lamp, that hung from a branch of the tree, was reflected in prismatic sparks. The hand was withdrawn and Bailey stared dreamily at the square pad of cotton-wool. Then the hand came again into view. This time it held a small phial which it laid softly on the seat, setting the cork beside it. And again the light flashed in many-coloured scintillations from the encrusting gems.

Bailey's knees began to tremble, and a chilly moisture broke out upon his forehead.

The hand drew back, but, as it vanished, Bailey moved his head silently until his face emerged from behind the tree. The woman was leaning back, her head resting against the trunk only a few inches away from his face. The great stones of the tiara flashed in his very eyes. Over her shoulder, he could even see the gorgeous pendant, rising and falling on her bosom with ever-changing fires; and both her raised hands were a mass of glitter and sparkle, only the deeper and richer for the subdued light.

His heart throbbed with palpable blows that drummed aloud in his ears. The sweat trickled clammily down his face, and he clenched his teeth to keep them from chattering. An agony of horror – of deadly fear – was creeping over him – a terror of the dreadful impulse that was stealing away his reason and his will.

The silence was profound. The woman's soft breathing, the creak of her bodice, were plainly – grossly – audible; and he checked his own breath until he seemed on the verge of suffocation.

Of a sudden through the night air was borne faintly the dreamy music of a waltz. The dance had begun. The distant sound but deepened the sense of solitude in this deserted spot.

Bailey listened intently. He yearned to escape from the invisible force that seemed to be clutching at his wrists, and dragging him forward inexorably to his doom.

He gazed down at the woman with a horrid fascination. He struggled to draw back out of sight – and struggled in vain.

Then, at last, with a horrible, stealthy deliberation, a clammy, shaking hand crept forward towards the seat. Without a sound it grasped the wool, and noiselessly, slowly drew back. Again it stole forth. The fingers twined snakily around the phial, lifted it from the seat and carried it back into the shadow.

After a few seconds it reappeared and softly replaced the bottle – now half empty. There was a brief pause. The measured cadences of the waltz stole softly through the quiet night and seemed to keep time with the woman's breathing. Other sound there was none. The place was wrapped in the silence of the grave.

Suddenly, from his hiding-place, Bailey leaned forward over the back of the seat. The pad of cotton-wool was in his hand.

The woman was now leaning back as if dozing, and her hands rested in her lap. There was a swift movement. The pad was pressed against her face and her head dragged back against the chest of the invisible assailant. A smothered gasp burst from her hidden lips as her hands flew up to clutch at the murderous arm; and then came a frightful struggle, made even more frightful by the gay and costly trappings of the writhing victim. And still there was hardly a sound; only muffled gasps, the rustle of silk, the creaking of the seat, the clink of the falling bottle and, afar off, with dreadful irony, the dreamy murmur of the waltz.

The struggle was but brief. Quite suddenly the jewelled hands dropped, the head lay resistless on the crumpled shirt-front, and the body, now limp and inert, began to slip forward off the seat. Bailey, still grasping the passive head, climbed over the back of the seat and, as the woman slid gently to the ground, he drew away the pad and stooped over her. The struggle was over now; the mad fury of the moment was passing swiftly into the chill of mortal fear.

He stared with incredulous horror into the swollen face, but now so comely, the sightless eyes that but a little while since had smiled into his with such kindly recognition.

He had done this! He, the sneaking wastrel, discarded of all the world, to whom this sweet woman had held out the hand of friendship. She had cherished his memory, when to all others he was sunk deep under the waters of oblivion. And he had killed her – for to his ear no breath of life seemed to issue from those purple lips.

A sudden hideous compunction for this irrevocable thing that he had done surged through him, and he stood up clutching at his damp hair with a hoarse cry that was like the cry of the damned.

The jewels passed straightway out of his consciousness. Everything was forgotten now but the horror of this unspeakable thing that he had done. Remorse incurable and haunting fear were all that were left to him.

The sound of voices far away along the path aroused him, and the vague horror that possessed him materialized into abject, bodily fear. He lifted the limp body to the edge of the path and let it slip down the steep declivity among the bushes. A soft, shuddering sigh came from the parted lips as the body turned over, and he paused a moment to listen. But there was no other sound of life. Doubtless that sigh was only the result of the passive movement.

Again he stood for an instant as one in a dream, gazing at the huddled shape half hidden by the bushes, before he climbed back to the path; and even then he looked back once more, but now she was hidden from sight. And, as the voices drew nearer, he turned, and, with stealthy swiftness, ran up the rustic steps.

As he came out on the edge of the lawn the music ceased, and, almost immediately, a stream of people issued from the house. Shaken as he was, Bailey yet had wits enough left to know that his clothes and hair were disordered and that his appearance must be wild. Accordingly he avoided the dancers, and, keeping to the margin of the lawn, made his way to the cloak-room by the least frequented route. If he had dared, he would have called in at the refreshment-room, for he was deadly faint and his limbs shook as he walked. But a haunting fear pursued him and, indeed, grew from moment to moment. He found himself already listening for the rumour of the inevitable discovery.

He staggered into the cloak-room, and, flinging his ticket down on the table, dragged out his watch. The attendant looked at him curiously and, pausing with the ticket in his hand, asked sympathetically: "Not feeling very well, sir?"

"No," said Bailey. "So beastly hot in there."

"You ought to have a glass of champagne, sir, before you start," said the man.

"No time," replied Bailey, holding out a shaky hand for his coat. "Shall lose my train if I'm not sharp."

At this hint the attendant reached down the coat and hat, holding up the former for its owner to slip his arms into the sleeves. But Bailey snatched it from him, and, flinging it over his arm, put on his hat and hurried away to the coach-house. Here, again, the attendant stared at him in astonishment; which was not lessened when Bailey, declining his offer to help him on with his coat, bundled the latter under his arm, clicked the lever of the "variable" on to the ninety gear, sprang on to the machine and whirled away down the steep drive, a grotesque vision of flying coat-tails.

"You haven't lit your lamp, sir," roared the attendant; but Bailey's ears were deaf to all save the clamour of the expected pursuit.

Fortunately the drive entered the road obliquely, or Bailey must have been flung into the opposite hedge. As it was, the machine, rushing down the slope, flew out into the road with terrific velocity; nor did its speed diminish then, for its rider, impelled by mortal terror, trod the pedals with the fury of a madman. And still, as the machine whizzed along the dark and silent road, his ears were strained to catch the clatter of hoofs or the throb of a motor from behind.

He knew the country well – in fact, as a precaution, he had cycled over the district only the day before; and he was ready, at any suspicious sound, to slip down any of the lanes or byways, secure of finding his way. But still he sped on, and still no sound from the rear came to tell him of the dread discovery.

When he had ridden about three miles, he came to the foot of a steep hill. Here he had to dismount and push his machine up the incline, which he did at such speed that he arrived at the top quite breathless. Before mounting again he determined to put on his coat, for his appearance was calculated to attract attention, if nothing more. It was only half-past eleven, and presently he would pass through the streets of a small town. Also he would light his lamp. It would be fatal to be stopped by a patrol or rural constable.

Having lit his lamp and hastily put on his coat he once more listened intently, looking back over the country that was darkly visible from the summit of the hill. No moving lights were to be seen, no ringing hoofs or throbbing engines to be heard, and, turning to mount, he instinctively felt in his overcoat pocket for his gloves.

A pair of gloves came out in his hand, but he was instantly conscious that they were not his. A silk muffler was there also; a white one. But his muffler was black.

With a sudden shock of terror he thrust his hand into the ticket-pocket, where he had put his latch-key. There was no key there; only an amber cigar-holder, which he had never seen before. He stood for a few moments in utter consternation. He had taken the wrong coat. Then he had left his own coat behind. A cold sweat of fear broke out afresh on his face as he realized this. His Yale latch-key was in its pocket; not that that mattered very much. He had a duplicate at home, and, as to getting in, well, he knew his own outside door and his tool-bag contained one or two trifles not usually found in cyclists' tool-bags. The question was whether that coat contained anything that could disclose his identity. And then suddenly he remembered, with a gasp of relief, that he had carefully turned the pockets out before starting, with this very idea.

No; once let him attain the sanctuary of his grimy little flat, wedged in as it was between the great factories by the river-side, and he would be safe: safe from everything but the horror of himself, and the haunting vision of a jewelled figure huddled up in a glittering, silken heap beneath the bushes.

With a last look round he mounted his machine, and, driving it over the brow of the hill, swept away into the darkness.

II MUNERA PULVERIS

(Related by CHRISTOPHER JERVIS, M. D.)

It is one of the drawbacks of medicine as a profession that one is never rid of one's responsibilities. The merchant, the lawyer, the civil servant, each at the appointed time locks up his desk, puts on his hat and goes forth a free man with an interval of uninterrupted leisure before him. Not so the doctor. Whether at work or at play, awake or asleep, he is the servant of humanity, at the instant disposal of friend or stranger alike whose need may make the necessary claim.

When I agreed to accompany my wife to the spinsters' dance at Raynesford, I imagined that, for that evening, at least, I was definitely off duty; and in that belief I continued until the conclusion of the eighth dance. To be quite truthful, I was not sorry when the delusion was shattered. My last partner was a young lady of a slanginess of speech that verged on the inarticulate. Now it is not easy to exchange ideas in "pidgin" English; and the conversation of a person to whom all things are either "ripping" or "rotten" is apt to lack subtlety. In fact, I was frankly bored; and, reflecting on the utility of the humble sandwich as an aid to conversation, I was about to entice my partner to the refreshment-room when I felt someone pluck at my sleeve. I turned quickly and looked into the anxious and rather frightened face of my wife.

"Miss Halliwell is looking for you," she said. "A lady has been taken ill. Will you come and see what is the matter?" She took my arm and, when I had made my apologies to my partner, she hurried me on to the lawn.

"It's a mysterious affair," my wife continued. "The sick lady is a Mrs Chater, a very wealthy American widow. Edith Halliwell and Major Podbury found her lying in the shrubbery all alone and unable to give any account of herself. Poor Edith is dreadfully upset. She doesn't know what to think."

"What do you mean?" I began; but at this moment Miss Halliwell, who was waiting by an ivy-covered rustic arch, espied us and ran forward.

"Oh, do hurry, please, Dr Jervis," she exclaimed; "such a shocking thing has happened. Has Juliet told you?" Without waiting for an answer, she darted through the arch and preceded us along a narrow path at the curious, flat-footed, shambling trot common to most adult women. Presently we descended a flight of rustic steps which brought us to a seat, from whence extended a straight path cut like a miniature terrace on a steep slope, with a high bank rising to the right and a declivity falling away to the left. Down in the hollow, his head and shoulders appearing above the bushes, was a man holding in his hand a fairy-lamp that he had apparently taken down from a tree. I climbed down to him, and, as I came round the bushes, I perceived a richly-dressed woman lying huddled on the ground. She was not completely insensible, for she moved slightly at my approach, muttering a few words in thick, indistinct accents. I took the lamp from the man, whom I assumed to be Major Podbury, and, as he delivered it to me with a significant glance and a faint lift of the eyebrows, I understood Miss Halliwell's agitation. Indeed, for one horrible moment I thought that she was right – that the prostrate woman was intoxicated. But when I approached nearer, the flickering light of the lamp made visible a square reddened patch on her face, like the impression of a mustard plaster, covering the nose and mouth; and then I scented mischief of a more serious kind.

"We had better carry her up to the seat," I said, handing the lamp to Miss Halliwell. "Then we can consider moving her to the house." The major and I lifted the helpless woman and, having climbed cautiously up to the path, laid her on the seat.

"What is it, Dr Jervis?" Miss Halliwell whispered.

"I can't say at the moment," I replied; "but it's not what you feared."

"Thank God for that!" was her fervent rejoinder. "It would have been a shocking scandal."

I took the dim little lamp and once more bent over the half-conscious woman.

Her appearance puzzled me not a little. She looked like a person recovering from an anæsthetic, but the square red patch on her face, recalling, as it did, the Burke murders, rather suggested suffocation. As I was thus reflecting, the light of the lamp fell on a white object lying on the ground behind the seat, and holding the lamp forward, I saw that it was a square pad of cotton-wool. The coincidence of its shape and size with that of the red patch on the woman's face instantly struck me, and I stooped down to pick it up; and then I saw, lying under the seat, a small bottle. This also I picked up and held in the lamplight. It was a one-ounce phial, quite empty, and was labelled "Methylated Chloroform." Here seemed to be a complete explanation of the thick utterance and drunken aspect; but it was an explanation that required, in its turn, to be explained. Obviously no robbery had been committed for the woman literally glittered with diamonds. Equally obviously she had not administered the chloroform to herself.

There was nothing for it but to carry her indoors and await her further recovery, so, with the major's help, we conveyed her through the shrubbery and kitchen garden to a side door, and deposited her on a sofa in a half-furnished room.

Here, under the influence of water dabbed on her face and the plentiful use of smelling-salts, she quickly revived, and was soon able to give an intelligible account of herself.

The chloroform and cotton-wool were her own. She had used them for an aching tooth; and she was sitting alone on the seat with the bottle and the wool beside her when the incomprehensible thing had happened. Without a moment's warning a hand had come from behind her and pressed the pad of wool over her nose and mouth. The wool was saturated with chloroform, and she had lost consciousness almost immediately.

"You didn't see the person, then?" I asked.

"No, but I know he was in evening dress, because I felt my head against his shirt-front."

"Then," said I, "he is either here still or he has been to the cloak-room. He couldn't have left the place without an overcoat."

"No, by Jove!" exclaimed the major; "that's true. I'll go and make inquiries." He strode away all agog, and I, having satisfied myself that Mrs Chater could be left safely, followed him almost immediately.

I made my way straight to the cloak-room, and here I found the major and one or two of his brother officers putting on their coats in a flutter of gleeful excitement.

"He's gone," said Podbury, struggling frantically into his overcoat; "went off nearly an hour ago on a bicycle. Seemed in a deuce of a stew, the attendant says, and no wonder. We're goin' after him in our car. Care to join the hunt?"

"No, thanks. I must stay with the patient. But how do you know you're after the right man?"

"Isn't any other. Only one Johnnie's left. Besides – here, confound it! you've given me the wrong coat!"

He tore off the garment and handed it back to the attendant, who regarded it with an expression of dismay.

"Are you sure, sir?" he asked.

"Perfectly," said the major. "Come, hurry up, my man."

"I'm afraid, sir," said the attendant, "that the gentleman who has gone has taken your coat. They were on the same peg, I know. I am very sorry, sir."

The major was speechless with wrath. What the devil was the good of being sorry? and how the deuce was he to get his coat back?

"But," I interposed, "if the stranger has got your coat, then this coat must be his."

"I know," said Podbury; "but I don't want his beastly coat."

"No," I replied, "but it may be useful for identification."

This appeared to afford the bereaved officer little consolation, but as the car was now ready, he bustled away, and I, having directed the man to put the coat away in a safe place, went back to my patient.

Mrs Chater was by now fairly recovered, and had developed a highly vindictive interest in her late assailant. She even went so far as to regret that he had not taken at least some of her diamonds, so that robbery might have been added to the charge of attempted murder, and expressed the earnest hope that the officers would not be foolishly gentle in their treatment of him when they caught him.

"By the way, Dr Jervis," said Miss Halliwell, "I think I ought to mention a rather curious thing that happened in connection with this dance. We received an acceptance from a Mr Harrington-Baillie, who wrote from the Hotel Cecil. Now I am certain that no such name was proposed by any of the spinsters."

"But didn't you ask them?" I inquired.

"Well, the fact is," she replied, "that one of them, Miss Waters, had to go abroad suddenly, and we had not got her address; and as it was possible that she might have invited him, I did not like to move in the matter. I am very sorry I didn't now. We may have let in a regular criminal – though why he should have wanted to murder Mrs Chater I cannot imagine."

It was certainly a mysterious affair, and the mystery was in no wise dispelled by the return of the search party an hour later. It seemed that the bicycle had been tracked for a couple of miles towards London, but then, at the cross-roads, the tracks had become hopelessly mixed with the impressions of other machines, and the officers, after cruising about vaguely for a while, had given up the hunt and returned.

"You see, Mrs Chater," Major Podbury explained apologetically, "the fellow must have had a good hour's start, and, with a high-geared machine, that would have brought him pretty close to London."

"Do you mean to tell me," exclaimed Mrs Chater regarding the major with hardly concealed contempt, "that that villain has got off scot-free?"

"Looks rather like it," replied Podbury, "but if I were you I should get the man's description from the attendants who saw him and go up to Scotland Yard to-morrow. They may know the Johnnie there, and they may even recognize the coat if you take it with you."

"That doesn't seem very likely," said Mrs Chater, and it certainly did not; but since no better plan could be suggested the lady decided to adopt it; and I supposed that I had heard the last of the matter.

In this, however, I was mistaken. On the following day, just before noon, as I was drowsily considering the points in a brief dealing with a question of survivorship while Thorndyke drafted his weekly lecture, a smart rat-tat at the door of our chambers announced a visitor. I rose wearily – I had had only four hours' sleep – and opened the door, whereupon there sailed into the room no less a person than Mrs Chater followed by Superintendent Miller, with a grin on his face and a brown-paper parcel under his arm.

The lady was not in the best of tempers, though wonderfully lively and alert considering the severe shock that she had suffered so recently, and her disapproval of Miller was frankly obvious.

"Dr Jervis has probably told you about the attempt to murder me last night," she said, when I had introduced her to my colleague. "Well, now, will you believe it? I have been to the police, I have given them a description of the murderous villain, and I have even shown them the very coat that he wore, and they tell me that nothing can be done. That, in short, this scoundrel must be allowed to go his way free and unmolested."

"You will observe, doctor," said Miller, "that this lady has given us a description that would apply to fifty per cent of the middle-class men of the United Kingdom, and has shown us a coat without a single identifying mark of any kind on it, and expects us to lay our hands on the owner without a solitary clue to guide us. Now we are not sorcerers at the Yard; we're only policemen. So I have taken the liberty of referring Mrs Chater to you." He grinned maliciously and laid the parcel on the table.

"And what do you want me to do?" Thorndyke asked.

"Why, sir," said Miller, "there is a coat. In the pockets were a pair of gloves, a muffler, a box of matches, a tram-ticket and a Yale key. Mrs Chater would like to know whose coat it is." He untied the parcel, with his eye cocked at our rather disconcerted client, and Thorndyke watched him with a faint smile.

"This is very kind of you, Miller," said he, "but I think a clairvoyant would be more to your purpose."

The superintendent instantly dropped his facetious manner.

"Seriously, sir," he said, "I should be glad if you would take a look at the coat. We have absolutely nothing to go on, and yet we don't want to give up the case. I have gone through it most thoroughly and can't find any clue to guide us. Now I know that nothing escapes you, and perhaps you might notice something that I have overlooked; something that would give us a hint where to start on our inquiry. Couldn't you turn the microscope on it, for instance?" he added, with a deprecating smile.

Thorndyke reflected, with an inquisitive eye on the coat. I saw that the problem was not without its attractions to him; and when the lady seconded Miller's request with persuasive eagerness, the inevitable consequence followed.

"Very well," he said. "Leave the coat with me for an hour or so and I will look it over. I am afraid there is not the remotest chance of our learning anything from it, but even so, the examination will have done no harm. Come back at two o'clock; I shall be ready to report my failure by then."

He bowed our visitors out and, returning to the table, looked down with a quizzical smile on the coat and the large official envelope containing the articles from the pockets.

"And what does my learned brother suggest?" he asked, looking up at me.

"I should look at the tram-ticket first," I replied, "and then – well, Miller's suggestion wasn't such a bad one; to explore the surface with the microscope."

"I think we will take the latter measure first," said he. "The tram-ticket might create a misleading bias. A man may take a tram anywhere, whereas the indoor dust on a man's coat appertains mostly to a definite locality."

"Yes," I replied; "but the information that it yields is excessively vague."

"That is true," he agreed, taking up the coat and envelope to carry them to the laboratory, "and yet, you know, Jervis, as I have often pointed out, the evidential value of dust is apt to be under-estimated. The naked-eye appearances – which are the normal appearances – are misleading. Gather the dust, say, from a table-top, and what have you? A fine powder of a characterless grey, just like any other dust from any other table-top. But, under the microscope, this grey powder is resolved into recognizable fragments of definite substances, which fragments may often be traced with certainty to the masses from which they have been detached. But you know all this as well as I do."

"I quite appreciate the value of dust as evidence in certain circumstances," I replied, "but surely the information that could be gathered from dust on the coat of an unknown man must be too general to be of any use in tracing the owner."

"I am afraid you are right," said Thorndyke, laying the coat on the laboratory bench; "but we shall soon see, if Polton will let us have his patent dust-extractor."

The little apparatus to which my colleague referred was the invention of our ingenious laboratory assistant, and resembled in principle the "vacuum cleaners" used for restoring carpets. It had, however, one special feature: the receiver was made to admit a microscope-slide, and on this the dust-laden air was delivered from a jet.

The "extractor" having been clamped to the bench by its proud inventor, and a wetted slide introduced into the receiver, Thorndyke applied the nozzle of the instrument to the collar of the coat while Polton worked the pump. The slide was then removed and, another having been substituted, the nozzle was applied to the right sleeve near the shoulder, and the exhauster again worked by Polton. By repeating this process, half-a-dozen slides were obtained charged with dust from different parts of the garment, and then, setting up our respective microscopes, we proceeded to examine the samples.

A very brief inspection showed me that this dust contained matter not usually met with – at any rate, in appreciable quantities. There were, of course, the usual fragments of wool, cotton and other fibres derived from clothing and furniture, particles of straw, husk, hair, various mineral particles and, in fact, the ordinary constituents of dust from clothing. But, in addition to these, and in much greater quantity, were a number of other bodies, mostly of vegetable origin and presenting well-defined characters and considerable variety, and especially abundant were various starch granules.

I glanced at Thorndyke and observed he was already busy with a pencil and a slip of paper, apparently making a list of the objects visible in the field of the microscope. I hastened to follow his example, and for a time we worked on in silence. At length my colleague leaned back in his chair and read over his list.

"This is a highly interesting collection, Jervis," he remarked. "What do you find on your slides out of the ordinary?"

"I have quite a little museum here," I replied, referring to my list. "There is, of course, chalk from the road at Raynesford. In addition to this I find various starches, principally wheat and rice, especially rice, fragments of the cortices of several seeds, several different stone-cells, some yellow masses that look like turmeric, black pepper resin-cells, one 'port wine' pimento cell, and one or two particles of graphite."

"Graphite!" exclaimed Thorndyke. "I have found no graphite, but I have found traces of cocoa – spiral vessels and starch grains – and of hops – one fragment of leaf and several lupulin glands. May I see the graphite?"

I passed him the slide and he examined it with keen interest. "Yes," he said, "this is undoubtedly graphite, and no less than six particles of it. We had better go over the coat systematically. You see the importance of this?"

"I see that this is evidently factory dust and that it may fix a locality, but I don't see that it will carry us any farther."

"Don't forget that we have a touchstone," said he; and, as I raised my eyebrows inquiringly, he added, "the Yale latch-key. If we can narrow the locality down sufficiently, Miller can make a tour of the front doors."

"But can we?" I asked incredulously. "I doubt it."

"We can try," answered Thorndyke. "Evidently some of these substances are distributed over the entire coat, inside and out, while others, such as the graphite, are present only on certain parts. We must locate those parts exactly and then consider what this special distribution means." He rapidly sketched out on a sheet of paper a rough diagram of the coat, marking each part with a distinctive letter, and then, taking a number of labelled slides, he wrote a single letter on each. The samples of dust taken on the slides could thus be easily referred to the exact spots whence they had been obtained.

Once more we set to work with the microscope, making now and again an addition to our lists of discoveries, and, at the end of nearly an hour's strenuous search, every slide had been examined and the lists compared.

"The net result of the examination," said Thorndyke, "is this. The entire coat, inside and out, is evenly powdered with the following substances: Rice-starch in abundance, wheat-starch in less abundance, and smaller quantities of the starches of ginger, pimento and cinnamon; bast fibre of cinnamon, various seed cortices, stone-cells of pimento, cinnamon, cassia and black pepper, with other fragments of similar origin, such as resin-cells and ginger pigment – not turmeric. In addition there are, on the right shoulder and sleeve, traces of cocoa and hops, and on the back below the shoulders a few fragments of graphite. Those are the data; and now, what are the inferences? Remember this is not mere surface dust, but the accumulation of months, beaten into the cloth by repeated brushing – dust that nothing but a vacuum apparatus could extract."

"Evidently," I said, "the particles that are all over the coat represent dust that is floating in the air of the place where the coat habitually hangs. The graphite has obviously been picked up from a seat, and the cocoa and hops from some factories that the man passes frequently, though I don't see why they are on the right side only."

"That is a question of time," said Thorndyke, "and incidentally throws some light on our friend's habits. Going from home, he passes the factories on his right; returning home, he passes them on his left, but they have then stopped work. However, the first group of substances is the more important as they indicate the locality of his dwelling – for he is clearly not a workman or factory employee. Now rice-starch, wheat-starch and a group of substances collectively designated 'spices' suggest a rice-mill, a flour-mill and a spice factory. Polton, may I trouble you for the Post Office Directory?"

He turned over the leaves of the "Trades" section and resumed: "I see there are four rice-mills in London, of which the largest is Carbutt's at Dockhead. Let us look at the spice-factors." He again turned over the leaves and read down the list of names. "There are six spice-grinders in London," said he. "One of them, Thomas Williams & Co., is at Dockhead. None of the others is near any rice-mill. The next question is as to the flour-mill. Let us see. Here are the names of several flour millers, but none of them is near either a rice-mill or a spice-grinder, with one exception: Seth Taylor's, St Saviour's Flour Mills, Dockhead."

"This is really becoming interesting," said I.

"It has become interesting," Thorndyke retorted. "You observe that at Dockhead we find the peculiar combination of factories necessary to produce the composite dust in which this coat has hung; and the directory shows us that this particular combination exists nowhere else in London. Then the graphite, the cocoa and the hops tend to confirm the other suggestions. They all appertain to industries of the locality. The trams which pass Dockhead, also, to my knowledge, pass at no great distance from the black-lead works of Pearce Duff & Co. in Rouel Road, and will probably collect a few particles of black-lead on the seats in certain states of the wind. I see, too, that there is a cocoa factory – Payne's – in Goat Street, Horsleydown, which lies to the right of the tram line going west, and I have noticed several hop warehouses on the right side of Southwark Street, going west. But these are mere suggestions; the really important data are the rice and flour mills and the spice-grinders, which seem to point unmistakably to Dockhead."

"Are there any private houses at Dockhead?" I asked.

"We must look up the 'Street' list," he replied. "The Yale latch-key rather suggests a flat, and a flat with a single occupant, and the probable habits of our absent friend offer a similar suggestion." He ran his eye down the list and presently turned to me with his finger on the page.

"If the facts that we have elicited – the singular series of agreements with the required conditions – are only a string of coincidences, here is another. On the south side of Dockhead, actually next door to the spice-grinders and opposite to Carbutt's rice-mills, is a block of workmen's flats, Hanover Buildings. They fulfil the conditions exactly. A coat hung in a room in those flats, with the windows open (as they would probably be at this time of year), would be exposed to air containing a composite dust of precisely the character of that which we have found. Of course, the same conditions obtain in other dwellings in this part of Dockhead, but the probability is in favour of the buildings. And that is all that we can say. It is no certainty. There may be some radical fallacy in our reasoning. But, on the face of it, the chances are a thousand to one that the door that that key will open is in some part of Dockhead, and most probably in Hanover Buildings. We must leave the verification to Miller."

"Wouldn't it be as well to look at the tram-ticket?" I asked.

"Dear me!" he exclaimed. "I had forgotten the ticket. Yes, by all means." He opened the envelope and, turning its contents out on the bench, picked up the dingy slip of paper. After a glance at it he handed it to me. It was punched for the journey from Tooley Street to Dockhead.

"Another coincidence," he remarked; "and, by yet another, I think I hear Miller knocking at our door."

It was the superintendent, and, as we let him into the room, the hum of a motor-car entering from Tudor Street announced the arrival of Mrs Chater. We waited for her at the open door, and, as she entered, she held out her hands impulsively.

"Say, now, Dr Thorndyke," she exclaimed, "have you got something to tell us?"

"I have a suggestion to make," replied Thorndyke. "I think that if the superintendent will take this key to Hanover Buildings, Dockhead, Bermondsey, he may possibly find a door that it will fit."

"The deuce!" exclaimed Miller. "I beg your pardon, madam; but I thought I had gone through that coat pretty completely. What was it that I had overlooked, sir? Was there a letter hidden in it, after all?"

"You overlooked the dust on it, Miller; that is all," said Thorndyke.

"Dust!" exclaimed the detective, staring round-eyed at my colleague. Then he chuckled softly. "Well," said he, "as I said before, I'm not a sorcerer; I'm only a policeman." He picked up the key and asked: "Are you coming to see the end of it, sir?"

"Of course he is coming," said Mrs Chater, "and Dr Jervis too, to identify the man. Now that we have got the villain we must leave him no loophole for escape."

Thorndyke smiled dryly. "We will come if you wish it, Mrs Chater," he said, "but you mustn't look upon our quest as a certainty. We may have made an entire miscalculation, and I am, in fact, rather curious to see if the result works out correctly. But even if we run the man to earth, I don't see that you have much evidence against him. The most that you can prove is that he was at the house and that he left hurriedly."

Mrs Chater regarded my colleague for a moment in scornful silence, and then, gathering up her skirts, stalked out of the room. If there is one thing that the average woman detests more than another, it is an entirely reasonable man.

The big car whirled us rapidly over Blackfriars Bridge into the region of the Borough, whence we presently turned down Tooley Street towards Bermondsey.

As soon as Dockhead came into view, the detective, Thorndyke and I alighted and proceeded on foot, leaving our client, who was now closely veiled, to follow at a little distance in the car. Opposite the head of St Saviour's Dock, Thorndyke halted and, looking over the wall, drew my attention to the snowy powder that had lodged on every projection on the backs of the tall buildings and on the decks of the barges that were loading with the flour and ground rice. Then, crossing the road, he pointed to the wooden lantern above the roof of the spice works, the louvres of which were covered with greyish-buff dust.

"Thus," he moralized, "does commerce subserve the ends of justice – at least, we hope it does," he added quickly, as Miller disappeared into the semi-basement of the buildings.

We met the detective returning from his quest as we entered the building.

"No go there," was his report. "We'll try the next floor."

This was the ground-floor or it might be considered the first floor. At any rate, it yielded nothing of interest, and, after a glance at the doors that opened on the landing, he strode briskly up the stone stairs. The next floor was equally unrewarding, for our eager inspection disclosed nothing but the gaping keyholes associated with the common type of night-latch.

"What name was you wanting?" inquired a dusty knight of industry who emerged from one of the flats.

"Muggs," replied Miller, with admirable promptness.

"Don't know 'im," said the workman. "I expect it's farther up."

Farther up we accordingly went, but still from each door the artless grin of the invariable keyhole saluted us with depressing monotony. I began to grow uneasy, and when the fourth floor had been explored with no better result, my anxiety became acute. A mare's nest may be an interesting curiosity, but it brings no kudos to its discoverer.

"I suppose you haven't made any mistake, sir?" said Miller, stopping to wipe his brow.

"It's quite likely that I have," replied Thorndyke, with unmoved composure. "I only proposed this search as a tentative proceeding, you know."

The superintendent grunted. He was accustomed – as was I too, for that matter – to regard Thorndyke's "tentative suggestions" as equal to another man's certainties.

"It will be an awful suck-in for Mrs Chater if we don't find him after all," he growled as we climbed up the last flight. "She's counted her chickens to a feather." He paused at the head of the stairs and stood for a few moments looking round the landing. Suddenly he turned eagerly, and, laying his hand on Thorndyke's arm, pointed to a door in the farthest corner.

"Yale lock!" he whispered impressively.

We followed him silently as he stole on tip-toe across the landing, and watched him as he stood for an instant with the key in his hand looking gloatingly at the brass disc. We saw him softly apply the nose of the fluted key-blade to the crooked slit in the cylinder, and, as we watched, it slid in noiselessly up to the shoulder. The detective looked round with a grin of triumph, and, silently withdrawing the key, stepped back to us.

"You've run him to earth, sir," he whispered, "but I don't think Mr Fox is at home. He can't have got back yet."

"Why not?" asked Thorndyke.

Miller waved his hand towards the door. "Nothing has been disturbed," he replied. "There's not a mark on the paint. Now he hadn't got the key, and you can't pick a Yale lock. He'd have had to break in, and he hasn't broken in."

Thorndyke stepped up to the door and softly pushed in the flap of the letter-slit, through which he looked into the flat.

"There's no letter-box," said he. "My dear Miller, I would undertake to open that door in five minutes with a foot of wire and a bit of resined string."

Miller shook his head and grinned once more. "I am glad you're not on the lay, sir; you'd be one too many for us. Shall we signal to the lady?"

I went out on to the gallery and looked down at the waiting car. Mrs Chater was staring intently up at the building, and the little crowd that the car had collected stared alternately at the lady and at the object of her regard. I wiped my face with my handkerchief – the signal agreed upon – and she instantly sprang out of the car, and in an incredibly short time she appeared on the landing, purple and gasping, but with the fire of battle flashing from her eyes.

"We've found his flat, madam," said Miller, "and we're going to enter. You're not intending to offer any violence, I hope," he added, noting with some uneasiness the lady's ferocious expression.

"Of course I'm not," replied Mrs Chater. "In the States ladies don't have to avenge insults themselves. If you were American men you'd hang the ruffian from his own bedpost."

"We're not American men, madam," said the superintendent stiffly. "We are law-abiding Englishmen, and, moreover, we are all officers of the law. These gentlemen are barristers and I am a police officer."

With this preliminary caution, he once more inserted the key, and as he turned it and pushed the door open, we all followed him into the sitting-room.

"I told you so, sir," said Miller, softly shutting the door; "he hasn't come back yet."

Apparently he was right. At any rate, there was no one in the flat, and we proceeded unopposed on our tour of inspection. It was a miserable spectacle, and, as we wandered from one squalid room to another, a feeling of pity for the starving wretch into whose lair we were intruding stole over me and began almost to mitigate the hideousness of his crime. On all sides poverty – utter, grinding poverty – stared us in the face. It looked at us hollow-eyed in the wretched sitting-room, with its bare floor, its solitary chair and tiny deal table; its unfurnished walls and windows destitute of blind or curtain. A piece of Dutch cheese-rind on the table, scraped to the thinness of paper, whispered of starvation; and famine lurked in the gaping cupboard, in the empty bread-tin, in the tea-caddy with its pinch of dust at the bottom, in the jam-jar, wiped clean, as a few crumbs testified, with a crust of bread. There was not enough food in the place to furnish a meal for a healthy mouse.

The bedroom told the same tale, but with a curious variation. A miserable truckle-bed with a straw mattress and a cheap jute rug for bed-clothes, an orange-case, stood on end, for a dressing-table, and another, bearing a tin washing-bowl, formed the wretched furniture. But the suit that hung from a couple of nails was well-cut and even fashionable, though shabby; and another suit lay on the floor, neatly folded and covered with a newspaper; and, most incongruous of all, a silver cigarette-case reposed on the dressing-table.

"Why on earth does this fellow starve," I exclaimed, "when he has a silver case to pawn?"

"Wouldn't do," said Miller. "A man doesn't pawn the implements of his trade."

Mrs Chater, who had been staring about her with the mute amazement of a wealthy woman confronted, for the first time, with abject poverty, turned suddenly to the superintendent. "This can't be the man!" she exclaimed. "You have made some mistake. This poor creature could never have made his way into a house like Willowdale."

Thorndyke lifted the newspaper. Beneath it was a dress suit with the shirt, collar and tie all carefully smoothed out and folded.

Thorndyke unfolded the shirt and pointed to the curiously crumpled front. Suddenly he brought it close to his eye and then, from the sham diamond stud, he drew a single hair – a woman's hair.

"That is rather significant," said he, holding it up between his finger and thumb; and Mrs Chater evidently thought so too, for the pity and compunction suddenly faded from her face, and once more her eyes flashed with vindictive fire.

"I wish he would come," she exclaimed viciously. "Prison won't be much hardship to him after this, but I want to see him in the dock all the same."

"No," the detective agreed, "it won't hurt him much to swap this for Portland. Listen!"

A key was being inserted into the outer door, and as we all stood like statues, a man entered and closed the door after him. He passed the door of the bedroom without seeing us, and with the dragging steps of a weary, dispirited man. Almost immediately we heard him go to the kitchen and draw water into some vessel. Then he went back to the sitting-room.

"Come along," said Miller, stepping silently towards the door. We followed closely, and as he threw the door open, we looked in over his shoulder.

The man had seated himself at the table, on which now lay a hunk of household bread resting on the paper in which he had brought it, and a tumbler of water. He half rose as the door opened, and as if petrified remained staring at Miller with a dreadful expression of terror upon his livid face.

At this moment I felt a hand on my arm, and Mrs Chater brusquely pushed past me into the room. But at the threshold she stopped short; and a singular change crept over the man's ghastly face, a change so remarkable that I looked involuntarily from him to our client. She had turned, in a moment, deadly pale, and her face had frozen into an expression of incredulous horror.

The dramatic silence was broken by the matter-of-fact voice of the detective.

"I am a police officer," said he, "and I arrest you for – "

A peal of hysterical laughter from Mrs Chater interrupted him, and he looked at her in astonishment. "Stop, stop!" she cried in a shaky voice. "I guess we've made a ridiculous mistake. This isn't the man. This gentleman is Captain Rowland, an old friend of mine."

"I'm sorry he's a friend of yours," said Miller, "because I shall have to ask you to appear against him."

"You can ask what you please," replied Mrs Chater. "I tell you he's not the man."

The superintendent rubbed his nose and looked hungrily at his quarry. "Do I understand, madam," he asked stiffly, "that you refuse to prosecute?"

"Prosecute!" she exclaimed. "Prosecute my friends for offences that I know they have not committed? Certainly I refuse."

The superintendent looked at Thorndyke, but my colleague's countenance had congealed into a state of absolute immobility and was as devoid of expression as the face of a Dutch clock.

"Very well," said Miller, looking sourly at his watch. "Then we have had our trouble for nothing. I wish you good afternoon, madam."

"I am sorry I troubled you, now," said Mrs Chater.

"I am sorry you did," was the curt reply; and the superintendent, flinging the key on the table, stalked out of the room.

As the outer door slammed the man sat down with an air of bewilderment; and then, suddenly flinging his arms on the table, he dropped his head on them and burst into a passion of sobbing.

It was very embarrassing. With one accord Thorndyke and I turned to go, but Mrs Chater motioned us to stay. Stepping over to the man, she touched him lightly on the arm.

"Why did you do it?" she asked in a tone of gentle reproach.

The man sat up and flung out one arm in an eloquent gesture that comprehended the miserable room and the yawning cupboard.

"It was the temptation of a moment," he said. "I was penniless, and those accursed diamonds were thrust in my face; they were mine for the taking. I was mad, I suppose."

"But why didn't you take them?" she said. "Why didn't you?"

"I don't know. The madness passed; and then – when I saw you lying there – Oh, God! Why don't you give me up to the police?" He laid his head down and sobbed afresh.

Mrs Chater bent over him with tears standing in her pretty grey eyes. "But tell me," she said, "why didn't you take the diamonds? You could if you'd liked, I suppose?"

"What good were they to me?" he demanded passionately. "What did anything matter to me? I thought you were dead."

"Well, I'm not, you see," she said, with a rather tearful smile; "I'm just as well as an old woman like me can expect to be. And I want your address, so that I can write and give you some good advice."

The man sat up and produced a shabby card-case from his pocket, and, as he took out a number of cards and spread them out like the "hand" of a whist player, I caught a twinkle in Thorndyke's eye.

"My name is Augustus Bailey," said the man. He selected the appropriate card, and, having scribbled his address on it with a stump of lead pencil, relapsed into his former position.

"Thank you," said Mrs Chater, lingering for a moment by the table. "Now we'll go. Good-bye, Mr Bailey. I shall write to-morrow, and you must attend seriously to the advice of an old friend."

I held open the door for her to pass out and looked back before I turned to follow. Bailey still sat sobbing quietly, with his head resting on his arms; and a little pile of gold stood on the corner of the table.

"I expect, doctor," said Mrs Chater, as Thorndyke handed her into the car, "you've written me down a sentimental fool."

Thorndyke looked at her with an unwonted softening of his rather severe face and answered quietly, "It is written: Blessed are the Merciful."

G. K. Chesterton

The Honour of Israel Gow

I once planned a collection of detective stories which were to be models of "fair play": where each story was interrupted at a certain point with a note saying, as it were: now you have all the clues that the detective has. Can you solve it? Ellery Queen used to do something of the sort with his "Challenge to the Reader", and the early Queen stories were indeed as fair as could be. The project foundered, alas, because I could not find enough other stories that could be split in this way. Most of them, when I came to analyse them, were very far from being models of fair play.

One of the handful of stories that would have made the grade is "The Honour of Israel Gow", one of the finest of the early Father Brown stories, though by no means the best-known. I have written elsewhere of Father Brown's creator, G. K. Chesterton (1874–1936), and here would only wish to emphasize one often overlooked point: that the first and best of the Father Brown stories were written long before Chesterton himself became a Catholic.

A STORMY EVENING of olive and silver was closing in, as Father Brown, wrapped in a grey Scotch plaid, came to the end of a grey Scotch valley and beheld the strange castle of Glengyle. It stopped one end of the glen or hollow like a blind alley; and it looked like the end of the world. Rising in steep roofs and spires of seagreen slate in the manner of the old French-Scottish châteaux, it reminded an Englishman of the sinister steeple-hats of witches in fairy tales; and the pine woods that rocked round the green turrets looked, by comparison, as black as numberless flocks of ravens. This note of a dreamy, almost a sleepy devilry, was no mere fancy from the landscape. For there did rest on the place one of those clouds of pride and madness and mysterious sorrow which lie more heavily on the noble houses of Scotland than on any other of the children of men. For Scotland has a double dose of the poison called heredity; the sense of blood in the aristocrat, and the sense of doom in the Calvinist.

The priest had snatched a day from his business at Glasgow to meet his friend Flambeau, the amateur detective, who was at Glengyle Castle with another more formal officer investigating the life and death of the late Earl of Glengyle. That mysterious person was the last representative of a race whose valour, insanity, and violent cunning had made them terrible even among the sinister nobility of their nation in the sixteenth century. None were deeper in that labyrinthine ambition, in chamber within chamber of that palace of lies that was built up around Mary Queen of Scots.

The rhyme in the country-side attested the motive and the result of their machinations candidly:

> As green sap to the simmer trees
> Is red gold to the Ogilvies.

For many centuries there had never been a decent lord in Glengyle Castle; and with the Victorian era one would have thought that all eccentricities were exhausted. The last Glengyle, however, satisfied his tribal tradition by doing the only thing that was left for him to do; he disappeared. I do not mean that he went abroad; by all accounts he was still in the castle, if he was anywhere. But though his name was in the church register and the big red Peerage, nobody ever saw him under the sun.

If anyone saw him it was a solitary man-servant, something between a groom and a gardener. He was so deaf that the more business-like assumed him to be dumb; while the more penetrating declared him to be half-witted. A gaunt, red-haired labourer, with a dogged jaw and chin, but quite blank blue eyes, he went by the name of Israel Gow, and was the one silent servant on that deserted estate. But the energy with which he dug potatoes, and the regularity with which he disappeared into the kitchen gave people an impression that he was providing for the meals of a superior, and that the strange earl was still concealed in the castle. If society needed any further proof that he was there, the servant persistently asserted that he was not at home. One morning the provost and the minister (for the Glengyles were Presbyterian) were summoned to the castle. There they found that the gardener, groom and cook had added to his many professions that of an undertaker, and had nailed up his noble master in a coffin. With how much or how little further inquiry this odd fact was passed, did not as yet very plainly appear; for the thing had never been legally investigated till Flambeau had gone north two or three days before. By then the body of Lord Glengyle (if it was the body) had lain for some time in the little churchyard on the hill.

As Father Brown passed through the dim garden and came under the shadow of the château, the clouds were thick and the whole air damp and thundery. Against the last stripe of the green-gold sunset he saw a black human silhouette; a man in a chimney-pot hat, with a big spade over his shoulder. The combination was queerly suggestive of a sexton; but when Brown remembered the deaf servant who dug potatoes, he thought it natural enough. He knew something of the Scotch peasant; he knew the respectability which might well feel it necessary to wear "blacks" for an official inquiry; he knew also the economy that would not lose an hour's digging for that. Even the man's start and suspicious stare as the priest went by were consonant enough with the vigilance and jealousy of such a type.

The great door was opened by Flambeau himself, who had with him a lean man with iron-grey hair and papers in his hand: Inspector Craven from Scotland Yard. The entrance hall was mostly stripped and empty; but the pale, sneering faces of one or two of the wicked Ogilvies looked down out of black periwigs and blackening canvas.

Following them into an inner room, Father Brown found that the allies had been seated at a long oak table, of which their end was covered with scribbled papers, flanked with whisky and cigars. Through the whole of its remaining length it was occupied by detached objects arranged at intervals; objects about as inexplicable as any objects could be. One looked like a small heap of glittering broken glass. Another looked like a high heap of brown dust. A third appeared to be a plain stick of wood.

"You seem to have a sort of geological museum here," he said, as he sat down, jerking his head briefly in the direction of the brown dust and the crystalline fragments.

"Not a geological museum," replied Flambeau; "say a psychological museum."

"Oh, for the Lord's sake," cried the police detective laughing, "don't let's begin with such long words."

"Don't you know what psychology means?" asked Flambeau with friendly surprise. "Psychology means being off your chump."

"Still I hardly follow," replied the official.

"Well," said Flambeau, with decision, "I mean that we've only found out one thing about Lord Glengyle. He was a maniac."

The black silhouette of Gow with his top hat and spade passed the window, dimly outlined against the darkening sky. Father Brown stared passively at it and answered:

"I can understand there must have been something odd about the man, or he wouldn't have buried himself alive – nor been in such a hurry to bury himself dead. But what makes you think it was lunacy?"

"Well," said Flambeau, "you just listen to the list of things Mr Craven has found in the house."

"We must get a candle," said Craven, suddenly, "A storm is getting up, and it's too dark to read."

"Have you found any candles," asked Brown smiling, "among your oddities?"

Flambeau raised a grave face, and fixed his dark eyes on his friend.

"That is curious, too," he said. "Twenty-five candles, and not a trace of a candlestick."

In the rapidly darkening room and rapidly rising wind, Brown went along the table to where a bundle of wax candles lay among the other scrappy exhibits. As he did so he bent accidentally over the heap of red-brown dust; and a sharp sneeze cracked the silence.

"Hullo!" he said, "snuff !"

He took one of the candles, lit it carefully, came back and stuck it in the neck of the whisky bottle. The unrestful night air, blowing through the crazy window, waved the long flame like a banner. And on every side of the castle they could hear the miles and miles of black pine wood seething like a black sea around a rock.

"I will read the inventory," began Craven gravely, picking up one of the papers, "the inventory of what we found loose and unexplained in the castle. You are to understand that the place generally was dismantled and neglected; but one or two rooms had plainly been inhabited in a simple but not squalid style by somebody; somebody who was not the servant Gow. The list is as follows:

"First item. A very considerable hoard of precious stones, nearly all diamonds, and all of them loose, without any setting whatever. Of course, it is natural that the Ogilvies should have family jewels; but those are exactly the jewels that are almost always set in particular articles of ornament. The Ogilvies would seem to have kept theirs loose in their pockets, like coppers.

"Second item. Heaps and heaps of loose snuff, not kept in a horn, or even a pouch, but lying in heaps on the mantelpieces, on the sideboard, on the piano, anywhere. It looks as if the old gentleman would not take the trouble to look in a pocket or lift a lid.

"Third item. Here and there about the house curious little heaps of minute pieces of metal, some like steel springs and some in the form of microscopic wheels. As if they had gutted some mechanical toy.

"Fourth item. The wax candles, which have to be stuck in bottle necks because there is nothing else to stick them in. Now I wish you to note how very much queerer all this is than anything we anticipated. For the central riddle we are prepared; we have all seen at a glance that there was something wrong about the last earl. We have come here to find out whether he really lived here, whether he really died here, whether that red-haired scarecrow who did his burying had anything to do with his dying. But suppose the worst in all this, the most lurid or melodramatic solution you like. Suppose the servant really killed the master, or suppose the master isn't really dead, or suppose the master is dressed up as the servant, or suppose the servant is buried for the master; invent what Wilkie Collins' tragedy you like, and you still have not explained a candle without a candlestick, or why an elderly gentleman of good family should habitually spill snuff on the piano. The core of the tale we could imagine; it is the fringes that are mysterious. By no stretch of fancy can the human mind connect together snuff and diamonds and wax and loose clockwork."

"I think I see the connection," said the priest. "This Glengyle was mad against the French Revolution. He was an enthusiast for the *ancien régime*, and was trying to re-enact literally the family life of the last Bourbons. He had snuff because it was the eighteenth century luxury; wax candles, because they were the eighteenth century lighting; the mechanical bits of iron represent the locksmith hobby of Louis XVI; the diamonds are for the Diamond Necklace of Marie Antoinette."

Both the other men were staring at him with round eyes. "What a perfectly extraordinary notion!" cried Flambeau. "Do you really think that is the truth?"

"I am perfectly sure it isn't," answered Father Brown, "only you said that nobody could connect snuff and diamonds and clockwork and candles. I give you that connection off-hand. The real truth, I am very sure, lies deeper."

He paused a moment and listened to the wailing of the wind in the turrets. Then he said, "The late Earl of Glengyle was a thief. He lived a second and darker life as a desperate housebreaker. He did not have any candlesticks because he only used these candles cut short in the little lantern he carried. The snuff he employed as the fiercest French criminals have used pepper: to fling it suddenly in dense masses in the face of a captor or pursuer. But the final proof is in the curious coincidence of the diamonds and the small steel wheels. Surely that makes everything plain to you? Diamonds and small steel wheels are the only two instruments with which you can cut out a pane of glass."

The bough of a broken pine tree lashed heavily in the blast against the windowpane behind them, as if in parody of a burglar, but they did not turn round. Their eyes were fastened on Father Brown.

"Diamonds and small wheels," repeated Craven ruminating. "Is that all that makes you think it the true explanation?"

"I don't think it the true explanation," replied the priest placidly; "but you said that nobody could connect the four things. The true tale, of course, is something much more humdrum. Glengyle had found, or thought he had found, precious stones on his estate. Somebody had bamboozled him with those loose brilliants, saying they were found in the castle caverns. The little wheels are some diamond-cutting affair. He had to do the thing very roughly and in a small way, with the help of a few shepherds or rude fellows on these hills. Snuff is the one great luxury of such Scotch shepherds; it's the one thing with which you can bribe them. They didn't have candlesticks because they didn't want them; they held the candles in their hands when they explored the caves."

"Is that all?" asked Flambeau after a long pause. "Have we got to the dull truth at last?"

"Oh, no," said Father Brown.

As the wind died in the most distant pine woods with a long hoot as of mockery Father Brown, with an utterly impassive face, went on:

"I only suggested that because you said one could not plausibly connect snuff with clockwork or candles with bright stones. Ten false philosophies will fit the universe; ten false theories will fit Glengyle Castle. But we want the real explanation of the castle and the universe. But are there no other exhibits?"

Craven laughed, and Flambeau rose smiling to his feet and strolled down the long table.

"Items five, six, seven, etc.," he said, "and certainly more varied than instructive. A curious collection, not of lead pencils, but of the lead out of lead pencils. A senseless stick of bamboo, with the top rather splintered. It might be the instrument of the crime. Only, there isn't any crime. The only other things are a few old missals and little Catholic pictures, which the Ogilvies kept, I suppose, from the Middle Ages – their family pride being stronger than their Puritanism. We only put them in the museum because they seem curiously cut about and defaced."

The heady tempest without drove a dreadful wrack of clouds across Glengyle and threw the long room into darkness as Father Brown picked up the little illuminated pages to examine them. He spoke before the drift of darkness had passed; but it was the voice of an utterly new man.

"Mr Craven," said he, talking like a man ten years younger, "you have got a legal warrant, haven't you, to go up and examine that grave? The sooner we do it the better, and get to the bottom of this horrible affair. If I were you I should start now."

"Now," repeated the astonished detective, "and why now?"

"Because this is serious," answered Brown; "this is not spilt snuff or loose pebbles, that might be there for a hundred reasons. There is only one reason I know of for *this* being done; and the reason goes down to the roots of the world. These religious pictures are not just dirtied or torn or scrawled over, which might be done in idleness or bigotry, by children or by Protestants. These have been treated very carefully – and very queerly. In every place where the great ornamented name of God comes in the old illuminations it has been elaborately taken out. The only other thing that has been removed is the halo round the head of the Child Jesus. Therefore, I say, let us get our warrant and our spade and our hatchet, and go up and break open that coffin."

"What *do* you mean?" demanded the London officer.

"I mean," answered the little priest, and his voice seemed to rise slightly in the roar of the gale. "I mean that the great devil of the universe may be sitting on the top tower of this castle at this moment, as big as a hundred elephants, and roaring like the Apocalypse. There is black magic somewhere at the bottom of this."

"Black magic," repeated Flambeau in a low voice, for he was too enlightened a man not to know of such things; "but what can these other things mean?"

"Oh, something damnable, I suppose," replied Brown impatiently. "How should I know? How can I guess all their mazes down below? Perhaps you can make a torture out of snuff and bamboo. Perhaps lunatics lust after wax and steel filings. Perhaps there is a maddening drug made of lead pencils! Our shortest cut to the mystery is up the hill to the grave."

His comrades hardly knew that they had obeyed and followed him till a blast of the night wind nearly flung them on their faces in the garden. Nevertheless they had obeyed him like automata; for Craven found a hatchet in his hand, and the warrant in his pocket; Flambeau was carrying the heavy spade of the strange gardener; Father Brown was carrying the little gilt book from which had been torn the name of God.

The path up the hill to the churchyard was crooked but short; only under that stress of wind it seemed laborious and long. Far as the eye could see, farther and farther as they mounted the slope, were seas beyond seas of pines, now all aslope one way under the wind. And that universal gesture seemed as vain as it was vast, as vain as if that wind were whistling about some unpeopled and purposeless planet. Through all that infinite growth of grey-blue forests sang, shrill and high, that ancient sorrow that is in the heart of all heathen things. One could fancy that the voices from the under world of unfathomable foliage were cries of the lost and wandering pagan gods: gods who had gone roaming in that irrational forest, and who will never find their way back to heaven.

"You see," said Father Brown in low but easy tone, "Scotch people before Scotland existed were a curious lot. In fact, they're a curious lot still. But in the prehistoric times I fancy they really worshipped demons. That," he added genially, "is why they jumped at the Puritan theology."

"My friend," said Flambeau, turning in a kind of fury, "what does all that snuff mean?"

"My friend," replied Brown, with equal seriousness, "there is one mark of all genuine religions: materialism. Now, devil-worship is a perfectly genuine religion."

They had come up on the grassy scalp of the hill, one of the few bald spots that stood clear of the crashing and roaring pine forest. A mean enclosure, partly timber and partly wire, rattled in the tempest to tell them the border of the graveyard. But by the time Inspector Craven had come to the corner of the grave, and Flambeau had planted his spade point downwards and leaned on it, they were both almost as shaken as the shaky wood and wire. At the foot of the grave grew great tall thistles, grey and silver in their decay. Once or twice, when a ball of thistledown broke under the breeze and flew past him, Craven jumped slightly as if it had been an arrow.

Flambeau drove the blade of his spade through the whistling grass into the wet clay below. Then he seemed to stop and lean on it as on a staff.

"Go on," said the priest very gently. "We are only trying to find the truth. What are you afraid of?"

"I am afraid of finding it," said Flambeau.

The London detective spoke suddenly in a high crowing voice that was meant to be conversational and cheery. "I wonder why he really did hide himself like that. Something nasty, I suppose; was he a leper?"

"Something worse than that," said Flambeau.

"And what do you imagine," asked the other, "would be worse than a leper?"

"I don't imagine it," said Flambeau.

He dug for some dreadful minutes in silence, and then said in a choked voice, "I'm afraid of his not being the right shape."

"Nor was that piece of paper, you know," said Father Brown quietly, "and we survived even that piece of paper."

Flambeau dug on with a blind energy. But the tempest had shouldered away the choking grey clouds that clung to the hills like smoke and revealed grey fields of faint starlight before he cleared the shape of a rude timber coffin, and somehow tipped it up upon the turf. Craven stepped forward with his axe; a thistle-top touched him, and he flinched. Then he took a firmer stride, and hacked and wrenched with an energy like Flambeau's till the lid was torn off, and all that was there lay glimmering in the grey starlight.

"Bones," said Craven; and then he added, "but it is a man," as if that were something unexpected.

"Is he," asked Flambeau in a voice that went oddly up and down, "is he all right?"

"Seems so," said the officer huskily, bending over the obscure and decaying skeleton in the box. "Wait a minute."

A vast heave went over Flambeau's huge figure. "And now I come to think of it," he cried, "why in the name of madness shouldn't he be all right? What is it gets hold of a man on these cursed cold mountains? I think it's the black, brainless repetition; all these forests, and over all an ancient horror of unconsciousness. It's like the dream of an atheist. Pine-trees and more pine-trees and millions more pine-trees – "

"God!" cried the man by the coffin, "but he hasn't got a head."

While the others stood rigid the priest, for the first time, showed a leap of startled concern.

"No head!" he repeated. *"No head?"* as if he had almost expected some other deficiency.

Half-witted visions of a headless baby born to Glengyle, of a headless youth hiding himself in the castle, of a headless man pacing those ancient halls or that gorgeous garden, passed in panorama through their minds. But even in that stiffened instant the tale took no root in them and seemed to have no reason in it. They stood listening to the loud woods and the shrieking sky quite foolishly, like exhausted animals. Thought seemed to be something enormous that had suddenly slipped out of their grasp.

"There are three headless men," said Father Brown, "standing round this open grave."

The pale detective from London opened his mouth to speak, and left it open like a yokel, while a long scream of wind tore the sky; then he looked at the axe in his hands as if it did not belong to him, and dropped it.

"Father," said Flambeau in that infantile and heavy voice he used very seldom, "what are we to do?"

His friend's reply came with the pent promptitude of a gun going off.

"Sleep!" cried Father Brown. "Sleep. We have come to the end of the ways. Do you know what sleep is? Do you know that every man who sleeps believes in God? It is a sacrament; for it is an act of faith and it is a food. And we need a sacrament, if only a natural one. Something has fallen on us that falls very seldom on men; perhaps the worst thing that can fall on them."

Craven's parted lips came together to say, "What do you mean?"

The priest had turned his face to the castle as he answered:

"We have found the truth; and the truth makes no sense."

He went down the path in front of them with a plunging and reckless step very rare with him, and when they reached the castle again he threw himself upon sleep with the simplicity of a dog.

Despite his mystic praise of slumber, Father Brown was up earlier than anyone else except the silent gardener; and was found smoking a big pipe and watching that expert at his speechless labours in the kitchen garden. Towards daybreak the rocking storm had ended in roaring rains, and the day came with a curious freshness. The gardener seemed even to have been conversing, but at sight of the detectives he planted his spade sullenly in a bed and, saying something about his breakfast, shifted along the lines of cabbages and shut himself in the kitchen. "He's a valuable man, that," said Father Brown. "He does the potatoes amazingly. Still," he added, with a dispassionate charity, "he has his faults; which of us hasn't? He doesn't dig this bank quite regularly. There, for instance," and he stamped suddenly on one spot. "I'm really very doubtful about that potato."

"And why?" asked Craven, amused with the little man's new hobby.

"I'm doubtful about it," said the other, "because old Gow was doubtful about it himself. He put his spade in methodically in every place but just this. There must be a mighty fine potato just here."

Flambeau pulled up the spade and impetuously drove it into the place. He turned up, under a load of soil, something that did not look like a potato, but rather like a monstrous, over-domed mushroom. But it struck the spade with a cold click; it rolled over like a ball, and grinned up at them.

"The Earl of Glengyle," said Brown sadly, and looked down heavily at the skull.

Then, after a momentary meditation, he plucked the spade from Flambeau, and, saying "We must hide it again," clamped the skull down in the earth. Then he leaned his little body and huge head on the great handle of the spade, that stood up stiffly in the earth, and his eyes were empty and his forehead full of wrinkles. "If one could only conceive," he muttered, "the meaning of this last monstrosity." And leaning on the large spade handle, he buried his brows in his hands, as men do in church.

All the corners of the sky were brightening into blue and silver; the birds were chattering in the tiny garden trees; so loud it seemed as if the trees themselves were talking. But the three men were silent enough.

"Well, I give it all up," said Flambeau at last boisterously. "My brain and this world don't fit each other; and there's an end of it. Snuff, spoilt Prayer Books, and the insides of musical boxes – what – "

Brown threw up his bothered brow and rapped on the spade handle with an intolerance quite unusual with him. "Oh, tut, tut, tut, tut!" he cried. "All that is as plain as a pikestaff. I understood the snuff and clockwork, and so on, when I first opened my eyes this morning. And since then I've had it out with old Gow, the gardener, who is neither so deaf nor so stupid as he pretends. There's nothing amiss about the loose items. I was wrong about the torn mass-book, too; there's no harm in that. But it's this last business. Desecrating graves and stealing dead men's heads – surely there's harm in that? Surely there's black magic still in that? That doesn't fit in to the quite simple story of the snuff and the candles." And, striding about again, he smoked moodily.

"My friend," said Flambeau, with a grim humour, "you must be careful with me and remember I was once a criminal. The great advantage of that estate was that I always made up the story myself, and acted it as quick as I chose. This detective business of waiting about is too much for my French impatience. All my life, for good or evil, I have done things at the instant; I always fought duels the next morning; I always paid bills on the nail; I never even put off a visit to the dentist – "

Father Brown's pipe fell out of his mouth and broke into three pieces on the gravel path. He stood rolling his eyes, the exact picture of an idiot. "Lord, what a turnip I am!" he kept saying. "Lord, what a turnip!" Then, in a somewhat groggy kind of way, he began to laugh.

"The dentist!" he repeated. "Six hours in the spiritual abyss, and all because I never thought of the dentist! Such a simple, such a beautiful and peaceful thought! Friends, we have passed a night in hell; but now the sun is risen, the birds are singing, and the radiant form of the dentist consoles the world."

"I will get some sense out of this," cried Flambeau, striding forward, "if I use the tortures of the Inquisition."

Father Brown repressed what appeared to be a momentary disposition to dance on the now sunlit lawn and cried quite piteously, like a child, "Oh, let me be silly a little. You don't know how unhappy I have been. And now I know that there has been no deep sin in this business at all. Only a little lunacy, perhaps – and who minds that?"

He spun round once, then faced them with gravity.

"This is not a story of crime," he said; "rather it is the story of a strange and crooked honesty. We are dealing with the one man on earth, perhaps, who has taken no more than his due. It is a study in the savage living logic that has been the religion of this race.

"That old local rhyme about the house of Glengyle – 'As green sap to the simmer trees Is red gold to the Ogilvies' – was literal as well as metaphorical. It did not merely mean that the Glengyles sought for wealth; it was also true that they literally gathered gold; they had a huge collection of ornaments and utensils in that metal. They were, in fact, misers whose mania took that turn. In the light of that fact, run through all the things we found in the castle. Diamonds without their gold rings; candles without their gold candlesticks; snuff without the gold snuff-boxes; pencil-leads without the gold pencil-cases; a walking stick without its gold top; clockwork without the gold clocks – or rather watches. And, mad as it sounds, because the halos and the name of God in the old missals were of real gold; these also were taken away."

The garden seemed to brighten, the grass to grow gayer in the strengthening sun, as the crazy truth was told. Flambeau lit a cigarette as his friend went on.

"Were taken away," continued Father Brown; "were taken away – but not stolen. Thieves would never have left this mystery. Thieves would have taken the gold snuff-boxes, snuff and all; the gold pencil-cases, lead and all. We have to deal with a man with a peculiar conscience, but certainly a conscience. I found that mad moralist this morning in the kitchen garden yonder, and I heard the whole story.

"The late Archibald Ogilvie was the nearest approach to a good man ever born at Glengyle. But his bitter virtue took the turn of the misanthrope; he moped over the dishonesty of his ancestors, from which, somehow, he generalized a dishonesty of all men. More especially he distrusted philanthropy or free-giving; and he swore if he could find one man who took his exact rights he should have all the gold of Glengyle. Having delivered this defiance to humanity he shut himself up, without the smallest expectation of its being answered. One day, however, a deaf and seemingly senseless lad from a distant village brought him a belated telegram; and Glengyle, in his acrid pleasantry, gave him a new farthing. At least he thought he had done so, but when he turned over his change he found the new farthing still there and a sovereign gone. The accident offered him vistas of sneering speculation. Either way, the boy would show the greasy greed of the species. Either he would vanish, a thief stealing a coin; or he would sneak back with it virtuously, a snob seeking a reward. In the middle of that night Lord Glengyle was knocked up out of his bed – for he lived alone – and forced to open the door to the deaf idiot. The idiot brought with him, not the sovereign, but exactly nineteen shillings and eleven-pence three-farthings in change.

"Then the wild exactitude of this action took hold on the mad lord's brain like fire. He swore he was Diogenes, that had long sought an honest man, and at last had found one. He made a new will, which I have seen. He took the literal youth into his huge, neglected house, and trained him up as his solitary servant and – after an odd manner – his heir. And whatever that queer creature understands, he understood absolutely his lord's two fixed ideas: first, that the letter of right is everything; and second, that he himself was to have the gold of Glengyle. So far, that is all; and that is simple. He has stripped the house of gold, and taken not a grain that was not gold; not so much as a grain of snuff. He lifted the gold leaf off an old illumination, fully satisfied that he left the rest unspoilt. All that I understood; but I could not understand this skull business. I was really uneasy about that human head buried among the potatoes. It distressed me – till Flambeau said the word.

"It will be all right. He will put the skull back in the grave, when he has taken the gold out of the tooth."

And, indeed, when Flambeau crossed the hill that morning, he saw that strange being, the just miser, digging at the desecrated grave, the plaid round his throat thrashing out in the mountain wind; the sober top hat on his head.

Ernest Bramah

Smothered in Corpses

Ernest Bramah (the pen-name of Ernest Bramah Smith, 1868–1942) first attracted notice with his delightful Kai-Lung stories, mock-Chinese tales of the shaggy dog variety which have had their admirers ever since. His detective was Max Carrados, a wealthy bachelor whose blindness did not prevent him from solving baffling crimes: an interesting variant on the "different-from-Sherlock" theme with some interesting insights resulting from Bramah's own temporary blindness, though I personally find these stories unsatisfying as mysteries. In place of a Carrados story I have chosen a tale which hilariously spoofs all those frantic adventure yarns of the early years of the century – notably those of Sax Rohmer and the evil Fu Manchu. Bramah's own introduction to the story follows.

The author of the following story deems it permissible to himself to explain that the work was projected, and, indeed, almost completed, as a 120,000 word serial of feuilleton scope, when a much-advertised competition for stories of not more than 4000 words in length came under his notice. Not to be deterred by the conditions, he at once set himself to the formidable task of reducing his manuscript to one-thirtieth of its original length. The result must, of course, be regarded purely on its merits, but in the writer's own opinion the process of compression has, if anything, keyed up the action to an even tenser pitch, without in any way detracting from the interest of the plot or circumscribing the wealth of incident.

I THE END OF THE BEGINNING

WHERE HAD IT come from?

I, John Beveledge Humdrum, general practitioner, of 305A, Hammersmith Road, Kensington, had come down to breakfast on that eventful July morning expecting nothing more exciting than the eggs and bacon with which my excellent man Perkins had regularly provided me on similar occasions for the past eleven years.

Imagine my surprise, therefore, on throwing open the door of the book-case that contained my sparse collection of medical works, in order to consult *Abernethy on Biscuits*, to be confronted by the doubled-up corpse of a young man of distinguished appearance, wearing a suit of evening clothes of the most expensive cut.

My thoughts flew back to the events of the previous evening in an attempt to unravel the mystery. Had anything remarkable happened? And then I remembered an incident, trivial enough in itself, which might supply a clue. At about eight o'clock I had received a professional summons, notable as being the first in my career. A heavily-veiled woman wearing a complete set of massive ermines had descended from a magnificently-appointed motor-car before my door. In response to her impassioned appeal, delivered with a marked Castilian accent, I had accompanied her to a miserable tenement dwelling in a sordid Limehouse slum. Here, after I had reluctantly given a pledge of secrecy and permitted myself to be blindfolded (even to this day the mingled aroma of Enigma Vanishing Cream and frying spaghetti vividly recalls the scene), I was taken to the bedside of my patient, a fair-haired boy of three or four. A villainous-looking Chinaman who was in attendance gave me to understand, partly by signs and partly in pidgin English, that the child had swallowed a bone button. Being unacquainted with the exact treatment of such a case I recommended his removal to the nearest hospital. As there was nothing more to detain me I left at once, overwhelmed by the passionate gratitude of my mysterious caller; but as I glanced back at the corner of the disreputable street, I saw a face charged with diabolical hatred watching me from the grimy window of the room I had just quitted. It was the visage of the aged Chinaman, who, but a moment before, had been bowing to me with true Oriental deference. As I looked, rather puzzled to account for his strange behaviour, a terrible explosion shook the ground, the front of the house disappeared, and a singed pigtail fell at my feet.

Recalling all this I was on the point of ringing for Perkins in order to question him, when something caused me to hesitate.

It was well that I did so. The next moment the double doors of the French window that overlooked the bustling turmoil of Kensington's busiest thoroughfare were flung frantically open and there sprang into the room a young girl whose dazzling beauty was, if possible, heightened by the breathless excitement under which she was labouring.

"Dr Humdrum," she exclaimed, throwing aside the luxuriant crimson opera cloak that had hitherto concealed the supple perfection of her lithe form, "save me! Help me!" and a look of baffling terror swept across her mobile features.

"Certainly," I stammered, bewildered for the moment by this strange intrusion into the dull routine of my commonplace existence, "but first let me have your name and address for entering into my caller's book."

For reply she dragged from her finger a ring set with a cluster of diamonds that had once, as I was afterwards to learn, graced the crown of an Eastern potentate, and with impulsive generosity flung it into the coal-scuttle.

"Call me Erratica," she murmured, with a slightly different look of terror contorting her lovely features. (And here, for the sake of brevity, I would remark that during the first seven weeks of our strange friendship she either shook with terror or shivered with apprehension whenever she spoke to me or I to her.) "Seek to know no more. Only save me!"

I was at my wits' end. She had already, with a gesture of loathing, hurled out of the window the glass of sal volatile which I had poured out for her, and that exhausted the first-aid remedies with which I was familiar.

"Save you from what?"

"From my enemies. I saw them knocking at your door. That is why I came in by the window."

"Would it not have been more prudent – " I began.

"Hush!" she whispered, tapping her exquisitely-modelled musical comedy teeth with her shapely Italian forefinger. "They are at hand. Play your part well." Then, with unsuspected strength and a knowledge of the arrangements of my modest apartment that staggered me, she tore open the door of the book-case, flung the corpse that it contained on to my dissecting table, and without a moment's hesitation took its place and pulled the door to after her.

"Open in the name of the law!"

Rather perturbed as to what the fair creature required me to do, I obeyed the summons and was relieved to see before me the burly form of Inspector Badger of the Detective Service, an officer with whom I was well acquainted.

"Rum case, that of the murdered prima-donna, Dr Humdrum," he remarked affably. As he spoke he took a seat on the corner of the dissecting table and thus, luckily enough, overlooked its grim burden in the glance of keen professional scrutiny that he cast round the room. "I thought that I'd just look you up and see if you knew anything about it before I ordered any arrests."

"Murdered prima-donna!" I stammered. "I haven't even heard of it. Surely you don't suspect – ?"

"Suspect you?" said the Inspector with a hearty laugh. "Why, no, sir; but as it happens a bone button, wrapped in a sheet of paper bearing one of your prescriptions, had been used to gag the poor creature with. That and the yard of pigtail tied round her neck are our only clues as yet."

At the mention of these details I could not repress a start, which would scarcely have escaped Badger's notice had he not been engaged at the moment in taking a wax impression of my boots.

"Tell me all about it," I remarked, with all the nonchalance I could muster. "I have heard nothing. Who is she?"

"Señora Rosamunda de Barcelona, the celebrated Spanish singer," replied the Inspector. "She left Covent Garden at half-past eleven last night, alone and wearing a crimson opera cloak."

"Surely that was rather late to be shopping," I interposed, with the happy inspiration of diverting his attention. "Would not the market then be closed?"

"I understand that there is a sort of play-house there, where a lot of these foreigners appear," he replied guardedly. "By the way now – "

Possibly the compromising garment lying on the floor between us would not have caught Badger's eye had I not endeavoured to kick it beneath the table. However, the thing was done.

"Ah, my old M.D. gown of the University of Ploughhandle, Ga., USA," I explained, with a readiness that astonishes me to this day, as I followed the direction of his glance. "I use it as a dressing-gown."

"Very natty too," he remarked. "Well, at seven this morning the Señora was discovered propped up in the vestibule of the Hotel Majestic, stabbed in eleven places."

"And the opera cloak?" I felt impelled to ask.

"The opera cloak had disappeared."

I rose to indicate that the instalment was almost complete. The Inspector took the hint.

"I'll look you up later in the day if anything really baffling turns up," he promised as he walked towards the door. Suddenly he paused and faced the bookcase.

"What was that, sir? Didn't you hear a noise in the cupboard?"

"Search it by all means if you wish, Badger," I replied with the utmost sangfroid, "but it only contains my zinc ointment, ammoniated quinine and – er – a little bundle of odds and ends. As for the noise – they have the chimney-sweep in next door."

"I shouldn't think of doubting your word, sir," said the Inspector.

Then very coolly he locked the cupboard door without opening it and slipped the key into his pocket. "A mere formality, but just as well to be on the safe side," he observed.

When I returned to the room – I accompanied Badger to the outer door myself – I stood for a moment considering the new complication.

"Deuced awkward!" I muttered, walking towards the book-case.

"That will be all right, sir," interposed the soft voice of Perkins behind me. "The key of my wardrobe fits all the locks in your sitting-room – except that of the tantalus, I should say," and he held out the indicated object for me to take. Under what circumstances my exemplary man had made the discovery I did not stop to investigate, but I have no doubt that he had conscientiously listened to every word of one if not of both conversations that morning.

I did not lose a moment in unlocking the door of the book-case and throwing it widely open to release my fair visitor.

But the many-clawed hand of improbability had by no means relaxed its grip on my shoulder.

The cupboard was empty !

In speechless bewilderment my gaze went round the room from one familiar object to another in a vain attempt to solve the mystery. There was only one possible place of concealment there. I snatched away the coverlet that hid the stark outline on the dissecting table.

Imagine my surprise to see before me the corpse of the elderly Italian anarchist who had offered me a throat pastille on the grand stand at Hurlingham a month ago!

II   IN THE THICK OF IT

In spite of the passionate insistence with which Sybil (as I had now grown to call her) had reiterated that I should think of her no more, there were very few hours of the day or night that she was absent from my thoughts.

The all-too-brief moment that I had held her in my arms when I rescued her from the burning dope den in Montmorency Square had settled my fate for ever. The emotion that swept over me when I found that we had been decoyed together into the abandoned radium mine in Cornwall had, if anything, deepened the conviction; and when I discovered that it was she and no other who, at such tremendous risk to herself, had sent me the anonymous warning that saved me from being drugged and tattooed beyond recognition in the Bond

Street beauty specialist's salon, I admitted that something stronger than myself was shaping our destinies.

The baffling enigma of Sybil's identity would alone have been sufficient to keep her continually in my mind, even if I had been disposed to forget. One morning, after I had vainly sought for a week, I discovered her. She was in charge of a novelty counter in the bargain basement of Harridge's stores, and so perfectly in harmony with her surroundings that it seemed impossible to suspect her of playing a part. Yet the same evening I caught her demure look of recognition across the table of a Cabinet Minister at a dinner given in honour of a popular Ambassador. And had not Slavonski, on the memorable occasion of the Incog. Club raid, referred to her as "our trusty associate Mademoiselle Zero"? but, on the other hand, Inspector Badger had placed himself unreservedly under her guidance when she steered the river-police motor-launch in pursuit of the desperate "Hi-Hi!" gang. It was all very puzzling to me, plain John Humdrum, M.D., and when I now look back over that period I see that Sybil's friendship kept me very busy indeed.

Possibly something of the sort flashed across my mind one morning when I found on my breakfast table a note addressed in Sybil's characteristic hand. It was postmarked "Express Aerial Service. Tokio to Aberdeen," and franked "Urgent and Frantic" in violet ink. Stamps of the highest possible value were affixed wherever there was an inch of space in the dear girl's usual lavish manner. The enclosure, like all her business messages, was brief but decided.

"A great danger threatens," it ran. "Meet me at twelve to-night in the Mummy Room, British Museum. – Sybil."

Unfortunately it was not dated.

It was, therefore, in a rather doubtful frame of mind that I presented myself, shortly before midnight, at the formidable closed gates in Great Russell Street. A printed notice, read uncertainly by an adjacent street lamp, informed me that the galleries closed at six.

As I stood there in indecision an official emerged stealthily from the shadow of an angle in the wall, where he had evidently been awaiting me.

"That's all right, sir," was his welcome assurance, after he had flashed the light of an electric torch several times all over me. "The young lady has arranged everything."

Without further explanation he led the way across the broad moonlit forecourt and then through several lofty galleries. Pausing before a massive door he unlocked it, pushed me inside, and I heard the fastening close to again with a soft metallic click.

Never before had the mysterious gloom of that ghostly rendezvous of the long-forgotten dead seemed so shadow-laden.

Sybil – it was she – came towards me with a glad cry.

"You are here!" she exclaimed. "How splendid; but I never for a moment doubted it."

"But why *here*?" I ventured to inquire, in my obtuse blundering way. "Would not Moggridge's or the Azalea Court of the Frangipane have been more up-to-date?"

She gave me a reproachful glance.

"Surely by this time you know that I am the most hunted woman in Europe, my good man," she answered with a touch of aristocratic insouciance. "My footsteps are being dogged by anarchists, vendettaists, Bolsheviks, Czecho-Slovaks, Black Hands, Hidden Hands, Scotland Yard, the Northcliffe Press and several of the more ambitious special constables. This is literally the one spot in London where we are safe from observation."

"How wonderful you are!" was wrung from me. "But will you not tell me what it all means?"

In her usual cryptic fashion Sybil answered one question by another.

"Will you do something for me?"

"Can you doubt it?" I asked reproachfully.

"I don't," she replied. "But all so far is insignificant compared with this. It will demand the reticence of a Government official combined with the resourcefulness of a District Messenger boy. This packet must be delivered to-night to the Admiral of the Fleet, stationed at Plyhampton. The fate of the navy, the army and the air service are all bound up in its safe arrival."

"I am ready," I said simply.

"A yellow motor-car, with one headlight green and the other red, will be waiting for you at the corner of Tottenham Court Road and Oxford Street," she proceeded rapidly. "You will recognize it by the driver wearing a crimson opera hat – that being the secret badge of the male members of our Society. Get in and the rest is easy."

Even as she spoke a sudden look of terror swept across her features.

I followed her agonized glance to the nearest mummy case. It was, the label stated, that of an Egyptian priest of Mut, named Amen-Phat, but the pair of steely eyes that I encountered looking out of the painted mask were those of the Hindoo waiter who had upset the discarded toothpicks into the poisoned dish of caviare at the Grand Duke's reception.

I turned to convey my suspicions to Sybil, but to my surprise she had disappeared, and when I looked again the gilt face of Amen-Phat had resumed its accustomed placid stare.

One thing was clear. In my hand I held the fateful packet directed to the Admiral of the Fleet, and my duty was to find the driver of the yellow car and to make a dash for the coast at all hazard.

As I strode towards the door I recalled the ominous sound of re-locking that had followed my entrance. Was I in a trap?

Whatever had taken place, however, the door was no longer locked. It yielded to the pressure of my hand, but only for a few inches. Something was holding it from the other side. I exerted my strength and in another moment I had made a sufficient opening to allow my passage. The nature of the obstruction was then revealed. At my feet lay the body of a man. A ray of green light fell upon his features, rendering them ghastly and distorted, but it needed no second glance to assure me that the corpse was that of the mysterious Ethiopian "minstrel" who had so inexplicably greeted me as "Uncle Sam" in the Empire promenade on boat-race night.

III THE BEGINNING OF THE END

Little more remains to be told.

I changed cars seventeen times between London and the coast. The loss of time was considerable, but it wiled away the monotony of the journey, and as a precaution, together with the badness of the road, it was effectual in throwing our pursuers off the track. Their overturned car was found the next morning in a lime quarry below the road near Dorsham. Beneath it was the body of the Greek curio-dealer with the Scotch accent who had sold me the cinquecento dagger with the phial of cholera microbes concealed in the handle. By his side lay the form of the old-looking young gallery first-nighter. Even to this day my frontal bone carries the scar of his well-aimed opera-glasses, on that occasion when, in the stalls of the Hilaric during the Royal performance, nothing but Sybil's presence of mind in flinging open her umbrella had saved me from a fatal blow. Both were crushed almost beyond recognition.

Dawn was within an hour of breaking when my seventeenth car – a taxi-cab of obsolete pattern – broke down in the quaint old High Street of Plyhampton. Leaving it to its fate I went on alone to make inquiries, and soon learned, to my delight, that the superdreadnought *Stalactite*, the flag-ship of the Admiral, was lying at that moment moored to the end of the pier. Truly fate, which had played us many sorry tricks in the past, was on our side that night.

Despite the earliness of the hour, the Admiral, Sir Slocombe Colqumondeley, received me at once in his state-room, a magnificent apartment upholstered in green and gold. As his eyes rested on the superscription of the packet I handed him he could not repress a slight start, but before he had finished the reading of the message his face had grown strangely tense. For a few minutes he paced the salon in deep thought, then turning to an instrument he transmitted a series of commands in quick succession. I have since learned, though I little suspected it at the time, that the tenor of these orders was for every ship of the fleet to clear for action.

Shaking off his preoccupation Sir Slocombe turned to me with an engaging smile.

"So you are my daughter Sybil's young man, Dr Humdrum?" he exclaimed, with bluff sailor-like heartiness. "Well, well; we must see what we can arrange after this business is over. How would Surgeon-Major of the Fleet suit you; eh, what?"

A few minutes later I was leaving the pier, more bewildered by the turn events had taken than I would care to admit, when a tall, dignified officer, with grey mutton-chop side-whiskers, approached me.

"Pardon me, but did you enter Plyhampton in a taxi-cab numbered XYZ 999?" he inquired courteously.

"I did," I replied, referring to the details which I had taken the precaution to jot down on my cuff.

"Then it is my duty, as Warden of the Port, to put you in irons," and he beckoned to a master of marines.

"On what charge?" I demanded with some hauteur.

"The driver of the taxi has been found stabbed to death with his own speed lever," he explained gravely. "Inside the vehicle was the dead body of the notorious international spy known to the secret police as 'Mr A.' He was disguised as an elderly Chinese seaman, and was wearing, beneath his tunic, a forged Order of the Crimson Hat of Siam."

"Is it possible?" I gasped.

"Well, frankly, it doesn't sound it," he admitted with unofficial candour; "but that isn't my affair."

"I am Dr Humdrum," I said, producing my stethoscope," and I live at 305A Hammersmith Road, Kensington. Surely – "

"That is quite satisfactory," he replied, throwing the handcuffs into a lee scupper that stood open. "Accept my apology. Hold an inquest on the bodies as soon as you conveniently can and you have my assurance that you will hear nothing further of this unpleasant business."

We are seated in the Piazzo d'Esperanto at Mentone. Sybil's head is nestling on my shoulder.

"Had we better not explain to them now, darling, exactly what it was all about?" I venture to suggest.

"No, dearest; I don't think we better had," replies Sybil, watching the play of the deep blue against the distant haze.

Melville Davisson Post

The Angel of the Lord

The Uncle Abner stories of Melville Davisson Post (1869–1930) cannot be described as models of fair play, but in them the power of the writing and the personality of the detective for once override such considerations. Post's picture of the Virginia backlands and the Wrath of God personified in Abner have a sort of grandeur that is unique in the genre.

Uncle Abner was not Post's first venture into crime fiction. In the 1890s he had written of an unscrupulous lawyer named Randolph Mason, who exploited loopholes in the law to defeat the ends of justice; Post was a lawyer himself, and the stories are supported by references to real cases – indeed, they brought about changes in the law. Monsieur Jonquelle, Prefect of Paris Police, was another French sleuth, and quite an entertaining one, but it is for the Uncle Abner stories that Post is revered.

I ALWAYS THOUGHT my father took a long chance, but somebody had to take it and certainly I was the one least likely to be suspected. It was a wild country. There were no banks. We had to pay for the cattle, and somebody had to carry the money. My father and my uncle were always being watched. My father was right, I think.

"Abner," he said, "I'm going to send Martin. No one will ever suppose that we would trust this money to a child."

My uncle drummed on the table and rapped his heels on the floor. He was a bachelor, stern and silent. But he could talk . . . and when he did, he began at the beginning and you heard him through; and what he said – well, he stood behind it.

"To stop Martin," my father went on, "would be only to lose the money; but to stop you would be to get somebody killed."

I knew what my father meant. He meant that no one would undertake to rob Abner until after he had shot him to death.

I ought to say a word about my Uncle Abner. He was one of those austere, deeply religious men who were the product of the

Reformation. He always carried a Bible in his pocket and he read it where he pleased. Once the crowd at Roy's Tavern tried to make sport of him when he got his book out by the fire; but they never tried it again. When the fight was over Abner paid Roy eighteen silver dollars for the broken chairs and the table – and he was the only man in the tavern who could ride a horse. Abner belonged to the church militant, and his God was a war lord.

So that is how they came to send me. The money was in greenbacks in packages. They wrapped it up in newspaper and put it into a pair of saddle-bags, and I set out. I was about nine years old. No, it was not as bad as you think. I could ride a horse all day when I was nine years old – most any kind of a horse. I was tough as whit'-leather, and I knew the country I was going into. You must not picture a little boy rolling a hoop in the park.

It was an afternoon in early autumn. The clay roads froze in the night; they thawed out in the day and they were a bit sticky. I was to stop at Roy's Tavern, south of the river, and go on in the morning. Now and then I passed some cattle driver, but no one overtook me on the road until almost sundown; then I heard a horse behind me and a man came up. I knew him. He was a cattleman named Dix. He had once been a shipper, but he had come in for a good deal of bad luck. His partner, Alkire, had absconded with a big sum of money due the grazers. This had ruined Dix; he had given up his land, which wasn't very much, to the grazers. After that he had gone over the mountain to his people, got together a pretty big sum of money and bought a large tract of grazing land. Foreign claimants had sued him in the courts on some old title and he had lost the whole tract and the money that he had paid for it. He had married a remote cousin of ours and he had always lived on her lands, adjoining those of my Uncle Abner.

Dix seemed surprised to see me on the road.

"So it's you, Martin," he said; "I thought Abner would be going into the upcountry."

One gets to be a pretty cunning youngster, even at this age, and I told no one what I was about.

"Father wants the cattle over the river to run a month," I returned easily, "and I'm going up there to give his orders to the grazers."

He looked me over, then he rapped the saddlebags with his knuckles. "You carry a good deal of baggage, my lad."

I laughed. "Horse feed," I said. "You know my father! A horse must be fed at dinner time, but a man can go till he gets it."

One was always glad of any company on the road, and we fell into an idle talk. Dix said he was going out into the Ten Mile country; and

I have always thought that was, in fact, his intention. The road turned south about a mile our side of the tavern. I never liked Dix; he was of an apologetic manner, with a cunning, irresolute face.

A little later a man passed us at a gallop. He was a drover named Marks, who lived beyond my Uncle Abner, and he was riding hard to get in before night. He hailed us, but he did not stop; we got a shower of mud and Dix cursed him. I have never seen a more evil face. I suppose it was because Dix usually had a grin about his mouth, and when that sort of face gets twisted there's nothing like it.

After that he was silent. He rode with his head down and his fingers plucking at his jaw, like a man in some perplexity. At the crossroads he stopped and sat for some time in the saddle, looking before him. I left him there, but at the bridge he overtook me. He said he had concluded to get some supper and go on after that.

Roy's Tavern consisted of a single big room, with a loft above it for sleeping quarters. A narrow covered way connected this room with the house in which Roy and his family lived. We used to hang our saddles on wooden pegs in this covered way. I have seen that wall so hung with saddles that you could not find a place for another stirrup. But tonight Dix and I were alone in the tavern. He looked cunningly at me when I took the saddle-bags with me into the big room and when I went with them up the ladder into the loft. But he said nothing – in fact, he had scarcely spoken. It was cold; the road had begun to freeze when we got in. Roy had lighted a big fire. I left Dix before it. I did not take off my clothes, because Roy's beds were mattresses of wheat straw covered with heifer skins – good enough for summer but pretty cold on such a night, even with the heavy, hand-woven coverlet in big white and black checks.

I put the saddle-bags under my head and lay down. I went at once to sleep, but I suddenly awaked. I thought there was a candle in the loft, but it was a gleam of light from the fire below, shining through a crack in the floor. I lay and watched it, the coverlet pulled up to my chin. Then I began to wonder why the fire burned so brightly. Dix ought to be on his way some time and it was a custom for the last man to rake out the fire. There was not a sound. The light streamed steadily through the crack.

Presently it occurred to me that Dix had forgotten the fire and that I ought to go down and rake it out. Roy always warned us about the fire when he went to bed. I got up, wrapped the great coverlet around me, went over to the gleam of light and looked down through the crack in the floor. I had to lie out at full length to get my eye against the board. The hickory logs had turned to great embers and glowed like a furnace of red coals.

Before this fire stood Dix. He was holding out his hands and turning himself about as though he were cold to the marrow; but with all that chill upon him, when the man's face came into the light I saw it covered with a sprinkling of sweat.

I shall carry the memory of that face. The grin was there at the mouth, but it was pulled about; the eyelids were drawn in; the teeth were clamped together. I have seen a dog poisoned with strychnine look like that.

I lay there and watched the thing. It was as though something potent and evil dwelling within the man were in travail to re-form his face upon its image. You cannot realize how that devilish labor held me – the face worked as though it were some plastic stuff, and the sweat oozed through. And all the time the man was cold; and he was crowding into the fire and turning himself about and putting out his hands. And it was as though the heat would no more enter in and warm him than it will enter in and warm the ice.

It seemed to scorch him and leave him cold – and he was fearfully and desperately cold! I could smell the singe of the fire on him, but it had no power against this diabolic chill. I began myself to shiver, although I had the heavy coverlet wrapped around me.

The thing was a fascinating horror; I seemed to be looking down into the chamber of some abominable maternity. The room was filled with the steady red light of the fire. Not a shadow moved in it. And there was silence. The man had taken off his boots and he twisted before the fire without a sound. It was like the shuddering tales of possession or transformation by a drug. I thought the man would burn himself to death. His clothes smoked. How could he be so cold?

Then, finally, the thing was over! I did not see it for his face was in the fire. But suddenly he grew composed and stepped back into the room. I tell you I was afraid to look! I do not know what thing I expected to see there, but I did not think it would be Dix.

Well, it was Dix; but not the Dix that any of us knew. There was a certain apology, a certain indecision, a certain servility in that other Dix, and these things showed about his face. But there was none of these weaknesses in this man.

His face had been pulled into planes of firmness and decision; the slack in his features had been taken up; the furtive moving of the eye was gone. He stood now squarely on his feet and he was full of courage. But I was afraid of him as I have never been afraid

of any human creature in this world! Something that had been
servile in him, that had skulked behind disguises, that had worn the
habiliments of subterfuge, had now come forth; and it had molded
the features of the man to its abominable courage.

Presently he began to move swiftly about the room. He looked out
at the window and he listened at the door; then he went softly into
the covered way. I thought he was going on his journey; but then he
could not be going with his boots there beside the fire. In a moment
he returned with a saddle blanket in his hand and came softly across
the room to the ladder.

Then I understood the thing that he intended, and I was motionless
with fear. I tried to get up, but I could not. I could only lie there with
my eye strained to the crack in the floor. His foot was on the ladder,
and I could already feel his hand on my throat and that blanket on
my face, and the suffocation of death in me, when far away on the
hard road I heard a horse!

He heard it, too, for he stopped on the ladder and turned his evil
face about toward the door. The horse was on the long hill beyond the
bridge, and he was coming as though the devil rode in his saddle. It
was a hard, dark night. The frozen road was like flint; I could hear
the iron of the shoes ring. Whoever rode that horse rode for his life
or for something more than his life, or he was mad. I heard the horse
strike the bridge and thunder across it. And all the while Dix hung
there on the ladder by his hands and listened. Now he sprang softly
down, pulled on his boots and stood up before the fire, his face – this
new face – gleaming with its evil courage. The next moment the horse
stopped.

I could hear him plunge under the bit, his iron shoes ripping
the frozen road; then the door leaped back and my Uncle Abner
was in the room. I was so glad that my heart almost choked me
and for a moment I could hardly see – everything was in a sort
of mist.

Abner swept the room in a glance, then he stopped.

"Thank God!" he said; "I'm in time." And he drew his hand down
over his face with the fingers hard and close as though he pulled
something away.

"In time for what?" said Dix.

Abner looked him over. And I could see the muscles of his big
shoulders stiffen as he looked. And again he looked him over. Then
he spoke and his voice was strange.

"Dix," he said, "is it you?"

"Who would it be but me?" said Dix.

"It might be the devil," said Abner. "Do you know what your face looks like?"

"No matter what it looks like!" said Dix.

"And so," said Abner, "we have got courage with this new face." Dix threw up his head.

"Now, look here, Abner," he said, "I've had about enough of your big manner. You ride a horse to death and you come plunging in here; what the devil's wrong with you?"

"There's nothing wrong with me," replied Abner, and his voice was low. "But there's something damnably wrong with you, Dix."

"The devil take you," said Dix, and I saw him measure Abner with his eye. It was not fear that held him back; fear was gone out of the creature; I think it was a kind of prudence.

Abner's eyes kindled, but his voice remained low and steady.

"Those are big words," he said.

"Well," cried Dix, "get out of the door then and let me pass!"

"Not just yet," said Abner; "I have something to say to you."

"Say it then," cried Dix, "and get out of the door."

"Why hurry?" said Abner. "It's a long time until daylight, and I have a good deal to say."

"You'll not say it to me," said Dix. "I've got a trip to make tonight; get out of the door."

Abner did not move. "You've got a longer trip to make tonight than you think, Dix," he said; "but you're going to hear what I have to say before you set out on it."

I saw Dix rise on his toes and I knew what he wished for. He wished for a weapon; and he wished for the bulk of bone and muscle that would have a chance against Abner. But he had neither the one nor the other. And he stood there on his toes and began to curse – low, vicious, withering oaths, that were like the swish of a knife.

Abner was looking at the man with a curious interest.

"It is strange," he said, as though speaking to himself, "but it explains the thing. While one is the servant of neither, one has the courage of neither; but when he finally makes his choice he gets what his master has to give him."

Then he spoke to Dix.

"Sit down!" he said; and it was in that deep, level voice that Abner used when he was standing close behind his words. Every man in the hills knew that voice; one had only a moment to decide after he heard it. Dix knew that, and yet for one instant he hung there on his toes, his eyes shimmering like a weasel's, his mouth twisting. He was not afraid! If he had had the ghost of a chance against Abner he would have taken it. But he knew he had not, and with an oath he threw the saddle blanket into a corner and sat down by the fire.

Abner came away from the door then. He took off his great coat. He put a log on the fire and he sat down across the hearth from Dix. The new hickory sprang crackling into flames. For a good while there was silence; the two men sat at either end of the hearth without a word. Abner seemed to have fallen into a study of the man before him. Finally he spoke:

"Dix," he said, "do you believe in the providence of God?"

Dix flung up his head.

"Abner," he cried, "if you are going to talk nonsense I promise you upon my oath that I will not stay to listen."

Abner did not at once reply. He seemed to begin now at another point.

"Dix," he said, "you've had a good deal of bad luck . . . Perhaps you wish it put that way."

"Now, Abner," he cried, "you speak the truth; I have had hell's luck."

"Hell's luck you have had," replied Abner. "It is a good word. I accept it. Your partner disappeared with all the money of the grazers on the other side of the river; you lost the land in your lawsuit; and you are to-night without a dollar. That was a big tract of land to lose. Where did you get so great a sum of money?"

"I have told you a hundred times," replied Dix. "I got it from my people over the mountains. You know where I got it."

"Yes," said Abner. "I know where you got it, Dix. And I know another thing. But first I want to show you this," and he took a little penknife out of his pocket. "And I want to tell you that I believe in the providence of God, Dix."

"I don't care a fiddler's damn what you believe in," said Dix.

"But you do care what I know," replied Abner.

"What do you know?" said Dix.

"I know where your partner is," replied Abner.

I was uncertain about what Dix was going to do, but finally he answered with a sneer.

"Then you know something that nobody else knows."

"Yes," replied Abner, "there is another man who knows."

"Who?" said Dix.

"You," said Abner.

Dix leaned over in his chair and looked at Abner closely.

"Abner," he cried, "you are talking nonsense. Nobody knows where Alkire is. If I knew I'd go after him."

"Dix," Abner answered, and it was again in that deep, level voice, "if I had got here five minutes later you would have gone after him. I can promise you that, Dix.

"Now, listen! I was in the upcountry when I got your word about the partnership; and I was on my way back when at Big Run I broke a stirrup-leather. I had no knife and I went into the store and bought this one; then the storekeeper told me that Alkire had gone to see you. I didn't want to interfere with him and I turned back . . . So I did not become your partner. And so I did not disappear . . . What was it that prevented? The broken stirrup-leather? The knife? In old times, Dix, men were so blind that God had to open their eyes before they could see His angel in the way before them . . . They are still blind, but they ought not to be that blind . . . Well, on the night that Alkire disappeared I met him on his way to your house. It was out there at the bridge. He had broken a stirrup-leather and he was trying to fasten it with a nail. He asked me if I had a knife, and I gave him this one. It was beginning to rain and I went on, leaving him there in the road with the knife in his hand."

Abner paused; the muscles of his great iron jaw contracted.

"God forgive me," he said; "it was His angel again! I never saw Alkire after that."

"Nobody ever saw him after that," said Dix. "He got out of the hills that night."

"No," replied Abner, "it was not in the night when Alkire started on his journey; it was in the day."

"Abner," said Dix, "you talk like a fool. If Alkire had traveled the road in the day somebody would have seen him."

"Nobody could see him on the road he traveled," replied Abner.

"What road?" said Dix.

"Dix," replied Abner, "you will learn that soon enough."

Abner looked hard at the man.

"You saw Alkire when he started on his journey," he continued; "but did you see who it was that went with him?"

"Nobody went with him," replied Dix; "Alkire rode alone."

"Not alone," said Abner; "there was another."

"I didn't see him," said Dix.

"And yet," continued Abner, "you made Alkire go with him."

I saw cunning enter Dix's face. He was puzzled, but he thought Abner off the scent.

"And I made Alkire go with somebody, did I? Well, who was it? Did you see him?"

"Nobody ever saw him."

"He must be a stranger."

"No," replied Abner, "he rode the hills before we came into them."

"Indeed!" said Dix. "And what kind of a horse did he ride?"

"White!" said Abner.

Dix got some inkling of what Abner meant now, and his face grew livid.

"What are you driving at?" he cried. "You sit here beating around the bush. If you know anything, say it out; let's hear it. What is it?"

Abner put out his big sinewy hand as though to thrust Dix back into his chair.

"Listen!" he said. "Two days after that I wanted to get out into the Ten Mile country and I went through your lands; I rode a path through the narrow valley west of your house. At a point on the path where there is an apple tree something caught my eye and I stopped. Five minutes later I knew exactly what had happened under that apple tree . . . Someone had ridden there; he had stopped under that tree; then something happened and the horse had run away – I knew that by the tracks of a horse on this path. I knew that the horse had a rider and that it had stopped under this tree, because there was a limb cut from the tree at a certain height. I knew the horse had remained there, because the small twigs of the apple limb had been pared off, and they lay in a heap on the path. I knew that something had frightened the horse and that it had run away, because the sod was torn up where it had jumped . . . Ten minutes later I knew that the rider had not been in the saddle when the horse jumped; I knew what it was that had frightened the horse; and I knew that the thing had occurred the day before. Now, how did I know that?

"Listen! I put my horse into the tracks of that other horse under the tree and studied the ground. Immediately I saw where the weeds beside the path had been crushed, as though some animal had been lying down there, and in the very center of that bed I saw a little heap of fresh earth. That was strange, Dix, that fresh earth where the animal had been lying down! It had come there after the animal had got up, or else it would have been pressed flat. But where had it come from?

"I got off and walked around the apple tree, moving out from it in an ever-widening circle. Finally I found an ant heap, the top of which had been scraped away as though one had taken up the loose earth in his hands. Then I went back and plucked up some of the earth. The under clods of it were colored as with red paint . . . No, it wasn't paint.

"There was a brush fence some fifty yards away. I went over to it and followed it down.

"Opposite the apple tree the weeds were again crushed as though some animal had lain there. I sat down in that place and drew a line with my eye across a log of the fence to a limb of the apple tree. Then I got on my horse and again put him in the tracks of that other horse under the tree; the imaginary line passed through the pit of my stomach! . . . I am four inches taller than Alkire."

It was then that Dix began to curse. I had seen his face work while Abner was speaking and that spray of sweat had reappeared. But he kept the courage he had got.

"Lord Almighty, man!" he cried. "How prettily you sum it up! We shall presently have Lawyer Abner with his brief. Because my renters have killed a calf; because one of their horses frightened at the blood has bolted, and because they cover the blood with earth so the other horses traveling the path may not do the like; straightway I have shot Alkire out of his saddle . . . Man! What a mare's nest! And now, Lawyer Abner, with your neat little conclusions, what did I do with Alkire after I had killed him? Did I cause him to vanish into the air with a smell of sulphur or did I cause the earth to yawn and Alkire to descend into its bowels?"

"Dix," replied Abner, "your words move somewhat near the truth."

"Upon my soul," cried Dix, "you compliment me. If I had that trick of magic, believe me, you would be already some distance down."

Abner remained a moment silent.

"Dix," he said, "what does it mean when one finds a plot of earth resodded?"

"Is that a riddle?" cried Dix. "Well, confound me, if I don't answer it! You charge me with murder and then you fling in this neat conundrum. Now, what could be the answer to that riddle, Abner? If one had done a murder this sod would overlie a grave and Alkire would be in it in his bloody shirt. Do I give the answer?"

"You do not," replied Abner.

"No!" cried Dix. "Your sodded plot no grave, and Alkire not within it waiting for the trump of Gabriel! Why, man, where are your little damned conclusions?"

"Dix," said Abner, "you do not deceive me in the least; Alkire is not sleeping in a grave."

"Then in the air," sneered Dix, "with the smell of sulphur?"

"Nor in the air," said Abner.

"Then consumed with fire, like the priests of Baal?"

"Nor with fire," said Abner.

Dix had got back the quiet of his face; this banter had put him where he was when Abner entered. "This is all fools' talk," he said; "if I had killed Alkire, what could I have done with the body? And the horse! What could I have done with the horse? Remember, no man has ever seen Alkire's horse any more than he has seen Alkire – and for the reason that Alkire rode him out of the hills that night. Now, look here, Abner, you have asked me a good many questions. I will ask you one. Among your little conclusions do you find that I did this thing alone or with the aid of others?"

"Dix," replied Abner, "I will answer that upon my own belief you had no accomplice."

"Then," said Dix, "how could I have carried off the horse? Alkire I might carry; but his horse weighed thirteen hundred pounds!"

"Dix," said Abner, "no man helped you do this thing; but there were men who helped you to conceal it."

"And now," cried Dix, "the man is going mad! Who could I trust with such work, I ask you? Have I a renter that would not tell it when he moved on to another's land, or when he got a quart of cider in him? Where are the men who helped me?"

"Dix," said Abner, "they have been dead these fifty years."

I heard Dix laugh then, and his evil face lighted as though a candle were behind it. And, in truth, I thought he had got Abner silenced.

"In the name of Heaven!" he cried. "With such proofs it is a wonder that you did not have me hanged."

"And hanged you should have been," said Abner.

"Well," cried Dix, "go and tell the sheriff, and mind you lay before him those little, neat conclusions: How from a horse track and the place where a calf was butchered you have reasoned on Alkire's murder, and to conceal the body and the horse you have reasoned on the aid of men who were rotting in their graves when I was born; and see how he will receive you!"

Abner gave no attention to the man's flippant speech. He got his great silver watch out of his pocket, pressed the stem and looked. Then he spoke in his deep, even voice.

"Dix," he said, "it is nearly midnight; in an hour you must be on your journey, and I have something more to say. Listen! I knew this thing had been done the previous day because it had rained on the night that I met Alkire, and the earth of this ant heap had been disturbed after that. Moreover, this earth had been frozen, and that showed a night had passed since it had been placed there. And I knew the rider of that horse was Alkire because, beside the path near the severed twigs lay my knife, where it had fallen from his hand. This much I learned in some fifteen minutes; the rest took somewhat longer.

"I followed the track of the horse until it stopped in the little valley below. It was easy to follow while the horse ran, because the sod was torn; but when it ceased to run there was no track that I could follow. There was a little stream threading the valley, and I began at the wood and came slowly up to see if I could find where the horse had crossed. Finally I found a horse track and there was also a man's track, which meant that you had caught the horse and were leading it away. But where?

"On the rising ground above there was an old orchard where there had once been a house. The work about that house had been done a hundred years. It was rotted down now. You had opened this orchard into the pasture. I rode all over the face of this hill and finally I entered this orchard. There was a great, flat, moss-covered stone lying a few steps from where the house had stood. As I looked I noticed that the moss growing from it into the earth had been broken along the edges of the stone, and then I noticed that for a few feet about the stone the ground had been resodded. I got down and lifted up some of this new sod. Under it the earth had been soaked with that . . . red paint.

"It was clever of you, Dix, to resod the ground; that took only a little time and it effectually concealed the place where you had killed the horse; but it was foolish of you to forget that the broken moss around the edges of the great flat stone could not be mended."

"Abner!" cried Dix. "Stop!" And I saw that spray of sweat, and his face working like kneaded bread, and the shiver of that abominable chill on him.

Abner was silent for a moment and then he went on, but from another quarter.

"Twice," said Abner, "the Angel of the Lord stood before me and I did not know it; but the third time I knew it. It is not in the cry of the wind, nor in the voice of many waters that His presence is made known to us. That man in Israel had only the sign that the beast under him would not go on. Twice I had as good a sign, and tonight, when Marks broke a stirrup-leather before my house and called me to the door and asked me for a knife to mend it, I saw and I came!"

The log that Abner had thrown on was burned down, and the fire was again a mass of embers; the room was filled with that dull red light. Dix had got on to his feet, and he stood now twisting before the fire, his hands reaching out to it, and that cold creeping in his bones, and the smell of the fire on him.

Abner rose. And when he spoke his voice was like a thing that has dimensions and weight.

"Dix," he said, "you robbed the grazers; you shot Alkire out of his saddle; and a child you would have murdered!"

And I saw the sleeve of Abner's coat begin to move, then it stopped. He stood staring at something against the wall. I looked to see what the thing was, but I did not see it. Abner was looking beyond the wall, as though it had been moved away.

And all the time Dix had been shaking with that hellish cold, and twisting on the hearth and crowding into the fire. Then he fell back, and he was the Dix I knew – his face was slack; his eye was furtive; and he was full of terror.

It was his weak whine that awakened Abner. He put up his hand and brought the fingers hard down over his face, and then he looked at this new creature, cringing and beset with fears.

"Dix," he said, "Alkire was a just man; he sleeps as peacefully in that abandoned well under his horse as he would sleep in the churchyard. My hand has been held back; you may go. Vengeance is mine, I will repay, saith the Lord."

"But where shall I go, Abner?" the creature wailed; "I have no money and I am cold."

Abner took out his leather wallet and flung it toward the door.

"There is money," he said – "a hundred dollars – and there is my coat. Go! But if I find you in the hills to-morrow, or if I ever find you, I warn you in the name of the living God that I will stamp you out of life!"

I saw the loathsome thing writhe into Abner's coat and seize the wallet and slip out through the door; and a moment later I heard a horse. And I crept back on to Roy's heifer skin.

When I came down at daylight my Uncle Abner was reading by the fire.

Sir Arthur Conan Doyle

His Last Bow: an Epilogue of Sherlock Holmes

Our sampling of the mystery fiction of the Golden Age ends, as it began, with Sherlock Holmes. "His Last Bow" (1917) was the final Holmes story, and Holmes' parting words memorably express the change that had come. Sir Arthur Conan Doyle (1859–1930; he had been knighted in 1902) had written a great many other stories and novels in the intervening years, but he never created another character to match the immortal Holmes. I don't believe that any other mystery writer has, either.

IT WAS NINE O'CLOCK at night upon the second of August – the most terrible August in the history of the world. One might have thought already that God's curse hung heavy over a degenerate world, for there was an awesome hush and a feeling of vague expectancy in the sultry and stagnant air. The sun had long set, but one blood-red gash like an open wound lay low in the distant west. Above, the stars were shining brightly; and below, the lights of the shipping glimmered in the bay. The two famous Germans stood beside the stone parapet of the garden walk, with the long low, heavily gabled house behind them, and they looked down upon the broad sweep of the beach at the foot of the great chalk cliff on which Von Bork, like some wandering eagle, had perched himself four years before. They stood with their heads close together, talking in low, confidential tones. From below the two glowing ends of their cigars might have been the smouldering eyes of some malignant fiend looking down in the darkness.

A remarkable man this Von Bork – a man who could hardly be matched among all the devoted agents of the Kaiser. It was his talents which had first recommended him for the English mission, the most important mission of all, but since he had taken it over, those talents had become more and more manifest to the half-dozen people in the world who were really in touch with the truth. One of these was his present companion, Baron Von Herling, the chief secretary of the legation, whose huge 100-horsepower Benz car was blocking the country lane as it waited to waft its owner back to London.

"So far as I can judge the trend of events, you will probably be back in Berlin within the week," the secretary was saying. "When you get there, my dear Von Bork, I think you will be surprised at the welcome you will receive. I happen to know what is thought in the highest quarters of your work in this country." He was a huge man, the secretary, deep, broad, and tall, with a slow, heavy fashion of speech which had been his main asset in his political career.

Von Bork laughed.

"They are not very hard to deceive," he remarked. "A more docile, simple folk could not be imagined."

"I don't know about that," said the other thoughtfully. "They have strange limits and one must learn to observe them. It is that surface simplicity of theirs which makes a trap for the stranger. One's first impression is that they are entirely soft. Then one comes suddenly upon something very hard, and you know that you have reached the limit, and must adapt yourself to the fact. They have, for example, their insular conventions which simply *must* be observed."

"Meaning, 'good form' and that sort of thing?" Von Bork sighed, as one who had suffered much.

"Meaning British prejudice in all its queer manifestations. As an example I may quote one of my own worst blunders – I can afford to talk of my blunders, for you know my work well enough to be aware of my successes. It was on my first arrival. I was invited to a week-end gathering at the country house of a cabinet minister. The conversation was amazingly indiscreet."

Von Bork nodded. "I've been there," said he dryly.

"Exactly. Well, I naturally sent a résumé of the information to Berlin. Unfortunately our good Chancellor is a little heavy-handed in these matters, and he transmitted a remark which showed that he was aware of what had been said. This, of course, took the trail straight up to me. You've no idea the harm that it did me. There was nothing soft about our British hosts on that occasion, I can assure you. I was two years living it down. Now you, with this sporting pose of yours."

"No, no, don't call it a pose. A pose is an artificial thing. This is quite natural. I am a born sportsman. I enjoy it."

"Well, that makes it the more effective. You yacht against them, you hunt with them, you play polo, you match them in every game, your four-in-hand takes the prize at Olympia. I have even heard that you go the length of boxing with the young officers. What is the result? Nobody takes you seriously. You are a 'good old sport,' 'quite a decent fellow for a German,' a hard-drinking, night-club, knock-about-town, devil-may-care young fellow. And all the time this quiet country house of yours is the centre of half the mischief in England, and the sporting squire the most astute secret-service man in Europe. Genius, my dear Von Bork – genius!"

"You flatter me, Baron. But certainly I may claim that my four years in this country have not been unproductive. I've never shown you my little store. Would you mind stepping in for a moment."

The door of the study opened straight on to the terrace. Von Bork pushed it back, and, leading the way, he clicked the switch of the electric light. He then closed the door behind the bulky form which followed him, and carefully adjusted the heavy curtain over the latticed window. Only when all these precautions had been taken and tested did he turn his sunburned aquiline face to his guest.

"Some of my papers have gone," said he, "when my wife and the household left yesterday for Flushing they took the less important with them. I must, of course, claim the protection of the Embassy for the others."

"Your name has already been filed as one of the personal suite. There will be no difficulties for you or your baggage. Of course, it is just possible that we may not have to go. England may leave France to her fate. We are sure that there is no binding treaty between them."

"And Belgium?"

"Yes, and Belgium, too."

Von Bork shook his head. "I don't see how that could be. There is a definite treaty there. She could never recover from such a humiliation."

"She would at least have peace for the moment."

"But her honour?"

"Tut, my dear sir, we live in a utilitarian age. Honour is a mediæval conception. Besides England is not ready. It is an inconceivable thing, but even our special war tax of fifty million, which one would think made our purpose as clear as if we had advertised it on the front page of the *Times*, has not roused these people from their slumbers. Here and there one hears a question. It is my business to find an answer. Here and there also there is an irritation. It is my business to soothe it. But I can assure you that so far as the essentials go

– the storage of munitions, the preparation for submarine attack, the arrangements for making high explosives – nothing is prepared. How then can England come in, especially when we have stirred her up such a devil's brew of Irish civil war, window-breaking Furies, and God knows what to keep her thoughts at home?"

"She must think of her future."

"Ah, that is another matter. I fancy that in the future, we have our own very definite plans about England, and that your information will be very vital to us. It is to-day or to-morrow with Mr John Bull. If he prefers to-day we are perfectly ready. If it is to-morrow we shall be more ready still. I should think they would be wiser to fight with allies than without them, but that is their own affair. This week is their week of destiny. But you were speaking of your papers." He sat in the armchair with the light shining upon his broad bald head, while he puffed sedately at his cigar.

The large oak-panelled, book-lined room had a curtain hung in the further corner. When this was drawn it disclosed a large brass-bound safe. Von Bork detached a small key from his watch-chain, and after some considerable manipulation of the lock he swung open the heavy door.

"Look!" said he, standing clear, with a wave of his hand.

The light shone vividly into the opened safe, and the secretary of the Embassy gazed with an absorbed interest at the rows of stuffed pigeon-holes with which it was furnished. Each pigeon-hole had its label, and his eyes as he glanced along them read a long series of such titles as "Fords," "Harbour-defences," "Aeroplanes," "Ireland," "Egypt," "Portsmouth forts," "The Channel," "Rosyth," and a score of others. Each compartment was bristling with papers and plans.

"Colossal!" said the secretary. Putting down his cigar he softly clapped his fat hands.

"And all in four years, Baron. Not such a bad show for the hard-drinking, hard-riding country squire. But the gem of my collection is coming and there is the setting all ready for it." He pointed to a space over which "Naval Signals" was printed.

"But you have a good dossier there already."

"Out of date and waste paper. The Admiralty in some way got the alarm and every code has been changed. It was a blow, Baron – the worst set-back in my whole campaign. But thanks to my cheque-book and the good Altamont all will be well to-night."

The Baron looked at his watch, and gave a guttural exclamation of disappointment.

"Well, I really can wait no longer. You can imagine that things are moving at present in Carlton Terrace and that we have all to be at our posts. I had hoped to be able to bring news of your great coup. Did Altamont name no hour?"

Von Bork pushed over a telegram.

"Will come without fail to-night and bring new sparking plugs. Altamont."

"Sparking plugs, eh?"

"You see he poses as a motor expert and I keep a full garage. In our code everything likely to come up is named after some spare part. If he talks of a radiator it is a battleship, of an oil pump a cruiser, and so on. Sparking plugs are naval signals."

"From Portsmouth at mid-day," said the secretary, examining the superscription. "By the way, what do you give him?"

"Five hundred pounds for this particular job. Of course he has a salary as well."

"The greedy rogue. They are useful, these traitors, but I grudge them their blood money."

"I grudge Altamont nothing. He is a wonderful worker. If I pay him well, at least he delivers the goods, to use his own phrase. Besides he is not a traitor. I assure you that our most pan-Germanic Junker is a sucking dove in his feelings towards England as compared with a real bitter-Irish-American."

"Oh, an Irish-American?"

"If you heard him talk you would not doubt it. Sometimes I assure you I can hardly understand him. He seems to have declared war on the King's English as well as on the English King. Must you really go? He may be here any moment."

"No. I'm sorry but I have already overstayed my time. We shall expect you early to-morrow, and when you get that signal book through the little door on the Duke of York's steps you can put a triumphant Finis to your record in England. What! Tokay!" He indicated a heavily sealed dust-covered bottle which stood with two-high glasses upon a salver.

"May I offer you a glass before your journey?"

"No, thanks. But it looks like revelry."

"Altamont has a nice taste in wines, and he took a fancy to my Tokay. He is a touchy fellow and needs humouring in small things. I have to study him, I assure you." They had strolled out on to the terrace again, and along it to the further end where at a touch from the Baron's chauffeur the great car shivered and chuckled. "Those are the lights of Harwich, I suppose," said the secretary, pulling on his dust coat. "How still and peaceful it all seems. There may be other lights within the week, and the English coast a less tranquil place! The heavens, too, may not be quite so peaceful if all that the good Zeppelin promises us comes true. By the way, who is that?"

Only one window showed a light behind them; in it there stood a lamp, and beside it, seated at a table, was a dear old ruddy-faced woman in a country cap. She was bending over her knitting and stopping occasionally to stroke a large black cat upon a stool beside her.

"That is Martha, the only servant I have left."

The secretary chuckled.

"She might almost personify Britannia," said he, "with her complete self absorption and general air of comfortable somnolence. Well, au revoir, Von Bork!" – with a final wave of his hand he sprang into the car, and a moment later the two golden cones from the headlights shot forward through the darkness. The secretary lay back in the cushions of the luxurious Limousine, with his thoughts so full of the impending European tragedy that he hardly observed that as his car swung round the village street it nearly passed over a little Ford coming in the opposite direction.

Von Bork walked slowly back to the study when the last gleams of the motor lamps had faded into the distance. As he passed he observed that his old housekeeper had put out her lamp and retired. It was a new experience to him, the silence and darkness of his wide-spread house, for his family and household had been a large one. It was a relief to him, however, to think that they were all in safety and that, but for that one old woman who had lingered in the kitchen, he had the whole place to himself. There was a good deal of tidying up to do inside his study and he set himself to do it, until his keen, handsome face was flushed with the heat of the burning papers. A leather valise stood beside his table, and into this he began to pack very neatly and systematically the precious contents of his safe. He had hardly got started with the work, however, when his quick ears caught the sound of a distant car. Instantly he gave an exclamation of satisfaction, strapped up the valise, shut the safe, locked it, and hurried out on to the terrace. He was just in time to see the lights of a small car come to a halt at the gate. A passenger sprang out of it and advanced swiftly towards him, while the chauffeur, a heavily built, elderly man, with a grey moustache, settled down, like one who resigns himself to a long vigil.

"Well?" asked Von Bork eagerly, running forward to meet his visitor.

For answer the man waved a small brown-paper parcel triumphantly above his head.

"You can give me the glad hand to-night, Mister," he cried. "I'm bringing home the bacon at last."

"The signals?"

"Same as I said in my cable. Every last one of them, semaphore, lamp code, Marconi – a copy, mind you, not the original. That was too dangerous. But it's the real goods, and you can lay to that," he slapped the German upon the shoulder with a rough familiarity from which the other winced.

"Come in," he said. "I'm all alone in the house. I was only waiting for this. Of course a copy is better than the original. If an original were missing they would change the whole thing. You think it's all safe about the copy?"

The Irish-American had entered the study and stretched his long limbs from the armchair. He was a tall, gaunt man of sixty, with clear-cut features and a small goatee beard which gave him a general resemblance to the caricatures of Uncle Sam. A half-smoked, sodden cigar hung from the corner of his mouth, and as he sat down he struck a match and relit it. "Making ready for a move?" he remarked as he looked round him. "Say, Mister," he added, as his eyes fell upon the safe from which the curtain was now removed, "you don't tell me you keep your papers in that?"

"Why not?"

"Gosh, in a wide-open contraption like that! And they reckon you to be some spy. Why, a Yankee crook would be into that with a can-opener. If I'd known that any letter of mine was goin' to lie loose in a thing like that I'd have been a mug to write to you at all."

"It would puzzle any crook to force that safe," Von Bork answered. "You won't cut that metal with any tool."

"But the lock?"

"No, it's a double combination lock. You know what that is?"

"Search me," said the American.

"Well, you need a word as well as a set of figures before you can get the lock to work." He rose and showed a double-radiating disc round the keyhole. "This outer one is for the letters, the inner one for the figures."

"Well, well, that's fine."

"So it's not quite as simple as you thought. It was four years ago that I had it made, and what do you think I chose for the word and figures?"

"It's beyond me."

"Well, I chose August for the word, and 1914 for the figures, and here we are."

The American's face showed his surprise and admiration.

"My, but that was smart! You had it down to a fine thing."

"Yes, few of us even then could have guessed the date. Here it is, and I'm shutting down to-morrow morning."

"Well, I guess you'll have to fix me up also. I'm not staying in this goldarned country all on my lonesome. In a week or less from what I see, John Bull will be on his hind legs and fair ramping. I'd rather watch him from over the water."

"But you're an American citizen?"

"Well, so was Jack James an American citizen, but he's doing time in Portland all the same. It cuts no ice with a British copper to tell him you're an American citizen. 'It's British law and order over here,' says he. By the way, Mister, talking of Jack James it seems to me you don't do much to cover your men."

"What do you mean?" Von Bork asked sharply.

"Well, you are their employer, ain't you? It's up to you to see that they don't fall down. But they do fall down, and when did you ever pick them up? There's James – "

"It was James's own fault. You know that yourself. He was too self-willed for the job."

"James was a bonehead – I give you that. Then there was Hollis."

"The man was mad."

"Well, he went a bit woozy towards the end. It's enough to make a man bughouse when he has to play a part from morning to night with a hundred guys all ready to set the coppers wise to him. But now there is Steiner – "

Von Bork started violently, and his ruddy face turned a shade paler.

"What about Steiner?"

"Well, they've got him, that's all. They raided his store last night, and he and his papers are all in Portsmouth gaol. You'll go off and he, poor devil, will have to stand the racket, and lucky if he gets off with his life. That's why I want to get over the water as soon as you do."

Von Bork was a strong, self-contained man, but it was easy to see that the news had shaken him.

"How could they have got on to Steiner?" he muttered. "That's the worst blow yet."

"Well, you nearly had a worse one, for I believe they are not far off me."

"You don't mean that!"

"Sure thing. My landlady down Fratton way had some inquiries, and when I heard of it I guessed it was time for me to hustle. But what I want to know, Mister, is how the coppers know these things? Steiner is the fifth man you've lost since I signed on with you, and I know the name of the sixth if I don't get a move on. How do you explain it, and ain't you ashamed to see your men go down like this?"

Von Bork flushed crimson.

"How dare you speak in such a way!"

"If I didn't dare things, Mister, I wouldn't be in your service. But I'll tell you straight what is in my mind. I've heard that with you German politicians when an agent has done his work you are not sorry to see him put away."

Von Bork sprang to his feet.

"Do you dare to suggest that I have given away my own agents!"

"I don't stand for that, Mister, but there's a stool pigeon or a cross somewhere, and it's up to you to find out where it is. Anyhow I am taking no more chances. It's me for little Holland, and the sooner the better."

Von Bork had mastered his anger.

"We have been allies too long to quarrel now at the very hour of victory," he said. "You've done splendid work, and taken risks and I can't forget it. By all means go to Holland, and you can get a boat from Rotterdam to New York. No other line will be safe a week from now. I'll take that book and pack it with the rest."

The American held the small parcel in his hand, but made no motion to give it up.

"What about the dough?" he asked.

"The what?"

"The boodle. The reward. The £500. The gunner turned damned nasty at the last, and I had to square him with an extra hundred dollars or it would have been nitsky for you and me. 'Nothin' doin'!' says he, and he meant it too, but the last hundred did it. It's cost me two hundred pound from first to last, so it isn't likely I'd give it up without gettin' my wad."

Von Bork smiled with some bitterness. "You don't seem to have a very high opinion of my honour," said he, "you want the money before you give up the book."

"Well, Mister, it is a business proposition."

"All right. Have your way." He sat down at the table and scribbled a cheque, which he tore from the book, but he refrained from handing it to his companion. "After all, since we are to be on such terms, Mr Altamont," said he, "I don't see why I should trust you any more than you trust me. Do you understand?" he added, looking back over his shoulder at the American. "There's the cheque upon the table. I claim the right to examine that parcel before you pick the money up."

The American passed it over without a word. Von Bork undid a winding of string and two wrappers of paper. Then he sat gazing for a moment in silent amazement at a small blue book which lay before him. Across the cover was printed in golden letters *Practical Handbook of Bee Culture*. Only for one instant did the master spy glare at this strangely irrelevant inscription. The next he was gripped at the back of his neck by a grasp of iron, and a chloroformed sponge was held in front of his writhing face.

"Another glass, Watson!" said Mr Sherlock Holmes, as he extended the bottle of Imperial Tokay.

The thickset chauffeur, who had seated himself by the table, pushed forward his glass with some eagerness.

"It is a good wine, Holmes."

"A remarkable wine, Watson. Our friend upon the sofa has assured me that it is from Franz Joseph's special cellar at the Schœnbrunn Palace. Might I trouble you to open the window, for chloroform vapour does not help the palate."

The safe was ajar, and Holmes standing in front of it was removing dossier after dossier, swiftly examining each, and then packing it neatly in Von Bork's valise. The German lay upon the sofa sleeping stertorously with a strap round his upper arms and another round his legs.

"We need not hurry ourselves, Watson. We are safe from interruption. Would you mind touching the bell. There is no one in the house except old Martha, who has played her part to admiration. I got her the situation here when first I took the matter up. Ah, Martha, you will be glad to hear that all is well."

The pleasant old lady had appeared in the doorway. She curtseyed with a smile to Mr Holmes, but glanced with some apprehension at the figure upon the sofa.

"It is all right, Martha. He has not been hurt at all."

"I am glad of that, Mr Holmes. According to his lights he has been a kind master. He wanted me to go with his wife to Germany yesterday, but that would hardly have suited your plans, would it, sir?"

"No, indeed, Martha. So long as you were here I was easy in my mind. We waited some time for your signal to-night."

"It was the secretary, sir."

"I know. His car passed ours."

"I thought he would never go. I knew that it would not suit your plans, sir, to find him here."

"No, indeed. Well, it only meant that we waited half an hour or so until I saw your lamp go out and knew that the coast was clear. You can report to me to-morrow in London, Martha, at Claridge's Hotel."

"Very good, sir."

"I suppose you have everything ready to leave."

"Yes, sir. He posted seven letters to-day. I have the addresses as usual."

"Very good, Martha. I will look into them to-morrow. Good-night. These papers," he continued, as the old lady vanished, "are not of very great importance for, of course, the information which they represent has been sent off long ago to the German Government. These are the originals which could not safely be got out of the country."

"Then they are of no use."

"I should not go so far as to say that, Watson. They will at least show our people what is known and what is not. I may say that a good many of these papers have come through me, and I need not add are thoroughly untrustworthy. It would brighten my declining years to see a German cruiser navigating the Solent according to the minefield plans which I have furnished. But you, Watson," he stopped his work and took his old friend by the shoulders, "I've hardly seen you in the light yet. How have the years used you? You look the same blithe boy as ever."

"I feel twenty years younger, Holmes. I have seldom felt so happy as when I got your wire asking me to meet you at Harwich with the car. But you, Holmes – you have changed very little – save for that horrible goatee."

"These are the sacrifices one makes for one's country, Watson," said Holmes, pulling at his little tuft. "To-morrow it will be but a dreadful memory. With my hair cut and a few other superficial changes I shall no doubt reappear at Claridge's to-morrow as I was before this American stunt – I beg your pardon, Watson, my well of English seems to be permanently defiled – before this American job came my way."

"But you had retired, Holmes. We heard of you as living the life of a hermit among your bees and your books in a small farm upon the South Downs."

"Exactly, Watson. Here is the fruit of my leisured ease, the magnum opus of my latter years!" He picked up the volume from the table and read out the whole title, *Practical Handbook of Bee Culture, with some Observations upon the Segregation of the Queen.* Alone I did it. Behold the fruit of pensive nights and laborious days, when I watched the little working gangs as once I watched the criminal world of London."

"But how did you get to work again?"

"Ah, I have often marvelled at it myself. The Foreign Minister alone I could have withstood, but when the Premier also deigned to visit my humble roof —! The fact is, Watson, that this gentleman upon the sofa was a bit too good for our people. He was in a class by himself. Things were going wrong, and no one could understand why they were going wrong. Agents were suspected or even caught, but there was evidence of some strong and secret central force. It was absolutely necessary to expose it. Strong pressure was brought upon me to look into the matter. It has cost me two years, Watson, but they have not been devoid of excitement. When I say that I started my pilgrimage at Chicago, graduated in an Irish secret society at Buffalo, gave serious trouble to the constabulary at Skibbareen and so eventually caught the eye of a subordinate agent of Von Bork, who recommended me as a likely man, you will realize that the matter was complex. Since then I have been honoured by his confidence, which has not prevented most of his plans going subtly wrong and five of his best agents being in prison. I watched them, Watson, and I picked them as they ripened. Well, sir, I hope that you are none the worse!"

The last remark was addressed to Von Bork himself, who after much gasping and blinking had lain quietly listening to Holmes's statement. He broke out now into a furious stream of German invective, his face convulsed with passion. Holmes continued his swift investigation of documents while his prisoner cursed and swore.

"Though unmusical, German is the most expressive of all languages," he observed, when Von Bork had stopped from pure exhaustion. "Hullo! Hullo!" he added, as he looked hard at the corner of a tracing before putting it in the box. "This should put another bird in the cage. I had no idea that the paymaster was such a rascal, though I have long had an eye upon him. Mister Von Bork, you have a great deal to answer for."

The prisoner had raised himself with some difficulty upon the sofa and was staring with a strange mixture of amazement and hatred at his captor.

"I shall get level with you, Altamont," he said, speaking with slow deliberation, "if it takes me all my life I shall get level with you!"

"The old sweet song," said Holmes. "How often have I heard it in days gone by. It was a favourite ditty of the late lamented Professor Moriarty. Colonel Sebastian Moran has also been known to warble it. And yet I live and keep bees upon the South Downs."

"Curse you, you double traitor!" cried the German, straining against his bonds and glaring murder from his furious eyes.

"No, no, it is not so bad as that," said Holmes, smiling. "As my speech surely shows you Mr Altamont of Chicago had no existence in fact. I used him and he is gone."

"Then who are you?"

"It is really immaterial who I am, but since the matter seems to interest you, Mr Von Bork, I may say that this is not my first acquaintance with the members of your family. I have done a good deal of business in Germany in the past and my name is probably familiar to you."

"I would wish to know it," said the Prussian grimly.

"It was I who brought about the separation between Irene Adler and the late King of Bohemia when your cousin Heinrich was the Imperial Envoy. It was I also who saved from murder, by the Nihilist Klopman, Count Von und Zu Grafenstein, who was your mother's elder brother. It was I – "

Von Bork sat up in amazement.

"There is only one man," he cried.

"Exactly," said Holmes.

Von Bork groaned and sank back on the sofa. "And most of that information came through you," he cried. "What is it worth? What have I done? It is my ruin for ever!"

"It is certainly a little untrustworthy," said Holmes. "It will require some checking and you have little time to check it. Your admiral may find the new guns rather larger than he expects, and the cruisers perhaps a trifle faster."

Von Bork clutched at his own throat in despair.

"There are a good many other points of detail which will, no doubt, come to light in good time. But you have one quality which is very rare in a German, Mr Von Bork, you are a sportsman and you will bear me no ill-will when you realize that you, who have outwitted so many other people, have at last been outwitted yourself. After all, you have done your best for your country, and I have done my best for mine, and what could be more natural? Besides," he added, not unkindly, as he laid his hand upon the shoulder of the prostrate man, "it is better than to fall before some more ignoble foe. These papers are now ready, Watson. If you will help me with our prisoner, I think that we may get started for London at once."

It was no easy task to move Von Bork, for he was a strong and a desperate man. Finally, holding either arm, the two friends walked him very slowly down the garden walk which he had trod with such proud confidence when he received the congratulations of the famous diplomatist only a few hours before. After a short, final struggle he was hoisted, still bound hand and foot, into the spare seat of the little car. His precious valise was wedged in beside him.

"I trust that you are as comfortable as circumstances permit," said Holmes, when the final arrangements were made. "Should I be guilty of a liberty if I lit a cigar and placed it between your lips?"

But all amenities were wasted upon the angry German.

"I suppose you realize, Mr Sherlock Holmes," said he, "that if your Government bears you out in this treatment it becomes an act of war."

"What about your Government and all this treatment?" said Holmes, tapping the valise.

"You are a private individual. You have no warrant for my arrest. The whole proceeding is absolutely illegal and outrageous."

"Absolutely," said Holmes.

"Kidnapping a German subject."

"And stealing his private papers."

"Well, you realize your position, you and your accomplice here. If I were to shout for help as we pass through the village – "

"My dear sir, if you did anything so foolish you would probably enlarge the too limited titles of our village inns by giving us 'The Dangling Prussian' as a sign-post. The Englishman is a patient creature, but at present his temper is a little inflamed and it would be as well not to try him too far. No, Mr Von Bork, you will go with us in a quiet, sensible fashion to Scotland Yard, whence you can send for your friend Baron Von Herling and see if even now you may not fill that place which he has reserved for you in the ambassadorial suite. As to you, Watson, you are joining up with your old service, as I understand, so London won't be out of your way. Stand with me here upon the terrace for it may be the last quiet talk that we shall ever have."

The two friends chatted in intimate converse for a few minutes, recalling once again the days of the past whilst their prisoner vainly wriggled to undo the bonds that held him. As they turned to the car, Holmes pointed back to the moonlit sea, and shook a thoughtful head.

"There's an east wind coming, Watson."

"I think not, Holmes. It is very warm."

"Good old Watson! You are the one fixed point in a changing age. There's an east wind coming all the same, such a wind as never blew on England yet. It will be cold and bitter, Watson, and a good many of us may wither before its blast. But it's God's own wind none the less, and a cleaner, better, stronger land will lie in the sunshine when the storm has cleared. Start her up, Watson, for it's time that we were on our way. I have a cheque for five hundred pounds which should be cashed early, for the drawer is quite capable of stopping it, if he can."